Boundaries

A Novel

Douglas B. Carlyle

Other Novels by Doug Carlyle…

In Search of the Fuller Brush Man
&
Vinegarone

For Dad

I must thank my editor Sandra Hickman for her attention to detail, patience, and guidance.

Hugs go to Sarah Carlyle for the cover art.

Book 1

SIX MONTHS AGO…

The hospital emergency room was its usual organized pandemonium. Many dozens of people walked briskly in every imaginable direction, all of them strategically avoiding collisions with each other as they moved beds, stocked carts, and went about their business at hand. At the far end of the expansive white room, a distinguished, yet unconventional-looking man entered through two swinging doors. He was a man wearing a kilt, spats, a horsehair sporran, and a bottle-green shirt with a leather tie at the top. A black wool Glengarry topped his head.

One of the nurses greeted him with a catcall, followed by, "Beautiful legs, Dr. Mason."

Her whistle and her remark caught the attention of others in the ER.

Loarn Mason waved his finger at the nurse's face and grinned as he responded, "I was at practice, thank you very much, when Bartholomew called me in. The Sandia Pipers Society is planning to take first place at next year's competition." Mason scanned around the ER before asking, "Where is he anyway?"

The nurse pointed toward a work area at the other end from where she stood around which crowded several physicians.

"Ought to be in nine," she replied. "He has some psych case back there." The nurse studied Dr. Mason from head to toe and back then bore a mischievous smile as she said, "You should be a model. You're quite handsome for a Scottish senior citizen."

From behind, another nurse held a polished stainless steel tray below Mason's kilt while exclaiming loud enough for all to hear, "Ain't wearin' none!"

The staff, all close friends with Dr. Mason, laughed at the prank.

Mason smiled and patted the nurse on the back of her shoulder while playfully protesting, "This is blatant harassment!"

Soon, he proceeded toward room nine, dodging several techs and nurses as he made his way, finally stopping at the desk to chat with the other doctors.

"Good evening Roger, Ken, Bob. Looks like a normal Friday night. Do you know why Bart called me in?"

Two of the doctors glanced over at Mason, examined him from head to foot and smiled. The third responded while still studying a CT scan on a large screen, never even looking at Mason.

"He's got an unconscious female—some kind of unusual lab results and a head scan he wants to discuss with you. Right up your alley."

Just then, Dr. Bartholomew walked through the sliding door, looking tired after twelve hours on the floor. "Loarn, thanks for coming in." Bartholomew stopped in his tracks while struggling unsuccessfully to withhold a chuckle. "Looks like I interrupted you."

"Oh, no bother really. We had finished blowing the pipes, and were just about to sit down to some single-malt when you paged. What do you have?"

"When are you going to get rid of that pager and get a phone?" Bartholomew asked, shaking his head. "We might have been able to handle this an hour ago with a phone consultation."

"Ah, yes, treatment over the phone. No thank you, I prefer to *see* and *touch* my patients. Call me 'of the old school' if you must, but be damn sure you know where the door is when you do."

"No, Loarn, it's pointless to try to change you. Anyway, I have a female in her mid-40s who was flown in from Roswell. Witnesses said she was checking in at a motel when she passed out cold in the lobby. They said she was acting strangely prior to doing so. I can't find any trauma, but her scan shows some unusual findings—I'll let you draw your own conclusion. Also, her labs have some strange values unlike anything I've seen, but nothing can explain her current state. No sign of a bleed or stroke. Glucose is good. Cardiac function is great.

Respiratory effort is non-labored." Bartholomew made certain Mason was listening intently before continuing, "One more thing—she's transmitting."

Mason pulled his eyeglasses down on his nose so he could peer over them at Dr. Bartholomew.

"There is a device of some kind in one of her ears. It was actually causing interference with some of the instruments. Other than that anomaly, she looks healthy, she's attractive, and she has a huge rock on her ring finger. She's starting to come around, but her mental status is really altered. Also, she's somewhat combative so we have her physically restrained. I withheld drugs. I just can't figure out what her problem is, and we're buried, so I thought I'd let you work her up and determine a course of treatment."

"Do you know who she is?"

"Possibly. Roswell PD found an old California ID in her handbag that says her name is Diane Alders. She was traveling with another woman in her early twenties and a young child, but they aren't cooperating or at least they aren't giving the police all of the information we need. The child reportedly points at the ID and says 'momma,' and the younger woman says she is the child's nanny, and that they're from Hunt, Texas. They're still with the police in Roswell. I have a contact if you want to call them. The law enforcement guys suggest we not attempt to contact anyone except them at this point just in case they were fleeing someone, and I think that's good advice."

"Interesting. You are probably right. It sounds like she is in some kind of trouble on top of everything else. I'll have a look at her."

"You might want to put on some scrubs," Bartholomew said, smiling and pointing at Mason's legs. "Anyone in her condition waking up to those hairy monstrosities, and a man in a dress, will certainly start screaming."

THE FIRST THING DIANE noticed was the smell...an antiseptic smell, and all too familiar. She slowly opened her eyes to find herself in a white hospital room. *Oh, God...Not again!* was all she could think. When she tried to sit up, she discovered her hands and ankles restrained to the bed.

"Hello!" she shouted. "I'm dreaming again. You can turn off the nanocells, asshole!"

A man carrying a clipboard and wearing a short, white doctor's coat over his green hospital scrubs, came through the door.

"Good evening. You seem to be improving."

"Oh, so now I am supposed to be raped by you, too. Well get it over with while you can," Diane said as she began to fight the restraints.

Mason slowly approached Diane as a nurse poked her head in the door.

"Is everything okay doctor? Do you need me?"

"Everything is fine, but why don't you stick around for a few minutes?"

The nurse entered the room just as Mason turned his attention back toward the patient.

"I'm Dr. Mason. And you are?"

Diane hesitated for a moment before replying, "Who do you want me to be?"

Taken somewhat aback by her response, Mason raised his eyebrows and said, "I don't want you to be anyone but who you are. The information we have here is that your name is Diane Alders, and quite frankly we don't know much else about you. Can you verify that this is your name?"

"Where's Gigi...my daughter?" Diane demanded, still struggling with the restraints.

Mason took a seat on a stool as he flipped through the file given to him by Dr. Bartholomew before asking, "Is Gigi the child or the young woman?"

"Kiss my ass!" Diane replied, angrily. "How old do you think I am?"

Ignoring her unhelpful response, Mason continued, "I was referring to the approximately two-year-old child and young woman with that child. I have no idea how old you are, but I'd be pleased if you would give me that information."

"Figure it out yourself, you old fart," Diane said, blowing her hair out of her eyes.

"Do you know what day it is?" Mason asked.

Donning a coy smile, Diane replied, "The day after yesterday, I suppose."

Boundaries

"Do you know where you are?" Mason asked, unaffected by Diane's lack of cooperation.

"Now that's a stupid question."

Mason continued to jot down notes despite Diane's unhelpful responses.

"This place looks like a hospital, smells like a hospital, and you look like some washed out old doctor in scrubs."

Mason wasn't the least bit surprised by the patient's hostility and mistrust. He'd seen it quite often in cases where there was a head injury or some type of organic malady of the brain. Sensing that Diane needed some motivation so that she would answer his questions, Mason took a different approach.

"Well let's see then, back to your original question, both young ladies are at the police station in Roswell because neither of the adults involved have a believable story as to who is who, where you are from, where you were going, nor why. There is a minor mixed up in this, and if the police do not get some answers quickly, they will see that the little girl is placed temporarily with a foster family so that they are satisfied she is safe. The other young lady, as I understand it, is a foreigner from Spain here on a work visa so she will become a matter for the Immigration people to handle, and these days that can be most unpleasant. She says she is a nanny in your employ. Do you care to confirm any of this?"

"Why am I tied down to this bed?" The veins in Diane's neck were beginning to stand out as she tried to pull her hands free.

"You didn't answer my question," Mason said persistently.

Breathing heavily and starting to perspire from the fruitless struggle to free herself, Diane relaxed somewhat and said, "I think you should answer mine first. I have no idea where I am."

Weighing the valueless conversation that was taking place, Mason decided to eliminate some of the mystery.

"You are at the Trauma Center at the University of New Mexico in Albuquerque."

Diane was quiet as she mulled over what Mason said to her.

"Tell me, do you have any medical problems?"

Though she was about to burst with anger, Diane's reflex action was to begin laughing.

"Let's see if you think this is a problem: I nearly died three years ago, but my husband decided to keep me alive by injecting nanocells into my body, along with the dreams and thoughts of a surrogate female. Now he is manipulating me with his handheld computer, causing me to move from one reality to the next at his command. Today I am here, the next I am across the world someplace, then I'm being raped by thugs, then I am having a baby, then I am running a business, then I am making love under a waterfall to a man who looks like a GQ model. Do you want me to continue?"

Unaffected by the Diane's diatribe, Mason responded, "Fascinating. You say you nearly died?"

"Oh, yes. I was almost beaten to death."

After studying the examination notes of Dr. Bartholomew, Mason asked, "You certainly do not show any signs of a beating. How long ago did this beating take place?"

"Aren't you listening to me?" Diane replied in frustration. "I said it happened three years ago, and then I said I was nearly beaten to death. Duh!"

The subject was unpleasant for Diane to discuss, and she found it difficult to maintain eye contact with Mason as she continued, "Oh, did I tell you? That was around the time I got pregnant? The father was either my lovely husband, who had his vasectomy reversed as sort of a birthday present and then failed to tell me, or some Italian dude who took advantage of me when I was drugged out of my mind. I'm not sure which." She turned her head so as to look the doctor square in the eyes as she asked, "Are you confused? I know I am."

It took all of Mason's patience and training to maintain his professional demeanor while he explored the possibility that Diane's story was true, or partially or totally fabricated.

"Where did this beating take place?"

"On some remote island in the Indian Ocean off the coast of Thailand. I think it was called Maribella Island or something like that."

Boundaries

Mason began to lose his focus, and found himself fighting back a smile.

"It's okay," Diane said. "I know I'm only dreaming. I'll just tell you my whole life story, you can have sex with me, then Mick will flash me back to Hunt and my life will continue as if nothing had happened."

"Ms. Alders, I do not understand why you are so obsessed about being attacked and sexually assaulted. Let me assure you that you are safe here. Have you been sexually assaulted?"

"Maybe," Diane said as she again blew her hair out of her eyes.

"And the pregnancy you are speaking about produced the child who is now in Roswell?"

"Yes! You make it sound so…so clinical," Diane replied, looking critically at Mason.

"I'm just trying to get a detailed history. Have you had any other pregnancies, miscarriages, abortions, and do you have any other children?"

"Yes, yes, no, and no."

Mason sighed, frustrated with the dialogue as it were.

"Are you from a place called Hunt, Texas?"

Pausing to think first, Diane replied vaguely, "Sometimes I wonder."

"What is the last thing you remember?"

Diane stared at the ceiling for a long time before answering, appearing to truly be searching her memory.

"Yellow. I remember flashing yellow light." Her attention shifted from the ceiling back to Dr. Mason. "What was your name again?"

"Fascinating...you are a fascinating woman."

Mason set down his clipboard on a counter and folded his glasses into his pocket. He smiled and said, hoping to improve the rapport between them, "Let me properly introduce myself. I am Dr. Mason...Loarn Mason."

Diane began to laugh out loud. "Mick must have finally reached the end of a very long list of names for his dreams if he has to use Loarn Mason as one of them..."

"I am Dr. Loarn Mason," he said, ignoring the insult. "I am a neurologist on staff part time here at this hospital, and the rest of the time I am in private practice in Santa Fe."

The laughter slowed as Diane finally began to take Mason seriously.

"You passed out or had some type of episode, possibly a seizure, at a motel outside of Roswell. You have been unresponsive until just a short while ago. As I understand it, the young lady with you—she said her name was Carmen—was trying to put your limp body into a car and drive off when deputies arrived. Do you recall any of these events?"

Diane shivered.

"He sets parameters this way."

"He?"

"Mickey."

Mason jotted the name down on the clipboard, as he asked, "Your husband, Mickey?"

"I guess he's my husband, but I can't be sure about anything."

Crossing his arms, Mason asked, "He sets what parameters?"

"Nanocell parameters, of course. Are you stupid or something?"

"Forgive me Ms. Alders," Mason continued quite intently, his eyebrows furrowed. "But you have me at quite a loss at this point. That is the second time you have said *nanocells.*"

"Okay, listen closely. The nanocells control my mind and my body functions. They carry around information and feelings and dreams and memories and allow me to live. Without them, I die. Oh, and before I forget, do not screw with MADONNA."

Mason's facial expression suddenly became serious as he began to relate key words Diane spoke with his own past experience.

"Madonna? Why is it I suspect you are not speaking about the singer?"

"I hate her, don't you?"

Boundaries

Diane looked at the doctor for quite a while. Neither of them spoke. Finally, Diane pointed out, "I'm strapped to the bed and, I presume, naked under this blanket. Are you going to rape me?"

Mason looked at the nurse who returned the same puzzled look back. He picked up his clipboard, put his glasses back on and tried to get his evaluation back on track. "Ms. Alders, your behavior is quite out of the ordinary. Have you ever had a seizure?"

"If Mickey wants. He even makes me have orgasms."

"Have you ever had a head injury?"

"Probably. Oh, I forgot to tell you about my brain cancer."

Mason stopped writing and looked at his patient. "Brain cancer...?"

"Yes, brain cancer. Don't you believe me?"

"Ms. Alders, your tests show no signs or symptoms of cancer."

"Damn, guess he lied about that one too," Diane said snapping her fingers. Tears began to well up in her eyes.

"He...Mickey?" Mason asked, quickly taking notes.

"Yes...He, Mickey."

"So who is Gigi?"

"She's my daughter." Diane's voice now broke with emotion. "Please don't take her away from me."

Mason decided it was time to take a chance.

"Nurse, please remove the restraints from Ms. Alders."

Diane watched the nurse remove the first restraint then began to look more relaxed.

Once Diane was free, Mason asked, "Who is the young lady?"

"She is Carmen, my daughter's nanny. She was telling the truth."

"Can you explain why you have an electronic device implanted inside your left ear?"

"A what?!" Diane asked, as a look of fear came across her face.

"There is something implanted inside your left ear—something I am not familiar with. It's very small, yet visible in our scans. You might have felt it at some point."

"I've wondered what that was for the longest time. I always thought it was a pimple or a mole or something. I feel it sometimes when I put in my ear bud."

"No, your head CT shows it to be some type of electronic device, and it is transmitting a signal as we speak."

"What type of signal?"

"Well, we are not exactly sure. We hoped you could tell us."

"Maybe that's how he controls me," Diane said as tears began to stream down Diane's face. "Can you help me?"

"We will do what we can, be certain of that. Can I possibly contact someone in your family to see if they can answer some of my questions?"

He could see resistance in Diane's expression.

"I have no family…only my husband. Please don't tell him where I am…please…don't tell him. He'll kill me, I know he will."

"Are you speaking of your husband, Mr. Alders?"

"It's Rollins."

Mason suddenly looked like he had seen a ghost.

"I beg your pardon?"

"My husband's name is Mickey Rollins."

"Dr. Mickey Rollins?"

Mason put his clipboard down at his side.

"Yes, do you know him?"

Mason stood up and turned away from Diane accidentally letting the clipboard fall to the floor.

"Doctor, are you alright?" The nurse asked, walking over to face Dr. Mason.

"He did it!" Mason ran his hands over the top of his head and squeezed his eyes closed. "I cannot believe the son-of-a-bitch did it." Mason recovered his composure after a few moments. "Nurse, I think the patient is stable at this time. If you would excuse us, I will call you if I need you."

Boundaries

The nurse hesitated for a moment, and then dutifully left the room.

"If you need anything, use the call button and I'll be right back."

Once Dr. Mason was alone with Diane, he picked up the clipboard from the floor, turned to her once more, and put his hand on her shoulder.

"Ms. Alders, I think I can help you. I most certainly want to help you. I know your husband and his work very well. But before I can begin, I need to know as much as you can tell me about your history with Dr. Rollins, and in particular, any treatments he may have administered."

Diane was startled by the change in Mason's voice, which was now slow, deliberate and deadly serious.

"How much do you want to know?"

"I need to know every last detail."

Chapter 1

THREE AND A HALF YEARS AGO...

Constantine Strokas enjoyed his monthly new-business reviews as much as most men love sports. He had earned the right to be vain, and he carefully combed his silver, perfectly-coifed hair while standing in front of a gilded mirror in his office. One would think he was dressing for a trophy wife—or even a girlfriend 40 years younger than him. But tonight, he was a working late. Jerry Baker, his business partner, looked forward to these meetings with equal enthusiasm. The two had been associates, competitors, or partners for some thirty years, give or take a few, and today their corporate victories had brought them to the point where they now thrived on mentoring other men and women with the entrepreneurial spirit and energy they once had.

C & J LLP blended its investments with other like-minded venture capitalists in various futuristic endeavors. The selection of co-investors in each deal depended on the type of new business or direction the prospective entrepreneur was heading. Tonight's meeting was to be particularly specific, focusing primarily on a medical-related project dealing with restoration of memory and function in patients who are victims of Alzheimer's Disease, strokes, or traumatic brain injury. This late night conference call would bring together representatives from a Swiss Bank, and a group of investors from Hong Kong. Over the years, C & J had a policy when making a major decision to seek the expert advice of recognized leaders in the field under discussion. Tonight's subject matter experts were Dr. Loarn Mason, a medical veteran, Professor and Chief of Neurology at a prominent Level 1 trauma center, and young Dr. Ricardo Mendoza, a neurosurgeon practicing in Singapore, Manila, Hong Kong and Bangkok, and considered to be one of a new breed of doctors in the neurosciences.

Boundaries

Constantine and Jerry settled into their chairs, comfortably dressed in their casual golfing garb after a day at the links, each with his favorite mixed drink in hand—a side benefit of doing business by web link. Two women wearing only bikinis under unbuttoned men's long sleeve shirts, who were employed by the restaurant that occupied the top floor of the glass-faced building, set out some meticulously prepared hors d'oeuvres. The two eccentric post mid-lifers felt no guilt knowing that those on the other end of the conversation would not be dressed in such casual attire, nor would they be in the company of such nubile, young ladies.

The speakerphone beeped as each member of the call connected. Constantine turned on a recorder as he facilitated the discussion.

"Who do we have on the line?"

"Yes, this is Germaine with Patrice and Depak in Lucerne. How are you doing, Constantine?"

"Oh I'm doing quite well, especially since I beat Jerry today on the back nine."

A voice with a thick French accent chimed in, "Jerry, did Constantine cheat?"

"Of course he did," Jerry replied as he flipped his mouthpiece down to his lips. "He always cheats."

The phone broke with laughter on the other end.

There was a second beep. "This is Wei-ming in Hong Kong, good afternoon."

"Hello Wei-ming, Jerry and Constantine here, and we also have the people from Lucerne on the line. How's the weather today in Hong Kong?"

There was a slight delay in the response from across half a world.

"It is very pleasant, about 27 degrees, but it is raining. There is a super typhoon between here and Taiwan, and we are catching the edge of it."

Jerry interrupted, "It's hard to imagine 27 degrees being comfortable."

One of the parties in Switzerland was quick to respond, "You Americans need to catch up with the rest of the world and go Celsius."

"No, thank you," Jerry replied. "I'm quite used to calling 80 degrees comfortable."

There came subdued laughter from both continents. The phone beeped again.

"This is Dr. Ricardo Mendoza."

"Doctor, thank you for giving us your valuable time. We have Hong Kong and Lucerne on the line. Does everyone have a copy of Dr. Mendoza's background, in addition to his well-written, expert opinion on the proposal for the project called PicoPoint?"

"Yes, we do here in Lucerne."

"And, yes, I do as well here in Hong Kong."

"Very good, now all we need is Dr. Mason, then we can…"

The phone beeped one more time.

"This is Mason." His Scottish brogue was loud, and spoke over everyone else on the line.

"Dr. Mason, we are glad you could join us at this late hour on the West Coast. We have everyone on the line now. How are you Dr. Mason?"

"Like you say, it is late. Let us move along."

Mason wasn't one to mince words. Constantine and Jerry looked at each other, both making a 'grumpy' face.

"Very well then, does everyone have a copy of Dr. Mason's background, and well-documented, expert opinion on the project being discussed tonight?"

"Lucerne has them."

"Same in Hong Kong."

Finally, Mendoza replied, "I am well aware of my distinguished colleague and his opinion on this matter."

"Then, let's proceed directly to the point," Constantine continued. "Of course all of you probably know this conversation is being recorded. Dr. Mendoza, if I may summarize your position, you are advocating that the firms respond favorably to Dr. Rollins' proposal, and make a significant investment in his PicoPoint program. Can you explain please?"

Mendoza cleared his throat before speaking.

"Gentlemen, Dr. Rollins' program is absolutely unique. I am abreast of all major research activity in the field of brain function restoration. With the exception of the one we are speaking about tonight, each is pursuing much the same old solutions that many experts in the field have tried before. They will more than likely achieve the same results—meaning nothing revolutionary. What Dr. Rollins has proposed exhibits great promise. His theory seems sound. I have assisted him with some limited testing, and the results, thus far, exceed our expectations. He clearly needs substantial funding for more research, but I feel certain that within two years, maybe sooner, he can demonstrate a clear breakthrough. We all know there is a huge, worldwide market for a product such as this. I can see a significant return on your investment, and to show you my sincerity in this matter, I am willing to invest up to $20 million USD of my own assets in this project, providing you would allow yet another outside investor."

Jerry was the first to speak.

"Well, the good doctor certainly puts his money where his mouth is. That's an American phrase that I would be happy to explain for those who need help."

"We understand it quite well here in Europe, in fact that phrase has Old Latin roots."

"And I understand as well. In China, such logic dates back many thousands of years."

"It's bloody foolishness," Mason interjected.

Constantine continued the call, "Well that would bring us now to the opposing point of view which Dr. Mason has already hinted at."

Speaking clearly and succinctly, Mason said, "There is no hint about my point of view. Let me first object, as should we all, to Dr. Mendoza's own choice of words. We are treating PicoPoint as a *product*, and not a *therapy* as should be the case. Furthermore, this project, while its goals are certainly worthy, cannot be completed without breaching today's bio-ethical standards. Therefore, there is no possible way I can endorse it."

"Through the decades," Mendoza cut in, "old arguments such as this one would have scuttled much of the good medicine we practice today, Dr. Mason."

Mason objected, "If you will please hear me out without interrupting…this work will require a substantial number of invasive trials in humans, and I see no way to complete such trials within the framework of morals, ethics, and laws in any civilized society. May I also add, gentlemen, that the use of LSD as a stimulant will bury the project for years in one challenge after another. As a resident of Southeast Asia, Dr. Mendoza, nobody should know better than you, that getting caught possessing or using LSD in several of the countries where you practice, for medicinal purposes or otherwise, brings the death penalty. Gentlemen, your money will be sucked up, and actual implementation of PicoPoint will be delayed by legal and political wrangling that would choke an elephant. Contrary to my distinguished colleague, I wouldn't put a penny of my own money into the project."

There was a brief period of silence until one of the European investors rekindled the conversation. "Dr. Mendoza, what do you think about this human trial problem?"

There was a pause while Mendoza carefully chose his words. "My friends, let me strongly suggest that when having discussions about making investments in technological breakthroughs such as PicoPoint, we must cast aside concerns about politics, ethics and morality. We are no longer in the 'dark ages.'"

Mason immediately challenged the remark, pounding his fist on his desk or table near the telephone.

"We are not speaking of the dark ages here, rather very modern and controversial subjects. Did you even read Rollins' proposal? Let me just highlight a few lightning rod words and phrases such as '*harvesting* dreams;' how about 'mind *clones*;' and how about 'anecdotal *thought transfer?*' These words are highly charged. And then he says he controls it all with a process named *MADONNA*? You just invited every Christian and conservative politician to a public hanging. Here is where we must fundamentally ask who and what we are, gentlemen. How can we possibly make any decisions without first weighing goodness of purpose?"

"Loarn, you are overlooking the broad picture here and getting lost in the minutia," Dr. Mendoza said, becoming noticeably belligerent. "Step outside the tiny box in which you live for once, and take a serious look at where we need to go in our field."

"Believe me, my friend," Mason concluded, "I have taken that look, and this is not the direction in which we should go."

There was silence. Constantine and Jerry looked at each other with raised eyebrows. One could almost sense the reaction was similar on the other ends of the conference call.

Realizing this was a good time to put a halt to the discussion, Constantine remarked, "My good doctors, if neither of you have anything further to say regarding your written opinions on the matter known as PicoPoint, then I will leave you to your work, or leisure as may be the case, and bid you a good night."

"I have said my piece, and I hope this is the final conversation about this matter." barked Dr. Mason. The phone beeped twice signaling that he had disconnected.

Mendoza spoke up.

"I trust you will consider my statements very carefully. We have been debating the business opportunity of a lifetime. I know several investors who will jump at the chance to see PicoPoint become a reality if you walk away. Have a good day and evening, gentlemen." The phone beeped twice again indicating Mendoza was no longer on the line.

Constantine set down his notebook and turned off the recorder. "We have all heard the opinions of our experts and we have their written recommendations as well. As you know, Jerry and I will only support a project if there is complete consensus among the parties. If each of you will send me your decision by the end of your business day so that I have it first thing in the morning, I will send Dr. Rollins our response. Are there any questions or remarks at this point?"

"None in Lucerne. It sounds to us here like a controversial endeavor, though certainly not without merit. We will let you know today."

"This is Wei. I agree with Lucerne that it sounds like there is a lot of risk, but at the same it sounds very exciting. I know Dr. Mendoza well. He is highly respected in this part of the world. Let me also say that he is telling you the truth when he says he will not have any trouble finding investors for Dr. Rollins' project. I will discuss this with the Board here, and you will know our decision when you get to work tomorrow."

"Very good then, this is Constantine and Jerry signing off."

"Good day."

"Cheers."

Chapter 2

Diane Alders leaned dangerously forward in her chair, looking straight down, except for when she turned her head slightly to the left to talk more directly into the speakerphone. Her long, wavy, auburn hair swung back and forth with the turning of her head. Her elbows were on her desk, and her head was propped up in her hands as she scanned a contract. Both of her legs hopped up and down, out of phase with each other, and too quickly to count. Except for the thin pile of paper in front of her, no stack of paper anywhere in her office was shorter than nine inches. The room was illuminated by a combination of soft florescent light, and light from the rising moon over the Laguna Mountains east of San Diego that could be clearly seen from her window.

"Finally, on page 16 we have the usual signature page. Can you make sure I have Gunter's last name spelled correctly?"

"Yes, Diane, you have it spelled perfectly," said the distinctly Germanic voice on the other end of the conversation. "But one correction must be made. Dr. Schemff is General Counsel to the Management Board. He is no longer Deputy General Counsel as of two days past."

"Oh, my gosh! Oh, my gosh! I heard about that from Dieter, and I still missed it in the final draft! I can't believe I almost screwed this up. Good catch. I'll make that change and the others we spoke about and send a new copy to you in one hour. Rajeev and I will catch a plane Tuesday to meet with you and Gunter in Munich on Wednesday afternoon at 1400 hours CET."

"Yes, Diane, I am looking forward to this partnership. You know how to make a deal. Let me say between the two of us that Gunter feels good about it too, and he is most critical of all of our suppliers. I think he really likes Medico Techniq."

"Harald, I am looking forward to this, too. I am certain our business relationship will serve both of our companies extremely well. You have a good day."

"You, too. You go to bed now. It is a long time after midnight, is it not?"

Diane looked at the ornate, Black Forest cuckoo clock on the wall. "Three–fifteen in the morning, but the last four hours have been time well spent."

"I agree, Diane. Now, goodnight."

"Gute nacht, Harald."

Diane waited for the phone to disconnect completely, and then listened for another ten seconds to be sure Harald was no longer on the line. Once convinced she was by herself, she pushed her chair back several feet from the desk and jumped up.

"Yes, yes, yes!" She shouted, proceeding to march around her office waving her hands and jerking her arms back each time she shouted her victory cry.

Her celebratory dance went on for at least a minute. Finally, Diane stopped, ran her fingers through her hair, and exhaled before taking a moment to touch a picture frame containing a picture of her while in college with a smiling, handsome, pony-tailed man. She walked over to her office window and stared out at the lights on the street and the moon rising above the horizon. As her focus shifted from distant to near, she recognized two familiar figures reflected in the window—Rajeev Munshi, her boss, founder and CEO of Medico Techniq, and Susan Reed, the Vice-President of Human Resources.

Diane turned around and pointed both index fingers at her visitors while sporting a huge smile, saying, "Did it! We did it! We got the deal…three years, sole source, with an option to extend. It's gotta be worth at least a billion."

"Probably closer to two," Rajeev said, smiling. "Diane you're incredible."

"Great news, Diane." Susan chimed in. "There's nobody who can do the job like you can."

Diane flopped down in her chair, and put her feet up on the arm of a sofa. She picked up a soft drink that was probably more than a day old from a small coffee table and took a swig.

Boundaries

"God, this shit's flatter than me," she said, breaking up laughing.

Rajeev and Susan glanced at each other, unsure how to respond to their associate's behavior.

Diane stopped laughing, and then looked at her watch. She moved her right arm closer, then farther away to find that sweet spot where she could see the hands on her Rolex Cellini. Her eyes were bloodshot and yet moist from happiness.

Turning back to her guests, she asked, "So, what brings you guys here this time of night? Are you having an affair?" Diane again broke up laughing at her own joke.

Rajeev and Susan walked toward Diane's desk and took a seat.

"Diane, we need to talk," Susan remarked.

Diane stopped laughing and looked up at the ceiling, searching for a distant memory.

"Bobby Carnes...yes, Bobby Carnes said that to me just before he broke up with me back in 9th grade. Are you breaking up with me?" Diane started laughing uncontrollably again.

"Diane, like Susan said, nobody can do a business deal like you can," Rajeev said as he leaned forward.

Diane stopped laughing, and rolled her chair back to the desk. Her expression became serious.

"Okay, now that we have that settled, what the hell are you guys doing here? You're creeping me out."

"I have a new job for you," Rajeev said, taking Diane's hands in his.

Diane looked at Susan, then Rajeev, then Susan, then Rajeev again hoping someone would break the silence. Being the confident, marketing and sales executive that she was, she boldly moved the conversation forward.

"Good, after Wednesday I can turn my focus on whatever you want. Who are we going after next? Is it Siemens?"

Rajeev stopped Diane short. As he touched her hands softly, he explained, "You're not going with me Tuesday."

"That's a bit risky, don't you think?" Understating her true opinion, Diane continued, "I think it is best for the deal-maker to be at the signing, no offense…"

Now serious, Rajeev responded, "Ashad is going with me."

Diane jerked her hands away from Rajeev. If there was such as thing as a stare of death, she was delivering it to Rajeev. Her demeanor transformed from joy to anger.

"Since when is this how you reward your top executives? Let them get the deal, then screw them over! What the hell does Ashad Mohammed have over me? He's in charge of Middle Eastern accounts, not to mention being five years my junior!"

"Diane…" Susan tried to intervene.

"Stay out of this, Susan! This is personal between Rajeev and me!"

Rajeev hurriedly tried to gain control of the situation.

"We want you to take on a new position reporting to me—Executive Vice President for Corporate Strategy."

"Nope. Not interested. I already report to you."

"Diane…" Susan tried again to intervene.

Diane bit her lip and closed her eyes, hoping Susan wouldn't be there when she opened them.

"Diane!" Rajeev shouted.

She opened her eyes and focused on Rajeev.

"Do you see anything wrong with this picture?"

Usually armed with an answer to everything, Diane was caught off guard.

"What are you talking about?"

"Diane, it's after midnight…it's Monday morning." Rajeev was obviously upset. "You just spent another weekend at the office, and now it's…what…three o'clock?"

Still at a loss for words, Diane looked at Rajeev, somehow trying to find meaning it what he was saying.

Filling in the void in the conversation, Susan added, "Diane, you're working yourself to death. Rajeev and all the rest of us are so inspired by you. We cannot thank you enough for what you do for the company, but we're watching you burn up. You're too valuable for us to let that happen."

The dialogue still did not make sense. Diane cocked her head like a spaniel as Susan spoke.

"Diane, Bruce was my friend, too." Rajeev said, his voice breaking. "We all miss him. He wouldn't want you to live like this."

Diane was now firmly back in the conversation. Her voice dropped two octaves.

"What the hell does any of this have to do with Bruce?"

Susan's voice, in contrast to Diane's, was almost shrill.

"Diane, since Bruce died seven years ago, how many days off from work have you taken?"

"I don't know, Susan," Diane answered bitterly. "Why don't you tell me? I have a feeling you know the answer."

"Seventeen. You've passed up two sabbaticals. You've never taken a vacation. You've never been disconnected for more than two days at a time…"

"I take time off!"

Rajeev countered, "Time off means no cell phone and no laptop."

"I'm not sure where you two are going with this, but I'm very happy with my life, my job, and my career." Slapping her desk with the palms of her hands, she added, "I am, quite honestly, the best there is and if you don't like it, I'll be glad to resign immediately. I'll be hired by 8 am."

Rajeev took Diane's hands again. His voice remained calm and his intention focused.

"Diane, the new job is where we need you. Revenue growth in our current markets is going to flatten in the next five years. I need someone who can look beyond the industry we're in and find us some new direction. You are the perfect person for this job."

Hoping that some concession would gain her the upper hand, she replied, "Fine, I'll consider it. But, why can't this wait until next week?"

"Diane, there is no start for you...no finish. You are all 'go.' The change is effective immediately."

Rajeev finally released Diane's hands.

The conversation could have remained civil at that point, until Susan added, "We have a lucrative package that goes with the job."

Diane looked at Susan and lost control.

"Why on earth would I need more money? All I want is my job...all I have is my job." Her voice crackling with uncharacteristic emotion, Diane finished with, "You are such a bitch."

Susan stood up as she said, "Rajeev, I don't think I am doing any good here. Keep me posted. I'll talk to you later this morning."

Rajeev knew she was right. It was time to get Susan out of the conversation.

"Drive safely, Susan. Pull the door closed behind you." As Susan left the office, Rajeev looked at Diane, and immediately got back on message. "This is really a good opportunity for you."

Now that Diane was alone with her friend, she could open up.

"Why now, Rajeev?"

"Look at you, Diane. You are a beautiful, vivacious, intelligent woman. We are not getting any younger, you and I. How long have I known you?"

Feeling more comfortable with Susan gone, Diane leaned back in her chair and replied, "I think you and Magda showed up at our barbecue, what, ten years ago?"

"We crashed the party. You did not invite us," Rajeev recalled while smiling.

"It was an oversight," Diane said with a grin.

"Bruce cooked pork chops," Rajeev said, laughing.

"He didn't know how to cook for Muslims. He was raised in Bakersfield."

Rajeev chucked at Diane's remark.

"I know, but we got beyond that, did we not. Once we began talking, we found we had more in common than there were differences."

Diane smiled as she reflected on the cookout, adding, "You just wanted to ride on his Harley."

Boundaries

"I loved sitting on all that power." Rajeev put his hands in the air as if they were on handlebars, and made a rumbling sound. "It was almost erotic."

Diane laughed, then she turned to look at the picture of herself with her late husband.

Rajeev paused and took a breath before saying, "I never told you this. Bruce asked me, once, to take care of you if anything ever happened to him."

Diane looked endearingly at Rajeev.

"That's very sweet. I can imagine Bruce doing that. But I don't need anyone to take care of me."

"Perhaps not. Maybe that was a poor choice of words. Let me say this instead. I think you need some guidance from a friend. Diane, don't let life pass you by. Go have some fun. Take some time for yourself. What about going away with Mickey for a while? He certainly knows how to play hard and have fun."

Diane smirked unnaturally, and shook her head back and forth with great exaggeration as she responded, "Rajeev, you've been pushing me in front of the Mickey-mobile for two years or more. Now back off!"

"Hey, he's a nice, good looking, smart guy...and rich."

"He thinks about Mickey."

"He is in a rut, just like you are. You need each other. I can see it in his eyes and yours when the two of you are together."

"He hasn't called me in months."

"When did you last phone him?"

"Rajeev, I'm not a desperate woman...Jesus!"

"No, you are anything but desperate." Tears began to well up in Rajeev's eyes. "Don't get that way. Do this for yourself. I promise your career will be waiting for you."

The two stared into each other's eyes, then Diane stood up and walked around her desk to where Rajeev sat. Once he stood up, they hugged each other and cried.

Chapter 3

Mickey paced his breathing with his running stride as he finished the last mile of his morning run along the winding roads in the hills above the Banana Belt near his Sausalito home. After rounding the last turn, he came up behind his neighbor, Mrs. Grady, and her two golden retrievers just like he did nearly every morning he went running.

"Beautiful day today, isn't it Beth?" Mickey asked, conscious of letting unsuspecting walkers know he was passing them.

"Beau, Gracie! Don't jump on Mr. Rollins!" Beth shouted as her dogs lunged toward Mickey, wagging their tales frantically.

He reached down to pat their heads as he breezed past.

Pulling back on their leashes, Beth managed to reply, "Like always, Mickey. Are you doing okay?"

"Dandy, Beth. Just dandy."

The headwind blowing in from the bay was cool and humid, making Mickey work harder as he ran the final quarter mile against it. He tried hard to ignore the nagging pain in his knees, refusing to acknowledge his fiftieth birthday looming in the not too distant future, and the possibility that he was feeling some wear and tear in his otherwise extremely well-tuned body.

His residence could not be seen from the street because its three levels clung to the descending hillside. Once he turned into the driveway of his Mediterranean-style home of twenty years, a steep drop followed by a turn to the left led him out of sight. The home was considered modest by contemporary California standards, but the three bedrooms and study, gourmet kitchen, exercise room, three bathrooms, multiple living areas, pool, and four-car garage more than met Mickey's needs.

Boundaries

Actually, the assessed value of Mickey's circa-1980s home was over six million dollars. Three successful company start-ups, stock options, and wise—occasionally lucky—investments, put the good-looking bachelor on the list of the wealthiest individuals in America. Although his marital status always begged the question of his sexual orientation, these rumors never bothered Mickey, and he referred to those making all of the buzz as simply ignorant people having too much idle time on their hands—something that Mickey had never experienced. Since finishing his doctorate in electrical engineering from the University of Illinois, he filled any spare time he had studying his obsessions—medicine and nanotechnology. He never bothered to offer information about his short-lived marriage to his high school sweetheart during his college years. That tidbit could be construed in several ways, so he consciously decided to keep his personal life a mystery, knowing it would antagonize the busybodies.

Mickey's father had also wanted to become a physician, However, his life took several unexpected and fortuitous turns, and he ended up both a consulting geologist in the oil business and successful entrepreneur who raised and sold organic beef. Speculative acquisition of once-dying West Texas oil leases had turned "Dub" Rollins into a multi-millionaire in his own right. But, Mickey shunned the oil business calling it "old technology" and followed his own passion.

Mickey entered his house through the side door of the garage where he kept his Toyota FJ Cruiser, an Aston Martin DB9 Coupe with vanity plates OHOH8, his late father's mint condition 1961 classic E-type Jaguar, and his "beater" car—the hybrid Prius that he seldom used. Standing to the side of his cars were several racing bicycles, one mountain bike, and a vintage Norton motorcycle. Hanging on the wall of the garage were several mangled bicycle frames, or as he called them, 'remnants of his pursuit of a faster life.' One thing stood out—his garage was well organized and exceptionally clean from corner to corner.

The same tidy conditions continued as he entered his house. Mickey was not a messy person, but his housekeeper for the last 12 years, Maria Ochoa, was a voracious cleaner. In addition to cleaning his home and cooking for him, she kept up his award-winning flower gardens, and scheduled his appointments. She now was the closest thing he considered family, and she felt the same about him. In fact, she lived with Mickey in her own room on the lower pool level. Despite appearances, their relationship was outwardly platonic, but inwardly was very deep.

Maria greeted her employer and friend with her Hispanic accent as he walked downstairs from the garage.

"Don't you go drippin' sweat on my floor, Mickey Rollins!"

"I'll drip where I want to," he replied, guzzling a sports drink he grabbed from the refrigerator. After picking up a banana from a bowl in the kitchen, he continued, "In fact, I think I'll go park my sweaty ass on a chair and read email."

"You do that, and I'll be glad to get you the leather cleaner so you can do the clean-up after yourself."

Sparring was sport to Mickey and Maria. It kept life from being dull.

"Do you want your coffee now or after your shower?" She asked.

"Now, please, and thank you. I saw a message from Constantine in my email index earlier that I'm eager to read."

"Is this the 'big one?'" Maria quipped.

"Yep. Gonna buy you that 'charp Chevy' you always wanted," he replied, playfully mocking her accent.

Mickey referred to every new idea, and each answer to a proposal as 'the big one.' There were two or three every year. Buying Maria a car was the standing joke in the daily conversation since he could have easily bought her anything she wanted. As it was, she had the key to the Prius. But Maria nearly always walked the hilly mile to the local store for what they needed. It kept her looking and feeling young and trim, and she enjoyed the fresh air. Besides, Mickey was generous with other compensation in that he was already footing the college tuition for Maria's two children.

With the banana in hand, he grabbed a towel from the hallway pantry, wiped the sweat from his face, and headed to his study where he spent much of his time each day. Pushing the power button on a CD player, his inspiration was soon playing—*Lady Madonna* by the Beatles. His office walls were adorned with dozens of photos, along with his many diplomas, awards, letters, and certificates. There were shelves filled with trophies from rugby tournaments, bicycle races, marathons, and iron man competitions. Notably, his most recent trophy showing Mickey achieving an athletic victory was dated four years ago. That was because his research in recent years had completely consumed him, relegating references to competitive sports to the past tense. He now relied on running and his free-weights for all of his exercise.

"You play that song morning, noon, and night," Maria protested. "Play something else. Here's your espresso," Maria said, carrying the drink over to Mickey and carefully setting it on his desk. The demitasse cup and saucer with the periwinkle pattern had been part of a setting Dub had passed on to him from his grandmother's collection.

"Maria, you simply have no appreciation for good music," Mickey said as he tipped up the cup of dark, steaming liquid with the froth on top and took a big sip. He winced in exquisite pain. "Ah, the drink of the Gods."

"Don't talk blasphemy around me, Mr. Rollins," Maria said, putting her hands on her hips.

"Yes ma'am, Ms. Ochoa," Mickey replied, holding up his free hand.

Maria put the palm of her hand up to Mickey's, touching his for just a moment, then turned and left the room, grinning in delight from the exchange. He walked through his bedroom to the adjoining patio office that overlooked the bay, where he sat down at his desk, and began to quickly scan half a dozen or so emails before he got to the one from Constantine. He took a deep breath, let it out, burped banana, then opened the attachment, mumbling as he read.

"Dear Dr. Rollins, blah, blah, blah...much discussion...yeah, I'll bet...conferred with the other partners....blah, blah, blah...interesting in concept...blah, blah, blah...get to the point, asshole...Doctors Mendoza and Mason as consultants...blah, blah, blah, blah, blah...we have decided not to fund the project at this time!"

Mickey stood up from his chair and tilted the screen of the laptop so he could see the rest of the text.

"Concerns over ethical issues and science too close to the fringe!"

He took a sip of his espresso, then another, then another. His face was turned red with anger. After carefully set the cup back in its saucer, Mickey suddenly slammed the laptop closed, breaking off a piece from the corner of the case. He then took the entire laptop and threw it out a window that overlooked the bay, shattering the windowpane into thousands of small pieces—the laptop landing with a splash in the swimming pool on the terrace below. Grabbing a baseball bat that he kept handy when he wanted something to fiddle while working, he began pounding and smashing everything in sight. His diplomas fell to the floor as he beat holes into the walls in his study; the trophies exploding on impact with the bat. As he swung wildly, he shouted expletives.

"Stupid, ignorant bastards! Chicken shit sons-o'-bitches can't make a decent decision if their lives depended on it! God damn stupid, ignorant bastards!"

Maria came running into the room just as Mickey checked his swing. She looked at the destruction, and then, after a few moments assessing the situation, leaned against the doorframe with her arms crossed.

"Coffee too strong today? No? Then let me guess, there was a large flying insect in the room?"

"They won't fund the project," Mickey said after pausing long enough to catch his breath.

Looking for words to defuse the outburst, Maria joked, "Does that mean I get the Jag instead of a new Chevy?"

Mickey exhaled and dropped the bat as he stood in front of the picture on the coffee table that had stopped his swing. It was a picture of him and his close—very close—friend Diane. The picture was taken at Yosemite during their last rendezvous six months ago.

"Mickey?" Maria spoke softly and caringly.

He didn't verbally respond, but managed to glance over toward her.

"Mick, it's time you took a break. You haven't had a day of rest since you and Diane last got together."

Mickey nodded more or less in agreement.

Boundaries

Kicking at some of the broken items on the floor, Maria continued, "It's time you blew off some steam. Why, all you probably need to do is to get laid."

There was a long period of silence during which Maria walked over to Mickey's cup of espresso that had been miraculously spared, picked it up and took it to him. "Go away for a month or so. It'll take me that long to fix the damage."

"A vacation? You expect me to just drop everything and leave?"

Maria stood close to Mickey as she put her hand gently on his lightly whiskered face. Her touch supercharged the moment.

"Take a look around you. You don't react this way. This is not you. Where is that man with the iron will and discipline I went to work for all those years ago? Go find him and bring him home." Maria almost let her emotions run away as she spoke, before catching herself. "Can I trust you with a fresh cup of espresso?"

Mickey reached down and picked up his bat, causing Maria to become worried that he might start wailing away at the room again, or worse yet her. But, before she could say anything, he handed the bat to her.

"That would be good. Yes, another cup would be good. I'll be in the shower."

"I'll bring it to you." She waited for Mickey to turn and walk away, before leaving the room herself.

Mickey went to his bedroom to shed his running briefs and T-shirt, then sat to pull off is socks and shoes. Pausing for a moment to reflect on his academic and professional career, it only took that long for him to count his failures and rejections, as there had been so few. Slapping his thighs, he stood up and walked to the shower, closed the door, and turned on the hot water. The door was soon nearly opaque from steam. He added some cold water until the stream was a tolerable temperature, then he stepped under it, leaning forward with his hands on the shower wall as he let the water run over his head and body. Except for his breathing, he stood there motionless.

Maria knocked on the frame of the open door as she entered Mickey's space. She couldn't tell if he was in deep thought, or having what he referred to as a 'numb moment.'

"I have your espresso. It'll be over by the sink," She said, speaking in a soft voice. She looked at the fuzzy image of Mickey's naked body, obscured by the etched glass and fog. After all these years, Mickey no longer considered her presence in this situation an intrusion.

"Are you okay?"

"Dandy," he replied after a delay.

"Do you want to talk?" Maria asked, making one more attempt to show concern. She cared deeply about her employer and friend—more than he knew.

"Nope."

"Are you taking any calls today, or do you want me to take messages?"

"Nope."

Maria felt her heart sink. As she had done so often, she had thrown Mickey a lifeline, but he never even bothered to reach for it. Maria realized that the verbal exchange, as ineffectual as it was, was the best he was going to give her, so she turned and left the room.

It was twenty minutes, more or less, before Mickey became aware that he had been standing in the same position since the beginning of his shower. His hands tingled from being up against the shower wall for so long. He shut off the water, stepped out, and snatched the towel with *The Peninsula* embroidered on it—a souvenir from his travels. After briskly drying himself off, he grabbed his espresso, and returned to the study adjoining his bedroom where he plopped naked in an overstuffed, timeworn chair he affectionately called Momma. To avoid giving Maria an unintended show should she return, he dropped his towel strategically over his lap.

He sipped his espresso, taking the time to look around the room at the destruction he had caused. Maria was right. This was not how he handled disappointment. It was time to get away. Mickey took a few steps to his desk, picked up his mobile phone and returned to Momma. After scrolling through his directory, he dialed a number. The ring tone was distinctly not that of the States.

A sultry, female voice answered, "Good morning Mickey."

"Hey, sweet thing. I need to come see you."

Chapter 4

Diane loved to take walks along the beach near her Ocean Beach home that she and Bruce had purchased shortly after they married. Bruce grew up in Bakersfield, and later went to college at the University of California at Santa Cruz where he adopted his laid-back lifestyle…and met Diane. Diane's family farmed near Watsonville, and had a horse ranch in Gilroy that had been in the family for generations. Diane's older brother had been killed in an auto accident, and in spite of her father's encouragement to stay with the family in agriculture, Diane chose to pursue her own life saying she didn't want a job that gave her rough hands and where mud boots were the normal footwear. After she accepted a job in San Diego, she and Bruce realized they wanted to live in an environment like Santa Cruz—casual and free of so many of the headaches associated with contemporary towns. When she lost Bruce in a tragic accident, she continued to live in their two-bedroom home. The mailbox still said L'IL DABA on the side, which not only represented their initials, but also was the name they gave to their "l'il daba California."

Diane hadn't slept at all since the meeting with Rajeev and Susan. After sending off the corrected proposal to Harald as promised, she headed for home, stopping three times for coffee at different all night restaurants along the way. The career change Rajeev had proposed was not one she welcomed. Diane depended upon her job as a distraction from her otherwise empty life. She confided in her closest friends that God had played a trick on her and Bruce by allowing her to conceive a child, but not letting her carry the fetus beyond six weeks. After four pregnancies, each of which quickly ended in miscarriage, she and Bruce gave up trying. Eventually they even decided not to adopt as both of their careers were starting to hit full stride.

The brutal fact of the matter was simple—the pursuit of her career probably spared Diane's life. One fateful weekend, she chose to stay in San Diego for a meeting instead of going camping in the mountains with Bruce. He was killed on the way to the campground when his motorcycle struck another vehicle—a fate that likely would have been Diane's as well had she accompanied him. She continually fought off feelings that she betrayed her husband by not being with him at that fateful moment.

Shortly after Bruce's death, her father invited his *Gilroy Girl,* or Gigi, as he affectionately called her, to live back on the farm. Diane declined the offer citing her career ambitions. In truth, when she learned her father had developed cancer, she didn't want to be close to another death when that inevitable event occurred. Her mother sold the Watsonville farm and Gilroy ranch, and died two years later…of loneliness. Diane's job kept her two steps ahead of all of the ghosts and fears of a similar fate, or at least she had herself fooled into believing that was the case.

The chilly, morning breeze gusting off of the ocean blew Diane's hair to one side. The spray dampened her rolled up khaki pants and her yellow sweatshirt, and her feet were slightly blue from the cold ocean water. She had walked back and forth along the beach for about an hour when her cell phone rang. Hoping it was Rajeev calling to tell her to come with him to Munich after all, and that he had reconsidered the job change, she quickly glanced at the caller ID. It was Mickey. She took a deep breath before answering.

"Hey, Mickey, long time, no hear. How are things in Sausalito?"

"Morning, beautiful. Things are okay here…okay."

Diane immediately realized that Mickey lacked his usual enthusiasm. 'Okay' to him is 'end of the world' for most people. He was constantly optimistic, and always bouncing off of the walls. She boldly brought up a subject he always liked to talk about—his latest project.

"Still working on the greatest invention ever?" she asked, reasonably certain she knew what his response would be.

"No, that was last month. I'm onto something better now."

"So tell me about it," she said, grinning to herself at his all too expected response.

"Actually, I'd like to do just that...face-to-face. What are you doing tonight?"

Diane stopped in her tracks, unable to walk and, at the same time, cope with the emotions racing through her mind. Whenever she did anything with Mickey, her thoughts became cluttered with all of the what-ifs that came along with knowing him.

Her mouth betrayed her, "I'm free," she replied, grimacing as she rolled her eyes, and disappointed at her gut response.

"I can be there around four o'clock."

Diane cringed, but continued, "You driving? I know you could do it in your Aston."

"Yeah! That would be a real trip! Actually, I have lots of unused charter hours, so I'm going to fly down."

"Sounds good." Diane hated to ask the next question. "Are you spending the night?"

There was a pause before Mickey replied, "You want me to?"

Jesus, if he could just answer the question instead of me choose, she thought. Diane's eyes sparkled as she replied, "Don't make a hotel reservation." That was the perfect answer. That left *him* hanging. He'd either be heading back on the plane, or spending the night with her, and *he* would have to make the decision later.

"Dinner at Dick's alright?" he asked, referring to Dick's Last Resort—a restaurant where they went the night they first met.

"That'll be fine."

"Good, I'll call you when the aircraft is thirty minutes out."

"See you then. Bye"

"Later."

Diane hung up, then hung her head, allowing her hands to fall to her side. After not seeing each other for months, Mickey failed to take the time to ask how she was doing or if she needed anything. What's more, every time they got together, it was a foregone conclusion that they would end up in bed. There was a definite chemistry between the two of them, and she often mused about the dichotomy that Mickey would be the *perfect* man for her if it weren't for all of his *imperfections*. Nonetheless, the good in Mickey still far outweighed the bad by most measures, otherwise she would have ended their relationship a long time ago.

It was so odd that just hours ago, Rajeev suggested she should give Mickey a call—then he up and called her. Diane shivered, but wasn't sure if it was due to the chill in the air, or the twist of fate.

DIANE FOUND HERSELF HURRYING back to her house where she nervously tidied up the 1500 square-foot bungalow, even though it was every bit as clean as Mickey's house. Her office at Medico resembled the aftermath of a small typhoon, but Bruce had liked tidiness, and she carried on his legacy. She opened up the refrigerator to see what it contained. She was anything but surprised to find old deli sandwiches, old Chinese carryout, old yogurt, old apples, old everything. She emptied the contents into a bag, took it outside to the trashcan, then headed out to a nearby eclectic variety market. Since she and Mickey were eating out tonight, she limited her purchase to some 'round food' that they both enjoyed—a small round of Brie, round crackers, a round loaf of bread, caviar in a round jar, champagne for the evening, and eggs and donuts for breakfast.

Rosario, the owner of the market, was a long-time friend of Diane's who knew about her relationship with Mickey. She usually took time to chat with all of her customers—they were all more than customers to her. But she paid more attention to Diane than the others because she knew of the inner pain Diane felt as a result of Bruce's horrible death and her restlessness over the frenetic relationship with Mickey.

There was another attraction. Diane was drop-dead beautiful and Rosy was a lesbian. Rosy stayed with Diane and her parents when Bruce died, offering them comfort and support. When Diane's father died, she and her mother cried on Rosy's shoulders. When Diane's mother died, Diane again was not alone. Rosy was a compassionate and caring friend, and at one point a little more. After her mother's death, Diane lived with Rosy for two weeks. It was at the same time, however, that Diane encountered Mickey at a conference. That's when she realized her heterosexual drive was greater than her feelings for Rosy, and she moved home to L'IL DABA. Her relationship with Rosy was one secret that Diane intended to keep from Mickey.

When Rosy placed the sack of custard-filled, chocolate-covered breakfast donuts in the grocery sack along with the 'round food,' she smiled at Diane and said, "So Mickey is coming to town? It looks like you won't be alone tonight."

It was at that moment that it occurred to Diane she had just answered the question about the overnight arrangements.

After dropping off the groceries at the house, she headed to Robin's Place to get her shoulder length hair shampooed and trimmed. She didn't have an appointment, but Robin somehow always worked Diane into her schedule, because she and her husband had been close friends with Diane and Bruce by way of the local Harley-Davidson club. It was like that in Ocean Beach.

Once home again, Diane dusted the hardwood floors and every flat surface in sight. She then showered, and slipped into her jeans and muslin blouse. After putting on the finishing touches in front of a mirror, she found herself pacing anxiously around the house. She fiddled with the magazines on the tables, the candlesticks, the draperies, the books, and the bowls of faux fruit. To calm her nerves, she selected and sampled the right mood music for the CD player, but subsequently changed it twice. Mercifully, her angst was cut short when Mickey called an hour and a half earlier than expected.

Chapter 5

The Gulfstream 550 pulled to a stop and shut down its screaming engines. Its door dropped down, and a gorgeous, smiling, blonde flight attendant waved as three passengers deplaned, followed by Mickey. He looked trim and GQ-cover handsome in his plain white, untucked polo shirt, blue jeans and sandals, and sporting a few days growth of whiskers—very unassuming considering who he was. Diane met him inside the fixed base operations terminal where the two friends and frequent lovers embraced and held each other for a long time. Mickey inhaled traces of Diane's Ungaro perfume at the same time Diane inhaled Mickey's faint cologne. They took their time. It had been too long. They pushed back slightly before gazing into each other's eyes and sharing a passionate kiss.

If any ice needed to be melted, it vanished entirely when Mickey asked, "How are you, Diane?"

Those were the simplest and sweetest words Mickey could have asked, and the most unexpected. Diane gradually leaned into Mickey's arms as all anxiety about his arrival immediately vanished. Tonight's arrangements were now definitely settled.

"I'm doing great, Mick," Diane replied, a huge smile lighting up her face. "I'm doing really great right now." They kissed again.

She led him by the hand to her convertible Porsche Boxter S. Mickey tossed his backpack behind the passenger seat, hopped in, and the two sped out of the airport. Diane zipped onto I-5, then exited Carmel Valley Road, and drove to their favorite local haunt—Torrey Pines State Beach. Diane's red coupe squealed to a halt in the beach's parking lot. In short order, Mickey grabbed his backpack, took Diane by the hand, and proceeded to the trail where they had often strolled. After several minutes of chitchat, the conversation began in earnest.

"So how are things at Medico?" Mickey asked as they walked hand-in-hand up the trail.

"Rajeev wants a change," Diane replied, looking down at her feet as she spoke.

"Where's he going?"

"No. Not for him. It's for me."

Diane sensed Mickey might actually be interested and turned to face him.

"What kind of change is he talking about?" Mickey asked, putting his arm around her shoulder.

Before Diane could answer, her phone rang.

"Hang on to that thought, Mick."

She answered the phone and carried on her conversation with the caller as she and Mickey continued walking.

"Hello, this is Diane. Eric! What's going on? Uh huh…uh huh… Call Seattle. They told me they'd have it to you next week. If they're telling you something different, I'll handle it. Okay? You, too. Bye."

After putting her phone back into her rear pants pocket, Diane picked up the conversation where they had left off.

"Sorry, where was I?"

"Rajeev has a change for you."

"Oh, yeah. He's created a position for me to look for new businesses."

"Is it a good job?"

"Well, I like my current job…or I guess I should say my former job since Rajeev made the change effective this morning at three o'clock."

"It doesn't sound like he wants a change. It sounds like he made a change. Why at such a bizarre time?"

"I was at the office making the deal of the century…oh, you gotta hear this…I'm talking about a billion dollars, Rajeev thinks as much as two, plus three years sole source…"

"Sounds super—why three o'clock in the morning?"

Diane smiled as though she was holding onto a secret, and answered mischievously, "I'm getting there. I had been on the phone with Munich since eleven last night and…"

The ringing of Diane's phone interrupted her again.

"Just a minute Mick, let me get this. Hello, this is Diane. Ajit!" She covered the phone's microphone with the palm of her hand. "It's our Chief Corporate Counsel."

Mickey motioned for her to continue.

"Where are you? Where are you going? You gonna meet Rajeev in Munich? No. I'm not going. Talk to Rajeev. He's made a change. Just call him, Okay? You take care. I'll see you in Seattle in two weeks. Bye. You, too."

"Where was I?" Diane asked, again putting her phone back into her pocket. The imprint of it matched the worn outline left on her jeans.

Holding out his arms in frustration, Mickey replied, "You were telling me about your meeting with Rajeev."

"Right. So, I just landed the biggest deal in Medico's history. It's gonna bring incredible in revenue each year with an option after 3 years to…"

"Diane, what's the job, and why was he meeting with you at three o'clock in the freakin' morning?"

"I'm getting there!" She replied, now exasperated herself. "So, it's three o'clock in the morning, and I had just finished going over the details of the contract with the customer in Munich, when Rajeev walked in with the VP of Human Resources—a real bitch, I can't stand her—and Rajeev said he had a new job for me so I asked, 'What's the job?' and he said…"

Once more, Diane's phone rang.

"I'm sorry Mick, I had my phone off all morning and…"

Stopping in his tracks, Mickey said, "Now I'm here, so you turned it on?"

Diane looked momentarily puzzled.

"Hang on Mick."

With the phone to her ear once again, she said, "Hello this is Diane. Hey, Eric, what did they say? That's bullshit!" Diane shouted, gesturing angrily with her free hand. "I'll call them and get back to you. Right. Give me fifteen minutes. Right. I'll call you back. Bye."

"Mick, I'm sorry but I have to deal with this right now and…"

Mickey took the phone out of Diane's hand, turned, and hurled it out of sight into the woods. Diane watched with horror as her phone—her lifeline—disappeared with a crackle in the brush.

"What the Hell!" Diane shouted.

Now facing Diane and blocking the trail, Mickey replied, "Tell me about your meeting with Rajeev."

"Damn it, Mickey! You just tossed my phone! Go get it!"

"I'm more interested in what Rajeev had to say!"

"He said I'm working myself to death, alright?! Now go get my phone!"

Mickey looked at Diane, but didn't move. She put her hands on her hips and stared back at him.

"So, are you gonna get it for me, or do I have to climb down the freakin' hill to get it myself?!"

A couple of college-aged men walked by at that moment. One of them boldly asked, "Are you alright ma'am?"

"Piss off!" Mickey shouted, looking squarely at both of them.

The two scurried away, adequately threatened by Mickey's response.

Putting put his hands on Diane's shoulders, Mickey asked, "Babe, do you see anything wrong with this picture?"

Diane's eyes glazed over. It was déjà vu. Those were the same words that Rajeev said some fifteen hours earlier. She started to get upset and pulled away from Mickey.

"It's my job Mick! It's my life! He has no business fucking with me like this! I'm pissed off, the warehouse screwed up a delivery, and now you go and toss my phone into the woods! I've had it! It's one stupid problem after another."

"Diane!" Mickey began, pointing his finger at Diane as he spoke—something he knew that she couldn't stand.

She slapped his hand away, but he redirected it back at her anyway.

"Let me tell you what the problem is. The problem is the illusion that you have a life."

"Is this gang-up-on-Diane-day or something?" Diane shouted. "I think I would have seen that on my calendar!"

"I'm sure you would have. Probably between planning for today at midnight last night, and making your deal-of-a-century at three in the morning!"

There were a few moments of silence. Another couple walked quickly past them hoping to not get caught up in the fray. Diane finally put her arms around Mickey and buried her face on his shoulder.

"I can't change cold turkey like this, Mickey."

"Sure you can," Mickey said, warmly returning the embrace. "I'll help you."

"Mickey, you don't understand," Diane said, firmly closing her eyes in an attempt to stop the tears.

He held her tightly and kissed the top of her head as he said, "Let's go get your phone."

Diane leaned back and saw a look of sincerity looking at back her— something she needed badly. She moved close and kissed him on the lips. Mickey pulled out a handkerchief and gave it to her so she could wipe her eyes and nose.

AFTER THE TWO SEARCHED for about ten minutes, they found Diane's phone, ringing yet again, and showing five missed calls. They walked back down the hill to the trail, continuing until they found a picnic table. That's where Mickey pulled out a bottle of Merlot, a corkscrew, and two glasses from his backpack. Diane spent forty-five minutes taking care of business as they sipped the wine. He jotted down some notes for her on the paper sack that had contained the wine bottle, consulted with her, and helped her with dates and so forth. Eventually, the business was done and she hung up her phone for the last time.

"Now turn it off," Mickey said.

Staring at her phone, Diane took a deep breath, then asked, "Do you know CPR?"

"Come on...turn it off," Mickey said laughing.

Boundaries

Diane pushed a button on her phone, slid her finger across its screen, then it went dark.

"That's what Rajeev wants me to do."

"What's that?"

"He wants to shut me off," she replied, staring at the phone as if it was alive.

"Just for a while. You'll feel better," Mickey said touching her hand.

"What am I supposed to do?"

This was the invitation to segue that Mickey had been waiting for.

"Come with me. I'm going on a trip."

"Where are you going?"

"Oh, Southeast Asia, the Indian Ocean, Europe."

"Is this another one of your crazy vacations?"

"Therapy…hopefully for two."

"For how long?"

"Couple of weeks, maybe a month, maybe a few months. Whatever it takes."

With each question, Diane knew she was closer to getting on an airplane with Mickey. *Why can't I just say no?* she wondered.

"When are you leaving?"

"Tomorrow night."

Diane leaned back with her eyes wide open, and said, "I can't just up and leave like that!"

"Why not?"

She turned her head to look down the trail and rubbed her hands nervously on her thighs as she fought for an easy answer, but the truth prevailed.

"Mickey, we're good together for a day…even for a couple of days. I'm not sure we can be good for each other over a long period of time."

Mickey leaned over the table and took Diane's hands again.

"I think it's time you and I took our relationship to a new level. I know what you mean about the short times being good times." Holding her hands tightly, he continued, "I need more of you than a day or two. I think we are both in need of something more. I'd like to give it a try. What about you?"

"It'll cost us a fortune to leave tomorrow," Diane replied, trying to be practical.

"Diane, neither of us has to worry about money," Mickey said, shrugging his shoulders indifferently.

Diane bit her lip and avoided eye contact with Mickey. Quite honestly, she was afraid to go. More than that, she was afraid to get too close to Mickey, so she weaseled out of an immediate commitment with, "Can I let you know in the morning?"

Mickey smiled as he replied, "Absolutely."

He kissed his fingers then put them on Diane's lips. She returned his smile.

"Do you know what time it is?" He asked with a frisky tone of voice.

Diane's face lit up as she replied, "Does it start with a D?"

"Yup."

"Race you to the car."

THE WINE WAS QUICKLY re-corked and stored along with the glasses, then Mickey and Diane proceeded quickly to her car. He started off in the lead before she managed to trip him up and get in front. There were numerous Roller Derby hits along the way, but when they got to the car, both claimed victory. They hopped in and took off north toward Del Mar. An hour later they stood in line at a kiosk that sold Dippin' Dots. Since they first met, Dippin' Dots had become a tradition, as well as a symbol of their relationship—cold at first, but soon melting in one's mouth. Diane loved the sensation as they melted. Mickey had more of a scientific affinity for them.

They got their servings—Diane's a chocolate and Mickey's a vanilla—and soon strolled barefoot along Del Mar Beach, reminiscing about the times they have spent together. Mickey assured Diane she was making a smart decision to take some time off, and also assured her that Rajeev had only her best interests in mind as motives for his action. After a while, they sat on the sand facing each other with their legs intertwined.

Realizing he had helped her through a crisis, it was now her turn to meddle.

Boundaries

"So, Mick, tell me about your latest idea."

He grinned and pointed his spoon down toward the cup of vanilla Dippin' Dots in his hand as he answered, "You are going to find this hard to believe, but these little round sons-o'-bitches are what gave me my brainstorm."

"No, really?"

"Think about it. Spheres have no corners, therefore they have the best chance of fitting through small spaces."

"Okay. I follow you so far," Diane said as she wiggled on her butt cheeks to move closer to Mickey.

"So instead of ice cream, let's imagine dots made of elastomeric polymer."

"That's organic, right?"

"Correct."

"Okay. I'm still with you."

"Now, let's imagine these dots can be cryogenically reduced in size so that not only are they smaller than a red blood cell, they are sterile and otherwise bio-neutral."

"Yep. I'm good."

"Now, suppose these dots can be made into machines that can deliver information to and retrieve information from the brain."

Diane's eyebrows went up as she said, "Kind of Orwellian, don't you think?"

Following her response, Mickey lost his smile, as well as his enthusiasm. Looking down at the sand, he replied, "In as many words, that's what the venture capital guys told me this morning."

"I'm sorry," Diane said, touching Mickey's face to reassure him. "I didn't mean to sound so negative."

"I know. The whole thing sounds pretty far-fetched. But, it can work. I just need more time for testing."

Diane looked out at the ocean, then back at Mickey. Figuring it was a good time to change the subject, she leaned over and kissed him, then said with an inviting voice, "I know one thing you can deliver, and no testing is necessary."

"You just want me for my body. You never acknowledge that there might be a brain above these shoulders."

The levity in the response from Mickey was just what she had hoped for.

"Body now, brain later," Diane said with a nod then a kiss.

"Do you think Dippin' Dots are an aphrodisiac?" Mickey asked with a grin.

"Definitely. Now quit wasting time." Diane smiled ear to ear and licked her lips.

THEY MADE THE TRIP back to Diane's house in less than thirty minutes. She brought out her treats—caviar, Brie, bread and crackers—while Mickey poured the champagne. They sat on the back porch, feeding each other. Drinking was the hard part. They each had a difficult time putting their champagne glass to the other's lips and drinking without spillage. The challenge got more extreme as the number of glasses increased. When the giggling started, they spilled more than they consumed. Having downed one bottle, they opened another, drank most of it, and took what remained with them to the bedroom.

The two didn't immediately strip their clothing off. Instead, they made removing their clothes a well-choreographed slow dance. It had become one of their biggest turn-ons. Neither removed their own clothing. That was the pleasurable task for the other. Undressing took over twenty minutes and it was not a frenzied, unfeeling act. Mickey made sure he touched and kissed most of Diane's body as he removed her clothes, dropping them neatly into a pile on the floor. Diane did the same. They took their time looking at each other's bodies. The pride they took in staying healthy and fit rewarded them in times like these.

Mickey lay down first on his back. Without wasting any time, Diane spooned up next to him and draped her leg over his. She propped her head up on her hand, and began to play with the hair on his chest. He savored the moment.

"It's been a long time…too long. I forgot how beautiful you are," he said, pulling her head down to his for a kiss. Soon, Mickey began to show his arousal.

Boundaries

Despite the intimacy of the moment, Diane found it hard not to think about what Mickey had told her about his new project, and asked, "So, what kind of information do you transfer with these dots?"

"Now that's discouraging. I put my naked body in front of you, and you want to discuss organic chemistry."

Diane playfully punched Mickey in the ribs, as she pried on, "No...come on...I'm curious. Tell me why you're inventing this stuff. We'll call this foreplay."

Mickey smiled. His eyes were glazed and his speech was slightly slurred from the champagne.

"Alright, have it your way. Have you ever had fleeting thoughts or dreams that you wished you could remember, but couldn't?"

"Sure. Everyone has them."

"Well, I thought, wouldn't it be fantastic to capture these thoughts, and record them for playback on some type of media? Kind of like harvesting."

"Harvesting dreams?"

"Yeah. Harvesting dreams. It's become somewhat of an obsession for me. Many nights I find myself sleeping like Renaissance Men reportedly did hundreds of years ago—I sleep a while, wake up and take note of what I dreamed about while it's still fresh, then go back to sleep. Well, it turns out that harvesting is harder to do than I thought. That's when I discovered doing the reverse is relatively easy."

"What do you mean?"

"It's easier to plant thoughts in a person than to retrieve them."

"Okay. So, why would anyone want to do that?"

"For one thing, to help people with memory loss. Let's say someone has Alzheimer's disease. Medical science is looking for ways to stop the degenerative processes, but what then? Suppose the patient has a restored brain, free of disease, but it's been emptied of some or many memories. Let's say someone sustains a traumatic brain injury or has a stroke. This can result in not only memory deficit, but partial or complete loss of sensory and/or motor function. How can we restore some or all of these memories and functions within the remaining healthy part of the brain?"

"You can do this?" Diane asked, excitedly.

"Well, on a small scale. We've only tried it on a very limited basis."

Her business mind now functioning at full speed ahead, Diane asked, "Like, how limited?"

"You'll notice I'm flaccid now," Mickey said with a chuckle.

"That's okay. I'm talking to the predominant head right now—at least I hope that's the case. I'll get back to the other one in a minute. Now, tell me about your experiment."

"Well, there was this old guy in Manila—he was 97 years old. He was still speaking and had some idea of his surroundings, but for the most part he was no longer himself. Case in point, he couldn't tell us his birthday."

"So?"

"So we gave him a birthday."

"You did what?"

"We performed an anecdotal thought transfer."

"A what?"

"We planted a thought in his mind. After the procedure, we asked him his birthday and he told us—March 7, 1970—the date we gave him."

"I thought you said he was 97."

"True, he was. We gave him a nonsensical date to validate the test, and I chose that date."

"Isn't that, I don't know, unethical? I mean the guy now has the wrong birthday."

"God damn! It's a birthday!" Mickey responded, frustrated by Diane's reaction. "The guy's ancient and will die soon. What's the harm here? We proved that we could transfer a thought."

Diane waited for it all to sink in before saying, "I have to be honest, Mickey, the hair on my arms is standing straight up right now."

"No kidding. I have to pinch myself to be convinced I'm not dreaming each time I think about the possibilities."

"How long have you been working on this?" Diane asked, stroking the hair on Mickey's chest again.

"Started about five years ago and got real serious over the last two years."

"And you're just now telling me this?" Diane shouted as she tugged on some chest hair.

"Ouch! It was all fantasy until a few weeks ago when we did this test in Manila."

Brushing her hair out of her face, Diane asked, "What happened to turn the corner?"

"I spent a week with this old Asian doctor named Wu—the grandfather of a close friend. He knows more about the mind than anybody I know."

"What does he know that makes him so great?"

"You'll have to give me your body to get the answer," Mickey said with a mischievous grin.

"You'll answer my question if you want this body," Diane said, maintaining her advantage.

Mickey turned toward her and started to roll on top of her, but she pushed him back.

"I mean it. Talk!"

"You're freakin' Gestapo tonight," Mickey protested. "Okay, I had spent years trying to deliver a memory or function to a specific part of the brain. Wu told me that the mind has its own order."

"Lost me," Diane said, shaking her head back and forth. "You'll have to do better."

"Okay, dumbass, here's an example. Let's say we have a conversation about the first time we had dinner at Dick's." Mickey stopped abruptly. "Wait a minute. We were supposed to have dinner there, weren't we?"

"Now who's the dumbass?" Diane teased. "That's alright. This was better anyway."

"What beer did I drink at Dick's?" Mickey continued.

Diane looked across the room and shrugged her shoulders. "Shit, Mickey, I have no clue. Are you avoiding the answer?"

"No, I'm getting there. It was Grolsch."

"Okay. Now I remember. How could I ever forget a name like that?"

"Well the point is, you had forgotten. So I just gave you a name, and you placed that memory back in your mind with all of its related associations of that evening. If I ask you tomorrow what beer I drank at Dick's on our first date, you will immediately recall Grolsch. Did I force the information into your mind?"

"Well, no."

"Did I tell you where to put the information?"

"No again."

"That was my epiphany," Mickey said, sitting up straight. "Don't force information. Deliver data to the brain, provide some chemical stimulation, and let the brain itself make sense of the information. This is what I define as anecdotal thought transfer."

"What kind of chemical stimulation are you talking about?" Diane asked, curiously.

"That's proprietary."

"So is my ass unless you answer me."

"I'm reconsidering my invitation right now."

"Answer my fucking question!"

"LSD!"

"You're using LSD!?"

"Just small amounts. We're still looking for a more natural, gentler and legal stimulant."

Diane paused for a moment before asking, "Let me ask you this. I have vivid memories and vague memories. How do you plan to make a distinction?"

"My interest in sex is now anecdotal. Do you have any Viagra?"

"Vivid! Vague! Distinction! I'm waiting!"

Boundaries

Mickey was amused by Diane's persistence. "You're good, but I'm ahead of you. This was a big problem at first. Imagine all of your thoughts being first order, maximum amplitude. Your brain would literally fry. Essentially every light and outlet in your house is drawing maximum current and the main circuit breaker trips."

"So what do you do?"

"I control a parameter called 'schwa.'"

"Isn't that something in a dictionary?" Diane asked, sitting up herself.

Flopping back down onto the bed, Mickey replied, "Exactly. Grammatically, it's an unpronounced, lightly accented syllable. Physiologically, by modulating the schwa, I can control the neural message amplitude." He chuckled and added, "Just think, I'm solving some of the world's greatest medical problems with tiny ice cream balls and a little, unknown vowel sound. And the coolest thing is it's all controlled with MADONNA."

"I hate Madonna," Diane responded while doing a double take. "She's wild and unpredictable. You can't control her."

"I love MADONNA. She's always testing boundaries. Besides, have you seen her lately? She's a pussycat."

Diane sat in stunned silence. Mickey managed to make this sound all too possible—scary to be certain, but all too possible.

"How much more work do you need to do?" Diane asked.

There was no response.

"Mickey?"

It was no use. He had succumbed to the champagne.

Diane quietly rolled off the bed, and covered Mickey with a hand-sewn quilt that her mother had made. Chills ran up and down her spine as she mulled over Mickey's ideas. After slipping on a robe, she walked to the adjoining living room to place a call.

The phone rang on the other end, and a tired voice answered.

"Yes?"

"Rajeev? It's Diane."

Rajeev cleared his throat.

"Diane?"

"You know that new technology you want? I have it. It's the latest project Mickey is working on. You had a fantastic idea having me get together with him. I may have to blow the guy to get to the bottom of his work, but I'm onto a leading-edge, revolutionary product you will not believe."

Showing absolutely no emotion or enthusiasm, Rajeev responded, "Diane, it's one o'clock."

"Oh! Do you want me to call back in the morning?"

"No. I want you to take time off like we talked about."

"I'm going with Mickey on vacation. I'll have all the details when I get back."

"Fabulous."

"Rajeev, you won't believe this product. This is the greatest breakthrough since…"

"Good night, Diane," Rajeev said, hanging up his phone.

Diane looked at the phone in disbelief before putting the receiver back on the cradle. She sat on the sofa with her legs pulled up, and her chin resting on her knees as she pondered the possibilities. Reaching into a box on the end table, she pulled out a cigarette and a lighter. With one click, she was puffing on the one unhealthy vice she rarely allowed herself when she was at the peak of excitement.

"That stuff's gonna kill you."

Diane jumped at Mickey's voice behind her.

"You scared the shit out of me!" Diane shouted, exhaling the smoke from her one and only drag.

"Put that out and come to bed. I still have to make that delivery you were wanting."

She didn't require a repeat invitation.

Chapter 6

The donuts had been good, the coffee great, and the sex outstanding. Sitting on the porch, one could hear the waves pounding the beach. The sound was so inviting that Diane insisted they go for a final walk before leaving.

The morning sun was low in the sky, and the wind felt like it was at gale force as it blew the spray off the tops of the waves. People of all ages—more young than old—whizzed along the walkway on roller blades and bicycles, while others walked or jogged. After a short walk, Mickey sat on a bench. Diane joined him.

"So, are you going with me tonight?" Mickey asked, hoping for a 'yes.'

Diane took Mickey's hand and replied, "Yup."

"I promise you this much, it will be a trip unlike any trip you've ever taken," he said, quite relieved.

"I'm really looking forward to it," she said eagerly.

Mickey looked down the beach, then out towards the water. It was apparent he was avoiding looking directly at Diane.

"Remember that Asian doctor I told you about?"

"The wise old man, Doctor Wu?"

"Yeah. That one." Mickey hesitated briefly. "He has a granddaughter who specializes in exotic travel and pampering those with extreme taste for fun, excitement, and luxury."

Diane's instincts began to make her feel a little uncomfortable with where this conversation was going.

"Did she help you plan the trip we are going on?"

"Well, in a manner of speaking." Following a pause, Mickey added, "She's going with us."

Diane looked at Mickey long enough to realize he was serious, then jumped up and started to quickly walk away.

"I knew this was too good to be true!"

"Diane, wait a minute," Mickey called out, running after her. "Let me explain."

She stopped and turned.

"There's nothing to explain! You're planning a ménage à trois, and you think I'm going to be part of it! Well, it ain't gonna happen!"

"Diane, this woman is a professional."

"Oh, I'll bet she is!"

"She's a professional concierge, just like at fine hotels. She plans, she prepares, she takes care of every detail, she takes care of every desire, and she gets me the most for my time and money."

"Have you slept with her?" Diane demanded.

Mickey hesitated for only a moment before blurting out his answer.

"Yes."

"Let me get this straight," Diane began, taking a step closer to Mickey. She crossed her arms and shifted her weight to one leg. "You expect me to go on a trip to the far corners of the planet, leave my home, and leave my job so you can spend time with some whore? Is that how little you appreciate me?"

Mickey put his hands on her shoulders in a desperate attempt to calm her. "Look. I've been honest with you, so please, hear me out. If you want the greatest adventure in the world, this lady can deliver it. I've been on several trips with her, and each time I come home feeling ten years younger and completely refreshed. I can think clearly again. It would have been easy for me to go by myself, but I didn't want to. I wanted to go with you...to share one of these experiences with you. I wouldn't do this for anyone else."

"*For* me? Don't you mean *to* me? Mickey, you listen to me and listen closely. I've put up with a lot of shit from you for three years, and I know you haven't been a saint during that time, but right now I'm really hurt. The fact that you're finding pleasure with another woman repulses me."

Boundaries

"It's not just about the sexual experience, Diane. It's much, much more. Give it a chance. This is the type of vacation you need right now. You'll forget about Medico entirely and find out things about yourself you never knew. You'll explore yourself physically and mentally, and you'll find out who I am, who you are, and why we should be together."

"I'm afraid to find out any more about you, Mickey."

"Diane…"

"Why couldn't we just go to Paris and climb the Eiffel Tower or something?" Diane asked as she threw her hands into the air. "Why do I have to go to such bizarre extremes to 'find out things about myself'?"

"Because you have to explore the limits of your body, mind, and spirit to really get the answers, Diane. Our very definition as man or woman doesn't come easily. One must reach beyond the boundaries for it."

Mickey pulled Diane close to him. Slowly, very slowly, Diane acquiesced and reluctantly put her head on his chest. Her gut was telling her to run away and to run away fast. At the same time, a keen business instinct kept telling her that she had to go with Mickey in order to get the scoop on his project, regardless of the personal cost.

"You know I'll leave the second I feel the least bit uncomfortable. You know I'll do that. You know I can," she told him, all the while trying to convince herself of the same.

Tightening his hold on Diane, he replied, "We'll leave together if you don't enjoy every moment. If this isn't the best vacation you've ever had, we'll bail…together. I promise."

Diane pushed back so she could gaze into Mickey's eyes, hoping to find some reason to make her say no. After a long look, and with great trepidation, Diane gave Mickey his answer.

"Alright. Let's do it. But I want to know everything there is to know about this woman."

"Okay, that's fair," Mickey responded. "Her name is Sukhon Jiao. She goes by Suki. Her father was Chinese and her mother was Thai."

"You're speaking about them in the past tense."

"True. They died when she was young. I don't know the details. Her grandfather, Dr. Wu, raised her and that's how I met her."

"And you had a chance encounter, or did you find her number in a personal ad?"

"Well, I guess you could call it a chance encounter. I was in Suzhou three years ago discussing my work with Dr. Wu when she happened to stop in for a visit. Our meeting was purely coincidental."

"How old is she?"

"Twenty-nine, give or take."

"She won't tell you?"

"No, it's nothing like that. I just never asked her specifically how old she was."

Diane froze as something Mickey said finally soaked in.

"Wait, you've been seeing her for three years? Who came first, me or her?"

"I met her just before I met you," Mickey replied, knowing his answer would hurt.

"And you've been seeing both of us ever since?" Diane exhaled as the glow in her face vanished.

"That's right."

Diane looked out to the water before asking, "So tell me Mickey, who's leading in this race for your affection?"

"Look, there is no race. She provides entertainment and company. She's not someone I want to settle down with."

"What do you mean by that?" Diane asked, startled by his choice of words.

Mickey looked at his feet and let out a short chuckle.

"I never thought I'd be saying this, but I'm dreading turning fifty, and I'm dreading growing…aging…by myself. I'm scared, and I don't want to be alone."

"I'll be damned. There's a real person inside of you."

"Hey, what did Bette Davis say? 'Getting old isn't for sissies'."

Boundaries

Diane had never seen Mickey exhibit any type of vulnerability, and she found his new trait both enlightening and, at the same time, startling.

"You know, you're kind of cute in a pathetic sort of way," she said.

"Gee. Thanks."

"You're welcome."

"Still love me?"

"Don't push your luck."

"I thought so."

After an extended silence, Diane put her hands on Mickey's cheeks before saying, "For your sixtieth, we're going to climb the Eiffel Tower."

"Dandy," he replied.

The two kissed and fell into each other's arms. As always, Mickey took both Diane's heart and breath away. She'd given up a long time ago trying to explain to herself his unbridled magnetism.

"When do we leave, Mickey?"

"Actually, I've booked two adjoining suites on Singapore Airlines leaving in about fourteen hours out of San Francisco."

"Suites?"

"Adjoining."

"As in First Class?"

"Better than First Class."

"You're not having some sort of mile-high club fantasy, are you?"

"No. That's frowned upon. Besides, we did that on the overnight to Munich last year."

"I know! My ass had a purple line on it for two weeks from that frickin' bathroom lavatory! Wait a minute, you mean you have tickets and you didn't even know if I was going?"

"Well, Babe, your actions have always been a foregone conclusion."

"How do we get to San Francisco?"

"I have a charter flight for us in six hours."

"I can't pack that quickly!"

"Pack light. We'll buy what you need when we get there."

"What about you? You arrived with a backpack!"

"I left two bags in a locker at SFO yesterday."

"Jesus, Mick!"

"Let's get back to your place and grab a few things. After all, this trip is all about spontaneity. That's the way I like to travel. You're still coming, aren't you?

Diane swallowed noticeably, then nodded

.

Chapter 7

After eight hours of engine drone, Diane and Mickey were well into their third bottle of Cuvée Dom Pérignon 1996 as they cruised somewhere over the northern region of the Pacific Ocean. Despite many hours of flying ahead of them, they remained totally immersed in one another. The flight had been remarkably free of any turbulence other than a few moments of jitter as the jumbo jet crossed over the same path previously traveled by another airliner many miles in front of theirs. By now, the other passengers had settled into their fully reclined seats for some shuteye. Only Diane and Mickey remained awake, shunning the selection of in-flight movies in favor of conversation.

Since departing, they had munched on shrimp cocktail and bread and cheese plates for starters, feasted on wonderful salmon with vegetable medley for dinner, and managed to have room for chocolate silk cheesecake for dessert. The food and liquor were non-stop for anyone who remained awake.

Mickey brought Diane up to date on Maria's children. Danielle was now a junior majoring in pre-law at UCLA, and Benito was a freshman in engineering at Cal Tech. Diane often fought off feelings of jealousy toward Maria, but found it comforting that Mickey was so forthcoming about their life together in Sausalito.

She was in many ways envious of Mickey's philanthropy and generosity—something she wanted to emulate, but never took the time to do. Mickey had endowed a chair and contributed to graduate research at his own alma mater, and furthermore, provided for a memorial scholarship at the University of Colorado in Boulder to honor his father, William "Dub" Rollins. Diane had planned to make named contributions to UC Santa Cruz in memory of Bruce, but just couldn't seem to get it done. In so many ways, Mickey had fulfilled a lot of dreams, while Diane had focused almost exclusively on her whirlwind career.

"I still can't believe what I'm doing, Mick. How did those ticket agents know you?"

"I'm a good customer."

"I'm going to pay you back, you know. Fifteen grand for a single roundtrip ticket is a bit over the top, don't you think?"

"You're not enjoying yourself?"

"Mickey, this is fabulous. This is beyond my wildest dreams. But it's ridiculous. Business Class is one thing, but Suites?"

"It's a new feature. This is my first time to fly in a Suite. You get to share the experience. Consider this an introduction to our lavish vacation the likes of which you'll never forget."

Just as the flight attendant topped off her glass with champagne, Diane introduced a new topic.

"The ranch is for sale."

"Your family ranch? The one in Gilroy?"

"Yes. The new owner couldn't figure out how to make money breeding and selling thoroughbreds. He tried to make it a hobby, but you just can't do that. It takes all of your time, and you really have to know and love horses."

"So, buy it."

"You make it sound so simple. Didn't you hear what I said? It's a job...a full time job. Between that place and the farm in Watsonville, Mom and Dad worked fourteen to eighteen hours a day. It would have been twenty-four hours if my brother and I hadn't been there. Plus, I already checked, and the guy is asking a fortune for it."

"So, buy the ranch and make it a full-time job. You don't need any more money from Medico. Let your investments work for you and give ranching a shot. You know how to do it."

"Yeah, but it's not a one person job."

Diane realized after the fact that what she had just said could be misconstrued as a baited line. Apparently, Mickey realized it, too.

Boundaries

"You can hire a good ranch manager to help you. There are a lot of good ones out there. I hired one to run Dad's ranch."

After his response, Diane realized Mickey might have just permanently written himself out of her fairy tale. At the same time, Diane dwelled on his words, lost in a would-o', should-o', could-o' moment that only Mickey can create, just as he had so many times before.

"I suppose you're right. But, it's just not the thing for me to do right now."

"So why did you bring it up?"

Diane fumbled, but answered, "I guess I had just run out of things to say and I've had too much to drink, therefore my mouth spilleth over."

"I suppose you wouldn't be able to handle it anyway," Mickey said, putting his arms behind his head and looked at the ceiling.

"What do you mean I wouldn't be able to handle it?"

"Ranching is dirty and hard work. That's not your style."

"I did it for years! I know exactly what it's all about. You're trying to use reverse psychology on me."

"Forgive me. Perhaps I chose my words poorly. The ranch would simply be too much responsibility for you."

Diane gripped her armrests in an effort to keep her voice down—and to keep from choking Mickey.

"My job is all about responsibility."

"No, your job is all about accounts. That has nothing to do with responsibility."

Diane was nearly beside herself. "Mickey, you sit around in your own little world, and you have the balls to tell me *my* job has nothing to do with responsibility?"

"Fine. Then buy the ranch."

"I don't want to buy the ranch!" Diane yelled, her voice carrying throughout most of the aft cabin. The flight attendant heard it and came over.

"Can I get something for you Miss Alders?"

"Do you have any Valium?" Mickey asked with a smile.

Digging her fingernails into Mickey's hand, Diane answered in a masterfully controlled tone, "No, I'm fine for now. Thank you."

The flight attendant returned to the galley.

Mickey put his free hand on top of Diane's and looked at her.

"I think you have dreams that aren't coming true and you're hungry."

"What?"

"I think you are thinking, *gee, I wish I'd done this, gee I wish I'd done that,* and something inside of you is keeping you from achieving the happiness you long for so badly."

"You're absolutely correct," Diane replied, pointing a finger at him. "That something inside of me is called sanity."

Shaking his head, Mickey said, "Sometimes a little in-sanity can be a good thing. Just think about it. Some years ago, this person from Gilroy, whom everyone thought was a complete whack-o, decided you could make garlic-flavored ice cream. Was that a bad thing?"

Diane stared at Mickey, marveling at his line of thinking.

"Do you realize how often your line of reasoning comes back to frozen desserts?"

"Hey, why make life complicated?"

"Because life *is* complicated, Mick."

"No, it's only one's perception that life is complicated. It's up to that individual to debunk that myth. Have you ever stared at yourself in the mirror, wondering if it was you who was looking at the reflection of yourself, or if it was the reflection of yourself looking at you?"

Assuming she would eventually have to answer his riddle, she reluctantly replied, "Obviously I'm looking at the reflection because it's inanimate."

"Wrong. Your answer should have been, 'Mickey, it really doesn't matter, does it?'" he said with a playful grin.

Diane, realizing she had walked into a trap, crumpled a napkin and tossed it in Mickey's face.

"You shit! You tricked me!"

"No, you just made life complicated," Mickey said, tossing it back.

Staring a hole through Mickey, she said, "Jesus, I'm going on vacation with Forrest Gump."

"Quite the sage, wasn't he?"

"I suppose you liked Peter Sellers in his movie, *Being There*."

"Absolutely! Life was about the perception of 'now.' It bore no connection to the reality of the past, nor what the future might hold."

"Okay smartass. So you mean to tell me that you haven't learned anything from your past, and don't care about your future?"

"I look at it this way. The past used to be now, someday the future will be now, and now is definitely now. Therefore life is about now."

"Is our entire vacation going to be like this?" Diane asked, throwing her arms into the air.

"Like what?"

"Complicated!"

The flight attendant came over once again to check on the commotion.

"Can I get something for you Miss Alders? Perhaps some chocolates?"

"Yes, I think she needs some chocolates," Mickey replied on Diane's behalf.

"Very good, I'll be right back with them."

The flight attendant dutifully went back to the galley.

Diane called out to the flight attendant in an effort to stop her, but it was too late. With a frustrated sigh, Diane turned back to Mickey to chastise him. But, before she could get a word out, he took a drink of champagne and held his glass up to Diane.

"I'm not making it complicated, you are."

"Wake me up when we get to Tokyo," Diane said after taking his glass from him, and chugging the remaining contents. She then pulled a blanket up to her neck and turned away from Mickey.

Mickey leaned over to Diane and put his mouth close to her ear, then whispered, "Buy the ranch. It will be a defining moment in your life that you won't regret."

"Goodnight, Mick," Diane said, closing her eyes.

Stroking Diane's cheek softly, Mickey said, "If we've just experienced a lover's quarrel, I guess that's a good thing because it means we're in love."

Diane opened her eyes, surprised at Mickey's choice of words.

"Goodnight, Mick."

The flight attendant returned with a platter.

"Miss Alders, I have your chocolates now."

Chapter 8

Precisely at noon, and a deceptive two calendar days after leaving Los Angeles, Diane and Mickey arrived at the resort that would be their home for the next…however long it was going to be. Diane felt and looked tired. She generally traveled eastward to Europe. On the other hand, Mickey was used to the long flights to Asia and showed fewer symptoms of jet lag. The concierge for their trip had hired a driver in a Mercedes S-class to pick the travelers up from the airport at Phuket, and also had pre-arranged for check-in, allowing the driver to deliver them directly to their private bungalow on the cliff side of the resort where they were to be staying.

As the driver brought the car to a stop and shut down its engine, a door opened and out stepped a petite Asian woman…an incredibly gorgeous, petite Asian woman. Diane had anticipated the concierge to be dressed in some type of traditional Thai clothing. Instead, she saw a woman who looked as if she shopped exclusively on rue du Faubourg Saint-Honoré in Paris. Her white silk blouse—top buttons left open to show plenty of cleavage—and pink mini-skirt probably had Italian tags. Her stiletto heels were without a doubt Prada. She stood waiting for Diane and Mickey to approach her. Once they were within a few feet of her, she gave her guests a customary wai, her hands held together at her chest. Diane froze, staring at her adversary's perfect complexion, perfectly straight, black hair, perfect figure, and perky chest topping a no more than one hundred and five pound frame.

Mickey put his arm around Diane, something she appreciated greatly at that moment, as he began with the introductions.

"Diane, this is Suki. Suki, meet Diane."

Somewhat reflexively, Diane put the palms of her hands together in front of her chest in order to return the gesture because she didn't know how to verbally respond.

"No need to do that, Miss Diane. The wai is a custom in my country, not in yours. I am very glad to meet you at last." Other than having a slight accent, Suki spoke impeccable *British* English, coupled with an Asian flavor.

"Well, Suki, I'm glad to at meet you, too. It appears you have the better of me. Mickey hasn't told me much of anything about you."

Dripping with politeness, Suki said, "We will have a lot of time to get to know each other better." Looking toward Mickey, Suki asked, "Why did you not tell her more about me? We have no secrets, do we?"

Diane and Mickey knew the secrets to which Suki was referring. His past encounters with Suki were the three hundred pound gorilla lurking in the shadows.

"No, Suki, there are no big secrets," Mickey said. Carefully choosing his words, he added, "Diane is aware that we have been...*close* on occasion."

Diane couldn't come up with anything to say at that point. How could any woman in her position?

"Good then," Suki said smiling. "We can be honest with each other. That's the key to relaxing. We should never keep anything from one another. I promise to be your honest servant, Diane. Tell me what you want, and you shall have it." Most provocatively, Suki finished with, "Anything...anything at all."

Deciding it was the time to mark her territory, Diane stated, "I have everything that I want or need. I have Mickey."

"I understand completely," Suki graciously responded, her smile displaying perfect teeth to match the rest of her. "What more could a woman want?"

The two women looked into each other's eyes, transmitting a subliminal and temporary cease-fire. Suki reached out, taking Diane's left hand and then Mickey's right.

"Let me show you the place. I am certain it will exceed your expectations by every measure."

Boundaries

As she escorted the two into their bungalow, Diane couldn't help but notice that Suki was at that moment solidly between her and Mickey. She hoped this wasn't a harbinger of things to come.

The entire resort was nearly new, having been rebuilt on the same spot where the tragic tsunami waters had destroyed the previous one. There were no discernible signs of the horrors that took place in that disaster. The grounds were replete with garden after fragrant garden, koi ponds, statues, and waterfalls. The trio entered through a very heavy and ornate teakwood door into a large open space. The floor plan, conforming to the natural shape of the outcropping of rock, was something like a bird with wings spread out in flight. There was a large open living area straight ahead. Beyond that was a large enclosed patio with rattan furniture and two massage tables. Skylights let filtered sunlight into that room. Off to the left were a large bedroom with a California King-sized bed, and a sitting area with a bar and several chairs. The bathroom had a large vanity with his and hers sinks and twelve feet of mirrored wall. A huge Jacuzzi, with a waterfall along one side, was in a screened-in alcove overlooking a garden. To the right was the gourmet kitchen area, along with a much larger bar. The place was adorned with artwork from Southeast Asia having paintings of the sea as a theme.

Suki next escorted her guests to the patio. The view to the west defied description. There was nothing but blue water as far as the eye could see, with ornamental trees bordering the view. A cool breeze blew off of the water. The door to the left led to a stairway that meandered down to a private swimming pool and a cabana with yet another set of massage tables and another bar. The door to the right led to a smaller bedroom. In all, the bungalow was as large as a good-sized American home.

"What do you think? Isn't this perfect?" Mickey asked, taking a firm, excited grip on Diane's hand.

Diane looked all around one more time before turning to him and answering, "I've never seen anything like this. Is this all ours?"

"This is all ours." Mickey said before kissing Diane causing her to grin uncontrollably.

Pointing to the small bedroom off of the patio, Suki said, "That is where I will be staying. My clients usually like me to be close to them and available."

Diane's face took on an expression of surprise.

"Is there a problem?" Suki asked. "I can stay elsewhere if that is what you want me to do."

Diane sensed that Suki was sincere in her offer, but decided to keep things simple. She remembered the adage: *keep your friends close, your enemies closer.*

"No, I look forward to having you here with us. Mick has told me you have a lot to offer. I hope to experience all of it firsthand."

"I am sure you will not regret my company," Suki replied with an innocent smile. "Mickey, you told me a lot about Diane, but you understated her beauty."

Diane squeezed Mickey's hand in response to Suki's compliment. Mickey took Diane's cue, saying, "She's the best thing that's happened in my life."

Suki quickly and discretely absorbed the hurt caused by Mickey's unintended barb, then moved matters along.

"Mickey, the porter generally knows where things go. Could you stay here and help him with the unpacking while I take Diane to the beach for a look? There is plenty of wine and beer at the bar."

"Dandy! Okay with you Diane?"

"Absolutely, I think Suki and I need a little time to get acquainted." Diane decided to play the first card. "Suki, would you mind making me a Rhine wine and seltzer?"

"Chilled, on ice, or room temperature?"

"Chilled would be perfect," Diane replied, trying almost with success not to sound catty.

"My pleasure, Diane. In fact, that sounds good. I think I will have one, too."

Mickey was mesmerized by Suki's walk as she proceeded to the bar. Diane noticed this. She quickly pulled him against her body, embraced, and kissed him. Suki turned around to glance at her clients, catching them in their moment of passion as Diane had hoped. Mickey reacted to Diane's advance by picking her up and carrying her into the bedroom where he put her down gently on the bed. He wasn't bashful at all when he put his lips on hers, slipped his hands under her blouse, and cupped her breasts.

A few minutes passed before Suki returned to the bedroom with a tray of drinks. She knocked before entering the bedroom, but nonetheless found Diane and Mickey still passionately making out on the bed, their clothes were in disarray.

"Okay you lovers. Save that for later."

Mickey stood up, pulling Diane to her feet. She reached beneath her blouse and slipped off her light blue Victoria's Secret bra that Mickey had unfastened, tossing it at him. In doing so, she momentarily flashed her taut abdomen and her own perfectly round breasts at Suki, just to let her know what the competition looked like.

"Whew, that's more comfortable."

Unfazed, Suki handed Diane her drink, saying, "I hope you enjoy. This is a Riesling from my choice of German vineyards."

"That sounds wonderful. Thank you, Suki."

Suki handed Mickey a bottle, saying, "Here is your Kirin and lime."

"Outstanding, you remembered."

Now it was Diane's turn to swallow hard, uncomfortable with Suki's degree of familiarity with Mickey. The battle was clearly on.

"Shall we go?" Suki asked, holding out her hand to Diane.

Diane failed to take Suki's hand, instead gesturing toward the steps.

"After you."

Suki headed out the door without a moment of hesitation.

Mickey sensed the tension in the air, and said, "Diane, this isn't a competition. We're here to have fun. Give Suki a chance."

Diane turned toward him, fighting the temptation to bolt out the door and leave, throwing things at him as she exited. She took Mickey's hand holding the beer, and raised it in front of his face.

"Kirin and lime? Since when has this been such a memorable drink? Is this your Asian version of Grolsch?"

Mickey didn't outwardly respond. Privately, he was enjoying every moment of what was going on.

"Don't tell me this isn't a competition. I suggest you get it clear in your mind real quick just who your companion is on this trip, and who's the help."

Diane dashed out of the bungalow to catch up with Suki, meeting her about half way down the steps to the beach. Suki heard footsteps approaching, stopped, and turned.

Noticing Diane was empty-handed, Suki said, "You forgot your drink. Would you like me to go back up and get it for you?"

Diane hadn't realized she'd hastily left the room without her drink. She felt rather foolish since she had made such a point of having Suki make her the drink in the first place, but she wasn't about to send her back up to the bungalow.

"No, that won't be necessary."

"I have not had any of mine yet. Here, you take it," Suki said, trying to remain polite. She held the drink out to Diane, but her guest didn't accept it.

"Miss Diane, I get the distinct impression you do not want me here."

Diane moved to the step just above Suki so she was looking squarely down on her opponent.

"How many times?"

Suki realized she was in for a confrontation, and was ready for battle.

"How many times…what? Did he meet with me? Did he call me? Did he send email to me? Did we make love?" Suki got the desired increasingly hostile reaction from Diane with each of her questions.

Diane realized she didn't want to hear answers to any of the questions but one.

"Do you love him?"

Suki hesitated, then looked deeply into Diane's eyes as she replied, "I am a concierge. It is my job to make my clients comfortable and to satisfy all of their needs—each and every one. Love would simply get in the way of my obligation."

"Well I *do* love him. I won't let anyone, or anything, come between us, is that clear?"

Boundaries

"Have you ever told him you love him?" Suki asked pointedly.

"Of course I have," Diane replied, though uncertainly.

"That is very strange, because Mickey has often told me of you, and when I have pressed him as to whether or not you have told him that you love him, he always replies 'no'. Mickey does not lie to me."

"Listen to me. I don't want to be a topic of discussion between you and Mickey. Is that clear?"

"Your reaction just now would lead me to believe that you are not secure in your relationship with Mickey."

"Secure?" Diane laughed. "How can this arrangement between the three of us possibly make me feel secure in my relationship with Mickey? This isn't my idea of a vacation. I'm here only because Mickey asked me to join him."

"It would be a tragedy for you to have come all this way only because Mickey asked you to join him. You must want something from him. Maybe you are simply using him for your own personal gain?"

Diane squirmed ever so slightly at Suki's suggestion, and knew she was onto something. It occurred to her at that very moment that she and Suki might not be too dissimilar.

"In any event, your business with him is between the two of you. As for my business relationship, I am emotionally detached. I am here only to please my clients. On this adventure, that would be Mickey and, of course, you."

Suki took another drink while Diane ran her hands nervously through her hair. The score was now in Suki's favor.

Taking Diane's hand, Suki offered, "I would like the opportunity to make you desire to be here in Phuket with Mickey, and even perhaps with me. Let us go take that walk on the beach. It may take a while, but I sense that we will become very close friends. A walk will help you unwind from the trip. It must have been long and tiring. Please, trust me. I have no desire to get between you and Mickey."

Diane stood motionless with her hand still held by Suki. The conversation had left her speechless.

"Diane!" Mickey called out as he came walking down the steps. "You two haven't gotten very far."

In truth, he had no idea just how far the two had come in their brief relationship.

Mickey put his arm around Diane, then looked at Suki as he suggested, "Let me show her the beach."

Diane looked relieved by Mickey's proposal. Suki let go of her hand, set her glass on a post, then smiled graciously as she gave the two another wai.

"I think that is a good idea Mickey. Diane has something to tell you."

Diane realized she had been trapped. Suki was a master of both words and wit.

"Be back in thirty minutes," Suki said, picking up her glass. "I will have a hot bath and a fruit tray ready for the two of you."

"Dandy!" Mickey replied with anxious anticipation. He was apparently familiar with the hot bath and fruit tray treatment. Taking Diane's hand, he started down the steps with her in tow. "Wait until you feel this sand. There's nothing quite like it."

In short order, the two were removing their sandals and walking in ankle deep sand toward the water. Suki stayed behind, swaying back and forth on the landing, watching the two lovers while slowly sipping her drink. Once out of earshot, Diane pressed Mickey for some answers to questions that were troubling her.

"Mickey, is it me, or is Suki a practicing passive-aggressive bitch?"

"Thai people don't understand aggressive behavior, passive or otherwise."

"That's bullshit."

"No, that's the truth. If you were confrontational with Suki, you probably got no overt reaction. You would have received the same reaction from any Thai."

"Jesus I wish she had just slapped me or something."

"Why do you want her to hate you?"

"Because I hate her and that would make it easier!"

"You'll stress yourself into an anxiety attack before Suki blinks. She has total composure, and believe me, it can't be broken."

Boundaries

Having reached the water's edge, they began to walk through the lapping waves as Diane continued, "Mickey, what have you told Suki about me?"

"I've talked about you a lot. She knows we have dated over the last few years, that you are a successful business woman, and she knows how I feel about you." Mickey stopped and turned Diane so that she faced him. "I have told her many times that I love you, babe."

Diane reeled at Mickey's choice of words. Bruce had always called her 'babe', and she found herself affected more by that one word than the preceding three. She forced herself to continue talking.

"Is she pulling you away from me?"

"On the contrary. You'll find this hard to believe right now, but she's helped me find myself. She's exposed feelings I didn't know I had. All of my senses have become stronger, and she's made me realize how important you are in my life."

Diane buried her head against Mickey's chest before asking, "Have I ever told you I love you?"

"Not in words, but always in actions," Mickey replied, squeezing Diane affectionately.

Diane realized Suki had been right. She had never said those words to Mickey. Her undying love for Bruce had kept her from taking that step.

"Mick, I'm so sorry I haven't told you before how I feel about you."

Mickey kissed the top of her head as he said, "Suki says your spirit is trapped by the memory of Bruce, and maybe there's more healing that needs to take place. She's a good therapist, and I fully expect she could make you healthier physically and emotionally."

"That's a relief," she said sarcastically. "After seven years of on-and-off again antidepressants, I'm ready for a change."

Diane felt Mickey chuckle ever so slightly.

"So, what do I have to do?" Diane asked grudgingly.

"You'll see. Actually, it will come naturally. Just work with her."

"You promise I can trust her?"

"Absolutely."

Book 2

"I'm going to step out while you get dressed," Dr. Mason said, handing Diane a plastic bag with her personal belongings and clothing. "I'd like to continue this discussion in a friendlier environment, one more conducive to open dialogue as opposed to clinical evaluation. I also want to get you away from this very public emergency room and into a more discrete place."

"How do I know I can trust you?" Diane asked, clearly skeptical.

"You don't," Mason replied, shrugging his shoulders. "I'm acting on faith that when I leave this room, you will change into your street clothes and join me. The alternative is you can flee to who knows where, at which point you will resume the situation you left earlier tonight. Something tells me that would be a much worse scenario for you than sitting with me and letting me help you with your problem."

Diane chewed her thumbnail, nearly overwhelmed with suspicion. With a great deal of hesitation, she held out her hand to Mason and they shook.

Mason stepped out into the emergency room, taking a seat beside a desk in the middle of the same well-choreographed chaos he had observed earlier. After rubbing his bearded chin for a moment, he picked up a phone and dialed a number, while at the same time, looking around to see if anyone was listening. The phone rang for a long time before a woman's voice answered.

"This is Dr. Madden."

"Bev, this is Loarn," Mason said after clearing his throat, trying to conceal his conversation as best he could.

"Jesus, Loarn. Do you know how late it is?"

"Bev, I only call you at such an hour when it is either extremely urgent or extremely interesting. On this occasion it is both. Where are you?"

"I'm leaving Presbyterian now. I had to admit a patient."

"Well, good. At least I didn't wake you."

"Okay, okay. What is it?

"I need you to join me at the Trauma Center. I have a woman here who has been clinically altered and psychologically traumatized. I have some insight into her problem, however I can only tell you that her case is totally unique in medical science. I need your help with this one."

"What do you mean 'clinically altered'?"

"I cannot explain this over the telephone because it is so extraordinary. In fact, I am going to record the patient under an alias while I am waiting for you. She must not be located. Her safety is probably at risk."

After pausing briefly, Madden replied, "Alright, Loarn, I'll be there in a few minutes."

"Thank you, Bev."

Mason put the phone back in the cradle before scanning around behind him for a registration clerk. Locating one, he called out, "Krissy, please!" motioning for the clerk to come over. When she got to his side, he leaned in close, saying, "Room nine needs a new identity. This needs to be completely locked up tight immediately."

"Right away, Dr. Mason. Do you want to pick the name?"

"No, just pick something pretty," he replied with his usual, cordial smile. "You already have her ID."

Mason tapped his fingers nervously, as he watched the clerk head off to her computer terminal. Staring across the room at nothing in particular, he was deep in thought, recalling his involvement with Mickey Rollins years earlier. Shaking his head again in disbelief over the turn of events, he looked back toward room nine where he saw Diane through the sliding door, peeking out from behind the privacy curtain. He got up from his chair and returned directly to the room.

Noting that she was wearing only blue jeans and a sweater, Mason asked, "Do you have a coat?"

"I think I had a jacket," she answered, rummaging through her bag. "I guess it didn't make the trip to the hospital with me."

"Allow me to fix you up with something. It's quite chilly outside." Mason stepped out for a moment before returning with a lab coat, saying, "This will have to do for now."

"Outside?" Diane asked, looking puzzled. "Where are we going?"

"We need to get away from here. A hospital is a very likely place for someone to go looking if a person of interest is missing. First, however, we must wait here until I get you a new identity."

"No! You said I could trust you," Diane said, a noticeable panic in her voice.

"It's just temporary and for your protection. Also, there is another doctor who will be joining us in a few minutes. Her name is Beverly Madden."

"Oh." Diane's demeanor immediately changed and she stood with her arms crossed defensively, refusing to make eye contact with Dr. Mason.

He sensed the need to keep the conversation going, and asked, "How are you feeling?"

She continued looking away from him, but chuckled quietly, managing to respond, "Let's see, for starters, I'm scared shitless; you tell me I have been unconscious; I have something in my ear that's communicating with Mars or God knows where; my daughter is in jail miles away; and I suspect my husband is trying to kill me." Diane turned abruptly, facing Mason, before adding, "I'm doing great!"

"At least your sense of humor is still with you," Mason responded with a kind smile. "We'll get through this. Beverly is good at listening and sorting things out."

"What is she, a shrink?" Diane asked, appearing to shut down again.

Cocking his head as if to acknowledge Diane's point of view, Mason tried to reassure her, "She is, as a matter of fact, an excellent psychiatrist, as well as a personal friend and, I might add, a very pleasant woman on top of everything else. I think those are all good qualities given the circumstances."

There was a tap at the door to the room and the clerk appeared.

"Dr. Mason, here you go. I've taken care of everything as we normally do for a CAT-3."

"Thank you, Krissy," Mason said, taking the folder.

Boundaries

"What's a CAT-3?" Diane asked.

"That's what we classify an individual who is considered to be at extreme risk and whose anonymity we wish to protect," Mason replied, rifling through the file. His eyebrows peaked as he found what he was looking for. "Marguarite Escamilla," he announced.

"Who's that?"

"That is *you* until further notice, at least as far as this hospital is concerned."

"Do you think Mickey would actually kill me?" Diane asked, a chill running down her spine.

Mason shut the folder before taking a deep breath, appearing to give his response a great deal of thought.

"Let me put it this way. I have been following Mickey and his work for a long time. Some years ago, I voiced my objections to a new project he was beginning. As a result he failed to get the funding he was seeking. I thought that was the end of the project. The essence of it, as I understood from the proposal, sounds much like some of what you are experiencing—in particular when you mentioned nanocells. That was when I became alarmed. The connection became absolute when I heard your husband's name."

"You did everything but answer my question," Diane said.

"I truly think you are very valuable to him, so I doubt he would harm you in any way." Mason continued, "Actually, he would probably rather kill me."

Diane again withdrew in response to Mason's disturbing choice of words.

"When did you find out you may have been a subject of some type of physical alteration?" Mason inquired.

"Just yesterday. Maybe the day before," Diane said, sitting down. "I overheard Suki talking about it."

"Who is Suki?"

"She…" Diane put her hands to her face as her eyes began to tear. "She is me."

"What do you mean?" Mason asked, trying not to lead Diane to any answers.

"I can't explain it right now. It's a long and upsetting story."

"Is she a relative or a friend?" Mason asked cautiously, seeing the discomfort displayed in Diane's body language.

"She was a friend—my best friend ever." Diane buried her face in her hands. "I loved her. I can't believe what she did."

Mason waited for Diane to volunteer more information. When she remained silent, he asked, "Is she someone you would feel comfortable bringing into this situation at this time?"

"No," Diane immediately responded, shaking her head. "She's in love with Mickey and he has control of her, too. She's a part of this entire mess."

"Is she also a subject of Mickey's work?"

Yes...no...I don't know what to believe anymore. Mickey controls people with his charisma as much as anything."

There was another knock. A woman in green scrubs and a waist-length white lab coat peaked in.

"Am I interrupting?"

"Bev, come in. Dr. Madden, this is Diane Alders. Diane, meet Dr. Madden."

Madden, an attractive, middle-aged woman, had a congenial smile and held out her hand for Diane.

"Call me Beverly."

"Don't expect me to warm up to you just because you tell me your first name."

Dr. Madden's expression remained totally neutral as she responded, "I wouldn't expect you to. I certainly understand you would be cautious at this point."

"And don't think that agreeing with me and making nice will have any effect on me either," Diane said, continuing to circle her wagons.

"I'm only here to help, Diane." Madden's manner continued being fair-minded.

Mason intervened. "Diane, your situation is so entirely unique I need to have someone I can trust implicitly to help me help you. In your case, Dr. Madden is just that person. Please give her a chance. After all, you gave *me* a chance, did you not?"

Diane paced back and forth, her arms crossed, without saying anything. Her body movement said it all.

"Let me bring Dr. Madden up to speed. It should only take a few minutes."

"No!" Diane stated firmly. "You have to talk right here in front of me so I can listen to everything you say. If you want me to trust you, it has to start right now." With a look of urgency, Diane continued, "But before anything else happens, I have to go to the bathroom really badly."

"With your permission, we need a specimen to see what, if anything, may be in your system," Mason said in a clinical tone. "We took blood earlier while you were still unresponsive, but for some reason, you were not catheterized, and therefore, we did not get a urine sample."

"I can't trust anyone, can I?" Diane said, wrapping her arms around her chest for protection. "You people just take and take and take…"

Madden tried to put Diane at ease by walking over and putting her hand on Diane's shoulder as she said, "This is all routine. It won't hurt you."

Looking at the placement of Madden's hand, Diane took exception, saying, "I took psychology in college. I won't fall for the soft touch shit either."

Madden removed her hand. Mason again took control of the situation.

"Once Beverly and I review your situation, I would like very much for us to take a drive to an all-night restaurant that I frequent where we can just sit and chat. But first, we must take care of the urine sample. Please use the restroom around the corner. I need to take care of your hospital orders, Ms. Escamilla," Mason said with a smile.

"Do they have espresso at the restaurant?" Diane asked, fidgeting. "The nanocells need caffeine."

Looking confused, Madden asked, "The nanocells?"

"It is all part of the story," Mason answered, putting his arm around Dr. Madden's shoulder. "Now please, Diane, the urine sample."

"I never understood how you people handle someone else's pee," Diane said wearily.

The two doctors looked at each other before Mason sighed and responded, "Well I for one share your discomfort which is one reason I chose neurology. However, what comes out down there can help me understand what goes on up here," Mason said, pointing to his head. "So, can we please get this done?"

Diane looked at Dr. Madden, then asked, "You're not going to stand and watch me are you?"

Biting her lip to keep from smiling, Madden replied, "No, I'll be right here." Mason reached into a cabinet, pulled out a specimen cup, then tossed it to Diane who quickly snatched the cup in mid flight. Madden clapped her hands softly as she said, "Your reflexes are certainly good."

"You people are seriously deranged," Diane said, not impressed in the least by Dr. Madden's humor. "Let's see you catch it when I toss it back at you…full. With any luck, I'll remember to screw the lid on tight."

Diane proceeded to the restroom and closed the door, after which there was a very distinct *click* of a lock.

"You owe me big time, Loarn," Madden said, looking angrily at Mason. "I was looking forward to a good night's sleep until you dragged me in on this case. It'll take hours, if not days, to get her to open up.

"She has some very serious issues, Bev," Mason chuckled. "You're just seeing symptoms of a much bigger problem. Let me take care of the paperwork and I'll meet you back here in five minutes or so. Read these while I'm gone."

Mason handed Madden a file, then retreated to a desk where he logged on to a computer. She opened the file and began reading over the notes from doctors Mason and Bartholomew, reviewing the lab results from the blood work as well as X-rays and CT scans. She was astonished by what she read.

"Holy shit…what the…huh?"

After a few minutes, during which Dr. Madden poured over the information given to her, a voice came from behind, breaking the silence and startling her.

"Pretty fucked up, don't you think?" Diane asked, lobbing the filled specimen bottle into the air toward Madden, who managed just in time to turn and field it. "Good catch."

Quickly regaining her composure, Madden said, "There's nothing we can't help you with. We just need to talk with you some more to help us understand what's going on."

"Right…Bev."

The two studied each other silently for a moment, both suspicious of the other. Finally, Dr. Madden asked a question. "What's a nanocell?"

Diane rolled her eyes and twisted her mouth thinking of a good answer.

"Think…Dippin' Dots."

"I beg your pardon?" Madden asked, raising her eyebrows.

"Ice cream! Don't make things complicated."

Madden still didn't understand, but saw no value pursuing the matter any further without Mason.

Both Diane and Dr. Madden were relieved as Dr. Mason returned to the room. Passing through the privacy curtain, he merrily announced, "Alright, Ms. Escamilla. You may leave the hospital with us. Having said that, you are now officially under Dr. Madden's care, so you must remain with us, as you have not yet been discharged. Bev, I hope you don't mind that I named you as the consulting psychiatrist."

"No problem," Dr. Madden replied with a hint of sarcasm in her voice.

Mason wrote Diane's new, fictitious name on the label of the urine specimen bottle before saying, "We'll just drop this off with the charge nurse on the way out." Once that task was accomplished, Mason said, "Let's go," gesturing for Dr. Madden to follow.

The three got to the exit of the emergency room where Mason pressed a large stainless steel button on the wall marked 'Push for Exit' causing the double doors to swing open. As the three exited the hospital into a large, covered, garage-like area, an ambulance pulled up. While they waited for the ambulance to come to a stop, its red and yellow strobe lights continued flashing.

"This way," Mason said, giving Diane's arm a soft tug.

Diane didn't move. Her face was totally blank—the bright red and yellow flashing strobes reflecting eerily in her eyes.

"Diane?" Mason asked anxiously.

Without answering, she collapsed, falling unconscious into Mason's arms.

"Bev, go get help."

Chapter 9

Mickey and Diane returned a short while later from their walk along the beachfront. Suki met them at the door to the veranda where she handed each a blended fruit drink.

Diane still hadn't warmed up to her host, and hoped to catch her unprepared, saying, "I'm sorry. I hope these didn't have time to melt away in this heat while you were waiting for us?"

"Oh, no, Miss Diane. These are quite fresh. I made them just moments ago. It is my job to anticipate your needs, and to do so requires that I know where you are at all times."

Both ladies turned toward Mickey, finding him grinning.

"Can I speak openly here?" he asked.

Diane and Suki nodded.

"Suki, I am here with Diane. I love her. I invited her to come along in the hope we might develop a closer relationship. I trust you will help me?"

"Most certainly," Suki said, looking directly at Diane while she answered Mickey. "I will help you in every way possible."

Mickey put his hands on both of Diane's shoulders commanding all of her attention before saying, "Diane, I want this to be a new beginning for us. Give yourself over to me and to Suki. I am here for you and she is here for us. There's no need to feel uncomfortable about previous encounters between Suki and me..." Looking at Suki, he finished his sentence, "...Is there, Suki?"

"Encounters?" Suki replied. "I, too, am uncomfortable with this arrangement. You have to put yourself in our position. Since you are not female, there is no way you can understand our discomfort. We have both shared ourselves with you in many ways, including intimately, and that makes Diane and me adversaries for now. I am most capable of understanding her feelings. You must earn Diane's trust, just as I must earn her trust. All I can do is provide for your needs equally or perhaps in favor of Diane for a while until these feelings go away. If you find that unacceptable, you may wish to reconsider having me as your concierge on this vacation. I can quickly arrange for another person to take my place."

"You're right, Suki," Mickey answered. "Maybe I shouldn't have brought the two of you together like this. How quickly can you…"

"Wait a minute," Diane interrupted. Looking at Suki, she said, "Mickey says you're the best at what you do. Is that true?"

Looking at her own feet, Suki replied, "My humility forbids that I should make such a claim."

"Humility…I like that in a person," Diane said with a comfortable smile. "Do you think you can teach that to Mickey?"

"Humility exists within all of us," Suki responded, also looking more at ease. "One needs only find it. My work with each of my clients centers on discovering, and if necessary, healing the body, mind and spirit. It is through this process that one finds all of his or her inner qualities and decides what one's dominant and subordinate traits will be. One can then begin to realize what traits he or she has to reveal to others, including humility."

"So what you are telling me is that Mickey is completely hopeless," Diane chimed with perfect timing.

Mickey faked a stab to the heart as Diane paused to let everyone have a good laugh.

After pulling back the hair that was sticking to her face due to perspiration, Diane continued, "That person controls the schwa."

"I do not understand this word," Suki said with a puzzled look.

"You didn't tell her about schwa?" Diane's face beamed, as she looked Mickey.

"No."

"You saved that for me?"

"Well, I think I was drunk at the time, but, yes, you're the only one I've told."

Boundaries

A weight had been taken off Diane's shoulders. The fact that Mickey had confided in her and not Suki gave Diane a huge boost of self-confidence.

Taking Suki's drink in her own hand, Diane guided it to her own lips, taking a sip. She then looked at Suki, "Now you."

It was a pivotal moment in their blossoming relationship. As Diane raised her own drink, Suki lightly guided it to her lips, allowing Diane to have control. Suki took a drink from Diane's glass, and the two exchanged smiles. She then pulled out a chair for Diane. Mickey took a seat, too. The tension in the air was gone.

"What is this?" Diane asked, taking another sip. "It's marvelous."

Suki put her hand on Diane's head, an action seen by Thai people as a most personal form of contact, as she answered, "It is a fruit and herbal blend. The sweet flavor is pineapple. It celebrates the beginning of our journey together."

"So is your therapy all about herbs, fruit, massage, and things like that?" Diane asked.

"It is a very complex process, but, yes, those are some of the things you will experience. You left out one very important component," Suki added.

"What's that?" Diane asked most curiously.

"I have a shopping trip set for us on your third day here. We'll fly to Bangkok…just the two of us."

"Oh, yes, shopping can solve all the world's problems," Diane said. "What about Mickey?"

"Who is this Mickey person?" Suki asked with a naive expression.

"Hello?" Mickey said, waving his hand. "I am still a part of this trip, aren't I?"

"Oh, yes, you're the one with the penis. I forgot you were here," Diane responded lightheartedly.

The three laughed a genuinely good laugh. Shortly thereafter, Suki held out her arm in the direction of the bedroom, guiding the two to where she had set out drinks and fruit on a table beside the large tub.

"Let us rid you two of the stress of the long flight, shall we? Your therapy begins with a diet of fruit and lean meats. Alcoholic beverages are limited today and tomorrow. You can have what I provide for you, but no more. I will replace the effects of alcohol with herbal and fruit drinks, massage, music, and all the accompanying sensations. I promise you will not miss alcohol. I will combine hot baths with swimming in salt water, aromatherapy, and sauna, and we will begin to cleanse your body of all of the toxins and poisons within it. You will feel a change very quickly. As the poisons leave your body, they will be replaced with wholesome nutrients that will give you energy. The process is entirely natural, and will let your body and mind start to experience energy, as well as feelings that have been suppressed."

"There aren't any drugs or native concoctions in these drinks are there?" Diane asked, being somewhat skeptical.

"Everything is natural, as are the effects upon your body and mind. I will consume the same foods and drinks as you. Keep in mind, my diet has been what we are having now so you will not see much difference in me. You and Mickey, on the other hand, will experience quite some change I expect. What is your diet like at home, Diane?"

"It's certainly not fruit and herbs. It's whatever is easy and portable and for the most part, if I told you all the details, you would probably vomit."

"And you, Mickey? Is Maria taking the suggestions I made, providing a healthy diet?"

Mickey nodded his head, and then shook it, confessing, "She's done wonders with fruit. She puts it on her pizza and it's to die for. She hasn't figured out how to make her migas healthy, and to be honest with you, I won't let her change that little vice, and her enchiladas are her mother's recipe, and…"

"Enough!" Suki said, holding up both hands. She picked up the tray of fruit, and presented it to the two as she said, "Start eating."

"What are these?" Diane asked. The unusual shapes and textures of the fruits piqued her curiosity.

"These should be familiar to you," Suki said pointing at the bananas. "They are *gluay* or bananas, but these in particular are called *gluay nam wah* which I find particularly tasty." Pointing to the other selections as she spoke, she continued,

Boundaries

"The bumpy green fruit is a custard fruit or *noi naa*. This other green fruit that is smooth is guava or *farang*. You dip the pieces in sugar, then in pepper and then eat. The red fruit is *litchee*."

"That's my favorite, right after mango," Mickey said.

"Of course," Suki acknowledged. "But you like your mango with coconut cream and sticky rice, and that is a treat that will have to wait until later." Turning her attention back to Diane, Suki asked, "Have you heard the saying, you are what you eat?*"

"Yes," Diane said.

"You will begin to experience a difference in how your bodies taste."

"Taste?" Diane's eyebrows furrowed as she waited for Suki to clarify.

"Why, yes, the oils and fluids that come from our bodies carry much of the latent taste and smell of what we ingest. You will find a change in the way Mickey tastes and he will find a change in the way you taste. The interesting part is that even though each of you will be consuming basically the same foods and drinks, the body processes are unique to the individual, therefore, so are the tastes."

Mickey decided the conversation had become too educational. He squeezed Diane playfully as she craned her head to look back at him.

"So you see, Diane, I'll have to take notes. I'll map how you taste as I lick you all over your body, and write it down in a journal. It will be just like a photo album of our trip!"

Diane rolled her eyes in response to Mickey's all too predictable reaction.

"Suki, you say the diet will improve the taste of *all* the body's secretions?"

"Yes, even that one," Suki said with a wink.

Diane broke free from Mickey, picked up a piece of litchee, and fed it to him, saying, "Eat plenty. I don't plan to take notes."

"Feed me, baby!" He muttered with his mouth full.

The three took time to consume some of the fruit and drink. They appeared to be avoiding what came next, which was that at some point, they had to get out of their clothes and into the water.

"So are you ready to get wet?" Suki asked.

Mickey nodded, as did Diane in time.

"So, how does this work?" she asked, "…I mean, with the three of us?"

"That is up to the two of you. We must establish boundaries that set the ground rules for my time with each of you alone, each of you together, and when the two of you want to be alone. I assume unless you tell me otherwise, I will be with you only when you are together, and only then with your permission. The boundaries can change at your discretion during your stay. Given that I anticipate ours will become an increasingly spontaneous atmosphere, planning for such a change is not practical. Therefore, let me make it clear that I am available to serve either or both of you. You may partake of all of my offerings. You may partake of me, should you so desire. I can pleasure one or both of you. I am completely amenable, and have no preconditions. But, both of you have to be comfortable and honest with your choices in advance."

"My, this is complex," Diane said. "I dislike rules of engagement. I know in marketing, if someone tells me this is as far as you can go, I'll jump right over it." She looked at Suki and Mickey for verbal or visual signs to guide her through this, but there were none. "Well for now, I need some time alone with Mickey."

"I like that. I want some time alone with Diane."

The pecking order was established…for now.

"I certainly respect your decisions," Suki conceded. "Can I bring either of you anything else before I step out?"

"No, we're good for now," Mickey replied, reaching out and touching Suki thoughtfully as he made his remark.

"Yeah, we're good," Diane concurred. "Maybe you could freshen up our drinks?"

"No problem. No problem at all. There are large towels in your room as well as by the tub. I will set your drinks and treats alongside the tub within easy reach. You both have mittens and you will find my special soaps next to the towels. Let me advise you that the water is set at forty degrees. Since it is thirty-five degrees outside today, you may feel chilled when you step out. I will bring your robes later. If you will leave your clothes on your bed, I will see that they are laundered right away. If you wish to get dressed after your bath, your clothing has been put away in drawers or hung in the closets."

"Thank you, Suki, for taking care of all of these details," Diane said sincerely. "You'll have to forgive me, but please help me convert the temperatures."

Mickey said, "The water is about one hundred four degrees, and the outside temp today is about ninety-five degrees. The water will be a shock at first."

"Why so hot?" Diane asked.

"The temperature is very critical in opening your skin's pores and allowing the process of healing to take place," Suki said with the serious expression of a teacher. "It will also relax all of your muscles and joints so that when you get your massage later, you will experience the full effect without me having to use too much pressure. The water is slightly salty with the extra treatment I have mixed in with it. Also, the fragrance of the soap is lavender and that of the shampoo is coconut, which I find most enjoyable. If you desire something else I am most happy to provide it for you."

"Do we need to wear bathing suits?" Diane asked, flapping the collar of her shirt.

"I plan to be butt-ass naked," Mickey laughed.

Diane rolled her eyes.

"You have total privacy here," Suki said. "Only the three of us will see each other in the nude unless you wish to invite others."

"I think we'll just keep to ourselves for now," Diane said.

"I completely understand," Suki acknowledged. "Let me say for the record, Diane, you have nothing to be ashamed of. You are a very beautiful woman."

Diane had a momentary vision of Rosario who had paid her the same compliment many times. She looked deeply into Suki's eyes, searching for any possible subliminal motive.

"Thank you, Suki."

After Suki had everything in place, she paused briefly before departing for her room to ask one final question.

"Diane, do you mind if I get into something more comfortable?"

Judging by Mickey's expression, Diane realized 'something more comfortable' was probably closer to *nothing* than *something*. But, she decided not to fight any longer.

"Whatever you would like to do is fine with me, Suki."

"Call me when you are ready for your massage, or if you need anything." With that, Suki went into her room and closed the door.

"I'm so exhausted. I just want to go to sleep," Diane said as she put her head on Mickey's chest and her arms around his waist.

"You don't want to do that just yet. It's better to stay up as late as you can on your first day in Asia." He tenderly kissed the top of her head, and added, "You'll be able to doze off when Suki gives you your massage. Let's get into the water, and I'll give you a rub down."

"That sounds nice. But no sex right now, alright? I want to enjoy the sex, and I want to do things to you that I just can't do right now."

"I'm here for you," Mickey said, kissing Diane on the nose. "I'll probably get—no I am certain I will get—a hard-on. Don't be upset."

"I can think of worse problems." After a short chuckle, Diane continued, "Oh, Mickey, I can't believe we're actually here. This place feels like a dream. I'm…I'm in shock, I guess. It's been so long since I've relaxed and been away from the grind, I just feel lost. Then you heap the jet lag on top of that and I'm just a mental case. Promise me you'll take good care of me until I have my senses back so I can dominate you again."

"Your sense of humor is intact," Mickey replied with a laugh.

Diane stepped back a short distance from Mickey, closed her eyes and held her arms out from her sides, saying, "Undress me you pervert."

"Anything you wish, ma'am."

Mickey began the slow process of removing Diane's blouse, followed by her shorts and then her panties. He was distracted by something he heard.

"Listen," he said.

"What?"

Boundaries

Mickey scanned the room for a moment, then said, "The sound we hear isn't just the ocean. It's some kind of music, you know, that organic, brain-numbing mood music."

"You're right. I can hear some sort of music just above the sound level of the waves and the wind."

Getting matters underway once more, Diane unbuttoned Mickey's shirt and shorts, letting them fall to the floor next to the bed. His boxer shorts bulged in front.

"God damn, you have no control, do you?"

"See what you do to me?"

She reached into Mickey's boxers and stroked his penis, saying, "I hope the hot water takes care of your problem."

Finishing the task of removing his underwear, they, too, fell into the heap on the floor. The two lover's lips met as they embraced, holding their kiss for a long time. Mickey's hands roamed from Diane's neck, down her back, stopping when they held the cheeks of her butt. He pulled her closer to him, and she reciprocated. Their tongues met. When their lips finally parted, Mickey began kissing and sucking on Diane's left ear lobe.

Quivering, Diane said, "Okay, maybe I was premature with the no-sex rule. Ignore what I said."

"What about your dominance?"

"Oh, I'll dominate, alright. Now get your ass into that water."

Mickey took quick, deliberate steps into the hot water, pulling Diane behind him.

"Whoa, Mickey, this is hot!"

"It's supposed to be hot. The water at Ainsworth didn't bother you."

"I mean it. Slow down!" she shouted, pulling back on Mickey's hand.

Letting go, he waded neck deep into the water, saying, "Come on, Ms. Dominant. Get it over quickly."

She closed her eyes, then waded quickly into the tub to a point where the water reached her neck.

"Oh, my God. Oh, my God."

"You alright?"

"Dandy," was the only response Diane could muster.

Mickey smiled as he made his way over to one side of the tub where he pulled a lever creating a waterfall of steamy water. The tub was more like a small pool than it was a tub as it was close to twenty feet across and even longer in the other dimension. There were jets of bubbling water at half a dozen small areas around the rocky edge of the pool. He waded into water that was chest deep to a spot under the waterfall and came out completely wet, then ran his hands through his two-inch long reddish-brown hair. He then swam back to Diane, at which point he raised himself out of the water part way. The hair on his chest and abs pointed downward in a single direction like a well-manicured lawn. His pectoral muscles were clearly visible, and the muscles in his shoulders and arms bulged in an exaggerated fashion because of the shine from the water.

When Diane stood up to greet Mickey, the water level came to just above her navel. The shock of the relatively cool ninety-five degree air made Diane's nipples immediately hard and firm.

"Suki was right, it does feel cold outside of the water," she said, dipping back down.

"I liked it better when you were standing."

"Pig." Diane knew what Mickey was referring to.

"Have I told you today how beautiful you are?"

"Not yet. Don't make this the last time either. Maybe you'll get lucky tonight."

"Did you know that beautiful, large areolas such as yours are preferred by men?"

Diane shook her head back and forth.

"Now that's an interesting factoid. Where did you come up with that? CNN? Discovery Channel? The Man Show?"

"I read it somewhere. Accept it as the compliment it was intended to be."

"Think so?" Diane said, deciding to welcome the observation. "Are my breasts perfect?"

She moved close to Mickey so her breasts were at the same level as his face. Mickey needed no more prodding and was soon devouring them. She held his head against her chest, savoring the sensations.

"Completely perfect," Mickey said, stopping the kissing and fondling for only a moment. "They'd have to be to adorn this perfect woman."

"Keep going. Keep giving me compliments. Your score will soon be above zero."

"Just zero?"

"Yup, you were way negative about thirty minutes ago."

"Because of Suki?"

"Duh, yeah, because of Suki."

"So, are the two of you okay now?"

"Time will tell. Don't ever let me catch you alone with her."

"You have my word, babe." Cocking his head slightly, he continued, "Don't ever let me catch you alone with her either."

Diane stepped back from Mickey.

"What's that supposed to mean?"

"I saw the way you looked at her a few minutes ago."

"What do you mean 'the way I looked at her'?"

"I think you're attracted to her."

Diane's arms dropped from around Mickey's neck.

"Mick, don't start with me. I don't see anything in her. She's your friend and you are her client. I'm just along for the ride. Don't make me a part of your male fantasy."

"I beg to differ. I think this is becoming your fantasy."

"So you think I have a lesbian streak in me?" Diane said, reflexively crossing her arms.

"I didn't say that. I just think you are more attracted to Suki than you will admit. But, hey, this is your vacation. It's your turn to be what you want, when you want, with whom you want. The military used to call trips like this 'liberty' for a reason.

Maybe Diane was too tired to debate, or maybe what Mickey was saying was too close to the truth. Diane did find Suki to be incredibly attractive, and she thought she had seen a look in Suki's eyes just moments ago when they had exchanged glances.

"I'm going shopping with her. Do I have your permission to be alone with her then?"

"You can spend any amount of time you want with Suki, doing anything you want. As for shopping, that's a chick thing. I'm totally unqualified for that."

"I cannot believe you used the *chick* word," Diane said as she put her hands around Mickey's neck and lightly pressing her thumbs into his throat as if she were choking him. "If you object to us going shopping, why did you set it up?"

Mickey began speaking with a broken voice as if he was being strangled.

"I had nothing to do with your shopping date."

Diane removed her hands from Mickey's throat, and put her arms back around his waist, surprised by the revelation.

"That came as a complete surprise to me. It was all Suki's idea."

He sat back on the smooth, rock ledge while Diane straddled his hips.

"Why would she do that?"

"Because she is a professional at arranging entertainment. She knows you will enjoy shopping," he replied as his body began to respond to Diane's intimate position.

"Why couldn't you be a part of it?" Diane asked as she wriggled closer to make more contact with Mickey.

"Believe me, she'll take you places and give you a shopping experience that you will never forget. I wouldn't fit into that scene. She goes the distance in everything she does."

"You won't be jealous that she is spending time with me and not you...or us?" Diane asked, hugging Mickey playfully.

"I'm not threatened at all. I suspect this isn't the last time the two of you will want to go places without me. You have my permission to do so."

Diane looked indignant and pinched Mickey's nipples.

"Your permission? Does this mean you're already changing our rules of engagement?"

"You're an adult. You know what you want. Knock yourself out."

"I will," she said, kissing him. "But you still can't be alone with her. You'll have to beg my permission before she touches you."

"Can I get on my knees when I beg?" Mickey was hard now and moved into position to enter Diane's body.

She responded at first to his advance by licking her lips, then said, "I like it when you get on your knees."

Before the missile could launch, she retreated from Mickey's approach.

Giving her an affectionate, sudden squeeze, he said, "You're a serious tease, aren't you?"

Diane nodded just as their lips met again.

He leaned over and picked up one of the mittens as well as the bottle with the lavender-colored liquid. Changing positions with Diane, he encouraged her to lean back onto the ledge near the waterfall where the warm spray filled the air, spread some of the scented gel onto the mitten, and began to wash her body. He started with her neck, then moved to her arms and her chest. Mickey didn't avoid stroking Diane's breasts, but he made sure he didn't linger there either. She responded immediately and completely by lying back onto the warm side of the tub and putting her arms on the side of the pool making her full front entirely available to Mickey's pampering.

"This is divine," Diane said, her nostrils flaring. "The mittens are amazingly soft, and I've never smelled lavender like this before."

Mickey continued with the gentle washing as he said, "Suki probably laced it with another fragrance to make certain it would be unique. She likes to use honey."

"Does honey smell?" Diane asked, rhythmically moving her body in response to Mickey's gentle caress.

"Just enough to make a small difference," Mickey replied, pulling Diane's left leg out of the water and starting to washing it.

"Oh, yeah…right there," she moaned approvingly, as he softly stroked the inside of her left thigh. "Does she actually use honey?"

Mickey made one long, slow approach to the top of Diane's thigh exciting her to the point at which she bit her lip. Before reaching the summit, he turned back toward her knee.

"Yep. She gets it from Changmai in the North. Sometimes she mixes her soaps and oils with orange so the fragrance is like a Dream Bar. Did you ever eat those?"

"Here we go with frozen desserts again."

"Love 'em all," Mickey replied, making another slow approach up Diane's inner thigh.

"Now you're teasing me."

Diane slid down on the rock ledge hoping her pussy would make contact with Mickey's hand. He reversed directions before she succeeded.

"How do you stay slim?" she asked, trying to keep her mind off his assault.

"I think it's hereditary. Dad was trim. So was Grandpa."

Diane noticed a change in Mickey's hand movements as he mentioned his deceased father. The topic always evoked strong emotions. He never talked about it, just as he seldom spoke of any sensitive matter. She thought it best to change the topic of conversation.

"You know a lot about Suki, don't you?" After saying those words, she realized her choice of subject was probably just as poor as the previous one.

Holding her left ankle in one hand, he began washing her foot with the mitten, causing her to turn her head to the side while she again moaned contentedly.

"I know that she makes me feel good when I'm with her, just as I want you to feel good when you are with her."

Boundaries

Diane opened her eyes and said, "In case you didn't know, what you are doing is driving me crazy." Her eyes became intense, as she demanded, "Fuck me."

"I believe you have developed a potty-mouth since we were last together."

"I thought men liked that?"

"Not this man. Maybe all of your other boy-toys like that sort of talk."

Mickey stopped, put some more gel on the mitten, and then switched his washing to Diane's right leg.

"There are no others, Mickey."

"Saving yourself for me?" Mickey asked as his hand ventured up the inside of Diane's right thigh.

Diane's eyebrows peaked and she shrugged her shoulders as she replied, "Do you deserve a woman as good as me?"

Mickey's gloved hand finally made contact with Diane's pussy. Her shoulders fell and she closed her eyes again, moaning with pleasure.

"Do you deserve a man as good as me?"

"Stop talking and let's have sexual intercourse."

"Nope," Mickey said, stopping abruptly. "That does nothing for me. I liked it better when you said 'fuck me'."

Diane splashed water in Mickey's face. He took the mitten off, and grabbed the drinks sitting near the edge of the pool, quickly returning and interlocking his arm with Diane's as they shared their drinks with one another.

"There's a touch of honey in this drink, too," Mickey said.

"I thought I tasted something besides pineapple."

"It makes the drink a little sweeter while not adding anything unhealthy."

"Is she going to surprise us like this all the time?"

"She's good at it. Everything is a special treat. Once you think you know what she's doing, she adds a twist to it. The element of surprise brings with it a certain degree of eroticism."

Diane leaned forward and kissed Mickey before taking the nearly empty glasses and setting them near the edge of the tub.

Mickey assumed that was a cue, but asked naively, "Do you want me to have Suki make us another?"

"No, spoil me rotten."

The expression on Diane's face at this point was distinctly seductive. Mickey grabbed both mittens, soaked them in the hot water, then put some gel on them. He gently began stroking the side of her neck and her cheeks. She responded this time by putting her legs on either side of Mickey's. The invitation was anything but subtle and 'Johnson' was ready. Mickey continued to stroke Diane's arms, then her chest, then her breasts. She opened her eyes and looked into his. The message was clear. Mickey moved closer to Diane, and the two met intimately.

Mickey never stopped washing Diane with the mittens while he slowly and passionately made love to her. She caressed his chest and abdomen while rubbing his buttocks as long as she could until she returned her arms to the side of the tub, and arched forward toward Mickey—her body pulsing rhythmically, soon followed by his.

Chapter 10

Suki's gold bikini bottom was what one would expect to see on the French Riviera. Certainly the price exceeded the material in substance. The finely woven white silk top she wore stopped four inches above the navel and draped open at the bottom leaving no doubt there was nothing but flesh beneath it. The silhouette of her breasts formed the final outline of her body. This time, it was Diane who was mesmerized.

Suki kneeled down with her tray and replaced the empty glasses with new frozen drinks. Her silk top gaped open at the top.

"Do you like these? They are not your basic piña colada."

"They're beautiful," Diane replied, staring down Suki's beach top.

Suki was taken aback by the seemingly out of context remark, but smiled instantly once she realized Diane was not speaking about the drinks.

"I believe your personality has already begun to change."

Diane's skin, already pink from the hot water and hot sex, turned pinker.

"I'm sorry. That was wrong for me to say. I didn't mean to embarrass you".

"Since when is it wrong to pay a girl a compliment? It is very natural for you to notice such things."

Suki put her hand on Diane's shoulder as she spoke, sending a shiver down her back. She noticed her guests were exchanging glances and trying to conceal their smiles.

"Is something funny?"

Diane replied, "He thinks I am going to become physically attracted to you."

"So, are you?" Suki asked, unabashedly.

Finding herself unable to take her eyes off of Suki, Diane answered, "Suki, I can't do this now. Besides, Mickey and I just made love. I'm very content."

"Making love with someone is a wonderful thing, Diane. I could tell from your skin and your expression that the two of you had just made love. Judging from your facial expression and muscle tone of your body, I think you were satisfied."

"Could you see it in Mickey's expression, too?"

"No, a man is hard to read. They are less generous with their souls and feelings. They control their colors and expressions just like other male animals and make themselves look the way they want to be seen. Women, for the most part, are very transparent."

"So you can get inside my head, is what you're telling me? Well let me say it again in case you think I am thinking something else. I can't do this with you."

Suki was clearly as comfortable discussing the matter as Diane was not.

"Diane, there is nothing to *do*. You are who you are. You feel what you feel."

"Mickey said I wouldn't be able to break you."

"Oh, he told you about Thai people?" Suki asked, looking accusatively at Mickey.

"He said you have great self-control," Diane replied, dipping down to her neck in the water, apparently feeling somewhat vulnerable.

"You said this, Mickey?"

Mickey stood up, exposing his naked body to Suki for the first time in Diane's presence. His bold display evoked no visible reaction from Suki.

"No. I said you have total composure."

"That is more correct," Suki said analytically. "You see Diane, I do not have self-control per se. Rather, I am at peace. I am at peace with myself, my place, and my earth. And it is not a *Thai* thing. It has more to do with my Buddhist religion. The inner peace that I experience is what I hope you might attain on this vacation."

Diane reached up for Mickey's hand, pulling him back into the water, before countering, "I'm not buying it. Mickey just stood up naked in front of you and you didn't stare or even blink. That's self-control."

"No, Diane," Suki said, taking a seat at the edge of the tub with her legs dangling in the water. "That was nothing more than a naked man. I am at peace with a naked man. What he did was not intimidating or sexual. He was just naked."

"In any case, I'm not where you are in this whole control-peace thing," Diane replied, now appearing frustrated with the conversation.

Suki put her hands in the water, scooping it into her palms and pouring it over her shoulders—first one, then the other.

"Are you uncomfortable with a naked man?"

"Let's just say I am a private person in that regard."

"Are you uncomfortable being with a naked woman?" Suki asked, pulling her hair back seductively behind her shoulders.

Diane paused somewhat uncomfortably.

Mickey broke the silence.

"Rosario, perhaps?"

Diane stood up immediately in response to his suggestion. Her gorgeous naked torso now loomed above the surface of the water.

"You know about Rosy?" Her vocal and physical reaction was an immediate admission of their relationship and she soon realized it. Slipping back into the water, she turned away from Mickey and rested her arms on the side of the tub. "It was a phase. I'm over it now."

"There's nothing to be ashamed of," Mickey said, moving close to Diane and putting his arms around her.

"How did you find out?"

"Rosy called me to ask if we were in a committed relationship. She didn't want to take you away from me."

"How long ago?" Diane asked, shaking her head in disbelief.

"It's been a long time," Mickey replied.

Diane continued shaking her head as she said, "Oh, boy, the secrets that we all keep from each other. What did Suki say? 'We should be honest with each other…that's the key to relaxing'. Well, I'm really tense right now."

Suki waded into the water to be next to her guests, stopping beside Diane and touching her arm lightly.

"Now we have no more secrets."

Mustering a weak grin, Diane looked suspiciously at Suki, and said, "That's right, no more secrets… except the ones we choose to keep."

Nobody said anything, which was as much a statement of closure as it was the beginning of a new chapter in a book. Suki knew it was time for a peace offering, and reached for the drinks, handing one to Diane and the other to Mickey.

"I'm going to pass right now," Mickey said. "I need to get a run in before I crash and burn. Do the two of you mind?"

There was no direct answer to the question, but it was clear by the body language that Mickey was being encouraged to go away for a while.

"Being alone with Diane may change the rules that the three of us agreed to only an hour ago," Suki said with a look of desire aimed directly at Diane. "That being the case, I would like very much to wash your hair, Diane, if you would allow me."

Mickey slowly walked out of the pool. Neither Suki nor Diane noticed his naked body as he picked up a towel and went into the bedroom to dress for his run on the beach.

Diane waded over to the waterfall where she let the knife of water run over her head. Stepping back out from under the water, she swept the water off of her face with her hands before pulling her hair behind her ears. All the while, she never took her eyes off of Suki.

"Tell me about your name," Diane asked.

"What it means?" Suki asked. At the same time, she took off her top and bikini bottoms, tossing them onto the edge of the tub.

"Yeah," Diane replied, trying not to stare at her beautiful, naked host.

"Sukhon is a Thai name from my mother's family. It means pleasant smell. Jiao is a Chinese name from my father's family and it means lovely. I grew up in a family that loved gardens."

"That's so beautiful," Diane said, slowly approaching Suki. "It's so fitting for you."

"Do you like the smell of coconut?" Suki asked.

"I'm certain that I will," Diane replied.

Suki reached for the bottle with the pale yellow gel, poured some of it into the palm of her left hand, and rubbed her hands together briefly before standing up in front of Diane. She began to run her hands through Diane's hair ever so slowly. Reaching forward, Diane put her hands on Suki's hips for balance and closed her eyes. Pulling Diane's head against her chest, Suki began slowly massaging the shampoo into Diane's auburn locks. Diane wrapped her hands around Suki's waist, at the same time she burrowed her forehead into Suki's chest.

After a short while, Diane said blissfully, "This is really exquisite."

"I am glad you like it."

Suki couldn't be certain if Diane was enjoying the scalp massage or the fact that her head was being pushed back and forth between her perfectly formed, yet petite breasts. Diane ran her hands up Suki's back adding to the opposing force from Suki's hands on the back of her head. Suki found the physical sensation from Diane's acceptance to be stronger than anything she had expected.

"I don't spend a lot of time or money pampering myself," Diane moaned. "It doesn't take much to give me a real rush."

"You deserve to spend time and money on yourself—lots of it," Suki said, using her fingernails to massage Diane's scalp. "We are going to have a lot of fun, you and me."

As Diane's hands moved slightly up and down, caressing Suki's hips, she asked, "What about Mickey? I feel awkward spending someone else's money."

"Mickey never misses it," Suki said with a smirk.

"How does he pay for all of this? I mean, I know he's wealthy, but how does the transaction work?"

"That is not the kind of question I would expect from someone who is trying to relax," Suki replied, shifting her massage to Diane's temples. "Let me rinse you."

Suki dipped Diane back slowly until the knife of hot water met her head, slowly washing away the lather. When the water met Diane's hairline, she leaned back the rest of the way, washing all the suds away from her face. The water sheeted off of her body, catapulting off of her breasts.

Diane opened her eyes just in time to see Suki staring at her chest. Reflexively, and perhaps to elevate Suki's excitement, she turned away. In a moment, there were two mitten-covered hands washing her back. She noticed that while Mickey's touch had been firm, Suki's was light and otherwise defied description.

"Come on, how does he pay for all of this?" Diane persisted.

"Very well. He does an electronic transfer to my account for my personal services. We agree on a minimum and make adjustments as necessary depending upon what takes place. For everything else, including incidentals, we have a joint Black Card. It serves as a form of insurance. Should he choose to leave before we meet the terms of our agreement, there is a costly, preset penalty. You do contracts. I think you understand."

"Sounds like you have it covered," Diane acknowledged. "So, you have a joint account with him?" She asked curiously. "That takes a lot of trust. He doesn't even have one with me."

Suki reached around so that one mitten pressed lightly against Diane's belly, while pressing more firmly against her lower back with her other hand.

"Why would he not trust me? I am his complete servant, just as I am yours," Suki said as her right hand swiped below Diane's navel for the first time."

Diane's stomach tensed in response to Suki's action.

"I'm not so quick to trust another person."

Suki's left hand swiped lower, just to the top of Diane's buttocks before returning to the small of her back.

"You have been hurt by someone?"

As Suki's right hand swept lower than the last time, Diane tensed up yet again.

"Not hurt. I think it's a control thing. I have to be in charge of all aspects of my life."

Boundaries

Suki's left hand reached around Diane's where it joined her right hand, bringing their bodies intimately close. Suki's breasts now pressed against Diane's shoulder blades.

"I think one of the strongest demonstrations of trust has nothing to do with material control or money. It has to do with giving one's self over to another person entirely," Suki suggested, just as her hands moved up both of Diane's sides to the nipple line, before traversing across Diane's breasts, and finally moving precipitously back downward.

Before Suki's hands passed Diane's tan line, she turned to face Suki, stepping back far enough so that their breasts would not touch.

"On that point, I can whole-heartedly agree. But that degree of trust takes time, much more than the few hours we have known one another."

"I did not realize we were speaking of us," Suki said sporting a coy smile, "but, yes, we all have boundaries, do we not?"

There was a long pause while both Suki and Diane tested each other's resolve to stay aloof, rather than become more intimately acquainted.

After a few moments, Suki said, "Perhaps this is a good time to…"

"Suki! Please stop pushing and suggesting this and that for just a while…please!"

"I will be in my room," Suki said as she sulked, beginning to walk out of the tub. "Please let Mickey know where he can find me."

"Wait!" Diane said abruptly.

Suki stopped just as she took her final steps up to main floor.

"Can you please hand me my towel?" Diane begged.

Suki picked up the towel from the small table and unfolded it before holding it out for Diane to take as she, too, stepped out of the tub.

Diane wrapped herself, tucking a corner so the towel stayed in place.

"I don't want to hurt you Suki, honestly. I'm very tired, and this is all very new to me. I sometimes say things that don't make sense. In fact nothing is making much sense right now. Does that make any sense?"

"It is not unusual for a long trip like you have just taken to have profound effects on one's body and mind."

"Do you forgive me for being rude?" Diane asked, putting a hand on Suki's shoulder.

"There is nothing to forgive, Miss Diane. I am here to serve you."

"No!" Diane shouted. "I don't like this 'serve you' shit!" After calming down, Diane put her hands up to her face as she apologized, "Sorry for the outburst." She wiped a tear from the corner of her eye. "I don't like servitude. Somehow we have to be equals in this. Somehow we have to make this seem like we are nothing more than three friends on a vacation. I just can't function in a dominant-subordinate situation like Mickey has put us in, especially with another woman. I am one woman who detests subordination to anyone, and I can't…no, I won't do that to you."

"But I work for Mickey and he likes me to…"

"I can handle Mickey."

"He won't understand that…"

"I can handle Mickey," Diane said emphatically.

There was a long pause while Diane let go of Suki's hands and walked over to the edge of the tub where the two piña coladas had been left. She brought them over to Suki and handed her one.

"Peace?"

"You learn quickly," Suki said with a smile. "Friends?" She offered in return, holding her drink up in the air.

"Friends," Diane replied, finishing the toast.

Trying a different approach, Suki said, "It would give me great pleasure, my friend, to give you a massage, on that table in the warm sunlight, while you relax and go to sleep. Thirty minutes of sleep will do wonders for you."

"How about sixty? Would that be twice as good?"

"Forty-five."

"Deal!"

Suki took Diane by the hand, leading her to the massage table.

"Have you ever experienced Egyptian cotton, satin weave sheets?"

"Can you buy them at Target?"

"I do not recognize the name of this store—Target—but, my guess is no."

"Then I am absolutely certain I have never experienced cotton weave sheets."

"No. It is Egyptian cotton, satin weave."

"Forgive me…Egyptian cotton, satin weave."

"Once you lay down on these, you will never lay down on another fabric and be satisfied."

"You mean I will never be at peace with my sheets?"

"Be serious. You are making fun of me."

Diane fought to keep a poker face.

"Okay. I'm now very serious."

"Good. Now make yourself comfortable."

"Face down?"

"Always face down first. All of your stress is in your back. Massage the back for relief, massage the front to excite."

"Well, we certainly don't want to excite, do we?"

"Maybe another time," Suki said, amused by Diane's response. Just as Diane started to take her towel off, Suki yelled, "Wait!"

Diane stopped.

"You have to be dry to have the full experience. Wait here."

Suki hurried off to a closet to fetch a dry towel. When she returned, Diane took off her towel, then reached for the one in Suki's hand. But instead of handing it to her, Suki began to dry off Diane. Her passes with the towel were brisk and deliberate as she dried off every inch of Diane's body. It happened so quickly, Diane was unable to voice any objection to what had happened—not that she would at this point.

"Now, you can lie down," Suki said.

"You're sure?"

"Yes, lie down, please. You are making fun of me again."

Suki had a nervous smile, and she was extremely anxious to please her new friend.

Diane took her time stretching out on the massage table. She moved both up and down, and side to side. After a short while, she settled to a stop.

"Wow."

Suki clapped her hands with joy.

"You like Egyptian cotton, satin weave sheets, yes?"

"This is good. Yes, this is a good thing."

"They are made by Yves Delorme. You have heard of that company?"

"No. But I'll definitely have to look it up. I'm sure my company can find a way to sell these on the side."

"They have a store in Bangkok. We will go there together where I will buy you your first set of Egyptian cotton, satin weave sheets. Do you like Thai massage, Swedish massage, or another kind of massage?"

"Suki, I'm serious. I have no spa experience. I have never spent a nickel on a massage. Bruce….my husband…."

Diane unexpectedly stopped talking in the middle of a sentence.

Suki felt Diane start to choke up as soon as she mentioned Bruce's name. She knew Diane was tormented by his memory.

"I'll give you a light Swedish massage. It is relaxing. You need relaxation now."

Suki poured some very light, clove scented oil into her hands, warming it briefly, then spread it on Diane's shoulders and began to work it in. Diane didn't say anything, but Suki could tell the muscle twitching in Diane's body was a result of quiet sobbing.

"I want to know more about Bruce. Today is not a good day as there is already too much stress. Maybe in a few days. I want you to talk a lot about Bruce while I listen."

Diane's voice broke as she regained enough composure to respond.

"Thank you Suki. That would be a good thing. That would be like Egyptian cotton, satin weave sheets.

Chapter 11

After thirty minutes of running barefoot along the water's edge, Mickey looked ragged and felt just as bad. The high temperature and humidity left him dripping with sweat and very winded. He walked for the next ten minutes to cool down before getting a large beach towel plus two bottles of water from one of the property attendants along the beach. He then proceeded to do his usual fifty push-ups, followed by one hundred sit-ups, stretching and yoga. Finishing his routine after about forty-five minutes, he then slowly made his way back to the bungalow. It was only then that he realized just how exhausted he was.

Suki met him at the door, holding her finger to her lips with one hand, and pointing with the other hand to where Diane was sleeping, covered by a sheet on the massage table.

"Be quiet," she whispered. "Diane is taking a nap. She needs a short rest." Looking at Mickey from head to toe, Suki said, "I think you have gained weight."

"Eighty-five kilos…just eighty-five," Mickey said, disputing her remark.

Wrapping his towel around Suki's neck, he pulled her closer to him.

"Clearly, your weight and figure haven't changed at all for the worse."

He took his time examining Suki's nearly naked body, also from head to toe, with deliberate stops along the way.

"Let me see," Suki said, putting her arms around Mickey's waist and holding him tightly. "Yes. You feel the same. I suppose you are eighty-five kilos," she said, kissing him in the center of his chest.

"You're as beautiful as always, Suki. It seems like forever since Manila."

This was the first time Mickey had looked at Suki where there was a noticeable sign of passion in his eyes, and she reveled in his attention.

"One hundred days ago tomorrow, but I am not counting them."

The two hugged each other tightly as Suki closed her eyes, lost in the moment.

"What do you think?" Mickey asked, kissing Suki on top of her head.

"About what?"

She opened her eyes and stared deeply into his, hoping he had a surprise that involved her.

"Diane, of course. What do you think about Diane?"

"She is a very lovely woman," Suki replied once she realized Mickey's focus had again changed. "I think she is very different from me. She wants to be a very strong woman, yet she struggles with dominance. She needs to dominate, but she does not like it. She is not at peace with herself, nor is she at peace about the death of her late husband. She cried about him while you were gone. I told her I would listen to her talk about him someday soon. Do you talk to her about him?"

"Hell, no. The last thing I want to do when we're together for the few hours we typically have is plow through some sob story about how her husband got splattered on the side of a truck."

With a look of disbelief, Suki responded, "She suffered a terrible loss. That is a story that has to be told if the two of you are to become one someday. I think nothing would bring her closer to you than for you to listen to her heart."

"You mean you want me to put my ear on her chest? I can do that. In fact, I'd like to do that."

"Mickey, there are times when you talk like a boy instead of a man."

Disappointed by his lack of compassion, she firmly pushed him away from her.

Mickey didn't like Suki's criticism, and the flexing in his jaw muscles made that clear.

"Well to be honest with you Suki, I don't want to be her crying towel. I thought you would be better at that."

"I am very capable of doing that, Mickey, and I will. I see a demon in Diane that has to be released. She and I will become friends. We will become very close because I will be there for her in her time of need when she is ready to talk. You will remain on the outside. You cannot benefit from my work in this regard."

"Good, you do that. I'm tired of this ball and chain she's carrying around. I think she'll be ready to settle down and have a committed relationship with me once we get this thing exorcised."

Suki closed her eyes, put her hands together, and muttered something in Chinese.

"What are you saying?" Mickey asked.

"I was asking for strength so that I would not hurt you," Suki replied, reopening her eyes.

"I'm paying you a lot," Mickey said, pointing a finger at her. "I expect a lot in return."

"I liked it better when all you wanted from me was companionship and sex," Suki said, gently but forcefully pushing Mickey's hand to the side.

"You'll get your chance with that as well."

Suki folded her arms across her chest in a gesture intended to show that she was off limits.

"Mickey, is that you?" Diane asked in a quiet voice, while turning her head toward the door where Suki and Mickey were standing.

"How are you doing, babe? Suki says you're tired," Mickey said as he and Suki walked over to her.

Diane didn't move a muscle, but managed to smile as she said, "I'm zonked. I just melted on this table. Mick, you have to lie down on these sheets."

"Did Suki give you the ol' Egyptian cotton, satin weave sheet treatment?"

"You can almost slide on them they're so soft."

"I like them because they won't chafe my dick when I get a massage."

Diane's smile quickly vanished.

"I can't believe you destroyed my perfect image of these heavenly sheets with the thought of your chafed dick. Suki, hit him for me."

"As you wish, Diane."

Suki didn't waste any time. She was already upset by the private conversation she had with Mickey. Taking her right elbow, she blasted Mickey in the gut as hard as she could, causing him to double over from the unexpected assault.

"Suki!" Diane shouted, sitting up suddenly.

Though stunned, Mickey managed to say, "I'm okay. She does this to me all the time. We have this Clouseau-Cato relationship. Besides, she has to use her Black Belt for something."

Mickey quickly retaliated by slapping Suki on her buttocks with a particularly vicious *whack*, making her cry out. For the next few seconds, they exchanged looks indicating perhaps they had both had enough.

Diane urgently intervened.

"Are you ready for your massage, Mickey?"

She gestured toward the empty table.

"Sounds great," he answered, still keeping a wary eye on Suki.

After walking over to Diane and kissing her, he removed his sweaty running shorts—his only garment—and tossed them at Suki.

"Yuck, you're salty," Diane said, licking her lips and making a face. "I guess it's too early for your taste to have changed."

"Even after several days of good diet, Mickey will remain a bitter tasting person," Suki responded, angrily tossing his running shorts in a corner.

Diane wasn't sure if Suki was kidding, and certainly didn't want to get to any specific details. She could only imagine *what* of Mickey's she had previously tasted.

"Please, Diane, you should lie back down and relax while I work on Mickey."

Suki guided Diane back down on the table that was sitting parallel with Mickey's, and covered her with the sheet—hiding her naked body from Mickey.

"Face down or face up?" Mickey asked, sporting a shameless grin.

"Face down," both ladies relied in unison.

Mickey smiled approvingly at the return of some semblance of civility.

"I see the two of you found common ground while I was gone," he said while stretching out on the table, his sweaty body sticking to the sheets.

"Wait!" Diane said, raising herself up on her elbows. "You're supposed to be dried off first."

It was too late. What was done was done.

"Oh, Mickey..." Diane said disappointedly.

"He is in a mood right now, Diane," Suki said, putting her silk top back on and straightened her gold bikini bottoms. "Let me work the kinks out of him."

Suki draped a towel over Mickey's buttocks, which he immediately removed. Raising her hand high above her head, she came down hard on Mickey's right butt cheek making a louder sound than when he had spanked her. That got his attention. She once again draped the towel over his buttocks. This time he left it there. After squirting some vanilla scented oil into the palm of her hand, she proceeded to spread it evenly over his back from his neck down to his waist using firm pressure. She followed by kneading his back until she found a spot between his spine and his right shoulder blade that caught her attention.

"Look what I found," she said.

Placing her right elbow on the spot before pressing hard until the veins in her neck bulged.

Mickey's legs bent up at his knees as he winced in pain.

Diane looked on with concern

"What are you doing to him?"

"It is something like trigger point massage," Suki replied, dispensing relentless pressure to Mickey's back. "He gets pain that is referred from angry nerve bundles in his back, neck and thighs. Am I right, Mickey?"

"Yup!"

"He does not like what he calls foo-foo massage, do you Mickey?" Suki asked, moving her elbow ever so slightly as she forced it deeper into Mickey's trapezius muscle.

"Nope." Mickey replied, grabbing the legs of the table while squeezing to hide his discomfort.

"He thinks therapy requires pain. Am I telling your story correctly, Mickey?"

"Right on," he groaned.

After thirty seconds, Suki stopped what she was doing and proceeded to rub and knead Mickey's back again. Slowly she circled back to the spot she had been previously working on.

"What do you know, it is still reactive," she said, getting up on the table and straddling Mickey's buttocks.

Once again, she began to push her elbow into Mickey's back, this time with more force. His face turned red and he began to perspire heavily, but he never asked Suki to stop. Diane watched the process with amazement. After another thirty seconds of non-stop pressure, Suki once again began to rub and knead Mickey's back. Upon re-examination of the spot that had been the focus of all of her effort, she was satisfied.

"There. That is much better."

"I'm stressed just watching this," Diane said, turning onto her side and propping her head up on her arm.

"Not to worry," Suki said. "I did not feel any knots in your back."

"I'm glad to hear that." Diane replied, raising her eyebrows. "I don't think I would like to have that done to me."

Continuing to lightly massage Mickey's back and shoulders, Suki explained, "It serves a specific purpose. I also find enjoyment inflicting pain with my therapy…depending upon the client, of course."

Suki playfully poked Mickey in the back to make sure he knew she was referring to him.

"Humph," was the extent of Mickey's response.

Intrigued by Suki's ability to be both ever so tender or so very brutal, Diane asked, "So, tell me about your Black Belt."

"I practice an art called lotus self-defense. It fits in well with the rest of my lifestyle."

"Have you ever had to protect yourself?"

"On a few occasions, but my instincts prevent me from getting into trouble ninety-nine percent of the time."

"Have you beaten up a man before?" Diane asked excitedly.

"Yes," Suki replied, nonchalantly. "Does that surprise you?"

Mickey added, "She's killed a man before."

Suki administered an aggressive punch to Mickey's ribs.

Mickey recoiled, "Argh!"

"He's kidding, right?" Diane asked.

Looking at Diane with an unemotional countenance, Suki replied very seriously, "One must do what one must to do. It happened. It is not to be discussed further."

Diane was speechless. She had never been confronted with a situation like this before.

After pondering Suki's remark, she said, "I'm expecting to have nightmares tonight."

"Think of me as a bodyguard as well as a concierge," Suki said, showing no hint of remorse.

"Is there a reason I would need a bodyguard?" Diane asked, her face now showing concern.

"No. No particular reason. Nonetheless, just like anywhere, bad things can happen. I will not let them happen to me or anyone that I care for."

Suki got off of Mickey before reaching her hand under the towel covering Mickey's buttocks. He responded by parting his legs. Suki was now rubbing some*thing* or some*things* that Diane thought would be off limits.

"What are you doing?" Diane asked.

"I'm getting ready to stimulate paradoxical emotions. A moment ago, he felt pain. Soon, he will be feeling pleasure. Doing so stimulates his mind, causing an abrupt and complete sense of relaxation. Am I offending you?"

"Let's just say I have never watched another woman rub my lover's balls before."

"You didn't answer the woman's question," Mickey said, looking at Diane. "Do you want her to stop?"

"Yes!"

Suki stopped what she was doing, but kept her hand under the towel as if she were taunting Diane.

"I said stop!"

Diane got up off of her table and grabbed the towel away from Mickey's buttocks, exposing Suki's hand. In it, there were two round, black spheres.

"What are those?" Diane asked.

"Onyx," Suki answered.

"Onyx?" Diane was livid.

"I use these spheres to massage Mickey's back," Suki stated calmly. "It is best that they are the same temperature as skin. I leave them between Mickey's legs when I start his massage so they can begin to warm up, then I check the temperature of them to be sure they are ready."

"I'm sorry," Diane said, covering herself with Mickey's towel. "I guess I overreacted. I thought you were rubbing Mickey's..."

"Testicles?" Suki's eyebrows raised and her face sported a crooked smile.

"Yeah, those," Diane said, letting out a sigh.

"That would have been improper. We have an agreement."

"I know, but earlier you and I..." Diane noticed Mickey listening intently.

Mickey rolled over onto his back, leaving nothing to the imagination.

"You and Suki what...? I want to hear this."

Now Mickey had his own crooked smile.

Diane let her towel drop to the floor as she approached Mickey. Without even slowing down, Diane hopped up on top of Mickey as he reclined face up on the massage table. Suki watched, almost looking distressed, as Diane kissed and grabbed at Mickey, slowly working her way down Mickey's body until she reached her target.

He was initially startled by Diane's unexpected attack, but soon was reciprocating by fondling her head, shoulders, and breasts. Mickey found the few moments of oral sex, complete with a voyeur, to be exhilarating. What followed was not. Diane reached down for Mickey's scrotum, latching on with a firm grip causing him to let out a scream.

Boundaries

"What are you doing?" Suki shouted.

"Me?" Diane said with her own crooked smile. "I'm stimulating paradoxical emotions. A second ago he was feeling pleasure. Now, he's feeling pain." Looking directly at Mickey, Diane finished with, "Like it?"

"Stop!" Mickey shouted.

Diane let go and hopped off of him. Immediately, Mickey sat up with his legs hanging off of the table, his hands cupping his sore boys.

Diane grabbed her towel and flipped it over her shoulder. She looked back and forth between Suki and Mickey.

"Don't ever fuck with me like that again. Got it?"

There was stunned silence.

"I'm going to bed now. I hope the two of you are on better behavior in the morning."

With that, Diane walked briskly to the bedroom, slamming the door behind her.

"I guess I screwed that one up," Mickey said. "So, did you and Diane...?"

Putting her hand up to Mickey's face, she said, "Do not even suggest it."

With that, Suki headed off to her quarters, slamming the door behind her.

Calling out to an empty room, and deaf ears, Mickey said, "I'm really enjoying my vacation. I just want everyone to know that!"

Chapter 12

No man looked better than Bruce when he was on his Harley. They were made for each other. He bought his Fat Boy new two years before the accident. The airbrushed flame custom paint job on the fenders and fuel tank matched the locks of his long hair as it blew in the wind when he rode. Diane loved the feel of his hair tickling her face as she held onto his waist. As his hands gripped the mustache highway bars, the muscles in his arms bulged. When he would turn the bike just so, Diane could see the smile on his face reflecting in the mirrors. She would be lulled into a zone of comfort by the sun on her head, the rumble of the bike, and the feel of her husband in front of her. He used to tell her that nothing made him happier than riding two things—her and his Fat Boy.

Today was just another ride. Diane and Bruce were heading for the mountains. They packed all they needed in a sissy-bar bag—lightweight down sleeping bags, a small tarp and collapsible poles in the event of rain, some basics to eat, and a couple bottles of wine. Mostly, they needed one another. The weekend getaways were cherished, but becoming less frequent as Diane's sales job blossomed and Bruce's architectural designs became noticed. That made these trips much more important than ever.

There wasn't even time to brake. The produce truck in the outside lane of the cross traffic—the sight of it blocked by a line of stopped 18-wheelers—pulled out in front of them without any warning. In an instant, Bruce's body was wedged unnaturally between the cab and the hopper of the truck. There was no sound. Diane was suspended above it all looking down on the chaos as people ran to the scene of the accident. As she reached out to try to pull on him, his arms failed to reach back for her. He was motionless. Blood poured from his chest and his face. His eyes were open and looked back at her. That's when he whispered, "Where were you?"

Boundaries

DIANE WOKE UP KNEELING in her bed, screaming as she reached toward the ceiling. She trembled uncontrollably, her breathing was rapid, and tears streamed from her eyes.

Suki came running into her bedroom and cradled Diane in her arms.

"Diane! What is wrong?!"

"Oh, my God, it's happening again. I had another dream about Bruce dying and it was horrible."

Diane crumpled onto the bed. Suki left her just long enough to wet a washcloth, returning with it to wipe the tears from Diane's face.

"Am I really here, Suki? Is this real?"

"This is real, Diane. I am here. Everything is alright."

Suki lay down beside Diane, stroking her hair and holding her closely, while she buried her face in Suki's chest and let go of her emotions. Several minutes passed and nothing was said. After the hysteria turned to crying, and the crying turned to sobbing, and the sobbing turned into whimpering, Suki figured it was time to begin the healing process.

"Tell me about Bruce."

Initially there was no response from Diane.

"Tell me about Bruce."

"He died and I wasn't with him," Diane replied, choking out the words.

"No, that was an event," Suki said, trying to get the conversation back on track. "Tell me about Bruce."

After some hesitation, Diane began to open up.

"He was my big bear. When I was little, I had a Teddy Bear named Bud that I took everywhere. It was my companion and my comfort. Eventually I grew older and I forgot about him, or it, or whatever. The first time Bruce held me in his arms, I remember feeling the same comfort that I felt with Bud. I knew right then I would marry him. Bruce was so hairy, too. He had a beard…a real nice beard, and long hair that was always clean and in a ponytail or braids, except when he was riding his motorcycle. That's when he would let it blow in the wind. He used to let me braid his hair. I always wanted to braid my daughter's hair, but we never had kids, so Bruce had to put up with me brushing and braiding his. He never complained about me doing it."

She took a deep breath before continuing, "He had a few tattoos, but not too many. There were three big ones—one said *Diane*, the other said *Peace*, and the one on his back was a huge falcon with talons. When I used to hug his back, he would say his talons were grabbing me. I could almost feel them digging into my skin. He didn't want me get any tattoos because he said I was too beautiful to disfigure with ink."

Diane paused to wipe her tears again before adding, "Everything with us was effortless. He was always there when I needed him. He was so generous with his thoughts, and he talked to me like a friend all the time. God, I miss that the most, just talking and talking. We connected so well." She wiped her face once more with the cloth before putting her head back on Suki's chest.

"He sounds like the perfect man to me."

"Oh, he was," Diane replied. Suddenly, the tone of her voice changed as she went on, "But Daddy hated him. Daddy wanted me to come back home to the ranch after college and take over the businesses. I was the only child after my older brother died. Daddy disliked Bruce until the day he died and from that moment on, I lost all love for my father because he never accepted Bruce. Bruce went to his grave knowing my father hated his guts. So when Daddy died, I made sure I wasn't there." Diane began to tear up again, saying, "Now, I feel bad because I think I let him down, too." Diane rolled over onto her back, put her hands over her eyes, and became quiet until she said, "I think that's enough for now."

Suki put her hand over Diane's heart before saying, "Anytime you want to talk, Diane, I am here."

Diane turned to Suki and hugged her.

"What time is it?" Diane asked, raising herself up on her one elbow.

"It is about three o'clock in the morning."

"Where's Mickey?"

Boundaries

"He is probably out walking. He often goes walking at night. He has this fixation on dreams. He wants to get up and think about all the details of what he has just dreamed about, so he can write down all he can remember. He does not do that when he is with you?"

"You may find this hard to believe," Diane said awkwardly "but we haven't spent too many nights together, and when we do I'm usually so drunk I sleep like a rock. I wouldn't know if he gets up or not." Suki's query begged the question, "So he gets up at night with you?"

Knowing she had to be completely honest, Suki replied, "Almost every time we have spent the night together, he gets up and wanders off some place."

Diane just looked back at Suki expressionless as she struggled to grasp Mickey's multiple relationships.

"Would you like something to drink?" Suki asked.

"Sure," Diane replied as she was drawn back into the moment. "That's sounds good. Just some fruit juice, please."

"I have just the thing," Suki said with a smile.

She hopped out of the bed and hurried out to the kitchen. Diane followed, but just as she got to the door, she was caught by the magnificent spectacle of the light of the moon reflecting off of the sea. Walking out to the porch, she was met by a wonderful breeze and the smell of flowers. She shivered even though the air temperature was over 80 degrees.

Soon, Suki returned with two glasses of juice and gave one to Diane.

After taking a sip, Diane exclaimed, "Whew! That packs a punch. What's in this?"

"It is a combination of various fruit juices, plus a little grapefruit juice to take away some of the sweetness. Do you like it?"

"It's...indescribable," Diane replied. "Let's just say the sweet and the bitter blend perfectly together."

"It is a lot like two people in love."

Diane soaked in the breeze for a minute, before saying, "Suki, I've spent seven years trying to run away from my feelings about Bruce's accident.

Sometimes I feel it creeping up on me so I work harder or do anything and everything to occupy my mind. Then, the feelings go away, and I find myself feeling guilty that I let the memory of him get too distant, after which I obsess about that. Before I know it, the whole vicious cycle starts over again. I've never told anyone the things I told you tonight—nobody."

"Do you feel better having talked about him?"

"That's just it. I've never talked about him before. I've just avoided the entire matter. I don't know if I feel relief or sorrow or numbness or what. I especially can't figure out why I'm thinking about this now."

"Do you think it interferes with your relationship with Mickey?"

"Oh, absolutely. I'm so…I don't know…guarded I guess is the word. I just can't let myself go. I feel like I'm cheating on my husband."

Diane's lips puckered as she took another sip from her drink.

"If I finish this I'll be out walking the beach."

"There is nothing wrong with having wonderful, loving memories of Bruce *and* moving on with your life. The two of you shared many years together and many experiences and those should be cherished. You should be able to tell Mickey about those memories, and then let him process the information the way he wants. Bruce is inside of you and will be forever. If Mickey wants you and loves you, he has to get to know Bruce, too."

"Suki, we're talking about Mickey…Mickey Rollins," Diane said, grimacing at the very suggestion.

"Mickey is changing. He used to think of himself as a deity. Now he sees himself as mortal. That is a big change for a god."

Diane laughed at the reference.

Pulling Diane close, Suki pointed off into the distance and said, "Look, there he is now."

Way down on the beach stood a figure with its legs and arms apart, forming an "X". It was too far away to tell if the figure was looking toward the water or the land.

Boundaries

"It is Mickey's way of meditating—unconventional at best, but then we are speaking of an unconventional person."

"Are you sure that's Mickey?" Diane asked, squinting her eyes in an attempt to make out his features.

"Diane, I come to this place often, and I can tell you honestly that nobody else stands like that on the beach at three o'clock in the morning. I have seen him do it before. He says it allows him to soak up life's energy."

"Do you think Mickey is sane?" Diane asked curiously.

"Diane, we are talking about Mickey...Mickey Rollins."

The two burst out laughing.

When the laughter had subsided, Diane took another sip of her drink then chuckled before saying, "I can't believe I thought you were rubbing his balls."

"That was a terrible trick he pulled and I played along with him," Suki said, shaking her head. "I am truly, truly sorry."

"Well, I forgive you. And Suki, seriously, thank you for listening tonight. I can't tell you how much that meant to me. Whatever your relationship is with Mickey, I have to tell you it's been trumped by, I guess, your kindness."

Suki waited to respond, soaking up Diane's compliment.

"Mickey is a good man—not without his faults—but overall a good man. I can sense he is looking for something permanent. A man with his qualities, not to mention his bank account, will not be available long. I hope you and he find what you are looking for in each other."

"Until I met you, I didn't know there were other women in his life."

As the two sipped their drinks, the wind blew through the hair of both women while they contemplated the depth and candor of their conversation.

Finally breaking the silence, Suki said, "You do not have to worry about me. Mickey and I have an unemotional relationship. On the other hand, there are two people who weigh very heavily on his mind."

"And who are these mystery people?" Diane asked, anxious to hear.

"You do know that Mickey was married previously?"

"Yeah, he told me, but that was a long time ago."

"I have no doubt he is still in love with her."

"How do you know?"

"I just know. Trust me."

"Isn't she completely out of the picture?"

"Is Bruce out of the picture?"

"That's different," Diane said, bristling for a moment at Suki's comment.

"No, it is very much the same. He made an imprint on your heart that is permanent, just like she did to Mickey's heart many years ago. The feelings never go away. One must assimilate those emotions and feelings from the past with those of the present."

"I don't know if I agree," Diane responded, shaking her head. "So, who's the second one I need to worry about?"

"Maria."

"Maria?! She's his maid!"

"No, she is his manager, his secretary, his confidant, his cook, his caretaker, and his friend. She tends to his garden. She sees him nearly every day, and she would be foolish not to want him in every other way. She is, after all, a woman. Let us also not forget that she washes his underwear, and probably buys them for him as well. There is not a man alive who does not think fondly of a woman with that résumé."

Diane continued to look disbelievingly as she responded, "Naw....I can't see it. I can't be in competition with a maid?"

"Diane, above all, Mickey is first and foremost a very basic man, with very basic needs. Think about it."

"Oh Suki, you're creeping me out," Diane said, clenching her shirt with her free hand. "Now I'm going to have this insane paranoia about the ex-wife and the maid. My life is becoming a bizarre, cheap, paperback novel."

After setting down her drink, Suki turned to face Diane directly, put her hands on her shoulders, and said, "You can be the author of this novel—cheap or otherwise. Why else did you come with Mickey on this vacation?"

Boundaries

It was obvious to Suki that Diane was privately reflecting on her motives. That Diane wasn't entirely forthcoming made Suki suspect her true reason for accompanying Mickey was not 'love.'

"This is an opportunity to capture his love for you and you alone. This place where you are standing is a paradise. Where we are going in the days to come is even more incredible. These places will take your passion and emotions and multiply them many times over *if* you let them. You have to decide here, right now, if you are ready for the ride of your life and most importantly, if you are ready to take it with Mickey."

"Why are you saying this? Why are you doing all of this for me? You hardly know me, and I suspect, despite your denial, you probably love Mickey very deeply."

"You are wrong, Diane. I know you very well. It would scare you to know just how much we are alike. We are both women with all the same basic goals and desires and needs and traits. Remember our discussion last night about humility. All of our traits have been modified by our past to be dominant or subordinate, and that order is what makes us unique individuals. If you look only at our components, we are almost twins. You may wish to examine the hierarchy of your traits. The person you *were,* does not have to be the person you *are,* nor the person you wish to become."

Diane stood looking at Suki, her mouth open slightly, and asked, "Do you have a PhD in something?"

"When it comes to life, soul, and the mind, a Buddhist has more knowledge than someone with a PhD."

There was a long period of silence. Suki waived her hand in front of Diane's fixed eyes. Finally Diane spoke.

"Do you have something to drink that has alcohol in it?"

"Yes. But, let us take a walk instead. That would be better for you."

"I'm not dressed to go out," Diane said, pointing to her panties and t-shirt.

"Diane, you are at a resort, on a beach. It is the middle of the night. I am dressed the same way."

Suki went into her room and grabbed two pairs of short shorts from a bureau.

"Here, put these on. I sleep in them sometimes because they fit comfortably. What color do you want?"

"Fit comfortably? You mean they're big enough for my ass, don't you?" Diane asked with a smile.

Suki gave Diane's rump a playful pat, as she clarified her remark.

"There is nothing *big* about your ass."

"I'll take the light blue," Diane said, taking the pair and quickly stepping into them.

"That is a good color for you," Suki said, putting on the canary yellow shorts.

Without warning, Suki went to the bar, removed a chilled Australian white wine, and put it along with a cork screw and some glasses into a small wicker basket.

"What happened to 'no alcohol'?"

"So I changed my mind. I am a woman. Please note that there are only two glasses, and one of them is not for me."

"You mean…?"

"Correct. We are going to interrupt old Mickey-boy. He will want to see you."

"How do you know?"

"After his nighttime wandering and meditation, he is probably the most wonderful, affectionate, and caring man you will ever know."

Once again, Diane was faced with the fact that Suki knew Mickey very well—better in fact than she knew him. But, there was nothing she could do other than take the comment in stride.

Suki interlocked her fingers with Diane's, and the two strolled down to the beach where Mickey was still standing spread-eagled. He was facing the water and the moonlight illuminated his face. His shirt was unbuttoned. His hair blew in the breeze. He looked completely at peace, and completely disconnected from the moment and his location.

Boundaries

Pulling Diane close, Suki whispered, "This is very delicate. You need to gently bring him back to reality. Is there something you say to him that he especially likes to hear or that you can be certain will get his attention?"

Diane thought for a moment, but soon smiled and replied, "Yeah. I've got something that should stir him."

"Get as close to him as possible without touching him, then start whispering. Get a little louder each time you repeat it. He should come around. Good luck. See you guys in the morning."

Suki set the basket on the sand. Without another word, she headed back to the bungalow.

Mickey was hardly breathing and his head was lower than usual because of his stance. Diane stood practically eye-to-eye with him after she eased up close to him. Leaning forward, she whispered, "Dippin' Dots." There was no reaction. She leaned forward again and whispered a little louder, "Dippin' Dots."

It took a few moments, but Mickey opened his left eye, looked at Diane, and mumbled, "It's not nice to interrupt someone who is meditating. But for you, and only you, I will always make an exception." He smiled and then slowly let his arms down to his side, grimacing as he moved his legs to stand upright.

"Are you alright?"

"Just moving kind of slow. I used to try the lotus position, but it took me hours to get to the point where I could walk afterwards."

"Oh, it's that *I'm-going-to-turn-fifty* thing, isn't it?"

Mickey gave Diane an unappreciative look.

"Do you want me to feel sorry for you?" She asked, putting her arms playfully around his waist.

Mickey put his arms around her shoulders. Their lips met and they kissed.

"Do older men turn you on?"

"No, just you."

"You were supposed to answer, 'You're not old.'"

"Sorry. I left my script up in the bungalow."

The two hugged again as Mickey blew into Diane's ear causing her to tremble.

"What's with the Dippin' Dots?"

"Suki told me to whisper something in your ear that would stimulate you. I narrowed it down to a short list of, 'Hey dude, want a blow job?' or 'Dippin' Dots.'"

"Well you chose right," Mickey said laughing. "'Blow job' wouldn't have done a thing for me."

Rolling her eyes, Diane said, "You lie like a rug."

She grabbed Mickey's ribs, making him jump. That led to a chase along the shoreline, ending when Diane finally succumbed to Mickey's pursuit. Reaching around her from behind, he held her closely. For the next few moments, the two said nothing, but simply shared the intimacy of contact.

"I think Rajeev is right. You need to take the new job so I can spend more time with you."

Diane was startled, but tried not to show it. This was not something to which Mickey had ever alluded.

"What would you do with me if we had this additional time?"

"I don't know. I guess I have this feeling when I'm with you that we belong together from now on."

Diane froze. Mickey's statement sounded like a proposal of marriage in so many words, and yet he left out the very words that would have made it perfectly clear. She was scared to death to ask him to clarify what he had said. Instead she changed subjects.

"There's wine in the basket."

The relief in Mickey's expression was unmistakable.

"That would be great."

He held out his hand. Diane took it. Together, they walked back to where the basket had been left on the beach not too far away. As Mickey sat down, Diane got down on her knees and opened up the basket.

Boundaries

"Look, it's a huge sheet! Feel it," she said, rubbing it against her cheek. "It's one of those Egyptian cotton things. Help me spread it out."

Mickey took two corners and assisted Diane with stretching it out, creating what was to become their king-sized pallet. Next, he opened the wine and began to fill their glasses. While he was doing that, Diane discretely looked up and down the beach to determine if they were alone. She only had a few moments to ponder her next course of action before Mickey turned around. After hastily removing her clothes, she stretched out on her right side. Mickey turned around, almost spilling the wine from both glasses as he looked down at Diane who was now in a most seductive pose. After burying the stems of the glasses in the sand so they wouldn't spill, he removed his shorts and shirt. He grabbed the glasses of wine, gave one to Diane, and soon was lying next to her. A few moments later, he was lying on top kissing her passionately. The breeze was suddenly warm.

Parting lips with Diane just long enough to utter a few words, Mickey said, "God I love these sheets."

From atop the hill where the bungalow clung to the hillside, Suki looked out onto the beach, sipping a drink from a tall glass. While she watched Mickey and Diane closely, tears ran slowly from her eyes.

Chapter 13

The sky began to reflect the colors of dawn, though direct sunlight was still blocked by the hillside and the buildings of the resort. Mickey and Diane remained lying in the long shadow of their bungalow. They had thought enough to pull the sheet over the top of them before they fell asleep in each other's arms. From the clothes scattered around them on the beach, it was clear to the few passersby that the two were not dressed. The locals who walked pass the lovers left plenty of space between themselves and the two, sheet-covered bodies. Other visitors paid little or no attention to what they saw as a perfectly acceptable, albeit extreme, display of affection.

A small gust of wind blew some sand into Diane's face awakening her. After opening her eyes, she soon realized their privacy was a thing of the past.

"Mickey. Mickey! Wake up!" she said in a low voice.

"It's so wonderful to wake up and to see you," he said, slowly opening his eyes and smiling at his companion.

His remark had gone straight to Diane's heart. She was certain that most men would be unable to think quickly enough to come up with *that* perfect line right after a sound sleep. It had to be genuine.

"I love you, Mickey." The words were becoming easier for her to say.

"I love you, too, babe," he replied, pulling Diane close and kissing her.

It wasn't long before Mickey's passion turned physical once more. Before Diane could stop him, his head disappeared beneath the sheet and moved down her body—his lips leaving the nape of her neck then quickly moving south.

"Mickey! We're in public! There are people watching us. That's why I woke you up."

Poking his head out from under the sheet, he replied, "They're just jealous." Looking around, he observed, "See that fellow over there. He's staring at us."

"I know! And he's not staring at us, he's staring at me."

"He's staring at you?"

"Yes! And that's not a look of jealousy."

"Is he bothering you?"

"Duh?!"

"Okay, now I'm pissed."

After rolling out from under the sheet, he stood up stark naked and began walking toward the man.

"Hey, look at this!"

The man was startled and fell over his own feet trying to escape. He repeatedly shouted something back toward Mickey in a foreign language, but Mickey didn't stop his pursuit. The man finally managed to get to his feet and ran off to a neighboring resort. After waiting until the man was out of sight, Mickey turned and walked back to Diane.

She couldn't take her eyes off of him. He was quite the spectacle. It was easy for Diane to see past the outrageous nature of the moment. Mickey might be approaching fifty, but there wasn't an inch of his body showing any wear. The sunlight still emanating from low in the horizon only accentuated his muscular physique that much more. All of him was perfectly proportioned...even *that*.

"I can't believe what you just did. Hand me my clothes."

Mickey picked up Diane's shorts, panties, and shirt that were scattered about before moving to within a few feet of her. Pausing in a moment of reflection, he said, "I saw Jimmy Stewart do this once in a movie." With a sinister smile, he added, "Come and get them."

"Yeah, but Donna Reed was hiding in a bush. Come on, Mickey, give me my clothes."

"No, you have to come and get them."

"ARGH! You shit!"

Diane stood up with the sheet wrapped around her before starting toward Mickey.

"Not fair. No sheet, Diane."

"Bite me!"

Backing away from Diane as quickly as she moved toward him, he said, "Okay, I'm more than willing to do that, too, but you still have to drop the sheet."

Looking around to convince herself that there was some privacy remaining, Diane dropped the sheet.

"There. Are you happy now?"

Immediately, Mickey dropped Diane's clothes and rushed at her. Before she could react, he had her naked body over his shoulder and was running into the water.

"Mickey! Put me down! Take me back to the beach now! I mean…"

Before she could finish her sentence, both of them were under the rolling surf. Diane surfaced, pulling her hair out of her face and rubbing the salt water from her eyes.

"You are so freakin' dead."

"Why? Nobody can see you out here under the water."

"Damn it, Mickey. Are you out of your mind? I'm flashing the beach with the passing of each wave."

"Am I out of my mind? Absolutely! I am out of my mind over you," he said, pressing up against Diane, and wrapping his arms around her as he stole a kiss.

She tried to maintain her anger, but the feeling of the slippery salt water lubricating their skin as they embraced was a huge turn on.

Out of nowhere, Mickey said as he held her tightly, "I want you to buy your family ranch."

"You want to do what?" Diane asked, pushing away from Mickey just enough so that she could look at his entire facial expression.

"I want you to buy your family ranch in Gilroy."

"We've already had this argument on the plane."

Mickey put his hands on Diane's shoulders reassuring her that he was serious. She may have disagreed with his proposal, but his offer took her mind off of the embarrassing situation in the water. They stood upright in the rough surf, totally naked, with the waves and troughs periodically exposing them from their knees to their chests.

"It wasn't an argument. It was a discussion, and I think it was a good ice breaker."

"No. When it was *my* idea, it was a bad idea. Now that it's *your* idea, it's a good idea. Nothing's changed Mickey."

"I told you to buy it!"

"And I told you it was more than one person could handle!"

"You were right," Mickey said, dropping his hands from her shoulders. He reached for her hands, holding them tightly, and continued, "I thought about this last night and I realized if I wanted to be a part of your life from now on, the ranch would be a good place for me to start."

Diane was at a loss for words. First, Mickey had told her he wanted to be with her *from now on.* Now, he was inserting himself into one of her greatest fantasies—regaining ownership of her family ranch. It was surreal.

"Alright, Mickey, we'll talk about it," Diane replied, waiting for the sky to fall.

There was an odd stalemate as both waited for some kind of further deliberation regarding his proposal. Neither folded, but neither raised the ante.

Finally breaking the deadlock, Diane said, "Now, can we get back to the beach so I can get some clothes on?"

Mickey picked up Diane like a bride going across the threshold of the honeymoon suite and proceeded to carry her back to the beach. She slowly put on her clothes. Having neglected to dry off first, the process somewhat difficult. Mickey put on only his shorts, choosing to wrap his shirt around his neck. The sheet was rolled up quickly and tossed into the basket, with the wine bottles and glasses placed on top. Mickey took the basket in his right hand, holding out his left for Diane. She was at a loss for words, but the smile that spread across her face indicated that Mickey might for once be on the right track.

The two lovers entered the porch of the bungalow where they experienced the overwhelming fragrance of coffee.

"Espresso?" Suki asked, approaching them with two small cups and saucers on a tray.

"How did you know?" Diane replied, stopping in her tracks.

"I just know," Suki replied in trademark fashion. "Here, sit on the porch. The view is marvelous and the breeze is quite cool this morning. Of course you already know this since you were frolicking about with nothing on. Remember, Mickey, we have spoken before about this type of behavior."

"Did we do something wrong?" Diane asked as they walked to the table and chairs outside.

After pulling out Diane's chair for her, Mickey took a seat himself before replying, "Oh, the locals don't like seeing my naked ass on the beach."

"It is just not appropriate," Suki said, correcting Mickey.

She served Diane, then Mickey their cup of espresso.

"Guess we need to find another beach," Mickey said, sipping from his cup.

"Maybe we just need to behave," Diane responded, siding with Suki who in turn smiled and nodded in agreement. "Thank you for the welcome, Suki," Diane continued, holding her cup in the air. "This is wonderful," she said, taking a sip. "It's exactly what I was looking for. Will you join us?"

"I would love to," Suki replied without hesitation. While Suki turned and walked back to the kitchen, Diane took time to observe the wrap-around garment that loosely covered her body. "I like what you have on. What's it called?"

"It is a simple three-piece sarong. I have it up over my shoulder now," Suki said as she placed her cup of espresso on the table. "You can also wear it low," she continued, undoing the sarong from her shoulder, thereby exposing the matching swirling patterned bra and panties. After re-tying it around her hips, she said, "I placed one for you on your bed for when you change after breakfast."

"Really? I can't wait."

"It is a different color and pattern. The color I chose for you goes better with your natural skin tone and it picks up the color in your eyes. The pattern is more subdued. I think that matches your personality."

"What did you set out for me that matches my personality?" Mickey chimed.

"I cannot say such things."

"See, she's a diplomat as well as a concierge," Diane said.

Suki raised her cup to acknowledge Diane's gesture. Then as quickly as the friendly banter had begun, the conversation turned unfriendly.

"So, did you spy on us last night?" Diane asked.

Suki was unfazed, absorbing the sharpness of the question, and answering it with complete control.

"Diane, you are an amazing woman. You drink as much as your man—in this instance, Mickey. You like sex on top and on the bottom. You like sex multiple times. You like to give and receive oral sex. You are at ease with your sexuality, and are very confident as long as you have the dark of night in which to hide. Then daylight comes and you become..." Suki looked at Diane and pointed, "...this."

"This?"

"You become a vulnerable woman."

"Why do you see me as vulnerable?" Diane asked, setting her cup down.

"Because you asked if I was watching you last night when, in fact, all along you knew that I was. What is more, you are trying to change the point of action from you to me—I did not watch. Quite the contrary, you performed."

Diane wriggled uncomfortably realizing Suki was right on target with her observation.

"Why does that make me vulnerable?"

"Because you do not have the courage to say what you mean. You wanted me to see you and Mickey making love all night long on the beach—being passionate, being together, you possessing him. You felt the need to make a point to me. When you have something to prove again and again, you are a vulnerable person. You are unable to accept the faith in your relationship with Mickey I have told you repeatedly you comfortably have."

Diane stared at her cup of espresso.

"Did it excite you to know I was watching you?" Suki asked, quickly looking back and forth between Diane and Mickey.

He restrained himself to just half of a smile, while she initially gave no physical or verbal response.

Exhaling loudly, she said, "Does that make me a pervert?"

"No," Suki replied. "That simply means there is a lot more to Diane than either she or the rest of us know about, and I think we need to help her unveil her mysteries."

Suki looked deeply into Diane's eyes almost as if she wanted to crawl inside of her body.

"You are continuing your process of self-discovery."

Mickey picked a bad moment to change the subject.

"What's for breakfast?"

Both women looked at him with disdain. If Mickey had one enduring quality on this vacation it was that he was able to bring Suki and Diane together again and again.

"Mickey, we are at a very pivotal moment for Diane, and you are thinking only about your stomach." Pointing toward the kitchen, Suki continued, "There is a selection of fruits, cheese, and breads as well as more espresso. Help yourself. Please, opt out of this conversation."

"She's right, Mickey. Go treat yourself to something to eat," Diane said, echoing Suki's response. Turning back to Suki, she said, "I'm sorry I acted so childish a moment ago. You were correct. I was hoping you would see us on the beach. Will you forgive me for being so competitive?"

Touching Diane's hand, Suki said, "Look, I am as competitive as you. That can be an outstanding trait. Remember our discussion last night?"

"Yes, I do. I think this is a good time to get over my sensitivity about you."

"I am your friend, Diane, not a foe," Suki said, smiling sincerely.

Comfortable once more, Diane asked, "Would you help me with my sarong? I've never worn one."

"I will be more than happy to help dress you," Suki said, taking Diane's hand in hers. "But I have a rule. Bathe each morning to get yesterday off of you. Every day starts new and fresh. So before the sarong, you will need a bath. I hope you will allow me to indulge you?"

Suki set her cup down and propped her head on her hands most seductively.

Diane instantly picked up on Suki's message and her skin noticeably flush.

"Hey, Mick, maybe you should skip eating and instead take your run now? Come back in, let's say, two hours or so."

"I was just at the beach. Maybe I'd like to stay here and watch. This sounds interesting."

Suki and Diane both glared at Mickey signaling his suggestion was not an option.

"Go. This is girl time," Diane said, waving her hand and shooing Mickey away. "Boys aren't allowed. We'll get to you later."

"We?" Mickey asked, his eyebrows perking up.

Realizing her choice of pronoun was unintentionally plural, Diane decided simply not to discuss the matter.

"Mick!" She said, pointing her finger toward the beach.

Taking the less than subtle hint, Mickey walked to the bedroom. A short time later, he came out wearing his running shorts and his shoes, and carrying a bottle of water.

"I just want you to know that I'm thoroughly enjoying my vacation."

Diane stood and kissed him as he passed.

As he walked past Suki, she swatted him on the butt then reminded him, "Remember to use the sunscreen I left for you."

"Don't need any sunscreen. I'll be running too fast," Mickey said, smiling brightly. "Have a wonderful time ladies," he said after slipping out the door.

"He never listens to me," Suki said as she looked at Diane.

"Well, that's another of Mickey's behaviors we both have experienced," Diane replied, chuckling.

ONCE MICKEY WAS GONE, the feeling in the room immediately became palpably different. Diane sat back down and stared at Suki to the point of making her feel self-conscious.

"Is there something you want to say?" Suki asked.

Diane grinned nervously, looking around the room at nothing in particular, before saying, "When I was young, I used to love Greek mythology. I read all types of books and I used to dream about being a mermaid and later a siren. Have you heard of a siren?"

"Of course. I, too, was once a young girl with an imagination."

"I always imagined sirens as being the most beautiful and seductive of women—and not only physically beautiful, but their voices were like music," Diane said, uneasily playing with her cup. "Of course they represented peril to the passing sailors, but they were just too irresistible, causing many to fall victim."

After standing up and walking behind Diane, Suki said, "I know exactly what you are saying." She put her hands on Diane's shoulders, massaging them gently while continuing, "I have a slightly different interpretation, however. There is no peril here. There are no victims. What is more, we are not men."

"I've known you for less than a day, Suki, and I see you as one of these sirens," Diane said, keeping her eyes closed. "Part of me says to run away, now! The other part of me..." Turning her head, she kissed Suki's hand. Self-conscious about what she had just done, Diane said, "I'm sorry. That just happened."

"You are not the only one feeling this way. Besides, you are on vacation. Compulsive and even inexplicable behavior is allowed."

"Compulsive? Inexplicable? Is my behavior that far off?"

"Perhaps I chose my words poorly. What I meant is that nothing is taboo right now. You see, from my perspective, you, too, are such a siren."

"But, I was describing you, Suki."

"And at the same time, you were describing yourself."

Suki began massaging Diane's temples and lightly stoking her cheeks with her fingers. She began to hum very softly, causing Diane's breathing to slow to nearly a complete stop as she melted into her chair. Minutes passed, but no words were spoken, until finally Suki bent over, put her lips next to Diane's ear, and whispered, "Now, come with me to the bath."

By now, Diane was following Suki's every command. They walked to the bedroom and stood next to the large waterfall bath. Suki began to disrobe, but Diane quickly stopped her.

"No. I get to do this," Diane said, removing Suki's sarong, eventually exposing her waist, then her hips and legs.

She was breathtaking. Diane reached behind Suki and unfastened her top allowing her breasts to hang freely. She bit her lip trying to restrain her desires, but found the strength she needed to move around behind Suki where she slipped her hands inside of Suki's panties, slowly worked them off of her. They landed on the floor and Suki stepped out of them.

Suki stood there motionless, fully aware Diane was studying her from behind.

After mapping every inch of Suki's body, Diane said, "Do you know you could be described as a work of art?" Then, Suki turned around. Diane's mouth dropped. "I spoke too soon. You are a work of art."

"I like that you undressed me," Suki said, reaching for the buttons of Diane's blouse.

She unfastened all of them before moving behind her and slipping off the blouse. Then, just as Diane had done, she slipped her hands into Diane's shorts and panties, working them off until they were on the floor. Suki's facial expression showed that she, too, was mesmerized by what she was looking at. Diane now turned around. Suki fought to stay in control.

"Mickey is a very lucky man," Suki managed to say.

After a moment of hesitation during which she couldn't take her eyes off of Diane's body, Suki took Diane by the hand and led her into the water. They waded in and floated toward the waterfall.

"Where are the sponges?" Diane asked, scouting around the edges.

"I put them away earlier, but that does not matter. For your bath, I use my hands. I need to feel the changes in your skin texture and muscle tone."

"What makes you think I am going to let you touch me with your bare hands?" Diane asked, a noticeable shiver of expectancy running through her body.

"I just know," Suki replied, with a now characteristic wink and a smile.

"You seem to *know* a lot."

"I know, among other things, that there comes a point in the life of every man and every woman when the temptation to pursue extreme sensations through the touch of another human being becomes an uncontrollable desire."

After reflecting for a moment, Diane began laughing.

"Did I say something funny?"

"I had a flashback of my roommate in college. She was taking some type of psychology class, and for a research topic, she studied the subject of touch. She would have casual meetings with her friends—both men and women—and she would study the responses she got during the conversations when she would touch the other person on the hand or on the shoulder or some other part of their body, and then when she wouldn't touch them at all."

"What did she find out?"

"Oh, my God. The simple act of her touch would bring out emotions, feelings, deep thoughts, and conversations, whereas the same people would be relatively cool without her touch."

"Your roommate learned a very valuable lesson, one that you will rediscover this morning. Now turn around and let me wash your back."

Complying without hesitation, Diane stood up so that she was above the water line from the waist up before closing her eyes in anticipation. Suki poured a cool, blue liquid out of a bottle into her hands then quickly rubbed it over Diane's back. She began to knead Diane's back with her fingers. Soon she was concentrating on a spot just above one shoulder blade.

"Oh, look what I found."

"Guess that's left over from sleeping on the beach," Diane said, wincing slightly. "You're not going to hurt me are you?"

"No. Remember, I only cause pain in those who deserve it...like Mickey. I will work this out very gently, but I need to apply some pressure."

Boundaries

Suki reached her arm around to Diane's front, putting her hand flat against Diane's chest between her breasts. She pressed Diane firmly back against her own naked chest, as she used her thumb to massage the tight mass she had discovered. The liquid that Suki had put on Diane's back caused an exhilarating lubrication between their two bodies.

"There, it is already going away," Suki said proudly.

Diane wiggled slightly, lost in the moment.

"Are you alright?"

"Great," Diane replied, grinning with her nostrils flaring ever so slightly. "I'm just enjoying this sensation you are giving me now. What do I smell? I can't put my finger on it."

"It is a spicy smell of cloves mixed in the soap, along with a small amount of camphor oil. The combination opens the pores for cleansing in addition to healing them. Later, I will apply a cream to your skin to enhance its moisture and softness.

"Why do you use all of these different scents and lotions?"

"The different scents keep your mind alive, continually challenging your senses. As for the different lotions, creams, oils, and soaps, each treatment contributes its own component toward your therapy. There, I think the knot is now gone."

Suki began to move her arm from its place on Diane's chest, taking her time as her hand traveled across a breast. Diane grabbed Suki's hand and held it there. Suki brought her other hand up to Diane's uncovered breast and pressed her body tightly against Diane's back.

"With touch comes talk. Is there more you would like to tell me, my friend?"

Unable to resist the invitation, Diane replied, "I want to tell you all about Rosy."

Suki began to softly rub Diane's belly

.

Chapter 14

Mickey arrived back at the bungalow two hours after he departed, as Diane had asked. He looked anything but refreshed. His running shorts were completely soaked in perspiration, and his skin was red from the combination of exertion and sunburn. He made his way to the refrigerator, and took out a bottle of water that he quickly began to consume. Realizing he was alone, he looked around the room for signs of Diane and Suki. Finding only empty espresso cups, he checked the bedroom where he discovered the two asleep, spooning in bed—Diane holding Suki. Their naked bodies were partially covered by a sheet. For a moment, Mickey thought about joining them in bed, but he stopped short, choosing instead to return to the living room. Deciding to take advantage of the privacy, he looked around for his phone, locating it on the bar countertop. After stepping out onto the porch, he took a seat before dialing a long-distance number.

"Gretchen? It's Mickey Rollins. How's the world's sexiest banker doing tonight? Yeah, well it's only nine o'clock here, and you get paid well to take care of your wealthy clients. Besides, I need you now. No, not that way. Hey, I want you to work a deal for me. There's a horse ranch for sale in or near Gilroy. They breed and sell thoroughbreds. I don't know the name of the ranch, but the previous owner's name was Fontaine, so you can probably figure it out through a title search. Can't be too many like this for sale. Price? I'd guess something around thirty. Yes, million. I want you to lock it up for me. You heard me. Get in touch with the broker, and tell him you have a very interested cash customer, but he has to sit on it for two or three weeks until I get back. If he balks, tell him I'll offer a five percent premium to the asking price if they wait. Assure him I'm good for the money. I'm in Phuket. Yeah, we did, didn't we? You animal. Do you talk to your husband like that? You lying bitch. So, you got me covered? I'm deadly serious.

Don't lose the deal. Call me if you have any trouble. Take care. Maybe next time. Alright, bye."

Just as he flipped his phone closed, two hands came across Mickey's shoulders causing him to jump.

"Did I interrupt you?" Suki asked.

She walked around to the chair in front of Mickey and sat down, crossing her legs. She was wearing nothing but her birthday suit.

Mickey looked up and down at Suki's body before saying, "I'm certainly glad the furniture out here has cushions. I wouldn't want there to be wicker marks left on that beautiful ass."

"Were you talking to another of your lovers just now?" Suki's normally smiling face looked unusually harsh.

After a brief pause, he replied, "She's my banker."

"The one with the blond hair and the butterfly tattoo on her bum?"

"Gotta hand it to you Suki, you have a great memory."

"You lied to me. You told me she was single."

"She could have been single when you met her. She's been married and divorced five times."

"I wonder why?"

Not about to be threatened by Suki's inquisition, Mickey said, "You've changed Suki. When did you become righteous?"

"Do you know what a treasure you have found?"

"Are you speaking of Diane?"

"Yes, Diane."

"That's why I brought her here."

"You have brought many women with you to Asia, Mickey."

"True, but this one's broken and needs to be fixed."

"Broken? Fixed?"

"You know—the dead husband thing."

Suki quickly stood up and put her hands up to her mouth, aghast at Mickey's cold-heartedness. Grabbing a nearby towel, she wrapped it around herself, saying,

"Mickey, I do not think I can do this with you this time. You need to find another…"

"I thought I heard voices." It was Diane, who was joining them on the porch. She was wearing the sarong that Suki had bought for her. "Look. I figured it out. Six years of college and an MBA weren't for naught." Noticing Suki's unhappiness, Diane asked, "Is something wrong?"

Suki was quick to recover her composure. It was almost as if the conversation that had taken place between Mickey and Suki had not taken place.

Replacing her frown with her usual smile, she said, "You look beautiful Diane. What do you think, Mickey?"

"Dandy."

Suki went on to say, "I'm upset with Mickey. Look at him. His sunburn is very bad. Now I need to take care of this before his skin is damaged further. Can you help me?"

"I think we need to let him suffer in silence," Diane replied, shaking her head back and forth. "He brought this on himself."

"Unfortunately, Diane, I am sure you know that Mickey cannot suffer in silence."

"Oh, poor little man got sunburned," Diane said unsympathetically. "Okay, what do I do?"

"He first needs a bath, if you can take care of that. I will bring you a special healing cream to use."

"Can I just give him the short version, or does he need a long version of a bath."

"He needs, and most certainly deserves, *only* a short version. Keeping him in the water for too long will just aggravate his problem. Clean him up—I know that is a tall order—and we will continue on the porch when you are done. No monkey business."

"Did someone say monkeys?" Mickey asked with his smart-ass grin. "I like monkeys."

"Did you get sunburned on purpose?" Diane asked, taking Mickey's hand.

Boundaries

"Oh no," Mickey replied while putting on a most unbelievable expression. "I am completely surprised that the sun was this strong so early in the morning."

Diane let go of Mickey's hand so that she could give him a disapproving push. Reaching the bedroom, he took off his shorts, socks, and shoes. The contrast between the whiteness of the skin on Mickey's mid-section against his sunburned stomach and thighs was almost laughable.

"Look at you. You're a lobster."

"Yeah, but I'll bet you've never seen a lobster hung like this one."

"Possibly. But the lobster is a hell of a lot smarter. Now, get in the water."

Mickey shuddered as if he was startled Diane's command.

"I mean it. Don't be a shit today. You and I had a wonderful night, but I woke up with a short memory."

Wading into the water, Mickey said, "It appears that you and Suki had a wonderful morning as well."

"Yes, we did. What took place is between Suki and me."

"When I saw both of you in bed together, I would say there was nothing between you and Suki."

"Ha, Ha. Let me tell you something Mickey, nothing beats snuggling with a woman."

"That's what I have always said. Are you coming in?"

"Nope. I'm clean, refreshed, happy, and all traces of you are off of and out of my body."

"Sounds like Suki gave you the royal treatment."

"That she did. And you know what else, we had this incredible exchange that did not involve bodily fluids—something called con-ver-sa-tion."

"Con-ver-what?" Mickey said, cocking his head like a cocker spaniel.

Diane splashed water at Mickey in retaliation for his lack of sensitivity.

Just then, Suki entered the room, saying, "Okay boys and girls. Here is a bottle of cream that Mickey needs to rub on and rinse off. Mickey, did you understand those very simple instructions?"

"I can't reach my back".

"Mickey, you're pathetic," Diane said, crossing her arms in disgust.

"No, I just think I need a little TLC. I'm sort of feeling left out of this love affair the two of you have going on."

"So, now that you find there is a bond between Suki and me—a bond that you helped arrange, I might add—you feel threatened?"

Diane started to untie her sarong, but Suki stopped her.

"No Diane. You are ready for the morning. I will take care of him, if that is alright by you."

Suddenly, Diane was faced once more with the very thing she had hoped to avoid. Best case, it was the ménage à trois—nothing more than the physical tryst she had predicted. But the situation had become much more complex—practically a Nash equilibrium. In less than twenty-four hours, Suki had won over Diane's heart, partly due to her charm and magnetism, and partly due to the void in Diane's life that was ready to be filled by a worthy suitor. Furthermore, her feelings for Mickey were still trumped by the memory of Bruce, as well as her quest for information about Mickey's latest project. Lastly, there wasn't enough genuine *love* between her and Mickey to warrant stopping Suki from becoming more physically and perhaps emotionally involved with him.

"Diane? Are you alright? Diane?" Mickey asked, noting that Diane's mind was wandering.

Snapping back into reality, Diane replied, "Yeah. Okay, Suki. Go ahead and do what you have to do." It was clear that Diane's response was less than honest.

"Is something wrong?" Suki asked, trying sincerely to show concern as Diane began to get emotional. Suki helped her into a chair, just as Mickey jumped out of the water, put his shorts back on, and went to Diane's side.

"Talk to me, babe," he said, taking Diane's hand and kneeling beside her.

With closed eyes, Diane said, "I feel kind of suspended in space right now. I'm trying to find something to hold on to, and what I have is the two of you."

Her remark left Mickey and Suki exchanging looks as she openly confided in them.

Boundaries

"I don't mean that negatively. I know what I said sounded that way. I'm just not used to the hunger for human touch and interaction, let alone affection and love—not since Bruce died anyway. I was so devastated by that event, that since then, I have kept everyone at arm's length...even you, Mick. I haven't been entirely honest with you. I mean, you're great, and you're fun, and our sexual relationship just blows me away. I really mean it. But, that's kind of shallow, don't you think?"

"Shallow is good. I can do shallow."

"And then you open your fucking mouth and say something stupid like that! I wonder if you really give a shit about me."

Mickey tried to defend his statement, but Diane cut him short.

"So while I'm in limbo, I meet Suki. Suddenly I find myself experiencing feelings that have been dormant for years and my juices start to flow again. At the same time, I struggle with the relationship that the two of you have with each other. I'm scared to death that at any second, the bond I have with either one of you will be ripped away."

Suki and Mickey stood silent, trying to understand.

"Suki, how do you do what you do and remain detached? Are you without feelings?"

"Do I have feelings?" Suki replied, sitting back in shock. "Each time I leave a client, it is as if a piece of me dies. At first, I could only think about the fun and excitement—and, of course, the money. Later, after I had experienced so many exhilarating times, and after the money became more than I could ever spend in my lifetime, all I had to look forward to was the individual with whom I was spending time. That is when I realized I had to get out of this job sooner, rather than later. I had a rule that I would not get emotionally attached to a client. I was true to myself until I became involved with the two of you. Never before have any of my clients become attached to me, nor I to them. They arrive, I serve, and they go. They take a piece of me with them each time. I have had to be vigilant and remain very detached in order to continue doing what I do. I am finding that increasingly hard to do because, like you Diane, I have the hunger you describe."

Again, there was a period where the three were silent.

"So what's your story?" Diane asked Mickey, waiting for him to make his contribution to the lonely-hearts club.

Mickey gave a lot of thought before answering her question, but he knew he had to show he could confide in his two companions. "It's a Yin-Yang thing."

"A what?"

"You know; Yin-Yang—but not in the sense that the two of you are opposites. Rather, the relationship I have with Suki represents one set of behaviors, and the relationship with you, Diane, represents another set of behaviors, and the two sort of complement each other. My *story*, as you put it, is that I am not entirely comfortable with either relationship. Therefore, I bounce between the two of you."

"Why don't you focus on getting one relationship right and stay with it?" Suki suggested.

"Yeah. She's right you know," Diane agreed.

Nervously running his hands through his hair, Mickey sat up against a wall, rested his arms on his knees, and said, "I lied about being afraid of turning fifty."

Diane and Suki looked at each other, wondering where the conversation was going. It was very unlike Mickey to open up, but the door appeared to be swinging wide open for once.

"I'm afraid to love someone—I mean really love someone."

"But, you said you love me," Diane said, a look of desperation on her face as she feared that her relationship with Mickey could be falling apart before her eyes.

"You know the old saying—that words are cheap. I say it, but I always wonder if I mean it."

"So, do you love her?" Diane asked, point toward Suki.

"No. She scares the hell out of me, too."

"I do not understand, Mickey," Suki said, now wondering where she stood with him. "What are you saying?

"I guess my problem goes back many years. My mother suffered from cancer for several years before dying. It was a long, agonizing death. I thought my father was Superman through the whole thing—always there, always caring. He really set an example that the rest of humanity should follow.

"The night she died, I was at the hospital with my father. Mom was telling us repeatedly that she was so tired…so tired. I knew it was the end. Dad told me to get something to eat so he could be with her for a while. I did as he asked. I guess I needed to get out of the room anyway. When I came back to the room, mom was no longer breathing. Dad was sitting in a chair, staring off into space." Tears began to roll down Mickey's cheeks, as he continued, "He sat there in his chair saying it was for the best. I just went off on him."

He looked up to make sure Diane and Suki were paying close attention as he continued, "Then he said something that has both mystified me and crippled me to this day."

"What was that," Diane asked, engaging Mickey in deep conversation.

"He said 'Beware of EVOL.' At first I thought he said evil, but he made sure I understood him to say E-V-O-L. He told me to be certain I understood the distinction between EVOL and LOVE. I asked him what this EVOL thing was and he answered that it is anti-love. He said it is pervasive and everywhere, affecting everyone to some degree. I thought he was full of shit—I mean, it's just LOVE backwards, right? But he was deadly serious and persistent with his explanation."

"I am still not following you, Mickey," Suki said with a puzzled expression.

"Basically, as he described it, you do something believing that you are doing it out of love, but in fact whatever it is you are doing is very self-serving and hurtful to the other person. To him, it was almost as if EVOL was sentient. He told me, 'the ultimate act of love is to be capable of letting go of a loved-one, and to know when that is what you must do.'

"I said to him, 'Dad, you just gave up. You let her die.' And he replied, 'Yes, son, because that's how much I loved her.' At the time, I thought he had lost his mind."

Wiping a tear from his eye, Mickey added, "I never spoke to him again. I know now I was wrong. His words have haunted me for all these years. I have it in my mind that if I love somebody deeply enough, I may have to end his or her life some day. At the same time, I question if my words and actions are really expressions of love, or this anti-love thing he warned me about. I know I am being completely stupid about all of this, but my obsession over love/anti-love has forever had me questioning my true motives when it comes to relationships."

There was a long pause before Mickey asked, "I suppose neither of you have ever had false motives in any of your relationships?"

His question struck a chord with both Diane and Suki.

"So now I am blessed with two wonderful women. Three years ago, I figured it would be helpful for me to have a superficial relationship, so I began dating you, Suki. However, each time we were together, I became increasingly attached to you, and I found myself more and more unable to have that superficial relationship. Now, I find each time we are together, I must quietly, but deliberately, retreat to safe harbor. That safe harbor is you, Diane."

Diane swallowed quite visibly, absorbing the revelation that, buried in his ranting, he *did* have strong feelings for her after all.

"You are all I could hope for in a woman, but I am competing with a dead man—Bruce. So when we spend time together, I eventually feel overwhelmed by his presence. I see the torment in your eyes—the same torment I saw in my father's eyes that night so many years ago. I doubt if I love you the way you deserve to be loved, and I find that I have to withdraw from you because I'm reminded how closely death and love are tied together."

Responding coldly to Mickey's candor, Diane said, "I'm not dying, and I don't think you're going to kill me, so what's your problem?"

Mickey's face showed strain. He shook his head, and replied, "And then you go and open *your* fucking mouth, say something stupid, and I wonder if you give a shit about *me*."

Mickey got up and walked quickly out the door and down to the beach without saying another word.

Suki and Diane looked at each other in disbelief.

"Suki, did this really happen? Did we just have an emotional revelation by the one and only Mickey Rollins?"

"It all makes sense now," Suki replied, taking a seat on the bed.

"What's that?" Diane asked, sitting next to her.

"I probably should not tell you this, but Mickey has been asking me to help you with your feelings for Bruce. I thought his motives were very selfish, very disingenuous."

"What a coward!" Diane said, her face red with anger.

"Maybe not," Suki answered, taking Diane's hand. "I think he really cannot deal with grief and loss himself. When he finds himself face-to-face with your past, it upsets him."

"So it's my fault that he can't have a relationship with me? I doubt that, Suki."

"There is no blame here, Diane, no fault. Yes, he is wrong to have me fix a relationship for him. But, he is a man after all, and we all know that men have trouble confronting deep personal issues. I think we just found a window into Mickey's mind, and he is as screwed up as we are. Right or wrong, he is blaming his father for the fact that he cannot have a warm, honest and loving relationship with one of us. Love can be very complicated."

Diane took Suki by the shoulders and begged, "Please do not tell Mickey love is complicated. He'll go off on some tangent about that. I did circles with him about the complications of life on the flight over here. He had me looking for a parachute."

"Diane, he is changing before your eyes. This is your opportunity. Go to him. Go to him now."

"What should I say?"

"Just talk and listen. See where it goes. If I am not mistaken, there may be a very different Mickey Rollins somewhere out on that beach."

Diane reflected on the situation for a moment before asking suspiciously, "So he wanted you to work out my issues about Bruce?"

"I think Mickey deserves the benefit of the doubt."

"Believe me, Suki, I have nothing but doubt right now," she responded, going to the closet, pulling out a suitcase, tossing it on the bed, and starting to pack.

Immediately, Suki got off of the bed and started out the door.

"Where are you going?" Diane asked.

"I'm going to check on Mickey," Suki replied, opening and readjusted the towel that was wrapped around her, making sure in the process that Diane knew she had nothing on beneath it.

"Of course, this opens the door for you."

"I am not the fool this time, Diane. Mickey wants one of us. If you will not be there for him, I will be."

Diane turned away from Suki, continuing to throw her clothes into the suitcase. Suki proceeded out the door toward the beach. Diane turned to see if Suki was really gone, and then began to cry as she continued packing. Eventually, she stopped what she was doing and leaned over the bed. Her tears dripped onto the sheets as she propped herself up on her arms. After a few moments, Diane made a fist and began pounding the bed.

"Damn it! Damn it! Damn it!"

She stood up straight and took a deep breath. After finding a towel, she dried her eyes and face as well as she could, then bolted for the back door, running down the steps to the first landing. There, in a chair, sat Suki. She was composed, her legs were crossed, and she was smiling. Diane almost fell as she came to an abrupt halt.

"How did you...?"

"I just know," Suki replied with a nod. The two exchanged pained looks for a few seconds before Suki motioned towards the beach, saying, "Now go find Mickey."

Struggling with emotion, Diane clasped her hands, interlocking her fingers, and held them under her chin almost as if she was praying.

"Thank you, Suki. Thank you."

Suki nodded again as she said, "You are welcome, my friend. Now go."

Diane didn't waste any time. She raced down the remaining stairs to the beach, looking right and left for Mickey. It wasn't long before she spotted a man dressed only in shorts sitting in the sand about a hundred yards down the beach.

Boundaries

She walked anxiously toward him. When she got to within a few yards, Mickey turned and looked at her. He was expressionless.

Diane sat down facing him. She entwined her legs with his just as she had done a few days earlier on the beach in San Diego and then she waited in vain for Mickey to say something…anything. It did not take long for her impatience to get the better of her and she decided to break the ice.

"I never spoke to my father again after Bruce died. It was as if I blamed him for the accident."

"I always took you for a smart person," Mickey answered, looking into Diane's eyes. "Maybe I was wrong."

Diane took the barb; perhaps it was deserved.

"There was a lot of unfinished business between my father and me. What about with you and Dub?"

"If you only knew how much," Mickey replied painfully.

Diane took Mickey's hands. She waited until he again made eye contact with her before saying, "That's just it, Mick. I do know how much."

That was all it took. Mickey's eyes glazed over, as did Diane's. They melted in each other's arms, crying quietly together for a long time. After a while, they wiped one another's tears away. Mickey managed to speak, though with a somewhat broken voice.

"Did I tell you I'm really having a good time on my vacation?"

"I'm having a great time, too," Diane chuckled, her voice also breaking. They kissed and held a long embrace.

"Diane?"

"Yes, Mick?"

"I would be honored if you would let me help you set up a memorial of some type in Bruce's name."

Diane's heart almost stopped.

"Oh, Mick, I'm not sure I can go through with that."

"I know. But maybe we can…together."

Diane looked like a captured animal desperately looking to escape.

"You don't need to decide now…nothing now. Just know that I will be there for you when you are ready."

A particularly large wave broke at the shoreline, and the water rushed up onto the beach surrounding both of them.

"I think that was a sign," Diane quipped, fanning her sarong.

The two got up on their knees, and Diane put her arms around Mickey, pulling him close to her body. She kissed him generously.

"I love you Mickey. I really do."

Returning the embrace, he replied, "I love you too, babe."

Book 3

"Loarn, she's coming around."

Dr. Mason got up from his seat and hurried over to the cot in Exam Room 9 where Diane once again was under observation.

"Diane, this is Dr. Madden. Can you hear me?"

As the two doctors stood over her, Diane slowly opened her eyes—her gaze was initially expressionless. Dr. Madden felt Diane's wrist to assess her pulse and at the same time pulled open her eyelids to see how they responded to the room light.

"It could have been a seizure. She seems almost postictal and yet nothing quite like I have seen."

"Don't leave me," Diane said softly as she reached for Dr. Madden's hand, pulling her close.

Madden was quick to notice Diane's complete change in demeanor from one of exaggerated caution to sudden dependence.

"Diane, you had some sort of event, perhaps a seizure. You were unresponsive again for nearly fifteen minutes. Have you had this happen in the past?"

Slowly, Diane replied, "Yeah, I have a lot of seizures—at least that's what Mickey calls them."

"How often?"

"Maybe once a week—sometimes more often, sometimes less."

"How long have you been having these events?"

"I guess since I had my head injury."

"That was about three years ago," Dr. Mason added.

"Does anything in particular bring them on?"

"No. They just happen," Diane replied, now becoming more lucid. "Fortunately, I'm always at home with Mickey when they occur."

The two doctors looked at each other, reacting to Diane's comment.

"That is very unusual, would you not agree, Beverly?"

"At best, it's extremely rare that seizures would have such a consistency. It's as if there was an environmental or situational factor tied to her home."

"Exactly my point. Are you listening to her speech? Have you noted her ability to respond rationally to your questions? This is not a postictal state after a seizure. The patient is quite normal." Dr. Mason tilted Diane's head to the side, looking inside her ear with an otoscope. "This device bothers me...it bothers the hell out of me."

"So you don't think I had a seizure?" Diane asked. "Because, this is how I feel whenever I have one—I blank out, then come back to reality."

"Have you ever fallen as a result of a seizure?" Dr. Mason asked.

Diane thought for a while before answering, "No. It's funny. Except for this time, I've always been sitting or lying down."

"Loarn, could that just be an incredible coincidence?"

"That would be far too incredible—always at home, always lying down or sitting...I'm sorry."

"Diane?"

"Yes, Dr. Madden?"

"Do you take any medications for seizures?"

"Mickey gives me Dilantin."

"Loarn, did you do a test...?"

"Phenytoin level was normal. She does not appear to be taking any. Nor is there any trace of other drugs."

"But he gives me the medication. I take it all the time! I'm not making this up!"

"Diane, I'm certain you take something," Mason said. "Perhaps it's a placebo."

"What does the pill look like, Diane?" Madden asked.

"It's a little capsule thing. I take three a day. The bottle says they are 100 milligrams."

"Do you have them with you?"

"They would be in my bag if I have them." Diane reached for it and began to paw through the items inside. "You know, I don't remember packing them…in fact, I don't remember packing at all. Wait, here they are. No, that's the others."

Diane handed Dr. Madden a bottle.

"This says lithium," Madden said, holding the bottle up for Dr. Mason to see. "Do you by any chance have a bipolar disorder?"

"Yeah, at least that's what Mickey says."

"Why didn't you tell us?"

"You never asked me. Here…here's the bottle I was looking for."

"Beverly, it's a perfect ruse." Mason took the bottle of pills out of Diane's hand. "We need to have these checked. A capsule is the perfect placebo. It could contain anything and be manufactured anywhere. I would wager the lithium is a placebo as well." Mason reached out for Diane. "Sit up and let's see how you do."

Diane sat up with her legs hanging off of the bed.

"Do you have any medical problems other than those you have told us about?

"I can't think of any."

"What can you tell us about your head injury? We need you to be as specific as possible."

"Oh gosh, there's so much to tell," Diane replied, running her fingers through her hair. "The injury was to the front of my brain—they called it a blunt force injury. I don't recall anything of the first year after the accident, and I have partial amnesia of events prior to the injury. Mickey and my neurologist say I had severe behavior problems that required heavy sedation."

"That would be consistent with an injury to the prefrontal cortex. All of your emotions, feelings, behaviors, and so forth are controlled there. When were you pregnant with your daughter?" Madden asked.

"Mickey tells me that I conceived Gigi when I was on the same vacation in which I was injured. I don't remember anything of the pregnancy." Beginning to tear up, Diane continued, "It's so sad. I wanted to have a child for so many years. Then, when I finally have a full-term pregnancy, I can't remember anything about it."

"Did you have a c-section?"

"No, it was a normal delivery," Diane said, exposing her belly. "See, I don't have a scar."

Doctors Mason and Madden exchanged looks as Diane's medical history kept getting more and more mysterious.

"Diane?" Dr. Madden asked tentatively, "Are you certain Gigi is your baby…that you didn't adopt and you just don't remember?"

"No, she's all mine," Diane answered very defensively. "She has my eyes, my hair color, my dimple, and she looks just like me when I was her age." Diane noticed that Madden still had a look of doubt. "I'm not lying! Why don't you believe me?!"

"Is your daughter developmentally and physically normal?"

"Damn it! I hate the way you guys talk about people—especially my daughter. Yes, she's perfect in every way."

"Diane, please bear with us. I know this is hard for you, but you hold all the answers," Madden said, trying to ease Diane's concern. "It's a very interesting detail if, as you say, you have a perfectly normal child who was carried full term to birth by you while you were recovering from such an injury. Sedatives sometimes can have profound effects on fetal development. Seizures themselves can cause harm. I guess you were—and Gigi is—very lucky."

"You told me earlier you were not sure who her father is." Mason said.

"I just said that earlier. I suppose I was being a shit. Mickey is her father."

"Did you have any extreme weight gain with your pregnancy or abrupt loss afterwards?"

"No, Dr. Madden. As soon as I was able to function on my own after Gigi was born, I recall pretty much being back to my old self. I don't recall any weight gain or loss."

"And yet you were confined to a bed during your pregnancy, unable to move."

"Yeah...weird, huh?"

Weird wasn't exactly what Madden and Mason were thinking. Entirely inconsistent with the facts was a better description.

"Okay. Who is your neurologist?"

"He's a visiting doctor from Asia. Mickey consults with him all the time. He's the same one who took care of me right after the attack. His name is Ricardo Mendoza."

"You don't say!" Mason reacted as if he had solved the puzzle.

"Do you know him, Loarn?"

"Of course. This all makes sense now. He was a partner with Mickey in a project, the purpose of which was to reinstate memory, thought, and bodily function. I was part of an assessment committee that was asked to evaluate the project for venture capital funding. Mendoza is a complete, arrogant ass—pardon my expletive. I would have nothing to do with it for the reason I feel we have before us. It required extensive human testing. Diane, I am afraid you may be part of such a test."

"You mean to tell me I'm unknowingly taking part in some sort of experiment?"

"Loarn, I think you're being too hasty with your conclusion."

"Perhaps, Bev. Diane, there was another doctor associated with Mickey—an old Chinese man named Wu. Did you ever have any dealings with him?"

"Nope. Never heard of him before," Diane replied, shaking her head.

"Odd, the three worked very closely on the project until Wu's untimely death."

"Are you talking about Chi-feng Wu—the man who spent his entire adult life documenting emotions and self-knowledge?"

"I knew that would interest you, Beverly."

"He passed away when we were at the conference in Toronto three years ago. Everyone was talking about him."

"There was that rumor…what was it?" Mason asked, scratching his beard.

"He was about to release the final volume of his work, *The Harvesting and Replacement of Emotions and Other Conscious Phenomena.*"

"That sounds like a bestseller," Diane quipped.

"You should be particularly interested, my dear. The 'rumor' was that there had been a breakthrough in a technique called 'beta immersion.'"

"Isn't that some type of educational method? I mean, I have heard about immersion programs in school—Spanish immersion, for example, to teach children the language."

"That's one form of immersion—one that he carefully distinguished from his work by calling the former alpha immersion. Alpha is based on intense exposure," Dr. Madden said, taking a seat on the cot next to Diane. "Another example is listening to recorded material that interests you as you sleep. It could be a language, or math, or music…just about anything. But that has very questionable and highly variable success."

"So what's different with his method?"

"That's something nobody ever found out. He died before the final draft was released, and reportedly, no manuscript was ever located."

"Did somebody take it?" Diane asked.

"It would be useful only to someone who could read Mandarin or a person who had a good translator." Madden stared off in the distance as she marveled at perhaps being close to Wu's work. "Not only did he write in his native tongue, he reportedly encrypted his work with references and riddles that could only be interpreted by someone who knew him well…perhaps a relative or close friend. One would need these references to make any sense of what he was writing."

"Did he have any relatives?" Diane asked.

Mason and Madden looked at her, noting she was now asking the questions.

"Hey, I like mystery novels."

"Locals said he had a granddaughter who was very close to him. She vanished after his death and nobody has been able to find her. There aren't even any pictures of her. She reportedly lived a very different lifestyle from him that made her very wealthy, but also gave her a darker side. Loarn, what was her name, anyway?"

"Jing...Ling...Jong..."

Diane's eyes got wide as she said, "Jiao?"

"That's it!" Mason, exclaimed. "Her name was Jiao. How did you know?"

"My friend, Suki. Her name is Sukhon Jiao."

"My God," Madden said, putting her hands on both cheeks. "Do you know her?"

"She's been at my side constantly, ever since before the injury." Diane clenched her fists as a feeling of betrayal overwhelmed her.

"Convinced now, Bev?"

Madden looked at Diane and Dr. Mason as she said, "I need coffee."

"You'll probably need something stronger than that," Diane surmised. "If Suki is the granddaughter of the man you are speaking of, then he didn't die...I killed him."

Mason rubbed his forehead while saying, "Diane, our conversation is private. We are not the police. Can you possibly have any more surprises for us? If so, we need to know."

"Just one."

Diane reached into her bag and pulled out an object covered with a silk cloth that was closed at the top by a drawstring. She opened the drawstring and retrieved a leather-bound book with two Chinese characters on the cover before handing it to Dr. Mason.

"Could this be the manuscript you're looking for?"

Chapter 15

A little more than an hour had passed since the three were together at the waterfall Jacuzzi. Suki was no longer in the chair where Diane had last seen her. Instead, Mickey and Diane found her reading on the porch. Once she saw them, she stood up—her face showing concern.

"This is very bad."

"What's bad?" Diane asked.

"Look at both of you," Suki said, stepping closer. "Mickey is now more sunburned and you have a little sunburn as well. Into the bath water, both of you."

"Suki, Mickey's going to help me set up a memorial for Bruce," Diane blurted out, paying no attention to Suki's concern.

"Really?" Suki replied, pleasantly surprised.

"Yep," Mickey said, putting his arm around Diane. "We found some common ground. I think we're good."

Suki scanned the expressions on her friends' faces, seeing what one might call 'true warmth.'

"That is wonderful. I am happy for both of you," she continued, sounding most sincere. "I am quite certain nobody has eaten anything as of yet today. You are both falling behind your nutrient curves."

"Oooh, the nutrient curve," Diane and Mickey responded in unison.

"Yes, the nutrient curve," Suki said seriously. "It is very important that you fill your bodies with the right things so we can eliminate the wrong things."

"Can we discuss this elimination thing a bit further?" Mickey asked, his voice dripping with sarcasm. "I don't quite follow you."

"You are making fun of me again. I try very hard to take care of you, and you make fun of me."

"She's right you know," Diane said.

Boundaries

"Damn, can't I be right just once?" Mickey responded, snapping his fingers.

"No!" Diane and Suki responded simultaneously.

"In addition," Suki continued, "we need to discuss plans for the next few days. You have some choices to make. Of course, there should be a lot of room for spontaneity on the calendar, with only a few planned events."

"I'm sorry I got it all wet," Diane said, pointing at her sarong. "A wave surprised us."

"Waves have a way of doing that around here. Let me help you get this off, and I will be sure it is properly cleaned."

Once the sarong was off and neatly folded in Suki's arms, Diane walked to a mirror and stood in front of it. "Oh, my gosh! You're right. I did get some sun."

"If you'd been naked or at least topless, you wouldn't have as many of those unsightly demarcations from pink to white."

"You mean I would be burned to a crisp like you?"

Suki put the sarong in a cloth bag for the laundress to take before saying, "Mickey, sometimes I wonder if you are truly the brilliant person you tell me you are."

He made a silly face to scoff at Suki's comment.

She continued, "Alright you two, now get on with it. There is a creamy soap in that bottle I prepared earlier. You need to apply it all over, and then rinse it off completely. Be quick about it. Standing in the water for too long will dry your skin more. Meet me on the porch when you are done."

After slipping off his shorts, Mickey held them out for Suki. She looked at him and rolled her eyes as she snapped them out of his hand. "Those go in a very different bag."

The persistent bickering between the two left Diane grinning.

Diane took Mickey by the hand and together they waded into the Jacuzzi. She cringed as the hot water made contact with more and more of her body. Mickey showed no pain until the water reached his groin.

"They'll be hangin' low today, I'll tell you that."

Diane laughed, knowing exactly to what he was referring.

The two lovers went about purposefully applying the cream on each other's body and rinsing it off just as Suki had instructed them. Neither showed any indication of arousal. They climbed out and dried each other off gently, taking care not to rub too hard on the other's sensitive skin. Suki had set out clean shorts and tops for both of them—brand new outfits that she recently purchased. They dressed and joined Suki on the porch where she had set out a wonderful spread of fruit, breads, jams, cheeses, and meats.

"Suki, where did you get these?" Diane asked, running her hands down her new clothes. "I love them."

"I am glad you like them," Suki answered, getting up from where she was sitting. "I bought them the other day when Mickey told me you were coming. I have several more outfits for you."

"I'd ask you how you knew my sizes, but I am sure that you would simply say, 'I just know'."

Pulling out a chair for Diane to sit in, she said, "Actually, Mickey gave me your sizes."

"Mickey, you know my sizes?"

"Does that surprise you?" he asked.

"Well, yes actually. But it's a very pleasant surprise."

"Espresso?" Suki asked the two, holding up a carafe.

Diane sat down and quickly held her cup up to Suki. Deliberately making her hands tremble, she jokingly said, "Please, now!"

Suki held the carafe toward Mickey.

"No thank you. I'll stick with some juice this morning."

"Are you feeling alright?" Diane asked, wondering if he might be ill.

He responded by putting his hand on his stomach and rubbing lightly. "Just a little out of sorts. I think I had too much of a run on an empty stomach." He looked up at Suki. "...and perhaps a bit too much sun. I'll feel better after breakfast."

Suki passed a basket of croissants to Diane, saying, "Here, take one and pass it on to the man whose nutrient curve is way off."

"Oh, Suki," Mickey said grinning, "You love the taste of victory, if ever so much in the Busch League."

Suki held up her cup of espresso as if to toast Mickey, then picked up a plate of butter and passed it to Diane. "Would you care for some?"

"Yes, and is that honey?" Diane pointed to a small flask with a dark liquid.

Suki nodded.

"From Changmai?" Diane asked.

"Yes, that is correct. I have my own special supplier. She is wonderful." Suki noticed Mickey was not eating. "Would you like some meat or cheese?"

"That sounds good. I need to get something in my stomach," he continued, holding out his plate. "So tell us about your ideas for entertainment."

Suki sat back and smiled. "Well, I have a lot of special experiences for you. Today, we are going to an art exhibition on the beach. Tonight we will have free time for rest and relaxation and whatever else might happen."

"I like the 'whatever else might happen' part," Mickey interrupted. "That's always a good activity."

Diane reacted by kicking Mickey playfully under the table.

"May I continue now, Mickey?" Suki asked.

He nodded, rubbing his shin.

"Tomorrow, you have a dim sum lunch at a small, local restaurant I have selected, followed by a free afternoon sight-seeing. Then, in the evening, I have an incredible nightclub experience for you at a new spot called R U Hot?"

"Obviously referring to the warmth in one's heart, I suppose?" Mickey injected.

Now it was Suki who kicked Mickey under the table.

"Damn! If you and Diane keep doing that, we may not be doing much of anything."

"The day after is girls' day in Bangkok where we plan to spend enormous amounts of your money, shop, and indulge ourselves in whatever we want."

"How are we traveling there?" asked Diane.

Reaching over to a table and grabbing her backpack, Suki pulled out a photograph of a small jet. "We are flying."

"What are we going to do with Mickey? Should we lock him up?" Diane asked with a wicked grin.

Mickey kicked her playfully under the table.

"Ouch!" She yelped, sticking her tongue out at him.

Suki's eyes squinted in a manner most evil, and sported her own devilish grin as she perched her chin on her hand. "I have arranged for some therapy for him with one of the local girls while we are gone; completely and painfully physical. He might possibly become a Monk after the experience."

"Oh, I love those monkeys."

"Do not talk blasphemy around me, Mr. Rollins," Suki replied, again kicking Mickey under the table.

"Stop that!" Mickey couldn't help but have a déjà vu moment. "Excuse me, Maria."

"Did you mean to call her Maria, or did that just slip out?" Diane asked.

"Forget it," Mickey said sporting one of his typical boyish looks. "Maria said the same thing to me just the other day."

"In any case, I suggest you stop trying to anger all greater powers," Suki said, trying to defuse the situation.

Diane had a final thing to say, "And I suggest you not mention Maria any more on this trip."

Before Mickey could respond with a remark that would certainly be fatal to the peace in the room, Suki finished summarizing her plans.

"Finally, after our day of shopping, we leave on an overnight cruise to a very private island off the coast."

Mickey and Diane looked at each other, grinning favorably in response to Suki's agenda. Diane took a sip of her espresso before pressing for some details.

"Tell me about the art show. I should let you know that I minored in art in college."

Boundaries

"This is an art show unlike any I suspect you have gone to," Suki said mischievously. "It is both an exhibition of the artist as well as his or her canvas."

"So, isn't it always about the artist and the canvas?" Diane asked, shrugging her shoulders with indifference.

Shaking her head, Suki replied, "In this case, the canvas is the human body."

Diane was amused, but at the same time lost in translation.

"Mickey, did I ever tell you that Bruce and I met in art class. One project in particular was about sketching nudes. I was the female subject while he was the male subject. That's how we first met."

Diane could tell from the look on Suki's face and by Mickey's snickering that she was missing the point.

"Okay, I guess I still don't get it."

"Diane, the body *is* the canvas. It is a body painting exhibition," Suki said, casually taking a bite of her croissant.

"Body painting—not a painting of the body?" Diane's eyes opened wide. "You mean…"

Taking a sip of her espresso, Suki answered, "Yes. And you and I are going to be participants."

Shaking her head, Diane said, "Suki, I'm not much of a painter. I mainly did pen and ink."

Suki coughed, nearly choking on her croissant. It was clear from Diane's response that she was still missing the point.

"Diane, we are not going to be painters. You and I are going to be the canvas."

Diane's eyes opened even wider as she exclaimed, "What?!"

"You and I will be painted, along with many others. It is an annual event here that fortunately coincides with your visit. The artists come from all over the world. Our artist will be Uma Goss from Austria. She is the best. I told her I was available, and that I had another subject as well. She paints me at various exhibitions each year."

"You've done this before?"

"Yes, many times. It is a lot of fun. I have won this contest twice...well, I should say, she has won this contest twice with me as her subject."

Diane looked for Mickey to intervene. But when it was obvious he was all for Suki's idea, it was clear she was on her own.

"You expect me to let someone paint my body in front of a group of strangers? How many are we talking about?"

"Oh, hundreds. Perhaps thousands—and I am counting just those in attendance. This particular exhibition usually is televised in Asian and European markets. It is a very large event, not to mention a fundraiser. As in past years, the proceeds are being collected for children orphaned by the 2004 tsunami. You do like to help out with charities?"

"Suki, I'm not comfortable with this."

"Why? You are beautiful, Diane. You will be a magnificent canvas, and Uma will turn you into a masterpiece. She has incredible ideas, and as I said, it is a lot of fun, not to mention one of the most erotic experiences you will ever have. Besides, you cannot lie around on the beach today with the beginning of a sunburn. So, a day off will be a good thing."

"Mickey, help me out here...." Diane pleaded.

"I think it's a dandy idea," he responded, taking a bite of cheese. "What am I going to do?"

"You are a judge," Suki replied, reaching for the meat and cheese plate.

"Yes!" He shouted, jumping up. "When do we start?"

"Mickey!" Diane shouted, now looked frantic.

Putting her hand on Diane's to calm her, Suki explained, "Look at it this way. You do not know any of the people who will be at the show, and they do not know you. Moreover, the paint offers one a certain degree of anonymity."

Diane stared at the table, not knowing how best to respond.

"Would you like a different artist?" Suki asked, not yielding to Diane's modesty.

"Suki, I'm forty-three years old. All the women there are bound to be a lot younger. I don't think I could stand the embarrassment."

Boundaries

"Diane," Suki answered, sitting back and enjoying another sip of espresso. "I am only one set of eyes, but believe me when I say you will give all the women there a challenge...a very big challenge."

Looking intently at Suki, Diane tried to in vain to grasp the compliment.

Sensing Diane was still not sold on the idea, Suki offered, "I will be with you the entire time."

Tossing out a desperate question, Diane asked, "Why isn't Mickey being painted?"

Suki laughed, while Mickey grumbled, "I got painted last year."

"And...?" Diane asked, shocked at the revelation.

"It was a celebration for our elephants," Suki said, fighting to regain her composure.

"A what?" Diane asked, flustered by being the only one in the room not familiar with that experience.

After taking another sip of espresso to help her stop laughing, Suki continued, "We celebrate elephants here in Thailand. They are such wonderful, sweet animals and a huge part of our culture. Last year at the celebration, there was a body painting exhibition with men posing as elephants."

A smile slowly formed on Diane's face. "You mean...?"

Diane looked at Mickey for validation, and he responded by nodding. She began laughing hysterically.

"It wasn't that funny," Mickey said without any expression.

Suki got up from the table and went to her room, returning to the others holding something behind her back.

"I made this just for Mickey. I knew he wanted to remember the event for all time."

She pulled out a framed photograph of Mickey at the contest, and handed it to Diane. Following just a brief glance, she could barely breathe as she was laughing so hard. Her previously pink face was now beet red, and the veins bulged in her neck and forehead. Tears began to stream down her face.

"I'm sorry. Oh, my gosh. I've never seen anything like this in my life." She carried on laughing as she handed the picture to Mickey.

Mickey looked at the picture and chuckled as he said, "She didn't tell me that all the rest of the dudes weren't circumcised. Try being an elephant when you're circumcised. It just doesn't work."

Mickey joined in with his own laughter, partly due to the contagious effects of Diane's hysteria. Suki got wrapped up in the moment as well.

"Suki, I can't thank you enough for this picture. It will go on my office wall along with all my other trophies."

Diane's laughter slowed to the point at which she could talk again. "Did you win?"

Leaning forward with his arms on the table, Mickey answered with a poker face, "Not even in the top ten!"

Diane and Suki began laughing again.

"Some fucking Aborigine with the biggest dick I've ever seen won the thing. I'm pretty proud of ol' Johnson here, but I looked like Elmer Fudd standing next to these guys."

At that point Diane just lost it, falling to the floor, buckled over and holding her stomach.

"You're going to give me a complex if you don't stop laughing."

Correcting Mickey, Suki clarified, "He was not some 'fucking Aborigine with the biggest dick.'"

"No?" Mickey argued.

"No," Suki said, "he was from Burma."

Tossing a crumpled napkin at Suki, Mickey said, "Thanks for that little tidbit. I feel much better." He got up and walked over to Diane who was still out of breath on the floor, and held out his hand to her saying, "Arise, oh Ye, who partaketh of said trunk with delight."

Diane reached for his hand and pulled herself up with his help. They hugged before he helped her back into her chair.

"Well now I know what to do whenever you are in a funk. I'll just whip this photo out."

"Oh, my gosh," Diane said, fanning her face with her hand. "That has got to be the funniest thing I have ever seen. Are they going to do elephants again at this year's exhibition?"

"It is not the theme, but some artist invariably does one."

"I have to see one. Please, take me to see one," Diane said, continuing to fan herself.

"I can show you one right now," Mickey said, standing up.

"No. Please don't," Diane responded, holding her hand up to Mickey. "We could never make love again without me laughing. Just…please, sit back down."

Suki again took Diane's hand, and asked, "So, will you do it with me?"

"Oh, what the hell," Diane replied, burying her head in her hands. "What a great memory. So when do we start?"

"As soon as we finish eating, we can take care of some preparations and then we will go to the resort down the beach that is hosting the event."

"So how long does it take her to paint a person?"

"It depends on what she wants to do, but she may take a good part of the day."

"That long?"

"This is art. It cannot be rushed."

"What are these preparations you mentioned?"

"We need to be shaved."

"Suki! You're kidding, right?"

"No, hair distracts from the painting. We have to shave from the neck down."

Mickey was quick to volunteer his services, saying, "I can shave you. I've been shaving for years."

"No, Suki said, nixing the idea. "This is something only girls can do. It is far too personal."

"I'm not shaving down there, am I?" Diane asked, shaking her head.

"Yes, but let me clarify. I will shave you, and you will shave me. It is much easier and safer that way."

Continuing to shake her head, Diane hesitated to ask, "Well, are there any more surprises?"

"No. None that I know of. Having said that, there could always be things that happen unexpectedly." Suki grinned, devilishly.

"Tell you what, I'll do it. But we're going to have to shave Mick, too. I think he needs to share in the experience."

"If there is time, we will do him. But he is not as important as a subject in the show."

"You know, I keep getting the hint I am unimportant to just about everything that's going on here."

Diane leaned across the table, kissing Mickey on the cheek before saying, "Oh, Mick, I'll do it to you later if we can't get it done today."

He grunted in acknowledgement, looking briefly at Diane before flashing the picture of his painted body at her causing her to laugh once again.

Suki quickly removed the dishes and food from the table, putting everything away, then taking Diane by the hand and leading her to the Jacuzzi tub. Mickey followed to watch. Neither Diane nor Suki minded if he was there. One hour later, except for the coif on their heads, they were completely clean-shaven. After quickly dressing, the three headed to the neighboring resort.

THERE WAS NOT MUCH of a crowd there yet when the trio arrived. Suki explained that the painting took place in the afternoon with the judging that evening. The artists and their participants worked inside a large tent that was sectioned off so the both artist and those being painted had some privacy. The tent also provided shade, and individual fans could be turned on or off to keep everyone cool as needed, yet not spoil the artwork as it unfolded. The three continued to a corner of the tent where a map showed Uma to be located. Uma spotted Suki first.

"Guten Morgen, Suki!" Uma waved from several meters away.

Boundaries

As the three friends approached, Suki replied, "Grüss dich, Uma. Wie Gehts?"

Diane was amazed at Suki's seemingly fluent German.

"Danke, gut." Uma replied.

Uma and Suki hugged each other and exchanged kisses on the cheek.

Suki pulled Diane close, and said, "Das hier ist meine Freundin, Diane. Sie kommst aus den Vereinigten Staaten."

Uma reached out and shook Diane's hand, as she asked, "Sprechen Sie Deutsch?"

Diane traveled in central Europe enough to know some of what was being said—the usual greetings, a polite introduction and lastly the most humbling question, *do you speak German?*

"I'm very sorry, but I don't speak much...I speak hardly any German."

Uma cocked her head to one side momentarily before smiling a huge smile, displaying plenty of white teeth.

"That is fine. I speak English a bit okay. I think we can talk alright, do you think so?"

"Yes, we will do just fine," Diane said, relieved that language would not be a barrier. "You speak marvelous English."

Uma walked up to Mickey, and gave him a hug and a kiss on the cheek before saying, "How is my elephant doing?"

"I wondered if you would recognize me from looking at my face."

Everyone laughed.

"I saw a photo of the elephant painting this morning, Uma," Diane said. "It was incredible."

"It was my first elephant, and my last. It is too hard to paint. The trunk kept on going up and down and up and down." Uma demonstrated with her arm.

Diane had one final laugh, saying, "Yes, I've noticed that problem, too."

"Oh, it can be a good thing at the right time, yes?" Hopping up and down with excitement, Uma asked, "Tell me that I get to paint you like I can paint Suki, yes?"

"Yes, Suki talked me into it," Diane replied, showing less enthusiasm than Uma would have liked.

Uma backed away, studying Diane head to foot, and walking completely around her before saying, "Oh, Suki. I am very sorry. This is a disaster."

"What is the problem, Uma?" Suki asked with concern in her voice.

"This Diane is so beautiful, that I think she may win better than you this time. Will you be mad if that is happen?"

Suki looked at Diane with delight as she said, "See? I told you."

A man with a scruffy beard approached with three children in tow—two walking beside him, and an infant in his arms. Suki held out her arms and the man put the baby in them.

"Oh, Uma, is this the baby? She is so beautiful. She looks just like Joop."

Uma put her arm around the man, then said, "Joop this is Miss Diane from America. We will paint her today and Suki. Miss Diane this is my husband Joop, and my son Menno who is age six, my daughter Ineke who is age four, and my baby Lulu who was born six months now."

"Das Baby hat Hunger," Ineke said, taking her mother's hand.

Uma stroked her baby's head, responding, "Hat meine kleine Lulu Hunger?" Motioning toward Diane, Uma said, "Ineke, sag Hallo zu Diane, bitte."

"Hallo," Ineke replied, looking up at Diane with a huge mile and big blue eyes.

Diane knelt down and said, "Hallo, Ineke."

Motioning again toward Diane, Uma said, "Menno, begrusse Diane, bitte."

Diane was immediately smitten by Menno, who reached over to give her a big hug as he said, "Hallo."

Menno pointed at Mickey and smiled as he inquired, "Dumbo?"

"Oh my, he remembers," Uma said, giggling. "He said you were painted like Dumbo in the book. He probably should not have been at that contest, but uh…"

Shaking Menno's hand, Mickey said, "Dumbo has to leave now." Looking at Suki and Diane, he asked of them, "You two are now officially contestants and I am a judge, so there is nothing between us. Understand?"

Boundaries

Suki and Diane mimicked zipping their lips closed.

Pointing to the curtained-off area in the corner, Uma said, encouraging her subjects along, "Come now and sit. We will talk ideas about us for a while."

The baby became a little restless forcing Suki to hand her to Uma who then took a seat toward the back of the workspace, unbuttoned her blouse and bra, and put Lulu up to nurse.

"We will have to work now a little around the baby's schedule. Joop will help with the painting so we can get it done for tonight."

"Joop will be painting?" Diane asked nervously.

Uma bit her lip as she looked at Diane, then Suki.

"Well for me to get both of you painted today, I must have some help because Lulu will take time from us so will this be alright? Joop is very good painting."

"This is Diane's first time for body painting," Suki explained. "She is nervous."

Uma gave Diane a confident look before saying, "You will not be afraid of your body. I think you will be a beautiful canvas to paint. Joop paints with me all the time. He sees a lot of women so not to be nervous. You are art, not sex."

Diane wiggled a little and nodded unconvincingly, trying hard to fit into the scene. It was obvious she was still uncomfortable with what was about to take place.

Sensing her discomfort, Joop set out to reassure her. He, too, spoke with a heavy accent as he said, "We do Suki all steps first so you watch. You then know what we do. I do big painting parts and Uma does the hard work and details. I will not paint all parts that you do not like."

Diane looked at Joop's eyes and watched his body language as he spoke, finally interpreting him to be completely harmless.

"I'll be fine," Diane said. "This will be a lot of fun."

There was a short period of silence until Uma decided to try breaking the ice with some friendly chitchat.

"Do you have babies?"

"No. No babies," Diane answered, somewhat startled by the question.

Uma rocked back and forth as she nursed, while Suki helped herself and Diane to a bottle of water.

"Do you have a husband here with you?"

Diane frowned and shook her head. "No, no husband."

Uma continued searching for something that could be considered positive. "Do you have a boyfriend?"

"Yes," Diane answered with a nod.

Having finally struck a positive note, a smile crossed Uma's face just as Suki followed up with, "Diane is with Mickey."

"You are the girlfriend of Mickey Rollins? I am sorry I did not understand earlier. I told Joop last year to be good to me or I would run away with Mickey. I painted the elephant on him last year. I hope you do not mind." Uma smiled as she reflected for a moment. "He is a well-endowed man, you know, but not a good elephant. You are a lucky woman," Uma concluded with a wink.

Diane smiled after a few moments once she realized what Uma was speaking about.

For whatever reason, Diane pulled the plug on all the upbeat conversation when she offered, "My husband died in an accident seven years ago."

Uma looked as if she had been shot with a gun. It was clear she had led a sheltered existence and nothing quite that horrible had ever happened to her. Suki had a shocked expression as well, wondering why on earth Diane changed the conversation at that point.

"I am uncomfortable to say that I am lucky," Uma responded, stroking the top of Lulu's head. "I have wonderful husband and three children and I am…just happy. I do not know a lot of sad. I do not like sad."

Following a deep breath, Diane acknowledged Uma's remark, "Yes, you are very lucky."

Taking a huge leap of faith, Uma suggested, "I think some day you and Mickey will be married and you will have babies." She watched Diane closely, hoping for a positive reaction, but she continued down her pitiful path.

"I cannot have children."

Boundaries

Deciding it was time to steer away from the subject, Uma said, "I have an idea. I think I will paint you and not talk questions any more. I think that is smart, yes?" Uma shifted Lulu to her other breast.

Diane bent over before giving Uma a hug, saying, "You asked perfectly normal questions. I look at myself in the mirror every day, wondering why I am not married and why I don't have children. I just never take the time to find the answers to those questions."

Uma excitedly stood up, still nursing Lulu, and said, "Diane, please take off your clothes now and let me look at you. I have an idea."

Diane hung her head low with embarrassment, but slowly took off her blouse, shorts, and finally her thong, handing each of them to Suki who neatly folded them. Lastly, she crossed her arms across her chest for cover.

"No, no. Please. Let me look at you. You should be proud of this magnificent body, not scared."

Diane bit by bit dropped her arms and looked up at Uma as she methodically studied every square inch of her body.

"Yes....yes. That will work. Yes. Oh, yes," Uma said to no one in particular.

Pulling Suki closer for support, Uma put her hand caringly on Diane's face, saying, "I want you to listen carefully to what I am about to tell you. I think this is an idea for you."

Diane looked at Uma nervously, and Uma made certain she had Diane's complete attention. Her expression was as serious as that of a surgeon explaining a medical procedure.

"I see a sad person inside of you. I think you are hurt and sad, but you hide your pain. You hide it a long time."

Diane gave a fragile nod.

"A lot of people in the world are hurt and sad also. They are a lot like you, but different. Do you know what I am saying?"

Suki looked on patiently as Diane nodded again.

"I am going to paint you sad. You will be sad and in pain. But then we will wash off the sad paint as part of the exhibit, and there will be a beautiful, wonderful, happy person that is painted underneath. Do you know what I am saying?"

Diane nodded again, more enthusiastically this time. Suki took Diane's hand and squeezed it hard, excited about Uma's description of what she planned to do.

"You know the caterpillar that is hairy and bumpy and not very happy to be a caterpillar, and then it turns into a beautiful butterfly? It does that thing called morpho…morphs…uh."

"Metamorphosis," Diane added, finishing Uma's sentence.

Uma put Lulu over her over her shoulder to burp her and said, "Yes, that is what I want to say—metamorphosis. It turns beautiful and flies away. It is free and with a new life to look forward to."

Diane smiled as she reconciled in her mind just what Uma was describing. "The painting you're suggesting is a metaphor for change—good change."

"That is going to be wonderful, Uma," Suki added.

"Here, please hold Lulu."

Uma handed her baby to Diane and grabbed a sketchpad and pencil. Diane cradled the baby too closely without much thought of what she was doing. It wasn't but an instant before Lulu took an immediate liking to Diane's left breast. She silently mouthed *ouch* as Lulu tried for dessert.

"Lulu, no!" Uma said, wiggling her fingers between Lulu's lips and Diane's nipple, breaking the suction and stopping her. Uma laughed awkwardly and rolled her eyes saying, "Put her over your shoulder or she will eat you."

Diane struggled with the extreme emotions of what had just happened between her and Lulu. For just a few short seconds, she experienced a small, intimate part of motherhood. Smiling, she managed to get out a few words. "She's so sweet."

Uma was already too absorbed in her work to pay attention to what Diane was saying. She began sketching as she intently examined Diane's body.

"What about Suki?" Diane asked.

So that Uma could continue to draw, Suki answered, "I am always a garden."

"I can't wait to see it," Diane acknowledged.

Boundaries

Uma began barking out instructions, first waiving for Joop to come over. "Joop, komm her!" He walked up to her and paid close attention. "Zuerst, bemalst du ihren ganzen Korper mit goldener Farbe."

Joop nodded his head. "Ja...okay."

She continued motioning toward Diane with her hand as she spoke to Joop in her native tongue. "Nimm die wasserfeste Farbe, die nicht wasserloslich ist. Dann will ich, dass du sie mit dunkel grauer wasserloslicher Farbe bemalst. Ich werde die melanchonlische Szene auf den grauen Deckanstrich malen. Wir werden dieses Jahr wieder eined bunten blattreichen Garten auf Suki malen."

Joop nodded again. "Ja, gut."

She then gave the sketchpad to Suki, took Lulu from Diane, and handed the baby to Ineke, saying, "Ineke, nimm deine Schwester Lulu und lass sie mit Spielzeuge spielen."

"Ja, Mama." Ineke took the baby aside where she could play with some toys.

"Menno!" Menno reported for duty. "Hilf Deinen Vater mit der Farbe."

"Ja, Mama." Menno ran after his father.

Uma ended with a final command to everyone, clapping her hands with authority as she said, "Alle an die Arbeit!."

She then turned to Diane. "You will stand over here with Joop. He is going to airbrush the base coating—it is a very bright color. Then I paint a new beginning on you. After that dries, Joop will airbrush a top coating—something dark and gray. That is where I paint the sad images and the pain. We also paint your hair. Do you have questions?"

Diane shook her head at first, but then changed her mind. "What if I have to go to the bathroom or have a drink?"

"Yes, the question is good," Uma replied, pointing her finger in the air. "Just let me know and I help you take care of that so the paint is not disturbed and we have to start again." Turning to Suki, Uma gave her instructions. "I will start on you so we can have two projects, so come here to me."

"Are you alright with this?" Suki asked, checking with Diane one last time.

"Sure. I think it will be fun—certainly it is a first."

With that, Suki and Diane moved to opposite corners of Uma's section of the tent, and the work began in earnest. Both women were asked to stand on a pedestal. Uma and Joop moved up and down on ladders, as necessary, and at other times, rotated the subjects in place keeping their 'canvas' in one relative position. The base coat took nearly ninety minutes to complete. Diane gulped hard several times as Joop painted places on her body that she herself seldom saw and rarely touched. When it was done, she found herself staring at Suki who was now entirely green.

"I can't believe what I'm seeing," she said, looking at her own arms and legs. It frustrated her that she could not see all of her body in the same manner as she was able to see Suki's. She was certain of one thing, however. All of her body that she could see was a brilliant gold. "Do you have a mirror?"

"No. No mirrors," Uma said quickly, before anyone else could answer.

"The color is striking," Suki offered, reassuring Diane. "You are a most perfect shade of happiness and life. You have to trust Uma."

Uma checked on Lulu to see if she was still sleeping, and looked out to find the whereabouts of Menno and Ineke. Satisfied they were safe, she changed places with Joop. "I can tell you what I am doing as I paint you, but you cannot have an opinion now because you are a canvas. You are what I make you."

Objecting to Uma's unilateral approach, Diane said, "Something I should tell you is that I am a woman who likes control."

Uma didn't respond directly to Diane's statement. Instead, she put on a new paint bottle and fresh airbrush before making a request of Diane, "Please, hold your arms out away from your body."

Diane hesitantly followed Uma's command, doing so as she continued to press her point. "Did you hear what I said a moment ago? I said I am a woman who likes control."

"I like woman who is strong and likes control," Uma acknowledged, glancing briefly at Diane's face before continuing with her painting. She looked over at Joop and gave him some further instructions. "Sei sicher, dass die Konturen der Stengels und der Blätter ihren naturlichen Kurven folgen."

"Ja, ja," Joop acknowledged, without stopping or turning away from Suki.

Persisting with her attempt to micro-manage what was taking place, Diane again said to Uma, "I think I should have some input into what is taking place, especially since this is my body."

The distraction caused Uma to raise her eyebrows and think for a few moments before she responded, "Diane, I think there was a woman once named Mona Lisa. She had eyes and a nose and a mouth. An artist met her and suggested that she be painted on a canvas. He painted her for a long time and ends up with a masterpiece. I do not think he ask her every ten minutes, 'Hey Mona Lisa, come look at how I paint you and tell me if you think it is what you like.'"

Diane was bold enough to challenge Uma's logic, suggesting, "I think Mona would have said, 'Hey Leonardo, can you do my mouth differently?'"

Resuming her painting, Uma closed with, "And maybe a masterpiece would be lost or forgotten in an attic in some awful place instead hanging in front of millions each year at Le Louvre." There was a purposeful pause following Uma's response allowing Diane to think. "You are too important to be lost in attic. Mankind needs you to stand still and be painted, not talk a lot."

Suki could be heard giggling in the other corner. Diane decided to once again become a willing participant, but had to get back at Suki for laughing.

"At least my ass is gold and not green."

Suki let loose, laughing. Uma simply smiled.

Uma painted small details on Diane's body with hand brushes, while she used an airbrush for the larger areas, creating the desired effects and pictures she had in mind. After two hours, she was satisfied with the result.

"Gut, ja?"

Joop walked over and put his arm around his wife as he replied simply, "Gut." She kissed him.

Diane watched in awe at how the couple lived their lives and worked in unison. They reminded her of her and Bruce.

The break in the work was brief, and soon Joop looked at Diane and said, "Now I paint the dark paint, and paint your hair too. Okay?"

"Uma, I need to…you know…"

"Ah, yes, Suki you come too. Good time we all go toilet."

Uma handed both Suki and Diane robes to cover their bodies for the short journey to the Loo. Joop took some time to make a snack for Menno and Ineke that they quickly gobbled down. Uma returned just in time for Lulu to wake up crying and hungry.

"Okay everybody, we take longer break than plan. Sorry but you have to stand, no sitting."

Joop quickly changed and cleaned up Lulu, and handed her to Uma who sat in her chair, nursing the baby for ten minutes or so before changing breasts and nursing some more. The entire time Lulu was enjoying her lunch, Joop and Uma studied Diane and Suki, and conversed at length in German or Dutch or both. They asked Diane and Suki to come closer, then walk away, then turn left, then turn right. Uma put Lulu on her shoulder and burped her for a while, achieving the desired result after rubbing her back. She then handed Lulu to her son so he could share the responsibility of caring for his young sister.

"Menno, nimm deine Schwester Lulu und lass sie mit Spielzeuge spielen."

"Ja gut, Mama," he obediently replied, but not as enthusiastically as Ineke had earlier. He took Lulu outside to play, and Ineke followed.

Uma clapped her hands once more, commanding, "Okay ladies—Suki you will be over here with me, and Diane you go with Joop to there and we get more work done."

Diane and Suki switched pedestals and the work commenced once again. Joop sprayed what could only be described as a macabre dark gray paint all over Diane's body and in her hair. With the help of the paint, he pulled Diane's hair into an unnatural, wind-blown and harried look. Uma in the meantime worked feverishly on Suki, transforming her into a forest of leaves and flowers, some in brilliant colors, others in pastels. When she was finished, Suki was gorgeous.

"I'm jealous," Diane said, lightheartedly. "Suki is beautiful, and I am all gray."

Boundaries

Rejecting Diane's remark, Uma replied, "You are gray now and you are about to be painted even more sad and more pain. You will be beautiful later. Very beautiful." Looking at Suki, Uma ordered, "You cannot move now until the show. Water only from straws in bottles. You know how this is done."

"Ja, Eure Hoheit," Suki acknowledged verbally, and without any great amount of movement. Uma responded with a stately nod, as would any 'queen.'

After spending several minutes preparing a palette of different colored paints, Uma grabbed a hand full of brushes, then walked over to Diane where she studied her closely, staring methodically at her every feature.

"I'm all one color. What on earth are you looking at?" Diane asked, wondering what Uma was going to do next.

As she continued to look at even the smallest features on Diane's body, she explained, "I study all of your body's texture. You have spectacular lines and curves. I am looking for bumps and dimples, but I do not see any. That is almost impossible. Even Suki has bumps and dimples."

"I do not!" Suki protested.

"They are cute bumps and dimples," Uma replied, glancing momentarily at Suki.

Again turning her attention back to Diane, she continued, "I could see a few when I paint the first layer, but now with more paint they have disappeared. I like to incorporate bumps and dimples into the smallest elements of my work. It puts all of your body to work. Now, because I can no longer find the flaws, I have to paint more shadows and texture. You are hard woman to paint when you are so flawless. Are you...maybe I say...thirty years old?"

"You're kidding, right?"

"Maybe thirty-two or thirty-three?"

"I am twenty!" Suki hollered from across the room.

Uma looked into Diane's eyes, smiling widely. She obviously knew how old Suki was, and understood the need to adjust her idea about Diane's youth.

"You age well."

"Thank you, Uma." Diane replied at the flattery. "You're my new best friend."

Uma began to paint. No longer using an airbrush, she used only small hand brushes employing tiny strokes. She said nothing as she labored, taking only two more breaks to check on her children and to nurse Lulu.

For hours, Diane tried to focus on Suki's body that she was modeling for her—turning and swaying like a tree in the wind—hoping the distraction would take her mind off of the beginnings of leg cramps and general soreness caused by standing in so few positions for such a long time. All the while, Uma coached Diane to assume some slightly different poses from time to time in order to alleviate the growing discomfort.

Finally, the work was done. Uma walked around Diane time and time again looking and staring. Joop joined her as she started to get tears in her eyes.

"This is good. I think I put all my feelings into this painting. Diane, I think I put all of your feelings into this painting, too."

Suki also walked around Diane and, like the others, became quite emotional.

"Suki you do not cry or I will have to do you again so stop now." Suki fanned her eyes to try to dry them.

"Now Diane," Uma coached, "take a small step forward with your right foot and squat down some...a little more...more...good. Now put your right arm down to the right with your palm facing to front." Diane continued following Uma's instructions despite her discomfort. "Now put your left arm up over your head like you are a wave that is breaking." Diane, again, did as she was asked. "Now look up to the left...little bit more...not so much...there."

Menno and Ineke returned, each carrying a bottle of water, and pushing the baby in a stroller. Ineke moved behind her father with a frightened look on her face of which everyone, including Diane, took note. Menno pointed at Diane's chest. "Ko Phi Phi Don?"

Putting her hands to her face, Uma shouted with joy, "Ja, Menno! Oh, this is good. Even Menno can see what I painted."

Boundaries

Ineke reached around from behind her father and pointed at Diane's belly. "Ko Phi Phi Ley?"

Uma jumped for joy. "Ja, Ineke!"

"Somebody tell me what is going on!"

Suki explained to Diane what everyone was admiring. "The painting depicts the tsunami disaster. Your right hand," Suki continued, pointing as she spoke, "is aimed at Banda Acer in Indonesia near where the earthquake started. Now there is a wave coming up your arm." Suki's hands moved in the direction the wave traveled. "Your breasts are the breaking waves as they hit the islands—there were two waves, you know—the water traveled between Ko Phi Phi Don and Ko Phi Phi Ley." Suki walked from Diane's right to left as she continued her graphic description. "One side of your body is painted with the bodies and debris that were pushed in front of the rushing walls of water, and the other side is painted with the bodies and debris that were pulled out to sea. Your left arm is the killer waves as they leave. Your legs are the sad faces of the survivors reaching up to the victims. Your face is the sadness and pain we all feel." Suki walked behind Diane. "Oh my, your back...your back is the faces of dead people." Suki looked at Uma. "This is really powerful, Uma. The details are incredible."

The artists shared a few moments of silence before Uma announced, "Now we go to the show. You will stand like this for a long time and let people look at you. That is all you have to do. After everyone has seen you, we then set up the water jets that will wash all of the sad off from you revealing happiness and a new beginning. At least that is what I hope will happen. If not we just have big mess of paint."

Everyone laughed, which was good because the levity was needed.

"Diane, one more drink and go to toilet before we go. Okay?"

She responded without hesitating, "Yes, please."

Twenty minutes later, Diane and Suki were on display along with sixty-eight other painted people. They stood on pedestals, brightly illuminated by the sun that was getting low in the west. Fans blew on some of the subjects to keep them cool or to blow their hair in a particular direction. Uma had seen to it that Diane and

Suki were among the lucky ones who had fans. One by one, then in small groups, then in larger groups, the spectators filed past each subject. They lingered at some displays more than others and many took photographs of the subjects. Television reporters and their cameramen walked past, speaking with the artists as close-up images were being broadcast to unknown destinations.

Diane watched as people filed past her. Without exception, the people who viewed her became distraught. Old people, middle-aged people, young people. People with yellow skin, people with dark skin, people with white skin. Some cried openly, while others simply had tears in their eyes. They got as close as they could, studying Diane, examining her with almost microscopic concern. Many returned again, and again. They lingered in front of her. As the crowd around her grew, some spectators pushed at each other to get a closer look. Diane could see out of the corners of her eyes that most of the spectators were attracted to Uma's two exhibits, with Diane stealing the majority of the audience from Suki.

Then, there they were—the judges, including Mickey. Each walked around Diane time and time again; all except Mickey. He just stood there, staring—his lips apart. Diane wanted desperately to know what he was feeling. Was he feeling what others were feeling—pain and sorrow, maybe even discomfort at what Uma had painted on her? Was he upset to see her painted and naked in front of so many people? Could he, in any way, be feeling all of the emotions that she was feeling herself?

After nearly forty-five minutes of posing, the judges completed their review of the contestants, including Diane, and Uma announced that it was time—time for the water. Joop quickly positioned four towers, each on a tripod base, and connected them to a water source. Uma gave him a nod, and as the water spray began, the pedestal on which Diane posed began to turn ever so slowly. Hundreds of spectators watched. They began to point. They began to talk, louder and louder.

The flashing from cameras was nonstop. Over the next five minutes, Diane's pedestal rotated ten times, after which Uma signaled for Joop to stop the rotation and turn off the water. The response from the spectators was difficult to describe. Initially there were *oh's* and *ah's*, then some clapping, then louder applause, then cheers. There was an outpouring of emotions, but it was clear from where Diane stood looking out at the throngs of people, that they approved of the transition.

She could now see her arms were bright gold. What she was unable to see, because of the water dripping into her eyes, was that all of her was now bright gold. What's more, she was covered with scenes of a happier life in the islands—families, children, local attractions, noteworthy landmarks, sea life, beautiful gardens. Diane began to cry herself, caught up in the emotional outpouring of those looking at her transformation from ugly duckling to beautiful swan.

The spectators could have studied her for hours, but after just twenty minutes, Joop and Uma came to her aid. Diane could hardly walk because she had been in the same position for so long. They helped her off of the pedestal, put a robe around her and walked her back to the tent. Once there, they gave her water to drink and comforted her. It was clear to them that hers were tears of joy, not pain.

Another artist came to the tent to retrieve Uma so she could be recognized for her floral work that was painted on Suki, and her thematic design that was Diane. Uma had stolen the show once again. She received overwhelming accolades from the judges, but it was the applause and sincere testimonials from the spectators that was the judgment Uma truly cherished. After a short ceremony, Uma, Joop, their children, and Suki returned to the tent where they told Diane the good news.

Uma walked up to Diane and kissed her on the lips. "I hope someday you will let me paint you again. You are a beautiful woman inside and outside. You helped so many people today…so many children. You helped take away a lot of pain. You are their hero."

Diane embraced Uma, then Joop, then Menno and Ineke. She stood in front of Uma and held both of her hands. "Uma, this sounds corny, but I woke up today a widow in mourning, even after so many years, and I will go to bed tonight a healed woman. How can I ever thank you enough?" They hugged tightly for what seemed like an eternity.

Turning to Suki, Uma offered her thanks, "My friend, as always you are a work of art. I hope you will let me paint you at the festival in Austria this summer. You are a spectacular canvas."

"Just let me know when and I will be there," Suki replied, hugging her comrade goodbye. "And, thank you for painting my new friend. She is a no longer a caterpillar."

Mickey burst into the tent, running over to Diane saying, "You can't imagine the impact you've had on the people outside. They're going nuts over you and they want you to go back out there." He gave Diane a gentle hug and kissed her.

"No. I'm tired now," Diane responded, shaking her head. "I just want to get my skin back."

Uma put her arm around Mickey and said, "You are a lucky man. Take good care of these beautiful women. Now, each of you, listen to me closely. Suki's paint will come off in the shower. Diane needs to have the oil put on her body. That can be a fun part. Letting your man...and your special friends...rub oil on you to get your paint off. Now go. Auf wiedersehen!" One more round of hugs and kisses and everyone parted company.

THE THREE MADE THE short walk back to their bungalow in just a few minutes. Once inside, Diane made a beeline for the bedroom where she removed her robe and stood in front of a mirror admiring the artwork.

"Did anyone take pictures of the top layer of body paint that was washed off? I have to see that. Did anyone?"

Suki stood next to Diane and reassured her, "Uma or Joop always takes pictures. Knowing her, they will be on her website by tomorrow. You were spectacular. I have seen a lot of her work, and I must say I have never seen anything as beautiful, nor as moving, as what she did with you."

"Let me get my camera," Mickey said, stepping out of the room.

Diane turned and removed Suki's robe, admiring her friend's artwork before it, too, was washed off. "You're beautiful, too. You're not mad that she used me for her thematic design, are you?"

"Not at all. I think this was good for you."

Mickey came running back. "Alright ladies, out on the porch and start posing."

Boundaries

Suki grabbed a white sheet from a drawer, and quickly walked outside where she draped it over a tree limb that extended over the porch.

Giving a 'thumbs up,' Mickey remarked, "Good idea—nice background. Love those Egyptian cotton sheets."

For the next several minutes, Diane and Suki took turns posing for pictures, separately, then together. After a while, the camera beeped.

"Oh, oh…card full. Guess that's it."

Suddenly, Mickey noticed that Diane was a little wobbly and asked, "Are you alright?"

Diane looked at Mickey with a blank stare, but didn't answer. Suki took one look at her and knew what was happening.

"Is she sick, Suki?"

Taking Diane by the hand, Suki replied, "She will be fine. We just need to get this paint off of her and I will need your help. We must all get into the shower."

Mickey followed the two to the bathroom where there was a large shower off to the side with multiple rainfall nozzles—a shower built for two or more. Suki adjusted the water to a temperature she found comfortable then helped Diane under one of the showerheads.

"Mickey, go to my room and bring back the large, black bottle of oil."

Mickey ran off to fetch the oil while Suki went to the waterfall tub, grabbed the bottle of soap left there earlier, then returned, joining Diane in the shower. Suki pulled Diane's face so she could look at her.

"Diane, talk to me."

"I'm good," Diane said with a weak voice. "I just feel really tired."

Suki felt relieved that Diane was able to answer questions, but knew she needed to act quickly.

"We are going to rub oil all over you to get the paint off. Just enjoy the attention and let me know if you feel like you need to sit down."

Mickey came back with the oil, handed it to Suki, then stood there staring at the two painted women in the shower.

"What are you waiting for," Suki asked. "Get your clothes off and help me."

Mickey removed his clothes and climbed in.

"Can I do her front?"

"No! This is not sex. This is for Diane. We need to get the paint off of her. Diane, hold your arms out to your side. Mickey, you do her back, I will do her chest and belly. She will feel better in a few minutes once her skin can breathe."

Mickey would not take the situation seriously. He glanced over Diane's shoulder and caught Suki's attention.

"Can I do your front?"

"No!" Diane shouted, firmly. "Focus!"

"Well, look who is back on the mother planet," Suki said.

Diane stood with her eyes closed as four hands rubbed oil all over her body, turning a once incredible work of art into a smeared mess of gold and other colors that slowly revealed the flesh beneath. At the same time Diane's flesh was re-emerging, Suki's paint washed off under the water without the use of oil, returning her to her own natural beauty.

"Mickey, is this like the ultimate male fantasy?" Diane asked. "You're in a shower with two beautiful women." Mickey smiled and thought for a while about an appropriate and mindful response. Diane reached behind her and felt for his penis that was beginning to give the only honest answer Mickey could muster. "God you are so predictable."

"Excuse me, but what do you expect," Mickey replied, as he stopped rubbing Diane's back for a moment. "You should always consider my erection the ultimate acknowledgement of your beauty and sex appeal."

Rejecting his comment, Suki faked putting her finger down her throat and gagging. The ladies began laughing.

"Hey, I am at a true disadvantage here. I have a libido gauge, while the two of you don't. You can't possibly tell me the two of you don't find this to be arousing."

Suki continued to rub oil on Diane's chest, mixing it now with some of the soap, and not giving any response to Mickey. Diane on the other hand did something so spontaneous that it shocked both Mickey and Suki. She put her arms around Suki, pulled her chest against hers and kissed Suki on the lips. It wasn't a short peck—their lips were locked for a long time and Mickey could see that tongues were touching.

When they finally separated, the look in their eyes was as intense as Mickey's now spectacular erection.

The last words out of Diane were, "Hold me tight…both of you. I love you guys. Thank you for tonight. I will never forget it."

Chapter 16

The morning sun broke through the clouds and shined through the bedroom window, casting its warm glow on the extra large bed. The wind coming off the ocean blew the curtains inward with considerable force. The waves could be heard crashing against the beach…if only there had been someone to listen. Mickey was asleep, naked and lying on his stomach—his favorite position. An Egyptian cotton, satin weave sheet covered only his legs. Diane was asleep on her right side, her bare back pressed against Mickey, and her left arm draped across another naked, supine body—that of Suki's. There were no longer any traces of paint on their skin.

The ringing of a phone broke the silence in the room, awakening Suki, who carefully wiggled out from under Diane's arm before dutifully answering it. On the line was a desk clerk delivering a message. Suki jotted down a note on a pad of paper from the desk before placing the receiver back on its cradle. Afterward, she took a few moments to look at her bedmates, allowing herself to have a private, uncontrollable smile, before retreating to her room to get dressed.

Twenty minutes later, a breakfast of fruits, croissants and assorted condiments was on the table, and hot espresso filled her cup. Diane approached Suki wearing panties and an unbuttoned shirt of Mickey's. Suki found her stunning, even early in the morning, although she limped slightly, and was not at all upright. Diane slowly leaned down, kissing Suki on the cheek as she begged, "Espresso…now."

After returning the kiss, Suki said, "Momentarily. Are you in pain? You look crooked."

"I hurt everywhere," Diane said as she slowly sat in a chair. "I think posing at the show killed my legs and arms, then, you know, our group activity in the shower, that killed my neck and back." Diane rubbed her arms and legs, then said, "My skin is super sensitive today."

Suki brought Diane her espresso, and she immediately savored the first sip with her eyes closed and her nostrils flared. Hers was an expression of pure contentment.

"Your skin will be better by tonight. All that paint took a toll on it." Suki walked around behind Diane and began to rub her shoulders, saying, "As for your muscles, I will give you a complete body massage after breakfast."

Diane closed her eyes as she relished Suki's tender touch.

"Was last night real?" Diane asked, taking another sip. "Did the three of us do what I think we did?"

"Completely and truly real, and yes," Suki replied, again sporting a forbidden smile that Diane was unable to see.

Diane cocked her head to one side so her face touched Suki's hand. "Yesterday changed my life."

Suki paused for a moment, accepting Diane's remark, before continuing to rub her shoulders while listening to her declaration.

"No, I am very serious. Do you think the feelings will last?"

"That is entirely up to you."

Diane slowly sipped her espresso, lost in the memory of the previous day and night. "Gosh I hate it when people make me accountable for answering my own question. That puts so much responsibility on me."

In keeping with Diane's observation, Suki didn't respond causing Diane to let out a sigh.

"I feel like seven years of hell have been washed away along with that paint. I know that sounds so stupid and trite. I just can't explain how good I feel. I mean, years of therapy and group counseling and antidepressants and pounding of pillows haven't begun to help me as much as what Uma did for me."

While massaging Diane's shoulders, Suki continued to listen as she analyzed her feelings.

"I have about fifteen friends who need to be painted. How do I make an appointment for them to meet Uma?

Suki laughed softly at Diane's remark.

"Last night was wonderful, too," Diane added as she caringly kissed Suki's hand. She was now thinking about the shower for three. "I've never done things like that before."

"You certainly seemed to know what you wanted."

"Maybe," Diane replied, shrugging her shoulders. "Maybe *you* knew what I wanted." Diane paused for a moment, obviously recalling one particular vision. "And of course we both knew what Mickey wanted…"

Suki let the last remark fall unanswered. If Diane could have seen her expression she would have known that Suki wanted to say more about what had transpired between the three of them.

"As for Uma, she does not take appointments. Besides, what worked for you may not work for others."

Diane continued to enjoy the final moments of caressing that Suki was giving her shoulders.

"There is a message for you to phone your boss, Rajeev," Suki said as she sat down. "He says it is urgent and he wants to have a conference call between himself, you and a man named Gunter Herff."

"When did Rajeev call?" Diane asked, her now eyes wide open.

"He phoned two hours ago and left a message. Since you and Mickey are on vacation, I have all phone calls to the room phone screened. Do you know this man Gunter Herff?"

"Yes," Diane answered anxiously. "He's the Chief Executive of a very important account. I was supposed to meet with him on Wednesday before my boss decided to put me on another career path." Diane looked for her watch, but it wasn't on her wrist. Putting her arms in the air in frustration, Diane said, "What the hell time is it? For that matter, what day is it?"

Boundaries

It is just before seven o'clock in the morning on Saturday." Suki calmly took another sip of her espresso before adding, "Drink your coffee. You need to be calm if you are going to telephone your boss and an important customer."

"What time is it in Munich and in California?" Diane asked, now looking completely confused.

Suki looked at the ceiling for a moment as she did the translations of time and space in her mind. "We are six hours later than Munich. There, it is in the very early hours of the morning, today. We are fifteen hours later than California. It is still Friday there and about four o'clock in the afternoon."

Diane shook her head. "How does anyone keep this shit straight? I need to call my office right now."

"Would you like me to arrange a call for you?" Suki asked as she put her hand on Diane's in an effort to ease her tension. "There is a videoconference facility here on the property, or you can just use a conference phone in one of the rooms.

Diane looked around the room as if she was trying to get her bearings, and then she held her cup out to Suki.

"No. I just need a refill and my cellphone. I should be able to call the States from here, right?"

"There should be no problem." Suki took Diane's cup and made another espresso. "You can dial direct. You just need to dial '001' first, or on some phones you must hold the '+' symbol, then dial '1' and the number."

Diane located her handbag across the room, retrieved her mobile phone, then returned to the table where she took another sip of fresh espresso—the temperature of the drink causing her to grimace. She turned on the phone and noticed the message indicator. Listening to an automated message, she said, "Great, I have twenty-eight unheard messages," then she disconnected before proceeding to dial Rajeev. She stopped after holding down one key for just a moment. "Crap! I always use speed-dial for Rajeev." She thought for a minute. "I'll just call the switchboard." She dialed again. Soon there was ringing on the other end. After a few rings, a voice answered.

"Good afternoon, Medico Techniq, this is Raul, how can I help you?"

"Raul, this is Diane Alders."

"Ms. Alders, how are you? It's been a while since we've seen you."

Diane was relieved to have gotten through. "I'm in...I'm on vacation. Can you connect me with Rajeev?"

"Certainly. You be safe."

"Thanks." There were a few more rings, then another voice.

"This is Mr. Munshi's office, Ella speaking, how may I help you?"

"Ella, this is Diane," Diane replied, sitting up businesslike in her chair.

"Diane! We've been so worried about you. Is everything alright?"

Looking puzzled, Diane replied, "I'm fine. Why would you be worried about me?"

"You just disappeared! You never leave without telling us where you are going. For that matter, you never go anywhere unless one of us has made the arrangements. This is so unlike you. Are you sure you are alright?"

Diane held the phone away from her and glared at it as if she was glaring directly at Rajeev's secretary, Ella.

"I'm perfectly fine. I decided to take some time off."

There was a pause.

"You? Time off?" Ella lowered her voice to a whisper. "There's a rumor that you're with Mickey?"

"Is that really any of your business?" Diane asked, shaking her head in disbelief. She listened to a rustling noise on the other end of the conversation. "Is Jenny listening to this conversation as well?"

There was another pause, then a voice in the background responded.

"Hello, Diane."

Diane smiled at the sudden interest shown in her personal life by the secretaries in the executive office.

Ella came back, "We've started a pool here that has you marrying Mickey."

"Ella! I will not have my personal life be subjected to betting like it's the NCAA Finals." Diane reflected for a moment, smiled, then asked, "What are the odds looking like?"

"Forty to one you'll come back married."

Grinning, Diane asked, "And where do you have your money?"

Ella made a high-pitched humming noise, then playfully avoided answering the question.

"Rajeev will speak with you now. Bye."

The phone was quickly transferred once again.

"Ella?!"

Diane was frustrated that her question went unanswered. Soon a familiar voice came on the same line.

"Diane?"

"Rajeev, you called?"

"Thank God you are safe!"

"Why is everyone so worried about me?" Diane again was puzzled.

"You never go away like this."

"Rajeev, you told me to go away!"

"Yes, like I've told you a hundred times, but you have never listened to me until now!"

"I called you the other morning at home and woke you up. Don't you remember? I told you I was going away with Mickey."

"Ah! That explains why my phone was under the mattress! I must have put it there when you woke me up from a sound sleep. I looked for the damn thing for half a day. The housekeeper finally located it when she heard a ringing from my bed. Where are you, anyway?"

"I'm in...I'm on vacation. You don't need to know where I am." Diane thought for a moment about Rajeev's question. "Hey, you must know where I am, after all, you called me at the resort where I am staying."

"No, I called Mickey's house and spoke with someone named Maria who said she could get in touch with him. I assumed you were with him, but she wouldn't say one way or the other. She's a very good personal assistant, I must say. I asked her to relay a message and, voilà, here we are. Did you hear that Herff wants to speak with both of us?"

"Yes. What's that all about?"

"This is most interesting...almost laughable...almost terrifying."

"What's that?" Diane asked as she closed her eyes expecting to hear that her billion-dollar deal was in jeopardy because of something that had happened at the meeting she did not attend.

"Gunter called me a while ago to tell me he was sitting at home with his wife and some friends, drinking wine and watching television. He said they were watching some special program about body painting that had been recorded earlier in the day—some kind of exhibition in Thailand or something—and he said he saw someone who looked like you."

Diane let her forehead hit the table as she listened.

"I thought to myself, how could Gunter possibly think that was you—especially if you are being painted? You would be impossible to recognize. And then it occurred to me that anyone whose body is being painted, must be nude."

Diane rocked her head back and forth on the table. Suki looked on, worried that Diane was getting bad news.

"So I said, 'Gunter, you must be mistaken. That does not sound at all like my Executive Vice President of Marketing, mentor to all women, and close personal friend of nearly a decade.' He went on to say that he was almost certain it was in fact you—that the subject was an American on vacation in Phuket, and the artist was some Scandinavian woman named Inga."

Diane pounded the table with the fist not holding the phone as she said, "She's Austrian, and her name is Uma." There was a long period of silence. "So, is this the point in our conversation where you tell me I'm fired?"

"Actually, there is some good news to all of this."

"Oh, do tell me. I cannot wait, master."

Boundaries

"It turns out that both he and some of his friends lost family members or acquaintances in the tsunami, and they were quite moved by the painting that was...you. He said your waves impressed him."

Diane put her forehead in her hand while saying, "Oh, Lord, please take me now."

"He thought the likenesses of Phi Phi were very graphic."

"You can stop now, Rajeev."

"He went on to say that he, his friends and their companies will contribute a total of two-hundred thousand Euros to the charity that was to benefit from that event."

"Two-hundred thousand Euros?!" Diane exclaimed, sitting bolt upright.

"Yes. You must have marvelous waves."

"Bite me, Rajeev."

"He also said he looks forward to meeting you at the next quarterly review. It appears I have no choice but to put you back on the account, and Ashad will have to take another role."

"Yes!" Diane shouted, jumping up. She grabbed her sore back, then managed to form an evil grin. "So, how did Ashad take the news?"

"Oh, Ashad is happy with the change. I gave him your raise."

"Rajeev!"

"So tell me, Diane, who is the girl painted with the floral designs that I see standing next to you?"

"That's my friend, Suki. She's...what do you mean 'see standing next to me'?"

"I had to be certain it was you that Gunter was looking at. After all, why should we labor over a mistaken identity, especially if large sums of money are at stake? Fortunately, he recorded the program and sent me a short excerpt. I've never seen you so...colorful, so...vibrant. From different angles, the shapes I see are..."

"Oh, Rajeev, please stop looking at it. I'll never be able to talk to you face-to-face again."

"I think we can use this for an advertisement campaign next year. I'm sending it off to the promotions group for their comment."

"Rajeev! Oh, my God, what would the Board say?"

"Good idea. Let me send each of them the file. I'll let you know their comments. This is certainly a new approach to customer relations."

"Rajeev, don't! You're having entirely too much fun with this. You can stop now."

"I think I will freeze one still shot and make it the desktop background on my laptop. I can arrange all of my icons around your…"

"Rajeev! Do you have anything worthwhile you want to say?"

Rajeev was laughing. "No, I think that just about covers everything, figuratively speaking, of course." Rajeev laughed harder.

Diane found it hard not to be amused, but refused to laugh.

"So, is there a conference call with Gunter?"

"Oh, no. Of course not. I just wanted to make sure you phoned me. I had to use the proper bait so I could tell you the news about the generous pledge from Herff. Please let me know when you plan your next surprise exposure."

"Goodbye, Rajeev."

Rajeev laughed as he bid, "Goodbye, Phi Phi."

With that, the phone call ended. Diane pressed the disconnect button on her end and then dropped the phone on the table. Suki was desperate to find out what the conversation was about.

"Is everything alright?"

Diane sat back in her chair and ran her hands through her hair, then buttoned up her shirt in a futile attempt to show some belated modesty.

"Anonymity you said?"

Suki's eyebrows furrowed. "Oh…"

"Yeah…*oh*. Nothing like having a client seeing you naked."

"Happens to me…every time," Suki jokingly responded while shrugging her shoulders.

Boundaries

Crossing her legs self-consciously, Diane responded, "You know what I mean!"

Suki tried to diffuse the situation. "Maybe your features are distinctive."

"Yeah, right...my waves."

Suki tried to hold back, but her laugh finally escaped. Shortly, Diane was laughing, too.

Mickey joined the two wearing only his boxers. Unlike Diane, Mickey looked like he had just rolled out of bed.

"My nutrient curve is sagging. What's for breakfast?"

"The usual," Suki said, pointing to the table. "You just have to open your eyes."

"Oh...fruit...yum," Mickey said, squinting at the table in an exaggerated manner. "How about bacon and eggs or some spicy migas?"

Suki twisted her mouth before asking Diane, "How is Mickey tasting these days?"

Diane thought for a moment, then smiled, replying, "Actually, surprisingly good...kind of sweet." Looking back at Suki, she asked, "What do you think?"

"I'll have to agree," Suki replied, taking a bite of fruit.

Mickey sat down, having listened attentively to the lady's exchange. Having been instantly enlightened, he said, "I think I'll have a double order of fruit," as he grabbed two forks, and put on his *Jack Nicholson* smile. Suki swallowed what was in her mouth just before Mickey raised one eyebrow in an evil manner and said, "I watched you swallow that way last night."

Suki and Diane looked at each other, shaking their heads in disgust.

"Seriously, Mickey, and I realize that is a stretch," Suki began, "you should have a light breakfast this morning. We are going to a local café for a lunch of dim sum and tea. So, you two eat up while I set out your clothes for the day." After getting up, Suki kissed Diane on top of her head and said, "Meet me on the lower landing for your massage." Affectionately stroking Diane's shoulders, she continued, "I will bet your Mr. Herff pays very close attention to you in the future." Suki further ruffled up Mickey's messy hair as she passed by him.

"Who's this Herff guy?" Mickey asked as he watched Suki exit to the bedroom.

"He's my billion-dollar CEO. He saw the body painting exhibition on television."

Mickey smiled. "Flashing the clientele? Bet that helps the market share."

Diane kicked him under the table.

"I'm going to stop sitting next to you if you keep kicking me."

"It's not funny!"

Chuckling, Mickey replied, "No, it's freakin' hilarious, actually."

Suki passed through the room and went down the steps to the lower landing. Diane got up from the table without saying a word and followed, leaving Mickey to enjoy breakfast alone.

"I just want everyone to know I am really enjoying my vacation," Mickey chortled.

JUST BEFORE NOON, DIANE Mickey and Suki arrived by car at a small, unremarkable storefront marked Café Sumalee. Mickey held the door open as Suki and Diane stepped out. The women were dressed in similar, incredibly stylish, pastel colored, lightweight skirts and tops. The three sat down at a long table with five other people—three were Asian; the other two, European. A breeze blowing briskly off of the ocean kept the room a comfortable temperature. Suki introduced herself and her friends to everyone. She spoke Mandarin to two, Korean to another, and German to the Europeans who were actually from Italy. In spite of the variety of nationalities, they all managed to communicate in some shared language. With the addition of Diane and Mickey to the table, they began speaking in English.

Curious about the languages that were spoken, Diane asked Suki, "I am impressed with all the languages you are able to speak—and so fluently. How many languages do you know?"

After thinking for a moment, Suki replied, "Well, I am fluent in Thai, Chinese—both Mandarin and Cantonese—Japanese, Vietnamese and Korean. I am competent in French, Dutch and German, and I can speak some Hindi. So ten in all."

"No, that's eleven. You forgot English," Diane said, impressed with Suki's answer.

"Yes, eleven." Turning to Mickey Suki asked, "Mickey, how many languages can you speak?"

Mickey knew he was being set up to look like the ugly-American, but he went along with the conversation anyway.

"Two—Californian and Texan."

"You forgot Illinoisian," Diane said with a smirk. "That's three."

Continuing, Mickey added, "Then, of course, there is British, Irish, Australian…"

Diane kicked Mickey under that table.

"You have got to stop doing that." Mickey decided it was time for payback. "So, Ms. Linguist, how many languages can you speak?"

Diane was ready for his question and quickly replied, "I speak the universal language—Woman."

The other guests laughed out loud at Diane's response, and she soaked up the attention.

"Actually, I took a sum total of six years of French."

The Italian men took note and attempted to initiate a conversation with Diane in French.

Obviously unable to understand their entire exchange, Diane relented, "I'll just stick with Woman. My French is a little rusty."

Shortly, the Italians, both incredibly handsome young men in their late twenties or early thirties, were conversing in their own tongue and becoming increasingly excited. They soon stopped and smiled—their eyes on Diane. One decided to elaborate.

"My friend here thinks that he knows you from some place. I told him he uses that pick-up line too much and besides you are with a man—your husband, I assume?"

Mickey bristled, making sure he had full claim on Diane.

"Yes, I am Diane's husband."

He lied so effortlessly that Diane briefly felt shivers run down her spine.

"So how do you think you know my wife?"

The two Italian men looked at each other before one replied, "I was at this body painting exhibition yesterday and…"

Diane turned to Suki and put her hands around Suki's throat as if to choke her.

"Anonymity! You said…anonymity!"

"I think I said a certain degree of anonymity…" Suki responded, laughing.

Without thinking, Diane stood up and shouted so that more than just her table could hear her.

"Alright, everybody! Yes, I was the one whom Uma Goss painted yesterday at the charity event! Yes, I was naked in front of God and all of humanity with Phi Phi painted on my chest!"

Diane abruptly sat back down after what she had just blurted out sank in. The entire café burst out laughing and applauding. Diane couldn't help but get caught up in the laughter herself.

Bottles of sparkling water and plates were set out for the new guests. Mickey wasn't sure he liked the attention that was brought to Diane, but the cat was out of the bag, and there wasn't anything he could do about it. One by one, a dozen or more of the café's customers came over to Diane and gave her an emotional hug. They offered their stories about the tsunami, as well as their recommendations about what to eat. Diane's embarrassment gave way to other emotions as people from all over the world who were eating there accepted her with open arms. Four of the patrons had the local newspaper with them and asked Diane to autograph the picture of her that was published on page 2. Mickey expressed his displeasure by nervously tapping a knife on the table.

The Italian man who had been at the exhibition soon became emotional as well. When the others in the café had resumed eating, he waited until he had Diane's attention then explained himself.

Boundaries

"I lost my older sister on Phi Phi Don. We never found her body."

He stared at Diane's chest. The sheer blouse covering Diane's braless chest didn't hide his memory of the illustration of Phi Phi Don.

"She was staying right about there…"

He reached across the table and put his index finger on Diane's breast just left of her right nipple. Diane gasped and her eyes got as big as silver dollars.

Mickey jumped up and grabbed the man's hand, not realizing he was still holding the knife he had been tapping. The café came became instantly silent waiting for all hell to break loose.

The man knew immediately he had overstepped his bounds.

"So sorry, I am so sorry. That just happened."

Mickey reflexively released the grip he had on the Italian man's hand, changing it to a handshake, put the knife back on the table and forced a smile to defuse the situation. He slowly sat back down and relaxed.

"I'm glad we understand each other."

Rudely inserting herself into the moment, Suki said, "What just happened here was an example of international outpouring of love and people finding common ground, being stopped short by the usual American cowboy diplomacy."

"Piss off, Suke," Mickey replied, deliberately slurring her name and pointing his finger in her face.

"Guys!" Diane shouted, putting her hands up as if to separate the two.

After a moment the Italians excused themselves, paid their bill, and left the café. Shortly after them, the Korean and the two Chinese men left as well, leaving Mickey, Diane and Suki at the table alone. It wasn't long before the table was cleaned up and another five people took their place. They introduced themselves to the trio. Mickey worked hard to be more civil with the new patrons and, thankfully, nobody mentioned body painting.

The servers pushing trays began circling the table. First, was the cart with the steamed dumplings. Next, there was the cart with various buns and spring rolls. Then came the carts with the exotic dishes and the deep-fried and heavier food, and, finally, the sweet cart with sponge cakes, custard tarts, sesame balls, and sweet rice cake. Diane sampled everything—everything that is except the chicken's feet. Mickey and Suki ate those as well. Several varieties of hot tea were served. All eight at the table exchanged lively conversation and amusing stories. After an enjoyable and filling lunch, Mickey, Diane and Suki returned to the bungalow.

UPON RETURNING, MICKEY WENT out on the porch by himself. Shortly, Diane joined him and then so did Suki. Diane thought it would be appropriate to bring up the subject of Mickey's earlier actions, but wanted to be alone with him.

"Let's go for a walk," she suggested.

"I'm stuffed."

Mickey knew what she wanted to discuss and was reluctant to talk about it.

"Let's just sit and be fat, ugly, unhealthy Americans," he said, looking at Suki to be sure she heard him.

Suki's nostrils flared—her only response to his remark. But, that was enough to let him know he had connected.

Diane persisted, "No, let's go. I want to talk."

She took Mickey's hand. His face clearly showed he was pouting, but she wasn't going to take no for an answer.

"Suki, we'll be back after a bit."

It took every bit of courage Suki could muster to respond in a manner that didn't show the hurt she was feeling, but she managed to pull it off.

"Enjoy yourselves. I will be waiting for you."

Now she was not only competing with Diane for Mickey's affections, but she was competing with Mickey for Diane's. The emotional pain was exquisite to be sure. To make things worse, she had insulted Mickey earlier at the cafe. That was something he never took well.

She was watching Mickey and Diane walk down to the beach when suddenly Mickey's mobile phone rang in the bungalow. She managed to locate it before the call went to his voicemail and answered.

"This is Mickey Rollins' phone. May I help you?"

"Hi," said a perky, female voice. "This is Gretchen. Is this Diane?"

Suki knew Gretchen…only too well.

"Hello, Gretchen. This is Suki."

Gretchen's voice turned squeaky.

"Suki? Let me talk to Mickey, hon."

She showed no interest in speaking with Suki.

"He is not here right now. Can I have him call you?"

"Are he and Diane having a good time? I sure wish they would get together permanently. God, I hope she gets him locked up as *Mr. Alders* really soon before I do something stupid and knock you off so I can replace you as his mistress."

Suki squeezed her eyes closed in an attempt to remain composed.

"Yes, Gretchen. They are having a wonderful time."

"Well, this ranch Mickey wants to buy for Diane ought to win her heart. It's her old family ranch. He says she's wanted it for years and it's for sale. Let me tell you, he's going to have to fork out the bucks—a lot more than he thought. They have an offer for thirty-seven million and the owner signs tomorrow afternoon. God, Mick's a sweet guy. Tell him I have to make an offer by nine o'clock tomorrow morning so he has to call me tonight. I don't care what time. Can you get him that message, honey?"

"I will give him the message the moment that he returns."

"Thanks, hon. By the way, I liked watching you and Mickey doing…you know…making love. It had all the entertainment value without me having to do any of the dirty work. Besides, it looked like you enjoyed yourself. I'm sure he did."

"Goodbye, Gretchen. It was nice speaking to you one last time."

"I beg your pardon?"

Suki disconnected. Just then, there was a knock at the door to the bungalow. A man announced that it was housekeeping. Suki let him in and he scurried about collecting trash while a team of women began cleaning everything in sight. Suki very discreetly turned off Mickey's phone and dropped it in the trash cart.

DIANE AND MICKEY MADE it to the waterfront holding hands. They found two unoccupied, isolated folding chaise lounge chairs and made themselves comfortable. Mickey took his shirt off. Diane did the same.

"Don't you think the neighbors will fuss?"

"Nah," Diane said, shrugging her shoulders. "We're just fat, ugly, unhealthy Americans anyway."

Her remark managed to get a smile out of Mickey. They both reclined in their chairs. After a few minutes, Diane began to pry.

"What got into you back at the café?"

Mickey put his hands behind his head, avoiding the question.

"Wow, this sun is brutal."

"I know, so talk fast," Diane said, agreeing with Mickey, but she persisted in her attempt to understand him. "What were you thinking?"

Looking at Diane, Mickey replied, "A man put his hand on my wife's breast...in public, no less. Countries have gone to war over things like that."

"Mickey, first of all, it's my body, not yours. Secondly, I'm not your wife. Finally, he wasn't a threat. He was trying to convey a feeling...tell us his story."

"Nope. He touched your tit. Besides, that's not the point. You are mine for the touching, not his—not even for the looking."

Mickey's comment shocked Diane. "You're kidding, right?"

"No. I'm dead fucking serious. You might as well know right here and now that I'm terribly possessive when it comes the women in my life."

"And yet, you have a relationship with Suki who we know is..."

"She's not a part of this conversation."

Diane got up and went to Mickey's lounge chair. She sat straddling his hips with her breasts dangling in front of his face.

"These are all yours and only yours."

Diane could tell there was something much deeper going on.

"You're not telling me everything. Talk to me, Mick."

It was apparent that unless he planned to toss Diane onto the ground, he was going to have to provide more information.

Boundaries

"Diane, I love you so I will bare my soul to you, but please don't share this with anyone." Mickey added a melodramatic pause. "I have a real insecurity problem." He waited for that to sink in. "I'm very jealous and possessive to the point of excess."

Diane just listened. Nothing he said came as news to her.

"That's why I broke up with Laura."

Immediately, Diane was completely engaged in the conversation.

"Who's Laura?"

"My first and only wife. I told you before that I was married once…a long time ago."

Diane was somewhat taken aback that the conversation involved an old flame.

"Right, but you never gave her a name."

"Well it's Laura. She was very talented, very attractive, very athletic, and men were just drawn to her."

"And…what's the problem? She sounds a lot like me, actually."

"I know," was all Mickey could say.

Debating for a moment how to respond, Diane sat up straight and asked, "So I am a problem for you in the same way that Laura was?"

"No, I am a problem for you," Mickey replied, avoiding eye contact.

Her eyebrows perked up.

"Okay. Earth to Mickey. Come in Mickey. I am not receiving you. Don't you think I should be the judge of that?"

"No, actually I don't. I became so possessive about Laura that I made myself believe she was a bad person so I could divorce her. In reality, I wanted her to get away from me so that she could become everything that she deserved to be. I was in her way."

Diane thought a moment about what Mickey said, then responded with, "So, you chose for her, just like you are choosing for me, now. You didn't even respect her intelligence enough to let her decide to stay with you or to leave you, and here you are repeating history."

"It was better that way."

Trying to control the level of her voice so that she didn't sound like she was scolding Mickey, Diane said, "Better for whom?" Then, she took her interpretation of what Mickey had said one level further. "So, you don't hate her."

After exhaling at length, he responded to Diane's point.

"I convince myself that I do."

Diane flashed back to what Suki had told her the other day—that Laura was a threat. She had to know just how big of a threat.

"Where is Laura now?"

"She's a long way off. I haven't seen her in years. I've sort of lost track of her."

Diane studied all of Mickey's facial expression and body language and could tell he was not completely forthcoming.

"Cut to the chase, Mickey. Do I have to worry about her?"

"No! You're missing the whole point. I'm having a difficult time not being a possessive asshole."

"Well that episode at the café would certainly support your concern. I'd think you could learn something from your past."

With a worried expression on, Mickey asked, "Can you love me this way?"

"I can love you a lot of ways…even if you are a little possessive." Diane put on a natural, warm smile. "Just don't start any world wars or impact foreign relations. Better yet, maybe you can change." She stroked his hair, as she continued, "Besides, you're sharing me with Suki and that doesn't bother you."

"She's no threat. When the contract period is up, she's gone."

He may as well have slapped Diane across the face.

"What do you mean, 'She's gone?'"

"Like…gone. We go one way, she goes another. That's it. C'est fini."

"What if I don't want her to go away?" Diane asked, a sudden feeling of panic rushing through her body.

"She always goes away. Her's is pay-as-you-go companionship."

Boundaries

Truly unnerved by now, Diane said, "Well, it can be different from now on. We'll remain close friends."

"Babe, you don't want to be friends with Suki. You use her for her knowledge and skills. You let her entertain. When it's time to go, you turn and walk away."

Thinking there might be a connection, Diane said, "She's just like Laura."

"No! She's not like Laura!" Mickey barked, thoroughly annoyed.

Realizing she had hit upon something, she pressed on.

"Yep, you used her and then you turned and walked away. She was nothing more than your first mistress. You just happened to be married."

"Don't ever talk about Laura like that!" Mickey shouted as he grabbed Diane violently by the hair while looking enraged.

Diane slapped Mickey's hand away with such violence that he pulled her hair before he could release it from his hand.

With an ever-so-threatening look, Diane began to chastise Mickey as she had never done before.

"Mickey. That's one time. You get one chance. Because you are such a sick, pathetic excuse for a man, I'm going to forget what you just did. But if you ever— do you hear me, EVER—even come close to becoming violent with me again, I'll castrate you and then I'll leave you to die. Is that clear?"

Mickey held his arms out to his side submissively.

"Sorry, sorry. This is just a very sensitive subject. Like I said, it's a problem. I wanted you to know. Don't be mad that I told you. You should be glad I was open and honest."

He resembled a dog that had just been whipped, but Diane still wondered, "I'm going to ask you one more time. Do I have to worry about your ex-wife?"

"No, absolutely not," he replied, putting his hands on her shoulders. "She's way in the past and way out of my life now. You're all I want, Diane."

"That's all I wanted to know." Diane wanted to believe Mickey, but she had had enough. She wiped sweat from her forehead, then said, "I'm dying out here in this heat. Let's go back up."

Thinking for a moment, he replied, "I'm going to stay here for a few more minutes." At least Mickey now made eye contact with Diane. "I need to be introspective and just let what went on here soak in for a while."

"I'm sorry about some of the things I said earlier. I do love you, Mick."

"Exorcism."

"What?"

"Exorcism. Maybe I need an exorcism."

Diane smiled at him and then said, "No, you just need to tweak your schwa."

Mickey returned the smile.

"Good. That was good. I'll get right on that schwa-tweaking."

She leaned over and kissed him on the lips, then got up, pulled on her shirt and headed for the bungalow.

ARRIVING A SHORT WHILE later with her shirt still unbuttoned, Diane was dripping with perspiration. Suki met Diane at the doorway with a frozen, blended fruit drink. She stopped and smiled approvingly, touched by Suki's well-timed attentiveness.

Suki could tell that Diane was upset and opened the conversation by saying, "Sometimes a disagreement is a good thing. It helps to clear the air."

After taking her drink and rubbing the glass on her forehead, she took a swallow of it, then replied, "I'll tell you, Suki, that man has more baggage than Samsonite. And you know something? You were right on target about his ex-wife. He's still in love with her after all these years!" Diane took another sip. "What do you know about her?"

"Really not much, but I can hear in his voice, the few times he has mentioned her, that he still cares for her." Suki could tell Diane was still upset. "I do believe that is the extent of it. She is but a memory. You, on the other hand, are the real thing. I think it is more an issue of closure."

Still quite disturbed, Diane said, "Well, I need to find the bitch and drive a stake through her heart. That ought to give him some closure." Realizing she needed to get off of the subject, she continued, "There, I feel better just saying that." She set her drink down and took Suki by the hands. "Suki, Mickey says we can't be friends when the vacation is over. I want to be friends with you after we leave. Can we do that?"

It was obvious from Suki's reaction that this was an atypical remark from a client. Suki thought a long time, but eventually managed a graceful reply that could not be interpreted as any type of commitment. "I would very much like that, Diane. You are a wonderful person. I am just not sure how that would work."

Trying to decipher the cryptic response, Diane continued, "Friends, you know. We pick up the phone and call each other, we send each other emails, we visit one another from time to time, we name our daughters after each other..."

Laughing, Suki asked, "Is this where we cut the palms of our hands with a knife and mix our blood together?"

Returning the laughter, Diane replied, "Yes...no. Let's think of some other way to make a bond." Diane put her hand on Suki's cheek and said, "I mean it. I never want to lose you, Suki."

Searching for middle ground on which to land, Suki responded, "Let us see what transpires over the next few days. Are you sure I am not getting in the way of you and Mickey?"

"What do you mean?

"This trip is about you and Mickey. I am a catalyst for your enjoyment, nothing more. When the vacation is over, it should be time for me to move on. That is the way Mickey likes it."

Lacking appreciation of Suki's point of view, Diane countered, "Maybe that's the way Mickey likes it. That doesn't mean that's the way I like it. I am, after all, an entirely separate person from Mickey."

"I think you and Mickey may someday be the same person—maybe soon."

Quickly reading between the lines, Diane asked, "You mean Mickey and I may someday be married? I think you're very optimistic, Suki."

"I would rather be considered a romantic. Diane, despite the fact that he treats you like you are his prize possession, you just discovered he still has feelings for his ex-wife, and he was just now less than a gentleman in an argument, you have returned to your bungalow and have not yet started to pack your bags to leave him." Suki stopped for a moment to allow what she just said to Diane to sink in. "You find too much in him to let him go. He is already a part of you, and you are a part of him."

"How did you know?" Diane asked as she stared at Suki.

"I just know," Suki replied, with her inevitable coy smile.

Diane didn't have time to respond before Mickey interrupted the conversation by bursting up the stairs and into the room.

"I'm brilliant. I am absolutely brilliant."

Diane and Suki exchanged looks that said to each other the conversation they were having would have to continue later, but that it would definitely have to continue.

"What's that Mick?" Diane asked.

"Okay, both of you have to sit down." Mickey guided them to a sofa and had them sit side by side. As he began pacing back and forth nervously, he said, "Well, I probably did a bad thing, but maybe not. Diane you have to listen to everything I am saying before you start throwing things."

Diane crossed her arms and put her chin on one fist as if it were protection from whatever kind of news Mickey was about to unload.

"Does that mean I can throw things at you whenever I want to?" Suki asked, trying to lighten up the mood.

"Good, humor, I like that," Mickey said, momentarily stopping and pointing at Suki. He again began to pace. "I need a beer."

He jogged off to the refrigerator and grabbed a Kirin.

"What, no lime?" Diane asked.

Mickey pointed at Diane.

"Good, more humor. This is good."

Mickey began pacing again, staring at the floor about two steps in front of him. He stopped directly in front of both women, turned and looked at them as he held his arms out.

"Diane, I'm buying the Gilroy ranch for you."

Boundaries

The reactions by Diane and Suki were diametrically opposite from one another. Diane cautiously reacted in surprise and joy. Suki reacted in surprise and horror. Diane was the first to say anything.

"You mean my family's old ranch?"

"Bingo. That's the one."

Suki covered her mouth in an attempt to keep from screaming.

"Why would you buy my ranch? Don't you think that I'm capable of buying my own ranch?"

Mickey's arms fell to his side and his smile began to fade. One could tell his mind was conjuring up another angle to the announcement.

"It's a birthday gift."

"It's not my birthday."

"Fine. Then, it's next year's birthday gift. Give me a break. Now, listen to what I want to tell you. The ranch is just a part of the deal. Can you just sit and listen?"

Diane found it hard to hold her tongue, but she decided to let Mickey continue. "Go on, I'll shut up…for now."

Mickey's face brightened up again, but Suki continued to stare into the distance with her hand over her mouth.

"Suki, you listen too."

Suki looked at Mickey, but wanted to run and hide somewhere.

"Diane, you want the ranch, right?"

"Yes. I want to buy my own ranch with my own money."

"Yes. Good. You want it," Mickey said, struggling to keep his train of thought. "The rest are details at closing." He took a deep breath. "Suki, you want a career change in the near future. Isn't that what you said?"

"I believe I have said that I may not be doing the concierge work too much longer. As for a career change, I have not made any plans for that as yet."

Mickey struggled again as the responses from both ladies were in both cases anything but a firm 'yes,' but he continued, "Diane, we both know the ranch will require a lot of help—a good business person and organizer to make things work."

Diane and Suki sat speechless, not sure where the brainstorm would sprinkle next. Standing there, holding his hands out, palms facing upward, Mickey was expecting simultaneous epiphany. Instead, there was silence.

"Don't you see? It's perfect. It's a perfect match. Suki can have a new beginning, and you Diane get a trusted business manager."

Diane and Suki looked at each other, but words never left their mouths. Mickey decided to push his point one more time.

"The two of you can run the ranch in Gilroy!"

Diane finally responded, "We both know a lot about stallions…"

It wasn't long before the chortling began, followed by all out laughter. Diane got up from the sofa and hugged Mickey.

"Mickey, sometimes I don't know if I should slap you or just love you." She kissed him on the lips before he could say something to ruin the mood. "Why would you go and do something like this?"

"Because I like making you happy."

Suki watched as the two melted in each other's arms, realizing she had to make at least a partial confession about her role in the ranch deal.

"It will cost you more than thirty-seven million dollars to make Diane happy."

"What?" Diane and Mickey responded.

"Gretchen called while the two of you were on the beach. Mickey, you need to call her right away. The ranch is under contract."

"Who's Gretchen?"

"Mickey's banker."

"How do you know that?"

Diane could tell from Suki's expression that Gretchen was probably another skeleton.

"Jesus, Mickey. Is there anyone from the States you haven't brought here? Was I the last one to finally get to the top of your list?"

Feeling guilty about her prior intentions, Suki continued to cover for Mickey saying, "Diane, it is nothing like that. She called on Mickey's phone. I answered.

She explained who she was and the situation. To be honest, I was not going to tell you, Mickey."

"Why wouldn't you tell me about this?"

Mickey realized Suki had just lied to avoid another embarrassing revelation at a pivotal moment. He nonetheless was puzzled.

Suki covered her eyes with her hand. Diane sat down next to her in an effort to console her. Mickey wasn't ready to forgive.

"I am ashamed of what I did. It was the wrong thing to do." She took her hand away from her eyes and looked at Diane and Mickey. Tears filled her eyes. "I was afraid the two of you would buy the ranch, settle down, and I would never see either of you again."

Mickey made the mistake of opening his mouth.

"Duh, yeah. That would have been the desired outcome."

"Mickey! We're not dumping Suki!"

"No, Diane, Mickey is right. We have an arrangement. I have broken a vow I made long ago to never become emotionally involved with my clients. I have no business interfering the way that I have and especially for selfish reasons."

Mickey stood with his arms crossed. Diane waited impatiently for him to put Suki at ease. When it was obvious that he would not, she did it herself.

"Suki, I'm the one who is emotionally involved with you. You feel what I feel. You aren't to blame."

Mickey threw his arms up in the air, shouting, "Shit! I've known you for three years and you run into the arms of a woman, no less, whom you have known for three days!"

"Mickey, you brought us together. Take some responsibility for a change. Maybe this isn't just about you!" Diane wiped the tears from Suki's cheeks, giving her ample attention as she said, "Mick, I apologize for assuming this Gretchen woman was another girlfriend. I owe you a little more consideration than to think you have slept with every woman in the world."

Mickey took a deep breath. Nobody spoke for a long time. It was a complete stalemate. Diane pulled Suki into her arms and held her closely. Suki waited for

Mickey to blow her story. Mickey waited for Suki to come clean, which certainly would have resulted in everyone going home on separate planes. He ran his hand through his hair before walking to the sofa.

"Hey, make room."

He slipped in between the two, sitting in the middle and put his arms around both of them. They each put their heads on his shoulder.

"We can sort through all of this. There are at least two good brains among the three of us."

Suki couldn't resist the temptation.

"Three if you count yours, Mickey."

"Three and a half if you count ol' Johnson here," Mickey said, pointing at his crotch. "You both have told me more than once that he does most of my thinking."

"Old Johnny boy wasn't thinking last night, Diane said, closing her eyes and kissing Mickey on the ear. "He was too busy doing."

Mickey looked to his right. Suki looked into his eyes. The mutual thank yous were quietly exchanged.

Breaking the few moments of quiet, Suki announced, "Guys, I have another confession to make."

Diane and Mickey cringed.

"I threw away Mickey's phone. Does the job offer still stand?"

"I guess we won't be interrupted, then," Diane replied, snuggling up to Mickey. "I think the job is a good fit for you. It's yours if you want it."

Mickey proudly smiled as he interlocked his fingers behind his head—his proposal may come to pass.

"Have I told you two how much I'm enjoying this vacation?"

Chapter 17

The sign outside the nightclub bore the letters *T-C?* in bold, colorful script. Westerner's more often used the popular translation—R U Hot?—when sending each other text messages about the club. "T'es Chaude?" was a new nightclub with a twenty thousand baht cover charge that delivered on its promise to keep out anyone but the most serious and wealthy party-goer. A sign on the door exclaimed, "Pas d'armes! Pas de lois!" which Diane interpreted for Mickey to mean *No Weapons! No Laws!* The owner was Genevieve duCoeur, a young, French woman who was known locally and afar to be driven to great extremes of fantasy. Her pewter-colored Maybach, with jade inlaid initials GduC on both rear doors, was parked in front as a statement and watched closely by three visibly-armed men.

Suki had seen to the proper attire for the evening. She and Diane were dressed in the chic, warm weather, tropical nightclub fashion—sheer, cotton wrap-around gauze tops with distinctive floral prints, sans bras, stretch-denim capri pants, and their choice of Jimmy Choo sandals. Mickey was Gucci from head to toe.

"Suki, is this place safe?" Diane asked, stopping outside the front door. "I'm a little intimidated, to say the least."

"You will be safe. You are with me," Suki replied, taking Diane's hand in hers.

"What about Mick?" Diane asked, looking behind her.

"He has to fend for himself."

Suki smiled as she said something in Thai to two giant bouncers stationed at the door. They held it open for the three to enter without any question. Mickey paused after he entered, wondering if Suki had finally exceeded his thirst for adventure, but soon followed as Suki and Diane disappeared around a turn.

The atmosphere inside was immediately overwhelming, not only in sound, but also in tempo, visual effects, temperature, and smell. Mickey managed to catch up with Diane and Suki as they were being seated at a round table with nine other people. Mickey smiled awkwardly as he was seated near the same two Italian men with whom, earlier in the day, he had had the altercation. The two apparently had got gotten lucky as they were in the company of two beautiful women, or rather girls. Neither of the young women looked to be over sixteen, but nobody had nametags, and nobody showed identification. One girl looked to be a toe-head, blue-eyed, Scandinavian, while the other had honey-colored skin and black hair. *Don't-ask-don't-tell* took on a whole new meaning.

The Italian man who had lost his sister in the tsunami was the first to speak. He had to raise his voice loud enough to be heard over the music.

"We meet again, my friend. Remember me? The name is Jep." He reached out to shake Mickey's hand, laughing as he continued, "I know in here you do not carry a knife."

Standing his ground, Mickey shook Jep's hand as he responded, "Yes. How could I possibly forget you? The name is Mick, and I don't need a knife."

Jep reveled at Mickey's response. "I like you, Mick. Please forgive me for my actions earlier today."

Mickey interpreted Jep's apology to be as genuine as a nine-dollar bill.

"Allow me to introduce my friends. You, of course, remember Gio." Gio extended his hand to Mickey, before waving at Suki and Diane. Jep gestured to the dark skinned girl as he said, "This is Ka. She is from Hawaii." There were the usual nods and salutes. "Next to Gio is Ingrid. She is from Denmark." Again, there were nods and salutes. "On the other side of Ingrid are Tors, Eef and Katelijne who are travelers from the Netherlands. And last, let me introduce Sankara and Lat who are a couple from Turkey." There were the final waves and nodding of heads. "Mick, can you introduce your women to the rest of us at the table?"

Boundaries

Mickey didn't much care for Jep, but he was determined not to make an ass of himself again. He went out of his way to be cordial to both of his dates, as well as the company before him.

"The lovely ladies who accompany me are Diane and Suki." Mickey gestured accordingly. There, again, were greetings all around.

"Diane is your wife, correct?" Jep asked, as if to question Mickey's assertion earlier in the day.

Diane answered, "Yes," and nothing more.

Suki watched the entertainment as everyone postured.

Smiling at Diane, Jep acknowledged, "Of course, that explains the ring. Wait a moment, there is no ring?"

"I leave my valuables in a safe place when I travel," Diane replied quickly.

"But your Cellini? You still wear that?"

Diane was unwavering.

"I find knowing the time to be very important to my orientation when I am traveling."

The other part of the Italian tag team, Gio, continued with the questions.

"Mick, have you been here before?"

"Here, Phuket?"

"No, here T'es Chaude?"

"No, he and Diane have not been here," Suki replied, making her presence known.

"Then you are in for one incredible experience, Mick," Gio said. "I strongly urge you to stay close to what is yours and to protect it." He looked around the table at the others. "I say that to each of you."

"They are well cared for," Suki said, defending her friends.

Jep spoke in Italian with Gio for a moment before responding to Suki's claim.

"Of course, they are. Your reputation in the martial arts precedes you."

"You will be well served to respect my reputation," Suki replied.

Nodding respectfully at Suki, Jep gestured for one of the waiters to come to the table. Making a circling motion with his hand, he called out, "Sambuca for everyone."

Just as everyone at the table cheered, Suki held up her hand and shouted loudly, "Stop!"

The waiter and others looked for Suki to explain.

"Sambuca is best served after food."

Jep and Gio nodded in agreement.

"We should start with Ouzo," Suki said with absolute authority.

The others at the table again cheered with approval—it was an easy crowd to please. Suki's suggestion was not challenged and the waiter left to fetch the group their drinks.

"Isn't Ouzo like gasoline?" Diane asked, tugging on Suki's arm.

"It is a national beverage in Greece," Suki replied. "Appropriately for us it is a licorice-flavored drink that will help to cool us down in this room."

Taking note of what Suki said, Mickey asked, "Why is it so warm in here? Can't they afford air conditioning?"

Obviously, there were other people at the table who had been to T-C before. Katelijne leaned forward so she could be heard above the pounding music.

"The temperature is just part of the experience," she said. "It affects your senses and makes your entire being more receptive to what takes place."

"Everything about this place affects my senses," Mickey acknowledged as he looked around.

Leaning in towards the group, Sankara elucidated, "That is how it works. Your ears are filled with the music. The music is piped into the walls and floor and ceiling and tables so that you feel it. The lights change color and flash to stimulate your vision."

"What's that smell?" Diane asked, leaning in so to be heard.

Speaking for the first time, Ka answered, "It is nutmeg incense."

Looking peculiarly at Ka, Mickey asked, "Nutmeg? Isn't that used by some people as a..."

"...hallucinogen?" Suki said, completing Mickey's question. "Yes, Mickey, you are correct."

Diane began to look extremely worried, and Suki set out to reassure her.

"Not to worry, it is just in the air—just enough to accentuate the experience."

Bowing over toward Suki, Mickey asked, "I assume everything here is legal?"

The other guests exchanged glances—an indication that the question was not to be asked unless one was prepared for the worst possible answer.

"What's behind those?" Diane asked, pointing to the curtains behind each table.

Gio leaned back in his chair as he pulled open one set of curtains, revealing a small room that was little more than a very large mattress with pillows, covered by, of course, Egyptian cotton, satin weave sheets.

"It is just in case you cannot wait until you get home..."

"Suki, can I have a word with you?" Mickey asked.

Excusing herself to follow him, Suki said to the others, "We will be right back. Diane, can you continue with the conversation for a moment while I discuss something with Mickey?"

Looking anything but relaxed in her response, Diane replied, "Uh, okay. You're not leaving are you?"

Bending over toward Diane, Jep replied, "Do not worry. You are now safe with me." His smile showed what appeared to be more than the usual number of teeth.

Diane sucked her head into her shoulders like a threatened turtle.

After pulling Suki over to a corner, Mickey looked around to see if anyone was listening. With a manufactured smile, intended to make it appear to Diane that he was comfortable—which he was not—he asked, "Suki, what's going on here?"

She put her arms around Mickey's waist, holding him closely so he could hear her as she replied, "I told you, do not worry. This place is perfectly safe and everyone here is very well behaved. T-C will stretch your senses to their limits. It is one enormous aphrodisiac—everything about it. You will see. It will be fun. Work with it. Get into it. Let your body go."

Looking over at the table, and specifically at Jep, Mickey said, "Mr. Ferrari over there has undressed Diane five times from where he sits at the table. It's making my skin crawl."

Suki smiled and said, "It is supposed to."

Mickey looked back at her a bit puzzled.

"Katelijne has undressed you ten times from where she is sitting," Suki added. Seeing the waiter return, she took Mickey by the hand, leading him back to the table.

The lights shifted from a peach color to a blue, making sharp edges and shapes difficult to see. The waiter passed out the drinks, first to the women at the table, then to the men. Suki signed a ticket just as Jep leaned over to her, asking, "Did you just buy all these drinks?"

"No. Mickey just did," she replied with a mischievous grin.

Mickey sat back as he contemplated what this was costing him.

Putting her hand in his right, front pants pocket and turning it inside-out, Suki announced so that all could hear, "Your Black Card is on file here tonight. Have a wonderful evening because you are paying top dollar for the experience." As she looked up at Mickey with her big brown eyes, Mickey found it impossible to take issue with her. She picked up her glass and held it in the air, then looked around the table before saying, "I think I can safely say that Mickey is the only one sitting at this table who is of Irish heritage."

Everyone easily nodded in agreement.

"For that reason, he will give the first toast."

Mickey didn't expect, nor want the honor, but again he didn't want to appear gauche, so he picked up his glass, looked around the table and gave it his best.

"It's better to spend money like there is no tomorrow, than to spend tonight like there is no money."

Everyone cheered and took a drink. Nearly all made some type of face indicating that the Ouzo was every bit 140 proof.

Boundaries

"What's that taste?" Diane managed to ask, despite having a hard time talking.

Leaning in, Eef suggested, "Try closing your eyes when you drink it. You can taste licorice and anise and sometimes coriander or cloves or mint depending on who makes the Ouzo."

This time with her eyes closed, Diane took another drink. She quickly sat the glass down and grabbed her blouse and began fanning it for air.

"I think I'm on fire!"

Several at the table laughed at her as she licked her lips.

"My lips are burning, too."

"So, tell us, what do you taste?" Eef asked, leaning in once again.

"Cloves, definitely cloves," Diane replied, taking in some deep breaths. "I wouldn't know coriander even if there was a label on it." She began to smile as she said, "Wow, what a rush," then slowly opened her eyes to see the rest of the people staring at her.

Taking his turn to make a toast, Jep stood up and said, "My friends, guests, beautiful ladies, and of course the man with the Centurion Card..." He held his glass towards Mick at that point. "...May we all meet Oscar Wilde before the night is over."

All at the table cheered and drank except Diane and Mickey who participated half-heartedly because they didn't quite understand what all of that meant.

Mickey wasn't going to be a victim of a joke, and since he didn't understand the Oscar Wilde toast, he had to ask the question, "Hey, Ferrari. Help out a stupid Yankee and assume for the moment I'm more naïve than I appear. What's with the Oscar Wilde thing?"

"Mr. Centurion, you may be a Yankee, but so far I do not think you are stupid. Do you like to drink?"

"Occasionally." Mickey replied, not taking his eyes off of his nemesis.

"So did Oscar Wilde, Vincent Van Gogh, and Ernest Hemingway. We will probably see all of them before the end of tonight's festivities."

Mickey smiled and nodded, now realizing what the toast meant. Jep sat back down.

Diane leaned over to Mickey and said, "I still don't get it."

"He's talking about absinthe."

Searching through years of memories, Diane stared at the table.

"Where have I heard of that?"

Putting his hand under Diane's hair and affectionately rubbed her neck, he replied, "You've probably heard about it in Santa Cruz."

"Yeah." Diane nodded slowly. "I think Bruce talked about it. Is it an herb or something?"

"Well, yes and no," Mickey replied, shaking his head ambiguously. "Absinthe is a rare liquor and difficult to buy. It's green, but it turns white when it mixes with water. One of the main herbal ingredients is wormwood."

"That sounds hideous," Diane said with a grimace.

"One of wormwood's derivatives is thujone and that is similar to THC."

"Ah, yes." Diane finally had connected. "The active ingredient in marijuana."

"I hit a chord with you?" Mickey chuckled.

"Yes, but I haven't played that chord in a really long time," Diane said with a smile and a nod.

"The individuals Jep mentioned had very storied abuse problems drinking absinthe. It has been said by some that it made them hallucinate. It has been said by others that it gave them their creativity"

"Are we going to be drinking that?"

Sipping his Ouzo, Mickey replied, "Guess we'll see what happens. Something tells me if it can be served anywhere, it can be served here."

Diane took another drink of her Ouzo. Her face didn't twist or contort as much this time. Instead, she was lost in reflection.

"I love licorice, and I used to chew clove-flavored chewing gum. It was so many years ago."

She had a smile that indicated those experiences were very important.

"Are these memories you have with Bruce?"

Her eyes became misty and her smile was warm as she replied, "No. The marijuana was with Bruce. But, it was Daddy who used to buy me licorice and clove-flavored gum at the pier when we went to San Francisco."

She didn't say any more. She didn't need to. She put her head on Mickey's shoulder and watched the others at the table.

It struck Mickey that this was the first time since knowing Diane that she had been able to mention Bruce without melting down. For that matter, it was the first time she had offered any pleasant memory of her father. Whatever was taking place, whatever he had done to bring this about, however Suki had contributed to this profound moment, regardless of the money he had spent, it was, as the saying goes, priceless.

Diane kissed Mickey on the cheek before saying, "I guess between the nutmeg and the absinthe, you'll be able to make all kinds of memories with me tonight." She noticed that Mickey became very pensive, as if perhaps he wasn't clear what she was saying. "You know, anecdotal thought whatever it was…like the old man in the Philippines that you treated a few months ago, except you won't need LSD."

Mickey put his fists to his head and began pounding. Everyone at the table noticed. Even Jep was concerned.

"Hey Centurion man, this is just the Ouzo. Wait at least until we get to the Raki and Sambuca before you start acting like that!"

Diane grabbed Mickey's hands in alarm, and asked, "Mick, what's wrong?"

"You solved it!" Mickey replied with an unbelievable look of elation on his face. "You just solved it!" Mickey grabbed Diane by the cheeks and kissed her. "Chemical stimulation. How to do it…legally…more gently."

Gio mocked the moment, kissing Jep on the cheek before saying, "Mick, go behind the curtain if you want to do her!"

Suddenly, Mickey felt a passion for Diane that he had never felt before. He ignored everything the others were saying.

"We shouldn't talk about this anymore here. Oh, Diane, you just took my work to a new level. You just took us to a new level."

Jep threw an ice cube at Mickey to get his attention.

"You said *work* here at this club. That word is forbidden."

Diane was shocked by Mickey's reaction to what she had said, but considered he might be, in part, responding to the atmosphere and not so much about her remark.

After guzzling the remainder of his drink, he signaled for the waiter to come back over. The well-dressed young man responded immediately.

"Get me your boss. I want a bartender and someone to prepare food parked here at this table. Go tell him. And bring everyone at this table another round of Ouzo."

The waiter was quick to reply, "Yes sir, but…"

"No buts! Now tell your boss to come over."

Suki tried to get Mickey's attention, saying, "Mickey, you cannot just go and ask for…"

Mickey put his finger on Suki's lips to silence her.

"Tonight, I forbid anyone to say 'cannot' or 'do not.' Is that clear to everyone at this table?" Mickey looked around and all at the table acknowledged him in one way or another. "Good, this is a night for celebration! I want all of you to have a grand time!"

After just a minute or so, the waiter returned with a bottle of Ouzo. He brought everybody's glass back up to full. Afterward, Mickey held up his glass again. Once everyone had their glass in the air, he offered another toast.

"Let us promise to forgive tomorrow our behavior tonight."

The drinks went down more smoothly this time.

After a few more minutes, a tall, sultry woman made her way to the table along with the waiter. Judging from the looks and salutations she was getting as she walked through the crowd, she was not just anybody.

Finally reaching the table, she inquired, "May I ask who requested a waiter and cook?"

She spoke clear English, with the most beautiful French accent.

Mickey raised his hand.

"And may I be so privileged as to have your name?"

Standing up and moving closer to her, he replied, "Mickey...Mickey Rollins."

Following a pause of a few seconds, during which both Mickey and the woman sized each other up, the woman continued, "Good evening. I am Genevieve, the owner."

He held out his hand to receive Genevieve's, saying, "My pleasure, certainly."

She gently placed her hand in his. There was a certain amount of energy that passed between them at that moment. Mickey could only hope it was not too obvious.

Genevieve was gorgeous. She had brown eyes, auburn hair, high cheekbones, a prominent nose, lips that would give the Pope an erection, and a body that belonged on the cover of a lingerie magazine.

Mickey finally had to let go.

"Can you fulfill my request?"

She could have said yes or no, but that was not her style. Genevieve smiled wryly and replied, "I can fulfill any request." As her eyebrows rose up and her mouth twisted into a half-smile at one corner, she re-emphasized, "*Any* request."

Mickey's eyes were unfaithful to him at that moment.

Suki realized she needed intervene before Diane reacted to Mickey's bad behavior.

"Genevieve, let me introduce you to the others since Mickey is too rude to do so."

After walking over to Suki and kissing her on the cheek, Genevieve said, "How are you Suki? It has been too long. We must get together soon and discuss old times."

Diane was impressed that the two knew each other.

Though possibly not genuine, Suki's response was at least polite. "Yes, we must do that. Of course you have met my friend, Mickey, the one admiring your cleavage."

There were chuckles from those at the table, even Diane. Mickey looked at his feet—guilty as charged.

"Next to me is his wife, Diane, who is watching Mickey as he looks at your cleavage."

There were more laughs.

"On the other side of Mickey is Jep who is looking at Diane as she watches her husband admire your cleavage."

Now the laughter was a roar.

"Alright, enough!" Mickey protested.

Genevieve came to his rescue. "For those of you who are new to T'es Chaude?, part of the fun of my club is window shopping. Who knows, one might find something that one must try on."

Pretending to ignore Genevieve's not-so-subtle remark, Suki finished the introductions.

Genevieve shook hands with some of the guests and hugged the others. She then leaned onto the table, putting all of her much-discussed cleavage on display for anyone who dared to look, as she said, "Since you are such special guests, I will open up one of my loft-suites to you. I assume money is not an issue?"

Mickey shook his head.

"You will find the arrangements to be much more than spectacular, and I will offer you your own bartender and food service as Mickey requested. If that is acceptable, please, accompany me upstairs."

ALL TWELVE MEMBERS IN the party followed Genevieve up a sweeping staircase to the second floor. It appeared there were a number of suites, each looking out over the rest of the club floor from a balcony. Upon entering their suite, ahead and to the left was a bar, manned by a slight, Thai gentleman. Behind and to the left was a serving area with a door that must have lead to a dumbwaiter connecting with the main cooking area downstairs. Another round table, larger than the one Mickey and the others were sitting at before, occupied the middle of the room, and scattered about the room were posh lounge chairs. The room was decorated with sculptures and paintings of people in various poses—all in the nude. But the one thing that spoke louder than any of the rest of the features in the loft was off to the right. There, separated only by padded shelves containing towels, oils, creams and individually packaged sex toys, were two huge beds. Their purpose required little strain on one's imagination. Genevieve walked around the entire room so that the guests were able see a full 360-degrees as they watched her.

When she returned to the main door, she turned to Mickey and asked, "Does this satisfy your request?"

He didn't want to appear overwhelmed, so his reply was subdued.

"We'll see how it works out. Why don't you check back with us in an hour or two?"

Genevieve knew Mickey was full of crap, but she decided to amuse his ego. After all, he was a top-paying customer.

"Your bartender is Sriroj. He goes by 'Roj.' Your hostess answers to 'Nell.'"

"Does she speak English or only her own language?" Mickey asked.

"All of the languages that she fluently speaks are her own language. I'll leave it to you to decide which is her native tongue."

Turning his charm on full throttle, Mickey smiled and replied, "I accept that challenge. I hope to see you back here in a while."

He extended his hand once again and she placed hers softly in his. He raised her hand to his lips and kissed it. Genevieve deliberately showed no significant reaction to his gesture. Instead, she smiled, turned and departed.

With Genevieve gone, Roj approached the group, asking, "Can I replenish anyone's glass of Ouzo?"

Jep continued as spokesman for the group.

"Mick, can we use the services of your friend Suki? Perhaps she can best recommend our choices for drinks and food—things that are specialties to the region."

"It's entirely up to her. I don't own Suki."

Suki sat down next to Tors and crossed her legs before replying, "I would be glad to order. I think we should drink cocktails with our food, then we can drift back into the hard liquor later as the mood warrants."

While the conversation over food and drink was taking place, Mickey lost his seat next to Diane as Jep took it instead. Mickey noticed that most of the couples were splitting up much as they might at a formal sit-down dinner so he tried not to think anything more about the situation. But, of all people to sit next to Diane and engage her in conversation, he trusted Jep the least.

Suki gave Roj and Nell the group's choices in Thai, then explained to the assemblage of new friends what she had requested.

"For drinks tonight, we are going to cool down a little with some cocktails. I have chosen my favorites for their sweet flavor and their kick. The first round will be Singapore Sling, the second will be Blue Hawaiian, and we will end our cocktails with a Bird of Paradise Fizz. The meals are all Thai so they will be spicy hot. Drink plenty of water. One of the dishes is kaeng phanaeng kai, which is a chicken dish with coconut curry. There is also kaeng matsaman, which is a beef curry that is cooked with peanuts, potatoes, chopped red onions and a thick coconut cream sauce. There is kaeng som nom mai dong. This is hot and sour fish ragout with pickled bamboo. Then, we will have pla see siad haeng thawt, and that is a deep fried, semi-dried pla see fish. All of this is served with generous portions of chopped lemon grass, peanuts, bean sprouts, green beans, sour mango and chopped makrut, and also khao suay rice and jasmine rice. For hors-d'oeuvres we will have spring rolls and sushi.

Tors put his arm around Suki.

"I like a woman who knows what she wants to eat."

His innuendo didn't go unnoticed.

"I have not had nearly enough to drink that I would find that remark, or your flirting, the least bit amusing."

Suki gently, but purposefully removed Tors arm.

He shrugged his shoulders, acknowledging Suki's rebuke.

"Perhaps later."

She half-heartedly grinned, but made no explicit response.

As Mickey was watching Tors with amusement, he felt a hand reach into his front right pants pocket, causing him to jump slightly. He turned and saw Katelijne.

"Your pocket was still turned out from earlier," she said.

He was startled by what she was doing, too much so to attempt to make her stop. She reached much farther into his pocket than was necessary to accomplish the task she set out to do. When she grabbed her target, her objective was clear.

"There, is that better?"

Mickey turned around, and in doing so not only pulled her hand out of his pocket, but also concealed from Diane and Suki the groping that had taken place.

Putting on a mischievous smile, Katelijne said, "You cannot tell me you did not like that? Part of you certainly responded the way I would have expected."

Mickey turned around nervously to see if Diane was watching only to find that both she and Suki were leaving together, deep in conversation as they exited the room. Katelijne wasted no time continuing her pursuit.

Putting her arms around Mickey, she asked, "How attached are you to Diane?"

Mickey debated being rude and removing her arms, but chose instead a more diplomatic, verbal approach.

"We are inseparable."

Katelijne's facial expression clearly said that she didn't believe him, but she reluctantly put her attack on hold.

"Check with me later when the absinthe takes effect."

Intending to remain true to Diane, Mickey replied, "I'll send you a post card."

THE LADIES ROOM UPSTAIRS was private and was there for exclusive use by the patrons given a pass to the suites. Diane was happy to have a few moments of relative quiet and time alone with Suki.

"I haven't been to a meat market like this one in a long time, Suki."

Suki entered a stall and closed the door before responding, "It is just that for the patrons who are interested in changing partners for the evening. For others, the temptation is all that is needed to make things exciting. Needless to say, there are some interesting people if you can get past the façades."

Upon entering her stall, Diane stopped to look at what appeared to be a computerized toilet.

"Suki, what am I looking at?"

"What you have before you is the latest in toilet technology. They come from Japan. There is a heated seat as well as several washing and drying functions to keep you feeling and smelling fresh."

"Oh, my God. I've heard of them, but I've never seen one. I thought there were squat pots over here."

"Yes, there are. I can take you to one if you like."

"No. I'm just making talk." Diane took a seat. "Oh, my gosh. I can't feel it. It's the same temperature as my ass…well, figuratively speaking." After relieving herself, Diane asked, "Okay, now what do I do?"

"Do you see the spray symbol?"

"There are several of them. Which one?"

"Well, depending on what you did, there is a front spray and a back spray. That should require no further explanation. Both options have a warm air-drying cycle. You can also have pulsing water if you want."

Diane made her choices and after a few blissful moments, said, "Suki, come back in about thirty minutes or so and get me."

Both ladies laughed at Diane's reaction to the new experience. Finishing what they had come in to do, they met at the sink.

"Now that was a new experience," Diane said, blushing. "I have to tell you, I want to buy one of those and send it home."

"I have never bought one on a shopping trip, but I am willing to try to please you any way I can."

Diane finished washing her hands, then said, "I wonder why I even did this. My hands weren't a part of the act."

Boundaries

She dried her hands on one of the cloth towels that were stacked in a blue, porcelain basin. Once used, she tossed it into a wicker basket.

"Suki, how do you know Genevieve?"

"She is an old friend of mine," Suki replied after pausing for a moment. "We went to university together and shared an apartment for several years."

"Forgive me. I must have missed that along the way. I didn't know you went to college."

Somewhat hurt, Suki replied, "Yes, I am just a concierge after all."

"Now that's not fair. I didn't mean it that way."

Continuing to dry her hands, Suki explained, "We got our undergraduate degrees in International Studies at the Université Marc Bloch in Strasbourg, then we got our business degrees from INSEAD at Fontainbleu."

"I am impressed," Diane said, leaning against a wall. "I am totally and completely impressed. You are such a worldly person. You have lived in all these different countries, you know so many languages, and you went to college in France. I am envious, you bitch," Diane said with a playful expression on her face.

"I will consider that a compliment, though perhaps your choice of words could be softened somewhat." Suki returned the smile.

"So after college did you guys stay together?"

"We had similar vocations, but we took different paths. They cross now and then. We are not as close as she would have you believe. You did detect some sarcasm in her voice earlier, did you not?"

"Yeah. She was a little fake. She certainly is beautiful. She had Mickey wrapped around her little finger. So is she also a concierge like you?"

Suki gave Diane a look that said she was asking too many questions, but answered, "She was for a while. She occasionally takes on a client. Mostly she is involved with commerce and, of course, she has her club. Let us simply leave it at that."

"Got it." Diane nodded. "Next subject."

THE TWO REJOINED THE group in the suite just in time for Mickey to bring them their Singapore Slings.

"Ladies, your drinks. Suki, let me be the first to congratulate you on your choice."

Diane took a sip and winked with approval.

"Oh, yeah. A couple of these and I'll be naked on the…"

Diane stopped short as she looked across the room at one of the beds. It was occupied by Gio and Ingrid who were making love for all to see. Diane grabbed Suki's arm and whispered, "Excuse me for being so Victorian, but do we watch them or ignore them?"

"You do as you like," she responded, casually taking a drink as she looked on.

Diane blushed and turned her back as she looked at Mickey.

"Well, this takes pornography to a new level." Then she noticed Mickey was watching. "You pervert."

He pointed at the spectacle.

"I think watching them is part of the turn on for them."

Diane refused to look.

"Mickey, promise me that no matter how drunk I get, no matter what I say, you will not let me do that."

Mickey was amused by her prudishness.

"I was about to say the same thing to you."

Diane rolled her eyes knowing that Mickey could make love in the middle of a baseball diamond during the seventh inning stretch if the opportunity arose.

"That's alright. I think Katelijne already has a reservation with me for later."

"Dead man," she replied, pointing a finger in his face. "You could be a dead man leaving in a plastic bag."

The threat triggered a laugh from Mickey who was beginning to enjoy the club.

Suki grabbed Diane, saying, "Come along, we should get some food. You will love it."

Boundaries

The hours passed during which Diane, Suki, Mickey and the others continually consumed the foods that were put before them, along with the Blue Hawaiians, then the Birds of Paradise Fizz, then the Raki, then the Sambuca. Like the Ouzo, the Raki was flavored with anise. The Sambuca was served with the traditional three roasted coffee beans floating on top that symbolized romance. Jep and Gio also asked that theirs be served flaming.

With each new food and drink, the conversation became livelier, and the barriers slowly disappeared. They talked and they danced. More and more, the dozen mixed and shared their lives. As the body heat in the room increased, shirttails were pulled out and shirt buttons were undone. Skin was exposed. Hands and lips touched those of others.

Tors hit on Suki several more times, each time unsuccessfully, but it provided a lot of entertainment. Diane spent a long time talking to Ka about her home island of Kauai. She and Bruce had spent their honeymoon in Princeville on the north side where he also got in some surfing. Lat and Sankara used the bed, but covered themselves with a sheet for privacy, much to the disappointment of the others in the group.

Genevieve visited with the group from time to time to check on things. She chatted mainly with Mickey when Katelijne did not have him trapped in a corner. Both Diane and Suki kept an eye on him, but they felt comfortable as long as he was in view. Once when he left the room for a while followed shortly by Katelijne, there were a few anxious moments. But, he returned to the group in a short enough time that neither Diane nor Suki felt he could have gotten into much trouble.

Genevieve joined the group one more time. On this occasion she asked Roj to prepare for the absinthe. That became quite a ceremony. The twelve guests plus Genevieve took up seats at the round table while Nell set out tall glasses. Roj added a shot of the liquor to each glass and then placed an absinthe spoon on top of it that contained a sugar cube. Nell followed and slowly poured ice water onto the cube, turning the drink first a milky green color and eventually opalescent. As each glass turned creamy white, the group applauded, and in turn, each took a drink as soon as their glass was prepared, again to applause. If ever there was an embodiment of the word 'concoction,' this drink was it.

The measure of one's sobriety at this point became their ability to say the sixty-two syllable traditional name of Bangkok—Krung Thep Mahanakhon Amon Rattanakosin Mahinthara Ayuthaya Mahadidolak Phop Noppharat Ratchathani Burirom Udomratchaniwet Mahasathan Amon Piman Awatan Sathit Sakkathattiriya Witsanukam Prasit. Even with Suki's coaching, it was all but impossible for a non-Thai to repeat. Suffice it to say, nobody except Suki and Roj could pronounce it clearly. After all the drinks that had been consumed, few made it past the first half dozen or so words, but it nonetheless became the party challenge. Suki even said she would dance naked on the table for all to see if anyone said it correctly, and would have sex with anyone, man or woman, who could say it two times sequentially—both wagers on which she felt comfortable that she would not have to make good.

The first round of absinthe provoked little change in the group. After the second round, new personalities began to evolve. The dancing became much more physical and animated. Diane began to feel as though the room itself was in motion. The music pounded in her head. The pulsating lights made everything in the room move in fits and spurts. The changing colors morphed people's expressions into something fearful, and then back to something joyous. After the third round, her skin felt like it was on fire. She could see herself dancing with Jep, but at the same time she was not sure if it was him or just her imagination.

She felt hands on her body—first two hands, then four, maybe more. She couldn't be sure. They came from behind. They came from the side. They came from the front. When she looked, she saw nobody attached to the arms, only the hands. The hands groped at her body and pulled her blouse from her shoulders. She opened her eyes and saw Mickey. He was dancing with her—he never, ever danced. She closed her eyes and continued to dance, feeling more and more like she was on fire. She opened her eyes and spotted a pitcher of water that she picked up, held over her head and slowly poured it over her body as she spun around in a circle, drenching herself from head to toe. The cool water failed to stop the flames she felt and she began spinning faster to try to get the air to move around her body.

She saw the faces of Ka, then Lat, then Gio, then Mickey and all the others as she turned and turned. They were looking at her, and then they were not. She wasn't sure who was in the room any more. The room kept spinning faster and faster and faster. Then it went dark. She didn't know if the lights had gone out or if she was holding her eyes closed. There were voices—she thought she heard Bruce, then her mother and father. She could feel bodies. She felt the smoothness of the Egyptian cotton sheets. At times she was certain she felt the weight of a body on top of her. She felt her body being penetrated in many ways—visually, aurally, and physically. She was unable to make her arms and hands move in a purposeful manner. She was certain that she felt the flesh of a person on top of her, then it was beneath her, maybe both simultaneously. She felt hands and lips on her body, and at other times, her hands and lips felt the flesh of others. She thought that her eyes were open and that she saw the shapes of men, then women. The music accentuated the frenzy. The tastes were exotic. The smells were all sweet. The sensations were exquisite. But nothing was certain, nothing at all. It was just happening and one thing was definite, she didn't care.

Chapter 18

Mickey awakened to the familiar sound of waves and looked around the room to see the familiar surroundings of the bungalow. He checked under the sheets and found himself in his boxers, then looked elsewhere on his bed and took inventory of his companions, expecting to find Diane and Suki. He was stunned to see he was in the company of Genevieve. Her body was soaked in blood and her skin was cold and pale with a bluish tint. Her throat had been cut deeply from ear to ear, and her eyes were open and staring at him. She was lifeless. Suddenly, roaches began pouring out of her mouth. Mickey jumped out of bed and fell over a chair while shouting meaningless words.

"Mickey, are you alright?" It was a welcome voice—it was Diane's.

He poked his head up from behind the chair over which he had stumbled and saw Diane sitting upright up in bed, dressed in a t-shirt and the shorts Suki had given to her the other evening when she found him meditating on the beach.

"What is going on? Is everyone okay?" Suki asked as she came running into the bedroom.

"Fuck."

That was all Mickey could come up with as he held his head and fell back onto the floor.

"I'm going to die—right here, right now. Death by absinthe. That will be my epitaph."

"I told you to stop at three" Suki said as she kneeled over him.

"Three what?" Mickey asked, holding his hands over his eyes.

"Glasses of absinthe."

Mickey took some deep breaths to ward off an increasing sensation of nausea.

"How many did I have?"

"I lost track at six," Suki replied as she kneeled down and rubbed Mickey's belly. "What were you screaming about?"

He burped, then pointed to the bed where Diane had laid back down and pulled the covers over her head.

"Genevieve was dead in that bed. Blood everywhere. Roaches. Just your usual hallucination."

After getting up and walking to the bed, Suki pulled up the covers.

"It is not Genevieve, it is Diane."

Diane showed few signs of life but managed to utter some words.

"No, it's not. Diane died last night along with Mickey."

"Oh, you two are such sissies!" Suki said, laughing at the two. "I anticipated you would be feeling this way today so I fixed a little something for you that will quickly cure your hangover."

"I'll take two of them," Diane managed to say, "even if they're suppositories."

"Give me three, and make them large," Mickey followed.

Suki departed the bedroom leaving Mickey and Diane lying motionless save for their breathing, and returned with two glasses, each containing an opaque liquid with a straw protruding from the top.

"Okay, here are your remedies. Take three big draws through the straw. Repeat every five minutes until it is all gone."

"Can I take six hits of this?" Diane asked as she turned onto her side.

"No!" Suki said adamantly. "You take three. The first three will keep you from throwing up. The second three will clear up your vision and dizziness. The next will clear your head."

Mickey took three sips through his straw.

"Does anyone have a shoe I can lick to get the taste of this shit out my mouth?"

Diane took one sip then gagged, "No more."

"Drink it, now!" Suki insisted.

Diane reluctantly took two more gulps.

"So, Suki, how much did last night cost me?" Mickey asked, rolling onto his back.

"Oh, no. No details this morning. Just rest comfortably knowing that many others are in the same condition as you and Diane thanks to your generosity. You paid handsomely for the experience."

"Humph," Mickey replied. "What's the saying—'blindness, vomiting, debauchery; for everything else there's the Black Card.'" He managed to open his eyes and look at Suki. "I never—repeat never—want to see that place again. Do you understand what I am saying?" He then sat up and walked over to the bed where he sat down next to Diane's limp body.

Diane now opened her eyes.

"Suki, I have little memory of what happened last night and I have no idea how we got back to the bungalow. Can you fill in the blanks?"

The response was deliberately vague.

"Everyone partied; everyone had a good time; both of you were brought home by my drivers as pre-arranged at the time I set for them."

"How did I get into these clothes?" Diane asked, picking at her t-shirt.

"My guys can do more than drive."

"So much for modesty." Diane remained nervous. "Why can't I remember much after the food was served?" Diane stared at the ceiling. "I remember the Raki. I sort of remember the Sambuca—yeah, Jep and Gio set theirs on fire. I kind of remember the first absinthe. Then, I remember dancing and the lights going out."

Mickey filled in some blanks.

"You had your eyes closed."

"How do you know?"

He flopped back on the bed and looked into Diane's eyes.

"'Cause I was looking at you just like this when we made love."

"Tell me we didn't," Diane said, closing her eyes and grimacing.

"Yup, we did," Mickey said with a nod. "Right along with everyone else. It was a regular, freakin' orgy."

"I made you promise…" Diane said, pulling Mickey's ear.

He kissed her on the forehead.

"Hey, there were no rules by that point, and if I hadn't been on top of you, ol' Ferrari would have been. As it was, he had you half undressed on the bed."

"You didn't hit him or anything, did you?"

"Hell, I couldn't feel my arms. Last I saw, he was just standing there watching us."

Diane crossed her arms over her head.

"Oh, my gosh, I've lost all self-respect. Suki, what have you done to me? I haven't acted like this since I was nineteen. I'm supposed to be a respectable, forty-something-year-old, college-educated business executive. I guest-lecture at a private women's college for Christ's sake!"

Suki brought the drinks over to the two again.

"Do not blame me. I just created the environment. You are the ones who chose to fulfill your desires. Now drink some more."

After taking three more sips of his remedy, Mickey looked at Suki and said, "Somebody could have been hurt."

"No," she replied, taking exception. "There was never any danger. Genevieve and I chaperoned all the activities. Nobody was ever at risk."

Diane opened one eye as she looked a Suki.

"Somehow I don't see you and Genevieve as chaperones."

She then sat up and took three more sips of her drink.

"We took time catching up on each other's lives while we watched."

Lying back down on the bed, Diane started to giggle.

"Now I remember," she said, turning quickly to face Mickey. "You danced with me!"

"No, it had to be someone else," Mickey said with a confused look. "You danced with every man in the place and half of the women."

"No," Diane responded, shaking her head. "I distinctly remember opening my eyes at one point and seeing you. You poured water on my head!"

"No, *you* poured water on your head," Mickey protested.

After a short pause, Diane said, "You're right. I did. But, you did dance with me, I know it."

She nuzzled up against Mickey's body.

"Diane, I don't know how to dance."

"Mickey, you were dancing." Suki chimed in. "You were good. Even Genevieve commented on how good you were."

Diane pulled Mickey closer. He wasn't going to argue the point any more. Mickey rolled over and looked into Diane's eyes.

"You looked terrific in that wet shirt last night."

Diane gently pulled the hair on Mickey's chest in response and they kissed.

"Come on you two. Both of you need to shower, get dressed, and eat. Diane and I have a plane to catch in two hours. And Mickey, you have a date with one of my associates."

"Can't we just stay here today?" Diane whined.

"No. This is our big shopping day. You will have fun and you can relax on the flight. I need to do your manicure and pedicure. Once you have your shower and finish your drink, you will feel like a new person. Trust me."

Mickey and Diane still didn't respond, nor did they move.

"You can rest tonight on the boat. It will be a nice, leisurely overnight cruise. Now get going! Be sure to use hot water!" Suki shouted, clapping her hands.

THE SHOWER LASTED MAYBE ten minutes and was just that—a shower. Suki set out a very nice outfit for Diane to wear and nothing more than shorts for Mickey. They dressed, finished off Suki's remedy, and reported for breakfast. The two looked and acted like completely rejuvenated individuals.

Unlike his initial condition, Mickey was almost bouncing when he asked, "What's in that potion you gave us? I have an old Jaguar that could use a couple of quarts of it."

"I am afraid that is a trade secret," Suki replied, taking note of the difference in his demeanor. "My, both of you look happy and healthy now."

She studied him a little longer and stroked his chin and cheeks as he passed by.

"You need to shave your stubble. It is beyond fashionable."

"Why is it when Harrison Ford has stubble, it's sexy, but when I have stubble, it's stubble?"

"Because you are not Harrison Ford…not even close," Suki replied with brutal honesty.

"Ouch!" was the only reaction he could muster.

"But I still love you," Diane said, feeling it was necessary to be somewhat gentler.

"Wait, something is coming to me," Mickey said, sitting down and sporting a devilish grin.

He slowly, deliberately, and accurately rattled off the traditional name of Bangkok—all sixty-two syllables—twice. Diane clapped her hands in recognition of his accomplishment while Suki simply smiled.

"So, when's payment?" Mickey asked.

"What you are speaking of was last night's offer. It does not apply to today."

"That's pretty chicken shit, don't you think?" Mickey said, pointing his finger at Suki.

"Mick, it's not like we need to win a bet to get Suki to be frisky with us."

"That's not the point. There is a matter of principle at stake here."

Changing the subject to get off of the matter of the wager, Suki began describing the day.

"Diane, we are going to the Ratchaprasong Shopping District in Bangkok. The shopping there is among the best in the world."

Indicating the futility of his lost argument, Mickey threw his hands into the air.

Diane poured herself and Suki an espresso, deliberately ignoring Mickey, then handed Suki's to her, saying, "It sounds wonderful."

Mickey held out his hand in vain for a cup.

"Thank you Diane. Anyway, you will find all the major fashions there, jewelry, watches, home décor, and of course, Egyptian cotton, satin weave sheets, and a brand new toilet."

After pouring himself a cup of espresso, Mickey sat down laughing.

"A toilet? You flew halfway around the world so you can buy a toilet?"

"No, I accompanied you halfway around the world so I could fulfill my wildest dreams, find out things about myself I never knew, and explore myself physically and mentally. Isn't that what you said would happen?"

"And that includes buying a toilet?"

"As I was saying," Suki continued, "We will have a very full day. The plane leaves here at nine o'clock. We meet a limousine at the airport that will take us to the shopping district. I have a short list of stores for us to visit in Gaysorn, Erawan, and Central World. If we have any extra time, we can go to Amarin Plaza. Lunch will be the most wonderful sushi, and, as I said earlier, I will do your manicure on our way to Bangkok and your pedicure on the way home."

"How will you tote around all of your bounty, especially the toilet?"

"Mickey, leave it!"

Diane was beginning to get perturbed by Mickey's irritating questions.

"Except for the smallest of items, Mickey, or those that we wear home," Suki clarified, "I will have everything shipped back to Diane's address of choice."

Diane put her arm around Suki, saying, "Now that sounds like a full day. I can't remember when I last went shopping—I mean *really* shopping. Let's eat and go!"

"Do you feel up to it now? Just a half hour ago you were telling me you were dead."

"I'm great," Diane replied with a mouth full of croissant. "Let's get going."

"Ahem!" Mickey cleared his throat to get some attention. He pointed at himself. "Et moi?"

"You get Soup," Suki said with a smile as she helped herself to a croissant.

"I beg your pardon?"

"Soup. Actually, it is Soupy. Her real name is Supavadee, but you may call her as I call her—Soupy."

Mickey waited for more information, thinking that Suki might stop eating long enough to fill in some blanks, but no more came. "So, what does Soupy do?"

"Yeah, what does she do?" Diane asked with equal interest.

Taking a sip of her espresso, Suki explained, "It is very simple. I told her she could do anything that did not involve sex. The rest is up to Mickey."

"So, I can play cards with her if I want to?"

"Absolutely," Suki replied.

"And I can feast on brie and crackers with her?" Mickey asked Diane.

"I guess so."

Mickey explored a little further. "And maybe she can give me a massage?"

Suki answered, "A proper massage."

"Of course, a proper massage." He paused for a moment before exploring, "My definition of proper or yours?"

"Mine," Diane answered. "No body fluids."

Mickey thought for a minute more, then asked, "And we are speaking of your definition of 'no body fluids', or mine?"

"None!" Diane answered.

"Okay. I think that's pretty clear."

There was a knock on the door, and Suki gestured toward Mickey.

"That would be for you."

"For me?"

"Yes. You. This should be your companion for the day."

"Soupy?"

"Yes! Now go answer the door."

"I'm hardly dressed to answer a door. What if it's the Prime Minister?"

"You are dressed properly for your visitor. Now go answer the door!"

Mickey took a final sip of his espresso and then headed toward the door. Stopping half way there, he teasingly said, "I haven't brushed my teeth yet."

Diane and Suki simultaneously yelled, "Door!"

A smiling Mickey, having totally frustrated his companions, finished his journey to the door and looked out the peephole. He saw nothing. There was another knock on the door, and once more he looked, but saw only shrubbery on the other side of the walkway. He inhaled deeply and opened the door. His expression gave away his feelings at that moment. Standing before him was a seven-eights scale version of Suki wearing a lavender wrap around dress and matching stilettos. Mickey's momentary excitement gave way to his apparent concern that Soupy might be under eighteen years old—an arrangement not uncommon as witnessed just last night.

"Hello. My name is Soupy. You should be expecting me."

The visitor didn't waste any time, quickly and purposefully stepping past Mickey as she walked over to Suki. After giving her a hug, they exchanged a few sentences in Thai. Suki then took the newcomer to meet Diane—an extremely important gesture since Diane had to be comfortable leaving Mickey alone with this woman. They shook hands, Soupy paid Diane several compliments and all appeared to be well. While all of this was taking place, Mickey helped himself to another espresso.

Finally, Soupy turned her attention to Mickey, looking at him somewhat seductively and asked, "So, you are the object of my attention today?"

"How old are you?"

"I am twenty-three," Soupy replied with a smile. "Would you care for a younger woman?"

"Absolutely not. I just want to make sure you're…old enough."

"Old enough for what?" Soupy asked.

"Yes, old enough for what, Mick?" Diane asked with piqued curiosity.

"We are waiting," Suki added.

"Now, let's all think about what's taking place here," Mickey began in a defensive tone as he sat down at the table. "I wake up, innocently minding my own business in my room for which I am paying dearly, and I find that I am part of a temporary arrangement, mind you, made by someone other than myself, with a twenty-three year old, attractive young lady, and I am being questioned about *my* intentions? This has entrapment written all over it."

Soupy made sure everyone was aware that she knew the rules.

"Remember, Mickey, no sex. I am just here to make you happy and comfortable while Diane and Suki go shopping."

"I may just sleep for six hours."

"You are in control of what takes place," Soupy responded. "If that is what you wish to do, I will see to it that you are comfortable and left alone."

Mickey grumbled unintelligibly.

"Sorry, Soupy," Suki said. "You may have an easy day. Should you need to reach me, call my mobile phone. Charge anything you want to the room."

Mickey grumbled again.

Soupy hugged Suki once more and said something to her in Thai, then walked over to Diane and asked, "Are you okay with this?"

She waited for Diane to respond in some positive manner.

"You must not worry. I will take good and proper care of him."

Diane tried hard to feel secure with the situation, but in reality, all she could do at this point other than refuse to go shopping, was trust Mickey and hope for the best. She went over to him and gave him a long kiss, ending with, "I love you. See you tonight."

Mickey held her hand for just a moment before saying, "Love you, too." Looking deeply into her eyes, he said, "You know, you don't have to buy everything you want."

After thinking for a moment, Diane said, "Yes, I do. I never go shopping and I have a lot of catching-up to do." She kissed Mickey one more time.

There was another knock at the door.

Suki grabbed her handbag and alerted Diane, "That will be our driver. We have to go now."

Diane held onto Mickey's hand as long as she could, then she, too, grabbed her handbag and joined Suki at the door. Closing it behind them, the two were quickly whisked away.

Soupy waited until the sound of the car disappeared, then sauntered over to the door and double locked it. She then turned and slowly walked most provocatively back to where Mickey was sitting, stopping about two feet in front of him, at which point she pulled on the tie at her waist, turned around once and allowed her dress to gape open. After wiggling her shoulders, the lavender dress fell to her feet in a pile. Except for her stilettos, she wore nothing.

"You never asked how old I was before," Soupy said as she sat down on Mickey's lap, straddling him.

She planted her lips on his and locked in. Mickey gently caressed Soupy's back as they kissed.

Eventually coming up for air, he responded, "You never looked like this before. Besides, the arrangements were a little different those times."

"So you have more than one set of rules?" She asked with a devilish smile.

"Does a chameleon have more than one color?" Mickey replied, stroking her hair.

Kissing the nape of Mickey's neck, Soupy asked, "So, why are you like this? Why can't you settle for one woman?"

"I'm trying…desperately, can't you tell?" He replied, cupping her breasts.

"Diane looks like a wonderful person. She is certainly beautiful."

"True. She is both."

Soupy grinned as she wiggled against Mickey's crotch, noticing that she had achieved the intended response to her affection.

"If you give me $5000 US I will not tell Diane that you lied to her. I will not tell her you knew me from previous visits, and that you have had sex with me against my will."

Mickey kissed her again, making sure he had her full attention.

"Suki doesn't know about our past. If we just enjoy ourselves this afternoon, I may give you a nice tip, and I won't tell Suki you broke your promise. She might let you live."

It was clear that Mickey's threat of Suki's wrath trumped that of her own, causing Soupy to momentarily lose her smile. But, she regained it, and running her hands through his hair, relented, "Okay, checkmate. You win…but only this time."

She stood up and took off her stilettos tossing them to the side, then picked up her dress, folded it neatly, and laid it on the sofa. "So, what do you want, Mickey?"

"Undress me," he replied as he rose to his feet.

She dutifully removed Mickey's shorts, putting them on the sofa next to her dress. He was standing at full attention in more ways than one.

"That took all of ten seconds. Now what do you want?"

Mickey picked up Soupy in his arms and took her to the waterfall tub. There, he carried her under the falling water, drenching both of them at the same time.

"It's bath time."

He put Soupy down so she was standing upright in front of the waterfall.

"Suki told me a moment ago that you had just bathed—just in case I wanted you to be clean. She thinks of everything, you know." Soupy reached for a bottle of soap, but Mickey quickly took it from her.

"She's right. I am clean. It's bath time for you. Turn around and face the water."

Soupy slowly complied with Mickey's request, but in addition to facing the other way, she bent over, presenting herself to Mickey for his further enjoyment. Mickey pulled her hair slightly, raising her back into a standing position.

"No. A bath. Just a bath. I want to feel you."

Mickey reached both arms around Soupy's body, feeling her breasts and stomach, rousing a moan.

"Diane has much larger breasts than mine. Why do you need to feel of me?"

Mickey paused for a moment, struck by the direct question.

"There's entertainment value in what I am doing," he answered, continuing his fondling.

"When did you last have sex?"

"A few days ago."

Soupy turned to face him and grabbed both of Mickey's hands.

"Then why did Suki tell me you had sex with Diane last night?"

"Oh, yes, that."

Holding him away from her slightly, Soupy said, "Mickey, listen to me. Suki asked me to 'fluff' you today, nothing more. I can take you all the way to the top, but not all the way. Do you know what I am saying?"

Mickey grunted.

"She also told me this is going to be your last time to be with another woman outside of her and Diane."

"She did, did she?"

"Yes."

"And you believe her?"

"She is not the one to believe. You are."

"So, this is my final test to see if there is any hope of me becoming faithful," Mickey said, shaking his head.

Soupy studied Mickey for a few moments before replying, "Something like that."

Mickey didn't say anything else.

"I am here for you Mickey. You are paying for my time today. I have no other appointments. If you want to have sex with me, I am yours. If you want me to blow you, I will do that. I will do anything...anything. But, if you want to behave in a more appropriate manner, and I think that is best for you, now is the time for you to change."

"Very well, then, I think you should leave now," Mickey said with a serious expression.

"Excuse me?"

Putting his hands on her waist, he said, "You know I have no self control. So I am asking you to leave."

Soupy hesitated before asking, "You are joking, right?"

"No. I'm very serious. If I'm going to change, I have to change now."

"Nobody else has to know, Mickey. Just one more time? I could make the experience a lasting memory," she said, reaching for something of Mickey's that was hard and pointing her direction.

Backing away from her, he said, "You're right, Soupy. Diane is a wonderful woman. I don't want to blow it with her. You need to dress and leave. Don't worry, you'll be well paid."

Soupy paused a little longer thinking Mickey would surely change his mind, but he eventually turned, exited the tub and took Soupy by the hand to escort her out. He dried her off and she exchanged the favor, then he slipped his shorts back on and handed Soupy her dress and stilettos.

Looking at him one more time, she asked, "Are you sure?"

He smiled and replied, "Yes, I'm sure."

She asked no further questions, got dressed, then went to the refrigerator and helped herself to a cola. Opening the door to the bungalow, she turned and faced Mickey one final time, saying, "Last chance…"

He nodded and blew her a kiss.

"Goodbye, Mickey," she said as she shrugged her shoulders and closed the door behind her.

Mickey took a few moments to reflect on what had transpired and wondered if he really was on a new course. Realizing he would have to be tested to truly know if he had changed, he set out to reward himself with food and drink. He loaded a plate with several types of breads, cheeses, and meats, then took them out to the table on the porch. In a second trip to the kitchen, he returned with a fresh glass of orange juice, butter and jams, then made a small sandwich from part of a sesame roll, took a bite and leaned back to enjoy himself.

The sun shined brightly through the screen onto him and the breeze blew lightly, almost creating a chill. Just as he settled into the moment, the phone rang from across the room. He got up and walked over to the phone. Caller ID indicated it was Suki.

"Hello. What have you done to Diane?" Mickey asked.

"This is Diane, you dork. I just wanted to say how much I love you."

Mickey detected a certain degree of sarcasm in her voice.

"You're coming back, aren't you?"

"Of course, I am. Hey, Suki just got a phone call from Soupy. She said you told her to leave. I'm impressed. I figured she'd be naked and on top of you within five minutes after we left."

Mickey scanned the room as if he was looking for a hidden camera. He wasn't sure how to interpret Diane's statement. Either he was extremely predictable, or Soupy spilled the beans, or both. He tried injecting humor into the conversation.

"Don't be impressed. Maybe I just came fast."

Diane's laugh was anything but genuine.

"So, are you at the airstrip yet?" He asked.

"We just pulled up." Getting the conversation back on track, she asked, "You lied to me again. She's another one, isn't she Mick?"

"It was not my idea that we get together. It was Suki's arrangement, remember?"

"And like all the others, you've slept with her, too."

"We might have done the Floating Market together sometime in the past."

"Is that a new position?"

Mickey didn't respond, figuring there was no positive outcome from the discussion that was taking place.

"Suki said she knew nothing about it."

"Soupy and I made arrangements on the side. Suki's innocent."

"What do you know? I think I heard an admission—you're even cheating on the mistress. I think that's a new low for you."

"Hey, I told her to leave. I'm making a fresh start toward sainthood."

"Mick? Take out a sheet of paper, find a pen, and start writing names of all the women in your life—past and present. I want the whole list. I'm tired of this one-name-at-a-time bullshit. I don't care if it's four or forty-four, I want a list of names. For that matter, so does Suki."

"It's really a much shorter list than you might think…"

Boundaries

"Names, Mick. It'll make for interesting discussion tonight on the boat."

"Diane, I love you…"

It was too late. The phone was already disconnected. He tossed the phone onto the kitchen counter with a bang, causing it to slide off into the sink. As he headed back out to the porch, he was stopped short by another knock on the door.

"Go away, Soupy. I'm in enough trouble."

There was another knock.

"God damn," he mumbled.

He walked quickly to the door, anger showing in his face, and pulled it open. To his surprise, it wasn't Soupy—it was Genevieve. She was wearing a perfectly filled, floral halter, and tiny cut-offs that stopped way below her navel. She was carrying a wicker basket. The neck from a bottle of champagne poked through the cloth that covered the top.

"Suki told me last night that she was taking Diane shopping in Bangkok for the day. Would you like some company? I brought some food and beverages for us share."

"Genevieve, I…"

Before Mickey could finish what he was saying, his uninvited visitor entered the bungalow, and set the basket on a table.

"This is really lovely…quite lovely. I have not been here since the tsunami. They have done a marvelous job rebuilding the place." After walking to the window overlooking the ocean, she said, "Yes, this is what I remember most—the spectacular view; that and the sea breeze. Suki chose wisely."

Mickey was dumbstruck by her exquisite French accent, and his mind was going a hundred miles an hour debating how to handle the situation.

"Genevieve, I don't feel comfortable being alone here with you."

She walked over to Mickey and put her arms around him.

"You were extremely comfortable with me last night. Have you forgotten so soon?"

"Having a few drinks and dinner is one thing."

Now he was struggling with his desires, and Genevieve knew it.

"Besides, Diane was there."

"Yes, I suppose you could say she was there," Genevieve said with a snicker. "She was asleep. I do not think she remembers very much today."

"I am very certain she was awake when I made love to her. I vividly remember staring into her eyes."

As if to recreate what had actually happened, Genevieve looked directly into Mickey's eyes as he looked deeply into hers. A chill went down his spine as he experienced déjà vu. Leaning forward, her lips met his with a more than familiar kiss.

"Is your memory of last night changing?" She asked with a sultry voice.

Suddenly Mickey realized it was Genevieve with whom he had made love in a fit of drug induced passion.

"Suki said nothing happened. She said I was with Diane."

Shrugging her shoulders with indifference, Genevieve replied, "Suki and I had a discussion about you. She owed me a favor. I told her the payment. The absinthe created the perfect situation. As far as anyone knows, you made love with Diane. That is all that anyone needs to know. You and I, on the other hand, know the truth."

"Did Diane have sex with anyone at the party?" Mickey asked, pulling away from Genevieve.

She shrugged her shoulders once again and replied, "I do not know. I was occupied."

"I think you have a selective memory," Mickey replied, having a problem with her response.

"Maybe I will remember later. Let's go to the beach and lie in the sun together, you and me. We can partake of our treats there."

"No. I want you to leave," he said in a firm tone of voice.

Ignoring him, Genevieve turned and walked to the porch where she sat down, tore a croissant in half and buttered it.

"Could you bring me some water or a cup of café?"

Boundaries

Mickey walked over to Genevieve, took the croissant from her hand, and threw it on the floor saying emphatically, "I told you to leave."

Suddenly, Mickey was startled by a man standing outside the porch window holding a camera with a long lens. When he realized he was spotted, the photographer ran.

"Who the fuck was that—one of your people?"

Genevieve calmly buttered the remaining half of the croissant, and after taking a bite, replied, "I think it would be devastating to Diane if she were to know what happened last night. She would cry if she found out you and I made love. She would be most upset if she discovered that she was violated by one, maybe two, maybe three men last night. I think she most certainly would leave you if she saw the picture of you kissing me a few moments ago when you invited me over for breakfast after they left for shopping. That would explain why you banished the young nymph. You simply exchanged a much younger, less experienced girl for a mature, all too experienced, woman. There was nothing noble about your gesture."

Mickey knew where this quid pro quo was going.

"What do you want from me to make you go away and be quiet? Money?"

Smiling malevolently, she replied, "I see you understand me. Now tell me about PicoPoint."

Chapter 19

The jet had been airborne for only a few minutes when Suki began working on Diane's nails. The two had the small, chartered jet to themselves. Diane's chair faced Suki's with the small table separating them.

"Give me your hands. There is not much time for your manicure."

Suki's eyebrows rose up at the sight of Diane's hands.

"These look terrible. You bite your nails."

"I bite them when I'm nervous."

"It would appear you passed nervous a long time ago."

"He's such a rat. I told him we wouldn't be good together more than a day. I told Rajeev that Mickey only thinks about Mickey. The biggest room in his house has to be his closet, and it must be full of skeletons."

"He is a rat undergoing reform," Suki commented as she began cleaning and filing Diane's nails. "These are so bad, we may have to finish them on the return trip and do your pedicure tonight on the boat."

"You don't care, do you?" Diane asked, obviously perturbed by Suki's seeming indifference.

Continuing to work on Diane's hands, Suki replied, "I believe that I have very different expectations of Mickey than you. I expect him to come, attach, detach, and then leave."

"I forgot this doesn't bother you since you do this sort of thing all the time."

"'This sort of thing?' Let us set the record straight. I have six regular clients—three are men, two are women, and one is a gay man who is not sure which way he wants to go. It is a very tight circle, a very small circle, and a very closed circle."

"Six? How can six customers give you the lifestyle that you have?"

Boundaries

Casually waiving the nail file at Diane, Suki replied, "You are a businesswoman. You should understand. I have no business expenses—I repeat, zero. The client pays for everything. Suffice it to say, none of my clients live in poverty, and they can afford my outrageous fee. Only two of them are gainfully employed—and I include Mickey in that number, so I use my definition very liberally. They pay dearly for my time. I work at most twenty weeks a year, and make a comfortable seven-figure income. As with the others, I am used to Mickey coming and going. You on the other hand want a new husband."

Diane realized Suki was spot on, but felt compelled to clarify her motive.

"Do you want to know why I am here with Mickey, I mean why I am *really* here?"

"Please, tell me," Suki replied, continuing to work on Diane's nails. "I am tired of talking about me."

"Promise me you won't tell Mickey?"

Suki stopped filing again, looked peculiarly at Diane, and said, "We are not teenagers, Diane. Talk!"

Easing into her response, Diane explained, "He has a new business venture that needs funding, and I want my company to partner with him. I'm researching his work so we can make an informed decision."

"Oh, so you are conducting business while you are on your back? We have more in common than I previously thought."

"Don't even try to put us in the same category, Suki," Diane shouted, jerking her hand away from Suki.

Taking Diane's hand back forcefully, Suki said, "It is simple, Diane. You are using your body in order to achieve your own personal gain, just as I do."

"Yeah! But you're a slut!" Diane yelled, pulling her hand away again.

"Well, you are a bitch!" Suki shouted back, throwing the nail file onto the table between them.

The two sat back in their seats, pouting, as they each stared out opposing windows. For the next few minutes, neither of them spoke a word, nor did they exchange glances. Eventually, with near synchronized timing, they both began to look at each other out of the corners of their eyes, began smiling, and ultimately laughing.

Finally holding out her hands to Suki, Diane asked, "Are you going to finish?"

"No," Suki replied, biting her lip. "They are quite hopeless…at least during this flight. I will finish them later."

"Since we're alone, is there anything you want to tell me about last night that you might not have wanted to say in front of Mickey?"

Suki crossed her legs and leaned back into a comfortable position before replying, "Last night was the party of the century for you. You should have been there for all of it."

"That's what is bothering me," Diane said with a chuckle. "I wasn't with it the entire time. I really don't like being out of control."

"I forgot. You mentioned that a few days ago. You should look at the night as letting your body and mind have an adventure."

"Alright, but I would like to remember some of it!"

"What would you like to know? I can answer any questions."

"Did I pass out last night?"

"No. You were very active last night. You danced like no woman I have ever seen. You must like to dance. You are very good."

"Did I dance with Mickey?"

"When he could get you away from Jep, yes, you danced with Mickey."

"So Jep had me cornered?"

"On the contrary, you were pursuing him. You felt his attraction. Did you know that his father is a top executive of an Italian automaker? He is one of the most desirable men in the Mediterranean, and I do believe he was very attracted to you."

"Suki, I could be his mother."

"You are not that old, and he is not that young. The two of you showed a great deal of chemistry."

"I don't want chemistry with Jep. I want chemistry with Mickey!"

"You could have both."

"I don't want both! I want one good man for the rest of my life. Is there a word for monogamy over here?"

"Of course. Monogamy means having one husband or one wife. It does not necessarily mean having one man or one woman in your life. At this time, I think you can understand this definition very well."

Diane looked at Suki as if she didn't appreciate the reality check, but moved the conversation forward—cautiously.

"I need you to tell me the truth. I know I had sex with a man last night. You know how it feels."

Suki nodded and grinned.

"It was Mickey, right? I mean, you said Jep was pursuing me. And I seem to remember seeing lots of faces and feeling lots of hands on my body. Was that the absinthe?"

"There were lots of faces and lots of hands last night," Suki replied, putting a hand on one of Diane's for reassurance. "You were dancing. You removed some of your clothing as you danced, as did all of the others. It was part of the excitement everyone was experiencing. There was a lot of touching and fondling and kissing. But, in the end, the group last night was surprisingly respectful of one another. Neither Genevieve nor I had to intervene."

"You gave me a long answer that did not answer my simple question. Did I have sex with Mickey last night?"

"Yes," Suki said with a nod. She suddenly changed subjects, "So Mickey wants money for PicoPoint?"

"What's PicoPoint?"

Suki put a finger in the corner of her mouth as if perhaps she had said too much.

"That is his new project; the one you are speaking of funding."

Diane was stunned.

"You know about it?"

Without hesitation, Suki answered, "But of course. He is, after all, working with my grandfather and another doctor on the project. I know quite a bit about what is going on. I am no expert, but I hear things."

"So you get two corners of the triangle—Mickey's and your grandfather's."

Shaking her head to the contrary, Suki said, "No, I know pieces of information from all three."

"You know the other doctor?"

"He, too, is one of my clients." Suki paused to let that sink in. "Mickey doesn't know that. Promise you will not tell him. It is best that we keep it that way."

"We aren't teenagers," Diane responded, playing back Suki's earlier response. "Is he the gay one?"

"Oh, no," Suki answered with a smile.

Deciding to pry into Suki's knowledge of the project, Diane asked, "So, the technology Mickey is speaking about isn't science fiction or anything?"

After studying Diane for a moment, Suki continued, "I can tell you a few things. First, it is not science fiction. Second, my grandfather is nearly eighty years old, and I have never seen him so excited, yet at the same time so secretive. I think they are on the cusp of making a huge medical breakthrough."

Sensing a distance developing between herself and Suki, Diane quickly followed, "What is the other doctor saying?"

Suki again appeared reluctant to speak too openly, but offered, "Diane, it is my direct experience that the three principals in this project each make a distinct contribution and that none of them hold an overwhelming amount of knowledge about the project. They must work as a team or nothing works at all. Mickey told me some months ago that they split up the project in this manner so that no one party could steal the entire project. It is funny, but the more they work together, and the more success they have, the farther they pull away from each other. I sense tension developing between them, and it is not wise, nor safe, for you to acquire too much knowledge about this project."

"Not safe?"

"There are some men and women who do not always hold life as sacred, especially if it stands in the way of wealth or power. I know of situations where people have been harmed for much less than what is at stake here."

After looking at Suki for a long time, Diane said, "Based upon what you are telling me, you, too, should be at risk."

"I am," Suki said without hesitating. "I do not want you to be in the same situation."

"And yet you still have a close relationship with all three men."

"There is a certain amount of security they each feel if I treat them as I always have and not as if one of them has any monopoly on my person. If they were to sense that the balance I have struck has shifted in favor of one, I am afraid of what might happen. Be certain that I am constantly evaluating my position in these relationships."

Suki turned the questioning back toward Diane.

"What about you? What do you know of the project?"

Diane now felt a certain degree of paranoia, but she thought it would be safe to mention what she had heard of Dr. Wu's work.

"I know a few things. First, there is something called anecdotal thought transfer. Mickey says that was your grandfather's contribution."

"Yes," Suki acknowledged. "He has defined how the mind works and how thoughts and actions are stored. There is a very specific order to everything. It has taken him decades to understand this. What else?"

Diane kept a wary eye on Suki, looking for any sign that she should stop talking. For whatever reason, she felt she could trust her. It was as though the knowledge they shared, as dangerous as it was, also brought them closer together.

Responding to Suki's question with just one word, Diane said, "MADONNA."

Suki's eyes opened wide as she said, "That is Ricardo's piece. That is how the strength of thought is controlled. I think the last letter "A" stands for attenuator or attenuation. How did you know about that?"

"Mickey told me. I think this is what he calls *schwa*."

A light went on in Suki's head as she recalled, "Yes, you mentioned that our first day together."

"Is Ricardo the other doctor?"

Suki took a deep breath, having inadvertently shared a name with Diane.

"Yes. He is the other doctor. You do not need to know his family name and I should not have told you his given name." After thinking to herself for a moment, Suki concluded, "So Genevieve was right."

"Genevieve?"

"She told me last night that Mickey knew all three pieces of the puzzle. I thought that was impossible…until now."

"What does Genevieve have to do with PicoPoint? Does she even know about it?"

Leaning forward as if someone might hear her, Suki said, "She has nothing to do with it per se. But remember when I said there are some men and women who do not value life, especially if it stands between them and wealth or power? She is just that kind of person. She knows about Mickey's work through her connections."

"Translation, she's slept with Mickey before, hasn't she?"

"No. I am certain they had not met until last night."

"So do you think she knows any details about it?"

"People listen very closely to what everyone is saying over here. The smart ones connect the dots."

Picking up on one particular word, Diane said, "Pardon the pun."

"Excuse me?"

"Dots…Dippin' Dots."

"What are Dippin' Dots?"

Realizing that might be a piece Suki was missing, Diane asked, "Are you certain you want to know?"

Suki held out her arms begging for the rest of the information.

"Those are the nanomachines that Mickey uses to deliver and retrieve information from the brain. I think that's his part of the project. I guess you can say that your grandfather is the conceptual architect, Ricardo writes the software, and Mickey builds the hardware."

"Do not tell me anymore," Suki said

"Do you think we're in danger?" Diane asked, suddenly looking worried.

"No, not directly."

Finding little comfort in Suki's answer, Diane asked, "What about Mickey?"

"Perhaps," Suki replied with reservation, her pause indicating to Diane that she was less than certain about her answer. "As long as Genevieve suspects that he knows all three pieces of the puzzle, she will try to get that information from him. She certainly will do him no harm. His knowledge is his greatest protection."

"Could the other principals in the project be in danger?"

"No, because my grandfather should not know all of the details, and besides, an old Chinese man will take secrets to his grave. As for Ricardo, I would not be a bit surprised if Genevieve is working for him in some capacity." After pausing to reflect a moment, Suki continued, "It is a good thing that we are leaving tonight. I think we have spent enough time in Thailand."

"Should we warn Mickey?"

"No. If we do anything indicating he might be hiding something, we might create suspicion. Perhaps we are just imagining things. Besides, Genevieve may not be interested in PicoPoint at all. She may just be interested in Mickey."

"So, what do we do now?"

"We go shopping," Suki replied with a grin. "We will land in just a few minutes. My guess is we are making too much of this." Suki stopped and reached out for Diane's hands. "Our overactive imagination began when you called me a slut." A smile grew across her face.

As the plane pitched nose down, beginning its descent into Bangkok, Diane leaned forward and kissed Suki, saying, "Forgive me, but what do you expect? After all, I'm a bitch."

Chapter 20

Mickey walked—no, more accurately, crawled—up the stairs from the beach to the bungalow following his run along the waterfront. Today was the hottest day yet of the trip and there had been sporadic tropical rain showers all morning making the humidity extremely high once the sun came out in the afternoon. His run was particularly vigorous as he tried without success to put Genevieve's visit, and the things she said to him, out of his mind. His ability to think clearly was still impaired because of last night's binge, and he found that his imagination was playing tricks on him to the extent that he was still seeing false images and hearing things, much as he had that morning. What he did know was that he didn't want any of Genevieve's words to be true. He also hoped that the red herring he gave to Genevieve about PicoPoint was enough to keep her out of the picture for the duration of the vacation, if not the duration of the project.

After Genevieve left the bungalow, Mickey scurried around to make sure there was no evidence that she had been there. The thought of admitting to Diane and Suki that she had dropped in crossed his mind, but he was certain he would not be able to consistently answer the litany of questions that would surely follow in a manner that could cover up any atrocities that may have taken place at T'es Chaude? In other words, his story—a collection of lies—would crumble.

He was hot, his skin was red once more for lack of sunscreen, and he was dripping with sweat. He grabbed a large bottle of water from the refrigerator, kicked off his shoes and socks, then went to stand under the streams of water in the shower. More than once, he felt a heightened sensation with the water falling on his skin. It felt as if there were bugs crawling all over his body, but he knew it wasn't real, and hoped the sensation would quickly end. It didn't. In time, he decided the water was for cooling only and stopped the shower, dried himself off, tossed the towel on the floor, and then flopped naked and face-up onto the neatly made bed. He put his arms under the pillow behind his head, and in just a few minutes, he was sound asleep.

HOURS PASSED BEFORE THE Mercedes limo pulled up to the front door of the bungalow early that evening. Out stepped first Diane, then Suki, both sporting new clothes, new shoes, and new sunglasses. Diane also wore a new watch on her right wrist where previously there had been her Rolex Cellini. They each carried two bags. Suki asked the driver to take the rest of the items into the bungalow and leave them inside the entry. She followed with instructions for him to return later to take the three vacationers to a waiting helicopter for the beginning of their journey to the island.

Diane stopped just outside the door where she was the first to notice an unfamiliar pair of sandals.

"Are these yours, Suki?" she asked.

Looking at the beige, average-size Chanel's, Suki replied, "No. I've never seen these."

"Are they Soupy's?"

"No, she wore lavender shoes that matched her dress, remember?" After putting her arm in front of Diane's body in an attempt to keep her from going in, Suki continued, "I know of one person who wears almost exclusively Chanel fashion—Genevieve."

All signs of happiness drained from Diane's face as she and Suki slowly entered the bungalow, expecting the worst case scenario—Mickey with yet another woman. They spread out and quickly canvassed the rooms and porch where they hoped they would find Mickey, until they reached the bedroom where they hoped they would not. Diane listened for a while, heard nothing, and then slowly opened the door. There, they found Mickey, alone, lying on the bed, asleep, and naked. The entire bed was in disarray, and there were two damp towels on the floor that Diane quickly snapped up. One had several long dark hairs attached. She looked at Suki just as her face turned fire engine red, then threw the towels at Mickey hitting him in the face.

"Asshole!"

Mickey jumped out of bed to find Diane chasing after him, striking him time and time again with her fists. He finally grabbed them both, subduing her and pinning her against a wall.

"What the hell is wrong with you?!"

She responded by firmly putting her knee into his groin, causing him to release his grip. Breaking free, she stepped over him, raced to the desk, and grabbed a letter opener. Quickly turning, she saw Mickey back on his feet, reaching for her. Fearing for her life at that point, she aggressively thrust the letter opener deeply into his chest. Blood poured from the wound as he fell backwards onto the floor. Diane began to scream hysterically. Instantly, she felt two hands on her body as she was being thrown forward.

"Diane! What is wrong?!"

Struggling against the hands that reached to hold her, she opened her eyes to see not Mickey, but Suki.

"I killed him...I killed Mickey."

She frantically looked around, trying to quickly get her bearings. She looked for Mickey, and the desk, and the bed. Instead, she saw the interior of a car—the Mercedes limousine that had earlier taken them to the airport. The vehicle came to a screeching stop at the side of the road.

"Diane, get a grip. You fell asleep. You must be dreaming. We are in a car. We have yet to reach the bungalow. Mickey is not even here."

Diane looked around in disbelief as Suki pushed the hair from her eyes. Focusing in on the friend who was trying to comfort her, Diane asked, "How do I know you are real? How do I know this is real?"

Bending over, Suki kissed Diane on the lips, before saying reassuringly, "I am very real." Lifting up Diane's right wrist so that she could see the new diamond-and-ruby studded Cartier watch, she added, "This, too, is real."

Diane put her head on Suki's shoulder for comfort as Suki said something to the driver in Thai, and he continued on down the road.

"I think you are finally due for a rest, my friend. You need the island."

Boundaries

"I need a brain transplant. Oh, my God. What a dream! Is this all a result of the absinthe, nutmeg, and all that other crap?"

"Perhaps," Suki answered as she caringly kissed Diane on the forehead. "More likely it is an accumulation of jetlag, sun, many days of activity, late nights and then, yes, maybe some of last night's recreation."

"I can't believe I dreamed of killing Mickey. I have never dreamed of killing anyone before...never. It was so horribly realistic."

"Why did you do it...in your dream?"

"He had slept with Genevieve. She was at the bungalow. She had left her shoes outside the front door."

"Your mind has many boundaries within which you live out your life—boundaries that have been set in place during the course of your life. Let us hope that particular one has not been damaged by absinthe."

Diane looked up into Suki's eyes with a frightened expression.

"I am just kidding, Diane. I am certain you are still your sweet, wonderful self."

The Mercedes pulled to a halt in front of the bungalow and the driver hurried around to Diane's side to open the door. Slowly and cautiously, Diane stepped out, still unsure if what was taking place was actually real. She grabbed two bags and joined Suki, as they proceeded toward the door. She was shocked just as was Suki, when they spotted a pair of beige Chanel sandals outside the door. They looked at each other as goose pimples rose up on their arms.

"Suki, how did I know these would be here?"

"I have absolutely no idea," Suki replied, dumbfounded.

Brushing her hair out of her eyes, Diane said, "This is the point in my dream when you tell me you know of only one person who wears Chanel sandals like these—Genevieve."

"That is precisely what I was thinking."

Diane's face turned red with anger once more, this time for real.

"Diane, remember the dream. Your actions do not have to be the same."

After taking several slow, deep breaths, her skin color returned to normal. The two opened the door, but unlike in the dream, Diane made haste directly for the bedroom, making no effort to be delicate when she pushed the door open. She soon let out a sigh of relief when she found Mickey naked, alone, asleep, with only one soiled towel on the floor and no other signs that anyone had been with him.

"The man has no modesty," Suki said, making light of the situation.

Grinning with joy that he was alone and perhaps innocent, she walked over to Mickey and awakened him with a kiss on the lips, causing him jump slightly.

"You'd think with all of your money you could afford to sleep in some shorts, or at least in underwear."

Squinting as he looked at her, he replied, "Did you like what you saw when you walked in?"

Diane nodded.

"There you have it." He got up, walked over to the small refrigerator in the room, and helped himself to a bottle of juice. Looking at Suki, who was staring at him, he asked, "What are you looking at?"

Suki was at a loss for words.

"Genevieve was here."

Both ladies were shocked by Mickey's candor.

"I'm not kidding. She knew the two of you were going to be gone so she invited herself over for breakfast." Mickey looked directly and accusatively at Suki, adding, "It appears that someone was speaking with Genevieve last night about our plans." Turning his attention back to Diane, he continued, "Her interest isn't me in case you were wondering."

"Well, that explains the shoes."

"What shoes?"

"She left her shoes at the door. I guess she was in a hurry to leave."

"No, I suspect she just wanted to leave her calling card," Mickey said with a serious tone.

Still doubting Mickey's story, Diane asked, "So why are you…" She pointed to Mickey's absence of clothing.

"Once I got rid of her, I went for a run, showered, and then took a nap in the raw. I don't know about you guys, but I'm dog-tired."

Mickey walked up to Diane and hugged her. She reciprocated with a kiss on his cheek.

"Missed you today," he said affectionately.

Diane smiled happily at Mickey's comment. It was an unexpected and spontaneous demonstration of his need for her.

"I missed you, too."

"I think it's best that we not have any further contact with Genevieve," Mickey said, looking over Diane's shoulder at Suki. "When are we leaving?"

"In a little over one hour," Suki said.

Walking over to Suki, Mickey asked, "Does Genevieve know anything about the island we're going to, or for that matter the rest of the trip?"

Suki was on the hot seat, but tried to give a reassuring, yet realistic response.

"I have not spoken to Genevieve about any such details. That is not to say that she is incapable of picking up our trail."

"Are you worried about PicoPoint?" Diane asked.

Mickey spun around and asked, "How did you hear about that?" Looking back at Suki, he answered his own question. "Let me guess."

Suki pushed her tongue against the inside of her cheek.

"That's just great. That's just fucking great. I suppose the two of you have tried to piece together this afternoon all that you know about the project. Am I right?"

"What do you expect from us?" Diane asked defensively. "We're both human, we talk, we both love you, and we're interested in what you do. Besides, you're the one who fell for the World's oldest form of espionage, so deal with it."

Taking a deep breath and putting his hands purposefully at his side as if to keep from striking someone, Mickey said, "Ladies, the project is very close to realization. In fact, with the epiphany I had last night thanks to Diane's remark about using nutmeg, I think I've resolved a huge barrier. This thing is big—I mean polio and smallpox vaccine big. The difference is that it can be used as a therapy or a weapon. I have to be careful. We have to be careful. I don't want any more discussion about the project, is that clear?"

The two women reluctantly nodded.

Nervously looking at Suki, Mickey asked again, "So, when do we leave?"

"I told you, in about an hour," she replied, frustrated at his repeated questions. "Everything is under control. You just have to take your essentials. Everything else of yours will be shipped back to the States and will be waiting for you when you arrive home. I have taken care of all that you will need at the island and at the next stop." Suki began to tear up and her stare burned a hole through Mickey as she pointedly asked, "So, you do not trust me anymore, do you?"

"What do you want me to say, huh?" Mickey asked as he moved face to face with her.

"Mickey, leave her alone," Diane said, moving to Suki's side and pushing him back with her right hand. In doing so, he caught a glimpse of Diane's new watch and slowly lifted her arm closer so he could see the new item adorning her wrist.

Taking this as an opportunity to change subjects, Diane asked, "Do you like it? It set you back $65,000 U.S."

Mickey moved her wrist in various directions to catch the light.

"It's a Cartier with a diamond bezel. I've always fantasized about owning one."

"It's beautiful. And don't worry about the money. You're worth ten times that much. I'm glad you bought it."

"It was her idea," Diane said, hugging Suki. "You should see what she bought."

Suki responded by running out to the living room, returning with a small bag, and announcing, "It's perfect for the moment." She pulled out a small item in a clear plastic tube, tossing it at Mickey. After twisting the top off, he pulled out a tiny pair of thong underwear with an elephant's face and trunk on front, obviously sized for a man.

"You have to be shitting me?" Mickey said, grinning as he put the underwear on.

Both ladies broke up in laughter at the sight. Mickey's essentials just barely fit into the small patch of gray cloth. Keeping with the frivolity of the moment, he began to bump and grind his hips as his audience cheered on.

Retrieving her purse from across the room, Diane pulled out some Thai paper currency that she shared with Suki. Both ladies took turns putting the money under the small straps on the sides of the thong. Diane even held one bill in her teeth while inserting it into the top of the underwear front as Mickey held it open. After a few minutes of revelry, it all came to an end.

Counting his earnings, Mickey said, "Gee, let's see here…four hundred and fifty Baht. Guess I'd better keep my day job."

Suki and Diane dried each other's tears of laughter.

Bringing everyone down to reality again, Suki said, "Okay you two, we need to pack what we are taking with us, and get ready to leave. We have a pretty tight schedule to keep."

"Can we show Mickey what we bought today?" Diane asked, hopping up and down with excitement. "We can pack at the same time."

"We probably can," Suki cautiously replied, but it was too late. Diane was already grabbing the boxes that were left at the doorway.

"I'm surprised this is all you came away with," Mickey said, sizing up the damage.

"No, this is all we brought back to the bungalow," Suki said, chuckling. "The rest we shipped back already."

"Oh…"

Diane opened several boxes, pulling out various items.

"Look at this dress, and this one." She laid them neatly on the bed. "Now, here are some blouses and pants," she continued as she laid them out in sets.

"What brands?" Mickey asked, actually showing some interest.

"Guy Laroche, Georges Rech, Féraud, Fendi…" Diane showed him the tags as she answered.

"Alright, I get the point. Top of the line stuff."

"Here are some things to sleep in," she said with a wink, holding the sheer pajamas up against her body. They were all but transparent.

"I like those best of all," Mickey said with a nod of approval.

"I thought you would." She next opened up a box, producing two handbags. "Gucci. Do you love me now?"

Mickey smiled, entertained by Diane's exuberance.

She reached into the last bag and pulled out a pair of sandals, followed by a pair of stilettos. With a most provocative look, she asked Mickey, "Ever made love to a woman wearing nothing but stilettos?"

Both shocked and amused by Diane's question, he answered, "No, but something tells me that is about to change."

"Can I take these with me?" Diane asked, holding the shoes up to Suki.

"Well, they are not exactly beach wear, but I suppose you can wear them around the bungalow on the island."

"Can I wear them on the boat?"

"Take them and we will ask the ship's captain. It might not be safe as I am not sure if your footing when wearing those will be adequate on the boat."

"I'm not planning to be on my feet when I have them on," Diane said, putting a finger on her lower lip and a coy expression on her face.

"What the hell did you guys eat?" Mickey asked, looking at Suki for an explanation for Diane's behavior.

"It was only sushi," Suki replied with a smile. "I guess it got her juices going."

Taking Suki's hands, Diane said, "No, it wasn't just the food. It was the entire afternoon. I haven't had this much fun shopping since…since I can't remember. I just let myself go and here you have it."

"Oh, I forgot about the rest," Diane continued.

Mickey took a deep breath, not sure what was about to be revealed.

"We purchased our first set of china."

"We? Like, yours and mine?"

"Yes. And of course we purchased lots of Egyptian Cotton, satin weave sheets."

"We did, did we? What about the toilet?"

"Yes, bought two, and they're on their way to my house as we speak. I also sent one to Maria as well—sort of a peace offering." Putting her arms around Mickey's neck, Diane closed with, "And, get this, we purchased round trip tickets to come back and visit Suki in six months. We're staying in Bangkok and Changmai next time."

"Alright…" Mickey replied tentatively.

"And we bought a round trip ticket for Suki to come to San Diego in three months to see us for two weeks."

Mickey swallowed hard on that announcement. It was clear now that the repercussions of the shopping trip would be felt for many months to come. Deciding it best not to dwell on that point, he said, "Quite a trip. Did you forget anything?"

"Actually, I neglected to mention these."

Diane pulled out another pair of boxes.

"I bought a Mikimoto black and conch pearl necklace and conch pearl earrings," she said as she proudly opened both boxes.

She handed one to Suki to hold, the other to Mickey, before pulling out the small gold studs she was wearing. Moments later, she had replaced them with two round pink balls, and followed by putting on the necklace. "Like them?"

"They look beautiful on you. Are you going to take them with us on the rest of the trip?"

"I think they will go perfectly with my stilettos, don't you?" Diane asked, sporting a completely diabolical expression.

Suki tapped Diane on her shoulder to get her attention, then pointed below Mickey's waist, saying, "Look, the elephant's trunk is getting bigger."

"I guess it's time for me to change into something that will deny your wanting eyes."

Quickly stepping out of the thong and into a pair of boxers, he gave the two lusting onlookers a brief, but impressive display.

"Well, now I am hot," Suki said as she fanned herself.

"Me too," Diane echoed, turning away from Mickey.

Chapter 21

It took every minute they were allowed to gather the things they wanted to take with them and pack up the items that were going to be returned to the States. Eventually, however, the task was done, and the three were whisked off in their Mercedes to a local airfield where they met up with a sky blue Bell/Agusta AB139 helicopter. It was a beautiful aircraft inside and out, one that was usually reserved for business executives, dignitaries, and celebrities. The guests climbed on board and were soon airborne, heading westward over the Andaman Sea. Diane marveled at the view from an altitude of one thousand meters. The Thai coastline was magnificent as it slowly disappeared and thunderstorms to the north put on an impressive show of lightning a safe distance away.

Looking curiously at Suki, Diane asked, "Could we just fly to the island?"

"Yes, we could. But, that is not nearly as romantic as the trip by boat. I am certain you will agree with me in the morning."

"Why are we flying to the boat, and why is it so far out to sea?"

"There is a loss of privacy when a boat, such as the one we will be on, comes to the coast. It attracts a lot of sightseers and perhaps some unsavory individuals we might not want to have see us. Also, we want to arrive at the island early in the morning. If we sailed from the coastline, we would be sailing with less favorable winds and against the incoming tide and that would add maybe four hours to the trip, which makes it just a little too long."

"You're right," Diane said, looking over at Mickey. "She thinks of everything."

Suki nodded, at the same time mouthing *thank you.*

"I hate to bring this up," Mickey asked nervously, "but how do you plan for us to get onto the boat? Does it have enough room for a chopper to land on it?"

"We jump," Suki replied with a calm expression that didn't match Mickey's.

"We what?" Diane and Mickey said simultaneously.

"We jump. The helicopter will descend to around ten meters from the water, move to about thirty meters or so from the boat, at which point we will jump in and swim the rest of the way to the boat." Reaching behind her seat, Suki pulled out some bags. "Here, put your clothes, jewelry, sandals, and other belongings into this watertight bag, seal it, and tie the lanyard to your ankle. I will go first, you simply follow me."

"What about sharks?" Diane asked, looking terrified.

"Swim fast," Suki replied, shrugging her shoulders.

Mickey added, "My suggestion is that you make sure you swim faster than me."

Without further discussion, Suki removed all of her clothing, sandals, and jewelry, put them in the bag, and then sealed it tightly. Soon, Diane and Mickey followed her lead. Diane took the extra effort to pack her special shoes and jewelry for the evening. No sooner had they finished than they felt the sensation of the helicopter descending and turning to the right. Diane looked out the window on the starboard side of the helicopter and her jaw dropped. There below them, was a beautiful, two-masted schooner much like what one would expect in a James Michener novel...only larger. It must have been fifty meters long from end to end. Its jib sails were deployed, but the main sails were folded away to keep the boat moving forward but only at a slow pace. The hull was a deep blue and the deck was made entirely of mahogany. It was a spectacular sight.

Grabbing both Suki's and Mickey's hands, Diane shouted, "Is that it?"

"Yes. That is your boat for the next twelve to fifteen hours."

"What's the boats name?" Mickey asked, equally impressed.

"*Je t'aime.*" Suki replied with a wink.

"I know enough French to know that means *I love you.* How did you find this boat?" Diane asked.

"It is a special charter vessel. Both I, and the man who owns the island to which we are traveling, frequently use this boat."

"May I ask this man's name?" Mickey inquired.

"Yes, you may ask, but I cannot tell you his name. He wishes to remain anonymous. I know him well, and I respect his privacy as much as he respects yours. He did not ask me to provide your names."

At that moment, Mickey did a poor job hiding his jealous feelings toward what was probably another client of Suki's.

"It was several years ago. He will not be on the island. He lives there only occasionally. Most of the time he lives in Monaco."

"I'm surprised that you no longer see him," Mickey replied. "After all, living in Monaco? Must be a rich dude."

"He got married. Some men do, you know?"

"He could still be seeing you, though."

"He loves his wife," she responded. "He is faithful to her." Noting Mickey's discomfort at that assertion, she continued driving the point home, saying, "That is possible, Mickey. You should consider these choices."

"Marriage, or being faithful?"

"Both," Suki answered, finally achieving her goal.

Mickey said nothing more on the subject, a fact that Diane noticed as well.

After putting on a headset, Suki spoke briefly to the pilot of the helicopter. Momentarily, they were circling the boat while descending in a downward spiral. The helicopter came to a rest, hovering a safe distance above the water, a short distance in front of, and to one side of, the path of the boat. Suki replaced the headset on a hook before pressing a button, opening the port side door of the helicopter. "Are you ready? All you have to do is jump feet first into the water. Be sure you have your belongings tethered to your ankle. Hold the bag in your arms against your chest when you jump in, then let it float behind you as you swim to the boat. The crew will lower a rope ladder into the water for us to climb."

Mickey nodded, and then Diane did the same. Without any delay, Suki tied the tether of her bag to her ankle, held the bag to her chest, stepped out onto the skid, and then hopped off. The sea was mostly calm, and the water was a deep blue. She landed with a small splash, surfacing in seconds. She waived, then moved out of the way so the next person could jump in.

Looking at Diane, Mickey asked, "Who's next, you or me?"

Diane pointed at him.

He cautiously stepped out onto the skid. No sooner had he got in position than he lost his grip. Mickey tumbled out of the helicopter, flipping in mid-air and landed with a flop in the water. He surfaced, looking up toward the helicopter where he saw Diane laughing hysterically. After looking at Suki, who was a few feet away, also laughing, Mickey chuckled and said, "That's gonna hurt."

Finally, Diane stopped laughing long enough to step out of the helicopter herself. She dropped straight into the water with almost no splash. It took a bit longer than Suki, but she eventually surfaced, pulling her hair out of her face and shouting, "Water up the nose!"

"Serves you right," Mickey shouted back at her.

The helicopter door closed, and while the three made their way to the boat, the large blue bird flew away. Four crewmembers, two men and two women, helped the guests climb up the rope ladder onto the boat. The male attendants provided the guests with large towels and took the bags from them. The female attendants returned with a pair of shorts for each of the new guests and skimpy, white muslin button-up blouses for the ladies. Soon, the travelers were dry and mostly clad.

"Your shirt," Diane said, motioning toward Suki, "it's not buttoned."

"Why bother?" Suki asked.

Diane shrugged her shoulders, realizing the casual nature of the trip, then handed her towel to the attendant.

Suki spoke Thai to the attendants and they responded with a wai, before returning to the rear of the boat with the other crewmembers. Moments later, a tall man with tan skin walked toward the three. He approached Suki first, giving her a hug.

"Diane, this is Captain Bates."

"Ma'am. It's a pleasure to have you as my guest."

He spoke with a noticeably European accent, mixed with a bit of Australian vernacular. He was a stout, handsome, weathered, forty-ish man with a perfect smile and long, sandy brown hair, and a full beard. His shirt was unbuttoned exposing copious amounts of curly, sun-bleached hair. Diane thought to herself that if she had pen, ink and paper, and was asked to draw a man-of-the-sea from this part of the world, her imagination would create a man who looked just like Bates. She noticed something else—there was something eerily familiar about him.

Diane held out her hand for him to shake, but he pulled it to his lips and kissed it. His hands were huge. His deep blue eyes were glued on hers, leaving only long enough to take a glimpse of her barely covered breasts, giving Diane a chill. She wasn't sure if it was a chill of excitement, flattery, fear, or a combination.

"And this is Mickey," Suki continued, pointing to Mickey, who was watching Bates suspiciously.

Bates slowly released Diane's hand and reached for Mickey. They exchanged a handshake, each gripping the other's hand as if to bend steel pipe. Neither flinched.

"You're Diane's mate?"

"That would be correct," Mickey replied, intending to make his dominance in the matter perfectly clear.

"You're a lucky man," Bates responded. His response didn't make either Diane or Mickey any more comfortable.

Once they had squeezed all the blood out of each other's hands, they released their grip.

"Good to have you on board," Bates said with a nod.

Mickey forced a smile.

"If there's anything I can do…," he shifted his gaze to Diane, "anything at all…let me know." With that, he returned to the stern of the boat.

Mickey was the first to make a less than kind observation about the ship's captain, saying,

"I think we should take our chances swimming back to shore."

"I don't know, I think he's kind of cute…in a Neanderthal sort of way," Diane replied, adding to Mickey's worries.

"He is the best long-boat captain in these waters," Suki said, trying to put the others at ease. "He is perfectly harmless. Nobody will touch him."

Diane said, "Nobody will touch him? We're out in the middle of the freakin' ocean!"

Mickey inquired, "Pirates?"

"Yes, pirates," Suki acknowledged.

"You're kidding, right?" Diane asked, snickering in disbelief.

"Not in the least bit. There are pirates in this part of the world and they particularly like yachts with wealthy individuals."

"Well, they're not getting much from us. We didn't bring a lot of valuables."

"What do you call that?" Mickey asked, pointing at her bag. "Your watch, not to mention your earrings and necklace."

Playing on Diane's emotions, Suki added, "They often are more interested in human bounty, particularly women, than they are money or jewelry. There is a significant human trafficking industry in this region."

"You guys could have just skipped all of these details, you know."

Only after Suki and Mickey began laughing did Diane realize she had been a victim of their sick sense of humor.

"Jerk," she said, smacking Mickey on the shoulder. Looking at Suki, she said, "I can't believe you went along with him—again!"

"Do not let what we said bother you. Now come with me," Suki said, taking Diane by the hand. "You have to see the rest of the boat."

Diane stuck her tongue out at Mickey as she was dragged away, to which he responded by swatting her on the butt as she passed by.

Walking to the front of the boat, past the forward cabin, the trio got a look at what would be their small slice of heaven until the next morning. There was a round teakwood table with cushion-covered chairs, surrounded by ice buckets containing various wines and champagnes. Just to the side was a table adorned with fruits, cheeses, meats, and breads. Just beyond the eating area was a very large mattress with a dozen or more overstuffed pillows—all covered, as one had come to expect by now, with Egyptian cotton, satin weave fabric.

A brisk wind blew across the bow from left to right, and in spite of being over water, the wind felt relatively dry. Two crewmen engaged electric winches and the two main sails were lifted to the top of their respective masts. There was a noticeable increase in the speed of the boat and it began to tilt slightly with the direction of the wind. Several dolphins paced the boat as it clipped across the waves.

Diane walked alone to the rail in front of the bowsprit and leaned into the wind, her hair blowing like a flag in the breeze as the boat literally sailed into the sunset. She closed her eyes and sucked the clean air into her lungs. From behind, Suki and Mickey stared at her magnificent silhouette. The outline of her body was clear to see through the sheer clothing she was wearing, and they were awestruck by her picturesque beauty.

"Wow. I've never seen her like this," Mickey said quietly to Suki. "Where's a camera when you need one?"

"Her diet is proper. Her skin is in excellent condition from my treatments. She is happy. She is in love. This is the result."

After a while, Diane turned around, sporting a huge grin, and said, "No bugs. There are no bugs out here. Is that because we're so far out to sea?"

"That is correct," Suki said, responding to her observation. "This is a bug-free zone. That is why you and Mickey can enjoy yourselves under the stars tonight wearing as little as you want."

"What do you mean Mickey and me? Where are you going?" Diane asked.

"I will be spending the night in the quarters with the rest of the crew," she replied, nodding toward the rear of the boat. "You will have two hostesses to take care of your needs all night long."

"You can't do that," Diane said emphatically as she walked back to Suki. "I want you here…with us." Looking at Mickey for support, she asked him, "You agree, right?"

"Well, I guess so," Mickey answered tentatively.

Looking back at Suki, Diane repeated her request. "I want you to be here with us…for drinks and food…and who knows. But please stay. I enjoy your company more than I can tell you right now. I need you. Will you do it for me, please?" Diane's begging stare burned a hole through Suki, as she added, "I'll pour you a wine, I'll make you a plate, I'll do anything you ask…"

"I'll cover your body with oil," Mickey added.

Diane jabbed him in the ribs.

"Fine, then. I'll cover *your* body with oil."

"Let's get her to stay with us, Mick. Don't scare her off or I'll have to hurt you!"

"People!" Suki said, putting her hands up. "In case you have not figured it out yet, I can be easily persuaded to accommodate your desires. I am here for you and, actually, I was hoping you would invite me."

Diane slipped her hands inside Suki's open blouse, put her arms around her, and squeezed her tightly while she looked over at Mickey, mouthing a kiss at him. He smiled and then pulled out two chairs at the table. Diane released her hold on Suki and they each took their places.

The hostesses quickly surrounded the three. They uncorked one bottle of each type of wine, left the reds on the table, and put the whites in the ice buckets.

Making good on her promise, Diane asked, "What will you have?"

Suki pointed at the white wine. One of the hostesses reached for it, but Diane held up her hand, stopping her. Instead, she stood up, walked to the ice bucket, pulled out the bottle and poured Suki a glass.

"Mickey, what can I get for you?"

"I'll take the same."

Diane poured Mickey a glass, then returned the bottle to the ice bucket and took her seat. She then reached for a bottle of Shiraz that was on the table, but a hostess beat her to it and poured her glass for her. Diane thanked her and the hostess acknowledged with a wai.

Suki made a request in Thai of the hostesses and one scurried off causing Diane to wonder if she had done something wrong.

Boundaries

"You didn't have to make her go away."

"No, no, she did nothing wrong. I told her you needed a pedicure. She will take care of that, after which she will finish your manicure that I left incomplete. She will be right back because she needs to get them done before it gets too dark."

"Now that's what I call decadent—wine, food, pampering, all at the same time." Diane sipped her wine. "Mickey, I thought you preferred red?"

After finishing a sip of his wine, Mickey replied, "What I really want is a col' beer."

Suki couldn't resist mocking Mickey with a frown, saying, "I feel so sorry that you have to drink white wine on a luxurious, private schooner in the middle of the sea with two beautiful women as we all sail into the night. It must be a terrible tragedy for you."

"Hey, this is true hardship," Mickey said as he winked. After swirling the wine in his glass, he took another sip. He was clearly relishing what was going on, especially the company of those sitting before him.

Diane reached across the table and touched Mickey's hand most tenderly. She bit her lip as she hesitated saying the words that were about to leave her mouth.

"Mick?"

"Yeah, babe."

Following a deep breath, she said, "Thanks for bringing me with you on this trip. I know I was sort of a bitch at first, but right now, I can honestly tell you I have never been on such a wonderful vacation. Everything from the basics—I mean food and drink—to the unique experiences…they are all incredible." Diane looked back and forth between her companions as she finished a sip of wine. "I think the best part about the trip is the company I'm with. I'm so comfortable with both of you."

"Comfortable?" Mickey asked.

Diane's eyes began to get misty, and she shook her head again to get the hair out of her eyes. "You guys are so great. I just feel I can be anything I want to be with both of you, and neither of you will judge me. I can also do anything I want, and there are no repercussions."

She put her feet up on a hatch, and then unbuttoned her blouse which the wind quickly blew open.

Suki pointed at Diane as she looked at Mickey, saying, "Oh, comfortable. Now I understand."

Mickey nodded as he finished his wine. It wasn't ten seconds before his glass was quickly refilled by a hostess.

Diane smiled, realizing she had finally gotten through to them.

"I am totally relaxed, very happy, and completely satisfied at this moment." Thinking perhaps she was being too serious, she continued, "So don't fuck it up."

Everyone laughed.

After her hair blew into her face again, Diane said, "Okay, this is going to piss me off. I need a clip of some sort."

Suki made a request of a hostess who reached into a large bag and, after a few moments of rummaging, produced a large hairclip that Diane used to pull her hair up onto the top of her head.

Mickey leaned forward and put his elbows on the table as he said, "I like your hair up like that. I mean not all the time, but, wow, you look…incredible."

"What do you mean?" Diane asked, raising an eyebrow. "Don't I always look incredible?"

"Oh, Diane, you're so incredible. You deserve a man like me."

Diane was quiet for a moment until her face began to light up at the thought of the jousting.

"I do, don't I. I guess that's why I *do* have a man like you." She waited for Mickey to look up into her eyes so that he knew she was serious. After holding the look for a few moments, she turned to look toward Suki and followed with, "And that's why I have a woman like you."

Suki held her wine glass up to her mouth and slowly licked the rim before pouring a small amount into her mouth.

Diane fanned her face with her hand and looked out to sea, away from Suki as she responded, "You sure know how to turn a person on."

Boundaries

Suki set her glass down and pulled her long straight hair into a ponytail. "Perhaps, but I have to try. All you have to do is to be you."

Diane was at a loss for words. Suki's was possibly the most profound compliment she had ever received. On top of Mickey's flattery, Diane was overwhelmed with a long absent sense of personal satisfaction.

THE HOURS PASSED. A hostess treated Diane to her manicure and pedicure while the three comrades took turns sharing stories, talking about the trip, and serving each other food and drink. One thing was noticeably missing—absent was the usual sarcasm and sparring that had become a regular part of the interaction among the three. Gone, too, were all defenses; gone were all barriers; gone were any remaining fears.

Mickey allowed himself a foot massage, something he was not known to do because his feet were particularly sensitive. While he was vulnerable, the ladies pressed him for the romantic history they had asked of him earlier in the day. That morning, the request had been a demand from Diane, but now it was more of an introspective discussion that opened a door into Mickey's mind, soul, likes and dislikes. Though neither Diane nor Suki believed for one minute that his list of dalliances was complete, it was nonetheless shorter than expected, and he never once mentioned Maria—a particular concern for Diane. She didn't know if it was good or bad that her name wasn't on his list.

One episode from Mickey's past, though, proved to be the comical highlight of the evening. Mickey took a sip from what was near the end of his sixth glass of wine as he began, "Then there was the Cheese Whiz gal."

"What's a Cheese Whiz gal?" Diane asked.

"What is Cheese Whiz?" Suki asked, even more confused than Diane.

Stepping in to answer, Diane replied, "That's the epitome of American junk food. It is processed cheese that is dispensed under pressure through the nozzle of a can. You can put it on crackers, or just your finger and lick it off if you want to. You can write with it, or make little flowers with it. It's art and food at the same time—the complete American package."

"It sounds awful," Suki said, sticking her tongue out. "Why would anyone do that to cheese?"

"Diane already answered your question," Mickey said. "It's art and food, which brings us to the Cheese Whiz gal."

"I have to hear this," Diane said as she sat up attentively, resting her elbows on the table.

"I'm going to try to get through this without throwing up. I was at a medical conference in the Bahamas a few years ago where there were the usual requisite social hours every evening. Well, the third night, I, along with three other guys, excused ourselves and went to a nightclub."

"A topless bar, right?" Suki asked.

"Hey, don't get lost in the semantics. Anyway, there was a special *goddess buffet* on the menu so we ordered it."

Diane put her hand up to her mouth and said, "Let me guess. The goddess was the main course."

"No, actually, she was the hors d'oeuvres. Here was this nymph of a girl, sans a single thread of clothing, decorated from head to toe with dollops and swirls of cheese in various flavors, colors and patterns. It was really quite creative."

"I expect you would describe that as being creative," Suki said. "I can think of other descriptions."

"Yes, I am certain you can, but this is my story so you can just sit there and listen."

Suki pretended to button her lips closed.

"She also came with sides of breads, crackers, vegetables like celery and even caviar. We would scoop cheese off of her and spread it on whatever and eat it. The more we ate, the more she would be exposed. It turned into a feeding frenzy. We must have looked like a bunch of hyenas fighting over carrion. She reminded me of the whipped cream girl on the cover of that '60s Herb Alpert album. I always fantasized about eating off that whipped cream just to see what was underneath."

Boundaries

Enlightening Mickey with a disappointing bit of history, Diane said, "I studied that photograph in a marketing class once. You know that was mostly a blanket and very little whipped cream."

"Next you'll be telling me there's no Santa Claus," Mickey said.

Suki had a look of disbelief on her face when she asked, "So was she naked when you were done?"

"Completely naked. We ate or licked every bit of that cheese off of her, even from places you couldn't imagine…"

"Oh, I can imagine," Diane said, nodding.

Mickey looked kind of pale and his face was contorted as he continued, "I have never been so sick in my entire life."

Diane and Suki laughed and applauded.

"I can't even look at a can of Cheese Whiz any more, let alone eat the crap."

"And you didn't have sex with her?" Diane pressed.

"That's the sad part. You get the girl along with the meal, but we were all so sick that we just left. I found out later that the owner of the club had been selling that very buffet for two years and he had yet to see one of the girls go home with a patron."

Leaning over to Mickey, Diane asked, "So if I had Cheese Whiz or whipping cream all over my body, would you eat it or run?"

He didn't have to think long before coming up with a gold medal response.

"Why ruin a perfectly good thing. I would prefer to eat you in the raw without being spoiled by any sort of topping."

Diane looked at Suki while she pointed toward Mickey, and said, "See, he does have good taste."

"I agree with him, completely, Diane."

Suki excused the hostesses, and they turned out all but one of the lamps on the deck as they left for their quarters. The winds remained steady, moving the long boat briskly through the water. The temperature had bottomed out at around eighty-four degrees. The combination of wind and temperature gave the air a soft quality that could hardly be distinguished from one's own skin. The countless stars in the moonless sky provided their own subtle ambient lighting.

"This is the best part of sailing," Suki said.

Diane and Mickey looked up and they, too, were amazed by the view. They also sensed that Suki was preoccupied with desires she would not discuss. This time it was Suki who stood up and walked to the bowsprit, letting her hair down so it would blow in the breeze. She knew she was being watched.

It wasn't long before she felt two hands wrapped around her waist and lips against her ear. She could tell instantly by the tenderness of the touch that they were Diane's. Diane had fulfilled Suki's silent wish that it would be she, not Mickey, who made the first move. Mickey's touch usually had purpose, whereas Diane's felt as if it was conveying feeling and energy.

Diane's nose and lips moved up and down Suki's neck as she softly said, "I love the way your neck smells. For that matter, I love the way your entire body smells. You always smell like some type of flower. Don't you ever sweat?"

Smiling in response to Diane's remark, Suki replied, "It is lilac. And yes, I occasionally sweat, but only when I am terribly excited. And remember what I told you in the beginning of your trip, what goes into one's body will change the flavor, and the smell, of one's body."

Diane gently inserted the tip of her tongue into Suki's ear, instantly creating as many goose pimples on Suki's body as there were stars in the night sky.

"Keep eating what you are eating. It works." After a few more moments of fondling, Diane asked, "What would you say if I told you tonight it's your turn?"

For the first time, Suki began to feel small beads of sweat form on her forehead. Still playing the role of an innocent, she replied, "What do you mean? My turn for what?" She knew only too well where Diane was going, but she wanted to appear vulnerable to see how she responded.

Diane kissed Suki's neck and sucked her earlobe before responding, "You know exactly what I mean. You have been here for Mickey and me all of these days and nights. You have done everything for us and remained a third party in this relationship. That just ended. Tonight will be your night for pleasure. Tonight is for Sukhon Jiao."

Chills ran up and down Suki's spine, and she felt herself breathing faster. "Should you ask Mickey? Perhaps he would prefer to be alone with you tonight."

Diane ran her hands up to Suki's breasts, lightly massaged her nipples while she continued to kiss and lick Suki's neck and ears.

"You have to be kidding. He won't be able to resist once he catches on. We're going to use him like the contents of a toolbox."

Diane carefully slipped off Suki's blouse and shorts, then her own. Once they were naked, she took Suki by the hand and escorted her to the bed, dropping their clothing into a pile nearby. Along the way, she picked up various massage oils and a bottle of honey left behind by the hostesses. Mickey watched as Suki lay back on the mattress. Diane grabbed her bag of personal items she had carried off of the helicopter, pulled out the pair of stilettos she had purchased earlier in the day, then carried them over her shoulder as she walked toward Suki. Kneeling down, Diane slipped the stilettos on Suki's feet. They fit perfectly. Suki looked puzzled for only a moment.

"I bought your size," Diane said with a satisfied expression.

Suki put her arms over her head as Diane motioned for Mickey to join them. He stumbled getting out of his chair, but fortunately, didn't have to take many steps before he was sharing the mattress with the ladies. Diane removed Mickey's shorts and tossed them over to the side with the rest of the clothing, then proceeded to straddle Suki's waist, grabbing a firm hold of the hands that were stretched out above her. Getting face to face with her, Diane asked, "What do you want, Suki? Name your pleasure."

"I can think of nothing you and Mickey could do that would cause displeasure."

Diane felt Mickey's hands on her shoulders from behind just as he asked, "Hey, how come Suki is wearing the stilettos?"

Chapter 22

The dim light of dawn peaked through some low clouds. The sound of waves slapping against the boat as it plowed along created a rhythmic tempo. In spite of the warm ambient temperature, the three were huddled under a marvelous down comforter. Diane opened her eyes and found her head resting comfortably on Mickey's bare chest. Her right arm was on his belly. It was comforting to hear his heart beating and to feel his breathing. She then realized the sensation of soft skin against her back and an arm and leg draped across her body from behind. There was warm breath on her neck. It had to be Suki. Diane was hesitant to move before capturing the moment in every way possible. Without awakening her lovers, she wanted to remember the feeling of their skin, the sounds of their breathing, the smells of them and the sea. Her senses were on high alert as she consumed all of the sensations.

After a few minutes, Suki began to stir. Not moving substantially, she, too, was absorbing every aspect of the moment, and she must have sensed that Diane was awake because she moved her hand to where she could cup one of Diane's breasts. Given the close proximity all three had with one another, Diane couldn't help but notice that Suki reached out to secure a hold on her body, not some part of Mickey's. It was a subtle, but terribly significant choice. Was it by design? Diane didn't know, nor did she care. The feelings she had at that moment for both Mickey and Suki defied qualification.

Mickey made a sound, but didn't stir. He was obviously far away in la-la land. Diane carefully and slowly rolled over onto her back just as Suki shifted her position in unison. It was as if the two women were in the same body. Their eyes met.

Suki propped her head on her hand. Her long hair hung down touching the mattress when it was not blowing gently in the breeze. She gently stroked Diane's abdomen, never taking her eyes off of her, as she whispered, "I am usually not at a loss for words."

Grinning ever so slightly, Diane whispered back, "You're telling me everything I want to know right now just being here and touching me." Diane lifted her head slightly. Suki went the rest of the way and their lips touched.

"Your face smells like me."

Diane nodded as she said, "I think I can say the same about yours." Both giggled. "What next, Suki? Where do we go from here?"

"Just be here, now. Let life just be about now."

Diane snickered in reaction to what Suki said.

"What is so funny?"

"I was recalling the flight over here. Mickey got onto this soapbox about how life should be about now. It all seemed terribly silly at the time, but now…now I think he was spot on."

Looking very serious as she brushed Diane's hair from her face, Suki said, "I know this sounds strange, but sometimes 'being here now' is the only way to make it to tomorrow."

"That sounds like something a great philosopher would have once said."

"I am certainly not a great philosopher, but I am happy that you liked what I said."

Jabbing Suki gently with her elbow, Diane asked, "Did you enjoy yourself last night?"

Blushing slightly, Suki replied, "Last night was…extremely satisfying. It was also full of surprises. You especially surprised me."

Now it was Diane's turn to blush. "There were a lot of firsts last night, Suki. You and I wrote some history."

"Diane, are you at ease with all that happened between us?"

"Absolutely."

"And you are alright with all that happened between Mickey and me?"

Smiling confidently, Diane replied, "You know, I am not the least bit threatened by what happened. In fact, it was so different watching the sex act instead of being the sex act. It was a huge turn on. Besides, I wasn't entirely on the sidelines."

"You must be speaking of the first time, because the second time…we know how that turned out."

"Yeah. The first time, the second time…" Diane giggled. "We gave Mickey quite a workout, didn't we?" Glancing over toward him, she added, "If he complains about anything, I'll kick his ass."

Mickey must have heard the ladies whispering because he opened his eyes and found both Suki and Diane staring at him. After yawning, he tried to lift the comforter and look beneath it.

Grimacing, he said, "I'm stuck to this thing."

Diane grabbed the comforter, ripping it off of him causing him to let out a yipe.

Looking back at Suki, she said, "What did I tell you?" Rising up and straddling him, Diane began playfully, but firmly, pounding on his chest with her fists as she scolded him, "Listen to your shit. I told Suki you would bitch about something. You're out in the middle of the freakin' ocean, on a beautiful boat, it's gorgeous weather, you're lying under what's probably a five-hundred-dollar comforter, your dick is coated with a dried mixture of me, Suki and yourself, we had a night that I, for one, will never, ever forget, and you wake up bitching. God damn you can ruin the perfect moment!"

Diane waited for Mickey to say something. She should have braced herself for disappointment.

"Well, I never thought it was possible, but I think the two of you stretched ol' Johnson."

Diane went limp. Suki kicked Mickey in the thigh.

One of the hostesses came forward with three folded robes. Suki slipped into one, handed one to Diane, and threw the other in Mickey's face.

Suddenly, Diane stood up, gasping with surprise. On the horizon, loomed the sharp, dramatic peaks of an island. Grabbing Suki's hand, she pulled her to the bowsprit.

Boundaries

"Suki, is that it?"

"Yes! That is our destination," Suki answered with a proud smile. "It is called Maribella Island. The owner named it after his wife."

Diane excitedly held Suki's shoulders from behind as she asked, "It's so cute and tiny. How big is it?"

Suki drew in the air with her finger.

"It is shaped like a trapezoid—about fifteen kilometers across in front, six kilometers across in back and about ten kilometers deep.

Turning back to look at Mickey, Diane asked, "Are you going to buy me an island?"

Mickey was coming forward to look for himself at the island, while carrying his robe over his shoulder. As he approached the ladies, he stumbled over one of the stilettos that had been cast to one side. The hostess who brought the robes appeared to be uncomfortable with his unabashed exhibition.

"Cover up!" Diane shouted.

Reluctantly putting on his robe, he replied, "Hell, I just bought you a ranch. Now you want an island? I'll put an island in your kitchen so you can learn how to cook."

Diane bristled, "First of all, I know how to cook, I just don't spoon feed you Mexican trash like your sweet Maria. Secondly, I'm buying the ranch, not you."

"Do you have a problem with Maria that you need to tell me about?" Mickey barked back in an unmistakably defensive tone of voice.

Suki had heard enough.

"Guys! Stop!" She shouted, stepping between the two, separating them like a referee at a boxing match.

In the calm that followed, the hostess spoke briefly in Thai with Suki, then turned and left.

"Did she go back to get a gun?" Mickey asked, belligerently.

"No," Suki replied, pointing at Mickey and taking a deep, slow breath. Her patience with Mickey's antics wearing thin, she continued, "The hostess informed me that we are about one hour away from our destination, and that they are making crepes for our breakfast. They will have them up here for us in a few minutes. I then thanked her for her kindness. I also told her there might only be one person eating because I may by that time have thrown both of you into the water for the sharks to eat!"

Mickey and Diane stood silently. Suki had never raised her voice until now.

"Mickey, do you love Diane?"

He responded with a simple nod.

Suki slapped him across his face with particular viciousness as she yelled, "Then say it!"

"I love Diane!" he replied, though possibly involuntarily.

Her face turning red with anger, Suki shouted, "Say it like you mean it…to her face!"

Managing to avoid a complete loss of words as a result of Suki's actions, Mickey turned toward Diane and said most earnestly, "You mean more to me than life itself. I love you."

Diane was surprised that he did as Suki asked, and even went the extra mile.

Turning next to Diane, Suki asked, "Do you love Mickey?"

"Are you going to slap me?" Diane asked as she grimaced.

"Wrong answer!"

Suki slapped Diane across the face, though not nearly as hard as she had done to Mickey. Diane, too, was now in shock.

Mickey grabbed Suki's hand and shouted, "Cut it out!"

Suki persisted. In an instant, she showed that she could easily protect herself by stomping on Mickey's foot hard enough to bring him to his knees. Looking back at Diane again, she shouted once again, "Say it! Say it to his face!"

Turning to Mickey, Diane cried out, "I love Mickey. I want to be with him forever." After walking over to Mickey and assisting him back to his feet, she asked, "What's going on?" at which point they held and comforted each other.

Nobody said a word for the longest time. Eventually, Suki leaned back against the wooden rail, studying the two while her skin color returned to normal, just as the red from Suki's slaps was developing on both Mickey's and Diane's cheeks.

After a few moments, she broke her silence, saying, "There. That is much better."

Putting her head on Mickey's chest seeking comfort, Diane said, "I thought you said Thai people never came unglued."

Mickey shrugged his shoulders.

"Thai people generally do not," Suki said with a coy smile. "You just got a taste of the Chinese warrior bitch. That, too, has been passed down from generation to generation."

"Well, I'm impressed," Mickey said, still struggling to find the right words.

"Yeah, I'm impressed, too," Diane agreed.

Suki took another deliberate, slow, deep breath, then smiled as if nothing had happened before saying, "I am looking forward to our breakfast together. I cannot wait until you see the island. But, now, I get to be the first to use the Loo." She quickly scurried off.

Mickey pulled Diane close to his body as he said, "That was really weird. Are you okay?"

"I'm in shock, but I'm okay. Is she bipolar?"

"Beats the hell out of me."

Diane looked down at Mickey's red foot and asked, "How about you? You took quite a licking."

"Oh, I'll be alright." Mickey paused, and looked into Diane's eyes. "You know something, I don't exactly agree with Suki's method just now, but I think she was giving me a wakeup call." He made sure he had a tender hold on her waist. "If I really love you as I say I do, I need to begin doing a much better job of showing it."

Mickey wiped the tears from her eyes, then pulled her tight and kissed her with an intensity he had never before exhibited.

Diane responded by squeezing Mickey tightly before saying, "No. I just want you to be Mickey. I don't think a person should have to change just to make another feel comfortable. I love you the way you are, Mick. Plus, I already have you as an adjective in my personal dictionary. If you change, then 'Mick' will mean something else."

She returned his kiss.

Backing away, she smiled at him and said, "You smell like sex, and it's not like when it's just you and me…if you know what I mean."

"I'll take care of that when she's through."

She put her hands on his face and said, "Don't rush. I'm not unhappy about last night. Last night was wonderful. It was a whole new expression of me that I think was dying to be released." Diane looked down for a moment to catch her thoughts, then back to Mickey's eyes. "For the record, I like having sex with a man better than with a woman. I think this is the proverbial flash in a pan."

Suki popped out of the cabin door and walked to the front of the boat. Wiggling anxiously, Diane said, "Bye."

It was now Diane who quickly shuffled to the toilet in the cabin, giving Suki a wide berth as she passed. Suki put on a fierce, albeit artificial, look as Diane dodged past, but ultimately, they managed to exchange smiles. Once Diane was out of sight, Suki confronted Mickey with a rather delicate observation.

"Mickey, call me suspicious, call me over cautious, call me not-minding-my-own-business, but last night, I noticed some new scars on your scrotum. Is there anything you want to tell me? Is everything healthy down there?"

"Gosh, you're observant. I was going to tell you at some point. I had my vasectomy reversed a few months ago. I'm back to shooting live rounds again."

Flabbergasted, Suki asked, "Diane knows about this, right?"

"No, she can't get pregnant. I thought you knew."

Suki's jaw dropped and she said, "You obviously did not listen closely to what she was saying, so listen to me now." Grabbing Mickey's ears, she said, "What she told me is that she has no problem conceiving. She just miscarries early in her pregnancy."

Mickey swallowed hard as the full impact of what had Suki just told him sunk in.

"Oh, Mickey, it will break her heart if she were to lose another baby. You have to tell her. She needs some kind of protection. Why did you do this?"

He paused for a moment before answering, "I felt old. I thought maybe someday I might want to have a child, and I didn't want to wait until the chances of having a successful reversal diminished. So I did it after I last saw you."

"You know what your problem is Mickey? You just said the word 'I' six times in your answer to my question," she said, barely able to remain composed.

"You're still on the pill, right?" Mickey asked, fidgeting restlessly.

"Oh, thanks for asking in advance," Suki said, shaking her head in disbelief. She waited until she was certain Mickey was completely unnerved before giving him a definite answer. "No, I am not. I never use oral contraceptives because I always use condoms except when I am with you. There was supposed to be no reason for me to use birth control, you selfish twit. Fortunately for you and quite by accident, the calendar is working to our advantage this week. Had this trip been next week the situation would be quite different."

Diane exited the cabin and turned to rejoin the others.

Acting quickly, Mickey said, "Suki, we can't tell her about this…not now."

"Mickey…" Suki's nostrils flared angrily.

"No, I'm serious. I'll tell Diane when the time is right. If there is some sort of medical issue, I'll take care of it."

"We could be speaking of a child, not a 'medical issue'."

Mickey put a finger over Suki's lips as he said, "We'll talk later. For now, we say nothing, do you understand?"

As much as Suki wanted to reveal the truth to Diane, she could think of no easy way to do it at this time, and in this setting, so she was compelled to hold her tongue.

When she approached, Diane noticed that Suki and Mickey were focused on each other, and not on the beautiful view that was before them.

"Guys, stop telling each other secrets and look at the island. It's spectacular."

Several birds met up with the boat—the first birds anyone had seen since leaving Phuket yesterday. Diane inserted herself between Suki and Mickey as they leaned over the rail with their faces piercing the wind. A casual observer would have noticed the change in the order from when the three met for the first time four days earlier.

THE CREPES WERE A welcome change from what had become the typical morning fare of pastries and breads, with meats, cheeses, and fruits. The plates had barely been cleared when a motorized dinghy approached the schooner to take the visitors, and later the crew, the remaining kilometer or so to the beach. The shoreline was dramatic in all respects. The water slowly became shallow with channels running through the multi-color coral, allowing the dinghy to navigate to one of several docks at the beach. It was obvious now that the draft of the big boat would have been too deep for it to safely come any closer to shore.

Mickey looked intently over the edge of the boat into the crystal clear water. As fish of varying sizes and every imaginable color combination seemed to look back at him, he said, "We're going to have to do some serious snorkeling today."

The beach itself varied from fifty to several hundred meters in depth before transitioning to a lush line of native foliage and trees. That line of green went as far as one could see in either direction until it disappeared with the curvature of the small island. Beyond and looming over the band of green was a precipitous formation of flatirons rocks. About two hundred meters down to the left of where the newly arrived guests were standing, water poured off of a cliff creating a picture perfect waterfall. Traversing the face of the rock were a series of wooden staircases climbing more than a hundred meters to the top of the precipice.

The three disembarked from the small craft and took several steps up the beach towards the tree line. Diane looked at the stairways as they rose from beach level to the top of the cliffs.

"Please tell me there is an elevator somewhere."

Suki spread her arms wide apart as she said, "As far as you can see, this island remains nearly unspoiled by humans. The structures on the compound use candles and lanterns for lighting. These buildings are made with materials harvested from this island. There are generators to provide power for some electrical appliances. Hot water comes from spring water that originates at the active part of the island where there is a volcano, then is cooled to a useable temperature. It is primitive elegance—and no, there is no elevator."

"A volcano?" Diane inquired anxiously. "There's a volcano on this island?"

"Of course. This entire region has a great deal of volcanic activity, but there should be nothing to fear. It is believed that this particular volcano last erupted around two thousand years ago and it does so on roughly a five-thousand-year cycle. Then again, volcanoes have been known to be unpredictable."

"Suki! Are you screwing with me again?"

She shook her head.

Looking at Mickey, Diane shrugged her shoulders saying, "Oh well, if it blows, it'll be over for us quickly."

"We'll be fine," he said. "Just think about all that the island has to offer."

"And if observing the marine life is not enough of a distraction," Suki continued, "there are over fifty species of birds on the island. Many of them are extremely rare."

"Alright," Diane protested. "I'm on overload now. Let's just get up to the top of the hill and get settled. Then we can go from there. Is that too much to ask?" She looked at the several locals in attendance, apparently hired staff of the owner, as they picked up the few belongings the three brought with them. Reaching for her bags, Diane said, "I can take my things."

"No," Suki cautioned. "By the time you get halfway up the hillside, you will be glad you have only yourself to carry."

"So be it. Let's go."

It took nearly fifteen minutes, including rest stops at three points, to climb the steps to the top of the rocks where the residence was located. Once there, however, it was clearly a trip worth making. The residence was a rambling place. Its outline was no particular shape. As soon as Diane entered the front door, she saw a trail of flower petals scattered about the floor obviously as a guide to one particular part of the home. There was a strong, sweet smell of the same flowers in spite of the open-air design with copious windows and doors, and a fair breeze they encouraged throughout the rooms. The décor could only be described as simple, yet elegant, with what appeared to be furnishings that were handmade of local timber, rock, or bamboo.

Diane locked hands with Mickey as they slowly made their way to the end of the trail where, as they had suspected, there was a lavish bedroom. But it was the views from the bedroom that made it spectacular, and there were windows on three sides to take advantage of what was to be seen. Because the home was on a jet of land, when the guest looked out the western-facing windows, there was a view of the volcano; to the north there was forest and the private pool; to the east was the view of the seascape with the Je t'aime anchored offshore.

Awestruck, Diane said, "I've seen places like this in travel magazines or on television programs, but I never imagined I would be standing in one. Mickey have you been here before?"

"I have never even heard of this place. Suki, you outdid yourself this time. Thank you. This is perfect."

Suki smiled, acknowledging her success.

"You will find all the clothing you need in the closet and drawers. The bathroom has all the necessary toiletries. The bar is over there. Someone will be along shortly with fruit and juices. Mickey, you mentioned snorkeling. Someone will be waiting for the two of you at the bottom of the stairs in exactly two hours. I suggest you take advantage of the shower and pool, have a light lunch, and then go snorkeling. Two hostesses, Li and La, will be available for all of your needs and you must take advantage of their massage. I have never had a better one. Dinner tonight will be an extravagant display of seafood. Afterward, I have a very special treat—my gift to both of you."

"Where will you be?" Diane asked, quickly noting that Suki herself was not specifically included in any of the plans.

"I have to discuss some business with Captain Bates. As such, I will be staying on the boat tonight."

"You know we want you to stay with us," Diane said, taking Suki's hands in hers.

Boundaries

"I know. But this needs to be a restful day and night and the two of you need to spend time together…alone. It hurt me a lot, what happened earlier on the boat. You did not come on holiday to fight." Staring intently at Mickey while she spoke, Suki finished with, "Time with one another today could be a turning point for your relationship. I should not be a factor in that. I will see you both tomorrow."

Chapter 23

"I refuse to climb those stairs again today," Diane said, tossing her fins, mask, and snorkel onto a chair just inside the door. Wasting no time, she flopped her bikini-clad body into a bamboo chair that was covered with a thick cushion.

"It's good for you," Mickey said, tossing his gear onto the same chair. "If you did this once a day, you could crack open chestnuts at Christmas with your butt cheeks."

"There goes another cherished, childhood image," Diane said, looking up at the ceiling.

"Can I get you anything?" Mickey asked.

"Water."

Opening the refrigerator, he asked, "Sparkling or plain?"

"Sparkling, actually."

Mickey took a bottle of Perrier over to Diane, en route twisting off the top, making a *pfsst* sound. Taking a seat in a chair facing her, he first sipped his own water, then asked, "Those fish were unbelievable, weren't they?"

"I just love parrotfish with those cute little faces," Diane responded. "Why aren't fresh water fish that spectacular?"

"They are, just in their own way."

"You think a mud-cat is as pretty as a damselfish?"

"You do have a point there," Mickey said with a chuckle. After a few moments while the two savored their refreshments, Mickey said, "Hey, stand up."

"Do I have to?"

"Yes."

Diane stood up and faced Mickey. He motioned with his water bottle for her to turn around which Diane did.

"You are so beautiful."

"A compliment, yet my breasts are covered. What's the occasion?"

"I'm serious, babe. You were a 'ten' to begin with. Now, I look at you and everything about you is so perfect."

"What's different?"

"Your eyes...your face. I see a light there that I didn't see when I landed in San Diego."

"Not even after Dippin' Dots?"

Mickey smiled. "No, not even after Dippin' Dots."

"This trip has been good...weird at times, but good. Let's face it, it's not every vacation that you have your asshole airbrushed by a stranger."

Diane walked over to Mickey, leaned over, and kissed him.

"You're right about that. I don't think that'll show up on the cover of *Conde Nast Traveler.*"

Pulling her chair closer to Mickey's, Diane sat down again. "Hey, we're alone now. Tell me some more about your project." Diane batted her eyelashes as if that might encourage him to be forthcoming.

"Let's see...it's been twenty-four hours since I suggested we not speak further about the project."

Before Mickey could say any more, one of the attendants, Li, approached. "Excuse me, massage for you, now, please," she said as she motioned toward the pool.

"Can this wait a while?" Diane asked her. Her request was met with a puzzled look from Li.

"Yes, you take off bathing suit," Li said with a pleasant expression. "Sorry, no English much."

That was an understatement. Li had no clue what Diane was saying. The other attendant, La, peeked her head in the door, sporting an equally innocent and enthusiastic smile, clearly indicating that she, too, expected both guests to respond to the call for a massage.

Diane gave Mickey a look indicating that she was still waiting for him to respond, and respond favorably, to her question.

"I think it's safe for us to have a massage and talk," he said. "What do you think?"

"I think I'm ready for a massage."

Diane stood up and took Mickey by the hand to the pool area where Li and La had set up two tables side by side. The two shed their swimming attire, then reclined face down onto their respective tables. In short order, their massages were underway and so was the response to Diane's question.

"So tell me, what did you learn about the project from Suki?"

"That I shouldn't ask any questions."

"Clearly you are not one to listen to sound advice, from Suki or from me. Now tell me something a little more substantive."

"She said you're the hardware guy."

"Sounds like an impressive role. So there are others involved?"

"Yeah. One's called *Brains* and the other is *Fingers*."

It was apparent neither Diane nor Mickey was going to be completely transparent.

"Long before there were USBs, serial ports, and parallel ports, the human body was blessed with evolution's greatest I/Os known as senses. Everything we assimilate enters our body through one of these systems."

"So let me guess, you need to hook up to them somehow, right?"

"Right. For hearing you need access via the 8th cranial nerve to the primary auditory cortex at each side of the brain, for sight you need access via the 2nd cranial nerve to the visual cortex above the cerebellum at the rear of the brain,…"

"Okay, I get the point. You know a lot more about anatomy and physiology than I know."

"…and so on and so forth for taste, smell, and the very complex somatosensory system—touch. Next you need to provide a high-speed connection to these I/Os. This is where the nanomachines come in to play. You create a PSP to each sensory input point…"

"What's a PSP?"

"A Primary Stimulation Path. As I was saying…"

Boundaries

"Am I interrupting too much?"

"Do you want me to answer your freakin' question or not?"

Diane laughed that she was able to get a rise out of Mickey.

"So there is a PSP to each sensory input point and these tie back to one central location where we can deliver photonometric data to the machines. The machines then travel in loops along the PSP to the sensory inputs where they deliver quantum information packets. The brain takes the information and does with it what it has always done—in short, it catalogues the data, deposits it for recall, processes it further as necessary, and establishes links to other information so that an image of grandma is associated with the smell of her cooking and other important matters in life such as that."

"Cold?" Li asked, referring to the goose pimples covering Diane's body.

"No...I'm fine."

Li proceeded to cover Diane up with a large towel anyway.

While her mind was spinning with the information Mickey had just given her, Diane asked, "Is that what you called anecdotal thought transfer?"

"You listen well."

"What about the nanomachines? Are they machines or cells or what?"

"The best answer is 'yes.' They are precisely controlled machines that contain many times more sophisticated information than a cell contains genetic code." Mickey took a moment before continuing, to check for any reaction from Diane that would make him stop short his explanation, then continued, "There are seven types of nanocells—alpha cells control motor activity, beta cells control memory, gamma cells control central nervous system actions, delta cells control autonomic nervous system actions, epsilon cells are the energy source, sigma cells control rest and tone, and lambda cells control emotions. You still with me?"

"This is deep, Mick. I am impressed."

"Within the lambda family, each cell has a Yin-Yang modulus. Lambda-1 deals with passion and compassion. Lambda-2 controls lust, desire and want. Lambda-3 controls anger and aggression. Lambda-4 modulates fear and comfort.

Lambda-5 is happiness and sadness. There are seventeen more, but I don't want to bore you. I'm sure you get the picture."

Diane propped herself up and took a drink of her Perrier before asking, "What's MADONNA? Is that schwa?"

"Damn, you do listen well. They are actually different features, and they are *Finger's* piece of the pie. He has developed an algorithm called MADONNA for setting the parameters of each nanocell. Without the algorithm, the patient could become something like Frankenstein when he was shown the torch. He becomes behaviorally wrong. The patient could fall asleep during a violent thunderstorm; eat bunny rabbits; find fire is soft to the touch. It's all environmentally driven.

"As for of schwa, think of it as 'gain.' This is how we set boundaries—limits if you will. If someone says to you, 'good morning,' you shouldn't immediately fall in love. If someone says to you, 'you have a little crumb on the corner of your lip,' you shouldn't pull out a .357 and blow his head off. MADONNA and schwa make the difference between a completely bipolar, schizophrenic, paranoid, homicidal maniac, and a normal person."

As she exhaled loudly, Diane asked, "I've been dying to know. What does MADONNA stand for?"

"Memory, Action, and Dyno-Opposing Neurological Neutrality Attenuator. Still impressed?"

"Now I know why you call it MADONNA." Diane paused to think, rubbing the mouth of the bottle across her lips. "Mick, what if I told you Medico would be willing to fund your research? I mean, it isn't entirely my decision, only my recommendation. The Board would have to approve of it, but I have a lot of influence with the Board."

"I'd tell you funding isn't the problem. The barrier is the testing phase. That has to involve human subjects and that means the FDA has to be involved as well as other medical advisors along with some fucking group of senators on some inane committee in Washington, not to mention your local Catholic priest and…"

"Calm down. I get the point. There are a lot of barriers. We can work on those one at a time. We have connections in academia and lobbyists in D.C. We may have a problem with the church, however, but we'll find a way to take care of that, too."

"Or…we can just do our research in Asia where the controls are few to none. Here, good science trumps politics. Then, we market a finished product to Europe and the Americas. Once they realize they are again behind the technology curve, hundreds of thousands, perhaps millions of consumers will beg for PicoPoint to return their sick or injured loved ones to a more normal life," Mickey said, his voice getting louder and louder.

"Tension?" La asked, referring to the knots developing in Mickey's shoulder as he spoke.

Diane got up from the table and walked over to Mickey, turning to Li and La in the process.

"Thank you. You may go."

"Okay. Dinner one hour," La responded.

With that, Li and La left the room.

"Relax, Mick, relax," Diane said, taking up where La had left off.

Slowly, she felt the tension in Mickey's shoulders lessen.

"Then there's the problem of finding a host."

"What is a host?" Diane asked, struggling to continue rubbing Mickey's shoulders and back as she analyzed each word he was saying.

She poured some more oil into the palm of her hand as she waited for him to elaborate.

"You can't just connect the whole works to a computer or something. You need something that works just as fast as the brain…and that has to be another human brain."

Diane swallowed hard as she asked, "What do you mean?"

"Let's put this in tech terms. Do you realize how many terabytes of information there are in the brain? Do you know the speed in gigaflops at which the brain must process this information? There's no macro level machine that can compare. So, you need to find a suitable host from which to extract—no that's too harsh a word—harvest the desired information." Noticing Diane had stopped her massage, Mickey asked, "You okay with this?"

"I'm alright. I'll start breathing again soon. Tell me, how do you find a host? Do you run an ad in the newspaper or something?"

"That's right. You'll find my advertisement on Craigslist under 'Very Personals.'"

The levity was good, and needed at this point. Mickey turned over so he could look at Diane.

"Actually, it doesn't get any more personal than exchanging a thought. It is intimacy in the highest degree. Let's use the two of us as an example. If I was to have a memory loss for some reason, I could regain the memories we share of Torrey Pines from you. If you were to have a memory loss, you could regain the memory of parrotfish from me. Now, multiply that by three hundred billion times over, and we have a whole brain."

"We certainly wouldn't want to use a brain from 'Abby Normal,' now would we?"

"Exactly. We have to be very purposeful in our selection."

"How does harvesting take place?"

"The donor has to undergo hypnosis. A subject is suggested, nanomachines begin hunting for synaptic action, capture it, assimilate it into quantum units, and then return the information to a port-of-call where it is transmitted by infrared signal at VFIR speed to the recipient." Mickey paused to let Diane digest what he just said. "There's one catch."

"What's that?"

"Harvesting is a destructive process. We don't fully understand why. It's very possibly the ultimate confirmation of the first law of thermodynamics, that energy is neither lost nor created, but rather it is simply transformed from one form to another—or in this situation, one person to another. Our estimate is that there is a two to five part per billion loss of host memory in a typical transfer. If we do a small transfer, it's really not an issue. If we do an extensive transfer or many small transfers, we're getting into some clinically significant numbers, meaning there is the potential for the host to suffer permanent memory loss or disability."

"I can see how that would be unacceptable."

"Why?"

"Well, it's wrong...don't you think?"

"If I choose to donate a kidney to someone I love, that's a five hundred thousand part per million loss. But, I may have saved someone's life."

"That's different."

"Is it, Diane?"

Struggling for an appropriate response, Diane replied, "Mickey, you're on a very slippery slope."

"Me? What happened to us? I thought Medico Techniq wanted a piece of the action. Change your mind so soon?"

Diane took a deep breath. After several moments of intense thought, she gave Mickey an answer to his question.

"No, the offer stands. I'll speak with Rajeev as soon as I get back in the office."

"I told you we shouldn't discuss the project. You're not sure about it now, are you?" Mickey asked, noticing that Diane was staring off into space.

"I was just thinking of a line I heard in a movie once. It went something like, 'Memory is a wonderful thing, if you just didn't have to deal with the past.' It occurred to me that none of this would be necessary if our past was not so important. Clearly we have to find a way to see your project to completion." Diane found herself holding onto Mickey tightly. "That's enough work-related talk for one day. Let's get into the pool."

THE EVENING APPEARED TO bring a relaxing end to what had been a rejuvenating day. There had been swimming and sunbathing, snorkeling, massage, conversation, a dip in the pool, and a fabulous, romantic, candlelight dinner for two on the patio overlooking the volcano in the distance. Diane was nonetheless unsettled about something.

"Do you think Suki will be alright on the boat?"

"Why do you ask?"

"I don't know. I guess I felt a little uneasy with Captain Bates and that whole pirate business. Let's face it, something could happen to Suki, and there would be nothing we could do. I mean, we can't exactly call 911."

"Something could happen to us. Suki may be better off on the boat."

"Oh, gee, thanks."

"Suki's a grown woman. She's very capable of taking care of herself should the need arise."

"It bothers me that she left us today when she was upset."

Mickey poured Diane another glass of chilled white wine, then said, "Look what she did for us. I think her tantrum this morning was well designed. It made me realize what I have, how special life is with you, and that I was wrong to take you for granted."

"Oh, Mickey, you're a sweetheart when you're drunk."

"Drunk? This stuff's like fairy pee. Tastes terrible, and there's not much of a kick."

"Thanks for refilling my glass."

"As any gentleman should do for his lady."

Li and La came out onto the porch carrying two large, wrapped boxes.

"Now special treat from Miss Suki. Have good night."

"How long did it take you to urinate in this wine bottle?" Mickey asked with a grin as he held the wine bottle in the air.

"Thank you, have good night," Li said smiling. Li and La turned and left the porch.

Diane bent over laughing.

"I can't believe you did that. What if they understood English, you shit?"

"What? Perhaps she's the fairy. That would have been quite a compliment."

The two had a long laugh.

"Let's see here," Mickey said as he picked up the box in front of him. "Could be socks…no, not too practical out here. Could be a gift certificate for Neiman-

Marcus…no, again, not too practical. Could be an assortment of sex toys—now that's a possibility!"

Mickey began tearing open the box, but stopped short of finishing the task.

"Wait. Just in case these go together in some manner, why don't we open the boxes at the same time?"

"I was waiting for my gentleman to return."

The two opened the boxes and each pulled out a pair of ostrich-skin boots, high socks, blue jeans, a snakeskin belt, a western shirt, and a Stetson.

"Where in the hell did Suki get these?" Diane asked, marveling at the unusual gifts.

"I have no earthly idea."

"So, are we supposed to wear these down the streets of Bangkok? What the…"

"Wait a minute, here's a note."

Mickey reached into the bottom of the box and pulled out a note that was rolled up and tied with a ribbon.

"It's probably the receipt showing how much she charged your Black Card to fly these things over from Dallas by private jet."

"Nope, not a receipt. It says, 'My Dear Friends,…' She must use this note over and over. 'I want you to know just how special you are to me. More important than that is the love you have for each other, now, and forever. My ultimate gift awaits you on the beach below. I will see you tomorrow morning. Love, Suki.'"

"Mick, I told you I am not walking down those steps again today."

"We have to."

"Bullshit!"

"Hey, she went to a lot of trouble to get these clothes. We need to see what she has in store for us."

"You think it's a rodeo?"

"Diane, get real."

"Mickey, I really don't want to go down those steps again."

"Come on, get dressed."

"Ugh!"

IT TOOK A FEW minutes, but soon the two were decked out in their Western best.

"I can't believe all of this fits," Mickey said, tucking in his shirt. "How does she do it?"

"She just knows," Diane responded, adjusting her hat and looking at herself in a mirror. "I haven't been in Western duds since I was a teenager. I forgot how good they feel and how sexy they make you look—especially a cowboy."

Diane walked over and finished tucking in Mickey's shirt for him. She reached her hand down deep into Mickey's pants and grabbed a hold.

"Whee, dowgie!" Mickey shouted. "Hang onto that saddle horn, girl!"

Diane turned Mickey around and kissed him.

"Come on, Roy, let's head to the beach."

"Right behind you, Dale."

Mickey tightened his belt, and then smacked Diane on the butt.

THE SECOND TRIP DOWN the steep stairway was painful. The muscles normally used for such descents were now screaming, and both Diane and Mickey had to hold on to the railing. Once the two had finally reached the bottom, they looked up and down the beach in both directions. To their right was a flag that hadn't been there earlier.

"Guess we'll head that way," Mickey said, gesturing to Diane with his hat in his hand.

"Thank you, kind sir."

As they began walking, Mickey took a few moments to look at the waves crashing on the beach and at the schooner still anchored offshore. He was caught by surprise when Diane picked up the pace, pulling ahead of him.

"Mickey…look at them…Mickey!"

Boundaries

Tied to a palm tree were two white horses, all tacked up to ride. Diane walked up to them and began patting them gently at first and then more playfully once she realized they would not present her any handling problem.

"They're beautiful. Look!" Diane said, pointing to the breast collars. "This one is Zeus, and this one is Hera."

Diane continued to hug and love all over both horses while Mickey stood with his hands on his hips.

"What are we supposed to do now...?"

Mickey was unable to complete his question before Diane had untied Zeus, mounted him in a single jump—without using her stirrup—and took off racing down the beach using her hat to encourage him into a fast gallop.

"Hey!" Mickey called out to no avail.

Even if Diane heard him, she wasn't coming back. The other horse, Hera, looked back at Mickey as if to ask him if he was going to get on, or just stand there.

"Alright, alright," Mickey said to Hera as he untied, then climbed on the steed. Hera required no encouragement—she was going after Zeus.

It was all Mickey could do to hold on and not fall off, but eventually he caught up to Diane and Zeus at a cove far out of sight of the Je t'aime. Diane had tied Zeus to a tree and was reading another note as she stood beside a large, four-poster bed.

"What does it say?" Mickey asked, tying up Hera.

"It simply says, 'goodnight'." Diane walked up to Mickey and held him closely. "I have never seen a more beautiful place. Just look around."

Diane understated the panorama in front of them. The sun was setting. Light danced atop the waves. The wispy clouds were pink, transitioning to orange as the sun lowered. The backdrop to this little holiday haven was the native trees and the flatiron rocks. The beach setting was perfect, private, and unblemished. Mickey walked over to a small table. On it were a few treats should they get hungry, and some champagne in an ice bucket.

After opening one of the boxes, Mickey exclaimed, "Look! Sticky rice with mango and coconut cream!"

He turned to look at Diane, only to find that she had stripped off her boots and clothes and was wading into the surf. She dove into a wave and began swimming to a group of rocks in the middle of the cove.

"Wait for me, Diane!"

Again, Diane was on a mission and that mission was to reach the rocks. As quickly as he could, Mickey removed his boots and clothing, and took pursuit of her. After a few minutes, he reached the rocks, finding Diane sprawled out on her belly, her head propped up on her hands as she looked into the sunset. Mickey took a seat next to her on the slippery smooth rock surface. The spray from the crashing waves blew into their faces.

The moment was perfect. It was every love story and romantic movie come together. Mickey found himself facing his destiny. What he had planned as a vacation, had now come to this.

"Diane, what are you doing for the rest of your life?"

She looked away from the setting sun toward Mickey.

"Will you marry me?" He asked.

She sat up and embraced him.

Chapter 24

Diane couldn't decide which evoked stronger feelings. On one hand, there was Mickey, the only other man besides Bruce to propose to her, sleeping next to her following an incredibly passionate night. On the other hand, there was a deep, subtle fear about Mickey's question that he had posed to her on the rocks…and her answer. Did she give him the answer he was looking for? Did she answer the question with only her best interests in mind? Would she change her decision? Would Mickey really make the commitment?

"You're thinking too hard," Mickey said, opening his eyes. "I can hear you breathing."

"What am I thinking?"

"You're probably thinking, 'I wish I had some round food for breakfast.'"

"You know, I would like a bagel or an English muffin. I might gag if I see another piece of fruit."

"Actually, you're more likely wondering why you didn't stay in San Diego."

"Would you have proposed to me in San Diego?"

"In time. The mood last night and this place were just perfect. I guess if we had gone to Dick's, I might have popped the question."

"Of course, Dick's. Idyllic island setting, I can see the similarity."

Mickey brushed the hair from Diane's face before asking, "What would you think if we had Bates marry us tonight?"

"On the boat?"

"Marriage at sea."

"Is that a real marriage?"

"No, not with his registry. But, it would be symbolic, and we could do the legal marriage when we get back to the States. We could invite some people, have a party, have the Eagles play for us…"

"Do they accept the Black Card?"

"I'm sure we could find agreeable terms."

"Can we invite Suki?"

"You mean to the ceremony on the boat?"

"No! To the real thing back home."

"Diane, do you really want Suki to come to the States? I think having her involved with us in the long run is a bad idea."

"Why, don't you trust yourself?"

"I think we're a little past that at this point. No, I was thinking more along the lines that life for three, over time, would be complicated."

"And you don't like complicated, do you?"

"Sometimes, complicated is unavoidable. But, if it can be avoided, why bring it upon yourself?"

"What's Maria going to say when you bring another woman into your life?"

"She'll be cool."

"I'd say she's going to be downright frigid. Talk about complicated."

"You think my relationship with her is more than platonic, don't you?"

"She's pretty, she's my age, maybe younger, and she lives with you. Let's face it, she's forgotten more about you than I know."

Mickey paused, took a breath, then said, "I'm going out on a limb with this one, only because I want to spend the rest of my life with you, in an uncomplicated and honest marriage. Here's the truth. Maria and I had a brief physical relationship for a few months over ten years ago. It just about ruined an otherwise good friendship. We decided to keep it out of the bedroom from that point forward. That was the end of the story."

After the shock had worn off, Diane reacted to Mickey's admission.

"I have two responses to what you just said. First, I really appreciate the truth, although I have to point out that you omitted her name from our discussion of your lovers the other night."

"I hadn't proposed to you at that point."

"That's really lame, Mick, but I'll overlook it. Second, how are things going to change between us? I mean, we're friends, and we've had sex. Are we no longer friends?"

"Of course we are, but in a different sort of way."

"That certainly doesn't make me comfortable. You call me complicated?"

"I guess you can say lovers can be friends, but the opposite isn't true."

"Is Suki a friend, a lover, or both?"

"None of the above, she's a contract employee."

"That's so much shit. I cannot believe you even said that about her."

"Diane, it's too early to have deep discussions like this."

"Just two minutes ago, you asked me to get married to you on a boat. It wasn't too early for that bombshell."

"Well, a bomb looks different depending if you're in the plane looking at the ground, or on the ground looking up at the plane."

"I swear Mickey, I'd like for once to have a conversation with you that doesn't include metaphors, or references to movies or frozen desserts."

"See what I mean? Before we became lovers, you would have thought that my analogy was clever."

"No Mick, I would have humored you, but I wouldn't have thought it was clever." Getting up from the bed, Diane said, "I need a break from this conversation. I'm going to take Zeus for a ride back up the beach. Chew on this while I'm gone—Maria goes. I'll see you in an hour or so back at the bungalow."

"I think you are making an unreasonable request based upon…"

"She goes, Mick."

"Do you want me to set things up with Bates for tonight?"

"We'll talk about it at breakfast," Diane said, putting on her clothes and boots. "I'll see you later."

"Diane…"

It was too late. Diane put a bridle and reins on Zeus, and headed north, back in the direction of the cove where the schooner was anchored.

DIANE AND HER STALLION hadn't traveled very far along the beach before they encountered the waterfall close to where she, Mickey, and Suki had first disembarked from the boat. It was a marvelous waterfall, originating high in the cliffs above the beach. The water fell several hundred feet before crashing onto the sharp rock outcropping, creating a spray that encompassed the trees in the small inlet. The sunlight created a rainbow in the mist. The entire setting looked enchanting, and Diane found herself drawn to it. She walked Zeus back to the entrance of the inlet before dismounting, tied him up, and walked the rest of the way to the base of the waterfall.

She made her way to where she could see the point at which the freshwater spring was born at the base. Suddenly, a movement in the spray caught her eye. It was a person. Looking closer, she could see it was a man showering in the waterfall. When he turned, Diane realized who he was. It was Captain Bates. She ducked behind a tree and turned away from the sight, hoping he hadn't seen her. Then, curiosity got the best of her, and she found herself peeking around the tree at Bates. She marveled at his body. He was a handsome, well-built man. From her vantage point, he clearly would have won first prize in the elephant body-painting contest. Diane felt ashamed that she was being a voyeur, but it was hard not to stare.

Without knowing he was being watched, Bates did something quite subtle that would change Diane's reaction to what she was seeing. All he did was turn around to face away from her. Diane's heart almost stopped. Tattooed on his back was a huge bird of prey with talons. From a distance, it looked exactly like Bruce's tattoo. The water pushed Bates long hair over his shoulders, and instantly Diane was looking at an effigy of her late husband.

Diane lost all ability to think rationally at that point and left her place behind the tree, approaching the base of the waterfall. Bates turned around once more and was startled to find Diane wading into the spring, completely dressed, and coming up to him with a look that could only be described as intense.

"I certainly was not expecting company this morning," Bates said, sporting a crooked smile.

"Let me see it."

"I beg your pardon?" Bates muttered.

"Turn around."

Bates did as he was told. Diane completed her advance to where Bates stood beneath the water, wrapped her arms around him, and put her forehead on his back.

"Is this a falcon?" Diane asked as she pulled back to look at it.

"You mean the tattoo?" Bates replied, enjoying the attention.

"Yes, the tattoo," she said, rubbing his back and his long hair with her hands.

"It's a Wedge-Tailed Eagle—Aquila Audax Fleayi—the largest bird of prey in this part of the World."

Bates paused as Diane again wrapped her arms around his body from behind.

"Ma'am, are you alright? You are soaking wet and still wearing clothes that Suki obviously went to great extremes to procure for you."

"Bruce used to talk like that. He was a bird-watcher and would tell me the genus and species of birds in Latin, just as you did. Please, let me hold you. I need this moment."

"I misunderstood. I thought your companion's name was Mickey. In any event, don't you feel this will be a bit awkward to explain if Bruce finds us like this?"

"You still don't understand. Mickey is the man I am with. Bruce is the name of my late husband. You remind me so much of him. Just let me stand here, holding you."

"I'm very sorry. Ma'am, you do realize who I am, don't you?"

"Be quiet. There's a woman coveting your body right now."

Bates slowly turned around, put his giant hands on Diane's shoulders, and pushed her back a short distance.

Diane looked at Bates from head to toe, her eyes opening wide as she unconsciously stared at the first uncircumcised man she had ever seen up close and personal.

"Miss Diane, I am the captain of your vessel, but I must warn you, I am first a man, and you are a beautiful and desirable woman. If you don't want this to become something you might regret, I suggest you turn and leave immediately. I, for one, am not a man who ignores an opportunity such as the one presented before me."

Diane ignored Bates' words of caution, overcome by the resemblance between Bates and Bruce. Her heart ached for it to be a dream come true, overpowering the mindless danger of the situation. She unbuttoned her blouse part way. Bates stopped her before she finished.

"Madam, let me get dressed. I think perhaps we should talk for a while."

Bates climbed out onto some dry rocks and proceeded to turn around, taking advantage of the slight breeze and shaking his arms.

"Are you trying to get me to stare at you or something?"

"Forgive me, madam, but remember how this encounter began. I was minding my own business, taking a shower, completely out of sight from anyone who might casually pass by, when you decide to go out of your way to burst into my private moment. And no, I don't have a towel with me. So, if you want to stare at me, have at it. If you find my only means to dry off offensive, then turn away or leave."

"I'm sorry. I wasn't thinking clearly…you have to understand…"

"Yes, I heard you. I remind you of your deceased husband. Well, get over it."

"What did you say?"

"I said, get over it!"

"How dare you speak that way about my feelings for my husband!"

"He's dead, madam. You need to move on with your life."

Diane turned to leave and began walking hurriedly from the pool of water back toward the beach. She stopped before she got out of Bates' line of sight, turned and came back to him, walking along the edge of the water.

"Do you know what your problem is?

"No, but I suspect you are going to tell me."

"You've never experienced a loss. You've never had someone you love die."

"You mean, such as my wife who died four years ago?"

"You call that a loss...? Your wife? I'm sorry. I didn't know."

"Four years ago. It was a diving accident off the coast of New Zealand. And your husband?"

"Seven years ago—motorcycle accident," Diane replied, hesitating at the frankness of the conversation.

"Could you hand me those shorts that are over next to you...by the knapsack?"

Diane picked them up and took them to Bates, stopping in front of him so she could take one final look at his body.

"I've never seen one that big before."

"The shorts, please."

Bates quickly put them on.

"And they say men ogle!"

"You must enjoy the attention."

"That part of me, madam, does not get a lot of attention these days."

"Oh, so you and Suki didn't..."

"No, Suki is my employer. We had some business to discuss last night."

"What kind of business do you do with Suki?"

"Suki is my employer. She pays me well. She pays me on time. She calls on me often."

"So, you're not going to tell me."

"You picked up on that rather quickly."

Bates pointed to a rock landing in the sunlight.

"Let's have a seat over there."

He walked over to it, made sure his footing was solid before helping Diane up.

"First, let me ask the reason why you are here?"

"On the island?"

"Well, more than that. Why are you on holiday with Mickey?"

"He often takes exotic vacations like this one. He asked me to come along."

"You strike me as an ambitious woman—one whom I would not expect to find on holiday on a remote island…unless you are in pursuit of something very important. So, once more, why are you here?"

"Well, I have a motive and a reason. First, the motive is to learn more about a project that Mickey is working on so my company can help bring it to market. As for the reason, we love each other, and we're going to get married."

"You are certain your motive is not the primary reason you are here?"

"Well…"

"As I thought."

Bates tossed a pebble into the water.

"I would say something now to the effect that you don't want to be too hasty, but then you have been a widow for seven years."

"What about you? Have you ever thought of remarrying?"

"I am married. She's anchored just offshore."

"You know what I mean," Diane said with a nod.

"Hyzy—that's my late wife—and I used to sail together; taking clients on long, private cruises. We thoroughly enjoyed ourselves. In so many ways, she is still with me when I'm on Je t'aime. I can think of no other way I'd like to live to be quite honest."

"That's very romantic. But, why did you criticize me a moment ago when I mentioned my late husband. It seems to me that you haven't moved on with your life either."

"That is a fair observation. Let me say that I have accepted what has taken place in my life. Can you say the same?"

"Yes…no…I don't know."

"Let me ask you something. Is there a part of your former life with your late husband that is a part of your life today? For example, I still sail on the boat that I shared with my late wife."

"I still live in our house, does that count?"

"Absolutely. Do you feel he is still with you in that house?"

Boundaries

"I don't know anymore," Diane said, staring off into the distance. "It's been a long time—seven years—and I think I am forgetting parts of him that I told myself the day that he died I would never forget."

"And you should forget some aspects of that person, that life, that relationship. It's natural to do so, and I would go so far as to say it is healthy to do so."

"Where are you trying to go with this conversation?"

"Ah, good question. You see, the helm of Je t'aime belonged to Hyzy. The boat was originally her father's. He used to sail all over these waters and taught her everything he knew about sailing and the boat itself. She was remarkable. She never once asked me to take the helm for her, and I never once requested it. My job was ropes and sails and so forth. Now that she is gone, while the boat was once *ours*, I stand today in the one spot that had been held only by her. So while I feel she is with me in spirit, the circumstances clearly reinforce that she is no longer of this earth."

"Bruce—that's my late husband—and I rode his Harley-Davidson all around the country."

"Your ship?"

"Yes, our ship, only with wheels. He always steered, I was always in back."

"Do you still ride his motorcycle?"

"No, it was destroyed in the accident, and I haven't been on one since."

"There is your first mistake. The first thing you should do when you get home is purchase a motorcycle just like the one the two of you rode together, only now, you will be the one in control."

"I don't think I could do that."

"I know you could."

Diane began to tear up as a result of the conversation.

"Do you want to know something funny?" Bates asked, trying to cheer her up. "The boat was originally named Aquila, just like the bird. One day, I was off in Brisbane taking care of some business when I came across this place that does tattoos. I thought, wouldn't it be wonderful to get a tattoo of a Wedge-Tailed

Eagle as a way of showing my dedication to our boat and our life together. So I had it done. It took the artist two bloody days. Well, unbeknownst to me, Hyzy decided during my absence to rename the boat to what it is now—Je t'aime. The evening I returned, after dinner, I pulled off my shirt and showed her my tattoo. I thought she was going to burst a gut laughing. When she finally got her wits about her, she took me by the hand to the stern and showed me the new name she had painted on the boat."

"What did you do?"

"I said there was still room on my ass and asked if I should have Je t'aime inked on it."

Diane began to laugh.

"Actually, we compromised and I had it inked on my shoulder with her name beneath it...Je t'aime Hyzy."

Bates leaned over and showed Diane that tattoo.

"Bruce had my name tattooed on his shoulder too...a lot like yours of Hyzy."

She moved close to Bates and kissed him on the cheek.

"You're a much different person than I originally thought, Captain Bates."

"Really, how is that?"

"At first, I was afraid of you. You seemed very rugged, very tough, very...a lot like a pirate, I thought. I didn't trust you."

"And now?"

Diane put her hand on Bates chest.

"You're a man I would like to know better."

"That is not likely to happen, madam. Before long, we'll be going our separate ways."

Diane stood up in front of Bates.

"When I want something, I get it. Got it?"

Diane finished unbuttoning her blouse and tossed it to the side.

She closed her eyes, imagining she was once again camping in the California mountains with Bruce, that they were alone, that they were sneaking as they occasionally did, a moment of discrete intimacy in a public place.

Boundaries

Bates stood and faced her. He lifted Diane higher onto a large rock so he could pull off her boots and pants. It was not long before she was naked. He then removed his shorts and the two lost souls slipped back into the water. Diane wrapped her legs around Bates waist and slowly slid down a wet, moss covered embankment. She had to maneuver slightly and then took several deep breaths as Bates began the long process of entering her. Once he reached the limit of what Diane could take, he began the rhythmic thrusting of his body against hers. She met his thrusts with those of her own. The water running between her back and the rock caused her to slide up and down almost as if she was weightless. Bates passionately squeezed Diane's breasts. She took his tongue into her mouth and sucked it hard as their bodies began pulsing as one.

As their bodies relaxed, Diane opened her eyes and looked at Bates. It was only then that she realized what she had done. As exhilarating as the experience with Bates had been, he wasn't Bruce, and she had betrayed Mickey. She felt sick to her stomach.

Bates had barely removed himself from Diane's body when there was a bone-crushing thud causing him to crumple onto the rocks—blood pouring from the top of his head. Two men stood over him; one held a club. Diane saw another figure—that of a woman—approaching her from the side. She walked quickly toward Diane.

"Where is Mickey?!" The woman shouted.

Diane momentarily froze with fear before realizing who was shouting at her. It was Genevieve. She bolted in the only direction that she thought offered her escape, took two steps, and then slipped on the rocks, viciously striking the front of her head on a large boulder in the process. Diane was dazed and could no longer stand, let alone walk or run. The two men pulled her up.

"I asked you, where is Mickey?!" Genevieve shouted louder this time.

Diane was barely conscious by now and unable to respond even if she wanted to.

"Help her remember," Genevieve commanded.

The two men took turns brutally striking and punching Diane about the head and torso with their fists.

"I will ask you only one more time, where is Mickey?"

Again, Diane was unable to answer.

"If she is here, he must be close by. Is she breathing?"

One of Genevieve's soldiers nodded.

Pointing toward the shoreline, Genevieve ordered, "Take her body and throw it on the beach next to the dead horse. We will wait for him. If Suki shows up, kill her, but I want Mickey Rollins alive."

Both men nodded, then took Diane's limp, naked body out to where the bloody carcass of the horse was sprawled on the beach and tossed her onto the sand. She was motionless. Genevieve looked at Bates, lying on the rocks. She took him by the arm and rolled him face down into the pool under the waterfall. After watching for a while, she was certain he would not be a problem.

MICKEY AND HERA SLOWLY made their way up the beach, following hoof prints left in the sand by Zeus. Suddenly, Mickey spotted an object ahead on the beach at the same time Hera began acting nervously. Mickey kicked her up to a trot and soon realized it was Zeus. Hera wouldn't go any closer.

Mickey dismounted and ran towards the horse's body.

"Diane!"

He finally got close enough to see her body lying next to Zeus on the opposite side from his approach. Mickey expected the worse—that she was dead. He slowly crouched down next to her and checked for signs of breathing and a pulse.

"Diane!"

Realizing she was still alive. He carefully rolled her over onto her back.

"Oh, my God," was his gut instinct remark as he saw Diane's black, blue, and swollen face and forehead. Those were Mickey's last words before he, too, was struck over the head. He fell forward onto Diane's body, but was able to get back up on his hands and knees. He didn't have to look for what had happened. It appeared before him when Genevieve stood over him holding the club. Her two accomplices stood by with their weapons drawn.

"It did not have to be like this, Mickey. All you had to do was tell me what I wanted to know the other day in Phuket. Instead you told me some bullshit story."

Genevieve kicked Mickey in the face, causing him to spit blood.

"You thought you could get me out of the picture long enough for you to disappear by sending me chasing after a lie."

She kicked Mickey in the ribs, causing him to fall over onto his side.

"Now we are playing for real, Mickey. You are going to tell me what I want to know, or Diane pays the price. She is still alive, but that can be a temporary condition. My men here would have a great time taking turns fucking her right here on the beach. Would you like that, Mickey?"

"Leave her alone, bitch!"

Genevieve bent down and took Mickey's chin in her hand.

"You have no idea how much trouble you are in, do you?"

"I said leave her alone!" Mickey managed to bark out again despite his pain.

"Or what?" Genevieve said, kicking Mickey in the stomach. She then nodded at her men.

Without hesitating, they rolled Diane over onto her belly. One of them drove the side of Diane's face into the sand with a knee on her neck while at the same time holding her around the waist so her buttocks were up in the air. Once in position, the other commenced raping her from behind.

"Are you enjoying this Mickey? All you have to do is tell me what I want to know about PicoPoint, and I will have them stop."

"Go fuck yourself."

Genevieve once again brought the club down on Mickey's ribs. He screamed in pain.

"You don't like Diane very much, do you? She must not like you either. She was fucking Captain Bates when I caught up with her."

The first man made groaning sounds indicating he was finishing his part of the assault. The two men looked toward Genevieve and she gave them a nod. They quickly changed positions and the second man began raping Diane.

"This can go on all day, Mickey. It can go on for many days. These men have a lot of energy and are deprived of pleasures such as this."

Mickey couldn't respond.

"I have another idea, when this man is done fucking your girlfriend, I think I will have them take her for a swim. Yeah, I'd like to see her swim for a while, how about you? Does she swim better face up or face down? I suppose we will have to try both ways."

The second man completed his part of the assault and pulled out of Diane's body just as Mickey opened his eyes. They let her body fall limp onto the sand again.

Mickey suddenly tried to get up and rush at the men, but Genevieve felled him with a blow to his right knee.

"Take her into the water!"

"Wait...." Mickey called out.

"Take her to the water and throw her in face down!"

Genevieve's men set their weapons on the dead horse's body, then did as they were ordered. It wasn't long before Diane's body was bobbing up and down on the waves.

"Wait, I'll do anything, just get her out of the water."

"No, you have it backwards. Start telling something worthwhile or she drowns."

"There's something called MADONNA..."

"Don't tell me Mendoza's part, I already know that! Tell me your part!"

"You know Mendoza?" Mickey asked, shocked that she knew his name in connection with PicoPoint.

"Mickey, Diane's dying, talk fa..."

Suddenly, there was a loud report from the tree line behind Mickey followed by a spray of bone fragments, blood, and brain tissue as Genevieve's head came apart, the result of high caliber gunfire. Her body fell backward onto the sand. Two more shots were fired, and Genevieve's men fell into the water. They both splashed in pain and struggled to get back to their weapons, but as they did so, their bodies were struck repeatedly by additional gunshots until they were floating motionless in the rolling surf.

Mickey looked up and saw Bates, undressed and blood running down his face, sprint into the water and pull Diane's body from the surf. He carried her to the beach, checked for breathing and a pulse, and then, finding none, began to resuscitate her lifeless body. Mickey got up, limped over to where the two were, and aided Bates in his efforts. After several minutes, Diane had a pulse and was breathing on her own, but she was still unconscious.

"Mickey!" Suki shouted, running down the beach toward the three.

She stopped short of where Mickey and Bates hovered over Diane, and examined the carnage before her.

"Is she alive?"

"Barely," said Bates.

"What happened?" Suki asked, as she held her hands to her cheeks, shocked and horrified by the scene.

"Genevieve found us," Mickey replied. "She wanted me to tell her about PicoPoint."

Full of rage, Mickey lunged at Suki, knocking her down. She immediately retaliated and after several kicks and punches, was on top of him in such a way that he was unable to move—her thumb pressed painfully into his throat.

Bates came to Suki's aid and held his gun to Mickey's head as he said, "I suggest you think hard before you make your next move."

"Did you tell Genevieve where we were going?" Mickey asked Suki.

"That would have been stupid. There is no reason I would do that."

"Then how did she find us?"

"She is a woman driven to extreme. If she wants something bad enough, she will stop at nothing to get it."

Mickey looked up at Bates and asked, "Did you lead her to us?"

Bates pulled the hammer back on his weapon.

"Stop!" Suki shouted. "He would never do that. I know him."

"How did she know Mendoza? Does she know your grandfather?"

"I am certain she has not met my grandfather. It is possible she has met Mendoza. He might have made a purchase from her."

Bates added, "You can almost be certain that if he needed young men or women for his research, she would be the best supplier."

"Supplier? Humans? For what purpose?"

"You know, his brain research," Suki said, her voice sounding guilty.

"He's doing human testing?"

"A lot. He has made great progress."

The three held their positions for a while until they realized no one would make a threatening move.

"Look, we have to get Diane some help. That is all that matters right now."

Suki slowly got off Mickey.

"The two of you need to get Diane up to the house. Do you still have a satellite phone and a GPS on your boat?" Suki asked Bates.

"Yes. Do you remember how to use them?"

"Not a problem. I will make some calls for assistance and have a helicopter come to the island to evacuate us back to Bangkok. From there, we can fly to whatever city is best for Diane's treatment—Hong Kong, Singapore, Manila."

"There's a heliport here?" Mickey asked.

"It is in a clearing about two hundred meters from the house. The owner frequently uses it." Suki looked at Diane. "How bad are her injuries?"

Mickey felt Diane's neck, then turned her head side to side, looked at her pupils, her ears, and pressed on her chest and abdomen.

"She obviously has a pretty severe head injury. At least her pupils are still equal and responding, and her breathing is normal. Her eyes, nose and mouth are full of sand. Her face is really beat up—probably some broken bones. I don't feel any broken bones in her chest, but that doesn't mean there aren't some internal injuries. She's in really bad shape. Those two men…both of them raped her."

"How about you?" Suki asked, putting her hand on Mickey's shoulder.

"I hurt everywhere."

"Sorry."

"And what's this I hear you...were banging Diane?" Mickey asked Bates.

"She had a need, I satisfied it," Bates replied.

Mickey tried to lunge at Bates, but Suki pushed him down. She then turned and brought her fist across Bates face knocking him into the sand. Stomping on his wrist, the gun came loose from his hand. Suki grabbed the gun, stood up over Bates body and fired two shots into the sand—one on either side of his head.

"If you ever touch her again, I will kill you, do you understand me?"

Bates nodded. Suki threw the gun at him, confident that her reputation for rapid and forceful self-defense would protect her.

"Now, both of you, get her up to the house."

"I'm not sure I can walk that far," Mickey complained.

Suki grabbed Mickey by the shirt and pulled him up.

"Mickey, this is all about Diane now. Nobody cares about you or your pain. Diane and I will leave from the heliport hopefully in two hours or so. I hope you are there when the helicopter leaves because I will not wait for you. Am I perfectly clear?"

Mickey nodded.

"Treat her with the utmost care, and put her in the bathtub with some ice. Be sure to rinse the sand from her eyes with fresh water and clean out her nose and mouth the best you can. I will try to get in touch with my grandfather. I am certain he knows of some natural therapies we can begin while we wait for help to arrive. He will know what to do."

"What about the bodies?" Mickey asked, pointing to Genevieve and the two men floating just off the beach.

Suki looked at Bates.

"My people will take care of the bodies and the horse. Tell them to come on shore. Tell them I told them to clean up the situation and to ask no questions. They have done this type of thing before."

Book 4

"Where did you get this book?" Dr. Mason asked.

"It belongs to Suki. I took it from her room when I left the ranch. She told me once that it was the written summary of her grandfather's research, and that it was guiding Mickey in his work to restore my memory. I hoped it might be useful to someone who could help."

"I can get it to Dr. Liaw," Dr. Madden said. "I'm certain she can at least give us an idea whether she can translate it or not."

"We have to be careful, Bev. It could be very dangerous if word of this project leaks out. Only give her parts from a couple of pages to look at to first see if she can make any sense of it."

"I'd offer to help, but I can't read Chinese. It's so weird, I can speak Chinese, but I can't read it. It was one of those unexpected quirks in the project."

"What do you mean?"

"Well, Dr. Madden, when Mickey and Dr. Mendoza were transferring thoughts and emotions and functions from Suki to me, they didn't realize that they were stored in her mind in her predominant language. Mickey says I first became aware of myself about four weeks into the therapy when, much to their astonishment, I began to speak in Chinese. By that time, they had transferred a significant amount of information from her to me. It would take several more weeks of thought transfer from before I would be capable of speaking in English. But listen to me, I'm Chinese…"

Diane began to comfortably speak in what Mason and Madden could only assume was Chinese.

"Remarkable!" Dr. Mason said, smiling like a new father. Noticing Dr. Madden was staring at Diane in total amazement, he asked, "Are you alright, Beverly?"

"Loarn, an hour ago, I thought there was nothing left that could shock me. Am I supposed to believe that Diane is the subject of this project you describe where memories, thoughts, and, I guess, functions are transferred from one person to another? The evidence of this is that she can now speak Chinese?"

"I've never studied Chinese," Diane said in an upset tone of voice. "Dr. Mason, I thought you said she was going to help. Get her away from me…now!"

"Ms. Alders, do you know what happens when a person has symptoms of bipolar disorder?"

"You're not listening to me!" Diane screamed, pounding her fists on the exam room cabinets.

Moments later, one nurse, followed by a second, and then a security guard came into the room.

"Dr. Mason, do you need help?" asked the first nurse.

"Excuse me," Dr. Madden interrupted. "You knock before you enter an examination room when I have a patient. Is that understood?"

The nurses and the guard looked at one another, puzzled by the admonishment.

"Do you need us, Dr. Madden?"

"What I need is for the three of you to leave. We are working with a patient, and things may get a little loud from time to time. If we need you," Dr. Madden looked directly at Diane, "and I am certain that we will not, I will call for you."

"Sorry, Dr. Madden."

The three left the room and closed the door.

"Beverly, can you describe, in the simplest of terms, the symptoms of a person with bipolar disorder for Ms. Alders."

"Yes," Madden replied. "Not what she is experiencing."

"You just think I'm some crazy bitch, don't you?"

"No. I think you're very frustrated and scared. Something has happened to you, and it has you so upset that before we can begin to help, we have to wade through all of these questions."

Diane paused to give Dr. Madden her due, then continued.

"Dr. Madden, open your notebook to a clean sheet of paper."

"Why?"

"Just do it, please."

She opened her notebook as Diane requested.

"Dr. Mason, hold my left hand."

Mason did as he was asked.

Diane reached into Dr. Madden's coat pocket and pulled out a pen, then began to write in the book. When she was done, she handed the book back to her.

"What did I write?"

Madden looked at the book, then began reciting, "I think you're very frustrated, and you're scared...has you upset...all of these questions. It looks like what I just said to you a moment ago."

"How would you describe my handwriting? Is it legible?"

Again, Dr. Madden looked at the book.

"Your handwriting is excellent, why?"

"I'm left-handed," Diane replied.

Dr. Madden looked at the book, mentally oriented herself to Diane's position and what had just taken place, then asked, "I don't follow you."

"I have pictures of me from before the beating. I am wearing my wristwatch on my right wrist. That would mean I was left-handed. I thought perhaps the photo was printed in reverse, but the person I am with has his watch on his left wrist, and he is right handed. In all of my pictures from before the beating, I am wearing my watch on my right wrist."

"Perhaps you're ambidextrous."

"No! It's because Suki is right-handed. I picked that up from her just like I picked up the Chinese."

"I guess that's possible," Madden said, hesitantly.

"I have never hurt anyone in my life, at least not to my knowledge. I know that Suki has killed before. I heard about that in Asia when I first met her. She used to drop it into the conversation from time to time over the years. It was sort of a sick joke. Yesterday, I remembered that I took a scalpel and stabbed her grandfather in the heart the first day of my treatment in Manila. Is it possible that I picked that up from her, too—I mean, the ability to kill a person? I think Mickey wants only the best for me, and Suki gave me a lot of good qualities, and I have to think I wouldn't be what I am today if it weren't for them. But, I also think there are parts of her that transferred to me that were unintended consequences. I don't think what they did was perfect. So, please tell me I'm not a murderer. Tell me someone else made me do it. Tell me I didn't have control. Please..."

"Loarn, what do we do. Has a crime been committed?"

Dr. Mason looked at both ladies and replied, "Well, as they say on television, we have no body. We don't know if the accusation is true, and if it is, the matter took place in another county. Therefore, I recommend we discuss this further over coffee and breakfast at the restaurant for which we were leaving earlier. Does anyone care to join me?"

Chapter 25

Chi-feng Wu looked like an archetypical, elderly Chinaman. He wore a traditional embroidered silk jacket with a Chinese twin-dragons pattern, Mandarin collar, frog buttons, white dragon silk pants, and black emperor slippers. A thin beard extended several inches below his chin. His face was thin, exaggerating its features, and his slight frame carried no more than one hundred twenty pounds. Despite his unimposing appearance, his very presence begat an air of authority and great wisdom. It was clear he was not a man to be trifled with.

Dr. Wu entered the lobby of the medical facility in Manila that dealt with brain injuries. There, a team of specialists had admitted Diane for treatment after she was evacuated from the island and subsequently stabilized at a hospital in Bangkok. He was unable to proceed through locked doors without introducing himself to a receptionist.

"My name is Wu, Dr. Wu. I am looking for Dr. Mendoza or Dr. Rollins."

"Yes sir, we are expecting you," the receptionist responded.

"I think not, otherwise the doors would not be locked."

"It is for security reasons, Dr. Wu. Please understand."

"No. I do not understand. Does it appear to you that I am a security threat?"

"Well, of course not, Dr. Wu."

"Then I suggest you unlock the door at once."

"One moment, sir, and I will have…"

Fortunately, the receptionist was spared additional agony when Mickey came out the door.

"C-F, thank you for coming."

Few people would be allowed to address Dr. Wu in such a familiar manner.

"It would appear you were involved in the altercation as well, Dr. Rollins," Wu said, noting Mickey's limp and his cuts and bruises.

"I'm fine, just some minor injuries here and there."

"You have taken me from my gardens. I have in the past left my gardens for other pursuits only twice—when my son passed away and when my wife passed away. You are like a son to me, and you say that you need me because someone you love is very badly hurt. If I can help you, I will offer all of myself to you."

Just then, Suki came through the door. She stopped in her tracks as soon as she saw Dr. Wu. It was then that the strain in their relationship became clear.

"Hello, Grandfather," Suki said, bowing her head and folding her hands behind her back in complete submission.

"Dr. Rollins, I will see to your friend shortly. First, I must have words with my granddaughter."

Wu tapped on the receptionist's desk with his knuckles.

"Is there a private room I can use—hopefully on this side of the razor wire?"

"Of course, Dr. Wu. There is a room just to the right as you walk past the door."

She stood up and presented Dr. Wu with a badge that had 'Visitor' printed on it in a bold font and at the same time presented him with a registration book that he was to sign.

"If you would, please?"

"I most certainly will not!"

Again, the receptionist was spared further distress when Dr. Mendoza walked through the door.

"Dr. Wu, welcome to my facility, and please accept my sincere apology. Veronica, the badge and signature are not necessary for our special guest. Make certain everyone on staff understands that."

"Yes sir, Dr. Mendoza."

"Gentlemen, I think we should meet at once in my office," Mendoza hastily proposed.

"Is there any change in her condition?" Mickey asked.

"No change, she's stable, but we need to proceed soon. Please."

Mendoza gestured toward the door.

"I must first speak to my granddaughter."

Mendoza was surprised by Dr. Wu's priority and lack of urgency.

"I assure you that we should proceed quickly, doctor. The patient has sustained a devastating brain injury, and she appears to have significant cognitive and motor deficits."

"And I assure you that I must speak to my granddaughter, and the longer we labor over this matter, the longer it will be before we can discuss our treatments for Dr. Rollins' dear friend."

One could imagine the posturing and strain between Roosevelt, Churchill, and Stalin at Yalta. Such as it was today in Manila between Mickey, Dr. Wu, and Dr. Mendoza. It was clear that each of the three held a key to the lock on Pandora's Box, and each was going to guard his to the bitter end.

"Very well, Dr. Wu," Mendoza conceded. "As soon as you are done speaking with Suki, please let the secretary just outside your meeting room know you are finished so she can escort you to where I will be."

Dr. Wu wasn't satisfied with Mendoza's proposal.

"I also wish to be alone with the patient for a while before we speak."

"But Dr. Wu, she is unconscious and heavily sedated. I can review my findings with you in short order once the three of us meet."

"I rely on my own assessment, Dr. Mendoza. Mine does not rely upon computers, models, or laboratory results. I must see and touch the patient."

It was clear from Mendoza's facial expression that he was already frustrated with Dr. Wu, but he also knew that the Chinaman had a very unique and deliberate way of dealing with patients, and that his method was not going to be swayed.

"Certainly, Dr. Wu. So, when you are done speaking with Suki, the secretary can escort you to me and I will take you to the patient."

"For the record, the patient has a name—it's Diane," Mickey said. "I don't want anybody to forget who she is or how much she means to me."

Dr. Wu put his hand on Mickey's shoulder in a gesture of kindness and sympathy, then Mendoza opened the door for his guests. Suki and her grandfather turned right into the small conference room. Mendoza closed the door behind them. Suki kept her eyes averted from her grandfather as she remained standing, her head bowed, her hands still behind her back, quietly hoping her grandfather would remain across the room from where she stood. Instead, he walked uncharacteristically close to her before speaking.

"It has been a long time, Sukhon, since we last spoke. Why is it I am not surprised you once again have brought embarrassment to this family?"

"Grandfather, I…."

"I am not ready to listen to answers to my questions! I did not raise you to live your life in such a way that it would continuously bring harm to others, let alone yourself. I raised you to follow a path that would make Buddha proud. You were given the best education, not to mention many promising opportunities, yet you squander it on what you call a career that is nothing more than the shameless sale of your body."

"Grandfather, please let me…."

"Once again, your actions have resulted in the injury of another person. I have yet to discover how many have died in this most recent escapade of yours, but I am certain I will soon find out, and that number will not be zero! As always, I will have to use my influence to ensure that these deaths remain unnoticed in order to protect what remains of our family honor."

"I was on vacation with Mickey when…"

"This time, you dare to tarnish the good name and reputation of Dr. Rollins. I forbid you to mention his name ever again. You are not worthy of mentioning his name! Here is a man whose work has a chance to return life and function to many people who are desperately ill or injured. What do you do? You let him use your body as a distraction from his work. His rate of progress has slowed greatly since the day he met you. I must sadly take complete responsibility for that unfortunate moment in time. It was I who introduced him to you in the hope he might steer you in a proper direction in life. Instead, it is you who has taken Dr. Rollins under a dark cloud."

By now, Suki was sobbing uncontrollably as her grandfather's words pierced her like knives.

"I pray for you Sukhon. I pray that someday soon, you will recognize the wrong path you have chosen. I pray that you will find the path of our spiritual leader. I pray that you will improve the lives of those you encounter. I pray that you will become a great leader of women and of men. I pray that when you leave this Earth, people will reflect upon your life as one of selfless giving. But I am growing old, so I must pray that these changes come soon, or I will never see the beginning of them."

Dr. Wu ended his verbal assault of Suki. He waited a while to hear if she had anything to say, but all she offered was silence. That being the case, he turned and left the room. When the door closed, Suki crumbled onto the floor, crying.

MICKEY AND DR. MENDOZA watched through an observation window as Dr. Wu meticulously examined Diane. Mendoza had taken her off of the ventilator earlier in the day, and she was now breathing on her own. Her face and head were still badly bruised. In fact, since the time of the beating, the bruising and swelling had slowly worsened. Wu paid no attention to the vast array of instruments monitoring Diane's body functions, preferring to instead exam her eyes extensively and probing all areas of her body with a sharp graphite stylus that he carried in a wooden case. In addition, he spent considerable time placing his hands on Diane's body, feeling it move, feeling texture, feeling temperature.

"The man is out of touch with technology, Mickey. He is a complete dinosaur," Mendoza said.

"If you think about it, he is completely in touch with the foundations of the technology you are so proud of."

"Why waste time? He will come out eventually, I should hope, and tell us what I already know. He is depriving the patient of care. You, Mickey, are depriving Diane of the expeditious treatment that she needs. Why I let you bring this old man into this case is beyond me. He has spent two hours with her. We should be well into the therapy by now."

"Well, I think you are going to find out what he has to say any minute. It looks like he is coming out."

"I will try to restrain myself from being too shocked by his revelations," Mendoza closed with an obvious sarcastic tone.

Dr. Wu left Diane's room and closed the door behind him.

"We can speak now."

Mendoza ushered Dr. Wu to an adjoining room.

"I would like some green tea, if that is not too much trouble," Dr. Wu requested, stopping just inside the doorway.

"Of course," Mendoza replied. "Mickey, can I get you anything?"

"Just water."

Waving at his secretary, Mendoza ordered, "Green tea and two waters. Be quick!"

She scurried off to meet his request, and the three took seats around a wooden table.

"So, Dr. Wu, what do you think?" Mendoza asked.

"I must have tea first. We can wait."

"I must tell you, Dr. Wu, I am a patient man, but my patience is wearing thin."

"I am sorry for you, my friend," Wu said, sitting calmly in his chair, observing Mendoza's body language. Turning to Mickey, Wu asked, "So, Dr. Rollins, how long have you known the patient?"

"About three years."

Wu looked at Mickey for a while before continuing, "Is she as physically active and healthy as she appears to be?"

"Very much so."

"Is she from a healthy family?"

"As far as I know, they were generally healthy. Her father died from cancer, but he was in his seventies when he died."

A secretary entered the room with a tray carrying an urn of green tea and several bottles of water. She sat it on the table and poured Dr. Wu his tea.

"Thank you, my dear. You are most kind."

She offered Mickey a bottle of water to which he replied, "Thank you."

Finally, she offered her boss a bottle of water. He was much less appreciative.

"You know I like only sparkling water. Please come back with the correct beverage."

The secretary hastily left the room.

"So, Dr. Wu, what did you find in your examination?" Mendoza pressed upon his guest.

Wu sat calmly sipping his tea.

"This is quite good. I think everyone should enjoy green tea several times each day. What do you think, Dr. Rollins?"

"I've never acquired a taste for hot tea."

"Do you drink café?"

"Yes, actually. Coffee and espresso."

"You should then try green tea. It is much better for the mind and the body," Wu continued while sipping his tea.

"Dr. Wu, we need to proceed. Do you have any observations you wish to share with us? If so, please get on with them," Mendoza said, showing obvious frustration with the pace of events.

"Yes, of course," Wu replied. "Tell me, Dr. Rollins, is the patient a career woman?"

"Yes, she's a marketing executive for a medical device company in San Diego. She's the best in her field."

"Of course, the best…yes. San Diego, you say? I have not been to San Diego. What can you tell me about where she lives?"

Jumping to his feet, Mendoza insisted, "Mickey, we need to begin the therapy. Dr. Wu is obviously not going to contribute anything more than what we already know."

"In what order do you wish to proceed with the therapy, Dr. Mendoza?" Wu asked.

Not wanting to show his hand, Mendoza answered with a question of his own.

Boundaries

"Where do you suggest we begin, Dr. Wu?"

"Emotions."

"Emotions?" Mendoza chuckled. "Why not motor functions?"

"Her motor functions will be fine."

"How do you know that?"

"I just know! The patient is experiencing something I have seen many times before. I call it 'eyes without a face.' She sees, but cannot understand. She lacks the capacity for self-knowledge at this point. Her injury is mainly to the front of her brain where emotions reside. Emotions are a fundamental mechanism of existence. Begin there, and you will successfully reconstruct the person you once knew. Begin elsewhere, and I cannot make the same promise.

"I disagree with you, Dr. Wu. Mickey, what do you want to do?"

"Hey, I'm just the hardware guy. But, if C-F says we start with emotions, I think we should start with emotions."

That wasn't the response Mendoza was looking for. Attempting to find a hole in Dr. Wu's proposal, he persisted with his challenge.

"Alright, let's boil it down further. What particular emotions do you want to target first?"

"Oh, that is quite simple, yes, quite simple. You appear to need early validation of your therapy so let me suggest these: anger, disgust, fear, joy, sadness and surprise."

"Why those?" Mickey asked.

"These produce the same facial expressions in all of human-kind. Reinstate these emotions and you will see rapid demonstration of success in the patient's face. She will no longer have 'eyes without a face.'"

Mickey and Mendoza exchanged looks.

"You know, Ricardo, I think he has a good proposal. A beta-immersion like this will yield quick results. That would give us proof of concept as well as a sense of viability for the ongoing reconstruction."

"Dr. Mendoza," Wu asked, "would you mind pouring me some more tea?"

In fencing, Wu's request would be called a 'coup de grace.'

"I'll send in my secretary," Mendoza replied. He then turned and left the room.

Mickey got up himself and poured Dr. Wu another cup of tea.

"Thank you, my friend." Wu sipped his tea and sat quietly for a while before continuing, "Dr. Rollins, the gardens where I spend my day were planted by my grandfather's grandfather's grandfather. It has taken until now for them to become full of color and full of life as one sees them today. Beauty and vitality takes time. That is an important concept that your young associate fails to grasp."

"That may be the case, C-F, but I can't do this without him."

"You would be surprised at what you can do with what only you and I know."

"Are you suggesting we stop working with Ricardo?"

"It is unfortunate that we are in the situation in which we find ourselves. Now is perhaps not the best time for us to part ways with Dr. Mendoza. But, in the future, when I am no longer of this Earth, all you will need is my book."

"What book?"

"You will know. When that time comes—and it will come—you will know."

There was a knock on the door. It slowly opened and Suki appeared.

"Forgive me Grandfather, but I saw Dr. Mendoza walking out of the room and he looked upset. Is everything alright with Diane?"

"You ask me to excuse your interruption, but not Dr. Rollins?"

"It's alright, C-F." Turning to respond to Suki, he said, "Diane will be fine. We just had a discussion about where to begin our work, and there was a disagreement about that one subject. But, rest assured, Diane is stable."

"Her injuries are not life-threatening?"

"Sukhon! Dr. Rollins just told you that the patient would be fine. I suggest you apologize for doubting his word."

"C-F, Suki and Diane are close friends. She is showing a concern for her well-being. I take no offense to what she is asking."

Suki was desperately trying to regain her grandfather's trust.

"Would you care for more tea, Grandfather?"

Boundaries

There was a long period where Dr. Wu was apparently examining all of Suki's motives for her offer, but he eventually responded, "Yes, child."

Suki poured his tea and smiled her first smile in a long time.

Wu watched Suki's expression and movements. There was a glimmer of a smile on his face, too.

"I see the face of your father when I look at your eyes, and then I see the face of your mother when you smile. They gave you their best qualities. You must cherish and protect them. I fear they will be harmed if you do not change the way that you live your life."

"Grandfather, I promise I will change."

"Yes, my child, as you have said you would do many times before."

"Grandfather, Diane is buying a ranch in California, near San Francisco. She asked if I would move there and manage the ranch for her."

Wu set his cup down in its saucer.

"Is this true?" He asked, looking at Mickey.

"Yes, C-F, that's one of the reasons we met with Suki on our vacation. I thought she would be great for the job."

There was a pause as Dr. Wu thought about what had been said.

"San Francisco, yes. There is a Chinatown there if I am not mistaken."

Suki saw that perhaps her grandfather was warming to the idea.

"That is correct. We could visit there, you and me."

"I would like to see this place called Chinatown," Wu said, a wide grin growing across his face. Suddenly, his expression turned serious and he asked, "What type of a ranch is this place you will be taking care of?"

"It's a ranch that breeds and sells thoroughbred horses," Mickey answered for Suki.

"Breeding horses? Child, what do you know about breeding horses?"

"Breeding horses is a lot like gardening, Grandfather. It is about carefully managing the pollen. You taught me everything about that."

Suki had struck home with her remark.

"Yes, and you were a good gardener," Wu said with pride.

"You were a good teacher," Suki said, feeling an intense sensation of relief.

"No, I am an excellent teacher."

The relative calm in the conference room was jolted when Mendoza returned. He immediately rushed to speak.

"Let's suppose we pursue Dr. Wu's choices for therapy. I can find you any number of suitable surrogates for motor therapy. Who do you suggest for emotion replacement? I would think you would want to be highly selective, am I right?"

Mendoza looked around the room at Wu, then Mickey, and then he noticed that Suki was in the room.

"Why is she here?"

Wu didn't hesitate to respond.

"I agree with you, Dr. Mendoza. The surrogate must be chosen carefully." He sipped his tea. "Dr. Rollins, as it is the case that Diane is a close friend of yours, I want you to close your eyes and begin describing her with adjectives you would use if you were to tell me of her for the first time. Pretend that you are an artist with a palate of colors and you have a blank canvas on which to paint her. Pretend that I am blind, yet you must make me see her come to life."

"Gentlemen, please, we don't have time for this nonsense!" Mendoza shouted.

Wu held up his hand.

"Dr. Rollins, please begin."

Mickey took a drink of from his bottle of water, closed his eyes, and started to describe Diane.

"She's intelligent, understanding, kind, incredibly beautiful, and sensual. She has a wild side. She's cunning, strong-willed, compassionate, loving, vivacious, caring, intense...."

"Stop," Wu said. "Dr. Mendoza, repeat your question."

"I said this was nonsense."

"No, I want your question!"

"I think I asked why she was here," Mendoza replied, pointing at Suki.

Dr. Wu looked at Mendoza, then at his granddaughter. "Can you possibly answer your own question?"

"What, her?" Mendoza shouted.

"Suki? Mickey echoed.

"Me?" Suki asked.

"I look at your canvas, Dr. Rollins, and I see my granddaughter."

"What are you asking me to do?" Suki asked, unsure of what might be in store for her.

Wu stood and walked to his granddaughter. He put his hands on her shoulders.

"Sukhon, you have an opportunity to do something great, not only for this individual, Diane, but also for mankind."

"You mean…"

"You could be the surrogate from which we heal your friend. There is no question that you are capable. There is no question that you are a perfect match for her. The only remaining question is, are you willing to give yourself to her?"

Suki looked at the others in the room. Nobody was going to help her with the decision. She was forced to reflect on what her grandfather had said to her, and about her, when they met earlier. Was this the time for her to answer a higher calling? It was as if her life was flashing before her eyes as she thought of things she had done with her life and things she wished she had done differently. It was, in the final analysis, her grandfather's desire that she be remembered for her selfless giving that swayed her decision.

"I will do anything I can for my friend."

Wu smiled and nodded at his granddaughter. Mickey got up and hugged her tightly. Mendoza was not happy with how they had reached this point, but at least now they would be able to proceed.

"Mickey?"

"Yes, Suki?"

"There is one more thing we must do for Diane."

"What's that?"

She hesitated for a moment before answering, "Remember, Diane might be pregnant with your child."

Shaking his head, Mickey said, "Suki, she was raped. The doctors in Bangkok said there was a lot of trauma."

"But did anyone check to see if she was pregnant? Was she treated?"

Mickey looked at Mendoza who shrugged his shoulders and said, "That wasn't our priority, Mickey."

"If she is pregnant with your child, maybe there is something that can be done. We have treatments here in Asia that are not available in the U.S. Maybe she could carry the child to term this time."

"That puts everything at risk," Mendoza replied. "We have far too much to concern ourselves with other than fetal development and the complications of a pregnancy. I can call a gynecological doctor to treat her for injuries as well as terminate the fetus if there is one."

"Is that what you want, Mickey?" Suki asked, "Because I do not think that is what Diane would want. I think it would fulfill her greatest dream to have a baby with you. This could be her only chance."

"It's out of the question, Mickey," Mendoza firmly asserted.

"What do you think, C-F?"

"Renewal of life is our primary purpose as a species. I suggest we consider the possibility that there are two patients, then as my wise granddaughter suggests, care for both of them."

Mendoza stormed out of the room in anger.

Chapter 26

"Certainly, Rajeev. Yes, I'll phone you daily with an update. No, as I said before, it's best that you stay in San Diego for now. I'll let you know if there is any reason for you to come to Manila. And Rajeev, thank you again for your kind words, and for your company's generous financial support. I know this is what Diane would have wanted. She's in good hands. Right. I'll phone you at the same time tomorrow. Goodbye."

Mickey sat back in the chair in his hotel room.

"Whew. That went better than I had expected."

"Did you say something?" Suki asked, stepping out of the luxurious bathroom wearing a posh, white robe with *The Peninsula* embroidered on it. Her hair was wet, but combed. "I just love these robes," she said, rubbing her hands over her sleeves.

"Diane's company agreed to fund all of the medical expenses and ongoing research needed for Diane's recovery for up to twelve months. Rajeev's really upset, but I think I have him calm enough to function. I didn't realize he was so close to her."

"Diane is the type of person who draws people close to her without expending any effort."

"You're right."

Mickey put his head in his hands.

"This has been a fucking nightmare, you know?"

Suki sat on the arm of the chair and put her arm around Mickey.

"We have all been through a lot. I am sorry your vacation turned out to be such a disaster. I never should have taken you to a place where Genevieve could find you. She used to be a wonderful person. But times change and so do people."

"I'll say this much, Bates is a good shot. I don't know what kind of a gun he had, but he sure finished her off quickly, as well as her bastard thugs."

"Let us not talk about that anymore."

"I was really helpless, Suki. There wasn't anything I could do to protect Diane."

"I know. They were very bad people, and they did things that normal people would not even consider. It is hard to defend yourself, let alone someone else, against that sort of person."

Suki pulled Mickey by the hand.

"You need to come to bed. It is two o'clock in the morning. We have to be at the clinic at eight, and you have to be able to think."

After undressing down to his boxers, Mickey began to shiver.

"I don't know if I'm getting sick or if I'm tired or both."

"Let me warm you up."

Suki opened her robe and wrapped it around Mickey, holding his flesh close to hers.

"I love this hotel. I remember our first time here. We were two rooms down the hall from this one."

Kissing Suki on top of her head, Mickey held up short.

"I can't do this Suki…I mean, Diane's not here."

"I am not asking you to make love. I am warming your body with mine. Now come to bed."

The two crawled under the covers together where Suki continued to hold Mickey tightly.

"You do not feel as though you have a fever. I think you are simply exhausted."

"Ouch."

"What?"

"You squeezed my ribs where Genevieve bashed me with that log."

"Sorry."

Boundaries

There were several minutes of silence before Suki asked, "Do you think Mendoza will cooperate with my grandfather and you to see to Diane's full recovery?"

"I'm certain he will, though his motives have nothing to do with Diane. It's all about money to him—success and money. He could give a rat's ass about the patient."

"Maybe you should consider doing your work without him."

"I can't do that right now."

"I think you could."

Looking over at Suki, Mickey said, "Your grandfather told me essentially the same thing at the clinic."

"He is right, you know. He is always right."

"He said something to the effect that after he's gone, he'll leave behind a book. It sounded to me as though it was a compilation of his work, including all of his new research."

Suki stopped stroking Mickey's chest for a moment, then said, "Grandfather finished his work on the mind ten years ago. There is nothing new. The only thing that can be considered remotely new is that I finished the book for him five years ago."

"You summarized his work for him?"

"Yes. He said he hoped it would change my course in life by challenging me with new revelations. I found it hard to take too seriously. I was younger then, and much less mature—a bit rebellious, I should say. So I made a game out of writing it, turning it into a puzzle. It took me four years to complete. He dictated and I wrote, at least that is what he thought. When we were done and I showed him the finished book, he found he was unable to make sense of all that I had put together. That was because I encrypted it with stories that my mother and father told me as a child, analogies of the flowers we grew in our garden, and the tales of an old fisherman we knew."

"I'd think he would have been really pissed off."

"Actually, I remember his exact words as if he had spoken them just this morning. He said, 'Sukhon, what I have told you is the secret to life itself, to one's own existence. It cannot fall into the wrong hands or be misused in any way. Since I will no longer be walking this Earth in too many more years, it is you who must protect what we know with your life. The clever way you have captured my thoughts has documented my work and spared me much worry at the same time.' Then, he thanked me."

"Maybe that's why your grandfather didn't object to you coming with us to the States. He said something to the effect that, when his life ended, the book would come to me, and that I would know what it was when I had it. Could he have been talking about you?"

"Your future lies next to you, my love."

Mickey was glad he had been shivering, because those words evoked a tremendous nervous shaking throughout his body.

"Are you alright?"

"Yeah, dandy."

Mickey pulled Suki's head tightly to his chest. It was clear to him now that the future to which Suki referred—the one he so dearly wanted with Diane— would forever have Suki engrained as a part in it. Entrapment was an inaccurate description for what Suki and Dr. Wu had done, but in truth, a trap it was, and Mickey had fallen into its web, taking Diane with him.

THE MORNING CAME QUICKLY and with it came the arduous commute from the hotel to the clinic. There was no such thing as an easy commute around Manila. The system of roads and highways were made for a population a fraction its size. The limousine only achieved what one could call full speed once it reached the highway heading south, beginning the forty or so kilometer drive to a place near Calamba in the Province of Laguna where Mendoza's clinic was located.

Boundaries

Dr. Wu remained at the hotel in Manila where he could relax before joining the rest at the clinic that afternoon when the real work would begin. The morning would be spent educating Suki on what to expect in the days and weeks ahead.

The limousine pulled to a stop at the clinic where a security guard opened the door for them. Suki stepped out and slowly made her way to the door, stopping along the way to admire the regional mountains and volcano, wondering when she would next see the light of day.

Mendoza met them at the door.

"Good morning, Mickey," he said, shaking Mickey's hand. "Good morning, Suki."

He proceeded to kiss her on the cheek.

Suki was wary of the Hyde-to-Jekyll transformation that had overtaken Mendoza since she had last seen him. As the three entered the building and walked to a treatment room, Suki asked, "Has something bad happened to Diane?"

"Quite the opposite," a jovial Mendoza replied. "She was quite active last night. In fact, she began moving her arms and legs so much we had to deepen her level of sedation. Her condition is what we would term combative."

"That is good, correct? I mean, she is moving. Do we even need to perform your procedure?" she asked, taking a seat.

If it weren't for the fact that Mickey, not Mendoza, answered her question, Suki might have climbed back into the limousine and left.

"Unfortunately, all of Ricardo's tests indicate the nature of Diane's injury affects her abilities in ways other than physical movement. Your grandfather himself said that her motor functions would return to normal. She might need physical therapy, but she will move normally again. It's her ability to reason, her rationality, and her memory that are going to be most significantly disabled. Your cerebral functions and thoughts will be a catalyst that will enable her to recover some of that on her own.

"We have to evaluate Diane for her deficits. Where there are most certainly voids, we need to make a replacement. Where her functions and memories are whole, we need to leave those parts of her mind untouched. Where there is a question, we need to decide if we should wait for time to heal the deficit, or if we should move forward. Let me make it clear, the point at which Diane is today, doing nothing is a terrible option."

Mendoza then added, "We have a lot of experience with the type of traumatic brain injury Diane sustained. Certainly, there is the option of waiting patiently for her brain to heal on its own, but the chance of that happening spontaneously is poor, and the prognosis for complete rehabilitation is worse. Our therapy offers the best chance for Diane to return to a completely normal life in the shortest possible time."

Mickey quietly reflected upon something Dr. Wu had said the prior day about his garden—that beauty and vitality took a long time. For the first time, he felt uneasy about administering the therapy on Diane, and using Suki as the host.

"Is it without risk?" Suki asked.

Mendoza and Mickey exchanged glances. They knew they had to be honest with her.

"Suki," Mickey replied, "there is always a risk when we explore a new frontier such as this. It'll be critical that we transfer not only the functions being extracted from you, but also the boundaries within which the patient can operate safely and appropriately. Ricardo has an algorithm that has proven in limited testing to work exceptionally well. That doesn't mean we won't hit a bump or two along the way."

"A bump?"

"Something unexpected that we will have to deal with," Mickey explained. "We'll have to slow down the process if that happens to analyze what we are up against."

Mendoza was surprised by Mickey's response, especially since he wanted to proceed as aggressively as possible.

"Everything you have told me concerns Diane. What about the risks for me?"

Again, the two doctors realized they had to be honest. The pause made Suki take a seat.

Boundaries

After taking a seat next to her, Mickey explained, "There's something we call diminishment. It's not exactly like degeneration, but the result is the same. Every function or thought you exchange with Diane will cause you to lose a very small amount of the same. Our data indicates the impact to you is probably not noticeable unless we, uh…"

Suki finished Mickey's statement, "…hit a bump?"

"Well, it's more than a bump. Our goal is to transfer a prescribed amount of a thought or function so that the diminishment is negligible. If we fail to achieve the target transfer, we will have to decide whether or not to complete it. If the transfer fails completely, we have to decide if we should repeat the process. Think of it as momentum. You are providing the initial push, but it is up to Diane to complete the journey by making the anecdotal connections. Our decision to complete or repeat an unsuccessful transfer is not a decision we will take lightly, and it would be very dependent upon the specific host."

"In what way would it depend upon me?"

"Think of it this way," Mendoza answered, "If the host is a strong-willed person, we might be able to transfer a significant amount of that attribute to a patient without the host experiencing any detectable diminishment. On the other hand, if we were to transfer the same amount of that attribute from a weak host to a patient, doing so could have profound effects."

Mickey put his hand on Suki's and squeezed it firmly before saying, "This is why you are such a perfect host. You are what we refer to as a 'high-boundary' host in virtually every aspect. You are in excellent physical health. You live your life to the extreme. You are highly intelligent. You are highly passionate. You are highly intuitive. I can put 'highly' in front of every descriptive you can think of. You have so much to give, if you will."

"It sounds like you feel as though you have control of the situation. But, based on what little I know of my grandfather's work, do you really?"

Mendoza chuckled and rubbed his hand over his head, then said, "Mickey, you told me she is intelligent. You should have emphasized that she is extraordinarily perceptive as well."

"So, you do not have complete control of the situation."

"Actually, you may know this part," Mickey answered. "Your grandfather postulates that it is possible, though improbable, that a beta immersion might result in an unexpected release of dopamine by the brain. This could cause the patient to experience a unique type of euphoria and a thirst for more of the function or thought to be transferred than we prescribe. In Ricardo's algorithm, the host controls the 'send' action. But, if the patient has a dramatic increase in the euphoria, the patient's 'take' action goes into high gear and can, in theory, overtake the 'send' action, putting control into the mind of the patient. This 'take' action is amplified by the patient's insatiable desire for more of what it sees as pleasant or satisfying. The more of the desired attribute the patient takes, the more he wants, much like a drug addict. According to your grandfather, the patient could theoretically deplete the host of all of the function or thought being transferred."

"The dopaminergic cascade. He told me of it."

"What else has he told you?" Mendoza asked, obviously unnerved that Suki knew as much as she did.

"Can you return the thought to the host, or at least the part that was excess?"

Mendoza and Mickey looked at each other for a moment, hoping the other would give the answer. Ultimately, Mickey replied, "A transfer of a single thought or function is one-way. The nanocells flip the information twice during the course of transfer. We have tried returning information and it appears that it is flipped only once during the reverse transfer. The result was disastrous."

Suki shrugged her shoulders, concluding, "I guess that would really suck?"

There was brief laughter at Suki's sense of humor in the face of such an ominous possibility.

"So, how do we begin?"

Mendoza went to a dry erase board and drew a picture of two brains and some arrows.

"This is your brain on the left and Diane's on the right. Last night, I surgically inserted into Diane's brain what we call canals that later this morning will be loaded with nanostructures called 'planters' that are made using Mickey's process. These will be the Primary Stimulation Paths. I also inserted a transceiver. Once you understand what we plan to do, and agree to embark upon this greatest of journeys with us, I will implant receiver canals outside your skullcap. We don't penetrate the host's brain, but I will have to shave your head. These, too, will be loaded with nanostructures called 'hunters'. Yours will be external Primary Retriever Paths that will join together at a transceiver that will be implanted in your ear, much like Diane's."

"Why is it a transceiver? Why a device that receives and sends? What would I receive and what would Diane send?"

"As for sending, other than the thought or function in question, several pieces of data are continuously transmitted—your pulse, your intracranial pressure, and your location…coordinates," Mickey answered.

"Why the location?"

"In the unlikely event that something goes terribly wrong and you wander off, we need to be able to locate you…quickly."

"And after you shave my hair, implant the canals, and have me showing up on air traffic control tower instruments, what next?"

"Actually, we would track you via cell phone towers, but don't tell the phone companies because, for now anyway, we are hacking into them."

"This sounds like a truly professional endeavor. I am feeling really good about this right now."

"So, back to your question," Mendoza quickly moved on, "We select the detail to be transferred, induce hypnosis in the host, and begin the therapy."

Mendoza wrote in abbreviated phrases as he captured everything that was being said on the dry erase board.

"Why do you call it therapy?"

"Therapy goes hand-in-hand with pharmacology," Mickey replied. "In this case, we give the patient low doses of lysergic acid diethylamide." Noticing his answer produced a visible distress in Suki, he clarified his point with, "It facilitates anecdotal assimilation."

"Naturally, I should have known," Suki said, sarcastically. "So, in addition to stealing telephony, you are illegally using LSD in this building?"

"We call it by its chemical name amongst ourselves. In more open conversation, we call it *catalyst*, but we never call it LSD," Mendoza said very clearly.

"There may be an alternative," Mickey confided.

Again, Mendoza was startled that Mickey was deviating from a previously agreed-upon script without consulting with him.

"It's new and entirely unproven. I haven't mentioned it to you because of this."

"What is it?" Mendoza asked.

"Not at this time, Ricardo," Mickey replied.

"So," Mendoza continued, his tone of voice showing disapproval, "Now comes the time when our partnership begins the process of dissolution."

"No! It's nothing like that. I just don't want to try anything new on Diane!"

"And you don't trust that I wouldn't do such a thing!"

Suki intervened, partially out of fear, saying, "Look, if you guys are going to start fighting, I will leave right now, and you will never lay a hand on me."

In a tone that left Suki still doubting his sincerity, Mendoza quickly walked over to Mickey and reached out to shake his hand, saying, "She's right, you know. We can discuss our future strategies at a different time, and of course in the context of a different patient and host."

Even Mickey felt unsure if he could trust Mendoza, and especially how quickly he produced an olive branch. But, he shook his hand anyway.

"So, Suki, now that this information has been given to you and you can make a more informed decision, are you ready to proceed?"

"There is one more question—how long will this take?"

Mendoza and Mickey looked at one another, but again, neither answered right away.

"A couple of days?" Suki offered.

Still, there was no answer.

Boundaries

"A week?"

Knowing that she would only believe an answer that came from him, Mickey replied, "This could go on a long time…perhaps months…even longer."

"Months!"

"Suki, it all depends upon the extent of Diane's injury and the rate of successful therapeutic transfer. Diane's condition is not completely understood. As it changes, we will have to adjust. This is our first endeavor of such magnitude. The success rate of transfer is something we will know more about once we begin. Finally, we don't want to cause any harm to you, so while we will move as quickly as we can, that may be slower than we would all like."

Suki stood up, grabbed a bottle of water and went to the window to look out, hoping her courage wouldn't founder.

"Please, no water just now," Mendoza requested. "No more intake by mouth until we are done with today's procedure."

Joining Suki at the window, Mickey put his arms around her from behind and said, "This is the best thing for Diane. I know the two of you are close. I can't think of a more ideal set of circumstances. Trust me…this is the ideal situation for everyone."

Her eyes filled with tears from fear. Suki knew, given what was explained to her, that she was undoubtedly the best candidate for being Diane's host. Nonetheless, the nature of the project was terrifying at best.

She let out a brief sigh before saying, "I suppose if I become cowardly later on, you can find someone else to be the host for Diane." She felt Mickey shaking his head.

"That's not the case. One host, one patient—at least during this preliminary work."

"Just a minor detail you were keeping from me?" Suki asked, somewhat angrily.

"No, it was an oversight."

"A rather large oversight!"

"You see, the bond between patient and host is more than physiological. At present, nanostructure data from different hosts are incompatible—sort of like different blood types. I'm working to solve this problem, but it may take another year of research."

What Mickey was unable to see, was the change in Suki's facial expression and the look in her eyes as if she had just had a momentous revelation.

"So, once we begin, you are stuck with me, perhaps forever."

Mickey squeezed her tightly, giving her all the reassurance she needed. Emboldened by this new revelation, Suki asked, "Dr. Mendoza, where do I go?"

THE CAR CARRYING DR. Wu arrived in the early afternoon as planned. A security guard opened his vehicle door and escorted him into the lobby of the building where the receptionist held the door open for him. He walked past her, stopping for just a moment to wink at her—a totally different interaction from the prior day. She acknowledged him with a smile, thankful there was not another confrontation.

"C-F," Mickey called out as he approached from down the hallway. "Join me in the conference room for a while. Dr. Mendoza will be along in just a few minutes."

"Yes, fine. I would like some green tea, if that is not too much trouble."

"It's being prepared as we speak."

"Excellent."

The two took seats in the conference room. Both looked extremely at ease—not what one might expect given the events that were soon to unfold.

"Tell me, Dr. Rollins, has Sukhon made her final choice in this matter?"

"Absolutely. She's been undergoing prep for the last three hours."

"What kind of preparations are you speaking of?"

"MRI, CT, blood work, x-ray, baseline EEG. The kind of tests necessary to map the skull and brain."

"What about the soul?"

"The soul?"

"Yes, the most important part. I hope Dr. Mendoza has not neglected that."

The secretary entered the room carrying the tea.

"Gentlemen, may I serve you some refreshments? We have hot green tea and some special snacks."

Dr. Wu nodded, continuing his conversation with Mickey.

"I am disappointed, Dr. Rollins, that you did not stress the importance of this to Dr. Mendoza. Certainly, I have discussed this with you many times."

"Yes, you have, C-F. But, I find the subject of 'soul' to be highly subjective, and I don't see how we can possibly get a handle on such a vague and nebulous thing. Even if we did, how would we use that information in reconstructive therapy?"

"The soul is a wondrous piece of each one of us that was never meant to be captured or quantified. The soul of a person is what takes all that we are, and nurtures us to apply it in a manner that is acceptable to a higher power."

"Are you confusing science and religion, C-F?"

"No, not at all, Dr. Rollins. That which we are is God-given. The choices we make in life are his will. Pictures of Sukhon's brain and information about her blood cannot tell me if her soul is prepared to act in Diane's best interest. Our work here will only be successful if she is completely ready to sacrifice all of herself without question and without hesitation. Only a good soul takes this path in life."

"Well, C-F, I have to say that we have made no evaluation of Suki's soul."

Dr. Wu sipped his tea, then said, "I expected as much. But, I am comfortable with this oversight since, in fact, I am the only person who can possibly make this evaluation. I will speak to her when I am finished with my tea."

"C-F, let me suggest..." Mickey was cut short when Mendoza entered the room.

"Dr. Wu, I am glad to see you. Your granddaughter is an outstanding physical specimen. I am completely certain this transfer will be a tremendous success."

"By what claim will you measure success, Dr. Mendoza?" Wu asked.

Mendoza started to answer Dr. Wu's question, then changed his mind.

"Dr. Wu, with all due respect, I refuse to enter into a philosophical debate with you, which is where I know you are heading with your question."

"Have you prepared your soul, Dr. Mendoza?"

"My soul? Prepared my soul for what?"

Dr. Wu took another sip of his tea, then looked at Mickey.

"And you, my friend, have you prepared your soul?"

Sitting up closer to the table, he responded, "C-F, I don't follow you."

"You and Dr. Mendoza are about to take on the work of God. Are your souls prepared to take on such a tremendous responsibility?"

"Dr. Wu, perhaps you should leave. I will…"

"Ricardo," Mickey said, interrupting Mendoza, "Dr. Wu wishes to speak with his granddaughter one last time before the procedure begins."

"That's out of the question!"

"And while he is doing that," Mickey insisted, "You and I will review our preparations."

"Dr. Rollins, if every step of the way we are one move away from checkmate, this will be an impossible task."

"Then I suggest you allow C-F to see Suki…now."

There was a long hesitation by Dr. Mendoza during which his face turned red. Eventually, he yielded, saying, "Dr. Wu, I demand that you respect the sterile field I have created around the host. You can get no closer than two meters. Is that understood?"

Dr. Wu got up from his chair, nodded at Mendoza, then left the room, but not before taking an extended look at Mickey as if he was making his point one last time.

Mendoza called the staff in the treatment room and informed them to allow Dr. Wu to see Suki, giving them very explicit instructions as to what he could and could not do. Once done with his directives, he slammed the receiver into its cradle.

"Do you want your name listed as co-author on our reports? Do you want to stand with me on stage when we announce our success? Do you want to share the wealth this breakthrough will bring? Mickey, this is Nobel material. Why are you wavering? What's wrong with you?"

Now it was Mickey's turn to flush with anger.

"Let's get this straight. You have nothing without me. You have nothing without Dr. Wu. The host's name is Suki, and don't ever again call her a specimen. The patient's name is Diane—soon, Mrs. Rollins."

"So tell me, Mickey, when this procedure is done, you will have two wives. How do you plan to explain that in your country?"

"The relationships will be clearly defined. Suki, knows where she stands with respect to Diane."

"You're kidding yourself, Mickey. You need to consider the two women as subjects, or your feelings will deny you that to which you are entitled."

"You worry about your problems and let me worry about mine."

The two stared at each other for several moments, obviously caught in a very precarious situation. Mendoza finally broke the silence when he tossed a sheet of paper across the table for Mickey to read.

"Here's a problem for you to worry about—Diane was pregnant. The obstetrics team's report is all there. They took care of the matter. You can see that the assault on her caused a lot of injury. There is a high risk of infection that we must constantly monitor during the reconstruction."

"The zygote," Mickey said, pointing at the document.

"I beg your pardon?"

"The report says that the team harvested a zygote from the tissue they removed. It had not yet attached to the uterine wall and according to the cellular division, it was at least five days old. That would make it my child. Where is the zygote?"

"It is in a protective media. I thought you might want to preserve it in case Diane can have children at a later time."

Mickey put the report down on the table and rubbed his chin.

"Diane will never be able to complete a pregnancy, but there is another possibility…"

Chapter 27

Hunt, Texas. Fifteen Months Later…

Pulling a calf has to be one of the messiest, but most gratifying jobs there is on a cattle ranch. Today, Toot had on his long veterinary gloves and had both arms well inside the back end of the reddish-brown cow.

"Sixto, feel for the head on the right side and push it around. I got the legs, but the head's turned towards you," he shouted to his foreman.

"Yessir, Mr. Toot," Sixto said, leaning into the side of the cow with his shoulder. "It's moving, sir. Can you feel it?"

"Push harder and down a little more," Toot replied.

Sixto leaned in some more. The cow let out a loud cry as if to say it was in pain, or at least, uncomfortable. But, she was hobbled and tied down securely so she couldn't get back up or move away from the men.

"How about now, sir?"

Toot got in position behind the cow, felt around inside her uterus, and slipped his hands over the calf's head.

"Okay, we're there. He's movin' out now."

As Toot maneuvered his hands all the way around the calf, it fairly quickly began to exit out the birth canal—so quickly in fact, Toot slipped backwards onto his rear end, the calf following him and landing on his lap.

"God damn! Guess these clothes are gonna get washed."

"It's a bull," Sixto soon noted. "A good lookin' one, too, Mr. Toot."

Pulling pieces of the amniotic sack from the calf, Toot looked like a proud father.

"He's got Dirt Bag's markings," he said, referring to the sire.

"Hopefully, he's not so mean."

Both men chuckled.

"Well, he'll probably get cut. We'll see how he looks in a few months."

The ranch had a bumper crop of bulls this year, and they weren't all needed for breeding. For now, that task was up to Dirt Bag and Thomas, the other champion bull named after the Tank Engine.

"Get him weighed, measured, and tagged right away. After she finishes, let her up. If things go normally with the two of them, turn them out in the morning. Call me if there's any trouble."

"Yessir, Mr. Toot."

Sixto called out to one of his cowboys and gave him instructions in Spanish. The young helper nodded and went off to fetch the items he would need to tag the new bull.

After getting to his feet, Toot removed the long, slimy gloves, tossing them into a nearby trashcan. He delicately pulled his t-shirt over his head, being careful not to get any of the remnants of the birth onto his face and head. With his shirt off, Toot revealed his firm, toned, and tanned torso, adorned with a few noticeable scars from occasional ranch or rodeo accidents. As he turned around, he nearly ran into Mickey who had been standing unnoticed at a distance, watching the birth take place.

"Well, that's typical," Toot said before spitting on the ground close to where Mickey stood. "I do the work and you watch."

"How you doing, Toot?" Mickey said, refusing to address Toot's remark. "Why don't you let Sixto and the boys do that?"

"You haven't changed a damn bit, Mickey," he replied, leaning up against a pen inside the large, well organized barn. "Ain't no job on this ranch I can't, or won't do from time to time. You ought to stay a while and do some real work for a change. The place is one-third yours...or have you forgotten about that?"

"No, I remember every quarter when my accountant tells me how the ranch is doing."

"Your accountant. An accountant's just as worthless as a freakin' lawyer. Just try pickin' up the phone some time, Mick. Let me tell you about how *I'm* doin' on *our* ranch."

"No, I figure you're doing a fine job without me."

"You're God damn right I am! Your daddy would be proud and so would mine." Toot turned to look away from Mickey in an effort to cool his rising temper, before asking, "So, how long has it been, Mick—three years, four years?"

"I think I was here…it's been a long time."

Toot walked outside the door to a pen where animals could be washed, picked up a hose, and began rinsing off his arms and face.

Mickey followed Toot into the pen, then asked, "So, how's your mom doing?"

There was a brief delay while Toot finished his barnyard shower.

"She's alive. Her mind's gone, but she's alive."

After walking to the edge of the pen, he put one of his feet on a fence rail. His boots were worn and had spurs—he always wore spurs.

"She don't even recognize me a lot of the time no more. Got her in a nice home up in San Angelo that deals with Alzheimer's people."

He wiped the water off of his face and flicked it to the side.

"Nice of you to ask. Thanks."

"Sixto's looking good."

"I hope I look that good when I'm fifty-eight."

"Can he still rope?"

"Best heeler in the state—my opinion, of course."

"And who's the best header?"

"You're lookin' at him, but what'd you expect me to say?"

"Your modesty impresses me. Do you get on bulls anymore?"

"Hell no. Last time I did that was two years ago. I got hung up and the son-of-a-bitch almost tore my arm off. Havin' a wreck like that was alright when Daddy was here to do some work, but now since he's passed, I can't lose time like that. Too damn much work around here."

Boundaries

"Been to Caddo lately?"

"Recaulked all the windows last winter. Ain't been there since."

Toot pulled the dip from his mouth and tossed it on the ground. Grabbing a small can of tobacco from his hip pocket, he quickly replaced it with a fresh pinch behind his lower lip.

"Want a dip?"

Mickey shook his head.

"So what brings you here, Mick? You ain't never been sentimental or nothin'."

"I need to move back for a while."

It was as if all the air got sucked out of the pen.

"You what?"

"I need to move back. Something's come up and I want to live here again."

Toot spit again.

"You're shittin' me, right?"

"Is the house still open, or do you live in it?"

"Me? Live in Dub and Ruby's house? That'll always be their place. I live in Number 2, just like always. So you think you want to live in their house?"

"Do you have a problem with me living in my parents' house?"

"Other than the fact that you never had residence there, and you ain't never done more than five days work here in your whole fuckin' life. You ask me if I have a problem?"

"Good, then I'll settle in tomorrow. I'd like you to meet the family. Why don't you come up to the house right now and meet them."

"You? A family?"

Toot spit on the ground again.

"I thought havin' a cow birth on me was the peak of my day. Now, you want me to meet your family? What are you talkin' about...a wife, kids?"

"I'm married and I have a daughter," Mickey said with a broad smile on his face.

Toot looked down at his boots and kicked the dirt. After gripping the fence rail for a few moments so hard that the veins in his arms and neck bulged, he managed to respond to the announcement.

"So, I guess that means you won, don't it?"

"There aren't any winners or losers, Toot. Everything can be the same. I just want to occupy the main house and settle back on the ranch. Maybe I can help out...if you'll let me."

"Guess you don't need to ask. We ain't one-third partners any more. I reckon we need to call Roger and make sure it's all legal and everything."

"Is Delaney still our attorney?"

Toot spit on the ground.

"Well, Mick, he sends you a letter concerning the estate and the trust every damn year. Don't you read your mail?"

"Not always."

"Yeah, right...not always."

RUB-A-DUB RANCH was supposed to be a quiet, retirement ranch for Ruby and Dub Rollins. Located in the Texas hill country in western Kerr County, it was five thousand acres of solitude—part rocky plateaus, part flat farmland, with two strong, all-season creeks that emptied into the Guadalupe River.

By age forty-five, Dub had become so successful as a geologist, he was able to run his consulting business from the ranch. Mickey was off to college, visiting on occasion and during the summer. Now it was time to transition to a new life for Dub and Ruby as they phased-out a previous livelihood.

But, retirement for Dub meant anything but rest. First came the house, then the barn, then the first of several additions to both. The sedentary ways of two retirees without any grandchildren quickly proved to be not enough of a diversion, so Dub decided it was time to try his hand at raising cattle.

As Ruby did for all of their married years, she took Dub's ideas and embellished them. Soon, Dub was raising and breeding a genetically-controlled, special breed of exotic cattle that, as Ruby insisted, would lead a pure, natural life.

By that, she meant they fed off the natural grasses of the land and drank only its spring water. They were given no chemicals, no drugs, and no supplements. They roamed freely in rolling pastureland. Local cattlemen initially called Dub a crank, but royalties from his oil investments kept him solvent while he developed a niche market, both domestically and overseas, for his special beef. Eventually, he became the envy of his peers, a favorite customer of his bank, and a generous philanthropist to the community at large.

Dub's project required extra help, and Mickey announced early on he wasn't interested in making the ranch a fulltime endeavor. So Dub hired rodeo star Clement Teudi to be his ranch manager. The growth necessitated the building of quarters for the ranch hands, then another house, called simply Number 2, for Clem, his wife, and son Marque, and even a cook for all the mouths. Marque followed in his father's footsteps for a while, becoming quite a success in the rodeo circuit. Rodeo announcers coined the nickname Rooty Teudi and, as his notoriety grew, his name was shortened even further to just "Toot."

Eventually, the operation grew to where the mature cattle were taken to another ranch named Out West for fattening and slaughter that was, as the name implied, a couple of counties west of the main ranch. The breeding stock, bulls and young cattle, that became Dub's passion, stayed at Rub-a-Dub.

After Ruby died following a short bout with cancer, Dub slowly lost interest in the ranch, turning the operation over to Clem, who had become his partner and best friend. Dub maintained ownership, but it was Clem and Toot who kept the ranch afloat. He set out to build a second retirement home to get away from all the work and responsibilities at his first retirement home—a beautiful log cabin on Caddo Lake in northeast Texas—but died of a heart attack before he spent his first night in it. Mickey and Toot finished out the house, named Back East, then left it as a vacation home that was seldom used.

Dub's will left thirty-three percent of his estate to Mickey, an equal amount to Clem, and the rest in a trust, the disposition of it to be made after Clem passed on. But, ranching is hard work, and it ages a man quickly. Toot was drawn back to the cattle operation as his father found it increasingly difficult to do it all by himself, and eventually he no longer participated in national rodeos, limiting his activities to more local, recreational events.

Where was Mickey during all of this? Well, that became the nagging question in Toot's mind. Mickey most certainly benefited financially from the ranch and the oil leases. But, he was nowhere to be found when it came to running the operation. While Toot was respectful of the fact that Mickey was the blood son of the founder of the ranch that he and his father helped to build into a successful operation, it irked him to no end that all the work and responsibility fell onto his shoulders. And work there was. Every hour of daylight and many hours at night were spent tending to the details and manual labor of Rub-a-Dub, Out West, and Back East. Toot used to tell his friends that he woke up one morning the son of a ranch foreman, an up and coming rodeo star, and a young buck with a host of local female suitors, and went to bed that night the foreman of that same ranch, having buried his own father atop Hooter Hill alongside his mother, Ruby, and Dub, up to his eyeballs in work, and no more time for rodeos, let alone women. Life, as Toot had known it, came to an abrupt halt.

As for the main house at Rub-a-Dub, it was a spectacle to behold for any gentleman rancher. There wasn't a lot of 'fluff'—even Ruby wouldn't have useless comfort in the home. Rather, the house had eighteen rooms, each laid out with a purpose, and most with more than the usual amount of glass to take in the natural grandeur of the hills, creeks, and trees that surrounded the property.

Following the deaths of Ruby and Dub, the house was used mainly as guest lodging and to host social gatherings and parties. Mickey never settled into a room he could call his own at the ranch, and Toot preferred to live in the foreman's house where he spent most of his years growing up. That Mickey wanted to occupy the main house now, weighed heavily on Toot's mind.

AFTER SHOWERING AND PUTTING on a clean shirt and pair of blue jeans, Toot reported to the main house where he quickly grabbed a cold, longneck beer. Heading toward the parlor, it wasn't long before he heard voices. There, he found Lupita, the cook and head caretaker for the past twenty-five years, serving her guests some of her special munchies and drinks. Mickey walked over to meet him.

"Toot, you finally made it. Glad you changed clothes. The ladies might have been a little repulsed."

"Wouldn't want to do that, now would we?" Toot answered, tongue in cheek.

Putting his hand on Toot's shoulder, Mickey guided him toward Diane.

"Toot, this is my wife, Diane. Honey, this is the man I told you about."

Toot extended his hand to Diane, but she was slow to respond. He noticed that she had a somewhat distant look about her.

"Pleased to meet you, Mrs. Rollins."

"So, is he the man that you told me works for you?" Diane asked Mickey.

"Yes, honey. Toot's the ranch manager."

It was proven on that night that Clem and Marie Teudi raised a true gentleman. Toot kept his smile, maintained his manners, and withheld his desire to beat the crap out of Mickey at that moment.

Diane finally extended her hand to Toot, and he gave it a delicate shake as he should with any lady.

"Your hands, they feel like leather," she remarked.

"Comes from years of hard work on this ranch," he replied.

"Mickey, how come your hands don't feel like his?"

"My work here has been different, babe. I handle the business end of the ranch."

Mickey's answer put Toot's resolve to the ultimate test.

Turning to Suki, Diane addressed her in Chinese. She got up off of the sofa and approached Mickey so he could introduce her.

"Toot, meet Suki. She's our personal assistant. And in her arms is our daughter, Gigi."

Mickey took the tiny girl from Suki's arms, after which she extended her hand to Toot.

"It is my pleasure to meet you, sir."

"Oh, you speak English?"

"Yes. Diane sometimes speaks to me in Chinese or another language. It is something we are working on."

"Working on?"

"Yeah," Mickey answered. "Diane's multi-lingual, and recently she's had some issues with getting confused about what language to use."

"Can she speak Spanish?" Toot asked. "We can always use someone who is good at speaking Spanish."

"Why is that?" Diane asked, again with a puzzled look.

Before Toot could answer what he thought was a perfectly legitimate question, Mickey broke in, "Toot, can I speak with you for a second?"

"I think that's a great idea, Mick," he replied, followed by a long swallow from his beer.

Mickey turned to leave. Toot was more polite.

"Excuse us ladies. Mick and I have a few things to discuss."

He took a moment to peek at the baby whom Mickey had handed back to Suki.

"Cute baby. She's got her momma's beauty already."

Toot was serious, and he didn't care if Mickey took offense to his indirect compliment paid to Diane.

The two stepped outside onto the patio where Toot closed the door behind them.

"I'll bet you have a couple of questions, don't you Toot? Let me explain about Diane's confusion. First…."

"Sounds like you've been feedin' her a lot of bullshit, Mick. Why don't you let me straighten things out? I'll personally take her around the ranch so she can see what really goes on here and who's really in charge."

"I need you to work with me on this Toot."

"Work with you? All I do is work, and you want me to help you with your charade?"

"Right after we got married, she had an accident that resulted in a head injury. She's been slowly going through rehabilitation, and she doesn't have all of her facts right."

"That's really chicken-shit, Mickey, even for you," Toot said before taking another drink from his beer. "You blame your lies and deception on some trumped up story about your wife? I think you've hit an all time low."

"I'm not lying, Toot. The injury affected her emotional stability and her memory. As it turns out, I've been working on a new therapeutic treatment to restore her to her original self. It just takes time. Along the way, she may not interpret things correctly. What you have in those instances are odd behaviors and statements like you saw tonight."

"You mean she thinks I'm some grunt on the ranch."

"Apparently she thinks you work for me."

"And she speaks Chinese?"

"She speaks a lot of languages—some very well, some not so well. She has some confusion about what language to use and in what circumstances."

Toot studied Mickey to see if he could get a good read on him, then asked, "Who's the Asian gal?"

"You mean Suki?"

"Whatever her name is."

"Like I said, she's our assistant. She's an integral part of the therapy."

"You mean she's a babysitter, don't you?"

"She cares for Gigi, yes."

"You need to get yourself a Mexican woman like the rest of Texas does. Lupita has a daughter that'll do you just fine."

"No, I want to keep Suki."

"Mick, I can count the number of Chinese in these parts on the fingers of my left foot. Get yourself a Mexican. You'll be a lot better off in the long run."

"That's not an option."

"An option? Sounds to me like you've already made up your mind on a lot of things, Mick. What else do you plan to change?"

"Well, now that you mention it, there are three things that need to change."

Toot sucked down the rest of his beer, then said, "Oh, this ought to be good."

"First, we have our own domestic help. Her name is Maria. She'll be coming to live with us, and I want her to do the cooking."

"No way. Lupita's been the cook here since the ranch started. If the boys don't get her menudo on Saturdays, there'll be another Alamo right out there in the front yard."

"Maria can cook those things if that's necessary."

"Won't work."

"It has to."

"I'm tellin' ya Mick, the guys on this ranch expect to eat certain foods, at certain times, prepared like their mommas cooked 'em when they were growin' up. Screw with that and there'll be hell to pay."

"Secondly, Diane wants space for about a dozen or so horses."

"This is a workin' cattle ranch, Mick, not some dude ranch. All the horses here are used to work the cattle."

"Diane owns a large ranch with thoroughbreds in California. She breeds, trains, and sells them. We need a small part of that operation here."

"Then buy fifty acres close by and set things up there. Don't go messin' up the operation."

"Finally, I need a greenhouse close to the main house."

"Why, you gonna grow orchids or somethin'?"

"There are certain herbs, spices, and flowers I need to grow as part of Diane's therapy. I need a constant, controlled source."

That was all Toot could take. He took his beer bottle and dropped it into a trashcan so that it made a loud noise.

"You know, Mickey, you mentioned Caddo. I think I'll head to Caddo for a couple weeks. I think I deserve some time off. After all, you're here to take care of everything now."

"I know I'm asking a lot of you, but in the big picture…"

Boundaries

"No, Mickey, you don't see the big picture. You never have. I run a successful cattle ranch and oil holding business, both of which are your daddy's legacy that he gave to us—both of us. It is all consuming. If I had time for horses or gardens or dealin' with a mutiny 'cause the guys don't get fed what they've come to expect over the years, I'd have already worked those things into my day...not to mention some sort of social life. As it is, I'm completely booked. I got up at five-thirty this mornin' only because I gave myself an extra half hour. Now, thanks to this little get-together, I'm going to bed a half hour later than normal. So you wanna do those things, go right ahead. Call me in Caddo day after tomorrow."

"Toot, maybe I came across a little too demanding. Let's talk tomorrow."

Before Mickey could finish, a strangely excited-looking Diane joined them on the patio. She gave Mickey a kiss, then, without asking, took Toot's hands in hers.

"I've never felt any like these before."

After a moment of squeezing his calloused hands, she closed her eyes, raised them up and rubbed the palms of Toot's hands across her cheeks. To say that Toot was bowled over was an understatement. His expression could almost be described as that of confusion, but there was also a hint of lust, and he concealed it poorly. The only person more affected by what she did was Mickey, and he was obviously displeased by Diane's interruption, and her ensuing flirting with Toot.

Again, being the consummate gentleman, Toot slowly and cautiously withdrew from Diane saying, "As I mentioned earlier, Mrs. Rollins, it comes from hard work."

"You can call me Diane."

"No, he should call you Mrs. Rollins," Mickey stated for the record.

Toot took a moment to revel in Mickey's discomfort before agreeing with him.

"Ma'am, it's not right for me to address a fine lady like yourself, especially one who is married, in anything less than a formal manner for now. If you don't mind, I'd like to keep calling you Mrs. Rollins."

It was clear from Diane's expression that she didn't fully understand why Toot answered the way he did, but her attention span appeared to be very short so she let matter drop.

"You were saying, Mickey?" Toot asked, trying to kick-start the conversation he was having before Diane arrived.

"I was about to say that perhaps I was too insensitive to your needs here. Maybe we can discuss our transition over breakfast tomorrow."

"Insensitive? Now that's a word I don't hear too often on this ranch."

Toot was continuing to enjoy Mickey's increasing level of discomfort. For now, anyway, he had managed to trump his reinvented partner's demands.

"Hey, Mick, if you're goin' back inside, would you mind transitionin' me another beer?"

"So, breakfast?" Mickey asked.

"Sounds great, Mick. See you in the kitchen at five-thirty."

Mickey was up against a wall for now, so he went along with the proposed time. He asked, "Sleeping in again tomorrow?"

"No, up at five; showered, shaved and dressed by five-thirty."

Mickey turned to leave the patio and fetch Toot a beer, but he met Suki coming out to join them.

"Where's Gigi?" Mickey asked, alarmed that his daughter wasn't with her.

"Oh, Lupita has her. They have already taken a liking to each other."

Mickey went inside to see what was going on.

Suki walked over to Diane, handing her a glass of Chablis, then to Toot, giving him another longneck beer.

"Thanks, Miss Suki. How'd you know I wanted another beer?"

"I just know," Suki replied.

"She does, too. Isn't she cute?" Diane asked, joining in.

Diane's choice of words wasn't particularly well thought out, but Toot found her to be increasingly amusing.

"Suki, check out his hands."

Diane watched as Suki began to completely disarm her new acquaintance.

Boundaries

"Could you open my beer?" Suki asked, admiring his hands.

She could easily have twisted off the top, but chose instead to let Toot pour on a little more Texas charm. He removed the top with a simple twist of his thumb and index finger.

"My, you are strong. Let me see your hands."

Toot handed Suki her beer, set his down, then turned his palms up.

"Wow. I have never seen anything like those. So rough...so big..." Suki said, glancing up to see his response.

A spicy remark like that from local Texas woman meant only one thing. But, Toot wasn't sure how to read Suki.

She took a drink from her ice-cold beer, then proceeded to shiver.

"Do you mind if I stand a little closer to you?"

Never giving him a chance to respond, Suki moved downwind from her victim.

"I think it is cold, do you?"

Actually, Toot thought, things *were* beginning to heat up...considerably.

"No ma'am. This is a fine, Texas night we have here."

"What is that cologne you are wearing? It smells unbelievable."

Toot was particularly moved by Suki's observation.

"Funny you should mention that, ma'am. It's actually some of my daddy's old English Leather. He must have bought a case of that stuff before he died. I use it now and then."

"If you wish to impress someone?"

"Perhaps."

"A woman?"

"I ain't trying to impress a man."

"A particular woman?"

"None at this time."

Suki stopped talking and took her time looking out across the pasture that was south of the main house.

"I have never been to Texas before. It is beautiful."

"That it is."

Toot didn't see what Suki was looking at because he was too busy looking at her from behind.

"I am glad you do not mind us coming to live on your ranch. You are most kind."

"No problem at all, Miss Suki. Fact is, I was just tellin' Mick that things were gettin' kinda lonely."

Mickey poked his head outside, and called out, "Ladies, I need both of you."

Gigi could be heard crying inside. Both ladies went to Mickey's aid, leaving Toot perspiring. He and Suki made eye contact as long as practical before she vanished into the house. He turned, propped his elbows on the patio railing, and rubbed the cold bottle across his forehead.

"Oh, Daddy, what am I gettin' myself into?

Chapter 28

The smell of hotcakes wafting through the air was unmistakable. It wasn't the smell of just any hotcakes—it was Lupita's hotcakes. Though Mickey was in the bedroom several long hallways from the source, the enticing scent of her cooking found its way to his nose, resurrecting memories of a past when he would spend weeks, and sometimes months, at his parents' home. There was something else— classic country music, just like that which used to play on the old local AM radio station Ruby and Dub always listened to.

Mickey turned over to look at the clock on the nightstand. It was five-fifteen in the morning, He knew if he was one minute late, Toot wouldn't let him hear the end of it. Racing against time, he pulled a fresh change of clothes out of a suitcase and hurriedly dressed. After quietly slipping into the bathroom, he poured water from his cupped hands over his hair, dragged a comb through it, then quickly shaved, managing to nick himself twice in the process. Before heading for the kitchen, he kissed a sleeping Diane softly on the cheek, then grabbed a pair of socks and headed down the hallway. Halfway to the kitchen, he realized he had forgotten his shoes and turned back to find some. After a futile two-minute search of the dark bedroom, he gave up and began his sprint to the kitchen one more time.

As he sprinted past what had been his father's office, something caught his eye, bringing him to a halt. On the floor, next to the fireplace, were Dub's old boots. Mickey grabbed them, then continued to the kitchen.

Lupita took one look at Mickey and began to laugh. He was quite the spectacle—small wads of toilet paper on his face, his hair unevenly parted, and his clothing wrinkled.

Mickey realized he looked the worse for wear, but at least he had beaten Toot to the kitchen. After taking a seat at a bar stool next to the kitchen island where he used to eat breakfast and read the local newspaper, all of his senses helped to put him into déjà vu overdrive—the cooking, the music, and Lupita's always-cheerful, motherly chatter.

Setting a cup of black coffee in front of him, she said, "You look like you fought with the wolves last night, and they won the battle."

Anxiously anticipating his first taste of her coffee, he asked, "Tell me, is it blended with chicory?"

"Do I cook with lard?"

A smile filled Mickey's face as he said, "Oh, Lupita, you're the greatest."

"You've been away too long, Mr. Rollins."

At that moment, Mickey was struck with the realization that she had always referred to him as Mickey and always addressed Dub as Mr. Rollins. It was an odd feeling now that he was Mr. Rollins.

"I'd have to say you're right. It's good to be back."

"You have a lovely wife and daughter. Your parents missed having grandchildren. You should have married and had children years ago."

"I never had the chance."

"No, Mr. Rollins, you never took the time. There was always Laura."

"Oh, come on, Lupita, don't start in on me when I have an empty stomach."

He savored a sip of Texas' finest coffee just as Toot walked in. His Wranglers were creased. His white, Ariat shirt was starched. His boots and belt were polished. He smelled of English Leather. After walking through the door, he removed his Stetson, revealing his close-cropped and neatly parted hair, and hung it on one of the hat racks located at each of the home's entrances. He wasted no time taking note of Mickey's appearance.

"I see you're dressed to impress this morning, Mick."

Mickey didn't care if he was dressed appropriately or not, he was too absorbed in the moment.

"You know how long it's been since I've had coffee with chicory?"

"Probably not since we were last graced with your presence?" Turning his attention to Lupita, Toot asked, "Boys fed?"

"Now why would you ask me a question like that? I've cooked three hundred sixty-five breakfasts a year, every year, for a quarter of a century."

"Oh, I don't know, thought you might have forgot or somethin'. After all, you're gettin' old. And don't start lyin'. You took two weeks off in '95."

"I'll forget you with a rolling pin upside the head if you go asking a stupid question like that one again," she replied, handing Toot an empty cup to make a point.

Still walking down memory lane, Mickey asked, "Do you know, I can remember the smell of Lupita's cooking like I was here yesterday?"

"Really?" Toot asked, taking a seat on one of the stools. "I'm surprised she cooked you anythin' at all. Did you tell her she was fired?"

"Fired!" Lupita shouted from where she stood at the sink. "Who said I was fired?" She asked, pulling the previously named rolling pin out of a drawer.

Though she participated in virtually none of the kitchen discussions that had taken place several times each day over the years, she served as a living archive of all that had ever been said in that room, leading one to believe she had the hearing of a young canine and the mental capacity of a savant.

"I never said she was fired!" Mickey insisted, knowing he was being thrown under the bus.

"Sure did. You said you were bringin' in another cook," Toot said, pouring himself a cup of coffee.

"Another cook?!" Lupita shouted, now sporting a wooden spoon in one hand and the rolling pin in the other.

"Lupita…" Mickey tried in vain to get out a believable explanation of the remark he had made to Toot last night.

"You don't like my cooking?"

"No, your cooking is spectacular. It's just that…"

"Somebody better start talking sense or I'll whoop both of you like I used to."

"Lupita, shut up and listen to me. Diane needs a special diet. I've had a woman living with us in California who's been with me for many years. She can make Diane the special food she needs. I don't want you to change what you do."

"You don't think I can cook for your wife? Does she dislike me because I'm Mexican?"

"No, it's nothing like that, it's just…"

"No, I've had enough. I'm leaving now. Mickey Rollins, you make me so mad, I could break this over your head," she said, waiving the spoon over him. "I'll come back and make lunch, and you had better have some answers!"

Lupita left the room as her tirade changed from English to Spanish.

"Thanks a lot, Toot."

"Hey, I don't like beatin' around the bush."

"Well you didn't have to just blurt it out. I mean it's not like I'm dumping her."

"Good. You have just over six hours to figure out what you're gonna say. I suggest you have your story straight."

Toot took a sip of his coffee, then picked up where Lupita had left off a moment ago.

"So why were you talkin' about Laura when I walked in?"

"Lupita said I should have remarried her and had kids long ago."

"She's right. You should have."

"Okay, Mister 'I'm-allergic-to-wedding-bells.' Whatever happened between you and Rachel?"

"Simple, Mick. She didn't like being number two. I had a ranch to run, and she got tired of always bein' in the shadows."

"Where's she now?"

"Married to Bobby Huisenfelter."

"You're shitting me? That dickhead?"

"That dickhead has become one of the biggest custom home builders in the region. He's doing a thrivin' business. They got two sons and a daughter. She was better off with him anyway."

Toot looked down at the floor where he saw Dub's boots.

"What are you doin' with those?"

"Oh, I couldn't find my shoes this morning so I grabbed Dub's old boots."

Toot shook his head, then sipped on his coffee, not saying a word.

"So, do you object? Is this some sort of nonverbal comment that I can't fill my dad's boots, or something?"

"Those are his Leddy's, Mick. Your daddy and mine worked hard for a lot of years before they got their first pair. You know how long Dub's first pair lasted?"

"No, please tell me this part of my family history," Mickey said sarcastically as he piled several hotcakes onto a plate, then smothered them with syrup.

"He bought his first pair in '88. Bought a pair for Daddy that same year as a gift. Both pairs lasted six years. That pair there is his second and last pair. That's an important—and expensive—part of your heritage right there you're plannin' to put on your feet."

"And you think that's some type of desecration, don't you."

"Hey, you said it not me."

"Well Toot, the difference between me and you is that I can fill my dad's boots and you can't."

Toot grinned as he turned and said, "No, Mick. The difference between me and you is that I won't try to fill my daddy's boots and you shouldn't."

"Is it going to be like this every day, Toot?" Mickey asked with a mouth full of hotcakes.

"Hey, if it's too hot around here, you know the way back to California. I mean, I was doin' just fine up until you showed up last night."

"Well, forget it. I'm staying."

"In that case, I figure you better come with me to my meetin' with Delaney at eight o'clock."

"You have a meeting?"

"No, I strongly recommend *we* have a meeting. I called him last night. He's real interested in the turn of events."

"You mean Diane and Gigi?"

"No, your supposed marriage. Names aren't important, just the piece of legal paper."

Mickey hesitated before replying, "I don't have it with me. It's packed somewhere."

"Figured a smart guy like you would have that sort of thing in a bank box somewhere. Anyway, a certified copy ought to be easy to come by. Until then, to give you a hint of what Delaney will say about that, 'He ain't got shit until he's got the paper in his hand.'"

Toot finished his coffee, then got up and headed for the door.

"Where are you going?"

"Got a meetin' in twenty minutes at the General Store."

"A meeting at six a.m.? With who?"

"Paul Duke."

"What about?"

"How's that any concern of yours?"

"Is he still married to Sarah?"

Toot grabbed his hat, then turned and pointed it at Mickey.

"Don't go there, Mick. She and Paul are happy. They got a good family. They're nice people."

"Huh…Sarah. I left her off the list."

"What list?"

"Oh, nothing. Hey, is she still as good looking as she used to be?"

"Do I need to remind you what it did to Dub when you told him she was pregnant with your child? Daddy told me once he found Dub cryin' like a baby in his office 'cause of you and all the shit you stirred up."

"Well, things got fixed."

"No! She had an abortion that your daddy arranged for her with a doctor up in Dallas, while he took Paul on a huntin' trip in Colorado. He should have just let Paul put a bullet up your ass."

"Like I said, things got fixed."

"You leave her the hell alone, Mick."

"Mind if I come along? After all, it's business that concerns our ranch."

"I'm not waitin' for you to clean up."

"Who's cleaning up? I am what I am."

Toot nodded, saying, "You got that right."

"MORNING BILLY, HENRY, JOHN, Jake. Solved all the World's problems yet?"

"Hell, Toot. That was a half hour and eight cups ago. You should have been here," Henry answered.

"Well looky here, if it ain't Mickey Rollins. I thought you had died," John said.

The group laughed at his remark.

"Sorry to disappoint you, John. Actually, I'm back."

"You had to have been here to be back, Mickey," Billy responded.

The four old men laughed again as did Toot. Mickey didn't.

Jake Woodson, the regional Farm Bureau agent, poured Mickey a cup of strong, black coffee and offered it to him.

"Guess if you're back, you'd better drink up."

"Thanks, Jake. Good to see someone around here still has manners."

The old men who had been chiding Mickey all reeled in unison from his remark.

"Hey, if you can't take the crap that's said here among your friends, ain't no use tryin' your luck outside. Pull up a chair, Mickey," Henry said.

"We got a new henpecked husband, gentlemen. Mickey, here, got himself married," Toot announced to the group.

"You don't say?" Billy answered. "Better teach her how to iron your clothes."

It was almost a given that the group would laugh at nearly everything that was said. Humor and laughter were a morning prerequisite, just like the coffee and the banter.

"Actually, we just arrived last night. I haven't even unpacked."

"I know what you're sayin', Mickey. I haven't unpacked yet, either, since Lorraine took me back," Henry said.

Billy pointed at him, "You're ahead of yourself, Henry. You're just packed for the next time she throws you out."

"So how long you been married?" John asked.

"About a year."

"Any kids yet?"

"One. A daughter named Gigi."

"Gigi?" Billy asked.

"As in 'GG'—those are her initials. They stand for Grace Gilroy. Grace was my wife's mother's name, and Gilroy was her hometown. Gilroy, California."

"That's the garlic capitol, if I remember right. Sure it doesn't stand for Garlic Girl?"

Billy's response drew more chuckles.

"No, Billy. It's really Grace Gilroy."

"Does your wife have a name?"

"It's Diane."

"That's a purdy name...couple of purdy names," Henry said. "Dub would have been tickled. Guess you guys'll be seeing Delaney mighty quick."

"Appointment's at eight," Toot replied.

"Figured it wouldn't be long before you got the lawyers involved. You boys ain't gonna fight over the place, are you?" Jake asked.

There was a long period of deafening silence.

"Well, we'd better get that roll of tickets over there, Henry," Billy said. "We got us a war fixin' to happen, and I figure twenty bucks a ticket could probably pay to pave half of the roads in the County."

Toot stopped the conjecture.

"Ain't gonna be no fight, fellas. Mickey and I are okay with the whole thing. We just gotta tend to the details. Besides, we owe it to the boys to make sure the Trust stays intact."

"Can't believe Dub left so much of his fortune to a bunch of Mexicans. He should have left it to me and the Bureau," Jake said.

Boundaries

"The Bureau would fall all over itself trying to spend all that money," Henry countered.

"Yeah, but I'd like to have had the chance."

A booming voice preceded a giant of a man coming through the door.

"No need to get up. Y'all keep your seats."

It was Paul Duke—all six feet and six inches of him.

Each of the men took turns greeting "Duke" while Toot handed him a cup of coffee. Duke took one drink from his cup, then almost choked as he caught a glimpse of Mickey out of the corner of his eye.

Wiping a drip of coffee from the corner of his mouth, Duke said, "I'll be God damn. Ain't seen you in a long time, Mickey. What brings you back?"

Before Mickey could answer, Toot did it for him.

"He got married. He's moving back into Ruby and Dub's place."

"No kiddin'?"

Duke's acknowledgement failed to capture the surprise felt by the entire group over what Toot had just announced.

"I thought I'd try to work things out with Toot and the business."

Jake was the first to take issue with Mickey's remark.

"I'm not aware that Toot needs any help. Son-of-a-bitch makes more money sellin' cattle to Japs, fancy restaurants, and tree-huggers than the rest of us can on the open market."

Billy seconded Jake's observation with, "Besides, all his cattle could fall over dead tomorrow, and he'd still be a millionaire with the price of oil where it is."

Duke, being a seasoned and educated businessman, pushed Mickey for more information.

"What about all those companies you started? Are they in trouble or somethin'?"

"No," Mickey replied. "I took each of them public and moved on."

"You done a lot of that movin' on, Mickey," Duke said, referring indirectly to Mickey's relationship with his father. "Oh, before I forget, pour me another cup. Sarah's out in the truck, and I told her I'd take her a cup of coffee."

Toot poured the cup as asked, and Duke added some cream and sugar, stirring the drink well.

"She's welcome to join us, Duke," Henry said. "I'll keep all these other dirty old men away from her."

"Other dirty old men? Let me ask Lorraine about the status of your knighthood, Sir Henry."

The group had another good laugh.

"No, she's out there logged onto the Internet on her damn iPhone, checkin' stock prices and doin' all kinds of computer shit I don't understand. Guess that's what I get for marryin' a woman twenty years younger and a whole lot smarter."

"Here, Duke, let me take her the coffee," Mickey offered. "I know you and Toot have some business to attend to."

"Mickey," Toot said, "I think you should be here for that discussion."

"Actually, we ain't talkin' rocket surgery or nothin'," Duke said. "Besides, it can wait a minute or two. Sarah'd probably get a kick out of seein' Mickey again."

Toot wanted desperately to keep that from happening, but there was no way to keep Mickey away from her without making a scene. Duke handed the cup of coffee to Mickey that he quickly carried outside before Toot could do anything to intervene.

Mickey walked up to the passenger side of the four-door late-model Dodge where Sarah's face was illuminated by the soft glow of her phone. She was as beautiful as he remembered. He tapped on the window to get her attention.

Sarah couldn't make out who her visitor was in the morning darkness, but she knew it wasn't Duke so she rolled down her window.

"Is that you, Jake?"

Before there was any answer, she recognized who was standing outside the door.

"Mickey?"

"Hey, Sarah. I brought you your coffee."

Sarah was frozen in place.

"Your coffee. Do you want it?"

"Mickey, you shouldn't be here."

"Sarah, it's coffee...just coffee."

"I doubt that, Mickey. It's never *just* anything with you. So, why are you here?"

"I've come back to live on the ranch."

"Ruby and Dub's place?"

"Does that surprise you?"

"Just doesn't seem right, I guess. That's a big place for one man."

"I'll be there with my wife."

Sarah turned her head back toward Mickey so violently, her neck cracked.

"You're...married?"

"Yep. Her name is Diane. You need to come by and meet her and the kid."

"You have a child, too?"

"Daughter, named Gigi."

Hiding the expression on her face with her hands, Sarah said, "So you're going to be a PTA dad after all? I thought you didn't want children. That's what you said, once upon a time."

"That was fifteen years ago, Sarah. People change."

"People do, Mickey. You don't. Thanks for the coffee," she said taking it from him, then closing the window.

Mickey realized it was pointless to try to talk to Sarah any further...at least for now.

"I'll see you around," he said, waving his hand as he went back into the Store.

Sarah didn't give an audible response.

MICKEY REJOINED TOOT AND Duke who were standing over in a corner by the meat counter. Their conversation was already underway.

"I can add another twenty-thousand square feet to the existing storage here, but to do it Out West will cost you a lot more—probably another fifteen percent."

"Yeah, but Duke, I hate slaughterin' then haulin' meat back here. It just makes the paperwork trail a nightmare, and these people are anal about records. If I build here, are you goin' to give me a break on the transportation?"

"Hey, diesel's out of sight, and I don't see it gettin' better, Toot. I can't make any commitment like that without workin' some numbers."

"Well, figure out what you can do and let me know. I have a meetin' with the bank next week. I have to move on this quick or I'm goin' to have to send cattle to auction."

"I could lease you more land right here, locally."

"I might could use some, but I really need to ship more finished beef out of here. I got people beggin' for more...close to twenty-five percent more. Keepin' 'em on the hoof at your place doesn't help the top line."

"You guys partners still?" Mickey asked, interrupting the discussion.

Paul explained, "Clem talked your daddy into splittin' the business up. He'd handle the animal end of things, while I'd handle all the transportation, any construction, and lease him grazin' land. We're still arguin' over who should do the cold storage. These customers of Toot's are a real pain in the ass. It's gotta be this temperature. They can't be stored more than so many days. Meat's gotta be RFID-tagged. The truck has to be loaded a special way. Blah, blah, blah. Now Toot wants to expand Out West, and I'm not sure it's worth my while."

"Oh, come on, Duke, it's always been a good business for you," Toot said.

"How much cost can you pass on to the customer?"

"Oh, maybe three to five percent."

"Better be five. I'll give you some figures tomorrow mornin'. Same time and place?"

"That'll be fine, Duke."

Before Duke could leave, Mickey got his attention.

"One more thing. That land you mentioned leasing, could I put some horses on it?"

"Horses?" Duke asked.

Toot tipped his hat back on his head waiting for Duke to begin his lecture.

"That's right. Diane wants to raise Thoroughbreds."

"I can ask Henry to start a fire over there in the stove, and you can throw your money right into it. That'll be a hell of a lot easier."

"She knows what she's doing."

"Mickey, Toot's runnin' a cattle business. Stick with the plan."

"This is more of a hobby than anything."

"Hobby? I ain't had a hobby since I was twelve. Best get that dumb ass idea out of your head. Sarah and I did Thoroughbreds for a while about twenty years ago. Hurt like a kidney stone. I know only a handful of people who ever made money at that."

"Was one of them called by the name of Fontaine?"

Duke rubbed his chin while he thought.

"As a matter of fact, that was one of those I'd put on the list as havin' done well in the business."

"That's Diane's maiden name. She and her parents raised Thoroughbreds in California. She's back in the business out there, and I want to help her start up a satellite operation here on the ranch."

Duke put his hands up in the air as he said, "You go ahead and do whatever you want to do. Just don't screw up the cattle business, don't go puttin' any more on Toot's plate, and spend your own damn money. You want land? There's a hundred and fifteen acres that borders your ranch to the south that's up for sale. Guy wants a fortune for it—he's waiting for a sucker. Maybe you're just the guy." Duke shook Toot's hand, then Mickey's before closing with, "Good to have you back, Mickey…I guess." They exchanged smiles. "Was Sarah glad to see you?"

"Let's just say I was the last person she expected to see today."

"Well, that goes for me, too."

Before Duke walked off, he noticed the boots on Mickey's feet.

"I'd recognize those Leddy's anywhere. That's wrong…just plain wrong."

He shook his head, then turned, waived at the others in the Store, and headed out the door.

"I SEE DELANEY'S MOVED up in the world," Mickey said, remarking on the attorney's new office in a renovated, 3-story Victorian home.

"Yep. He was in that place on Center Street for twenty-eight years. He's in practice now with his son and his daughter."

"You talking about Deborah Delaney?"

"No, I'm talkin' about Deborah Moffitt—Mrs. Charles Moffitt. You missed out on another one."

"Me? I thought you dated her for a while. In fact, I remember a time down at the creek..."

"No you don't. Erase that from your memory."

"I was with Teri Griffin. You were with Deb. You brought the beer Jimmy Baker bought for us, I brought the blankets..."

"Mickey...erase. We're fixin' to talk to her father. Quick, what's Delaney's son's name?"

"Gregory?"

"No! It's Gordon. Get the names straight. You gotta show this guy some respect."

Toot parked his Chevy truck outside the office. There were plenty of spaces as it was still early in the morning. They were met at the door by Roger Delaney himself.

"Mornin', Toot. Mornin', Mickey. Come on in. Coffee'll be ready in about five minutes, give or take. Y'all take a seat here in the parlor so we can chat a while."

Toot and Mickey took a seat on a sofa. Delaney sat in a high-back, black leather chair. A coffee table separated them. He crossed his long legs, Mickey and Toot copied him. It only took a moment for Delaney to notice them.

"Let me ask you something, Mickey. Is your return to the ranch symbolic of something?"

"No, sir. I just need a place to settle with my wife for a while so we can complete her therapy. As for my father's boots you're staring at—that everybody seems to notice before they take note of me—I'll be returning them to their place in his office about ten seconds after I get home."

"Read my mind. Now, tell me about this therapy. Toot said something about brain damage."

"We don't refer to it as…"

"…who is 'we,' Mickey?"

"My partners in the project."

"Is it therapy, or is it a project? I'm a bit confused."

"Both."

"So, back to these partners, do they have names?" Delaney asked, watching Mickey closely.

"Yes, and those names would be confidential at this moment."

"And why is that?"

"Because what we are doing is leading-edge…the first of its kind."

"Do you have your wife's permission to do this?"

"After a fashion. I have power of attorney due to her injury."

"Is she unable to function?"

"No, she does quite well now. There are still some refinements we must work on."

"So, when were you married? Was that before or after her injury?"

"Actually, we had a ceremony on a ship, before the injury."

"And what was the ship's registry?"

"To answer the question you didn't ask, I understand that the wedding on the ship was not a legally binding act. We had a legal marriage in California."

"Of course you did. I'm certain you can provide me with a certified copy of the license."

"You don't trust me, Roger?"

"Let me put it to you this way, Mickey. I had a trusting relationship with your father, and I have that type of relationship with Toot, here. You and I, on the other hand, aren't there just yet. Secondly, I doubt seriously if a marriage would be considered valid if, in fact, at the time of the marriage, the bride didn't have the capacity to know what she was doing. That's more like kidnapping, than marriage. I'd have to look into the matter as it probably varies from state to state."

Mickey sat forward, put his hands on his knees and said, "Roger, is this your version of chatting? Because if it is, I never want to be cross-examined by you."

Delaney laughed at Mickey's remark.

"I'm sorry to come across like something of an ass, Mickey, but you see, I promised your daddy a long time ago that after he passed, I'd make damn sure everything ended up the way he wanted it. We ain't talking about a couple hundred thousand here. That estate, plus the trust, is a big son-of-a-bitch. And, you know, he worded it so that Clem got a third, which he conveyed to Toot when he died, you got a third, the Trust got twenty percent, the first bride of either you or Toot gets ten percent, and the bride of the last of you two idiots to marry will get the remainder."

"Roger, you knew him. Why'd he do the will that way? I mean it's natural for a father to pass his estate onto his son."

"You know Mickey, that's right. I've lost count of how many family estates I've handled and Trusts I watch over, and almost without exception, a father passes his wealth on to his family. I hate to be the bearer of bad news, but he didn't think you could handle the ranch and the money."

"That's crazy, Roger."

"Is it? I look before me and I see two well-established men. Toot here has, quite frankly, done all the work since Dub and Clem died. He handles all the responsibilities of co-Trustee, requiring little guidance from me. He handles all the philanthropy. He's made money on the ranch every year. He's made money in the oil business every year. You, on the other hand, while you've made a success of yourself according to my research, you ain't been a part of the action here. You're off making money wherever you've planted your butt, and you've made no attempt to engage in the business with Toot. I'd say your daddy was a wise man. My only gripe with Toot here is that he took my daughter down to the creek that time."

Toot looked as though he had swallowed a tennis ball.

"Betcha didn't think I knew, did you, Toot?"

"No, sir."

"Other than that, he's been a real gentleman. Frankly, I always hoped he'd be the first one to get married so his family would have majority control. That may not be the case if, in fact, you have a legal marriage. To that end, if you would be so kind as to produce a certified copy of the marriage certificate at your earliest convenience, we could put this matter to rest."

"I'll see to that as soon as I get settled in, Roger."

"Thank you, Mickey. Now, how about that coffee?"

"I'll take care of that, sir."

"Thanks, Toot. See what I mean, Mickey? He's a real gentleman."

Toot got coffee for the three, then sat back down on the sofa.

Making small talk, Mickey asked, "So, how's Gordon doing?"

"Gordon, who the hell's Gordon? Do you mean, Gregory, my son?"

Mickey looked at Toot, who was staring away from Mickey at a painting on the far side of the parlor.

Chapter 29

"Why do I have to do this Mickey? I don't like talking to a lot of strangers."

"These people are all important contributors to your rehabilitation. They give us a lot of guidance, they fund my work, and they want to monitor your progress. Someday, the therapy you're experiencing could be available to others."

"Can't you just give them a written report or send them a video?"

"No, babe, they want to meet you in person."

"Couldn't you have given me some warning? I mean, you take me out to breakfast at a local restaurant, then I find out I have this meeting in San Antonio."

"There are set guidelines for what I can tell you in advance, just as I have set guidelines as to what they can ask you."

"Why? Why can't I just be me?"

"It's just some of the many controls we have in place to help validate the success of the project."

"Do you know the questions they're going to ask me?"

"For the most part."

"Why are we having a meeting now? I mean, we just got to Texas two days ago."

"Because it's been fifteen months since your fall, and that's an important milestone."

"How often will I have these meetings?"

"Four times a year. We have a firm schedule."

"Have you had meetings like this one before?"

"Yes, I have met most of these individuals previously at quarterly progress updates. This time, the group wants to meet you in person."

"Do we get to travel to other locations for the meetings?"

"No, at least not in the foreseeable future. I want you close to home."

"Is Dr. Mendoza going to be there?"

"No."

"Is Suki going to be there?"

"No."

"I really would feel better if she was there."

"Not this time."

"What about Gigi?"

"No. This doesn't concern her except for the fact that you have experienced a normal pregnancy and are dealing with motherhood extremely well."

"What about Toot? Is he coming?"

"No. He has nothing to do with your therapy per se."

"Per se. I think my whole life is nothing but per se."

Mickey pulled the brand new platinum-colored Land Rover, with the dealer-provided temporary license plates, into the parking lot and brought it to a halt.

"Aren't you going to park in the 'handicapped' parking?"

"Babe, you aren't handicapped. You need to stop thinking of yourself in that way. Right now, I need you to turn on your usual charm, and put away this frustration you're feeling."

Diane let out a blood-curdling scream that must have lasted for a good ten seconds, turning her face red, and scaring Mickey in the process.

"There, now I feel better. How's this for charm?" she asked, leaning over and kissed Mickey.

"Dandy."

His answer was less than honest, as he was concerned about Diane's diametric behavior—something she exhibited quite often. He walked around the vehicle and opened Diane's door for her.

"You know, the reason I could tear a phonebook in half right now is because of all that caffeine you pumped into me this morning."

"Just your usual espressos. You always have three."

"Can I answer the questions in Chinese?"

"No."

"French?"

"English. Please stick with English."

"Don't you want to impress them with my language skills?"

"Believe me, they'll be impressed the moment you walk through the door."

"Where's your laptop?"

"Don't need it."

"That's right. All you need is your iPad."

"What room do we go to?"

"Babe, you're nervous and asking a lot of questions. Just walk with me. Remember, focus on staying calm and being charming."

Mickey and Diane proceeded from the parking lot to the entrance of the elegant San Antonio hotel. As they approached the double, wooden and gilded doors, they neared a large, decorative water fountain at which point Diane slowed to a stop and developed a blank look.

"What's the matter, babe?"

"Do you hear that?"

"I hear the water fountain."

As soon as Mickey said those words, he realized Diane might be having an association with that sound. Diane crossed her arms, began to shiver, and soon tears ran down her cheeks.

"Mickey, something bad is going to happen."

"You'll be fine. Let's go inside."

"That sound. That means something bad is going to happen. Mickey!"

He wasted no time quickly escorting Diane through the door and into the hotel lobby. As soon as she was inside and surrounded by the sound of a cleaning crew vacuuming the carpet, she quickly began to calm down. After walking across the room to the far side of the lobby, Diane sat down in a chair where she could look out onto a courtyard.

"What was that all about?" Diane asked, embarrassed by her behavior.

"I think you may have a touch of post traumatic stress disorder. I'm not surprised."

"From the sound of water?"

"It could be. You fell in a pool at the base of a waterfall. That's where your injury occurred. The sound may have triggered a strong emotional response."

"Ya think?"

After letting Diane calm down some more, Mickey asked, "Do you recall anything about the accident?"

Diane took her time, but ultimately she responded, "No, nothing specific." Looking up from her chair, she asked, "Why won't you tell me more details about what happened? I feel like you're hiding things from me. This whole water fountain thing probably could have been avoided if you would just tell me more about my past."

"Diane, I've told you a hundred times, there's a method and order to what we're doing. We must proceed carefully. A lot of your memory will be restored spontaneously. It's possible at some point you may experience an event that will, for lack of a better description, shock you into achieving total or nearly total recall of your memories. Do you trust me?"

She closed her eyes for a moment to put herself into her calm space before answering, "You're right. I guess I just need to have patience."

"I love you, Diane."

Finally opening her eyes, Diane smiled and said, "I love you, too, Mick."

"Let's go," Mickey said, helping Diane to her feet. "The room is upstairs on the second floor. Just be natural. I'll coach you through the meeting. You'll do just fine."

"I need to stop off at a bathroom first."

"Sure, there's one over here on the left."

Mickey guided Diane in the general direction of the bathroom, at which point she took off on her own.

Minutes later, Diane exited her bathroom stall and stood face to face with her nearly full-length image in a mirror. She was dressed in a very professional-looking, gray jacket and slacks, with a white-collared blouse. After pausing to study her reflection in the mirror, she pulled out the hairbrush and cosmetic bag from her purse to do some touch-ups. When she had finished, she paused again...this time at length. There was something about the image staring back at her that looked so familiar, yet so out of place. She spent time trying to decipher what was simply the reversal of the image from left to right, but that didn't ease her anxiety. Then, there was the business attire that looked as if it was made just for her. Why did this look so perfect? But the one thing that stood out the most was her facial expression. It showed a lack of confidence, trepidation, and was inconsistent with everything else she was looking at and experiencing.

A voice spoke up from the doorway of the restroom.

"Are you Diane?"

"Yes, I am," she responded, somewhat startled.

"Your husband was worried about you. Are you alright?"

"I'm fine. I'm just a little nervous about a meeting I have to attend."

"You're Diane Rollins, correct?"

"That's right. How did you know?"

"I'm Margaret Pearce from the Baylor College of Medicine. I'm one of committee members who will be speaking with you this morning. Believe me, we're all excited to meet you. Don't worry about a thing." She smiled and finished with, "I like your suit."

Diane chuckled, "It's been so long since I've dressed like this. I have no recent memory of wearing a suit, but it looks like I should be in one all the time."

Dr. Pearce approached Diane.

"May I?" She asked, reaching for the collar of Diane's jacket.

Diane watched the doctor as she stepped behind her, then felt a tug.

"Tag. Obviously your husband is as useless as mine."

Grinning, Diane acknowledged the gesture.

"Thanks...and yes."

Both ladies laughed. Diane turned and reached out to shake Dr. Pearce's hand, but the moment was immediately and dramatically awkward because Diane held out her left hand—Pearce held out her right. It was at that moment that Diane realized for the first time she wasn't sure about her left and her right sides.

Dr. Pearce picked up on her confusion.

"It's alright, Diane. I've read your case file, and I know what you've been through. That you may have some physical disassociation is not uncommon. I find the fact that you are functioning and speaking as well as you are to be nothing short of a miracle. Your husband is waiting. You had better get back to him before he comes barging in."

Without giving the situation much thought, Diane leaned over and hugged Dr. Pearce, then left the room.

Joining Mickey, she was almost excited about her encounter. She handed Mickey the tag that had been removed from her suit.

"You're useless. You know that, right?"

"I don't follow you, Diane, but that doesn't matter. We're late."

"No, we're not. Dr. Pearce is still in the bathroom. She's late."

"Is that who that was?"

"Duh?"

"Did you tell her anything? Did she ask you any questions?"

"Yes, and yes. And guess what, my left and right are screwed up. When did that happen?"

"Look, I don't want you answering questions from strangers right now."

"Mickey, what happened to my left and right?"

"There might be a disassociation problem. Most likely it will be temporary."

"Mickey, I've been writing with my right hand for the last nine months best I can remember. Two minutes ago, I had a vivid memory of being left-handed. I think your definition of temporary differs from mine."

"The fact is Diane, you can write. Your handwriting is beautiful, and your spelling is perfect."

"Mickey, you don't get it do you? You once told me some stupid riddle, something like, 'If you look in a mirror, are you looking at the image or is the image looking at you?' You said it didn't matter…well it does. I'm that image in the mirror now, I'm not Diane."

"Let's go to the meeting, we can discuss this more later."

"I'm serious, Mickey, I want this shit fixed. I want to be what I used to be."

"That's my desire, too, babe. We'll get there."

DIANE WAS RELIEVED TO find only three people waiting in the room for her. They were joined, in short order, by a fourth person, who was at least a little familiar—Dr. Pearce. One by one they approached her and introduced themselves while Mickey stood close by.

The first to greet her was an older, silver-haired man.

"Good morning, Diane, I'm Dr. Jim Walsh from Toronto."

"My pleasure. What is it that you do?"

"I'm the Director of a hospital that treats individuals who have sustained a loss of memory or motor function. I've been retained by the company that is funding your husband's work—which is, of course, your therapy."

"It's nice to meet you."

Diane looked at Dr. Pearce who was next to Dr. Walsh.

"We've met already. What do you do at Baylor?"

"Hello again, Diane. I'm the Department Chair for neurological research. I, too, have been retained by the same company."

"I see. And what's the name of this company both of you are referring to?"

A third person from the group approached Diane. He was a Middle-Eastern man who appeared to be somewhat nervous.

"That would be my company, Diane. I am Rajeev Munshi, CEO and President of a company called Medico Techniq."

Diane extended her hand to Rajeev's outstretched one.

"It's a pleasure to meet you."

Rajeev didn't immediately let go of her hand after the initial introduction.

"Is there something wrong?" Diane asked.

"Have we met before? I feel that I know you."

This was the reunion that most concerned Mickey.

Boundaries

She studied Rajeev for a few seconds, but quickly responded, "Not that I remember, but then, of course, it's my memory that's the topic of discussion. Should I know you?"

Rajeev noticed Mickey glaring at him and took the hint.

"Perhaps I am mistaken."

Before Diane could move on to the final person in the group, Rajeev asked one more question.

"Have you heard of my company before, Diane?"

After a short pause, Diane replied, "No, I'm not familiar with that company. Should I be?"

Again, Rajeev took note of Mickey's expression.

"Maybe it is my ego working overtime. I thought everyone knew about my company."

He motioned toward the final member of the evaluation team.

"Allow me to introduce Dr. Gert Braune, my Chief Technical Officer."

Stepping forward, Braune said, with a strong German accent, "Hello. It is an honor to be here with you today."

"An honor? My, I didn't know I held such lofty status."

"Yours is a remarkable story. I would go as far as to say you are a walking medical milestone."

Taking particular note of Braune's accent, Diane asked, "Do you know a person named Uma?"

Braune replied, "But of course, Uma is a very common name in Central Europe. Might you be referring to one in particular?"

Diane thought for a moment, then replied, "There must be, otherwise I can't imagine why I would suggest such a name."

"Do you know her family name…a last name, perhaps?"

"No," Diane replied after a few moments.

"What did this person, Uma, do? How do you know her?"

"I can't remember. I just have a feeling that she is someone important to me. But, right now, I'm unable to paint a clearer picture."

Diane stared at Braune for a few seconds as if she was beginning to recall some bits and pieces.

"Painting—maybe she was an artist? Does that ring a bell?"

"No, I'm afraid not."

Smiling, Diane said, "Such is my life. I encounter dead ends like this all day long."

"And yet, you have made so much progress," Mickey said to the group, "and it is that progress which we are here to discuss."

Mickey took his coat off and placed it atop his iPad. After Diane and the others had taken a seat in the informal setting of the small conference room, Mickey began to answer questions to offer some detail regarding Diane's injuries, the therapy, and her progress.

"Dr. Rollins," Walsh began, "Can you give us more description about Diane's brain injury?"

"Of course. There couldn't be a more perfect subject for this therapy than Diane. The injury was sustained when Diane fell forward from a standing position onto a solid surface. There was immediate coup trauma to the frontal lobe of the brain, but fortunately no contra-coup trauma nor other direct trauma to any other part of the brain, or the rest of her body for that matter. The ensuing increase in intracranial pressure was mitigated by quick-thinking witnesses at the scene who used ice in a bathtub to lower her body temperature immediately after the accident. Diane was also exposed to an environment in which she inhaled the byproducts of certain plants and roots as they burned."

"Can you tell us what those were?" Walsh asked.

"No. Unfortunately that remains proprietary at this point."

Walsh and the others looked at each other and nodded.

"Continuing with her injury pattern, the injury itself was ischemic in nature caused by swelling, in addition to a bruising of the immediate area, both of which disproportionately affected the right side more than the left."

"So, as you reported, Diane suffered some emotional changes?" Dr. Pearce asked.

"Yes, and they were initially quite profound, largely involved in the mediation of emotions. She suffered from extremes, and, in spite of substantial progress, she remains on a small dose of lithium."

"Would you describe this as a bipolar disorder?"

"The symptoms were similar, but the etiology was quite different. It should be considered traumatic, rather than organic, in origin."

"Can you give us an example of these symptoms?"

"Certainly. I don't have to look too far. When we arrived at the parking lot outside just a short while ago, Diane resorted to screaming out of frustration over a conversation we were having. She followed the screams by giving me a very affectionate kiss. This pattern of dysfunction is typical and common."

"Can I say something at this point?" Diane interrupted.

Rajeev replied, "Of course."

Before Diane could continue, Mickey jumped in.

"I think it's best if we continue with the predetermined set of questions."

"I think, if you want me to stay in this room, you should allow me some time to talk," Diane responded emphatically.

Mickey didn't want the situation to turn into a meltdown, so he allowed Diane to have her say.

"Go ahead, babe."

"Do any of you find this entire situation outrageous? You're all speaking of me like I am a science project. You're addressing me in the third person...the subject, if you will...with a dysfunction. You say I have experienced some emotional changes. Well, one emotion still works. I'm hurt." Diane's eyes began to get somewhat misty. "I'm hurt by all of you—those of you who are asking the questions, and those of you who are just sitting there listening. If I scream out of frustration, consider what you would do if you were in my position.

"What's more, I ask to have questions answered, yet my dear husband doesn't bother to give me an answer. It's always 'not now,' or 'be patient,' or 'don't you trust me?' or some other bullshit answer. Then you sit down with him, and he eagerly answers all your questions. I think I deserve the same respect given to each of you, wouldn't you agree?"

Rajeev answered, "Forgive us, Diane. We were trying to find out more about you, and, at the same time, operate within a set of predetermined conditions. Perhaps Dr. Rollins could give us, and you, a little latitude?"

Mickey was clearly unhappy by being put on the spot, but he had no choice other than to accept Rajeev's suggestion.

"Alright, Diane, do you have a question you would like to ask?"

"A question? Try five thousand!"

"Well, let's begin with one and go from there."

"Why don't you begin by explaining to me and the group why I used to be left-handed and now I'm right-handed?"

"Nice segue, Diane. Actually, we were just about to get to that point. As Diane has pointed out, she now favors right-sided motor activity versus left-sided. It's true, as she says, that she used to be left-handed. As mentioned previously, the injury affected the right side of her brain more than the left. During restorative therapy, the left side of her brain became dominant. One result of this is that she now favors right-sided motor skills."

"Was there damage to the primary motor cortex?" Walsh asked.

"Yes, and the pre-motor cortex. So initially, she had trouble thinking about doing the things she was setting out to do, as well as the actions themselves. All of these processes had to be restored."

"Diane?" Braune asked. "Would you describe yourself as a positive person or a negative person?"

"Do you mean is the glass half-full or half-empty? I would say I have had very negative feelings since the accident, but I am feeling increasingly positive with time."

Pearce spoke up.

"Diane, what you just described is consistent with current theory that there is asymmetry within the brain. One such asymmetry in the frontal lobe is that the left side favors positive feelings and the right side negative feelings."

Taking Diane by the hand, Mickey continued, "Damage to the frontal lobe affects one's inhibitive control. This is precisely what you have experienced. Initially following the accident, you could be described as having violent behavior. That was controlled at first pharmaceutically. As time progressed and we made headway with your therapy, your behavior has become much more socially consistent."

"Socially consistent? What about just returning me to the way I was?"

"And how would that be, Diane? There is no fingerprint for your emotional behavior. All that exists is the memory held by those closest to you and their description of how you were."

"Including yours?"

"Yes, mine."

"And Suki's?"

"Yes, especially Suki's."

"Why don't I remember being this monster you describe?"

"Just as I have told you that you are not handicapped, you were not a monster either. You *were* in transition."

"Ah, yes, between here and there—that's me, alright."

"Another aspect of the left side of the frontal lobe is that it plays a greater role than the right in preserving new memories. Therefore, we have concentrated on supporting recent history for you. Events prior to the accident, and for that matter, prior to the second breakpoint of your therapy, are still largely not a part of your memory."

Diane shivered briefly.

"Is that why I can't remember being pregnant?"

"Most likely," Mickey answered.

Leaning forward, Rajeev asked, "Dr. Rollins, what is this second breakpoint you mention. Is it a milestone of some sort?"

"Absolutely. The first breakpoint is the point of self-awareness—in the simplest of terms, knowing that one exists. The therapy until that point is largely driven from external sources. At the second breakpoint, Diane began showing clear signs of having stitched together blocks of new, post-traumatic, memory into continuous periods of time and patterns of conscious behavior that fit social norms."

"Diane?"

"Yes, Dr. Pearce."

"Do you have any memory of your childhood, teenage years, or early adult life?"

"Bits and pieces. We own the same ranch in Gilroy where Mickey says I grew up. Yet, each day I'm there, I have only fleeting images of a past. It's a beautiful place. I'd like to remember what it was like growing up there...my parents...my brother."

"Do you recall anything about your years subsequent to growing up on the ranch?" Rajeev asked.

"Nothing I can actually describe. It's like my life was a six-hundred-page novel, and someone tore out all but every tenth page, then marked out most of the words on those pages."

"What do you recall of those pages?" Rajeev persisted.

"Rajeev, we know her memory is still being restored. I don't think it adds value to this discussion by focusing on the past."

"But Dr. Rollins, a person's memories are in many ways more treasured than..."

"Bakersfield," Diane interrupted. "There's something about Bakersfield."

"And what might that be? Have you returned to Bakersfield since the accident?" Pearce asked.

"I don't know what it is about that place, and Mickey hasn't taken me there. He says it's not time yet."

"Is that so?" Rejeev said, taking great notice of what Diane said.

"Yes, Rajeev, that's so," Mickey answered. "Restorative therapy is a process, not some arbitrary collection of actions."

"He's right, Rajeev," Walsh said.

"Diane, what can you tell me about this person named Suki?"

"She's my assistant in Diane's therapy," Mickey answered.

"I think he was asking me," Diane said, disturbed that Mickey had answered for her.

"The question isn't part of today's discussion."

"Why not?"

"This meeting is about you, Diane, not how you became you."

"But it's a very simple question, Dr. Rollins," Rajeev continued.

Mickey pulled out his iPad from under his coat and began jotting down what appeared to be notes, ignoring Rajeev's remark.

Despite Mickey's warnings, Diane offered a response.

"She's a very close friend who is with me almost every minute of the day. She is for my mind what a physical therapist is to an injured sports player. She is teaching me how to live a full life once again."

"And how is she doing this?" Braune asked.

"I don't quite know."

"Precisely," Mickey said. "Here's what I have to say, and then we must move on. In the course of Diane's treatment, she has taken on near savant tendencies. What's more, she has an unbounded ability to learn. Through hypnosis, she has a complete recall of all that is said to her. Suki is what one could describe as a mentor's mentor. She is extremely intelligent, she has a remarkable formal education, she is a high-achiever by every measure, and she befriended Diane during our trip to Thailand shortly before the accident. They became very close in just a short amount of time, and she volunteered to assist Diane in her recovery, regardless of how long it takes."

"But what makes her special?" Rajeev asked. "You could at least have found someone from San Diego."

"San Die…"

Diane quit speaking suddenly and a blank look came across her face. The group became restless as Diane essentially shut off. Mickey put his iPad back under his coat.

"What did you do to her? Rajeev asked, shocked by what he had just witnessed.

"I've essentially put Diane in 'stand-by.' Shutting her down in this manner creates the appearance that she is experiencing an absence seizure."

"Dr. Rollins, this is truly disturbing." Pearce said, holding her hands up to her cheeks.

"Can she understand what we are saying right now, Mickey?" Rajeev asked.

"She's completely shielded until I reset the instruction."

"She has no idea what you are doing to her, does she? She has no idea about the surgery and the transfer from Suki," Braune said, shaking his head.

"None, which is why we have to stick with the script. Rajeev almost blew it with the reference to San Diego," Mickey replied.

"Why can't we bring up San Diego, her job, and her husband, Dr. Rollins? Why can't we fill in those gaps in her past?"

"That's too far in her past, Rajeev, not to mention the fact that they don't exist as a part of host memory. They have to wait."

"I knew Diane for ten years. I worked with her and she was a close personal friend. I insist that I, too, should be considered as a person who could help restore Diane's memory."

"That isn't practical. As I've mentioned in my reports, the restorative therapy must come from tightly controlled sources. If two sources were to give mixed information, that portion of the restoration could generate unfortunate consequences."

Becoming obviously irritated, Rajeev argued, "Dr. Rollins, is it possible that you have another reason to keep these cherished memories from Diane?"

"I find your suggestion insulting, Rajeev. All I care about is Diane's best interest."

"And I find what is going on here to be totally unethical. You are controlling a human being...a person...with a device you hold in your hand."

"It has to be that way until we're done. You know what Diane is capable of doing."

"Does she have any idea what happened to Dr. Wu?" Walsh asked.

"None whatsoever. She has no memory of him at all."

"We should have reported it to the authorities, Rajeev," Braune said to his boss.

"Spare me your righteous bullshit, Gert," Mickey said. "You want to see this project through to the end as much as the rest of us."

"What if Suki tells them at some point."

Mickey shook his head.

"She'll be the first to tell you she's glad he's gone."

"And tell me, what of Dr. Mendoza? Where is he?" Rajeev asked.

"I've removed him from the project until we resolve an issue."

"So what you are saying, Dr. Rollins, is that you now are operating independently with no direct oversight."

"Is anybody in this room the least bit excited by the fact that I've taken a person who suffered a debilitating brain injury resulting in profound loss of memory and function, and she sits before you today, for all intents and purposes, a normal, healthy, adult female and a mother?"

"Perhaps we should stop where we are," Pearce suggested.

"Let me remind you that when I discussed the nature of this project with you at the onset, I told you then there would be no turning back once we started. We would go all the way or Diane could have permanent deficits."

"I'm afraid I regret having given you my support back then. If I had an alternative at this moment, I'd tell you to stop what you are doing immediately."

Rajeev got up and walked over to Diane where he passed his hand in front of her face, failing to register a response.

"Since I have none, I'm forced to let you proceed. Please take good care of my friend."

He took his seat once more.

"Thank you, Rajeev, for your not-so-enthusiastic endorsement and continuing support. I promise you will be pleasantly surprised at Diane's progress each and every time we get together.

"I also need to advise you that we've relocated to my ranch here in Texas. There is a lot of adjustment and settling in that we must do. I would ask you to have our next meeting in six months, with subsequent meetings once per quarter as you have previously requested."

"Why did you relocate, Dr. Rollins?" Pearce asked. "You had a perfectly marvelous home in Sausalito and the new ranch in Gilroy appeared to offer much for Diane's recovery, being a business as well as a recreational opportunity."

Mickey studied the members of the group before deciding to give them an answer.

"All I can say at this point is that the move has to do with Diane's safety."

"Her safety?" Rajeev asked with an alarmed tone.

"As I suspected a long time ago, the technology we are applying to Diane has far-reaching possibilities in the context of rehabilitation. Having said that, some of the technology we are using has an application in the intelligence and military setting. I have reason to believe that Dr. Mendoza was being seduced by large sums of money for information about our work"

"I don't quite follow you," Rajeev said.

"Consider the ramifications of being able to alter a person's memory—what they believe to be real or unreal, true or untrue, right or wrong. At the same time, consider the possibility of extracting information from a person without having to use torture in the conventional sense of the word."

"I see. And you say Mendoza was being seduced. Do you think he succumbed to selling information about this project to someone?"

"Not someone…three governments."

"Good Lord!" Walsh exclaimed. "I can't believe someone in the medical community would sacrifice his integrity for money."

"How much do they know?" Rajeev asked.

"Enough to be extremely interested. They've apparently been monitoring our progress for some time, and now that the effort appears to show a great deal of promise, I'm afraid they might intervene."

"How?"

"In the case of our government, they might prevent the therapy from going public, retaining it for military application only."

"What about the others?" Pearce asked.

"I suspect they will buy what they can and take the rest."

"I don't particularly like the word 'take,'" Rajeev said, wringing his hands.

"And you shouldn't," Mickey replied.

Dr. Walsh stood up from the table.

"People, I'm sorry to do this to you, but this activity has just gone far beyond anything we have discussed. I can't risk any involvement in something like this. You will have to forego my participation in this evaluation from this point forward."

"That's not possible," Mickey said. "The same people who are interested in the science behind this technology are also interested in anyone who knows about that science. That includes each and every one of you."

Rajeev stood up and shouted, "Dr. Rollins, this is preposterous! This is an outrage! You've taken money from my company on false pretenses! You've put all of us in danger! I'll see you in court over this!"

"Everyone, please, sit down. The last thing we need to do is bring a lot of publicity to the project. Public acceptance is the only thing that will keep the technology from going underground with the military or another government."

"But won't public acceptance require a considerable amount of publicity in and of itself, Dr. Rollins?" Braune asked.

"Exactly, Gert. In many ways, the best way to avoid being the victim of a misdeed is to be in a crowded place—to be in the spotlight. This is where Diane needs help from all of you."

Dr. Walsh started toward the door, followed shortly by Dr. Pearce.

"Please, doctors," Rajeev said emphatically, raising his hands in the air. "Please, stay and help us think this through. If Dr. Rollins is wrong in his assertion about outside involvement, then we have nothing to worry about. If he is correct, then as he said, it may be too late, so another few minutes of discussion shouldn't put anyone at more risk than may already be the case. Please, stay."

Walsh and Pearce stopped just short of the door and looked at each other, but failed to return to the table.

"I'll double your fee," Rajeev offered.

After a few moments, the two consultants returned to the table.

"Ah, integrity meets capitalism once again," Mickey said, smiling.

"Dr. Rollins," Pearce said, "if you want us on your side, I suggest you refrain from any further unflattering discourse. What do you have in mind for Diane?"

"She needs visibility. In the context of a patient recovering from a traumatic brain injury, I'd like to begin exposing her to the public as a spokesperson. We can begin to tell her story, though not any of the particulars of the remedy right now. Let's face it, if ever there was a 'poster-child' for a cause, it would be Diane. She's beautiful, she's articulate, and she has a personal experience to share. I'd like to establish a Foundation in her name that funds research in the treatment of memory loss. It'll need corporate sponsorship and seed money."

"And that's where I come in, correct?"

"We're on the same page, Rajeev. I also need a website and webmaster. Could you...?"

"Yes, I'll provide that, too."

"Good. Next, we need some speaking engagements. That's where the three of you come in," Mickey said, pointing at Drs. Pearce, Walsh, and Braune."

"What did you have in mind?" Pearce asked.

"Maybe three engagements with professional organizations each year, plus I'll get her involved with local women's groups, the Rotary circuit, and some venues in San Antonio, Dallas, and Houston."

"Do you think this is what Diane wants, Dr. Rollins?"

Mickey patted his coat covering his iPad and replied, "Of course, I know exactly what she wants."

"You disgust me, Dr. Rollins."

"Thank you, Rajeev. In two years, your Board will be rewarding you with disgusting sums of cash when your company buys my technology. Your shareholders will think you are a god."

Boundaries

Rajeev sat back in his chair, absorbing what Mickey had said, then responded, "Remember, Dr. Rollins, gods we are not. Don't stray beyond your mortal boundaries."

"Do you think there are any personal security measures you need to take for Diane's safety?" Walsh asked.

"Well, the ranch offers a fairly high level of security. The perimeter is very well fenced. There are cameras with night-vision capability placed strategically throughout the ranch due to problems with poaching. Every vehicle carries a high-powered rifle, and when on horseback, the hands on the ranch have a rifle in their scabbard and carry a handgun as well. In addition, there's considerable use of person-to-person and mobile radio communication around the ranch. I'll look into upgrading that as well as the security system at the house and the entrances, and I'll be hiring full time personal security for Diane, though the person will probably operate under the guise of a horse trainer or nanny. This is something I haven't worked out yet."

"And what if all this fails and someone gets a hold of Diane?" Rajeev asked.

Mickey took a deep breath before explaining, "Then, there's the 'Seattle Solution.'"

Braune looked at the others before asking, "I hate to ask, but what is that?"

"It's a fabled failsafe that was rumored to be a part of the source-code of a certain Seattle-based mega software company. Should there have ever been a true threat of piracy of their source-code, the owners of the company would run an executable program that would set all binary code, normally both '1's and '0's, to only '0's, effectively destroying whatever the thief was looking for."

"You can do this?" Braune asked.

Mickey patted his coat again.

"That's truly Machiavellian, Dr. Rollins." Rajeev said.

"Yep. It would really suck."

"And what would happen to Diane if that occurred?" Pearce asked.

"She would instantly return to the mental condition she was in right when we began our therapy."

There was a long period of silence in the room as the four guests sat looking at each other, at Mickey, and at Diane. Eventually, Rajeev broke the silence.

"We'll support you any way we can, Dr. Rollins."

"Dandy!" Mickey said, sitting forward with a huge smile on his face. "You can use Suki as your contact for scheduling. I'll write her number on the back of my card."

He quickly jotted down the number on four business cards and handed them out. The front of the card said,

Mickey & Diane Rollins, Owners
Bella Vista Ranch
Hunt, Texas
830-555-2635

Mickey reached under his coat and retrieved his iPad once more.

"So, is everyone ready for re-entry?"

The guests looked at each other, then Rajeev nodded. Mickey gave the face of the device a taps and strokes. Immediately, Diane's disconjugate gaze changed. She was now back of the group once more.

"Dippin' Dots?" Quickly realizing something had happened, Diane turned to Mickey and asked, "Did I have another seizure?"

"I'm afraid so, babe. It's time to go home now."

Chapter 30

It was seven-thirty in the evening, and Toot was looking forward to some of Lupita's home cooking, a couple of beers, getting his boots off, and setting down to watch some mindless television in the privacy of the ranch-style dwelling he had called home for most of his adult life. He drove his Chevy truck up the driveway to the main house where he could park it inside the garage like he often did when he had a lot of valuable equipment in it. He assumed he would need most of what was in the truck the next morning, and this way he wouldn't have to unload everything at the end of a long day's work. With any luck, Lupe, the groundskeeper and Lupita's husband, would wash it before dawn, much as he did any dirty vehicle, as long as it was at the main house.

Toot brought his truck to a stop and pressed the transmitter on the top console that controlled the right door of the three-car garage. As the door opened, he was surprised to see Mickey's FJ Cruiser. He pressed the transmitters to open the middle and left doors, and found Dub's old Jaguar in the middle bay, and Mickey's new Land Rover in the left bay.

"Son-of-a-bitch!" Toot yelled to himself, slamming the shifter into park and turning off his truck.

Before bolting through the door to the mudroom that connected the garage to the kitchen, he took a moment to admire the Jag, having not seen it in several years.

"Nice to have you home, Tweety," Toot said to Dub's canary yellow E-type—the name of which was the outcome of a contest held by the elementary school in Hunt back when Toot was still in high school.

He walked through the mudroom, taking off his boots and hanging his hat on a peg, then rushed into the kitchen expecting to catch Mickey by surprise so he could blast him for taking over the garage. Instead, he found an empty room. This was peculiar since he couldn't remember the last time there hadn't been anybody in the kitchen at this time of evening. Lupita was always cooking, and that often attracted Lupe, Sixto and the some of the older hands who would sit around telling stories about the day while praising her cooking. He knew he wouldn't find them elsewhere in the house because the policy was that none of the ranch hands were allowed past the mudroom or the kitchen unless they were accompanied by Toot himself. Hearing soft music in the living room, he eased that direction, unsure just who he would find, and what they might be doing. What he found was the one person he was least capable of handling—Suki…and she was alone. The subdued lighting in the room gave her an angelic appearance.

"Hello, Toot," She said with her soft accent, looking up from where she was sitting.

As if he was acquiring a target at a shooting range, Toot zeroed in on her. A moment later, she was up and walking over to him. She was wearing low-cut, red and black, log cabin-print pajama shorts that were barely held up by a loose drawstring, and a short, red vest that purposefully didn't go nearly far enough south—the combination of which revealed more of Suki's trim, athletic figure than Toot was prepared for. Once again, he was completely disarmed.

"Ma'am."

"I would rather you called me Suki, than Ma'am, Marque."

The only person to have called him by his given name was his mother. It felt wrong. She had made her point.

"Can I get you a beer?"

"Where's Lupita?" Toot asked, trying desperately to keep focused on what had been bothering him rather than the beautiful woman before him.

"She looked tired so I told her to take the night off," Suki responded as she came to a stop just in front of him—so close that it almost hurt Toot's neck to look down at her five-foot, three-inch frame. "I told her I could look after you. So, do you want a beer?"

"Where are Mickey and Diane?" He asked, his resolve quickly withering.

"You are not going to answer my question, are you? Follow me."

Suki slipped past Toot and headed for the kitchen while he stood frozen in his tracks.

"I can feel you staring at me," Suki said as she stopped, slowly turning around to find him standing motionless with his eyes glued on her.

"Sorry, Ma'am...I mean, Suki."

Toot grimaced as he demonstrated his lack of finesse in the situation.

She returned to where he was standing, grabbed one of his hands, and pulled him along with her to the kitchen, telling him along the way, "I don't bite...usually." Grabbing a beer out of the refrigerator, she said, "Here, you open it."

"Are you havin' one?"

"I have a glass of Chablis in the living room."

"I'm sorry. I didn't notice."

"You were not paying attention to details, were you?"

"Oh, I was payin' attention to details, alright, just not to what you were drinkin'."

There was a 'pfsst' sound as Toot twisted the top off of his beer. The two looked into each other's eyes for a few moments, deciding who would blink first. Toot struggled to remain a gentleman.

"You gonna tell me where Mickey and Diane are?"

"They had a long day. Mickey took Diane to San Antonio to see some doctors who are working with him on her case. She had one of her seizures while she was there."

"Guess she was in good company at the time. Is she okay now?"

"Oh, she is fine. She has these frequently. If you are around her long enough, you will see her have them. They are harmless—just a phase of her recovery. However, she usually needs to rest the remainder of the day. Mickey sometimes gives her a sedative, and usually I spend some time with her as well."

"So why aren't you with them?"

"They wanted some time alone tonight."

"How's their marriage...if I may ask?"

"Well, they are alone, and knowing Mickey, I doubt that they are watching television."

Toot nodded, acknowledging what she meant. It was difficult for Toot not to feel jealous over Mickey's good fortune.

"They are a good couple. They dated on-and-off for several years. I think they were both ready to settle down. Unfortunately, the accident has put a strain on them."

"Where's the little girl?"

"Gigi? She is asleep. She has not slept well during the move, and I think tonight she is exhausted. Can I make you something to eat?"

"I don't want to put you out, Ma'am...I mean, Suki."

"I would like very much to make you dinner. Lupita showed me where things are located. To be honest, she has your dinner prepared. I simply need to heat it up. All I need is my wine. Would you bring it here for me?"

"Yeah, sure," Toot said, briskly retrieving the glass from the living room. "Looks like you need a refill. Allow me," he said, pulling a bottle of Chablis from the refrigerator and topping off her glass.

He took a seat at the island while Suki pulled out a covered plate, put it in the oven, and set the temperature and a timer. She then joined him, sitting next to him at the corner. After a few awkward moments, Toot finally spoke up.

"Forgive me if I'm a little forward, but I gotta come right out and ask it. Do you work out, Suki? You've done real good keepin' in shape."

"Was that a compliment or an observation?"

"Both...Ma'am."

"I take excellent care of my body. I recently had some extra weight to lose, so I have been working out more than I typically do to get back in shape. Judging from your remark, I guess it is working. And you?"

"I don't work out, but I work hard. Result's the same."

"Not always. How tall are you, Toot?"

"I'd be six foot and two inches. I weigh one eighty-five, and I'm pushin' fifty years old."

"Good. I ask one question, and I get three answers."

"I don't like beatin' around the bush, Ma'am…Suki."

"What do you mean by 'beating around the bush?'"

"That's just slang, I guess. Means avoidin' somethin'. Life's short, no need to fill it with meaningless crap. Excuse my language."

"What is it that you are avoiding, Toot?"

He took a long drink from his beer, hoping for something intelligent, or at least, clever, to come to mind. Nothing did.

"So, Miss Suki, what exactly do you do for Mickey and Diane?"

"That is a very personal question, Toot."

"It can't be that personal…can it?"

Suki nodded.

"Let me narrow it down a bit. You said you spend time with Diane. What do you do?"

Suki studied Toot for a moment, trying to figure out where he was really going with his questions, but soon offered this, "I am a trainer. I provide physical therapy as well as emotional therapy."

"Okay, but I can pull out a phone book and find dozens of physical therapy people and shrinks within fifty miles of here. Why you?"

"Because I am the best there is, and besides, Diane and I have a special bond."

Toot studied Suki for a while, trying to figure out if there was some hidden meaning in her response. "Does she need all that stuff?"

Suki nodded again.

"You and Mickey have a special bond?"

"I have known Mickey for a long time."

"That's not exactly the answer to my question."

"Perhaps, but that is the answer I am giving you."

There was a period of silence while both of them tried to figure out what path the conversation should next take.

"The night we first met, you made it sound as though you did not have a girlfriend. Is that true?"

"That's correct, Ma'am."

"You are a nice and handsome man, Toot. I think that is a loss for you, not to have a woman in your life." Suki put her hand up to her mouth, "You are not gay, are you?"

"Uh, that's a big negatory on that one, Miss Suki," he replied, sucking down the rest of his beer.

"Can I get you another?"

Toot hadn't realized that he had chugged the remainder of his beer after that last question.

"Yes, Ma'am...Suki." After taking a deep breath out of frustration, he said, "I'll get the name right eventually."

She got up to check on his dinner, then grabbed another beer from the refrigerator and brought it to him. During her short circuit around the kitchen, Toot couldn't keep his eyes off of her.

Moving close behind him, she asked, "Do you mind if I ease your stress?"

Without waiting for his answer, she began to knead his shoulders, slowly working her way down his back searching for points of tension. Finding one, she reached around in front of him, pulling him back against her while she pressed her fist into the spot that had her attention.

"I don't feel no....argh..."

Suki pressed her fist hard into his back.

"Well, maybe I'm a little...ah...stressed...ah."

"Why do men deny their pain?"

"Pain's good. Means you work for a livin'. Anyway, I ain't in pa....ah."

"You can work for a living and not be in pain. Earlier you said that you do not 'work out,' but that you 'work hard,' and that the result is the same. The result may be muscle and a strong heart, but also there is a loss in your range of motion and a good deal of unnecessary discomfort. You just need a trainer. If you wish, I can be your trainer, too."

"I think Mickey would have something to say about that…ouch!!"

"Mickey has a lot to say about what I do, but he does not own me. I am free to do as I wish."

Suki continued for a few minutes massaging Toot's back. Soon, he began to move his shoulders up and down and side to side.

"You know, I do feel a little better."

"Just think of how good I could make you feel if you would let me."

"What'd you have in mind?"

"Oh, for you to get into some hot water, then a relaxing, full-body massage. Then, I need to work on your hands and your feet."

"Ain't nobody touchin' my feet."

"Are you ticklish?"

"Let's just say they're off limits and leave it at that."

"I am certain you would like what I would do for you. You will see."

"My hands are hopeless."

"They just need some care. Besides, they are too rough for my skin."

The bait had been cast in front of Toot, and he wondered if he should bite, or if he misunderstood Suki's intentions.

"There's a Jacuzzi just down from the deck," he said.

"I saw it. I was in it last night. But you need a shower first."

"I never took no shower before gettin' into it in the past."

"That was then. You are on a new path now."

Toot felt a sudden rush, and he couldn't be sure if it was excitement or anxiety.

He took Suki's hand from his chest, turned around, and said, "I didn't say nothin' about goin' down no new path."

Suki took her glass of Chablis and slowly licked the rim before taking a slow sip of the chilled, golden wine. A gunshot couldn't have made Toot blink after that.

"Of course. If I understand all of your negatives, all you want is dinner."

She walked over to the oven, put on some mittens, pulled out the hot, covered plate, and set it in front of Toot.

After removing the aluminum foil, she said, "And we need to do something about your diet. You need some vegetables and some fruit."

"I like what Lupita cooks."

"You do not have to stop eating what she makes. Just add some healthier items to your diet. I do not want to change you, Toot. I want to help you feel better."

Toot picked up a fork and pointed it at Suki, preparing to tell her he didn't need nor want to change his ways. But, as she stared into his eyes, she climbed up on a stool next to him, sat on her crossed legs and leaned onto the island allowing her vest to gape open just enough to give Toot a teasing look at what was underneath.

"You are pointing your fork at me. Do you plan to eat me?"

With her remark, he felt a warmth rush throughout his body, along with, he knew, came a flushed-red face. The only way he could think of responding to her assault on his senses was to stick his fork into a piece of Lupita's Carne Asada and put it in his mouth.

"Tell you what. I'll eat more fruit and vegetables if you'll eat more of Lupita's cooking. We'll meet in the middle…I mean, half-way."

Toot could feel his face getting redder as he stuck his fork into another piece of meat.

Suki responded with one of her heart-melting smiles, saying, "I think meeting in the middle is a good compromise, Toot." Leaning forward and taking the meat from Toot's fork, she added, "I am going to get some things ready outside, then I am going to take a shower. Instead of going back to your house, you are invited to join me."

She then placed the small chunk of meat into his mouth. It nearly stuck in his throat as he swallowed it long before he should have.

"You mean…?"

"I can wear a bathing suit, if you would like."

"Ma'am…I mean, Suki…I, uh…"

"Toot…this is a shower, a good soak in the Jacuzzi, and a nice, long massage. Nothing more."

"Sounds like we don't have no clothes on."

"Have you ever seen a naked woman before?"

"Well, yes Ma'am…dammit!"

"Well, I have seen a man naked before as well. So, there should be no surprises. Swimsuits and clothing simply get in the way."

The conversation was brought to a halt by the distant crying of a small child. Before Toot could get up—a reflex action brought on by years of watching what men do in Texas when a lady gets up from her seat—Suki was hurrying down the hall toward the sound of Gigi's crying. It was just as well that he didn't leave the kitchen counter because the bulge in his Wranglers gave away a lot of information.

Toot shoveled away his dinner, put the dishes in the dishwasher, and within a few minutes had the kitchen—and himself—pretty much back in order. He cracked open his third beer, and topped off Suki's wine just as she rounded the corner carrying Gigi. There was something primal, something so correct about that moment…a man, a woman, a child, dinner, a warm home. A lot of things that had been absent from Toot's life suddenly came together.

"Is she alright?"

"As I said earlier, she is out of sorts. The move has been hard."

"She sure likes you."

Suki brushed Gigi's blond hair from her eyes.

"She is my little girl." After giving Gigi a kiss on the forehead and a long hug, Suki asked, "Do you want to hold her for a while? I think she wants some juice. She craves it."

"Uh, I don't think…"

Before Toot could finish, Suki deposited the little girl in his arms. She looked at him curiously, but certainly she wasn't frightened.

Gigi's reaction didn't go unnoticed by Suki.

"My, look at you. You are a natural with children."

"Uh, I wouldn't say I'm a natural, but I ain't afraid. Gosh, she's so tiny. It's like holding a little puppy or somethin'."

"Here, Gigi. Here is your juice."

"What is that?"

"This is a blend of mango and orange juice. I make a different juice every few days. It helps her develop an appreciation for different tastes, and it keeps her digestive system working properly. She likes it more than the formula we are slowly eliminating from her diet."

Toot watched, transfixed on Gigi.

"She sure does like it. Looks like me drinkin' a beer."

"Except that she stops at one."

"I'll bet she wouldn't if given the chance. Let's just say she paces herself."

Toot carried Gigi into the living room and sat in a chair with her sitting in his lap.

"She looks like Diane...and like Mickey."

Suki's expression became solemn.

"Yes, I hear that all the time."

Her reaction didn't go unnoticed.

"Did I say something wrong?"

"Let us just say that Diane was incapable of being a mother when Gigi was born. For all practical purposes, I was Gigi's mother."

"She gets the glory, you get the work."

"Something like that."

"Been there."

"She is worth it, though."

"That she is. She sits on her own good, don't she?"

"She began sitting without help a month ago."

"Standin' yet?"

"Not yet, but soon. She wants to. She has a lot of drive."

"She can't keep her eyes open. Look at her."

Boundaries

Toot took the nearly empty bottle from Gigi, handed it to Suki, and put the baby on his shoulder. She pushed herself up to take a good look at him, smiled and burped, then put her head back down.

"I will say it again, you are a natural father. When I want a day off, I will call you, Toot."

"I'll do that. All you gotta do is clean the barns, count cattle, check the fences…"

"I get your point."

"Mickey ever hold her or feed her?"

"No, not very often. He is always working. Both he and Diane rely a great deal on me."

"Shame. Their loss."

"I agree."

"Mickey wants to hire a nanny for her."

"You gotta be kiddin' me, right?"

"No. I am supposed to begin a search for one right away. He gave me some very specific criteria, so it will take some time. He wants one within the next year."

"What kind of criteria? Warm heart, college educated, firm bosom?"

"Well, something like that. Plus, she must be proficient in equestrian, self-defense, and guns."

Shaking his head, Toot asked, "Who's stupid-ass—excuse my language—idea is that?"

"Diane wants to raise Gigi around horses."

"I can understand the horses thing, I guess…when she's old enough. But, what's with the self-defense and guns? I mean, she's cute and all, but I don't think she has to fight off the boys for a few years."

"Diane wants help with her horses, and Mickey wants some personal security for Diane."

"What the hell for? He hasn't been back long enough to piss off anyone except me. And Diane don't know nobody here."

"You should discuss this with Mickey. I probably should not have told you the things that I did."

"Think I will. Security. What a crock. We take care of our own security 'round here. By the time the law gets all the way out here, bad guys are long gone."

"Is she asleep?"

After moving ever so slightly to see if Gigi responded, Toot answered, "Think so."

"Let me put her back in bed."

"Do you have to?"

"What are going to do, hold her all night?"

"I don't know…maybe. Feels kinda good to hold a baby."

Suki decided to take advantage of Toot's captivity and his openness.

"What can you tell me about Mickey's first marriage?"

"To Laura?"

"Do you know her?"

"'Course I do."

"And how might that be? Can you tell me her last name?"

"Chase. Laura Chase. Mickey ain't never told you about her?"

"Why do you think I am asking you these questions?"

"Does Diane know about her?"

"Toot…So, what can you tell me?"

"Oh, boy. She's gonna be pissed. Let's just say although Mickey divorced her, Dub and Ruby never let go of her. She was always their daughter-in-law, and they kept thinkin' Mickey would see his way back to her some day."

"So where is she? Is she around here?"

"In a manner of speakin'. You heard about Back East?"

"That is the home in East Texas, right?"

"That's right. Caddo Lake. Beautiful spot. Dub called it his second retirement home. But, in reality, he built it hopin' Mickey and Laura would settle down there."

"Where does she live?"

"Couple miles up the road from Back East. Dub bought the Log Cabin Hotel and Resort close to the lake. Nice place. She ran it for him even after the divorce. Griped Mickey to no end to know his parents were hangin' on to her. After Dub died, she got title and keys to it, and added a market and beer garden beside it. I hear she makes real good money—smart woman, Laura. She's just been tendin' to it and Back East all these years, hopin' Mickey'd come back to her."

"What is she waiting for? She should have gone after him if she truly wanted him."

"She's stubborn, just like him. I took her out a couple of times, but he'd stole her heart a long time ago. They're waiting to see who twitches first, I guess. Anyway, it don't matter no more now, him bein' married and all."

"Does Mickey ever see her?"

"Oh, he'd wander up there on occasion. He'd be lookin' for peace and quiet, least that's what he said, and she'd be chasin' after him. It was really sad to watch. She said there was no other man for her except Mickey Rollins, and he never gave a shit…excuse my language. I think he liked the thought of being pursued…that he was so good, someone smart and pretty would throw her life away for him."

Suki stared across the room at nothing in particular as she softly said, "Just like Diane…just like me."

"Beg your pardon?"

"Oh, nothing. Is she pretty?"

Toot nodded, and said, "Just like a '66 Vette. Body with no end, waxes up pretty, and runs mighty fast. I owned one of them once."

"Do you still have it?"

"Nope. Sold it. Couldn't pull a trailer with it, and I'm too practical a guy." Toot rubbed Gigi's back, then continued, asking, "So, Diane don't know nothin' about Laura?"

"Mickey told us about her, but said she was 'out of the picture.'"

"Tell ya what—I don't want to be around when Diane and Laura get face-to-face."

"Maybe they will never meet."

"Suki, we're talkin' about Mickey here. If there's trouble or scandal anywhere within five-hundred miles, he'll find it…or it'll find him."

Chapter 31

There's something about the smell of lavender that makes a person entirely relaxed and allows one's mind drift off to nowhere. Couple that with the soft music that accompanies a massage, and the talented hands of a good masseuse, the sensations add up to nothing less than pure bliss. Such were the circumstances in which Diane found herself awakening. The comfort she felt prevented her from moving, and what she assumed to be cucumber slices over her eyes, kept her from seeing her surroundings. It didn't matter at that moment.

"Ummm. Right there, Suki," Diane said quietly as a pair of hands softly caressed her abdomen.

"No, stay sleep," an unfamiliar voice with a Creole accent answered.

Something suddenly felt wrong—very wrong. That wasn't Suki's voice Diane heard, and she certainly couldn't place the voice with anyone on the ranch. Curiosity finally overwhelmed Diane. She pulled off one of the cucumber slices, looked up and focused in on a young woman whom she had never seen before.

"Who are you?" Diane shouted while jumping off the table.

She looked around the room in a matter of seconds and quickly realized she wasn't in any place that was familiar.

"Where am I?"

"No, it's okay. Lay back down," the young woman attempted to persuade Diane, without success.

"Is there a problem?" It was Suki looking alarmed as she passed through the doorway.

"Suki, I'm so glad to see you," Diane said, running into Suki's arms. "Where's Mickey?"

"He did not return with you. You said you left him on the beach."

"What beach?" Diane asked, looking out the window for some type of validation of what Suki was talking about.

"Diane, are you feeling alright?"

"Suki, why am I here?" Diane asked, frantically looking about the room for any familiar, and expected, point of reference.

"Diane..."

"Suki, what are you doing to me? Where's Mickey? Where's Gigi? Where's Toot?"

"Come here and sit down."

Suki put a robe around Diane and escorted her to a chair where she took a seat. She was at a complete loss regarding Diane's irrational behavior.

"Who is Gigi?"

"Don't fuck with me, Suki!" Diane shouted, jerking herself free from Suki.

"Diane, calm yourself," Suki replied, trying in vain to ease the distress in her friend. "You spent last night with Mickey, and you came home this morning. Do you remember any of this?"

"Yes, but that was Maribella Island that we sailed to with Bates. What's this place?"

"Diane, we left there two days ago. We are on Mauritius now. We flew here yesterday. You spent one night on the beach at Maribella, and you spent the night on the beach here last night. Maybe you got the two confused. Does any of this sound familiar?"

"Yes...No! I don't know. This isn't right, Suki," Diane said, whimpering with tears streaming down her face. "I have a daughter named Gigi. Mickey and I are married, and we live on a ranch in Texas. Why am I here?"

It was clear from Suki's expression that she had no idea what Diane was talking about. All she could do was try to reorient Diane with reality.

"Diane, Captain Bates did marry you to Mickey on the boat the night before we left the island. But, you have no children. What's more, you live in San Diego, not Texas."

"No!" Diane let out with a scream.

Suki spoke in French to the attendant who hurried out of the room. She then put her hand on Diane's forehead to check her for a fever.

"I think you may be sick. Maybe it is malaria. Tell me how you feel."

"Suki, there's nothing wrong with me except I am not supposed to be here. I live in Texas. For that matter, you live in Texas with us. Where's Gigi?"

"Diane, I have never heard of this person."

With those words, Diane broke down sobbing uncontrollably.

"What's going on?" Mickey asked, arriving in the room behind the attendant.

Diane jumped up and ran to Mickey who took her in his arms.

"Mickey, where's Gigi? Why did you bring me here?"

"Babe, are you talking about yourself?" Mickey asked, totally confused by Diane's question. "Gigi—that's the name your dad used to call you, remember? You're right here."

Diane reacted by gripping his arms as she began hyperventilating to the point where she was gasping for air.

Suki quickly blended a drink and handed it to her.

"Here take slow sips of this."

"No...don't give...me any...drugs."

"It is a mild drink, Diane. It will help you calm down. Just take some small sips and slow your breathing down."

Mickey broke loose from her grip and took the glass from Suki, holding it up to Diane's lips. She spilled a lot, but managed to get some down.

"What did you do last night, Mickey?" Suki asked, clearly suspecting Mickey was the root cause of the present situation.

After helping Diane with another drink from the glass, Mickey answered, "We had a spectacular time. You outdid yourself once again."

"Why is she acting this way? Did you eat and drink what I gave you?"

"Just what you had prepared for us."

"What did you say to her?" Suki persisted, still waiting for an admission by Mickey that he was the source of Diane's distress.

"I asked her last night if she would like to try having a child with me."

Suki wondered if that was Mickey's backdoor way of informing Diane she might already be pregnant. It took all of Suki's inner strength not to tell Diane at that moment what she knew about Mickey's fertility.

Grabbing Suki and Mickey, Diane screamed, "No! We already have a child!"

"Babe, as much as that would make me happy, we don't have any children. We talked on the beach last night about having kids, or at least trying. You left kind of upset."

"Why was she upset?" Suki asked.

"Well, I told her we needed to sell her place in San Diego."

"Why?"

"We're buying the ranch in Gilroy, and we don't need three homes in California."

"Diane, is that what this is all about?" Suki asked.

"No! He never spoke to me about selling my home. Besides, I would never sell it any more than you'd sell your place in Sausalito. You're just trying to protect Maria, aren't you?"

"What the hell are you talking about, Diane?" Mickey asked.

"You're getting rid of Lupita and bringing Maria to the ranch."

"Where did you get a whack-o idea like that? How do you know about Lupita?" Mickey asked, completely surprised by Diane's familiarity with a name from Mickey's past.

"Toot's pissed off because you're making all kinds of changes at the ranch."

"I'm not making any changes because we don't live on the ranch. Get a grip. And, how do you know about Toot, anyway?"

"Because we live in Texas! Why are we here?"

"We're on vacation! We don't live in Texas!"

"Guys! Stop it!" Suki shouted, finally having reached her limit of what was taking place. "Mickey, wait outside until I come get you. I want to be alone with Diane."

"No way."

Boundaries

"Mickey! Do it!" Suki shouted, again, pushing Mickey toward the door.

"Five minutes. You get five minutes, then I'm coming back in here," he answered, exasperated by what was taking place.

All Suki did was point with her arm extended straight. The expression on her face said the rest. After a few moments, Mickey left the room, and Suki shut the door behind him.

"Suki, what's going on?" Diane asked, her breathing having returned to something one could consider normal.

After pacing a while and trying to think of what she was going to say to Diane, Suki took her by the hand and led her to a sofa.

"Come over here. We need to talk."

"Don't you remember living on Rub-a-Dub Ranch?" Diane asked, taking a seat next to Suki. "You're in love with Toot. You won't admit it, but I can tell."

Suki wondered where to begin. She had never seen Diane this way.

"Diane, do you remember when we first met in Phuket?"

"Yeah, that was a long time ago."

"Diane, that was last week."

"Suki, now you listen to me," Diane said, her face showing great strain. "Mickey and I are married. We have a daughter who was conceived on our trip to Phuket a year-and-a-half ago. I fell and sustained a head injury. I don't remember being pregnant, but you cared for Gigi until I could take care of her myself. We all moved to Mickey's parent's ranch near Hunt. Does any of this sound familiar?"

"Diane, I think you are pregnant. I think that may be why you are hallucinating."

"I'm pregnant again?"

"Diane, you told me you could never have a child. You and Bruce tried many times. Remember?"

"I know...I know we tried, and I always miscarried."

"So how is it that you and Mickey have a daughter?"

Diane thought for a long time, unable to clearly answer Suki's question in her own mind.

"I don't know, Suki. But it happened...it's true...we have a daughter. She's beautiful."

"I need you to be calm. What I have to tell you will probably upset you a lot. Mickey told me last week that he had his vasectomy reversed some time ago. He did not tell you, and you have been having unprotected sex with him. He thought you were unable to become pregnant. What he did not realize is that you can get pregnant. You just cannot carry the baby to birth. I think you are pregnant. That, in combination with the time change and all that we have done, could possibly be causing you to have these wild thoughts. They seem to be fantasies of the future—maybe the way you hope things will be."

"So he knocked me up, and that's why I'm having these thoughts?" Diane asked, simply unable to fathom what Suki was telling her.

"I believe that is the case."

"So Gigi isn't real?"

"No, at least not yet."

"You're telling me all the happiness I feel about being married, having a family, and living in Texas is all fantasy...all caused by Mickey getting me pregnant?"

"That is the only explanation I have for your behavior."

There was a long period of silence while Diane tried to make sense of what Suki had told her. Eventually, she asked, "So, are you pregnant?"

"Possibly. I should know next week."

Diane bolted toward the door.

"Where are you going?"

"To kill the son-of-a-bitch! She shouted, running toward the beach.

It only took a fraction of a minute for Diane to find Mickey standing at the poolside bar. Grabbing a serving tray off of the bar top, she hit him across the top of his head, making a racket that could be heard by everyone in sight.

"Asshole!"

"What's your problem!" Mickey shouted as he ducked before Diane could connect with his head a second time. He wrestled the tray from her hands and pushed her away hard enough that she fell to the ground.

Several men came to Diane's rescue and pinned Mickey against the bar. As he was forcibly held, Diane jumped to her feet, grabbed a sharp knife from the bar and plunged it into Mickey's chest…

DIANE ABRUPTLY SAT UP in her king-sized bed. Perspiration dripped from her face, her lips quivered, her body shook, and no words came out of her mouth. Her mind quickly produced one thought—*I'm back…again*. It wasn't long before she realized something else—she was having one of her terrible headaches.

"Do you want me to get you one of your pills and a glass of water?" Mickey asked as he sat up and put his arm on her shoulder.

"Oh, God, yes."

"Did you have another dream?"

"I guess you could call it that. It's that same one I keep having over and over. I just stabbed you to death. At least this time, Suki didn't get killed."

"Did you actually see me die?" Mickey asked as he walked to the bathroom for the medicine and a glass of water.

"Don't ask questions that require any thought…please."

"It's important, Babe. Did I die?"

Diane tried to think, then realized that she actually had very vivid recall of what had taken place in her dream.

"I woke up before you died."

"So, you didn't kill me," Mickey said, returning with the medication and water.

"It can't be healthy that I have dreams about killing you."

"As long as they're dreams, we'll assume you're working some things out."

"Remember when Suki and I came back from our shopping trip in Bangkok? I fell asleep in the car on the way home, and I had a dream that I stabbed you with a letter opener. There was a lot of similarity in the dreams. Is there a pattern here?" Diane asked before taking her medication.

"That was a long time ago. I'm impressed you remember that event since it was before the accident. That tells me your memory restoration is coming along nicely. So tell me, what did you use this time?"

Diane chuckled as she remembered the details of her dream.

"It was a knife used for cutting cheese."

"So, why'd you do it?"

"What? Stab you?"

"Yeah."

"Did you ever have a vasectomy?"

"No."

"You're sure?"

"I think I'd remember that."

"Well, in my dream, you had your vasectomy reversed and neglected to tell me. That's how I got pregnant with Gigi."

"So that's why you wanted to kill me? Because I knocked you up?"

"For starters. You also got Suki pregnant. That's why I stabbed you to death."

"Ah, but you didn't kill me. You came up short. You see, you're a good person."

"Umm. There's always next time."

The two embraced, then kissed.

"You taste like sweat," Mickey said.

"Murder turns me on."

They kissed again.

"Mick, I know I should simply be happy, but I still can't figure out how I gave birth to Gigi."

"Mendoza's people had some new techniques. They worked."

"That's it?"

"That's it."

"You're never going to tell me anything else about the pregnancy, are you?"

"Nope. Be happy."

"What if I asked Dr. Mendoza?"

"Don't."

"Why not?"

"He's out of the picture."

"Are you ever going to tell me what happened between the two of you?"

"Nope."

Getting up out of bed, Diane finished with, "I just love our conversations. We never discuss what's important to me. You can't continue to deny me information like this."

"Diane, just leave it. There are things that are best left unknown for now," Mickey said as she walked out the bedroom door. "I'm serious!"

It was no use. Diane wasn't going to listen to Mickey any more tonight. She was frustrated at the continual avoidance when it came to the subject of her pregnancy. For her to have carried Gigi to birth was nothing short of a miracle, and she was determined to find out how it was accomplished. Mickey was obsessed with his reconstruction of the mind, but Diane was equally obsessed with her seemingly impossible creation of new life.

She walked to the kitchen and poured herself a glass of orange juice, then proceeded to the porch for some fresh air. Once she had opened the door, she knew she had caught Suki and Toot at a most intimate moment. She watched—a tree partially obscured her view, and at the same time shielded her from them. She saw a passion between them…an overt affection, not just sex. It was the very thing she was missing with Mickey.

Chapter 32

Six Months Later…

Much to the surprise of the regulars at the General Store, Roger Delaney, and others familiar with the situation at Rub-a-Dub, Toot and Mickey actually found a way to cohabitate, avoiding a much-expected brawl. A lot of the success in the relationship could be attributed to Toot's diehard focus on ranching, allowing him no time for Mickey's outside pursuits. He also followed the advice of his father, which was to pick only good fights. He knew that a protracted battle with Mickey would probably cause more harm than good in the long run.

Mickey spent countless hours with Diane and her therapy. Yet, as her progress reached new milestones, he found time to make more of a contribution to the ranch. At first it was just an hour here and there, but that later turned into the occasional entire day working alongside Toot and the ranch hands. In a gesture designed to show Toot his sincerity in trying to make things work between them, he decided to leave Maria in Sausalito where she could tend to the home there until he decided what to do with it. The tension between him and Toot either disappeared, or was well hidden, and it was not uncommon to see the two together.

Diane became a good friend and neighbor in the region. Her outgoing personality made her a delight to everyone who met her, and with the help of a most unlikely ally, Sarah Duke, she developed a strong network of personal and professional contacts enabling her to tell her story. Mickey kept her on a fairly short leash except for when he was with her because of her ongoing seizure-like episodes. He was never too far away to tend to her with medication. His obsessive care-taking was viewed by most to be necessary. Oddly, she never had an episode except when he was around.

Boundaries

Suki was by Diane's side, contributing in her own way toward her friend's rebirth. She probably played the largest role as peacekeeper in the household with her passive demeanor, unceasing wisdom, and endless pampering of the other three figures on the ranch. She continued to give of herself to Diane and Mickey, and they willingly took all she could dole out. The chemistry between her and Toot continued to percolate, but they both realized, and for now accepted, that the discovery of any type of relationship between them would tear apart the extended family that now occupied the ranch. That being the case, they went to great lengths to hide their feelings.

All of this was soon to change with the introduction of a new face. After searching for months, Diane and Suki finally decided on a nanny for Gigi—a nanny with special talents and a mission, both of which were unknown to Diane. It had been an arduous task. Suki had created several short lists of candidates from which Diane could choose, and in the end, they selected Suki's favorite. Her name—Carmen Julietta Emmanuel de los Santos—was beautiful as it flowed off one's tongue; a beauty that was matched by what one saw on the outside, but masked darker qualities within her.

THE FAMILY LAND ROVER pulled to a stop at the top of the circular driveway leading to the entrance of the main house. Lupe hopped out of the driver's door, and quickly made his way to the passenger side of the vehicle where he held open the door for the new guest.

"Allow me to get the door for you, Miss Carmen," Lupe said, winded with excitement while trying to make an impression on the attractive, young woman.

"Gracias, Señor Lupe."

It was a made-for-television moment. Most people would climb out of a vehicle without a lot of show. Not Carmen. Each move was choreographed. First Lupe extended his hand, which she gracefully took. Then, swiveling in one continuous motion, she swung her legs out, planting her red, Italian-made pumps on the washed gravel drive. Knees deliberately together, she stood up, looking to either side as she did. She was wearing an ultra lightweight cotton-muslin top and pants. The sleeveless blouse was lavender—a color that accented her tan complexion and brown eyes—and was buttoned only below the bust, exposing ample cleavage and her navel. Under it, she wore a risqué, floral-patterned halter that had the same pattern as her pants. Her handbag sported the Christian Dior logo. After flipping her long, wavy, brown hair out of her eyes, she put on sunglasses for the short trip to the door. She was a Bond girl—trim, athletic, and drop-dead gorgeous.

"Let me get the front door for you," Lupe said, trying not to stare. "It should be locked."

"Is it always locked?"

"Uh, yes, ma'am. Most of the time it is locked. We also have an alarm. We never used to lock the door here. Sometimes I forget and Mr. Rollins gets mad, so I try to remember."

"Did Mr. Rollins tell you why he wants the door locked?"

"No, he didn't say much. He just said to be sure it is locked. I guess he is protecting the women who are here. I don't know. It was only men and my wife living here until recently, so we didn't much care."

Carmen slowly made her way up the steps behind Lupe, scanning the front exposure of the residence while making a memory of everything that she saw.

"It's beautiful; much nicer than what I saw in the pictures."

"Miss Suki said your family lives in a big home in Spain. What is the name of the region?"

"Cadiz."

"Yes, Cadiz. That's a pretty name. It sounds like one I would hear in a fairy tale."

Lupe began going through his pockets looking for something.

"Did you forget something?" Carmen asked, humored by Lupe's frantic search.

"Oh…uh…I think I left my card in the car. You know, a card key. I have to enter a code on a touch pad, or use my card key. I can never remember all those numbers so I need my card. Wait here for just a moment."

Boundaries

Lupe made his way back to the vehicle, his arms flailing as he limped down the stairs. The age of his bones betrayed the youth in his heart.

While Lupe rifled through the pockets and compartments of the SUV, an outline of a figure appeared through the etched glass on the other side of the door. It was Suki. The heavy wooden door opened, activating the characteristic *door-open* alert chimes of an alarm system.

Suki stood still for a moment, examining Carmen and her attire, before greeting her.

"Welcome to Texas. How was your trip?"

"Hello, Miss Suki. I'm actually quite exhausted."

She leaned forward and exchanged an obligatory hug with her new associate.

"Let me guess...Lupe cannot find his card key?"

"I feel so sorry for him because he wants so much to impress me. He's the sweetest man. In many ways, he reminds me of one of my uncles."

Lupe stepped out of the Rover and noticed the door was open.

"Hello, Miss Suki. I have the card key now. Thank you for getting the door. Miss Carmen, I'll bring up your bags."

"Thank you, Lupe," she answered.

"Take them to the Spirit Room, Lupe," Suki said in a voice loud enough that Lupe could hear from where he stood.

"The Spirit Room?" Carmen asked.

"Your room. It is named after the small creek that runs just outside of it—Spirit Creek. Local legend says its headwaters are near what used to be an Indian burial ground. Reportedly, there are occasional voices and the sound of footsteps coming from the creek."

"Have you heard them?"

"No. Not yet. They are supposed to be heard only at night, and I never stay in that room. But, I have no doubt that spirits do exist."

"That will help me sleep tonight," Carmen said, rubbing the goose pimples on her arms. "By the way, just a moment ago, you almost seemed a little surprised to see me."

"Oh, I was expecting you. I was not expecting you to be dressed in this manner."

"And how is that?" Carmen asked, puzzled by the remark.

"I feel your attire is entirely too provocative for your job."

"Mrs. Rollins never took issue with my dress in our interviews."

"In all of our video-phone interviews, you were dressed quite conservatively—more appropriate for the job."

After a few moments, Carmen said, "You are a sophisticated woman, Miss Suki. I can tell by the way you dress, the way you talk, and the questions you ask. I'm certain you and I can agree on how I should dress. I'm sorry if I offended you in any way. But in the end, isn't it Mrs. Rollins' decision that matters?"

Before Suki could respond, a voice from down the hallway called, "Carmen, you're finally here!"

Diane approached the two with Gigi in her arms. She had an air of confidence about her, and a walk that said she was the Lady of the House. She shifted the young girl to her left arm then extended her right hand to shake Carmen's, then moved closer to give her a kiss on the cheek.

"How were your flights?"

"Hello, Mrs. Rollins. As I was telling Suki, they were long…very long. We were delayed in New York, and it took a long time to get through immigration. But, I'm here now."

"I'll bet you're exhausted. And please, don't call me Mrs. Rollins. Call me Diane. If we are to be friends, we have to address each other as such."

"Certainly, Diane." Taking care to watch Suki out of the corner of her eye, Carmen added, "I'm sure we will become good friends."

"We're having a get-together tonight with some neighbors as a small welcome for you. It's supposed to start around seven o'clock. That'll give you some time to freshen up, and take a short nap if you want."

"And this is Gigi?"

"Yes, it is."

Boundaries

Diane turned so Gigi could see her new nanny, but the youngster quickly buried her face in her momma's shoulder.

"She's adorable. She looks just like you right down to the dimple."

Carmen noticed that Suki winced at her remark.

"I hear that all the time," Diane said proudly.

Suki stood to the side, experiencing a number of unexpected emotions. First, she was relieved that someone else would be able to help with Gigi. That was quickly followed by feelings of inadequacy and concerns that she might miss the day-to-day challenges of raising a small child. She was also overwhelmed by something almost foreign to her—a feeling of jealousy. There were fleeting visions of growing relationships between Carmen and the others. And while these developments were natural and could be expected, in Suki's mind, Carmen threatened *her* family, posing both emotional and physical threats to those she cared for, and she felt a rising urge to protect what was hers.

"Suki, would you please show Carmen to her room?"

"Of course."

"I'll see you later tonight. Suki will see that you're comfortable."

The last remark was unexpected, and although it was probably unintended, had the effect of making the playing field more level between Suki and Carmen than was likely the case. In spite of all Diane's restorative therapy, she still had a problem with the occasional poor choice of words and timing that was off cue.

Suki escorted Carmen to her room, which was in the same wing of the house as her own. The Spirit Room was actually more like a studio apartment than a single room. Ruby had designed it as her own get-away where she did her painting, and Diane and Suki had subsequently remodeled it for guests, and eventually, for anyone requiring a more permanent place to stay, such as a nanny. One entered the room at what was actually the loft, containing its own small kitchen and the living area. The room conformed to the slope of the terrain that ultimately became the bank of the creek, creating a second level downstairs where the bedroom and bath were located. The Spanish-American décor made for very comfortable accommodations. All of the furniture, pictures, mirrors and artwork came from Mexico. The bed was a four-poster, with sheer curtains to pull around it—a nice, and necessary, touch since there were expansive, curtain-less windows, on three sides of the bedroom. The bath, with a faux-rock tub and shower, was in a nook off to the side, giving the dramatic and very real visual effect that one was bathing along the rock bluffs that bordered the creek.

"All of your extra linens are in the cabinet over there. We have staff that will take care of your laundry. You only need to put it in the laundry bags, much like in a hotel. You should have plenty of room for your personal belongings in the drawers and armoire."

"This is the most beautiful room I have ever seen," Carmen said. Looking out the windows, she added, "It takes in the natural surroundings so wonderfully." Turning, she asked Suki, "Where do you stay?"

"We passed by my room. It is the one more or less across the hall. Gigi's room is next to mine. We share a connecting door."

"I would have thought as Gigi's nanny, I would have the room that connected with hers."

"I like my room. I asked to stay."

"That's only fair, I suppose. Where do Diane and Mr. Rollins stay?"

"They are in the master wing on the other side of the house. You need permission to go over there."

"Permission from whom?"

Suki was annoyed by the question, and it was reflected in her answer.

"Either Mr. or Mrs. Rollins, myself, or Toot."

"Toot?"

"He is the ranch manager. You will meet him tonight."

"Oh, yes. Mr. Teudi. Diane mentioned him during the interview. Is he married?"

"I do not see that his personal situation is any concern of yours. You are here as Gigi's nanny. Do your job, and never, I repeat never, become involved with anyone in this household on a personal basis. Do I make myself clear?"

Boundaries

"Yes," Carmen answered with a crooked smile and raised eyebrows. "Of course, I must become involved personally with Gigi. Wouldn't you agree?"

"To the extent that you must perform your duties in nurturing and educating her, I agree. Only never forget, you are an employee. You are not family."

"You mean, just as you are?"

Suki realized Carmen was going to be a challenge and most likely a difficult adversary. But continuing with the conversation at this point was not going to produce any peace between the two so she chose to leave. As she climbed the stairs to the loft, she saw out of the corner of her eye the reflection of Carmen in a mirror…watching her.

LUPE BROUGHT ALL OF Carmen's belongings to her room, then went about his business. She spent a short while putting away the contents of one of her three suitcases, then turned her attention to a well-deserved shower. Sixteen hours of airplane and airport grime had to go. She shed all of her clothes, tossing them defiantly into a pile on the floor instead of into a laundry bag as Suki had requested. After letting the hot water run in the waterfall shower long enough to create the sensation of a sauna, she stepped inside. For the next twenty minutes, she washed and shampooed her body from head to foot. The dirt and the tension of the day drained away, and she exited the shower feeling completely refreshed.

After drying herself off, she wrapped up her long locks in the towel and walked into the sunlight beaming through the west window. Still mesmerized by the beauty of the view, she watched as a dozen or so horses grazed in a nearby pasture. In the evening sun, the view of the horses, the hillside, the creek, and the white fences that divided groups of cattle was quite pastoral. The warmth of the sun shining on Carmen's naked body felt wonderful. The winter sun takes a long vacation in Shannon, Ireland where she had been attending school, and rain clouds darken many of the days in other seasons. This felt more like the Riviera. Stretching her sore muscles, she locked her hands together above her head and turned around to warm as much of her body as possible. The combination of the warmth and her jetlag began to make her drowsy and she lapsed into a lack of awareness as to where she was and what she was doing.

Suddenly, she realized the sun was partially blocked by shadows moving across her face. After opening her eyes and letting them adjust to the light, she focused in on the cause. It was two men on horseback.

OUTSIDE, TOOT AND MICKEY were on their horses, Mico and Biggun, riding to the barn down a rarely used short cut that passed alongside the house. Today, they weren't looking at the horses in the pasture.

"Damn." That's all Toot could muster.

"What?" That was all that Mickey could muster in return.

"Damn," Toot said a second time.

"I guess Diane bought new window treatments for the Spirit Room," Mickey replied, hoping humor might get the two gracefully out of the situation they were in. "Very realistic, don't you think?"

Toot was now at a complete loss for words, but he managed to tip his hat at Carmen. He didn't know what else to do. Even Mico and Biggun seemed to be taken aback by the figure in the window

Carmen was definitely a product of the post-Victorian era. Most women would have been terribly embarrassed to be seen even partially exposed to a stranger. Yet, here she was in her birthday best, standing before two men she didn't know, and she wasn't even the least bit distressed by what was happening. She was quick enough to see the discomfort that she was causing her voyeurs, and decided to make the pain last as long as possible. Capitalizing on her audience's lusting eyes, she slowly lowered her arms, allowing her hands to stroke her breasts before they continued down her waist. She winked, then did one of those pivots that only a runway model can do. Finally, she proceeded back to the bathroom, deliberately placing one foot in front of and slightly across the other as she walked. Despite the insulated glass separating them, Mickey and Toot thought they could hear a 'boom-da-da-boom-da-da-boom' as she walked.

"We're in serious trouble now, Mick."

"Nope. Not gonna happen. First thing we do when we get inside is let Diane know about this, and everything will be okay. She's pretty cool, and besides, this was an accident," Mickey said with false confidence. "We shouldn't have been on this path anyway."

"I'll let you tell her...be right behind you."

The two continued toward the barn.

"Who the Hell was that anyway?" Toot asked.

"I'm thinking that was Gigi's new nanny. If that's the case, her name is Carmen this, that, the other Santos, or something like that."

"Well, I'm in love."

"No, you're not."

"Yeah, you're probably right. I could be, though."

"Keep your cock in your pocket, Toot, or Diane will grab it and Suki will cut it off with wire snippers."

"Speak for yourself there, *Kimosabe*. Last I checked, you're the married one, not me. Oh, at least you claim that you're married. You still need to show me that marriage certificate."

The subject of the marriage certificate had become the brunt of frequent jokes. It was Toot's way of dealing with the unresolved and questionable arrangement between Diane and Mickey. He had to keep the pressure on Mickey to produce the document, and yet he had to be able to walk away when, each time, Mickey failed to do so.

"I'll get right on that, Toot. Can you put up the horses? I need to check on Diane."

"Not a problem."

"You'll be up for dinner tonight?"

"Yep. Seven o'clock, right?"

"That's right."

"I'll be there. Paul and Sarah are still comin'?"

"Oh, yeah. They won't miss your cooking."

"Hey, Mick?"

"What?"

"For what it's worth, I think Sarah's been good for Diane. I know it's been hard for you to keep things plutonic. The way you have dealt with the situation has come as a surprise to me. I figured the two of you would…well…anyway, it ain't happened, and I guess I just wanted to say I'm proud of you for leavin' her alone."

"See, a tiger can change his stripes."

"I wasn't worried about your stripes."

Mickey dismounted and handed the reins to Toot, who walked off to the barn with both horses. Mickey headed for the house. After taking off his boots in the mudroom, he eased into the kitchen expecting to find an unsuspecting prey with her back turned toward him. Sure enough, there she was—Lupita—working feverishly to get dinner ready, and she was facing away from him.

Having tip-toed to within a foot of his victim, Mickey shouted, "Okra!"

Lupita let out a scream, followed by a tirade in Spanish as she chased Mickey around the kitchen with a wooden spoon in one hand and a butcher's knife in the other. Only Lupe understood what she was saying when she let loose with a blue streak, and he would never provide a complete and accurate translation, preferring to say only that 'it was bad.' Mickey had developed a habit of scaring Lupita when he was much younger and still found it humorous, even though Lupita had long ago grown weary of the prank.

After three circles around the kitchen, Lupita finally stopped, resolving to only toss a stalk of celery at Mickey.

"One day Mickey Rollins, you will give me a heart attack, and then there will be blood on your hands."

"Hey, you looked like you needed some exercise."

"Someday, Mickey Rollins…," she said pointing the butcher's knife at him, then with one quick swipe, split a cucumber into two pieces for visual effect.

"Ouch," Mickey said, putting his hands in front of his zipper. "What's for dinner?"

"For you, dog food. For the civilized people who live here and their company, they will be starting with Miss Diane's favorite cold soup—gazpacho."

"Of course. That's why the okra."

"Si, and the tomatoes, and onions, and peppers, and parsley, and cucumbers."

"You really put all those ingredients in there?"

"They come fresh out of Lupe's garden," she answered with a sigh, giving one-half of a cucumber another whack. "Then we will have halibut for the main course because that is Mrs. Duke's favorite—especially when it is smoked the way Mr. Toot does it."

"How about lobster tail?"

"Yes, I bought some of those, too."

"For me?"

"No! For Miss Suki. She says it was a rare treat where she comes from, and she has taken a liking to it. She also had some of her fruits and vegetables shipped in overnight from that market in San Francisco. She said she would prepare them. I don't touch them."

Mickey went to the refrigerator where he pulled out a cold bottle of beer.

"Steak for the guys, right?"

"As usual—Rub-a-Dub Ribeye. However, I must say that I think Miss Diane and Miss Suki have a healthier diet than the men on this ranch do. And don't even think of drinkin' no beer at the table. You know the rules. You want beer? You guys have to drink it on the patio while Mr. Toot cooks. Miss Diane already has the bottles of her V. Sattui picked for tonight—three white and three red—and she told me the ones to get next if those get used up."

Such had become dinnertime at the ranch. Diane and Suki were very discriminating about what they ate and drank, and tried to influence what Toot and Mickey could ingest by making them go out of their way to get what they wanted. If beef was served, it had to be accompanied by the option of chicken or seafood. There were always fruits and vegetables taken from the garden, or flown in from one of the several produce markets Suki had found on the internet. Wine was the only alcoholic beverage served at the table other than an after dinner cordial.

What's more, the wines could only come from Diane's favorite vineyard in Napa—V. Sattui. By contrast, Mickey insisted on bottled beer from an ice chest, and since with that came water spots that aggravated Diane, beer had become an outside-only drink when company was being served.

To get relief from *Diane's Commandments*, as these and other rules of the house had become known, she agreed to letting Mickey attend a monthly 'Boyz Night' on Section Eight of the ranch where, on the last Saturday of the month, basically anything was allowed to happen. 'Eight,' as it was known to those familiar with it, was located on the most distant six hundred and forty acres of the ranch, and actually was created back in Dub and Clem's time as a place where the ranch hands could safely blow off steam without disrupting life at the main house. It was aptly named after the military term for 'unfit conduct,' and, in reality, was a rambling, old house made of cedar logs and rock cut from a local hillside, and a grand barn, both of which predated the Rollins' acquisition of the land. There was an endless supply of beer. Beef and wild game taken from the ranch were cooked over a pit. There were music, dancing, and girlfriends. The occasional lady of convenience spent the night. Dub and Clem looked the other way as long as nobody left Eight, and as long as everyone was at work at dawn Monday morning. Mickey and Toot usually went for a couple of hours, but were always home by ten o'clock. Diane and Suki went to Eight once, accompanied by Mickey and Toot, and vowed never to go again.

"Mickey," Diane called, entering the room with Gigi in her arms. "Do you know what time it is?"

"Is this where you tell me I'm late?"

"Yes. You're late! Not only that, you're filthy and you smell like cow."

She emphasized her point by coming up close, sniffing, and making an unpleasant face.

"We had a busy day."

"Well, busy yourself in the shower. Where's Toot?"

"He's putting up the horses. He knows to be here at seven. Heaven forbid we be late to Princess Carmen's inauguration."

"You think this is a big joke, don't you?"

"Usually when I hire someone, my life doesn't revolve around them."

"Well, your life revolves around mine, and mine revolves around our daughter's, and her life is about to be strongly influenced by Carmen, so get used to the arrangement."

"I'm not sure you have that correct, but we can discuss it later. Anyway, I already met her...sort of."

Diane picked up a stalk of celery, took a bite, then asked, "How's that?"

"Hey, monkey, how was your day?" Mickey asked, taking Gigi from Diane. He figured it might be safer to be holding Gigi when he told Diane about his encounter with Carmen.

"Mick, don't call her a monkey. She'll end up needing therapy someday because of it."

"I wanted to name you Cheetah, but Mommy wanted Gigi."

"Mick!"

"She named you after garlic."

Gigi had no idea what he was saying, but the attention provoked a huge smile.

"Mick! Come on. Stop it. Now tell me about Carmen."

"Did you put her in the Spirit Room?"

"Of course. That's where I said we would be putting her, unless, as usual, you weren't listening to me."

Gigi began to wiggle and smile with excitement as Suki entered the room.

"Hi, baby," Suki said, taking Gigi by her outstretched arms into her own, and thereby removing Mickey's defense. The two snuggled closely for a few seconds. "I heard you talking about Carmen. She is in the Spirit Room."

"Mickey said he met her already. Did she meet him when she first arrived?"

"Let me explain," he began. "Toot and I were coming back from the loading pen, and I wanted to show him where I needed some irrigation for my garden. I was thinking we could simply channel some water from the creek through a gate. Anyway, we were riding Mico and Biggun along the path by the creek when we saw her in the window."

"You didn't scare her, did you?" Diane asked. "I hope she was decent."

"Nope. She wasn't scared a bit...more like embarrassed. As for decent, if you consider naked to be decent..."

"Naked!" Both shouted in response to his revelation.

"Yep, as a jaybird. So, there were a few awkward moments. Toot swallowed his tongue. I had to do the Heimlich on him."

Diane took a seat at the table, buried her head in her hands, and said, "I can't believe this happened. Nobody ever rides along the creek. You said it was too rocky."

Suki seemed to relish the thought of Carmen's unplanned exposure.

"Call it a series of unfortunate events."

"Oh, my God," Diane said, looking up at Mickey. "Don't mention this tonight...please."

"I don't plan to bring it up. Toot, on the other hand, said something about being in love. He may still have a hard-on," he said, turning to Lupita. "Do you remember what a hard-on is?"

Lupita responded by chopping the remaining half of a cucumber with the butcher's knife.

"Mickey!" Both ladies shouted, again in unison.

The reactions by Diane and Suki to Mickey's remarks were not in and of themselves unexpected. What was becoming increasingly noticeable, however, was how Diane and Suki were becoming more and more indistinguishable in their mannerisms, reactions, habits, and words. Their last two simultaneous and identical responses might have been pure coincidence, but Mickey was beginning to wonder if this was a new byproduct of Diane's therapy. Furthermore, it wasn't just words and actions. Diane always called herself the queen of simplicity when it came to eating—craving 'round' food or carry-out. Now, her meals selections had more of a gourmet appearance similar to what Suki used to plan for her clientele. Her sexual desires were no longer just the basics. She had become something of a nymphomaniac with needs having to be satisfied by both Suki and Mickey—often together. Then, there were the physical changes. She was becoming a dominantly right-handed person, like Suki; her walk was different, more similar to Suki's; and her smile was quick and bright, like Suki's.

Diane began laughing indicating the worst of her reaction to the news was over.

"I need to have a talk with her to be sure she's alright. I don't want her to think we're a bunch of perverts. Things are strange enough around here as it is. Suki, can you help Mickey get ready? I don't want him to be late. We can't screw this up any more than it already is. I'll take Gigi with me."

"Certainly," she replied, reluctantly handing Gigi back to her mother. The reluctance to separate was mutual, and Gigi began to reach out for Suki and whimper.

"Suki can stay here. I can get ready without any help."

"No, I want things to be perfect tonight for Carmen. I want everything to go without a hitch."

"What makes you think something will go wrong?"

"I just know," Diane replied. "Come on Gigi, let's go get dressed and see Miss Carmen."

After watching Diane and Gigi disappear down the hallway and around a corner, Suki looked at Mickey and said, "This is harder than I ever expected it would be, especially now that Gigi is developing her own personality."

Lupita began humming as she always did in the past when she overheard something she thought she shouldn't hear, giving Mickey the opportunity to take Suki by the hand and head toward the master wing of the house.

"Bad timing."

"I am sorry, but I had to let you know."

"Duly noted. Now get over it. I need you to stay focused on your mission. This is about Diane, not Gigi."

Suki stopped dead in her tracks, and said, "You talk of this as though it were a military exercise instead of raising your family."

Ignoring Suki's remark, Mickey asked, "Have you noticed how much Diane is beginning to sound and act like you? It's remarkable. She's taking on more and more of your characteristics."

She jerked Mickey's arm until he turned to face her, saying, "There is one characteristic she will never have, I promise you that much."

"She'll have what I instruct you to give to her, that is unless you've found a way to control your mind during hypnosis. You're good, Suki, but not that good. Besides, you're addicted to the euphoria of the therapy, aren't you?"

Mickey was right. He had found a way to manage the dopaminergic cascade such that it produced a more rapid transfer of thoughts, but never became uncontrollable. A result of this was the speedy progress of Diane's therapy. However, a side effect that was produced by the process was a 'high' Suki craved. Also, there was another, more insidious side effect—she was beginning to experience some of the diminishment Mickey and Mendoza had warned her about, and the losses weren't as benign as they had promised. While Diane's will, drive, and inner strength blossomed, it was at the expense of the same qualities within Suki, and she was finding it more and more difficult to say 'no' to Mickey.

"We need to get you ready," Suki said, taking Mickey by the hand and leading him into the master suite. "Get in the shower, and I will set out your..."

Before she could finish her sentence, Mickey pulled her close and kissed her.

"You know I still love you, Suki."

Looking shocked and confused, Suki responded, "Excuse me, but how did we transition from 'focus on your mission' and 'you are not that good' to 'I love you?' I seem to have missed something."

"It's all the same thing, Suki. Sometimes I think you start to drift off course, and I need to give you guidance because I deeply care for you. Besides, I can't do this without you. I really need you to be with me...to be a part of us."

It had been a long time since Mickey had held her in his arms and used the word 'us,' and it had the effects of defusing the situation and relighting the candle. Those were the reactions Mickey had hoped for. His next kiss was met without resistance.

"Shower with me."

Suki paused to think before replying, "No. Not without Diane."

"She asked you to help me get ready."

"That has nothing to do with sex."

"Who said anything about sex? I just asked you to get in the shower with me."

"Mickey, you are a terrible liar."

"I didn't lie. We'll take a shower together. Now, if we just happen to have sex..."

"You see? That is a lie. I cannot do that to Diane. The three of us have an arrangement. Besides, she will be back here any minute."

"Maybe later?"

"No. Never alone, remember? Diane made us promise."

"Then why did she send us back here together alone?"

"Mickey, please. I cannot break my pledge to Diane."

"I could change her memory of that pledge. You'd have to help me."

"Absolutely not. You act like a spoiled child sometimes, Mickey. You persist with a request until you get what you want. You need to start acting your age for once."

Mickey immediately released Suki in response to her reference to his age—a terribly sensitive subject for him. Without saying a word, he turned and went into the master bath, closing the door behind him. There was nothing she could do to salvage the moment.

"MY, DON'T YOU LOOK good in that outfit. When did you get it?" Diane asked, making a circle as she critiqued Suki.

"Thank you. I bought it last week, remember?"

"Was I with you?"

"Yes, Diane. It was that at new shopping center just outside of San Antonio."

"Gosh, so much is happening, I can't remember things that just took place. What do you think about Carmen?"

Knowing Diane was probably looking for more positive feedback than she could honestly give, Suki felt it best to divert Diane's focus to another matter.

"Did Mickey get ready?"

"Not that I know of. At least I haven't seen him. Did you set his things out for him and herd him in the direction of the shower?"

Now Suki wondered if her new topic was any better than the last.

"I tried, but he seemed preoccupied about something. We were talking about it, and I forgot to place his clothes on the bed. That was about a half hour ago. I left him as he was entering the shower."

"What were you talking about?" Diane asked, her possessive streak beginning to show.

Lying enough to avoid anything resembling Mickey's attempts at plotting to have clandestine sex with her, Suki replied, "I cannot remember all of the conversation. However, it ended when I said something along the lines of 'he needed to act his age.' My comment did not go over well with him."

"Why did you say that?"

"You know how he is when things are not going his way. I think he just had a difficult day."

"I don't know what his hang-up is about his age. He survived fifty and he looks spectacular. A little gray on the sides, but it looks good on him. And physically, he's in great shape. A little softer than Toot, probably, but not everyone can have Toot's physique."

"You are most correct. Toot's body is one for the books."

"I guess you would know."

Assuming they had been discovered, Suki asked, "How long have you known?"

"Long enough to know you want to keep the matter private."

"We do, Diane. Please do not let Mickey know. I think he would be upset with me, and more so with Toot. One more thing, Toot does not know all the details of the relationship the three of us have together. It is important that what is between me, you and Mickey, remain in confidence between us. For now, he sees me as only involved with your therapy, and that I take care of Gigi…or at least I did until now. "

"Your secret is safe with me. I'm happy for you. So, how is he with you?"

Suki felt a certain amount of pride that she had what appeared to be a real, honest relationship with a man, albeit poorly veiled. Ironically, it was Mickey's own denial that Suki could be interested in any man other than him that kept him from realizing what was going on between her and Toot.

"Toot is exactly what you see on the surface. He is a sweet, kind, gentle, and caring man. He listens to me. He wants to please me. He cherishes Gigi. He takes pride in his work and this ranch. If he has one shortcoming, it is that he looks up to Mickey. I am at a loss to explain why, but he does. I suspect it has something to do with the fact that his father used to work for Mickey's father, and that order in life continues."

"Wow, does he have a brother some place?" Diane asked.

Diane chuckled at her own joke, but Suki was a little less amused because she thought she read more into her question than one unfamiliar with Diane's mind might think. After all, Diane's mind was now a lot like her own, and respecting the sanctity of another woman's special relationship with a man wasn't something about which she used to care.

"By the way, where is Gigi?" Suki asked.

"I put her down for a while. She's been quiet so I think she needed a short nap before dinner. Do you mind listening for her while I check on Mickey?"

"Not at all. I need to help Lupita prepare some dishes for the meal tonight anyway. I will keep an ear tuned for her. And Diane, thank you for being such a good friend."

"Absolutely, and thank you just the same, Suki," Diane ended, giving her a long, heartfelt embrace.

DIANE WALKED DOWN THE hallway seemingly oblivious to what had taken place between Suki and Mickey. Of more interest to her was the description that Suki had given of Toot. By that definition, he was what she had hoped to find in a husband, and realized Mickey fell short in several of the categories. Yet, there was something in what Suki had said about Toot. It sounded so real, almost as if she had experienced the same feelings once. Then again, how could that be, she thought.

Eventually arriving in the master suite, she found Mickey in the shower. He was standing under the water, his hands up against the wall with the water falling on his head. He wasn't moving, and Diane knew that meant he was in deep thought. She hesitated before breaking the silence.

"Mick?"

"Yeah."

"You alright?"

"Dandy."

"Do you want me to set out your clothes?"

"Dandy."

"I'm going to take the Jag for a spin. Be back in a couple of hours."

"Dandy."

He was having a fugue-like moment. Diane knew it would take physical contact to shake him out of it. She closed the bedroom door, shed her clothing, and stepped into the shower with him.

"Hey, Babe, what are you doing here?" Mickey asked, turning around to greet her..

"I've been trying to have a conversation with you for the last few minutes."

"You're kidding?"

"Nope. All you've been saying is dandy, dandy, dandy."

"Sorry. I hate when I get in these moods."

"You're not the only one."

"I love you, Diane. This has been rough. I know it's rough on you, too. But, to be in Dad's place, to walk where he walked, to ride in pastures where he used to ride, it just tears me up. It's like you said once, there was so much left unsaid. So much left undone."

"I love you, too, Mick. Everything is fine between us, right?"

"What do you mean?"

"I mean—us."

"Oh, yeah. We're...dandy."

Diane was pained by his answer. The word didn't exactly capture strength in their relationship she was hoping for. But then, Mickey wasn't the most outspoken person.

"Suki told me what happened."

"She did? I was just messing with her. I wasn't going to take her to bed without you. Surely you know I wouldn't do that. We made a promise."

"What are you talking about? She told me you were upset because you were pouting over needing to act your own... Oh, now I get it."

At least the foot Mickey put firmly into his mouth was a clean one.

"What I meant was..."

"No, Mick. No more lies. You were trying to fuck our little Thai friend behind my back, weren't you?"

"Nothing happened."

"Thanks to Suki and only Suki, I'm sure. Get your own clothes."

Without saying another word, Diane bolted from the shower and slammed the bathroom door behind her.

Chapter 33

Sarah Duke was a Bohnert, as in the Fairhope Ranch Bohnerts. The pedigree went back six generations to the acquisition of just over two thousand acres of South Texas land from the government in the 1850s when the land was still unsettled. Blood, sweat, tears and subsequent deals grew the ranch to several hundred thousand acres of agricultural farmland that gave many branches of the family the wealth they enjoyed today. The women in the family were expected to marry 'well.' Sarah certainly did when she met Paul Duke. The fact that he was a much older man was unimportant to the family. His name, status, and deep pockets were all that mattered.

Paul was a good man. The son and grandson of men who ranched and speculated in gas and oil, he was as Texan as a man could be. His personality was the only thing bigger. There wasn't a man with status in Texas or any neighboring state who couldn't call Paul by his first name and vice-versa. He and Sarah had six children. Their first, Paul Junior, was tragically killed in a motor vehicle accident his sophomore year of high school. Sarah was an emotional wreck for years, and to this day won't talk about it. Sammy was an officer in the Army, having graduated a decorated member of the Corps of Cadets at A & M. Next came Carla who was in medical school at Galveston. Austin was at Baylor where, at six feet four inches, two hundred twenty pounds, he was starting quarterback, not to mention Paul's pride and joy. The youngest children, twins Ella and Stella, were still in high school, but did part-time modeling for Saks, appearing in local television commercials.

Sarah was not the only one who wouldn't talk about Paul Junior's accident. Toot wouldn't either—he was the driver of the vehicle. PJ thought Toot hung the moon. He wanted nothing more than to be a rodeo star like his hero. They were returning from a rodeo in Mineral Wells, pulling a heavy three-horse slant with living quarters behind him. A drunk driver cut Toot off causing him to flip the rig. Paul, Sarah and Clem were behind them and witnessed the whole thing. Had it not been for the relationship between the families, there wouldn't be a partnership, let alone a close friendship.

Paul was stoic about the accident, never shedding a tear. Sarah was almost inconsolable. He found solace in his business; Sarah found hers in Mickey. She was lonely as Paul held all of his feelings within, while she was dying inside with nobody to share her emotions. Mickey, as always, was a predator with a keen eye for women in need who could easily succumb to his charms. After her remarkably well-concealed, three-month-long affair with Mickey, and subsequent pregnancy, she remained faithful to Paul and never saw Mickey again until his return to the ranch with Diane and Suki. That she could face Mickey at all, and be friends with Diane, lies in the fact that she took full responsibility for the affair. Dub was ready to disown Mickey entirely but for the fact that Sarah begged Dub not to be angry with him. He took the secret of the affair, pregnancy, and abortion to his grave. Only Clem and Toot knew about it, and they were sworn to secrecy—a vow they would never break, sealed with a gentleman's handshake.

Dinner tonight was the first time everyone had been together at the same time. Privately, each wondered how the evening would work out with so many secrets, so many agendas, and a new face—that of Carmen.

"GREETINGS," SUKI SAID TO the Dukes as she met them at the door. "Please come in and make yourselves at home."

"Suki, darling outfit. Where'd you get it?"

"La Cantera."

"It's perfect on you, don't you think, Paul?"

"I don't usually make a habit of complimenting other women's figures, but Suki, you look fabulous."

"I didn't say compliment her figure," Sarah said, jabbing Paul in the ribs. "I was talking about her outfit."

"See, Suki, I just can't stay out of trouble."

"Thank you both. Paul, the other gentlemen are on the porch if you would rather be with them instead of being in harm's way at the fashion show."

"I think I'll take you up on that," he said, making a quick exit.

As soon as he was out of the room, Sarah finished with the obligatory, "Men!"

"It is alright. I was not offended in any way. I like what you have on as well. You look so good in casual attire. Would you care for a glass of wine?"

"Thanks. I just like keeping things simple. And, yes, do you have a white?"

"Yes, one of Diane's Sauvignon Blancs."

"Perfect."

"Sarah! I'm so glad you're here," Diane said, joining the two. "Another night with only Mickey to talk to and I'd lose my mind."

"Now Diane, he can be a wonderful listener at times."

"Oh, I suppose, as long as he's not in one of his moods."

"Have you been feeling well lately?" Sarah asked.

"Do you mean, have I been having any seizures? Just two so far this week. But, I've been having the weirdest dreams, followed by headaches."

"What kind of dreams?"

"No. Not tonight. We need a calm day where we can laugh out loud about it."

"I'm going to the spa Thursday. Do you want to come with me?"

"I'll let you know. For the most part, Suki takes care of that sort of thing for me right here."

Suki approached the two with two glasses saying, "Sarah, here is yours, and Diane, I took the liberty of pouring a glass of red for you."

"Thanks. Say, Suki, would you mind giving Sarah a massage some day?"

"That would be no problem at all. Just name the time and place."

"Well, I don't want to intrude or anything."

"It is no intrusion whatsoever. I am a therapist among other things, and I am more than happy to work with someone other than Diane."

"Well, if you don't mind seeing a lot of stretch marks, I may just take you up on that offer. Can I pay you?"

"Oh, please, no. I just enjoy making people feel better. That is payment enough. Also, I have some treatments that do wonders for stretch marks."

The conversation was interrupted by the sound of footsteps. It was Carmen, and she was carrying Gigi. Two things visibly shook Suki: that Carmen had taken it upon herself to get Gigi, and that Gigi appeared to be so at ease with her new nanny.

"Was she awake?" Suki asked anxiously.

"Of course, and ready to party," Carmen replied as she tickled Gigi, evoking a giggle.

"Sarah," Diane began, "I'd like you to meet Gigi's new nanny, Carmen."

"I'm pleased to meet you. Talk about fashion, I love your clothes. And, your accent, it's divine."

"Just a little something I picked up on the way home from the airport. As for the accent, I am from Spain."

"See, Sarah, she calls this 'home' already."

"That's a good start," she replied, nodding in agreement.

The little something Carmen referred to was nothing short of spectacular. She wore skin tight Lady Wranglers that looked as though they had been painted on. Above them, she sported a trendy, pink, button-down, hand-sewn western shirt, complete with sequins on the cuffs of her sleeves. She had wasted money on the top three buttons as they were left undone. Judging from the cleavage shown to all, she wasn't wearing a bra. She walked in a pair of Lucchese boots that still smelled like new leather. Her belt buckle was a Montana Silversmith double heart.

"You really know how to dress Western, Carmen," Sarah said, almost blushing as she stared at the new resident of Rub-a-Dub.

"I call it, The Alamo meets Milan."

Diane and Sarah laughed heartily at Carmen's remark, adding to the distress that Suki quietly felt.

OUTSIDE, THE CONVERSATION HAD an entirely different perspective on life. Toot was cooking steaks on one side of an enormous grill, and lobster and halibut on the other. Smoke flavor came from his private source of hand-cut wood. The seafood was basted with his signature sauces, the recipes for which were unknown to anyone but the chef himself. His "Teskey's Saddle Shop" cap was turned backward atop his head, and his T-shirt showed ample perspiration from the effort he put into his grilling. The shirt read "Hooters VP of Recruiting'" on the front, and "No Cleavage Overlooked" on the back.

"Have you thought about how much you want to put up at the stock show auction?" Toot asked.

"Well," Paul replied, "We did twenty-five last year, and there's a bumper crop of seniors in the County this year lookin' for some college money. I figure thirty, maybe thirty-five."

"Seen that steer Shelby Heisler raised?"

"Big son-of-a-bitch, ain't he."

"Gotta be fourteen hundred pounds. He's solid, too, and she shows him good. Could be her year for San Antone and Fort Worth."

"I think you're right."

"What are you guys talking about?" Mickey asked, joining the conversation late.

"We're just talkin' about the stock show auction. It's next weekend and we always help out the kids. Grab yourself a beer."

Rummaging through the bottles of beer, Mickey half-seriously asked, "What, no Falstaff?"

Toot and Paul looked at Mickey like he was crazy.

"Just kidding. Anyway, you said thirty…like thirty thousand bucks?"

"Yep," Paul said without flinching. "Gotta problem with that?"

"No, I guess not. I'll just stay back and sit on my hands."

"Good idea," Toot replied.

"How's the horse business, Mickey?" Paul asked.

"Too early to call it a business. We bought the acreage next door that you told me about. Brought some horses out last week."

"I seen 'em. Pretty good lookin' stock."

"Tell that to Diane. She'd like to hear a compliment from someone like you."

"I'll be certain to give her my opinion any time. All I see is mares. Got any stallions yet?"

"Yeah, we got two here and two back at Terra Vista in Gilroy. The ones here are on the other side of the barn—either that or they got out, and they're at your place."

"Better not be, or the taxidermist is goin' to be mighty busy."

There was plenty of laughter with the thought of mounted horse flesh.

"Anyway, we'll be building a barn just for the horses starting next month as soon as Diane finishes the plans."

"Oh, Toot," Paul said, "That reminds me. Blaine called today. He can start on the new storage facility in two weeks."

"Glad you thought enough to tell me. Thanks."

"Hey, you didn't ask. Figured you weren't too excited anymore."

"Bullshit. I been waitin' on you. Figured you were wheelin' and dealin'."

"Well, I'm done dealin' and in truth I just plain forgot to tell you. He says it'll take him six weeks as long as there's good weather."

"That'll be fine. Just in time, too. I had to send forty head to auction last week, and I figured I'd have to send another forty in two months. That's perfect timin'."

"That's what partners are for," Paul said, shaking Toot's hand.

"Can you stick around after dinner? Thought you might want to go up to Eight for a bit with me and Mickey."

"I'll check with Sarah. Might go with you for a while. Can you take me home if Sarah leaves before we get back?"

"Not a problem."

WHEN THE COOKING WAS done, Toot took the covered platters into the kitchen so that Lupita could finish the preparations. While that was going on, he made a quick exit to the guest bathroom where he quickly washed up and changed shirts. The others began milling around the dining room at which point those who hadn't been formally introduced to Carmen were able to make her acquaintance.

"Paul, I'd like you to meet Carmen," Diane said. "She's the new nanny who will be taking care of Gigi."

Uncharacteristically at a loss for words, Paul managed to squeak out, "Ma'am."

"I am very pleased to meet you, Mr. Duke," Carmen replied, holding her hand out to shake Paul's.

Next, Diane escorted Carmen to meet Mickey.

"This is Mr. Rollins."

"Mr. Rollins, I recognize you from a photograph Diane sent to me. You look much younger in person."

Her handshake lasted a few seconds longer than necessary to greet her new employer.

It was all Mickey could do to avoid highlighting her compliment in front of Suki and Diane. Nonetheless, his facial expression said what he was thinking.

"Please, call me Mickey. I'm most happy to have you here at our ranch. Make yourself at home, and let me know if there's anything I can do to help you with Gigi."

Before either Diane or Suki could say something, Toot returned. He wasted no time introducing himself.

Approaching Carmen with an outstretched hand, he said, "Ma'am, you can call me Toot. You must be Carmen."

"Yes, we have already met."

"Oh, you mean earlier. Well, that was a bit awkward now, wasn't it?"

"No, not at all," she replied with a coy smile. "Was it awkward for you?"

There was nothing Toot could say to Carmen at that moment that was appropriate, so he winked and moved on.

After giving Suki a quick hug, he walked over to their guests.

"Sarah, you look great tonight, like always," he said as the two gave each other a mutual hug. He then walked over to Diane who carried Gigi. The child's two tiny arms reached for him. "Hey sweet pea. Come to Tooters."

The handoff was effortless as he took the child, managing to kiss Diane on the cheek in the process.

"Diane," Paul said, "I don't know why you need a nanny. After all, you got Toot here." He quickly nodded at Carmen and finished with, "No offense, ma'am."

"None taken, Mr. Duke," Carmen replied. "Toot appears to be marvelous with Gigi."

Mickey's feelings went from high to low in record time as he watched Toot seamlessly move among the women at dinner, not to mention his magical touch with Gigi.

There was a timely distraction as Lupita approached the group and announced, "Dinner is ready. Everyone please take your seats."

Diane took her seat at one end of the table where she usually sat. Mickey stood at the opposite end and waited for the others to find their places. Paul stood to his left. Mickey pulled out the chair to his right.

"Sarah?"

Breaking the rules of etiquette, Sarah replied, "No, but thank you Mickey. I'll just sit here next to Paul."

She quickly pulled out the chair on the other side of Paul which he pushed back in as she sat down.

Suki took up her place on the opposite side of the table from the Dukes where she pulled out a second chair, hinting to Carmen that she was to take that seat. Carmen, however, had a different plan as she passed the Dukes and Mickey, and instead of taking the seat Suki had pulled out for her, she sat in the open seat next to Mickey. There was nothing Suki could do or say at that point without making a scene.

Seeing the only remaining open place setting, Toot took his seat to the right of Suki, next to Diane. He held Gigi comfortably on his lap.

Finally, Mickey took his seat, and Lupita came out to serve the wine and dinner.

Paul broke the ice by asking what was on the minds of many at the table.

"So tell us about yourself, Carmen."

"What would you like to know?"

In his disarming fashion, Paul replied, "Oh, come on now, we don't bite here. Just start with where you're from and your family and see where the conversation goes."

"Well, my full name is Carmen Julieta Emmanuel de los Santos. My hometown is El Puerto de Santa Maria in the southwest corner of Spain. My father is Alvaro Domecq de los Santos. Our family has lived in El Puerto for 600 years. I have a twin sister and two brothers. Papa and my uncles own and operate The Province de Cadiz School of Equestrian Art. My mother is also named Carmen and she operates the family bodega."

"Good golly, you takin' notes, Sarah?"

"How did you find her, Diane?"

"Actually, Sarah, her name was on a short list of prospects provided to me by Suki. She did all of the research."

"Alright. Suki how did you come up with somebody half way around the world?"

"Her father and I have a mutual friend—the gentleman who owns Maribella Island."

This was the first time Diane had heard this little factoid. It sent a shiver down her spine.

"Let's hope that's not an evil omen of some kind."

"You have heard of this island?" Carmen asked Diane.

"Yes, it's had a significant impact on my life. That's the island where I had my accident."

"Now that's what I call a small world," Paul added to the conversation.

"Aside from that association, Carmen has excellent credentials for the job," Suki continued, trying to move off the subject of the island and accident.

"And what might those be?" Mickey asked.

"Mickey, quit prying," Diane said, chastising him.

"No, I am proud of my accomplishments. I recently graduated from Shannon College in Ireland where I completed my Bachelor of Commerce, and also received my diploma in International Hotel Management at Galway. I fulfilled my two-year professional placements at hotels in Salzburg and Dubai. I will eventually be employed by a hotel or property management company, but first I wanted a break, and to visit America. I felt this opportunity would be just what I needed for the next few years."

"Are any of these places near Texas?" Paul asked. The humor helped ease some of the tension in the room.

"Far East Texas, perhaps," Carmen replied, adding to the frivolity.

"So," Toot asked, "You know something about horses? I mean, it sounds like your family makes a livin' that way."

"I've taken several European awards for my riding, if that answers your question."

"Right, but you're talkin' about that English stuff, aren't you?"

"Let me guess, you think English riding is somehow inferior to Western riding."

"No, I'm just tryin' to see what kind of a rider you actually are."

"I feel quite certain I can ride better than anyone sitting at this table."

Like fans at a fight, the others watched as the punches became harder until Paul said, "Oh, oh, Toot. I see a rodeo on the horizon."

All but ignoring Paul's comment, Toot asked, "How long you been ridin'?"

"Since I was three years old," Carmen said confidently. "And you?"

"Started when I was five. Got my first buckle at eight."

"And this buckle is some kind of award?" she asked sarcastically.

"Yes, ma'am. It's like about ten of your trophies."

"Toot, that's enough," Mickey said, having heard his fill of the one-upmanship. "You two can sort this out another day. Let's say you're both accomplished riders and leave it at that."

Carmen and Toot stared at each other just long enough to let the other know that there *would* indeed have to be some sorting out of the pecking order as it related to equine expertise.

DINNER WAS NOTHING SHORT of spectacular. As always, everyone raved about Toot's talent with a grill. This time, they also complimented Suki for her fruit and vegetable dishes. Thankfully, the conversation eventually turned civil, masking the underlying hostilities that were brewing. Gigi was passed between Toot, Diane, Carmen, and Suki, then back to Toot again.

Perhaps it was the many glasses of Diane's chosen wines or perhaps it was because everyone had let their guard down, but the peace at the table was turned on end when out of the blue, Toot asked Carmen, "Ever shoot off of a horse?"

"Toot!" Diane shouted, now having heard all the competitive jabs she wanted to as well. "This is no way to treat a new member of the household."

"I'm sorry Diane, I just wanted to understand more about why we had to fly someone all the way from another country to take care of my little girl here."

"My little girl," Mickey said, correcting Toot. "My little girl."

"Figure of speech, Mick. Don't get bent out of shape or nothin'."

"I'd like to answer Toot's question, if I may," Carmen said before Toot and Mickey escalated their argument over possession any further. "I have competed and placed in European final events for Fifty Meter Rifle, Ten Meter Air Rifle, Twenty-five Meter Pistol, Ten Meter Pistol, Trap, Double Trap, and Skeet—all pre-Olympic trials. I can tell you about every part of the Anschutz, Steyr, and Walther firearms that I own. But, no, I have never fired a weapon while sitting on the back of a horse. I'm willing to learn. Would you like me to have them shipped over here so we can go shooting together?"

"I'm impressed," Toot said, absorbing the details that Carmen provided. "Do you hunt?"

"I have on occasion. It's not a passion of mine. How about you? What do you shoot with?"

"Ever hear of Winchester?"

"Of course. They're legendary."

Sitting back in his chair with a cocky grin, Toot said, "I have not one, but two Model 70s, one of which I carry with me at all times on the ranch."

"He can hit anything with those," Paul added.

"My trophy guns are my 1873 and 1894 lever action rifles."

"You own both of those?"

"Sure do. Want to see them?"

"Another time, perhaps, but I would certainly be interested in seeing them…even shooting them. What about handguns?"

"Nothing but Colt. I have a .45 automatic and a Single Action Army for show and for competition when we shoot and ride."

Carmen nodded, impressed by his collection.

"Well isn't this interesting?" Diane said awkwardly. "Who would have thought that it would be guns that brought Toot and Carmen together?"

Toot winked at the new member of the family, then said, "We're not together just yet, but it's no longer out of the question."

"What about children?" Sarah asked. "After all, it must have been that which put you on Diane's short list. It's clear you know how to dress, run a hotel, and shoot a gun. Tell us about the things in your background that make you suited to be the nanny for little Gigi?"

"I'm so glad you asked. You see, I have three nieces and a nephew between my two brothers. I have taken care of them each summer since they were two. They are now able to converse in their native Spanish, English, and French at their respective age levels. They are commended for their math and writing skills at school, and their behavior is exemplary. I am instructing them in piano and art. In addition, the oldest of them can now ride English at a basic level."

"What about your twin sister. You haven't mentioned much about her. Does your sister have any children?"

For the first time, Carmen appeared to be somewhat uncomfortable.

"My sister and I, surprisingly, aren't that close, and she has no children."

"I think my little girl here might be a wee bit too young for any type of riding, don't you think?" Toot asked.

Mickey had enough. "Toot, let me have her."

"Beg your pardon?" Toot bristled.

"Gigi—let me have her."

"Mickey, stop it," Diane said trying to intervene.

"Fine, then. You take her," Mickey responded.

"Mick, I don't think Toot meant anything by…" Paul said, trying to make peace at the table.

"Paul, I didn't ask for your opinion, did I?" Mickey said thoughtlessly.

"No, Mickey, you didn't. That's never stopped me in the past, nor will it in the future. I suggest you begin treating the people who care about you with a little more respect than what I've just witnessed."

Gigi felt the tension in the room and began to cry.

"Jesus, Mickey. When are you going to learn to keep your mouth shut," Diane said, disgusted with the collapse of an otherwise fabulous evening. "Here Toot, let me take her."

Concerned about Gigi, Toot handed her over to Diane, then said, "Paul, want to head out for a while?"

"Sounds good Toot. You still okay with that, Hon?"

"Sure, Paul. Have a good time."

"Alright everyone," Mickey pleaded, "I'm sorry I acted like such an ass. I apologize. Please, let's just let all of this pass and continue where we were before…"

Before Mickey could finish, Gigi threw up all over Diane's outfit. There wasn't any 'continuing' after that.

"Here, let me help," Suki offered.

"No, but thanks. We're going to get cleaned up together and call it a night. Sarah, you'll be able to get home without difficulty?"

"No problem."

"Paul, thanks for coming," Diane said with an apologetic tone in her voice.

"Absolutely, Diane."

"Toot, stay out of trouble. Suki, Carmen, I'll see both of you in the morning."

With that, Diane left the table with Gigi whimpering over her shoulder. She completely ignored Mickey.

It wasn't but a few moments before Paul and Toot departed for Eight, also ignoring Mickey as they left the room.

Sarah looked at Mickey for a few seconds, then said, "Mickey, sometimes life isn't about just you. When will you ever learn?"

Mickey shook his head, tried to reply, but nothing came out.

"Goodnight, Mick. Suki, it was wonderful. Carmen, it was a pleasure to meet you. Don't worry—things aren't entirely screwed up around here. Tomorrow, it will be as if nothing ever happened." Sarah took the time to walk over to Mickey and kiss him on the cheek before saying, "Get your shit together or you'll lose everything. Don't make the same mistake you made in the past."

Carmen and Suki could only imagine what Sarah meant, but it was very clear to Mickey.

It was quiet in the room for what seemed like an eternity. Eventually, Carmen stood up and said, "I've had a long day. I'm going to bed now. I will see both of you in the morning. Thank you for dinner. It was really…quite interesting." She then left the room.

Her choice of words was a perfect ending to an imperfect evening. It wasn't long before Suki and Mickey were alone and chuckling at the night's turn of events. He poured her one more glass of wine, and she returned the favor, then he stood and took her hand in his. Slowly, they walked down the hallway to the master suite.

Book 5

"I'd like to order a small stack of your whole wheat pancakes with pecans, a side order of bacon, and an endless cup of your wonderful coffee."

"Certainly, Dr. Mason. My, you're sure perky for three o'clock in the morning."

"It is simply a marvelous day, Joan. I didn't want yesterday to end, and I can't wait for tomorrow to begin. So here we are!" Mason said as he folded up the plastic-covered menu and briskly handed it back to the waitress.

"I hate you," Dr. Madden said.

"Can I hate him, too?" Diane asked. "I've never been a morning person. All day long, Mickey pushes caffeine into me. I find myself waking up in the middle of the night craving espresso, but I never have this much energy."

"Oh, and a glass of orange juice as well," Mason barked, finally completing his order.

He noticed the ladies weren't saying anything, and that the waitress was standing, holding her pencil and pad most patiently.

"I'm buying. Go ahead. Order."

Diane finally said, "Double espresso."

"Oh, come, come, come, come. Eat up. We have much to talk about."

"And a sprinkle doughnut."

Mason pulled his glasses down his nose, looking over them at Diane with displeasure.

"Ma'am?" the waitress with the twenty-year pin asked Dr. Madden.

"Do you have any Fruit Loops?"

"Just in those teeny boxes."

"Give me one of those, with skim milk, and coffee."

"I'll have your pancakes up right away, Dr. Mason. It'll be a while on the Fruit Loops," the waitress said, giggling at her own joke.

"No hurry. The bowl of them will be my second helping tonight," Madden replied dryly.

Joan left the table and scurried about behind the counter getting everyone's coffee.

"Were you speaking disparagingly about me—calling me a Fruit Loop, Dr. Madden?"

"Oh, no, Diane. However, I wonder about certain other company here at the table."

"Beverly, you're such negative person in the morning."

"Loarn, I'm fine in the morning. It's the middle of the night when I'm a bitch!" Madden looked around to see if her choice of words was heard beyond their table.

"Oh, I see. Well that explains a few things."

Dr. Madden crossed her arms, disapproving of Dr. Mason's remark.

"Tell me, Diane, you've mentioned a relationship between caffeine and the nanocells more than once—a sort of dependency it would appear. What can you tell us about that?"

"I don't know what it is exactly. All I can tell you is that for as long as I can remember, Mickey has pushed caffeine into me—particularly strong drinks like dark roasts and double espresso."

"How much do you drink in a day?" Madden asked.

"Always three espressos in the morning. Then, I have a steady dose of coffee, usually made from strong-roasted beans, all day long until I go to bed."

"Do you know why you are asked to drink so much caffeine?"

"Suki told me the other day that the nanocells need the stimulant."

"A machine…needing a stimulant?"

"That's what she said. She also made it sound as if they weren't just machines. There seemed to be an organic quality about them."

"Fascinating, don't you agree, Bev?"

"I agree that I need a stimulant right now."

"I'm back," Joan said. "Here's your double espresso, ma'am. Would you like some cinnamon on top?"

"No, I don't think so. Do you have any nutmeg?"

"I'll check. I know we use it for baking. And here's your coffee," Joan said, handing a cup to Dr. Madden.

"Spectacular."

"And here's your coffee and your orange juice, Dr. Mason."

"Perfect, Joan. Freshly squeezed, I presume?"

"Just like you like it," the waitress said, blushing. "Let me go check on your meat...I mean, your bacon..." Joan rushed off.

Madden leaned over the table.

"You flirt! Are you trying to pick up a waitress at an all-night diner, Loarn?"

"Oh, it's perfectly harmless banter, Bev. We play like this all the time."

"Yeah, I'll bet you do. Do you have her phone number?"

"No. She doesn't own a phone," Mason said with a big smile. "Instead, she gave me her address."

Madden tossed a crumpled napkin at Dr. Mason.

"I just remembered something else that Suki told me."

"What's that, Diane?"

"She told me that vitamin C is bad for the nanocells. I was never allowed to have citrus fruits or juices."

"Fascinating, don't you agree, Bev?"

"Loarn, if you say 'fascinating' one more time, I'm leaving. Nothing is fascinating this time of the morning."

"You're upset because I have a secret admirer, aren't you?"

"Not in the least, Loarn."

"Excuse me," Diane interrupted. "Is this get-together about me, or about the two of you?"

"Right," Mason acknowledged. "Where were we? Oh, yes. Diane, you mentioned when I was first talking to you that you ran some type of business. What is that, if I may ask?"

"Well, actually, I don't think that I do."

"You mean, you don't remember?"

"No, I do remember, but I think it must have been a dream. Suki told me that in order for Mendoza's algorithm to work, I had to have an experience. Since real experiences are not always practical, they had to produce at least some of the experiences in my dreams."

"Such as?" Madden asked.

"Take the emotion of sadness. I would have to experience something terribly sad. When my physiologic response met the parameters set in the algorithm, the program would set a boundary limit."

"Did this actually happen?"

"Oh, my God, countless times. I remember the dream I had in which Suki and Gigi died in a plane crash. I was hysterical with grief. Then I woke up. According to Suki, that was the time they set the boundary for sadness."

"How many emotions are we talking about, Beverly?"

"Oh, Loarn, it depends on how you want to group them. For example, if you talk only about emotions that drive action, there is anger, aversion, courage, dejection, desire, despair, fear, hate, hope, love, and sadness. Emotions that result in facial expression—these are universal, by the way—are anger, disgust, fear, joy, sadness, surprise. Emotions that are more or less instinctive are anger, disgust, elation, fear, subjection, tender emotions, and wonderment."

"What about happiness?" Mason asked. "Do you recall a dream that made you happy?"

"I remember one very vividly. I remember waking up once. I was in a hospital with Bruce looking down at me."

"Who's Bruce?" Madden asked.

"He was my first husband. He died in a motorcycle accident a long time ago...at least, I think he did. Anyway, in the dream, I had fallen at an awards banquet and sustained a head injury. When I woke up in my dream, he was alive. He had never died, never had a motorcycle accident. It was the happiest moment of my life."

"Perhaps that is where Mendoza set a boundary for happiness," Mason said.

"Possibly." Diane continued to sip her espresso as she reflected. "But for a split second, it was as if my dearest wish had come true. It was so strange. It appeared as though several of my dreams had been stitched together. I used to have this recurring dream about receiving an award, one where I would fall down while walking to the podium. I also used to have horrible nightmares about Bruce's accident. Occasionally, I would lie awake at night trying to convince myself that the accident was nothing more than a bad dream and that I would wake up and he would be alive. Is it possible that Mickey reached inside my subconscious and put these separate thoughts into one?"

"I would suggest there is no limit to what Mickey can do at this point." Mason said, before taking a drink of his coffee. "So, what do you remember about the dream in which you had a business?"

"Not much actually. Just bits and pieces, like you remember of your own dreams, I suppose. But, it seemed so vivid, so real. At the time, I was certain I ran the company."

"Do you remember the name of the company?" Mason asked.

"I believe it was called, PicoPoint."

Mason began to chuckle.

"What's funny about that, Loarn?"

"That's the name of Mickey's project. That was the name on the proposal I reviewed years ago."

"That makes sense," Diane said. "A few days ago, when I discovered something was wrong, I was probing around in Mickey's office and found an icon on his computer with the word PicoPoint. Until that moment, I thought it was the company in my dream. That was when he caught me holding the goods, so to speak, and everything began to unravel."

Boundaries

"You poor thing," Madden said, putting her hands on Diane's. "I can't imagine what you've been through. Most of us establish our responses to emotions over the course of a lifetime. We all must set our own boundaries for how we respond appropriately in all situations. But you…you've been through emotions boot camp. For you to have gone through the setting of boundaries for all of your emotions during the relatively short time since your accident is something I can't imagine. That's awful. It's criminal."

"What about Dr. Wu's granddaughter, Suki?" Mason asked. "She must have had a role in all of this."

Diane's face showed great pain.

"I don't know what my feelings are about her. I remember her as a friend…the greatest of friends. In another way, she's like an organ donor who just saved my life. So much of what I am today is made up of thoughts, movements and functions I lost, that she gave back to me. But, all this time, she was participating in the most horrific act of deception one can ever imagine by not telling me all that was happening."

"I now understand, Diane, why you questioned the reality of the hospital, of your illness, of me and Dr. Madden, and why you would question the foundation of your friendship with Suki."

"You know, they did it all without Dr. Wu. She knew everything. All Mickey needed to complete his work was Suki. That's a bond I, as only his wife, could never fulfill. Sharing Mickey physically with her didn't bother me nearly as much as finding out she was his partner in his project. I think she's more important to him than I am."

"Mickey was having an affair with Suki?" Madden asked, sitting back with a look of disgust on her face.

"I don't know what to call it. We took our vacation with her. Mickey already had a physical relationship with her, and I developed one, too. She's really a beautiful person in so many ways…so giving of herself. It kind of became a three-way marriage, and that's what it is today. I didn't use to be that way…I mean, being in a relationship where I shared myself with a man and a woman at the same time. I had a lesbian relationship once a long time ago, but I still consider myself for the most part to be a heterosexual woman. I'm not sure if I'm in a bisexual relationship now by choice, or if Suki has made me think that it's acceptable to be like that. Do you understand what I'm saying? I can't differentiate my thoughts and decisions from those Suki may have given to me."

The three looked up and noticed Joan listening intently to the conversation.

"Girl, don't let your man get away with that kind of stuff. If you want my opinion, you need to kick his ass."

"Uh, this is a private conversation," Madden said, startled by the intrusion.

"No, it's alright," Diane said. "Sometimes I need a real-world perspective and, with all due respect, I don't think I can get that from a doctor."

"I'm sorry. The conversation was so interesting that I simply couldn't help myself. Oh, we don't have any nutmeg. I'll go check on your breakfast, folks."

"Diane," Madden asked, trying to get back on subject, "the emotion that probably causes the most significant physical response is fear. Can you recall anything that may have been in one of these dreams which you consider as being most frightening?"

"Yep, just like it was yesterday. In fact, all of these dreams are simply overloaded with detail. They are as real as the three of us sitting here right now. This particular one involved a woman named Genevieve du Coeur."

"Was she a French woman, Swiss, Canadian?" Mason asked.

"French. Does it matter?"

"Oh, not really, I suppose. But, you mentioned that the dream was very detailed, so I assumed this little tidbit might have been revealed at some point."

Joan approached Dr. Madden and set her order before her.

"Here's your bowl of Fruit Loops, ma'am."

"Thank you."

"And here's your doughnut with sprinkles," Joan said, setting Diane's treat before her. "I'll be right back with yours, Loarn…I mean, Dr. Mason. I need both hands for it."

After the waitress left, Madden asked, "Loarn? She calls you, Loarn?"

"Well, Bev, I don't always want to be called 'doctor' in public. People with runny noses come over to me to ask about this and that right when I am trying to eat."

It was obvious from Madden's expression that she wasn't buying what Mason was selling.

"Here are your pancakes and bacon, Dr. Mason."

"Ah, thank you, thank you, Joan. And what about some..."

"Yes, your maple syrup. Here it is," she said, pulling out a small, exotic-looking bottle from her apron.

"Wow, that's the real stuff," Dr. Madden said, taking notice of the name on the bottle.

"Yeah. I keep a special stash here all the time just for him because I know Loarn—I mean Dr. Mason—really likes it."

"I have to tell you, Bev, the service here is impeccable."

Madden grinned as more and more about her long-time associate and friend was revealed, then turned her attention back to Diane.

"So, is this person real or fictitious?"

"Genevieve? Oh, she's real. I met her at a bar in Phuket."

"A bar in Phuket? You certainly get around."

"Loarn, quit acting like you know what you're talking about."

"I do, Bev. I've been to Phuket...several times, actually. It's marvelous! Having said that, there is no limit to how much trouble one can get into there."

"And that's exactly what happened. I went to this bar with Mickey and Suki where you could get all types of exotic drinks; there was nutmeg burning like incense; some people were doing drugs. It turned out Genevieve was interested in meeting Mickey because she knew about PicoPoint. She even met with him privately the day after our evening of partying, while Suki and I were shopping in Bangkok."

"Jesus," Mason said with a mouth full of pancake. "I thought the project was to be kept quiet. And nutmeg? That's right out of a Haight-Ashbury cookbook."

"Diane, just a moment ago, you made it sound as if PicoPoint existed in your dream, then told us it appeared as an icon on Mickey's computer. Now you say you heard about it while you were in Phuket—on the trip when you were injured. Am I correct?"

"Dr. Madden, how can I trust any of my memories? How can I differentiate a real memory from a dream anymore? Yes, I think I heard about it in my past, but it didn't become real to me until I saw it on Mickey's computer."

"But, you say Genevieve is real, and she was interested in PicoPoint."

"Your point is?"

"I'm just trying to understand what you think you know, and what you really know."

"Well, when you figure that out tell me the trick, because that's exactly what I'm trying to do!" Diane shouted, loud enough that the few other patrons in the restaurant took notice.

"Sorry, Diane. I don't mean to pressure you. Please continue telling us about Genevieve."

"She knew Dr. Mendoza and Mickey. Anyway, we left Phuket partly to get away from her—we just didn't trust her. We went to a private island, and that's where I fell and injured myself."

"So, what about the dream?"

"Well, we had planned to go on to Mauritius after the island, but we didn't make it. In my dream, we actually did."

"Phuket…Mauritius…you should have your own travel program on television."

"Well, my trips are the type that end up the basis of Friday night horror movies."

"What took place on Mauritius?"

"We were staying at a resort called the Oberoi. It was exquisite. The view of the ocean was indescribable. All the villas have thatched roofs. Mickey had us in the most expensive suite—the Royal Villa. He always went all out on his trips. It cost seventeen hundred Euros a night…whatever that is in dollars. But, oh, my gosh, it was spectacular. We had our own pool. The living room was as big as a small house. The spa treatments were to die for. The food...I can still taste and smell it."

"Was Suki with you?" Madden asked while stirring her cereal.

"Of course."

"Is it possible the taste and smell you remember is actually the taste and smell that she remembered?"

Diane began to break down.

"You see? That's a perfect example. I don't know. I don't know what's mine and what's Suki's."

Setting out to reassure Diane, Mason offered the following.

"Diane, regardless of its origin, every thought you have now belongs to you. You have to accept them for what they are."

"But, I want *me* back, Dr. Mason. I miss *me*."

"I understand your wish for things to return to the way that they once were, but I would be lying to you if I was to tell you that is possible. It may be, but you need to be strong enough in your resolve to complete the discovery of your condition; to accept all the good news and all the bad that will come as we move forward."

After taking a bite of her doughnut and sipping some espresso, Diane was able to continue with her story.

"How much do you want to know about this dream?"

"I have no other place to be. Do you, Bev?"

"No. Diane, just begin telling us about the dream. Say what comes to mind. Let us know the things that stood out...the things that were truly frightening."

Diane took a deep breath, then said, "The first two days were uneventful and very relaxing."

"You say two days, did it seem that long?" Madden asked.

"Absolutely. I remember the meals, the sex, the beach, and everything else that took place. My dreams—at least the ones in which I think Mickey has set a boundary—feel like real time. Well, not long after we arrived, Suki told me I was pregnant and suggested that she might be pregnant, too. I couldn't believe it. She said Mickey had his vasectomy reversed about six months prior to the vacation and didn't tell me. I have never been so angry in my life."

"Angry, you say?" Mason asked. "What did you do when you heard this?"

"I pitched a huge fit...made a big scene on the beach. I said a lot of unflattering things to Suki. Then Mickey showed up, and I had a cow. All kinds of people were watching us. It was really awful. At least I didn't get violent or anything."

"Bev, you said 'anger' was one of our basic emotions, correct?"

"That's right."

"Do you think that...?"

"...He was setting another boundary—maybe two in one dream? It's very possible. The scenario she's describing would just about push any woman over the limit."

"If I had a boyfriend who did that," Joan said, standing at the edge of the table, "I'd kill him dead. Gun...knife...bare hands. He'd be dead. There'd be a baby without a biological father. Permanently!"

"Thank you, Joan," Mason responded, "for your insight. Would you mind getting us all a refill?"

"Oh, certainly, Dr. Mason."

"Loarn, do something about her," Dr. Madden requested.

"Why, she just expressed what Diane was thinking at that moment, didn't she, Diane?"

"That's right, except Suki was going down with him," Diane said, sticking her knife into her doughnut and holding it up in the air. "So, Mickey takes off like a coward, and I head back to our bungalow with Suki chasing after me. I get inside and she slams the door behind us. All of the sudden these guys grab us— four of them. I figured Suki could handle them, but I was wrong. As I watched, one of the men held her, while another stuck a knife in her chest again and again and again. It just kept happening. I don't know how many times she was stabbed. The two men were covered with blood. I was covered with blood—I even remember tasting it. Then, as she was dying in the arms of the guy who was holding her, the other slit her throat from ear to ear nearly decapitating her."

"I figured I was next so I started to fight as hard as I could. When I spun around, there she was, sitting in a chair—Genevieve. She had this hideous smile, and was sitting with her legs crossed, completely poised, just watching. She said she was going to wait for Mickey to show up, but until then, her men were going to play with me. They cut off my clothes and tied me to the bed. Then they chopped off my hair, leaving only uneven chunks."

"Did they rape you?" Joan asked, holding a pot of coffee.

Dr. Madden jumped, startled at Joan's presence next to her.

"Joan! Just leave it on the table!" Madden shouted.

"Fine. What about her?" Joan asked, pointing at Diane. "Does she want another espresso?"

"Diane?" Mason asked.

"Yes, and another doughnut. I kind of killed this one," Diane said, picking up, then dropping some crumbs of her doughnut onto her plate.

Mason leaned forward scratching his beard.

"Diane, allow me to digress for a moment if I may. If Mickey is the father of your daughter, as you say he is, he obviously is not infertile. You've known him a long time. Did he at one time have a vasectomy?"

"No, not that I know of."

"So, the two of you used some kind of birth control on a regular basis up until the time Gigi was conceived?"

"I guess. I only have one child."

"You've never been pregnant before?"

"Not that I remember."

"How long were you and Bruce married?"

After a pause, Diane replied, "A long time."

"But, the two of you never had children?"

"I don't have any other children."

"So how is it you suddenly ended up pregnant with Gigi?"

Diane realized her story seemed to have holes in it, but she persisted.

"When I've wanted something for so long, and I finally get it, and it's so wonderful, I'm not about to consume myself with the kind of questions you're asking."

"Did you have any trouble losing your pregnancy weight after Gigi was born?"

Diane thought for a long time as she sipped her espresso, but finally answered Dr. Madden.

"Like I told you before, I didn't gain any weight during my pregnancy. Are you trying to trap me or something?" Diane asked very defensively. "Change the subject now, or I'm leaving."

Chapter 34

"Can I help you with anything, Diane?" Carmen asked.

"Tell you what. You get Gigi out of her clothes, and wash her up in the sink, while I get out of mine and hop into the shower for a few minutes."

"No problem. I'd love to do that."

Gigi happily went to Carmen's outstretched arms.

"Can I get you something to wear, Diane?"

"I have a couple of pajama outfits back here. They're in the top left drawer of her dresser."

"How about these?" Carmen asked, holding up a pajama set with pictures of horse heads on them.

"Perfect," Diane answered. "I used to rock Gigi every night, and occasionally I still do. I just got used to showering and dressing for bed back here so I wouldn't bother Mickey."

"That makes a lot of sense. By the way, thank you for having a dinner tonight for me. It was a very special introduction."

"You're either easily impressed or you're a good liar," Diane said with a grin.

"Nonsense. I had a wonderful time."

"I apologize for all of the competition around here," Diane said, unbuttoning her blouse. "It must be a man thing. Everyone thinks they have to compete for Gigi's love, and then Suki's love, and then my love. It just gets old after a while. There's plenty to go around."

"I felt sorry for Mr. Rollins," Carmen said, undressing Gigi on the bathroom counter. "I don't think he intended to come across the way that he did." Noticing that Diane was stepping out of the rest of her clothes, she asked, "Do you want me to give you some privacy while you take your shower? I can take Gigi into the bedroom."

"No. I've lost all sense of modesty since my accident. Besides, I'd like to have someone to talk to. It'll help settle me down."

Diane might have lost all modesty, but she wasn't exposed but for more than a few seconds before she stepped into the shower.

"As for my husband, he means well, but his actions and words often give one the impression he's in the game only for himself. Oh, and that thing tonight, when you said he looked younger in person than in the photos I sent to you? Go easy with the compliments. He doesn't know what to do with them. Pay him a compliment and he'll think he's engaged to you."

"Alright, I'll be careful," Carmen replied, chuckling. "Gigi has no problem standing by herself?" Carmen asked as Gigi stood on the counter laughing at her reflection in the mirror.

"She stands and walks very well so she's going to be into a lot of things. That's one reason I wanted you here sometime around her first birthday. There's so much to get into in this house."

"Is Suki too busy for her?"

"She has a lot going on as it pertains to my care. She can't have her hands full with two people."

"What does she do for you, if I may ask?"

"Oh, it's not a problem. There's still a lot of physical therapy I need as well as help with my memory issues." After pausing to think for a moment, Diane continued, "I thought I explained that to you during the interview."

"I must have forgotten. In any case, I would be glad to help in that capacity if you would ever need me to."

"Thanks, but then we're back to where we were when we started—a disproportionate burden falling on one person. Besides, Mickey won't let anyone else help with my situation other than Suki."

"There, little missy," Carmen said to Gigi, shaking her playfully in front of the mirror. "Now you are all dressed for bed."

The miniature version of Diane responded with a huge smile, showing a few top and bottom teeth as she laughed.

Boundaries

"Perfect timing, I'm done, too," Diane said, shutting off the water. She stepped out and grabbed a towel, wrapping it around her head, then grabbed a second towel and began drying off the rest of her body. Looking at Carmen in the mirror, she asked, "Could you do my back for me? I hate putting on my PJs when my back is wet."

Carmen took only a moment to run a towel up and down Diane's back a couple of times as she held Gigi in one arm. When she was done, she said, "You must work out. You have a marvelous body that any woman would be envious to have—and you have no bumps, no dimples, and no stretch marks that I can see either."

A distressed expression came across Diane's face as she absorbed what Carmen had just said to her.

"What did you just say?"

"You have no stretch marks. Certainly you've noticed that before? I mean, for recently having had a baby, one would never know you were ever pregnant."

It was so peculiar, but this was the first time anyone other than Suki, Mickey, or a doctor had seen her without clothes. Nobody else had ever made such an observation, and Carmen's was troublesome for Diane in more ways than one.

"Yes, the stretch marks. Suki has a remedy for those, I think. But, what else did you say?"

Carmen was puzzled by Diane's question, but she reflected for a moment then answered, "You have no bumps or dimples. Is that what you are referring to?"

Diane wrapped herself in a towel, then sat on a stool as a chill ran down her spine.

"Are you alright, Diane? You're covered in goose pimples."

"I think so. I've heard that expression before—bumps and dimples. There's something about it that's important in some way. Someone once was describing my body, and they said that I didn't have any bumps or dimples. It's like it was yesterday, but I can't think of who said it or why."

"I find that most interesting. I teach my nieces and nephew how to paint and do sketches of animals and people. I always tell them to take special note of texture so they can incorporate things like bumps and dimples of a person into their..."

"That's it!" Diane shouted, jumping to her feet.

"What, Diane?"

"I was painted...somebody did a painting of me...no, they painted my body," she continued, pacing frantically back and forth. "It was when I was on vacation—the one where I had my accident. Oh, my gosh. This is important."

Diane took the towel off of her head, tossed it into a hamper, and began rubbing her fingers through her hair.

"This is some type of breakthrough, Carmen. Mickey said I would have a breakthrough like this one day, and when that happened, a lot of my memory would suddenly return."

"That's incredible, Diane. Can you remember anything else about that event such as who the artist was?"

"No...no. I need to go check the Internet." After quickly climbing into her pajamas, Diane asked, "Can you watch Gigi? She needs a bottle, and then a story. She ought to go down without any problem. If you think she needs me, I'll be in the den."

"We're fine. Go look it up. I'll join you if I can."

Diane literally ran through the house to the den where she found the desktop computer she used for her presentations turned off. She clumsily fiddled with the several power switches necessary to get the computer and monitor to come on. It felt like an eternity, and she continued with her pacing as she waited for everything to come on line. Her Google homepage finally appeared, and she took a seat, typing and erasing several words while trying to narrow her search. She spoke softly to herself as she typed in a few chosen keywords.

"Let's see...Bangkok...no Phuket, body painting exhibition. When would it have been? Oh, yeah. Return...and voilà."

A long list appeared on the screen.

"Six hundred thirty-five results…great. Wait, what's this? Uma Goss. Bingo! I think that was her. Uma Goss wins yet another… Click. Yep, that's her. Look, she's holding a baby. Her name was Lulu. Wait a minute."

Diane saw a thumbnail image as she scrolled further down the page—an image that was profoundly familiar. She clicked on it. Suddenly, a nearly full screen version of the image appeared. It took her breath away. It was a photograph of her with the tsunami scene painted on her body. There was a link to 'more images' she next clicked on. What appeared was a portfolio of several dozen images of her body painting, from all angles, including full body shots and close-ups. As she studied the images, she began to experience the same intense emotions she felt at that time. Tears began to flow down her cheeks as she remembered the relief she felt when the sad images were washed away and she was left with a body covered with happiness. Suddenly, one memory flashed in her mind.

"Bruce…I was married. My husband's name was Bruce. He's dead. We lived in San Diego. That's why she did the painting."

Diane stood up, frantically trying to figure out who to speak to first and what she would say. She was overwhelmed with a sense of freedom and elation at her discovery. Yet, at the same time, she felt intense feelings of anger, fury, betrayal, and loss. Her head pounded with a pain unlike anything she ever experienced before as countless thoughts, visions, and feelings fell into place. Unknown to her, the nanostructures were fighting to maintain a prescribed level of control of her mind, set by Mickey, and the battle zone was her brain. She had to find him.

MICKEY TWISTED OPEN A bottle of beer, took a gulp, then flopped backward onto his bed.

"What a mess this night turned out to be."

"And whom do we have to thank for that?" Suki asked, pulling off his boots.

"Don't you start in on me, too," he said, rubbing the cold bottle across his forehead. "What's with Toot these days anyway?"

"Toot? What is wrong with you?"

"There's not a damn thing wrong with me."

"What was it that Sarah said, 'It's not just about you?'"

"That's a bunch of self-righteous crap."

"She said something else," Suki recalled. "She said, 'Don't make the same mistake you made in the past.' What did she mean by that?"

"Just Sarah pontificating."

"No, I believe she was trying to send you a heart-felt message. You just failed to listen."

"Fail? That's a mighty harsh word. Here's a news flash for you. I never fail."

Shaking her head in response to his remark, Suki continued, "Mickey, I need to tell you something, and I need you to listen to what I am saying."

"Why do I think I would rather have Gigi puke on me?"

Suki tossed Mickey's boots to the side, rather than setting them down nicely.

"That is not a nice thing to say, Mickey. I am your friend, and I want to help you."

"Whatever."

Lying down on her stomach next to him, she propped herself up on her elbows and began to tell him what he didn't care to hear in the first place.

"I think it is time to fill in some more of the blanks in Diane's memory."

"Nope," he replied succinctly.

"Mickey, she is ready. You know it would be better for her if you were to restore her memory methodically rather than if she were to have a spontaneous, complete restoration."

"Yeah, well the latter is unlikely to happen."

"Perhaps, but it could—especially now with the additional stimulation from Carmen's presence."

"I'd like a little stimulation from Carmen's presence, if you know what I mean. Damn near got some at dinner."

Biting her lip, Suki asked, "I cannot believe I am asking you this. What did she do to make you think she was attracted to you in some manner?"

"She played footsy with me practically half of dinner, and she put her hand on my leg twice."

"So, now you think she wants to sleep with you? Your imagination amazes me."

"Stranger things have happened."

"Mickey, we are talking about Diane. Seriously, I want you to restore some more of her memory…soon."

Sitting up in bed with his legs hanging off the side, Mickey defiantly turned away from Suki and said, "Things are going well. She fits in with the community. She's doing well with her seminars. She functions just fine around here. She's handling Gigi like any mother should. She seems happy to me. I don't see that there is any reason to hurry this along."

"What you are doing is wrong."

"That's strike two—I'm never wrong," he responded, never bothering to turn and face her.

"Bullshit, Mickey. You owe it to her to remove the boundaries that are preventing her from assimilating her past. That does not mean that she will withdraw from you if you do it right. In fact, I think she might be thankful. I can help you with her feelings toward you during this transition."

"Meaning you won't if I don't do as you say?" After pausing for that remark to sink in, Mickey continued with, "You're starting to sound like Toot. Everything is becoming a veiled threat."

"No, that is not the case. You are interpreting the constructive criticisms and guidance from your friends and those who love you to be threatening, when in fact they are not."

"And you know this because…"

"Because I am close to Diane. I am close with Sarah." She paused fatefully before adding, "And, I am particularly close to Toot."

Shaking his head, Mickey replied, "So, he's in your pants. It was inevitable, I suppose. Did this just happen, or have you been waiting to tell me?"

"That does not matter."

"Like Hell it doesn't matter!"

Spinning around in bed, he flipped Suki over onto her back, grabbed her by the hair with one hand, and squeezed her cheeks with the grip of his other as he forced her down onto the mattress.

"I love you. I love you more than you will ever know. I didn't want you to come live with us because I knew at some point I wouldn't be able to resist you. Then you fucking trapped me. It was like you knew this would happen. You set me up for a fall with your non-stop presence in my life. You sucked Diane into your life and bam, she goes down and there's nothing else I could do but drag your ass along with us."

That was all Suki could take. With a few sudden moves and twists with her body, she had Mickey pinned face down onto the mattress, his arm twisted painfully behind his back while she straddled him. Her blouse was torn open during the tussle.

"Mickey! You are the most self-centered piece of shit of a man I have ever known, but for some reason I love you too!" Tears poured down Suki's cheeks as she showed uncharacteristic emotion. "I have loved you since the first day I met you at my grandfather's house. Now let us be clear about one thing—it is *you* who sucked me into *your* life. Do you hear me! I have wanted to be with you so much, I was prepared to give all of my life to you just to be with you every day. I let you tap my mind. I let you use my body. I had your baby for you because Diane was unable to carry your child. I sit here day after day watching her try to be the mother that I should be, trying to be the wife that I want so much to be. What do I get for my effort, my pain, my struggles? I am ignored and blamed for all that you have done wrong—yes, you heard me. You!" Suki pounded the fist of her free arm into Mickey's back, screaming, "Are you listening to me?"

"I'm listening to you," came a voice in the doorway. It was Diane.

"Diane, I…" Suki tried to explain, jumping off the bed, but was cut off before she could finish.

"You what? You neglected to tell me that you had my baby for me? You simply overlooked the fact that you love my husband? It was an oversight that you're using me to get his love?"

Mickey stood up next to Suki, "Babe, listen to me…"

"Listen to you? You took my life from me. I was married," Diane began, crying as she spoke. "My husband's name was Bruce. We lived in San Diego. He died in a motorcycle crash, but it is you who killed his memory. You destroyed all of my memories, you son-of-a-bitch! You kept my past from me so I would stay by you because you knew I could never separate my feelings for Bruce from my feelings for you. Well that just got real simple. My love for Bruce is perpetual. My love for you is now just a memory." Diane picked up a porcelain Lladro figurine and threw it at him, smashing it against the far wall.

Mickey didn't waste any time. He ran to his desk where he grabbed his iPad. By now, Diane knew what this meant.

"No! Don't do it! No!!" She screamed.

It was too late. Mickey stroked the face of the device several times, after which Diane became quiet, then crumpled to the floor.

Suki ran to Diane's.

"No! Mickey, stop it! Leave her alone…please!" She cried as she cradled Diane's motionless body in her arms.

"Oh, my God," Carmen said as she watched horrified from the doorway. "Do you need a doctor?"

Surprised by Carmen's sudden presence, Mickey spun around and replied, "I am the doctor. She's having one of her seizures. She'll recover just fine after a while."

He walked over to his desk where there was a small black kit. Unzipping it, he pulled out a small vial, then drew up some of the medication in a syringe. He returned to where Diane and Suki lay, and as he injected it into Diane's arm, Suki looked away.

"Suki, let go. We need to get her into bed."

She heard Mickey, but she wouldn't release her hold on her friend.

"Suki, let go…now," Mickey insisted, the tension showing in his face.

Reluctantly, she let her arms fall to her side, releasing Diane, after which Mickey picked her up and put her in bed where she remained motionless, unresponsive, and totally unaware of anything that was going on. If it weren't for her breathing, it would be easy to believe she was dead.

"Are you sure there is nothing I can do to help?" Carmen asked, checking for those obvious signs of breathing.

"Why are you here, Carmen?" Mickey asked, slowly turning to face her as he snapped a safety cap over the end of the needle—the click sounding louder to Carmen than it really was.

"I'm sorry. I heard shouting, and I thought someone was hurt or in trouble. Diane…"

"How could somebody be hurt or in trouble in this house? This is just a normal, everyday home, Carmen. Do you understand?"

"Yes sir, Mr. Rollins," she replied hesitantly. "I only wanted to help."

"Call me Mickey," he said, walking over to Carmen and putting his hands on her shoulders."

Carmen kept a wary eye on the hand with the syringe.

"I appreciate your concern. Let me start by saying, you're not in any trouble. However, I don't ever want you back here without asking me first. Is that clear?"

"Yes."

"Diane undergoes frequent treatments here in the bedroom and in the office over there," he continued, nodding in the direction a room off to the side. "It's imperative that these treatments be conducted without interruption. Suki assists me, but nobody else is allowed back here when we are working."

"I understand. I'll respect your privacy."

"Good." Trying to end on a lighter note, he added, "I'm glad you're here, Carmen. I know Diane is, too."

"Thank you," she replied. Looking over at Suki, Carmen asked out of concern, "Is she alright?"

Mickey looked briefly at Suki who was still sobbing, before saying, "She's fine. I'm certain she's tired and stressed out. These are intense episodes, and Diane is Suki's closest friend, isn't she, Suki?"

He walked over to help her off the floor.

Finally, after regaining a little of her usual composure, she stood up, dried the tears from her cheeks, and replied, "That is correct. And, I am Diane's closest friend."

Carmen could tell by Suki's expression that there was a lot more going on than anyone was willing to divulge. She had to let them know one more detail before leaving.

"There is something important I think I should tell you."

Mickey and Suki anxiously waited for her to reveal what was on her mind, though probably for different reasons.

"After her shower, she had a revelation about her past. She said her body was painted at an exhibition on the island where she was injured. It seemed to have significant meaning to her. She left me rather quickly to follow up on what she remembered by researching the Internet. Did she tell you anything more?"

After a brief pause, Mickey replied, "This is part of a recurring fantasy. She often gets lost in various make-believe scenarios that are so real to her, she's certain they are true representations of her past. It's essential to her recovery that we not bring these events to her attention. If the memories are real, she will stitch them together in her own way. If they are not, in the morning she will have forgotten the episode. Don't mention it again. Understood?"

"I understand. Well, I'd best be going. Gigi's asleep, and I am very tired as well. I'll keep an ear out for her so the two of you can tend to Diane."

"Thank you, Carmen," Mickey said. "Sleep well. There will be a lot to do tomorrow."

Carmen left the room and Mickey closed the door behind her.

"What are you going to do, Mickey?" Suki asked, putting her hands up to her cheeks. "It has begun. She had a partial, if not complete, restoration. Who knows what the outcome will be?"

"Unfortunately, I think you're correct," he replied, walking over to the bed where Diane lay. "Has anything significant in her life taken place in the last…oh…ninety-six hours."

"Every day is significant for her, Mickey. They are significant to each of us. Why do you ask?"

"Will she miss any of it?"

Suki suddenly realized Mickey was planning something diabolical.

"No. You cannot do it."

"I'm afraid we have no choice at this point. Go make yourself comfortable on the table, and begin your relaxation exercises. I'll bring Diane to you in just a moment."

Suki was already exhausted. With each session, Diane's treatments were taking a greater and greater toll on Suki's body and mind as Mickey made 'fine adjustments' to Diane. This one in particular would prove to be extremely intense in that for the first time, it required Mickey to use Suki's mind to remove the memories Diane had spontaneously regained. For the heretofore untested extraction process to work, the nanocells in both women had to be reset in such a fashion that they temporarily reversed roles. The nanocells residing in Suki's body were initialized to be the *planters* and those in Diane's were the *hunters*. Mickey would then have to hypnotize Suki, instruct her nanocells to impart instructions in Diane's, isolate the new memories created in the last 96 hours, and transfer them to Suki. Ideally, Mickey wanted the memories destroyed, but just like other types of energy, they could not be terminated—only moved to another person or converted into some other form. Suki would now hold the memories and feelings Diane had spontaneously regained, and Mickey privately hoped both Suki and Diane would be strong enough to cope with the experience.

IT WAS AFTER TWO o'clock in the morning when Suki left Mickey and Diane in the master wing of the main house. As Suki passed by the main living room, she was startled to see the silhouette of a figure sitting on the sofa. She thought she recognized who it was.

"Toot?"

"Hey, it's me. Come on over."

She walked over, sat down next to him, put her head on his shoulder and began to cry almost inconsolably. Toot had never seen her get the least bit emotional before let alone break down in this manner.

"Suki, what's wrong, darlin'?"

Thinking quickly to fabricate a believable reason for her behavior that didn't divulge the true cause, she replied, "Diane had another seizure tonight. It was really bad."

Her crying became so intense, Toot wondered if Suki was in need of a doctor herself.

"Suki, pull it together. She has these things all the time. Was this one worse in some way?"

"Mickey says she might lose some of her short-term memory—something he called retrograde amnesia. He said it could be permanent."

"Does she need to go to a hospital?"

"No. Mickey took care of her," she continued. "She may be asleep until tomorrow afternoon. He says she needs rest."

After finishing, she cried to the point where she was unable speak.

Toot held Suki tightly for several minutes and just let her bawl. The few times in his past women had cried like this, being patient and caring in this manner was the best medicine.

Eventually, Suki stopped crying to the point where she said, "Toot, don't ever leave me."

"I ain't goin' nowhere. I'm right here."

"No, you do not understand. I feel emptiness in my heart. I feel a complete loss of love. It feels as though all hope is gone."

"Suki, what are you talkin' about? You talkin' about your family back in Asia? Are you homesick or somethin'?"

"I cannot explain it, but it is total loss. I think I feel the loss Diane feels."

"What loss are you talkin' about?"

As if it were an epiphany, Suki realized what was taking place. Every intense emotion associated with every moment Diane had had with Bruce and their lives together, had been forced into her body over a period of hours. The love and passion, the pain and anguish, and every feeling in between were of a greater magnitude than anything Suki had experienced in her life. She struggled to regain her composure, but she knew she wouldn't be able to do it by herself.

"I cannot explain it, Toot. Maybe I will understand tomorrow. All I know is I do not want to be alone tonight. Let me stay with you tonight, please."

"Hey, no problem. I'll get my stuff and be right back."

"No, I want to spend the night at your place. Carmen is here now. She will look after Gigi. I need to get out of this house tonight."

"You sure?"

Suki kissed him passionately. That was answer enough for Toot.

"Did Paul make it home safely?" Suki asked.

"That's a whole 'nother story. We went up to Eight for a while. Paul had too much whiskey to drink like he does some times. Then he made the mistake of callin' Sarah, and they got into an argument about somethin'. Long story short, he's spendin' the night up at the lodge. They'll sort it out tomorrow." The two stood up and hugged for a few moments, then Toot asked, "You need to get something to sleep in?"

"That would be a waste of time," she replied.

The two left the house by way of the mudroom adjacent to the kitchen. The door's alarm chimed its alert tone as the door opened and closed—the electronic door lock securing the door behind them. As they made their way down the walkway to Number 2, a figure appeared at the door from which they had just exited. It was Carmen.

Chapter 35

Despair: How Not to Run a Business…

Whump! Diane's eyes opened quickly in the near darkness.

Whump! It happened again. She felt herself falling for a moment before landing softly on what felt like a bed. Something didn't feel right. Partly out of fear, partly due to confusion, Diane stood up to discover she was standing in what appeared to be a small room. Turning around in an effort to gain her bearings, she knocked over a tray and a glass, breaking it on the floor. It wasn't long before she stepped on the shards, cutting one of her bare feet. With the pain, came panic.

"Somebody help me!" She shouted.

A door flew open exposing a familiar face—that of Suki's.

"Diane, what is wrong?"

Diane's face was void of expression.

"Diane, do you know who I am?"

There was a long pause while Diane blinked her eyes and scanned her surroundings.

After a few moments, she said with a great deal of uncertainty, "Suki?"

"Good, we have our first correct answer," Suki replied with a reassuring smile. "I told you not to take those pills with wine. When will you listen to me?"

Suki turned to a flight stewardess who had come to assist, spoke to her in Thai, and in short order, she was on her way. Diane began to shake uncontrollably causing Suki to pull a blanket off the bed and wrap it around her.

Soon, a voice boomed from no place in particular, "Ladies and Gentlemen, this is Captain Somak. I regret the turbulence we just experienced. We appear to have flown through the wash of another large aircraft that is flying some distance in front of us, also bound for Manila. We have deviated from the path we were on just slightly, and we should not experience any more bumps. Again, I apologize. Thank you for flying with us on Singapore Airlines." The voice then began to speak in another language, presumably repeating the same message.

"Suki, what's going on?"

After pulling closed the door to Diane's suite again, Suki replied, "Well to begin with, you are in a First Class Suite, and it is inappropriate to speak in such a loud tone of voice. People are trying to sleep."

Suki pushed a button on an armrest, illuminating the space with a faint glow. Diane found herself standing in what could only be described as lavish airline accommodations. Its elegance was tainted by a laptop computer that had fallen to the floor along with bits of food, spilled wine, and broken glass.

"Now do you know where you are?" Suki asked her confused-looking colleague.

"It looks like a plane, but I'm supposed to be in Texas," Diane replied, continuing to look blankly at Suki.

The stewardess returned carrying in one hand a tray holding an insulated pot and a cup and saucer, and in the other a plastic box with a red cross on it. All at once, something caught Diane's attention. It was the stewardess' nametag. It read "Soupy."

"I know you. I met you in Phuket. You stayed with my husband while Suki and I went shopping."

Now it was time for Suki and Soupy to look confused. Suki took the first-aid box from the attendant, allowing her a free hand to pour Diane a cup of very dark coffee. To this, Suki added a powder from a small vial, and after stirring the concoction, she handed it to Diane.

"Now sit back and drink this while I tend to your foot. Be sure to sip it slowly. It will taste sweet because of the herb I added to it."

After taking her seat, Diane asked, "Suki, why are we on an airplane?"

At first, Suki ignored Diane, preferring instead to examine her foot.

"This is a deep cut. You will need some stitches when we get to Manila."

With great care, she cleansed and bandaged the injury.

Boundaries

"Suki, why are we on an airplane bound for Manila?" Diane asked more emphatically.

Shaking her head, Suki looked squarely at Diane and answered, "We are going to Manila to negotiate the biggest deal of our careers. Pull yourself together, Diane. You had better not screw this up for us. We have both worked long and hard for this."

Rubbing her now throbbing foot, Diane said, "What are you talking about, Suki? We're supposed to be in Texas. Who in Manila wants cattle anyway?"

"You were dreaming about Mickey again," Suki replied, pulling her hair away from her face. "I should have guessed you would never get over him."

"Get over him? What do you mean?"

Suki studied her expression long enough to be convinced that Diane, for whatever reason, seemed not to know what she meant.

"Laura? His wife? Does the name ring a bell with you?"

"But, he's married."

"I know…to Laura."

"No, he's married to me!"

After checking to make sure the door to the suite was pulled firmly closed, Suki pointed her finger at Diane, the veins in her neck and forehead bulging, and said, "Listen to me. There is no Mickey in your life, nor is there Texas. You believed him when he said he was in love with you, you let him take you to bed a couple of times, and he fed you all of his stories about some mythical ranch he wants to retire on some day. It is all a bunch of lies. He is our largest private investor and nothing more. Now wake up!"

"No! It's not true!"

Spotting Diane's wallet on the floor, Suki opened it and pulled out a business card, flashing it in Diane's face.

"Does PicoPoint mean anything to you?"

After studying the card for a few moments, Diane asked, "PicoPoint? I've heard of that before. How do I know about PicoPoint?"

"We own PicoPoint! You are the President, CEO and part-owner. I am the co-owner, Executive Vice President and Chief Financial Officer."

It remained clear to Suki that she was still not getting through to Diane. Being careful not to step on any of the broken glass, Suki stood up, grabbed Diane by the wrists until they hurt and got right in her face as she proceeded to lecture her companion.

"Diane, I am tired of doing this with you. First, there were the problems with liquor, then it was pills, then it was your dalliances with Mickey and others, then it was all of the above. You are going to blow this deal for us and cost *me* a lot of money. I refuse to let that happen so pull it together…now! The only reason you are here to begin with is because you are the face of the company. You were the founder. But, if I had not carried you the last two years, we would have lost everything." Abruptly releasing Diane's wrists, she concluded, "When this trip is done, there will be big changes between us."

Running her fingers through her hair, Diane said, "Suki, this isn't right. I'm married to Mickey. We live on a ranch in Texas. I have a daughter. You live with us. I just know."

Suki angrily picked up the broken glass and trash from the floor in Diane's suite, finally picking up the laptop computer that she opened, setting it on a tray in front of Diane. Reaching into Diane's briefcase, she pulled out a spiral-bound document and set it on top of the laptop.

"Do you see these?" She asked as she opened the booklet. "This is your company—start reading. We have six hours until we land. You have four hours to be able to convincingly tell me you know what PicoPoint is all about. If you cannot do this, I will phone Sylvie as soon as we land and have her call the meeting off. I will make up some excuse for you, but I will not put you in front of our guests, or the rest of the staff for that matter, when you are in this condition."

There was no response, and Suki noticed that, again, Diane had a blank look about her.

"You do know who Sylvie is, right?"

After hesitating, Diane replied, "The name sounds familiar. I just can't…"

"Sylvie de Beers. She is our Chief Corporate Council you moron, and she does not like you. I cannot believe this. I have told you a hundred times she will stab you in the back if that is what it takes to move up the ladder. Have you forgotten that she, too, is rumored to have had a relationship with Mickey? She will protect his investment with your life if it comes to that. Of all the times to lose your mind."

"I haven't lost my mind!"

"Yeah, right. Tell you what, Sylvie set this whole thing up, and if you cannot perform as you need to, I am certain she will ask the Executive Council for your removal."

"I can't believe you're talking to me like this. It's as if you don't care. I'm your friend, Suki."

"You still are, Diane. Sometimes friends have to dispense tough medicine. For now, you need to focus on reality, and put your fantasies about Mickey far away."

"I know you think I'm wrong, but this right here, right now, seems like the fantasy. Maybe I'll read something that changes my mind. The first thing I need to do is find a toilet."

As Diane began to exit her suite, Suki put a gentle hand on Diane's face.

"I am with you, Diane. All I want it the best for you. But, I will not let you take us down. I will come back in a couple of hours to see how you are doing. Meanwhile, I am going to try to get some more sleep. I'll be right across the aisle."

Suki entered her suite and pulled the door. As Diane looked up and down the aisle, she saw nothing that looked the least bit familiar—that is except for one person, Soupy, who was standing at the end of the aisle in the First Class galley. As she approached her, Diane continued to have visions of Soupy wearing a lavender wrap-around dress and stilettos.

"May I get you something, Ms. Alders?"

"You don't know me?"

"Of course, I know you. You are one of our best customers. You travel this route and others in Asia frequently. We see each other about every other month. The clientele in First Class is a relatively small group. I try to remember as much as I can about my regulars."

Not sharing any of the same memories Soupy had of her travels, Diane asked about one in particular.

"Have we met in Phuket?"

"I have been to Phuket, yes. I go there once or twice per year. I do not think I have seen you there."

"Well, I was there," Diane insisted. "And you were there at the same time. I don't know why everyone is messing with my head, but I don't appreciate it. When I find out who's behind it all, I'll be back to see you."

"Long flights can have strange effects on some people. You haven't had much water to drink during the flight. You might be dehydrated. That could cause you to have delusions…"

"Delusions! Is that what you think is happening?" Diane turned and walked away. After taking just a few steps, she turned back to Soupy and said, "Just leave me alone. Do us both a favor, and leave me the hell alone!"

After closing the lavoratory door, Diane put her hands on either side of the sink and looked into the mirror. What she observed in her reflection was a tired woman. Her eyes looked tired and red. Her skin was pale with no evidence of being exposed to a lot of sun. Her hair was in disarray. She looked at the reflection, then away, then back at it again. She repeated this several times to see if it was really her reflection she was seeing in the mirror. Then she began to laugh quietly after having the strangest thought—was the reflection looking at her, or was she looking at the reflection? If nature's urge hadn't overtaken her giddiness, she might have become completely lost in the moment.

After sitting on the commode and relieving herself, she wiped, only to find the string of a tampon.

"I can't freaking believe this," she mumbled to herself. "This is about as much reality as a person can take. Why does this have to happen to me?"

She bent over, laughing quietly, but uncontrollably for a few moments.

"This can't be a dream. Dreams don't have tampons. Oh, shit. If this is real, I just made a huge ass of myself out there. Why am I sitting in a lav talking to myself?"

After taking care of matters, Diane stood up, straightened her clothing, then washed her face, brushed her teeth, and fixed her hair as best she could without a brush. She took a deep breath, then opened the door and turned to head back toward her suite. There was no way for her to avoid crossing paths with Soupy, so she decided to make amends. It was apparent from Soupy's expression and posture that she was expecting to be admonished again.

"I apologize for the way I spoke earlier. I was way out of line. I know you were just doing your best to take care of me. What I said was thoughtless. Will you forgive me?"

A huge smile came across Soupy's face.

"Certainly, Ms. Alders. You must be under a lot of stress in your position. Plus, long periods of travel wear on many people—even seasoned travelers. You are not the first person to become short with me. Is there anything I can do for you?"

"Perhaps you could bring me a double espresso?"

"Absolutely. I will have it out to you shortly."

The two shook hands, turned, and went in separate directions. As Diane limped back to her seat, another passenger stopped her.

"Excuse me, madam," said a stodgy-looking older character with a British accent. "My name is Dr. Ork. I gather from all of the commotion that you injured your foot in some manner. May I be of assistance to you?"

"That was quite a jolt a little while ago, wasn't it?"

"My, oh my, yes indeed. Two of them at that."

"Well, I did cut my foot, but my companion bandaged me up pretty well. She says I'll need stitches. Do you know of a hospital in Manila?"

"Oh, yes, but I'd steer clear of them if I were you. If I may ask, where will you be staying in Manila?"

"At the Peninsula."

Diane wondered why she answered the question so directly, since she had no idea where she was staying. The response was simply automatic.

"What a coincidence, so am I. An associate of mine will meet me at the airport to take me there. He is a physician as well, and he has access to suturing supplies, antibiotics, and other things I might need. Perhaps I can meet with you at the hotel and take a look at your foot. If I can take care of it there, it would save you a lot of unnecessary difficulty. What do you think?"

Diane studied the man. If it weren't for the fact that he had gray hair and a beard, a paunch, and the face of an old Biblical character, she might have considered his proposal the greatest pick-up line she had ever heard.

"Dr. Ork, you have a deal. Just let me make sure that's where I'm staying. If it is anywhere else, I'll let you know before we get off the plane. How is that?"

"Splendid. Now then, I suggest you take care of your foot until I see you later."

"That's my plan, right after I clean up all the broken glass that caused the problem to begin with. You have a pleasant rest of your flight."

"And you, too, madam."

Diane returned to her suite to find the entire mess cleaned up. It looked as if nothing had ever happened. Her flat bed was made back into a seat, her laptop and book were clean and set in a neat manner on the workspace, the bed linen was put away, a fresh pillow and blanket were beside the chair, and the floor was spotless. Now she felt really bad about how she had carried on earlier with Soupy. After taking her seat and buckling up, she retrieved her briefcase and opened it, quickly spotting her passport. She began fanning through the pages from back to front. As she did so, she was astonished at what was revealed.

Under her breath, Diane said, "Holy crap. Munich, Amsterdam, Hamburg, Berlin, Amsterdam again, London, Toronto, Vancouver, Taipei, Hong Kong, Tokyo, Bangkok, Manila, Singapore, Kuala Lumpur…it goes on and on. Shit, this is only going back six months. I must live on a plane."

"Here is your espresso, Ms. Alders," Soupy said, placing the steaming drink carefully on the table in the suite. Noticing that Diane was studying her passport, Soupy added, "As I said, you travel a great deal."

"No kidding," Diane replied before taking a sip of her coffee. "Can you see if Suki is awake for me?"

Soupy looked across the aisle to find the privacy light illuminated and curtains pulled. Turning back to Diane, she replied, "She does not wish to be disturbed. I cannot, by policy, disturb a passenger who wishes to be left alone to rest."

"Oh, forget it. I'll catch her later. Thanks for the espresso."

"Certainly, let me know if there is anything else I can do for you to make your trip a pleasant one."

Diane proceeded to turn on her laptop. After a while, a picture appeared across the entire screen—a picture of a two-masted schooner with a blue hull and a wooden deck, skipping along the water at full sail. The silhouette of a single man stood behind the helm.

Touching the figure of the man on the screen, she mumbled, "I know this person. I know this boat."

Suddenly a query window popped up requesting a password.

"What the hell?"

Diane looked around at nothing in particular as she tried to think of what to type. All at once, something popped into her mind. She typed, "BellaVista.' The query window closed and icons began to appear all across the screen where once there had been a picture of a schooner.

"How did I come up with that word?"

Now, Diane was even more distressed. It was a relief that she had more evidence that what was taking place was real. But, at the same time, she felt immense despair that what she thought was real—her marriage to Mickey, her daughter, and her life on a ranch in Texas—were, it appeared, nothing but a fantasy.

In the middle of the screen was an icon for a presentation that was titled, *PicoPoint*. She opened the file.

"Hum. Sixty-eight pages. Guess I'd better start from the beginning." Speaking softly to herself as she studied each page, she continued, "Let's see...company profile...started ten years ago. Founder...Diane Alders. Major venture capital investor...The Rollins Group. You're shitting me! Suki left Rollins and joined PicoPoint as co-partner, EVP and CFO...obviously Mickey wanted someone close to him to be close to me. Chief Technology Officer Gert Braune? Un-freakin'-believable...I know that name. Sylvie de Beers, Chief Corporate Council...also from Rollins...never heard of her. The company has sustained fifty-five percent sales growth year-over-year...pretty damn good. Sales last year were...Jesus! We have an international presence with factories in Quebec, Hamburg, Taipei, Bangkok, and Johannesburg. Expanding into Manila and Suzhou. Privately held. Proprietary technology. Yeah, but what do we make? Oh, my gosh, look at this. We make nanostructures for neurological therapy. Primary application...motor function, thought, and memory reconstruction."

Diane couldn't stop reading. The more she read, the more she discovered. The more she discovered, the more she was able to personally relate to the therapy the material discussed. As she combed through the presentation and the book, she realized she was not only a subject matter expert. Her level of understanding felt frighteningly intimate, yet she couldn't explain why she felt that way.

After two hours of reading, Diane was convinced she was the head of PicoPoint. She understood the organization and she understood the business. The question she was still unable to answer was, what was the meeting in Manila all about? Hoping to find more answers in her briefcase, she began going through its contents. First, there was a white envelope containing a banded wad of one hundred dollar bills. That was a lot of cash to carry overseas; probably barely legal. Why would she need all that money? Then she found a folder neatly labeled 'Manila Trip.' Bingo. That's exactly what she was looking for. It contained a letter of intent from the Board of Management of a group called MT Holdings Philippines to buy PicoPoint for $2 billion U.S. dollars, and there was a reference to a meeting that was to take place tomorrow. Suki had written and attached a note saying, "D—we cannot blink on this one. M says to hold out for $3.6 billion, nothing less. He will join us in Manila. –S."

Suki was right. Diane clearly remembered now that this was the deal of a lifetime. MT was Manila Technology, a holding company owned by four of Southeast Asia's wealthiest technology gurus—Wei from Hong Kong, Fong from Taiwan, Pachit from Thailand, and Cayuhon from Laguna. She was also well aware of the controversy that swirled around Wei and Cayuhon, suggesting they had dishonest dealings, though nothing was proven…yet.

Another sheet in the folder was an itinerary with some notes from a secretary named Carmen. The trip was one-way, with an open-ended return. The group was staying at the Peninsula in Manila. A limousine would pick up Diane and Suki at the airport and take them to the hotel. On yet another sheet of paper was the itinerary for "Mr. Braune." He would be flying in separately.

Diane had been so preoccupied with her reading, she hadn't noticed Suki was now awake, sitting in the suite across from her, drinking hot tea.

"I remember everything, now," Diane said. "Are you going to test me?"

Suki turned toward her and smiled, but didn't say anything. Diane was puzzled. After all, earlier it had been Suki who insisted she study the material.

Still trying to get a reaction of some kind from Suki, Diane asked, "There's just one thing that I can't figure out. If Sylvie is such an important figure in our organization, why can't I picture her? I mean, all the other names I recognize."

Again, Suki didn't say anything. Instead she glanced downward at Diane's open briefcase. When Diane looked, she saw a lavender envelope.

"That's funny. I don't remember seeing that before."

Diane sensed a non-verbal encouragement from Suki making her curious about the item. She reached for the envelope, opened it and pulled out a handwritten letter on lavender, personal letterhead of Sylvie de Beers. Slowly, she began reading its contents.

Dear Diane,

It is essential that you read every word of this letter from beginning to end without stop. Your life and health depend on it. Do not look toward Suki, as doing so will cause the letter you are holding to disappear.

My name is Sylvie de Beers. I am nothing more than a phantom image that exists temporarily in your mind. I am the creation of your friend, Suki. It is her thought that has brought me to life in your imagination. There are things that Suki wants to say to you, that she is forbidden to convey because of the control placed on your mind and hers by Mickey Rollins. I exist only as a medium through which she can communicate freely to you. In doing so, she can give you her message, embedded within this letter. This is the only way to reach you that is beyond Mickey's powers.

The flight you are on is part of a complicated series of dreams. PicoPoint is Mickey's invention. The material you read earlier describes in fairly granular detail how the process of the therapy works. You are the first complete human test subject, which is why you feel so possessed now by the technology. The therapeutic results have exceeded all expectations, but now Mickey is using the same technique to control you in ways Suki finds abhorrent. She wants to rescue you from his grip.

You sustained a brain injury. Mickey has used Suki as your surrogate to reconstruct the parts of your mind, thoughts, and abilities that were damaged in the accident. He hypnotizes her then directs her to send specific cerebral content to you. It is through me that she can now try to free you from this control. The outcome of her effort will be impossible to predict. There are things you can do that will help break you out of your mental bondage. The nanostructures thrive on caffeine. They suffer when exposed to the byproducts of citric acid. You must decrease the amount of coffee you consume, and begin drinking citrus drinks and eating citrus fruits, but you must do so only when Mickey is not around. He must not suspect anything. You should be able to slowly starve the nanostructures of their energy source, and at the same time build up enough metabolic change in your body to cause the nanostructures to slowly lose their capabilities and disassociate from you. Suki does not know the ultimate effect should this occur, as this is all highly theoretical. Nonetheless, you have to trust that she only has your best interest at heart.

Because I am a dream within a dream, bringing me to life is a tremendous drain on Suki, both physically and emotionally. I will appear to you in future dreams. You must trust me implicitly. Be aware, however, that Suki may not be able to create me in your mind very many times, so you must find a way to remember what is said to you each time I speak to you.

If this was not enough, I must give you a warning. Beware of Carmen's twin sister. She will bring great harm to all of us. You will know when she arrives. She was close with Genevieve. I can tell you no more.

Now, before you fold this letter and replace it in the envelope, reach into the back pouch of your briefcase. You will find a photograph of two couples sitting on motorcycles. You carried the photograph with you in your handbag when we were in Phuket together. You told me that the people on the other motorcycle in the picture were among your closest of friends. The man sitting in front of you is your late husband, Bruce. He was a wonderful husband who loved you dearly, as much as you loved him. Mickey has prevented the restoration of any memory of Bruce or your past in San Diego where the two of you lived happily.

Diane, you were an incredibly successful business executive at a company called Medico Techniq. You worked for a man named Rajeev. He has this picture and Suki will find a way for him to get it to you, but it will have to be done surreptitiously. Find this picture. It has the names and address of your friends on the back. They can help you. They will save you from Mickey.

Now replace the letter in the envelope and put it and the photograph back in the briefcase. They will disappear, as will I, for I am nothing more than a subliminal phantasm.

We love you,
Sylvie de Beers

Diane did as she was told. Shivering in horror at what she had read, she looked over at Suki to find tears streaming down her cheeks as she looked back at her. Suki's face showed a pain unlike anything Diane had ever seen in her before. When she looked back at the briefcase, the envelope and photo were gone.

AWAKENING TO THE SUBTLE fragrance of lilac, Diane once again found herself in familiar surroundings. She was in the comfort of her own bed. Egyptian cotton, satin weave sheets caressed her naked body. Scanning about the room, everything illuminated by the soft, filtered sunlight was as she remembered, and she found herself thinking, as she did so often, "What an unbelievable dream." As she lay there for several minutes, relishing the blissful feeling of safe-harbor, she struggled unsuccessfully to remember anything specific about her dream.

Alone in bed, she sat up and saw a pair of her panties, shorts, and a tank top set out neatly on the bedspread as Suki so often did for her. After quickly dressing, she walked to her dresser, habitually put on her watch and a necklace, then stood in front of a mirror for a moment. She vaguely remembered looking into a mirror in her dream. Fortunately, the reflection today was that of a remarkably beautiful and healthy-looking woman.

The search for others in the household ended when she found Carmen, much to her surprise, in the kitchen feeding Gigi breakfast.

"Say hello to Mommy," Carmen said in a squeaky voice to Gigi.

The little girl responded by holding out her arms and smiling. Diane bent over and kissed her daughter on the forehead.

"When did you get here?"

"I beg your pardon, Diane?"

"Did you get in overnight? I wasn't expecting you until Friday."

"I did arrive on Friday…yesterday. Today is Saturday. You had a reception for me last night."

Trying to avoid looking completely out of her mind, Diane replied, "Oh, of course. I guess I had a bit too much to drink."

She suspected she had another seizure, but tried to avoid bringing that up with Carmen.

"Are the two of you getting along without difficulty?"

"Absolutely. We are going to have fun today, aren't we, Gigi?" Carmen said to the child, now comfortable that she had managed to be convincingly oblivious to the prior evening.

The youngster, dressed in kitty pajamas, answered by saying something that sounded remotely like the word *fun*, and beamed a smile as she kicked her legs with excitement.

"You're going to be busy today," Diane said to Carmen, putting a reassuring hand on her shoulder as a she spoke. "Have you seen my husband?"

"No. According to Lupita, he left early this morning."

"Left for where?" Diane asked, now feeling slightly panicked.

"I have no idea," Carmen replied, shrugging her shoulders.

"Hmm. Maybe Suki knows. Have you seen her?"

"She is outside on the patio."

"I'll be out with her if you need me."

After grabbing an apple from a basket, Diane walked out onto the patio, and found Suki, wearing only bikini bottoms, lying face down on a comfortably-padded, sand-colored chaise lounge. Her bikini top was lying on the ground next to her.

Speaking softly, Diane approached Suki, and asked, "Suki, are you awake?"

"No," came a muffled response.

Diane took a seat on the lounge next to Suki as she said, "It's going to be hot today."

Suki groaned.

"Why are you so tired?" she asked, taking a bite from her apple.

"Rough night," Suki replied, exhaling loudly as she did.

"When did Carmen arrive?" Diane asked, wondering if Suki's response would agree with Carmen's statement.

"She arrived yesterday. There was a reception last night with the Duke's. Do you remember?"

"I had another seizure last night, didn't I?"

It was difficult to do, but Suki played along with Mickey's ongoing ruse. "Yes. It was a bad one according to Mickey. He had you pretty well medicated afterwards, saying you might have some amnesia. I am surprised you are awake so early."

After adjusting the lounge chair to a comfortable angle, Diane said, "I'm glad I woke up. I'm so tired of these insane dreams I have. I wake up feeling literally exhausted like I've been through a mental marathon or something. Last night's must have been a doozie."

"Do you know what day it is?" Suki asked.

Diane thought a moment, then replied, "I could swear yesterday was Tuesday and that this should be Wednesday. I have a feeling I'm off by a few days."

"Three, to be exact," Suki replied.

"Have you seen Mickey? I need to talk to him."

Diane's question brought Suki to her elbows.

"I assumed you knew something. He left a note on my desk saying he was going to Caddo for a few days. You did not know?"

"Caddo? Why would he go to Caddo? Why wouldn't he take me?"

Lupita walked up to the two carrying a tray with two cups and an urn.

"Here you are ladies, your morning espresso."

Diane started to take a cup, then sat back in her chair.

"Lupita, I'm sick of coffee. Could you bring me some orange juice instead?"

"Of course, Miss Diane, but you know what Mickey says about..."

"Lupita, I'm feeling a bit on the pissy side today. Would you just get me some juice...please?"

"Certainly. What about you Miss Suki? Coffee or juice."

"I think I would like a Virgin Mary this morning."

"My, what got into the two of you last night? One orange juice and one Virgin Mary coming up."

Suki reached across and touched Diane's hand.

"Oh, the two of you should put on some appropriate clothing," Lupita continued. Austin Duke is coming over after a while to pick up his father. He said that neither of his parents was at home this morning, and when he called his father, he told him he was at the lodge. Did Mrs. Duke spend the night as well?"

"No," Suki replied. "She left right after Mickey ruined everyone's evening."

"What did he do?" Diane asked.

"Oh, let me tell you later. He was just being Mickey. Anyway, Toot took Paul up to Eight for a while. I understand he drank too much, then had an argument over the phone with Sarah. It appears she is still not over it if she is sending Austin to retrieve him." Suki answered.

"Maybe she left already," Lupita said, heading back to the kitchen.

"Left for where?" Diane asked.

"Oh, Austin said she was heading out to see family this afternoon up at Noonday. Maybe she left early."

"What is Noonday?" Suki asked.

"That's a little town up in the Northeast part of the state," Lupita replied. "Known for sweet onions. In fact, you drive right by it on your way to Caddo."

Chapter 36

"Sarah?"

Looking in the direction of the voice that called her, Sarah spotted an elderly, yet familiar-looking waitress with an unmistakable voice.

"Sarah Bohnert Duke?" The woman asked again.

"Aunt Jo? Is that you?"

Sarah got up from her booth and quickly walked over to meet the woman in the middle of the diner. As the few other patrons watched, the two embraced for a long time. Both had tears in their eyes.

"I didn't know you worked here."

"'Course you don't. You never call. You never write. It's like you fell off the face of the earth after you ran off with that rich rancher. What was his first name?"

"Paul."

"That's right. Now I remember. Tall as a cypress, if I recall. How long you two been married—twenty years?"

"Longer than that."

"I can't believe it's you standin' here. Let me look at you…turn around."

"Aunt Jo, really…"

"No, do it," she persisted, twirling her hand in the direction she wanted Sarah to spin. "Spittin' image of your mother. Now, go sit down. I'll get your order in about ten seconds. I gotta tend to Alvin and these other people."

"Uncle Alvin? Is he here?"

Aunt Jo leaned over and said, "That's him in the corner booth."

"Can I sit with him?" Sarah asked, looking across the room at a smiling, silver-haired man who was staring out the window from his booth.

Boundaries

"No. Best not. I bring him with me and set him over there so I can watch him. Mind's gone...nothin' but salt 'tween them big ears of his. We got us a routine. He knows a couple of the waitresses and ol' Gene Long down at the garage, but he don't know nobody else anymore. He'll be ninety-three in September. Now go, sit on down. I'll be right there."

After taking her seat, Sarah dried her eyes, then watched as Aunt Jo went about her business. Soon she was refilling coffee cups of the other couple who was seated. After that, she set a bowl of mashed potatoes in front of Uncle Alvin, topped off his glass of iced tea, then tucked a big cloth napkin into his shirt and fed him his first bite. It wasn't long before he helped himself to the second.

Jo was Sarah's aunt on her mother's side. She, too, was a Bohnert. The difference in her fortune came when she met and married a handsome, but older farmer while she was attending college. Alvin was full of ambition, but for all intents and purposes penniless when they were married. The two had been together now over fifty years, but that bond had resulted in her being disowned by the "moneyed" side of the Bohnert family because she failed to fulfill her obligation of marrying a 'notable man of considerable worth.' Aunt Jo was now in her mid-seventies, but looked significantly older. Life was hard in Noonday if you're unlucky enough to spend your life there in the onion fields.

Sarah quickly recalled all of the women on her mother's side of the family. Aunt Jo was the only one of the five sisters to be married more than twenty years. That she and Paul had been married twenty-four was nothing short of a miracle, and Sarah wondered more each day if they would see silver. It was ever so clear that money couldn't always bring happiness to a marriage.

"There you go," Aunt Jo said, setting a glass of sweet tea in front of Sarah. "Alvin and I quit worryin' about you a long time ago. Figured you'd remember us some day."

Jo took a seat across from Sarah.

"So, tell me about the family. What are you doing these days?"

"You know we have a son, Sammy. He's a Captain in the Army. Right now he's deployed somewhere. He says he can't tell me where he is or he'll have to shoot me."

"Bet you're right proud of him. How old is he?"

"Twenty-three, and I am proud of him. But, I worry about him constantly," Sarah said, taking a sip from her glass of tea. "He turned into a wonderful young man. He's engaged to a woman who's a lieutenant stationed in Korea now."

"Good golly. I ain't never been more than ten miles from Alvin in fifty years. Hard to imagine how spread out people are these days."

"Carla is twenty-one and she's in pre-med at Galveston," Sarah doted, adding some more sugar to her already sweetened tea.

"Too bad your mama wasn't alive to meet her. It would warm her heart to know she had a granddaughter named after her."

"Austin's a sophomore at Baylor. He's the starting quarterback." Sarah took another sip from her iced tea before continuing, "He just turned twenty."

"I read about him in the paper up here," Aunt Jo responded, wiping up spilled sugar and cleaning a water ring with the rag she was carrying. "He's all over the sports section. He's a handsome devil."

"Yep, and big just like Paul. Then, the twins are eighteen. They're finishing up school this year. I think Ella's going to New York. She likes dance and acting. Stella wants to go to veterinary school at A & M."

There was a short pause as Aunt Jo waited to see if Sarah was finished. Eventually she said, "PJ would have been twenty-four, right?"

Sarah was uncomfortable with the topic, but she replied, "That's right. He was born nine months and two hours after Paul and I got married."

There was brief laughter followed by another pause as Sarah was overcome with emotion. Jo took her niece's hands in hers, and said, "I know it's hard honey, but don't go forgettin' PJ. You need to talk about him like he's still here. After all, he's still in your heart."

"I know," Sarah said tearfully. "But, it's just something I can't get over." She took a drink of her tea and wiped her tears with a napkin."

"I'm so sorry I didn't go to the funeral. Aunt Ellen told me about it, but I figured all the Bohnert clan would show up and there'd be a ruckus so I just stayed clear."

"That's okay," Sarah said. She then asked, "So tell me about you. How long have you worked here? Do you still farm? What about Dickie and Tom?"

"Hold that thought a minute. Alvin wants more taters."

Sarah looked over and saw her Uncle Alvin holding his bowl up in the air, but otherwise making no other attempt to communicate. He still had kind eyes and the most incredible smile. Aunt Jo wiped the corners of his mouth with his napkin, took his bowl, spooned in another few dollops of mashed potatoes, smothered them with gravy, and brought the bowl back to her husband. After pouring herself a cup of black coffee, she returned to the booth with Sarah.

"Well, this diner is my diner—I own it. Bought it fourteen years ago right after Alvin had his first heart attack. He couldn't farm any more so I had to go to work. We'd saved money all our lives so we bought this and named it the Possum Trot Grill."

"I love the name."

"And we still have the farm, but all we do is live out there. Tom does all the work with his kids and wife, Betty. Dickie's a meat-cutter at the big grocery in Tyler. He split with Liz eight years ago. He helps out some of the time. Mostly, we just take life one day at a time." Jo took a sip of her coffee then asked, "My gosh, what kind of a waitress am I? Do you want some lunch?"

Sarah's expression could best be described as that of a deer in the headlights, but she managed to squeak out a response.

"Actually, I'm meeting someone for lunch. Then we're going on to Tyler."

Jo looked disapprovingly and responded, "You ain't goin' to the old homestead are you?"

"Actually...yes."

"Why do you go and torture yourself like that? Just find yourself a contractor and fix it up. It looks real bad. Last time I drove by all the windows were broke out and the yard looked like some nature picture in National Geographic."

"The man I'm lunching with is an investor who is interested in buying the place," Sarah said, discretely squirming in her seat.

"Well, I reckon that's a better fate than just letting it fall apart. Still don't know why you don't go fixin' it up first. You should keep it for one of the kids. They don't know what happened, do they? All I gotta say is stay out of that room."

"No, I won't be going there."

The "room" Aunt Jo referred to was the upstairs master bedroom of the house in which Sarah was raised along with her two siblings. The house still stood, albeit in a state of disrepair, on five fenced acres about two miles from the edge of Tyler. It was more or less out of sight, ten miles out at the time it was occupied, but now that it was empty and falling apart, the locals wanted it either fixed up or razed.

"Way I see it, that place is yours. Ain't Paul's. Ain't your brother's or sister's place. It's yours. You did everything after it happened. Yep, I say fix it up, and give it to one of your kids. What's some investor want to do with it anyway?"

"I'm not certain," was the best answer Sarah could come up with.

She was a terrible liar, and Aunt Jo was catching on.

"What's his name?" Jo asked.

"Who?"

"The man you're meetin' for lunch."

"Oh…Craig."

Aunt Jo stared a hole through Sarah, pointed an accusing finger at her and said, "Craig, my ass. You'd better not be makin' the same mistake your mama made. You saw what it got her, and I suspect Paul's just as jealous as your daddy was. I ain't losin' no more family. Nope, not on my watch I ain't."

No sooner had those words left Jo's mouth than a Land Rover pulled up to the front of the restaurant and Mickey hopped out.

Now, unable to wiggle her way out of the predicament, Sarah said, "Here he is now," her feet nervously bouncing up and down under the table.

"Craig, glad you made it," she said meeting him several feet from the table with a business-like hug. "Did you have any trouble finding the place?"

Understanding the code, Mickey replied, "No problem at all. Your directions were perfect to the mile."

"I'd like you to meet someone," Sarah said, pulling him toward Jo. "This is my Aunt Jo. She owns this place, much to my surprise. Aunt Jo, this is Craig."

After shaking hands with Mickey, Jo asked, "I didn't catch your last name."

"Oh, Maxwell. Craig Maxwell."

"Well, pleased to meet you O'Craig O'Maxwell," Jo said, inflicting pain on Sarah's suitor with the obvious pseudonym. "Investor of some type, am I right? That's what Sarah said."

"That's correct. Residential and commercial real estate."

"I might be sellin' this place one of these days. Any real estate man good enough for my niece is good enough for me. Do you have a business card?"

The slope now was a slippery one.

"No…I left them at the office. I didn't bother to go back since I was planning to meet only Sarah."

"That's okay," Jo replied. "All I need is your phone number."

After exchanging the looks of chess players just before one says 'checkmate,' Mickey asked, trying to change the subject, "What's your specialty here?"

"Liar's stew," Jo replied, flipping the damp rag she held over her shoulder.

Mickey knew he was up against a wise, old woman. He tried humor to get beyond the moment.

"Do you have bullshitter's pie for dessert?"

Jo took a menu and slapped it against Mickey's stomach making a whack.

"Y'all are welcome to stay and have dinner. At least that way I can keep an eye on both of you." Taking particular aim at Mickey, she continued, "I don't know what your real name is, and I don't care. But, let me tell you one thing, that lady you're thinkin' about messin' with is just about all I got left of my baby sister. I may be old and bent over, but I'll whoop your butt in a blink if you touch a hair on her head. They'll be draggin' sloughs all over Texas lookin' for your body. Get my drift?"

"Uh, yes. I hear you loud and clear. By the way, the name's Mickey—Mickey Rollins."

Looking directly at Sarah, Jo said, "Shame on you for lyin' to me. Now sit down and order somethin'."

"I'm sorry, Aunt Jo. Mickey's my next door neighbor back home. We…"

"Married, too, I suppose?"

"Well, yes. His wife and I are friends."

"She knows you're here?" Jo asked, looking at Mickey. "For that matter, Paul knows?" she asked again, this time looking at Sarah.

There was silence.

"Figured as much. Tell you what, I think the best thing here and now is for you, Sarah, to go over yonder and sit by yourself and have dinner. You and I need to talk. Then you're comin' home with Alvin and me for supper. I'll steer you back home to your husband before you go and make a mess of your life like your mama did. As for you, Mister Gigolo, make dust. I want to see nothing but your rear license plate in about ten seconds."

"Aunt Jo, I can't stay."

"Can't? Or won't?"

"I have to leave. I'll see you again…real soon."

Jo took a long deep breath and her facial expression turned sad before saying, "Those were the same words I heard your mama say…her last words, mind you."

"I'll be just fine, Aunt Jo." Sarah gave her aunt a long hug, then took Mickey by the hand and pulled him along behind her as they left.

From the front porch, Jo shouted, "God save the both of you!"

Neither Mickey nor Sarah responded. Sarah climbed into her Silver Tahoe and took off like a bat out of hell. All Mickey could do at that point was head back to Hunt, or follow.

IT WAS ABOUT A twenty-minute drive on country roads—some paved, some not—before Sarah's vehicle came to a stop in front of a huge old antebellum house. Mickey pulled up behind her and got out. Matters were worse than Aunt Jo had described. The fence along the roadway had been partially knocked down. The grasses were high. Trees from years ago looked unkempt, and several new ones, contributed by passing birds, had sprouted in random locations. The barn leaned at about a fifteen-degree angle, and apparently wind had blown off a good part of its metal roof which was now scattered about to the west of the house. The implement shed was empty. Its contents now most likely adorned the lawns of thieves or unwitting buyers at auctions or flea markets. Every window in the house was broken. Even the window counterweights had been removed from the frames. It was hard to imagine this was once a prosperous, working farm.

Sarah got out of her SUV and forced a key into a rusty padlock on the gate. Surprisingly, it still worked. Mickey helped her lift the gate out of the way.

"Was this home?"

"No, Mickey, this *is* home," Sarah replied, defiantly.

Mickey realized this was going to be a tough conversation.

"Sarah, nobody lives here anymore."

"Nobody has to live here for this to be home," she said, spinning around and glaring at him. "Let me tell you right now, Mickey Rollins, don't say another bad word about this place!"

It was obvious that Sarah's feelings for the place were deep and whatever memories she had of it still left their indelible mark.

"Do you want to talk about it?" Mickey asked, trying to offer some level of comfort.

"Do you really want to hear what I have to say, or are you just making conversation so you can get into my pants."

"That's harsh."

"Oh, Mickey, don't give me any of your virtuous bullshit. I know you too well, remember? Jesus, I got pregnant by you in a church cemetery!"

"Hey, it was quiet and the landscaping was nice."

As anger ran through her veins, Sarah picked up a huge rock that was probably much larger than she could normally lift and put it at the end of the gate to keep it from blowing closed.

"My grandparents lived on a farm," Mickey said, hoping an anecdote would smooth things over. "It was a lot smaller, of course. They moved to town when I was seven. I cherish all the times I had there. The house and barn are still standing, and the same old couple who bought the place from my grandparents still live there. I went back once—remembered every square inch of the place. Of course, I remember that it felt a lot bigger to me back then. The railroad tracks alongside the property are gone now. I used to love to watch the trains go by."

It must have been an adequate ice-breaker for Sarah. She began to reminisce. For the next two hours, the two walked hand-in-hand from the barn, to the shed, to the house, and back again, over and over as she told story after story. She would tell a tale, then cry on Mickey's shoulder. He would hold her close. She would hold her head in her hands. Mickey would kiss her tears away.

Mickey was shocked to hear the details about the murder-suicide of her mother and father. When Sarah was twenty-two and her brother and sister were already married and out of the house, her father returned home unexpectedly one afternoon to find her mother in bed with one of the local bank presidents. He shot them both dead, then turned the gun on himself. The penalty for infidelity haunted Sarah especially since she, too, had wandered. She married Paul a few months later, not so much out of love, but in a desperate attempt to flee the memory of what had happened. Afterwards, she and the others abandoned the house after auctioning off all of its contents.

She was tortured by the place. Her emotions ran the gamut from the warmth of loving memories, to anguish and total despair. She finally became so distraught, Mickey gave her two of the Valium tablets he always carried with him for Diane. One would have been adequate. After giving her such strong medication, there was no way he could leave her alone.

"You can't stay here alone, Sarah. Why don't you come on with me to Caddo? We can get there in a few hours."

"I don't think it's right for me to go there alone with you," Sarah said as she stood held firmly in Mickey's arms.

Boundaries

Rubbing her back and pulling her closer, Mickey said, "I think we're past 'right' at this point. Besides, what else are you going to do?"

Sarah pulled his face toward hers and they kissed.

"Were you a little surprised I called you last night?" Sarah asked.

"More than a little," Mickey replied.

"I was just so mad at Duke. He takes me for granted," she continued as she put her head on his chest. "I had been planning to come up here for a few days anyway so I just thought, 'Screw him, I'm leaving now. He can make his own meals and do his own laundry.' I'm sorry I got all the way to Marble Falls before getting up the courage to call you."

"It was best we left in separate vehicles. We sure didn't fool your aunt, did we?"

"Oh, my gosh. I had no intention of running into her. I love her a lot. She was my mother's favorite sister. I think Mama felt sorry that Jo more or less got tossed out by the family. I never got the impression that Mama loved Daddy. I see Aunt Jo and Uncle Alvin together after all these years, and I see the bond they have. That's what Mama was looking for. I guess that's what I had always hoped for with Paul. Maybe in my next life."

"I can't believe you told her I was a real estate broker. I hate real estate dealings."

"And you're Irish, too," she said with a fake accent.

The two laughed out loud until Sarah started to rock a little in Mickey's arms. The medication was beginning to take effect.

"Feeling a bit light-headed?"

"Whew. That stuff you gave me is strong," she replied, spreading her legs a little more for stability as she clung to Mickey. "My call didn't wake up Diane, did it?"

"No. She had another seizure last night. I had to medicate her. Suki's watching over her today. Your timing was good. I needed to step away from Diane's situation for a while and clear my mind. Caddo's just the place."

"I'm truly impressed by the changes in you, Mickey. You're married, you have a family. You love your wife dearly and you take such good care of her— especially with her health problems. There was a time…" Sarah stopped before finishing the cut and paste of herself into his life. "Of course, here you are with me."

"We haven't done anything to be ashamed of, Sarah. We're just two people looking for some space."

"What about tonight, Mickey? What about tomorrow?"

On an empty stomach, the drug worked quickly, and it wasn't long before Sarah's movements slowed and her speech slurred. Mickey walked her to his vehicle, helped her into the front passenger seat, and turned on the satellite radio to a station that played soft, spa-like music. He then drove her Tahoe into the old barn and pulled the door closed with a loud squeal from the wheels supporting the decrepit wooden door.

When he returned, Mickey checked on Sarah's condition, finding that she appeared to be dramatically affected by the tablets he had given her earlier. He felt her pulse which appeared to be normal then brushed her eyelashes to see how far under she was. There was no movement. She was obviously heavily sedated. Then, with a twisted sort of reasoning that only Mickey could justify, he unbuttoned her blouse to check her breathing, exposing her pink bra…and more. Paul had said in jest once during a conversation about women's breasts among the 'guys' at The Store that he would never let Sarah get a 'boob job' because there was no need to change what was already a work of art. What he didn't know was that Mickey had already been to the same gallery.

It was no time before Mickey succumbed to his desires and undid the convenient, front clasp of Sarah's bra. He took his time admiring the breasts he had fondled and the nipples he had sucked years ago. The memories were vivid and their effect was apparent by the bulge in his pants. After checking to see that she was still unaware of what was taking place, he indulged himself once again for several minutes. When he had finished with the objects of his affection, he hooked the clasp, tucked Sarah's breasts back into position, and buttoned her shirt. There was no shame in his expression.

THE JOURNEY TO CADDO took another three hours and Sarah slept the entire trip. Mickey placed a pillow under her head and a jacket over her upper body so that she appeared to be sleeping while he stopped in at a local grocery to stock up on provisions. Once back on the road again, the drive to Back East took him another thirty minutes along a winding road that followed the shoreline. Nearing their destination, the early evening sun shining through the canopy of trees left long shadows across the road causing the vehicle's headlights to turn on. The driveway to the lake house was ambiguously marked, but Mickey remembered it vividly and turned down the three-quarter mile serpentine, caliche road. The soft dirt of the road showed no signs of recent tire marks giving him an unnecessary feeling of security. Nobody ever trespassed up at Caddo. Violators would be shot, and everybody knew that.

Mickey pulled up to the front door of the two-story log cabin that had been Dub's dream house, turned off the engine, and stepped out to complete solitude save the sounds of birds, the wind in the trees, and the lapping of small waves against the waterfront. His first order of business was to tuck Sarah away comfortably so that she would awaken to the splendors of a soft bed in the cabin. He unlocked the heavy wooden door, then returned to the Rover and picked up her limp body, carrying her up the flight of stairs to the large bedroom overlooking the lake. Once she was beneath the sheets of the bed and one of Ruby's rail fence quilts, he returned to the vehicle and unloaded the food, drink, and what few items they had brought with them from Hunt.

After opening windows throughout the house to get a good cross-breeze, Mickey returned to the bedroom where he found Sarah beginning to stir. He opened the blinds and the windows in that room, then sat down beside her and put his hand gently on her head. She opened her eyes and smiled at him.

"I had the wildest dream about us," she said with a timid expression. "Let's just say it made me horny."

Mickey knew it wasn't a dream, but he was surprised she had any recall of his earlier intrusion on her body.

"Valium has different effects on different people. It'll pass."

"Maybe I don't want it to pass," she continued, pulling Mickey's hand to her lips so she could kiss it. "Paul's on all kinds of medication for his diabetes and high blood pressure. Of course, he's too proud to take Viagra or one of those other drugs, and he has no imagination whatsoever. Do you know how long it's been since I've had a man inside of me? Do you know how long it's been since I've been satisfied…sexually?"

"I get the impression you would like me to answer with, 'not counting today.'"

She pulled him close and their lips met. Soon their tongues touched and the juices began to flow in both of their bodies. Mickey stood up and removed his shirt, tossing it onto a chair. He answered the evil expression on Sarah's face with one of his own. Sitting up so that she could unbutton her blouse, she stopped at the third button—it was matched with the fourth button hole. Something was wrong. She was an impeccable dresser. Sarah suddenly shivered with the fear that she had been violated in some way.

"My shirt's not buttoned right," she said, looking accusatively at Mickey. "This button should go into another hole. Did you sneak a peek at me while I was passed out?"

"I won't lie to you, Sarah. I got carried away and I unfastened your…"

He had made the mistake of getting too close to Sarah as he confessed his sin. It only took a split second for her to bring her right hand hard across his face. Mickey winced in pain. It was a good shot.

"You son-of-a-bitch!" She screamed angrily. "I would have given myself to you Mickey, but you had to take from me instead. I was wrong about you." As she stood up from the bed, she finished with, "You're the same selfish, sick asshole I knew years ago."

"Sarah, I…"

Boundaries

He was unable to finish before she let him have it again. His face was already pink from the last strike. This one might leave blue as well as she caught the corner of his eye.

That was enough for Mickey. In a fit of rage, he scooped up Sarah and tossed her over his shoulder while she pounded on his back.

"Put me down or I'll…!"

He had heard more than he wanted to hear. After stepping out onto the balcony that extended over the cove which served as both a swimming hole and a boat dock, he threw Sarah ungracefully into the water below. There were a few moments of splashing before she sank below the surface and failed to rise. He waited, but still she remained below the water.

Afraid that the drugs may have kept her from swimming, or that she injured herself when she hit the water, he ran down the steps out onto the shoreline and jumped into the cove where he last saw Sarah. After groping around for a few seconds, he felt an arm and was able to hoist her above water. He carried her to land and placed her on the lawn where she coughed water for a while before being able to speak. At least she was breathing.

"If I hit you again, will you throw me back in the water? I can't swim you idiot!" she shouted, finally able to lay flat on her back.

Mickey was still straddling her, the water dripping off of his head onto her face. He looked down at her heaving chest and watched her soaking wet blouse wrap itself around her breasts. She noticed him staring at her.

"Is this what you want?" She shouted, ripping her blouse open.

Buttons flew in all directions. She then unfastened her bra, exposing her bare breasts to him. Her nipples were hard as rocks due to the cool water.

He sat upright, still astride her half-naked body, and unzipped his pants as he asked, "Is this what you want?"

The seconds seemed like an eternity. Without warning, she grabbed Mickey and rolled him over so that she was on top of him. She removed her blouse and bra then unzipped her jeans. Collapsing onto him, they passionately and vigorously grabbed at one another's bodies. While their lips were locked together,

Mickey reached inside Sarah's jeans and grabbed her buttocks. However cold they had felt moments earlier, that cold was now gone, and was replaced by a heat the two had experienced years before.

It wasn't long before they had removed all of their clothing, and were making love on the front lawn of Back East. The act fulfilled a fantasy both had longed for since Mickey handed Sarah a cup of coffee the day after he returned to the ranch. Both were satisfied physically and emotionally at that moment. Neither gave any thought to the consequences of their actions.

THE TWO LAY NAKED in each other's arms on the lawn for a long time listening to the songs of birds, the wind in the trees, and the lapping of the water against the shoreline. There was a new sound, too—the beating of two hearts. There was no conversation, only soft strokes, long, soulful looks, and soft kisses. They knew their time together would be short, but they were determined to forge a memory that neither would ever forget.

They enjoyed each other in this manner until the shadow of the cabin fell across their bodies and the temperature began to drop. Eventually, they gathered up their clothing and walked back to the cabin. No sooner did Sarah turn the corner in the kitchen to the hallway leading to the stairs than she found herself face-to-face with a woman standing spread-eagled and holding a gun pointed directly at her face.

"Move and I'll blow your head off!" the stranger shouted.

Sarah froze in her tracks. She was joined a moment later by Mickey. He, too was startled by the intrusion, but in a different way.

"Laura?" Mickey called out to the woman with the gun.

"Mickey?" She replied, lowering her weapon.

Mickey grabbed a nearby tablecloth and wrapped it around Sarah before asking, "What the hell are you doing here?"

"I was about to ask you the same question," Laura replied, tucking the black pistol into her belt.

"Excuse me," Sarah interrupted. "Is anyone going to tell me what's going on here? Mickey, do you know this person?"

"Jesus Christ! I can't believe this is happening," Mickey said, pulling on his jeans over his otherwise naked body.

"Mickey!" Sarah persisted.

Gesturing toward Laura, Mickey replied, "Sarah, this is Laura...Laura Chase."

"And she's here because...?" Sarah asked.

"She takes care of the place."

Laura broke up laughing at that point.

"Busted! I don't know who you are lady, but you just got screwed by my husband."

"Laura!" Mickey objected loudly.

"Mickey?" Sarah said in response to Laura's remark.

"Sarah, she's psycho. Don't pay any attention to her."

"I'm a psycho, and that's why I have a key and take care of the place? Mickey, your bullshit lies get worse every time I see you."

"She's my ex-wife, Sarah. She just has issues with the 'ex' part."

"No, my lawyer has trouble with the 'ex' part, Mickey. So who's the girlfriend? Wait, I see a wedding band on her hand. Could she be married—like to someone else, I hope?"

"I'm going upstairs to get dressed and gather my things, Mickey," Sarah said, her face beet red with embarrassment. "Then I'm leaving. What's taken place here had better stay in this house Mickey. I mean it."

"Sarah," Mickey said, holding his hands up in vain as she ran up the stairs. Turning to Laura, he continued, "Your timing sucks. For that matter, you suck. When will you ever leave me alone?"

"Hey, I'm doing my job taking care of your father's vacation house, I find an intruder, accompanied by my husband who I haven't seen in, what, seven...eight years? And you have a problem with *me* being in the house?"

"Ex-husband, Laura!" Mickey shouted again. "Ex!"

"So, whose wife are you screwing now, Mick? I hope you aren't shitting to close to the back door, if you know what I mean."

"She's none of your business, Laura."

It seemed like only a few seconds until Sarah came back downstairs wearing the same outfit she had taken off on the lawn and carrying the rest of her belongings.

She stood facing Laura and said, "I don't know who you are, but you never saw me here, do you understand?"

"I understand you've been cheating on your husband," Laura replied.

Turning angrily toward Mickey, Sarah demanded, "Let's go, Mickey."

"Go? Go where? Laura was just leaving, weren't you?"

"No, actually I have some work to do around the place. But, if you concentrate on something else…perhaps sex…you won't even know I'm here."

"Mickey," Sarah said bitterly, "Let's go."

"Go? We just got here!"

"Then give me the keys," Sarah said, holding out her hand.

"Sarah, please stay here with me."

"The keys, Mickey!" She shouted.

He pulled the keys to his Rover out of his pants pocket and dropped them into Sarah's outstretched hand.

"I'll leave them under the driver's side mat. You can pick up your vehicle where I hope to find mine. Don't bother to follow…and don't call!"

With that, Sarah rushed out the door, slamming it behind her.

"Wow, the bitch has issues, don't you think, Mick?"

"Laura, I hate you. Please leave."

"If you need a shoulder to cry on, or some familiar pussy, I can…"

"Laura! Leave!"

"Jesus! Try to be a good wife and look what it gets you."

Chapter 37

By the time Lupita had returned poolside with the lady's drinks, Diane had assisted Suki with her bathing suit top, what little there was of it, and the two inseparable companions had finished rubbing some of Suki's homemade sunscreen on each other's skin. Diane didn't see the need to change her outfit, even though her shorts and top could be easily described by most as being too provocative for company—especially a young male guest. They were cut short, revealing, and the top was ultra shear leaving little of her upper body to the imagination.

"Miss Diane, Austin Duke just drove up," Lupita announced. Hoping Diane would heed her advice, she asked, "Are you sure you don't want to change into something else? I can get a robe for you, or maybe a different shirt."

"Why? Is he an Eagle Scout or something?"

Suki was surprised by Diane's cavalier attitude.

"You know what I mean. He's a young man, and you don't want him to get ideas."

"What kind of ideas are you worried about, Lupita?" Diane asked, being strangely argumentative.

"Oh, honestly. You know…man ideas."

"Do you know what she's talking about, Suki?"

Neither Lupita nor Diane could tell if Suki's eyes were open beneath the dark sunglasses she wore.

"Leave me out of this. If you want to flash the neighbor's son, that is for you to explain to his parents."

Suki wasn't going to tell Diane what to do, but she was beginning to notice Diane was exhibiting a behavior that was new—a more promiscuous side.

"Well that settles it," Diane said with an indifferent shrug of her shoulders. "Send him back, and bring us some salt and pepper. I'm hungry."

Lupita shook her head disapprovingly. Diane's remark even evoked a reaction from Suki who glanced toward Diane while tipping her glasses down enough so she could see over them.

It wasn't long after Lupita left to let Austin in that he walked through the French doors. Even the most recent pictures Diane had seen of him at Paul and Sarah's house no longer did him justice. He was a made-for-television quarterback with his huge smile and perfect teeth, his short, curly blond hair, gorgeous facial features, and piercing blue eyes, all atop a six-foot, three-inch muscular frame. He, too, was dressed casually, wearing corduroy cutoffs, a t-shirt, and sandals.

"Can I bring you something to drink, Austin?" Lupita asked.

"What are they having?" he replied, nodding in the direction of the two drinks on the table.

"A Virgin Mary, and the other is having plain orange juice."

"Could I just have some ice water?"

"Are you sure?"

"Yes, ma'am. I went running earlier, and I need to push some fluids."

"One water coming right up."

Seeing that Diane was staring at their guest, Suki decided to break the ice with at least a PG version of what Diane's X-rated mind was conjuring up.

"Hello, Austin! Great to see you again. Make yourself comfortable."

Austin pulled up a wooden chair with a plush cushion and made himself at home facing the two women.

"The last time we saw you it was last summer. You've really changed a lot, and for the better."

"Are you flirting with me, Suki?" he responded confidently.

"Was I flirting, Diane?" She asked, an index finger innocently pulling on her lower lip underscoring the obvious.

"You're a hussy, Suki. Besides, he's mine. Sorry, Austin, we've kidnapped you…oops, I mean man-napped you. Lupita's chaining your car to a tree as we speak."

He was used to the teasing verbal assaults, and he loved them. The grin on his face produced perfectly matching dimples on either side of his mouth.

Taking note of what Austin was wearing, Diane remarked, "I like your shirt."

He was wearing a deep red t-shirt with gold letters that read, "Thick and Juicy" on the front. After standing and turning around to display the backside, Suki read out loud, "Souquets' BBQ—Tongue Waggin' Good." What is BBQ?"

"That's barbecue, ma'am," he replied with typical Texas manners. "You've never had any?"

"Is that the sliced meat that Toot cooks until it is black before pouring that red sauce all over it?" Suki asked Diane.

"No, ma'am," Austin argued. "Your description doesn't do it justice. What Toot does to meat is the equivalent of what a maestro does with a symphony."

"What he means to say," Diane interrupted, "is yes, that's it. You've been served barbecue, you just haven't eaten any."

Making an unpleasant facial expression, Suki said, "I do not understand why you do that to meat. It should be lightly cooked, steamed, or eaten raw."

"Here is your water, Austin," Lupita said, returning with a tall tumbler, condensation dripping from its walls. "Let me know if you need anything else."

Turning back to Austin, Diane asked, "How do you pronounce the name?"

"Austin…it's like Boston."

"No, smartass, the restaurant."

Suki laughed out loud at Austin's quick wit and Diane's response.

"Oh, it's pronounced "suck-its." It's a Cajun name."

"I beg your pardon," Diane said, reacting excitedly.

"Cajun…it means more or less from Louisiana."

"No! I mean the name…it's 'Souquets?' Pronounced suck-its?"

"That's right, ma'am. It's a restaurant that's been serving barbecue dishes near the Baylor campus for generations. It's famous for its food as well as its name. The correct pronunciation should be the more French version "Soo-kays." But, the story goes, one summer, a Baylor fraternity began calling it "suck-its" and business took off. The rest is history. I work there on weekends in the off-season."

Diane couldn't resist, so she asked, "So, do you?"

"Beg your pardon, ma'am?"

"You know, do you…?" she finished as she pointed at his shirt.

"Oh, you know the joke, too," he replied, his face now turning red. "That's been the scandal around Baylor for years, I guess. Lots of people, particularly Baptists, have wanted to change the name."

"Diane," Suki intervened, "don't embarrass the boy."

"He's a man, Suki. I'm certain he can handle himself." Giving the young guest a sultry look, Diane finished with, "Can't you, Austin?"

The look and the come-on were almost more than Austin could take. Had he been alone with Diane, it's hard to say what he might have said or done. He quickly changed the subject to what he had come for in the first place—his father, Paul Duke.

"So, neither of you have seen Dad?"

"He spent the night up at Section Eight," Suki replied, reiterating what she had told Lupita earlier in the morning. "Toot said he was going to get him and take him home after he checked on a water level or flow some place."

"Probably at the Falls," he said, showing some familiarity with the ranch. "It hasn't rained in a while. I suspect he's worried."

"No," Suki, said, "He said something about 'way back at the headwaters.' Do know where that is?"

"I've heard about it, but I've never been there. Dad always said it was off limits. He said it was 'for adults only.' I guess I never qualified."

"Well, I bet you qualify now," Diane said.

"Diane…" Suki tried unsuccessfully once more to get her to stop flirting.

"I'll bet that's where we could all go skinny dipping."

"Diane, stop it," Suki said.

"Suki, he's not the least bit embarrassed. He's in college. He's a Pike for God's sake. He probably has a different girl in bed every night."

"Actually, ma'am," Austin corrected, "I have a steady girlfriend."

"Isn't that special," Diane said in a particularly catty tone. Pointing at his shirt again, she asked, "So, does she?"

Finally reaching the point where he truly was uncomfortable, he replied, "I think this shirt has done nothing but get me in trouble today."

"For the record, Austin," Diane said, flipping her hair suggestively, "I do."

He was speechless, but Suki wasn't.

"Pardon my friend here, Austin. She has a hormone problem today, and she needs to take a cold shower," she said with increasing volume.

"So, why don't you take it off?" Diane asked, one eyebrow raised.

"No, I think that would just cause more talk."

Standing up and walking over to Austin, Diane said, "Then let's trade. I'll give you my shirt, and you give me yours."

The request was so out of line, Austin didn't feel he needed to respond thinking she was not serious. But, before he could say 'no' to Diane's bizarre request, she had her shirt up over her head and off, dangling from one finger. Her girls were now there for Austin to see.

Suki jumped up and wrapped a towel around Diane.

"Austin, I am sorry about this. I do not know what has gotten into Diane today. Please keep this to yourself. I do not think your parents need to know about what just happened."

Austin was so startled it took him a while before he could respond.

"Believe me, I won't say a word. Hey, I need to leave anyway. If you see Dad, tell him I'm getting together later with some of the guys from the team, and we're taking the jeep out on the ranch. Also, tell him Mom left early today so he doesn't need to go looking for her."

He turned to leave, but before he reached the door, he looked back and said, "It was good to see both of you again. I won't tell anybody anything."

"Goodbye, Austin," Suki said.

Diane said nothing and finally appeared embarrassed.

In the time Suki had known Diane, she had never witnessed her demonstrate such an unrelenting obsession with sexual innuendo. More notably, this was the first time she had openly solicited the interests of another person—man or woman.

Once Austin was out of sight, Suki asked Diane, "What got into you?"

"I don't know. Was I out of line?"

"Out of line? You practically spread your legs for the boy. I was self-conscious for both of us, and that takes a lot. You never act like this…never."

Diane put her top back on, took her seat back on the chaise lounge, and reflected a moment before saying, "I acted like this with Guy Leroux."

Suki looked as if she had seen a ghost.

"How do you know that name?"

"What are you talking about?" Diane asked. "He owns the island…Maribella Island. He liked it when I flirted with him." There were a few moments while Diane rubbed her forehead as if she was in pain. "Did I meet him?"

"I do not know who you are speaking about," Suki said emphatically.

"We got together on the island…several times. He liked to watch as his wife and I…" The pain in Diane's head worsened. "I can see her so vividly. She was from Tunisia. I can smell his cologne."

Suki looked away from Diane in an attempt to conceal her reaction. Diane was correct—the names, the details, and the man's voyeur fetish. But, what she described were visions seen through Suki's eyes, not Diane's. Diane had never met the owner of Maribella Island. Could it be, Suki wondered, that when she created the image of Sylvie, and transferred the secret messages to Diane, she inadvertently transferred other memories as well? Or, could Mickey have lost control of the cascade in such a way that unintended information was sent to Diane. This might explain the dramatic personality change Diane exhibited versus just a day before.

"Suki, are these your memories?"

Diane's question was the ultimate test of Suki's allegiance to Mickey, and her devotion for Diane. She had to choose, and she had to choose now.

"We have discussed so many things since we met, Diane, I probably mentioned him to you at some point. He and his wife were clients of mine for about one year. He was a kind and generous customer. I probably told you about him while we were on the island."

Diane had no immediate reaction to what was said to her. But, after a few moments, she became bothered by Suki's initial denial and pressed her for an explanation.

"Why did you initially say you didn't know who I was talking about? Are you trying to hide something?"

Suki was spared having to respond by the sudden appearance of Toot who came rushing out onto the patio and he wasn't happy.

"Where's your stupid husband? He's supposed to be checking fences and nobody's seen him. He won't answer his phone. He doesn't show up."

"He's in Caddo," Diane replied.

"Caddo!" Toot shouted.

"That is right. He left a note on my desk sometime last night," Suki continued. "He was gone when I woke up."

Toot removed his sweat-stained Resistol hat, wiped the perspiration from his forehead onto his shirt sleeve, turned away from the ladies, and began mumbling expletives.

"This is just great, just freakin' great," Toot said, sounding frustrated. "I gotta be at the fairgrounds this afternoon to start settin' up for the auction day after tomorrow. Sixto and half his crew went Out West and won't be back 'til dark. Mickey has two guys tearin' down and buildin' a new fence for your horse corral, and he was gonna do their job and check the perimeter."

"So, don't check the fence," Diane said, oblivious to Toot's anxiety.

"Yep. Why not?" Toot responded, throwing his arms in the air showing the futility of the situation. "Just piss away everything, all our work, all our future. Who gives a shit anyway?"

"You're being kind of melodramatic, aren't you Toot?" she calmly countered.

"He is right, Diane," Suki said, siding with Toot. "Toot runs a complicated operation, and Mickey made a commitment to do something. Now he is not keeping up his part of the agreement."

Surprised at the statement, all Toot could say was, "Yeah…just what she said."

"Well, I'm sure he had a good reason! Get off his case!" Diane yelled, defending Mickey.

"I don't think chasing after his ex-wife is a good reason!"

Toot grimaced, immediately regretting what he had said.

Diane was initially aghast at Toot's proclamation. But, she could tell by Suki's pained expression there was at least some validity to what he said, and that she, too, was partly behind a well-kept secret.

"Ex-wife? Mickey's ex lives at Caddo Lake?"

Toot stared at his boots looking for divine, or any other type of guidance at that moment. His silence was affirmation that there was a link between Mickey, his ex-wife, and Caddo.

"And you knew?" Diane asked, looking directly at Suki.

Suki was at a loss for words. She had painted herself into a corner more than once this morning, and there was no way out this time.

"Weren't you the one who told me his ex-wife was a threat?"

"Yes, Diane. I was the one," Suki admitted.

"So, why would you keep this a secret?" Diane asked, her stare piercing Suki. "Why would either of you keep this a secret from me?" she asked, scanning both of them. "What's her name, Suki? You know it, don't you?"

"I just found out, Diane. I promise I wasn't trying to withhold anything from you."

"Her name!"

"Laura," Suki replied.

"Laura, what?"

Suki thought for a few moments, and it was apparent the last name eluded her, so Toot answered the question.

Boundaries

"Chase. It's Laura Chase."

It was more than Diane could take. Without saying a word, she broke into tears, ran out a gate at the rear of the patio and down the steps to a driveway. Finding one of the work trucks, she hopped in and took off toward the south end of the ranch that bordered the Duke's place. Neither Suki nor Toot rushed after her, but they knew one of them would have to go.

"Of all the things to tell her, Toot…why?"

"Me? Why didn't you tell her about our conversation the other evening? The whole Laura thing is a big no-no in this house. That was a subject for Dub and Ruby. Nobody else crossed that line. If Mickey wants to go screw his ex-wife, I wouldn't put it past him. But, it's not my place, or yours for that matter, to get in the middle of that mess!"

"I do not think he is with Laura," Suki said.

"Well then, why the hell is she freakin' out? Where the hell is he?"

"I have good reason to believe he is with Mrs. Duke."

Toot spit on the ground.

"Tell me you're jerkin' my chain."

Suki shook her head. Toot had to take a seat.

"She was not at home this morning. Austin called to see if she was here. He thinks she took off for a place called Noonday."

"Right. That's right. It's near where she grew up. She's got kin there."

"And it is supposed to be near Caddo Lake. Is that true?"

"Well, if you blink you'll miss Noonday on your way to Caddo. But, the two are in the same neck of the woods." Toot stared at the deck shaking his head as he said, "You're sure Mickey went to Caddo?"

"Am I being unfair to Mickey and Sarah to assume their simultaneous trips to the same part of the state are not pure coincidence?"

Toot wouldn't answer—he wouldn't even make eye contact with Suki.

"Is there more between Sarah and Mickey than a neighborly friendship?"

Knowing there was no way to escape Suki's inquisition, he finally answered, "We're speakin' about Mickey…Mickey Rollins. That's all I'm gonna say."

Toot didn't need to elaborate. She knew exactly what he meant.

"So, somebody needs to go to Caddo, and somebody needs to get Diane," Suki said. "Do we flip a coin?"

"Well, I'm not going to Caddo," Toot replied. "I got too much to do around here, starting with what Mickey was supposed to do today."

"I cannot go either. I need to stay where I can respond to Diane if she has any medical problems, especially with Mickey gone. Plus, I am not leaving Gigi alone with Carmen. It is just too soon."

"That's settled, then. Nobody's gonna rescue Mickey. If he screws up his life, that's his problem."

"What about Sarah?"

Toot sat back in his chair and pulled his hat down over his eyes as if that would make the entire problem go away. Fortunately, there was another possible solution. She was walking out onto the patio at that moment.

"Suki, have you seen this rash on Gigi's arms before?" Carmen asked, carrying the small, happy and smiling child toward her. "I think it just popped up."

Toot tipped his head up so he could see Carmen. Suki immediately knew what he was thinking.

"No, Toot."

"Why not? We both have things to do. She could be up and back in no time."

"She is new to the area. There is no way I would let her drive all that distance."

"So, fly her. There's an air strip not twenty miles from Caddo. I could call in a charter. It'd probably be at the Kerrville airport by the time she got there. Lupe could drive her that far. She gets Mick and hauls his silly ass back here."

As the dialogue between Suki and Toot was taking place, Carmen realized the conversation involved her. She set Gigi down, but instead of running to Suki's outstretched arms, she ran to Toot. He helped her up into his lap at which point the little urchin proceeded to crawl up his body until she was face to face with him so she could kiss him.

Boundaries

"Let me see them arms, girl," he said as she assumed a position straddling his chest. "Fire ant bites," he said, running his thumb over the red bumps with white pustules.

"What?" Suki asked with alarm in her voice.

"Fire ants. Was she outside this mornin'?"

Carmen walked over to see the rash again.

"How do you know?"

"Like I get fire ant bites about six times a day. Me and ants go way back. See the little pustules? That's what they look like. Plus there's a bunch of 'em. Little buggers wait until an army has crept up on you then they bite the piss out of you." He shook Gigi playfully and said, "But, you don't care, do ya'? You're my tough little cowgirl, right?"

Gigi nodded her head and gave him a hug.

Suki went to Toot's side to see for herself the rash on Gigi's arms. After looking at both arms carefully, she looked accusatively at Carmen and asked, "Where did you take her this morning?"

"We played in the front yard for a while," Carmen answered defensively.

"She has no business being in a place where she could be eaten by bugs! What will Diane say?"

"I didn't know there were ants in the grass!"

"Ladies!" Toot interrupted. "This is Texas. There are bugs everywhere. Everybody gets bitten. Now chill out. Everything's gonna be fine. She has a rash, not cardiac arrest or nothin'. Don't go gettin' Diane worked up over it."

"Well, she should not have bites like this," Suki replied taking Gigi from Toot. "Let me put some cream on it."

"She'll probably get a reaction from your cream," Toot said, sparring with Suki.

"You, Mister *Man*, go take care of the ants," Suki replied.

"I'll have one of the boys sprinkle some ant killer around the lawn, so y'all need to keep her out of the grass for a week or at least until we get some rain."

Suki and Carmen both nodded.

Gigi smiled while she tried repeating, "Missa Ma," and giggled at Toot.

"'at's right, sweat pea. I'm Mister Man." He gave her a kiss on her cheek. "I'm gonna go look for Diane. I'll either send her back or haul her back kickin' and yellin'—whatever I need to do." Pointing at Carmen, he instructed Suki, "Tell Lupita she needs to fly from Kerrville to Harrison County Airport in Marshall. She'll need to get a car from Lew Comstock. He'll give her directions from the airport to Back East. She might oughta get a return flight set up just in case Mickey tells her to take a leap. If he cooperates, she can come home with him. Any questions, call me."

"Where am I going?" Carmen asked, now thoroughly confused.

"Just follow me," Suki replied. "I will explain right after I take care of Gigi."

AFTER DRIVING FOR WHAT seemed like twenty minutes along a rugged, dirt road that followed the path of Menger Creek, Diane reached what could only be described as Eden. The creek lapped over a rock wall that was maybe thirty yards across, creating a sparkling waterfall. The spray shimmered in the sunlight. On either side of the creek, meadows of native wildflowers poked their pink, yellow, red and blue heads up over the grasses. The glassy creek above and below the waterfall reflected the tall hills that loomed not too far away. It was so peaceful and so incongruous from the problems in her personal life. She realized she must have reached it—The Falls.

A black, open-topped Jeep pulled up to the same spot on the opposite side of the creek from where Diane parked. Three young men hopped out, and Diane immediately recognized the driver as Austin. He recognized her as well and waved. Perhaps they were going swimming, she thought, and she felt like going for a dip as well. What better way to relax and try to put one's troubles behind?

She turned off the truck's chugging motor and quickly stepped out, looking forward enthusiastically to frolicking in the creek. She ran the few yards to the water, wading out to her waist, when she suddenly stopped in her tracks. At first it was the sound—that of roaring water. It pulled at distant memories, bringing pieces of them into the present. Then it was the sight of the men wading into the water and rushing toward her. Panic struck. She couldn't breathe. Her heart raced. She turned to run, but slipped on the rocks that lined the bottom of the creek and plunged into the water. As she came up gasping and choking, Austin grabbed her hands and pulled her up. One of his friends held her waist. The sheer and minimal clothing she had on clung to her skin, her breasts clearly visible through her soaking wet shirt. She was no longer Diane. She instead was a terrified woman defending herself. Her scream echoed against the steep rock wall of the hillside.

"Get her to shore!" Austin shouted.

The three pulled and struggled against Diane's thrashing body.

"Mrs. Rollins! It's Austin. Are you hurt?"

The face that looked back at him was unrecognizable. This wasn't the Diane he left at the house a short while ago. This was a frightened animal, and it was fighting for survival.

After getting her to shore, one of the men held Diane's legs and the other her arms while Austin sat on her and held her down. In trying to protect her from harming herself, they were unknowingly recreating her worst nightmare—the rape at Maribella Island.

"Diane, it's okay. It's me…Austin. What's wrong?"

She let loose another blood-curdling scream.

Trying to avoid attracting attention, Austin reflexively put his hand over Diane's mouth. With a sudden burst of strength, Diane managed to get an arm free from one of the young men's grip, and she brought her fist across Austin's face, drawing blood.

Austin was shocked and momentarily paralyzed by Diane's blow. Unfortunately, his friend holding Diane's remaining hand was not. He brought his huge right hand across her face with a fierce blow that would have hurt a strong man, let alone a woman. She was dazed and motionless afterward, all her resistance shattered.

"What the fuck did you do that for, Greg?"

"Who is this bitch?"

"She's my neighbor, dumb fuck!"

"What's wrong with her?" asked his friend.

"Hell if I know, Nate." Austin replied. "Mrs. Rollins…Diane, can you hear me?"

There was no movement, but Diane managed a muffled groan.

The sound of the waterfall became mixed with that of a truck engine, then that of wheels grinding to a halt on the dirt road. A cloud of dust blew across the men and Diane. The door of the truck swung open with great force striking Greg in the head sending him reeling onto the ground. A man jumped out holding a shotgun. It was Toot.

Nate instinctively tried to rush at Toot, but was stopped when Toot brought the butt of the Mossberg across his face, sending several teeth flying into the creek. Toot then repeatedly pumped the action of the gun and fired three shots— two toward Nate, and one toward Greg, both of whom lay sprawled on the ground. The twelve gauge slugs narrowly missed the men as Toot had intended. He then leveled the barrel of the gun at Austin's head.

"If she's dead, so are you!"

The look in Toot's face was enough to scare Austin to death.

"It ain't what it looks like, Toot, I swear. She…"

"Get off of her, now!" Toot made sure Austin understood every word that he slowly spoke.

"Listen to me, Toot. We were just going swimmin' and she jumped in, too, and…"

"Shut the fuck up, pick up your friends, and stand by the rear of the truck. I have enough rounds left to kill all three of you. Don't make me do it." He motioned at Austin with the barrel of the gun as he spoke.

Austin was quick to do as he was told. The three teammates huddled by the bed of Toot's idling Chevy.

Toot removed his hat. After dipping it in the creek, he went over to Diane, put his gun down, and poured some of the water onto her forehead. Carefully brushing her hair out of her eyes, he looked for any obvious injuries other than the black eye and large bruise that were forming on the left side of her face.

"Toot?" Diane said with a whimper.

The relief he felt brought tears to his eyes.

"Toot...the waterfall. Get me away from here. Just get me away," Diane said with increasing alarm in her voice.

He didn't need any further instruction. He grabbed the shotgun, helped Diane to her feet and assisted her into his truck. She crawled in the open driver's side door and scooted over to the center. Turning toward Austin, he said, "This ain't over. Get back on your place. Don't ever let me catch you on my ranch again or I'll kill you. Is that clear?"

"Toot, it's a misunderstanding. I swear..."

Toot wasn't in a listening mood. He forcefully brought the butt of the shotgun up into Austin's groin sending him to the ground in severe pain, then got in the truck with Diane at his side, slammed the door and sped away.

THE DRIVE FROM THE Falls to the old house at Section Eight would normally have taken fifteen minutes. Toot made it in ten. The otherwise lively place was deserted at this time of the week. Along the way, he had managed to pull a bedroll from the backseat of the truck and gave it to Diane to wrap herself in for warmth. It was clean, warm, and she couldn't help but notice that it smelled like him.

Her emotions were bouncing from one end of the spectrum to the other. She had, so far in one day, weathered the realization of her amnesia, experienced the disappearance of her husband under less than gallant circumstances, and survived a perceived attack by Austin and his buddies, a beating, and gunfire. Now, she found herself in the company of perhaps the one human being—the one man—she trusted more than anyone. There was no sound to conjure up horrid memories. There wasn't the persistent, personal invasion by Suki or Mickey. There was no feeling of being an unwelcome squatter in Dub and Ruby's home. There was, however, an overwhelming feeling of safety and comfort.

Toot effortlessly carried Diane into the unlocked cabin and placed her on a sofa. He then went to the freezer, dumped several handfuls of ice cubes into a plastic bag, and wrapped it in a towel. After returning to Diane, he kneeled next to her and gently placed the cold pack on her now purple and blue eye and cheek bone.

Taking her hand in his, he asked, "What went on back there? Did they…" He couldn't finish his question before choking up.

"I'm okay. My head just hurts…it hurts like hell."

"You need a doctor? I'll take you to town."

"No, I don't want anyone to know about his."

Toot smiled and said, "Well, that ain't gonna happen unless you have about four pounds of make-up."

"Looks that bad, huh?"

Toot nodded.

"Bet I look awful, don't I?"

"Diane, ain't nothin' could ever make you look awful. You're beautiful in and out." Tears came to his eyes again.

"What's wrong?"

Sitting down with his back against the sofa, Toot said, "When I drove up and saw them on you, I figured they'd, you know…they were attacking you."

She put her hand gently on his shoulder. He responded by reaching up and putting his hand on top of hers.

"I'm just glad you're alright."

"You know what's sad?" Diane asked, "I think it was all a huge misunderstanding."

"What do you mean?" Toot asked.

"I freak out at waterfalls. This is the second time that I can remember. The first time was right after we moved here. From what little Mick and Suki will tell me, I had my accident at a waterfall. That's how I sustained my head injury and this whole soap opera that's my life began. As soon as the attack was over today and you put me in your truck, I started to recall things…things that blessedly I had forgotten. Pieces of my past are beginning to fall into place. I think I was attacked at a waterfall by some men—maybe two or three. I think I was raped, but I can't remember for sure. I don't even recall if it was the same time when I fell. No one's ever told me the whole story. It must be gruesome."

"That or someone's hidin' somethin'."

"Yeah, or that. So today, I flipped out from the association of the sound of the waterfall. Austin and his friends just happened to be at the wrong place at the wrong time. I don't think they meant any harm, I truly don't, now that I think back on the whole thing. But, I reacted as if I was being attacked again. There was nothing but adrenaline pumping through my veins."

"I came this close to shooting all three of those pissants," Toot said, holding his finger and thumb slightly apart. "Talk about a misunderstanding. Paul's gonna kick my ass."

Diane stared at the ceiling while she stroked Toot's shoulder.

"There's something else I vaguely remember."

"What's that?"

"The whole thing—the first time—ended in gunfire. I don't know who was shooting or if anyone got shot for that matter. But, I do remember whatever was happening to me, ended at that moment. There was another hero in my life and it wasn't Mickey. Somebody saved me back then, just like you thought you were saving me today."

Toot glanced back over his shoulder toward Diane with one of his smiles.

She stroked his face and said, "You're a good man, Marque Teudi. Thank you."

There was no misunderstanding at that moment of the meaning behind the words, the looks, and the touches Diane and Toot exchanged with one another. He turned around and kissed her. She dropped the bag of ice and put both of her arms around his body pulling him close against hers. Moments later, her damp, skimpy top and shorts were on the floor in a pile with Toot's blue jeans. A lot goes on at Section Eight...more than anyone will ever know.

Book 6

"Alright, no more questions about Gigi…at least not here and now," Dr. Madden said to Diane in a conciliatory tone of voice. "You must love her a great deal."

"She means everything to me," Diane replied, gazing across the room. "Can I call the police in Roswell and speak with her?"

Mason had to swallow an unmannerly large bite of his breakfast before answering, "I see no problem with that, but we need to wait at least until a reasonable hour. Four o'clock in the morning is a little early for anyone, would you not agree?"

Still staring across the room, Diane was lost in thought. She hadn't touched her food. For that matter neither had Dr. Madden. Only Mason was eating, and he was half-way through his meal.

"Is anything wrong, Diane?" Dr. Madden asked.

"You know, it's said you eventually get used to living in a different time zone. I never got used to the time here. It doesn't feel like my 'home' time."

"What do you mean?"

"I always know the exact time in Bangkok and Hong Kong, for example. It should be late afternoon right now, not early morning."

Mason and Madden exchanged puzzled looks before he interjected, "Could be the caffeine."

"Maybe…maybe," Diane replied, still lost somewhere.

The conversation ground to a halt while Diane continued sipping her espresso and staring across the room. Mason glanced over his shoulder to see if she was fixing on anything in particular, but saw nothing except empty tables. He looked at Madden and they non-verbally told one another that she was fading.

"Are you tired, Diane?" Mason asked

She didn't answer. It was as if she was locked in thought. Mason picked up his knife, held it a few inches above the table and dropped it. The noise jolted Diane back into the conversation.

"I can't believe she has an evil twin. You've heard of that before, haven't you?"

"She, who?" Madden asked, totally puzzled by Diane's choice of subject.

"Carmen."

"The young lady who is in Roswell?" Mason asked.

"No, she *is* Carmen…I think. For some reason, I suddenly seem to recall that the first nanny we had who claimed to be Carmen was actually her sister Magdeliene."

"How do you know they were actually sisters? Did you see them together? How did you figure this out?" Madden asked.

"I think it was her tattoo."

"Carmen has a tattoo?" Mason asked.

"No, Magdeliene has the tattoo on her left breast. It's coming back to me now. When the real Carmen showed up, she showed us she didn't have one."

"The nanny showed you her breasts?" Madden asked, unnerved by the thought.

"Not exactly. When Magdeliene arrived, Mickey and Toot saw her undressed after taking a shower and they caught a glimpse of the tattoo."

"What became of Magdeliene? Madden asked.

"To be honest, I don't know."

"And who is Toot, again?" Mason asked.

"He's the other owner of the ranch…Marque Teudi."

"Time out!" Madden said. "Too many people, too early. Someone needs to draw some pictures or something. I'm completely lost now."

"Joan!" Mason called out to the waitress.

She quickly came to his side.

"Do you have some paper we can write on?"

"Certainly, hon. Does anybody need something more to eat? More coffee?"

All three held their cups in the air. It was becoming an arduous journey down the road Diane was taking them.

"Let me take your plates. I'll be right back with the coffee and some paper."

"While she's doing that, I need to pee," Diane said, indicating to Madden that she needed to let her out of the booth.

Mason motioned with his eyes to Madden for her to go with Diane. Diane picked up on his gesture.

"You've got to be kidding. I can't piss without her holding my hand?"

"You are still in our charge, Diane. I don't want you to have an unattended seizure."

"You're a lying sack of shit, you know that?" Diane asked as she headed off quickly for the ladies' room.

"Good job, Loarn." Madden said.

He motioned with his hands for Madden to tag along and she followed.

"Here's your coffee, Loarn, and a pad of paper."

"Thanks, Joan. Would you please hand me that bag over by the window?"

"This one?" Joan asked, reaching for Diane's colorful, woven shoulder bag.

"Yes, that one. Thank you."

Mason began to rummage through Diane's belongings, looking for anything that might be useful to the discussion.

"Is that legal?" Joan asked, looking on curiously.

Without stopping what he was doing, Mason replied, "Legal, yes; nice, no; ethical, definitely not. But, my friend here is quite the mystery woman, and I'm hoping something might…wait a minute…"

Mason pulled out a small notebook with a lavender cover. After quickly fanning through the pages, he was about the return the book to Diane's handbag when he spotted writing in the middle of what now appeared to be a journal. He quickly glanced at the first sentence at the top of a few of the pages.

Boundaries

I first met Sylvie on the flight to Manila. That's when she told me about Mickey...

Sylvie told me to beware of Carmen's twin sister Magdeliene...

Sylvie told me last night about Mendoza, saying I need to avoid seeing him at all costs...

I remembered today that it has been Sylvie who was telling me to avoid caffeine and to drink citrus beverages. Why do I crave caffeine? Why do I feel so liberated when I eat an orange?

Sylvie told me I can never be apart from Suki for any length of time. I could die without her. I have to find a way to ask her, why? Who will care for Gigi? I hope it's Toot...

Sylvie looked scared last night. She told me Suki would be unable to communicate for much longer. She's becoming forgetful and her health is suffering. She said he's onto her...

Mickey killed Sylvie this morning. I'll miss her...

Mason thought he heard voices coming from the direction of the ladies' room, so he quickly replaced the book in the bottom of Diane's bag. At his urging, Joan replaced the handbag on the seat from where she had earlier removed it.

"Did you read something bad? You look worried."

Mason shook his head, avoiding eye contact with Joan while he assimilated the tidbits he had read into something meaningful. He realized that he was wringing his hands and had to force himself to stop. He noticed something else— there was ink all over his hand. He must have accidentally uncapped a pen in

Diane's handbag. He knew he was on borrowed time. Once she discovered it, any trust she had in him would almost certainly vanish.

"Oh, my. She doesn't look well," Joan said.

Mason turned around and saw that Dr. Madden was helping Diane back to the table. Her skin was pale. He quickly stood to lend a hand, only to find that Madden was heading toward the door of the restaurant while he was trying to direct her back to the table

"Loarn, we need to get her back to the hospital. Her gait is unsteady, and she had a near syncopal episode in the bathroom."

"No. Not yet."

"Loarn!"

"Sit...both of you. Joan, bring Diane a large glass of orange juice."

Diane sat at the table and said, "I don't think I'm supposed to drink orange juice. Mickey forbids my eating fruit and drinking juices."

"Loarn, she may have an allergy. She probably knows something..."

"So do I," Mason said emphatically. "Joan, please, cold orange juice in a large tumbler."

"Be right back with it, Dr. Mason."

"Is she diabetic?" Madden asked.

"Just...work with me on this Bev, please."

With some reluctance, she decided it was best to follow Mason's lead in the matter.

"You will feel better after the juice. Your color is already returning to normal since you've taken a seat. Now that we are all back, please help us with the names as we were discussing a short while ago. By the way, did everything work as it should in the ladies' room?"

Rolling her eyes, Diane replied, "Do we have to talk about pee at the breakfast table? Are you always a doctor?"

"Yes, as a matter of fact, I am always a doctor."

Boundaries

Deciding it was best to nurture the conversation along, Madden said, "All was well, Loarn." Putting a friendly hand on their weakened patient's shoulder, she asked, "Now, about the names, Diane?"

Diane spun the ledger pad around so it was facing her and began to jot down names. The pen Joan had left wouldn't write.

"Shit," she said, tossing the pen across the table and starting for her bag.

"Wait!" Mason said in an unexpectedly loud tone of voice. "Use mine."

"Mont Blanc? Nice. Can I keep it?" Diane asked.

"I'm afraid not." After a brief pause, he continued, "It was a gift from my wife."

"Wow, an expensive gift from an adoring wife. Does she know you're hitting on a waitress?"

The question didn't settle well with Mason.

"I think I'll step out to the men's room for a moment."

Without saying another word, he got up and left the table.

"Wash your hands," Diane said, trying to be funny.

Mason had no reaction.

"Geez, what got into him?" Diane asked, spinning the pen with her fingers like she used to. "I forgot I knew how to do that."

The pen hit the table hard when Diane lost control of it, spinning freely and heading toward the table's edge. Dr. Madden quickly scooped it up.

"Dr. Mason's a widower, Diane. It's been a while since she passed away, but he's still grieving. Just give him a few minutes to get himself together."

"Oh, my gosh. I feel like such an ass."

"It was an innocent misstatement, Diane. I'm certain he confronts his loss frequently in his work. No harm was done. Now then, what about some names."

"Here's the juice, folks, and more coffee. Where's Dr. Mason?" Joan asked, setting Diane's glass before her.

"He'll be right back," Madden said while watching Diane down half of the glass of orange juice.

"Refills of coffee for the doctors," Joan said, pouring from her carafe. "And I'll be right back with the espresso."

"That will be fine, Joan," Madden replied.

After setting down her glass, Diane held out her hand and said, "Keep the pen. Do you have another one I can use?"

"Absolutely," she replied, pulling a pen from a pocket of her long, white lab coat.

"Do you want all the names?"

"Well, I'm sure I know about your husband Mickey, daughter Gigi, and Suki, your..."

"Best friend, worst enemy, lover, caregiver,..." Diane said, finishing Madden's remark.

"I suppose. Remember, those are your words, not mine. So, who's Toot?"

"Toot..." Diane took a long, deep breath. A smile graced her face. "Imagine Robert Redford and Matthew McConaughey rolled into one gorgeous hunk of man. He grew up on the ranch that he now co-owns with Mickey. There's some sort of weird estate issue, and the two are locked into this love-hate partnership. Anyway, if you could describe your ideal man, Toot fits that description. He's handsome beyond belief, kind, generous, thoughtful, marvelous with Gigi, wealthy yet humble, and strong. He has man-hands. They're abnormally large and rough, but they feel like silk rubbing over your breasts and butt." With her eyes closed, Diane rubbed her hands down her body as she described Toot's features. "And you know what they say about the size of a man's hands and the size of his penis?" Diane held her hands out on the table spaced a considerable distance apart. She opened her eyes to find Madden and Joan both staring at her with their mouths and eyes wide open.

"I think we've heard enough about Toot," Madden said.

"No, we haven't," Joan said, smacking the doctor on the shoulder.

"Yes, Joan. We have," Madden insisted.

"Oh, alright. Here's your espresso."

"Continue with the names, Diane."

"There's Mickey's ex-wife, Laura."

"I don't believe you mentioned her."

"Let's just say that until a few days ago, she was nowhere to be found, completely out of the picture, and yet, she was always there. Get my drift?"

"I think I understand. Mickey still has feelings for her."

"Big time," Diane replied with exaggerated hand gestures. "Then there's Paul Duke and his wife, Sarah. She's really sweet and one of my closest friends—at least until recently."

"What happened?"

"I'm not entirely sure. She's just become very distant. She barely speaks to me, and she avoids Mickey entirely. If I didn't know any better, I'd think they were having an affair or something."

"What makes you think they're not?" Madden asked.

"Oh, Sarah would never do that, especially with Mickey. Besides, she and Paul are inseparable."

"Okay, who's next?" What about the nanny, Carmen?"

"Carmen is perfect—great pedigree and Gigi loves her as much as she does Toot. Suki did a lot of research before choosing her.

"You mentioned Bruce. This is your ex-husband?"

Diane paused, drank the rest of her orange juice, then said, "No, he's my late husband. I'm still grieving, too, after ten fucking years, thank you very much."

"I'm sorry, Diane. I came across a bit callous. I didn't intend to be.

"Seems to happen a lot at this table."

"Diane, I…"

"Look, here's the original grief-stricken person," Diane said as Dr. Mason returned to the table. "Sorry, I was an ass. But, you missed the encore. Dr. Madden here was just an ass. Now it's your turn. Do you want to join the foot-in-mouth club? Any stupid questions you want to ask?"

"Just one," Mason said, sitting down.

"I can't wait. Go ahead, ask," Diane said, her voice dripping with sarcasm.

"Who's Sylvie?"

Chapter 38

Suki could see the bruise on Diane's face the moment she stepped out of Toot's truck and went running down the stairs toward her.

"Diane, what happened?"

"Stupid me, I slipped and fell in the water up at The Falls."

Toot waited to see if Diane was going to complete her story. She did fall, but there was more to it. After giving her ample opportunity to be entirely forthcoming, he did the job for her.

"She had a run-in with Austin Duke and a couple of his friends," he said, putting his arm around Diane's waist and helping her up to the house.

"What type of run-in, Toot?" It was clear from the tone of Suki's voice and the color in her face that she was furious. She stopped them on the steps to look at Diane's black eye.

"It was an innocent mistake, Suki," Diane replied, cutting Toot short before he could reply. "Don't make anything of it."

Brushing Diane's hair from her face, Suki quickly examined the swollen, black and blue cheekbone. When she pressed lightly on the raised welt, Diane grimaced.

"I am calling the Sheriff," Suki said, her voice quivering.

"No, you're not," Toot said.

"Toot, we are not letting this go unpunished."

"I took care of things. Now, let's get her up to the house."

Suki wasn't about to let the matter drop. Grabbing his shirt forcefully with a clenched fist, she asked, "I thought I heard gunshots at one point. Did you...?"

Without thinking, Toot removed Suki's hand with equal force then answered, "No. Came mighty close, but no."

Boundaries

She was startled by the unnecessary pain of his grip on her wrist, but managed to say, "If you shot at them, something must have been going on that…"

"Suki! Let's get Diane inside! We can talk about it there!"

There was something more going on—something much more. Suki yielded to Toot and Diane, letting them proceed up the walkway. Watching as they passed by her, she couldn't help but notice the attention Toot was giving to Diane. He was going out of his way to take care of her given that he was largely dismissing the entire episode. She noticed one more thing—neither of them looked her directly in the eye.

Lupita was the next member of the household to see Diane, and she immediately let off a near panic-stricken barrage in Spanish. Toot said something to her in Spanish after which she quickly quieted down and walked briskly to the kitchen. Once inside, Diane took a seat at the breakfast table. Toot pulled out another chair so she could raise her legs. Lupita returned, handing Toot a bag filled with ice that was wrapped in a towel. He gently placed it against Diane's face and head. Diane soon opened her good eye and noticed Suki was glaring at her, waiting impatiently for somebody to explain what happened.

"It was all a series of huge mistakes. First, I went to The Falls to get away— to run away from my idiot husband. By the way, has anyone heard from him?"

Suki shook her head. "We sent Carmen to go collect him."

"Carmen?"

"She has strict instructions as to what to do, and she will be in contact by phone. She might be airborne by now. Do you want me to try and call her?"

"You're flying her?"

"Hey, we wanted them both back ASAP," Toot said. "She don't know the way there, and Suki and I needed to be here. She'll find him and send him back. She can hitch a ride back with him or fly."

"Just what he needs—a cosmopolitan, Spanish nymphet, and a secluded cabin in the woods."

"Do you want to go get him yourself?" Toot asked.

"No! I don't even want to see him!"

"Diane, you do not know for certain that he is with Laura. I think he just took some time off. You need to give him the benefit of the doubt."

"Oh, I don't doubt for a minute he's up to no good."

"Do you want me to call Miss Laura to see if she has seen Mr. Rollins?" Lupita asked.

Diane was incredulous.

"You mean you know about this too, Lupita?"

"Si. I know about Miss Laura. I have her phone number if you want to…"

"No!" Toot stopped the conversation before it went any further. "Thank you, but no. We're not callin' Laura."

"I have got to get out of this place," Diane said trying to sit up. "It's turning into one giant freakin' conspiracy."

There was a roar of a truck out front. The noise stopped as suddenly as it began when the vehicle came to an abrupt halt on the circle drive. The silence was broken by a pounding on the door.

"It's Mr. Duke," Lupita said. "And he has Austin with him."

Toot put his head in his hand for a moment as he said, "Jesus, this is gonna be just great. Let him in Lupita."

She no sooner had the door latch released than Paul barged through the door and past Lupita. He looked bigger when he was mad, and he already had a head start on big.

"I got the Sheriff comin'. Better be a God damn good reason, Toot, for what you did."

Meeting him half way to the door, Toot said, "Calm down, Paul, or I'll toss your ass out right now along with Austin."

"You and who else!"

The two stood face-to-face, bowed up and ready to go at it right then and there when Diane stood up and yelled, "Both of you! Cut it out!"

The two cowboys remained head-to-head, each ready for the other to make a move. Diane went over to the two and pushed them apart.

"I mean it. Either break it up or take it outside! I won't have this in my house!"

Paul finally looked away from Toot long enough to see the huge bruise on the side of Diane's face and her black eye.

"What the hell happened to you?"

"Ask him," Diane said, pointing toward Austin.

"You didn't tell me Diane was involved in this!" Paul shouted at his son.

"You wouldn't listen, Dad."

"Did you do this to her!" He shouted, grabbing his son by the arm.

"No, it was Greg."

Paul was astonished by his son's admission of any involvement in Diane's injury.

"First of all, you need to apologize to Mrs. Rollins. Then you need to start explaining. I want one story before the Sheriff gets here…one story out of both of you."

Diane was furious at Paul's accusation and, pointing at her face said, "Whatever happened, I didn't deserve this."

"My son doesn't get into trouble unless there's a damn good reason. Now, what went on up there?"

That was all Toot could take. He grabbed Paul, spun him around and let him have it in the chin with his right fist. The many brawls Paul had been in as a youth were reflected in his reaction to Toot's punch. He barely flinched.

No sooner had Paul returned Toot's blow, than there was a flurry of fists and feet in both mens' faces and guts as Suki proceeded to pummel both into submission, sending them to the floor. She stood in front of Diane, muscles tightened, veins bulging, and poised to strike again. The room became totally silent as the shock of what had just taken place settled in.

Suki was the first to speak.

"We all want to know what happened and no one more than I. We will be civil about this, am I clear?"

As Austin pulled his father to his feet, Paul said while rubbing his chin, "Well, that got my attention."

In a gesture of peace, Paul held his hand out to Toot.

Toot reached up and as he got to his feet said, "I do believe without a doubt that's the first time a female has whooped my ass." Looking at Suki with a grin, he continued, "Where did our little Suki learn to do that?"

"Would you believe me if I told you I grew up with four mean, older brothers?"

"Not for one second."

"Then never mind." Turning back to Diane, Suki asked, "Now then, would you be so kind as to tell us all that went on up at The Falls?"

The face looking back at Suki was of a person who was in a different place…a different time.

"Diane, are you alright?"

"What happened to Zeus?"

"Zeus? What on earth are you talking about?"

"The horse—I was on Zeus; Mickey rode Hera."

"You mean on the island?"

Paul, Toot, Austin and Lupita exchanged looks. It was clear the conversation was significant only to Suki and Diane.

Suki approached Diane and took her hands, then asked, "Tell me Diane. Tell me everything you remember."

"I remember the night Mickey proposed. It was on Maribella Island. We were at the cove. You had made all the arrangements. We rode horses to get there."

It was happening. Diane was beginning to fill in a lot of blank spaces and Suki wasn't about to stop her. She eased her friend over to the sofa and sat down next to her. Soon, the others in the room had taken a seat and were listening.

"Mickey and I had an argument that morning. It was over something stupid…I can't remember what it was about. I was mad, and I rode off. I rode to the waterfall. Do you remember it?"

"Of course I do. It is a beautiful place."

"He was there." Diane stopped for quite a while searching…searching for details. "Bates?"

"Captain Bates, that is correct," Suki said smiling with approval regarding Diane's improving memory.

"He was taking a shower in the waterfall." Diane began to smile and blush. Looking around at the men in the room, she turned back to Suki and said, "I'll tell you later about what took place."

Her smile was shortly replaced by a look of horror.

"They came out of nowhere."

"They? They who?" Toot asked.

"Two men…and a woman. They hit Bates on the head with something. Did he live?"

"Yes, Diane. He lived."

"Thank God."

Diane began to anxiously rock back and forth on the sofa and ran her arms over her shoulders.

"Who was the woman?"

"Her name was Genevieve."

Nodding, Diane said, "Now I remember. We left Phuket to get away from her didn't we?"

"Yes, we did."

"Anyway, that's when I turned to run away, and I fell on the rocks. Is that what happened, Suki?"

"Yes, Diane. You have even told me more than we first knew. By the time we found you on the beach…"

"They killed Zeus, didn't they? I remember seeing a dead horse on a beach, but I couldn't move."

Suki touched Diane's hand tenderly. That was acknowledgement enough.

"What happened to those two men and the woman, Suki?"

Thinking quickly, Suki said, "They got away. They were gone by the time Mickey and I got there."

Paul decided he'd heard enough. "How does somebody get away? You're on an island, right?"

"We just didn't take the time to look for them. We had to get Diane off the island and to a hospital."

"Is that why you got so upset this morning at The Falls, Mrs. Rollins?" Austin asked.

"Yeah. Waterfalls do something to me. Then add into the picture a couple of guys running at me in the water, it was the whole nightmare happening again. So I tried to escape. That was when I fell into the water."

"And you hit your head when you went down?" Paul asked Diane.

"No, she didn't," Austin answered. "She was screaming. I thought she was drowning or something so the guys and I grabbed her and carried her to the shore while she was kicking and yelling and punching. We got on top of her to try to keep her from hurting herself, and she just turned wild. That's when she hit me in the face. Greg lost it right then, and he whacked her one on the side of her face."

"He did what?"

"Greg hit her, Dad."

"Why'd you let him do that?" Paul asked.

"It all happened so fast. I never imagined he'd do something like that. Then, Toot drove up on us. I guess he thought we were attacking Mrs. Rollins or something. If I was in his shoes at that moment, I'd have thought the same thing—I might even have reacted the same way."

"Shooting at people? I hope I'd have raised you better," Paul said.

Toot got to his feet, ready to go at it again, but Suki cut him off.

"No! I will not have any more fighting in this house!"

Pointing at Paul, Toot said, "I was gettin' on the high side of a fight, Paul. If I'd wanted to shoot anyone, this meetin' would be a whole lot different than it is. Just imagine a bunch of guys lyin' astraddle one of your daughters or your wife. Imagine them holdin' her hands and her legs. She's screamin'...she's injured. What would you do, Paul?"

"He's right, Dad. You always taught me to protect what I love."

"And that's just what I was doin'," Toot said as all eyes turned to look at him.

Diane and Suki were paralyzed by Toot's choice of words.

"Do you still want the Sheriff, Dad?"

"They're probably just about here anyway," Paul said.

"How is that possible?" Suki asked. "When did this happen?"

"Couple of hours ago," Austin replied.

"Where did you go after you found Diane?" Suki asked Toot.

"I went for some ice."

"We have ice here, Toot. Where did you go?"

"I took her up to Eight."

"Kind of out of the way, don't you think?" Paul asked, questioning Toot's actions. "If you were so concerned about her, why wouldn't you bring her back here?"

"I needed to get my thoughts straight," Diane said. "I was scared. I was hurt. I just told Toot to take me away."

Toot hoped Diane's response, though only partially truthful, was enough of a red herring to divert everyone's focus. It wasn't, and judging by the look Suki gave the two of them, he realized she knew the truth about what had happened.

"You will have to excuse me," Suki said to the group. "I need to check on Gigi." It was a gracious exit.

Paul got up, walked over to Toot and shook his hand. Then he went over to Diane and said, "I never knew what happened to you. It was always a big mystery and Sarah told me to stay out of it. I reckon you had a good reason to be scared. And Toot, you had a reason to do what you did. I just hope what Mickey's doing is helping you get where you want to go. I don't want us to have another near miss. Next time, somebody might get hurt."

"Austin," Toot said, "Sorry about what I did back there. I know now you didn't mean her harm. What about the kid whose teeth I knocked out?"

"Fortunately it was a bridge. He'll be alright once the swelling goes down."

"Tell him to give me a call if there's any money involved in getting his mouth put back together. I'll take care of it."

"Mr. Toot," Lupita called out. "There are two Sheriff's cars coming up the driveway. Wait a minute. Here comes a third one."

"Dammit, Paul, what did you tell them anyway?"

"I told them there was an assault, and a gun was involved. Guess they're taking it kind of seriously."

"You gonna tell 'em different now?"

"Let's you and I go out together and talk to them. Since I called them, let me start."

"Right behind you. Diane, you stay here. Austin, you come with us."

The three men walked toward the deputies, waiving, smiling and talking as if nothing had taken place. Lupita brought Diane's icepack to her, then quietly asked, "Are you going to be okay, Miss Diane?"

"Where did Suki say she was going?" Diane asked, looking disturbed by all that had taken place.

"She has Gigi out on the patio."

AS DIANE EASED TOWARD the patio, still holding the ice pack to her head, she spotted Suki walking slowly back and forth at the far end that overlooked the terrace separating the main house from Number 2. She carried Gigi over her shoulder. Diane's daughter looked so big now compared with just months earlier. Seeing that Gigi was asleep, she approached Suki very quietly and cautiously. When she stepped in front of Suki, she could see the tears streaming down her cheeks.

"I'm sorry, Suki. It just happened."

"So you are saying it was consensual."

"Uh, yes. But, in truth, I seduced him."

"Do not lie to me, Diane. I am sick of lies, and right now, I am sick of you!"

Gigi remained asleep in Suki's tight embrace. The two were truly at ease with each other. Diane felt they could continue with their conversation without waking the child.

"I don't have particularly strong feelings for him, Suki. It's more of a physical attraction. It's a…"

"…a detached feeling," Suki said, finishing Diane's thought.

"Yeah, a detached feeling. It lacks warmth."

"I know the feeling well. I perfected it, then I gave it to you."

"What do you mean, you gave it to me?"

Suki didn't want to tell Diane about her therapy. Not now. She had to tell her at the right time—when it would hurt the most.

"We have been friends and lovers now for several years. You are selecting traits of mine you wish to emulate. Your choices leave a lot to be desired."

"Wait just a minute. There are three legs on this stool. You're not entirely without fault."

Suki wanted so badly to tell Diane everything. She had to be quick to craft a response that made her point, without endangering her position in the home.

"I love Mickey, Diane. I have loved him since before you came into the picture. But, I realized my place in his life a long time ago, and it was second behind you. I was alright with the arrangement. As long as Mickey was in my life, I did not care about the circumstances. I even grew to like you…to love you. I could master the detachment."

Diane felt almost sick to her stomach at Suki's admissions.

"With Toot, I had someone who was mine for the first time in my life. I did not have to feel detached. I could let the warmth flow for once. It was spectacular."

"It still can be, Suki."

"No. It is over. This pain I feel is something I never want to experience ever again. All my love now goes to Gigi. She is someone who nobody can take away. I will always be here for her, and she can never hurt me. As for you and Mickey, I am here to serve as you wish, but there is nothing more."

"What's this 'serve you' shit? I hate that!" Diane said, loud enough to wake Gigi. "Why don't you just leave us? Go back to Thailand or something."

"Mommy," Gigi said, looking into the eyes of the person holding her.

"Unfortunately for you and me, Diane, we can never be separated. We will always be one. Our bond is now more than that of sisters."

"What are you talking about? You're nuts."

"Ask Mickey. He will explain it to you."

Diane shivered.

"Here, give her to me," Diane demanded. "Give me my daughter."

The look on Suki's face was ten times more chilling than it had been just minutes ago when she was clashing with Toot and Paul Duke. Diane had never seen anything like it.

"When you make that request in the future, Diane, you say, 'Give me Gigi.'" Never say to me, 'Give me my daughter,' is that clear?"

"You can have Toot, Suki. For all I care, you can have Mickey. But, don't ever touch my daughter again. I want you out of here. Pack your shit and leave. You have until the day after tomorrow."

Diane reached for Gigi, but Suki turned. Instantly, Diane yelled, "Give her to me!"

"Hey, hey, hey!" Toot shouted, approaching with two uniformed men. "What's the problem?"

"Tell her to hand over my daughter, Toot!"

"Here, Diane," Suki said, slowly turning around. She was smart enough to know it was unwise to make a scene in front of anyone in a uniform, especially when not in one's own homeland. "Here is Gigi," she said, finally and reluctantly handing the child over to Diane.

Gigi again reached back for Suki at the same time she said, "Mommy!"

It tore through the hearts of both women, but for completely opposite reasons. Diane ran back into the house with Gigi crying in her arms where she was met by one of the uniformed men. Suki turned away from Toot and the officers to hide her emotions. Toot walked up to her and put his arm on her shoulders, but she quickly twisted away from him.

"Suki, these men want to speak with you," Toot said.

"Why?" Suki asked, turning around and staring into his eyes for the truth.

"They have some questions," Toot answered.

"No! I don't care about them. Why were you with Diane?"

"Not now, Suki. Later."

She continued to glare at him hurtfully for a few moments before wiping the tears from her eyes. Being uncharacteristically disrespectful, she sat on the patio wall and waited for the officers to come to her. They soon did just that.

"I was not there at the creek," she began without being asked. "All I know is what Toot and Diane told me. If you have questions, ask them."

The two men looked at each other, then the one sporting a neatly creased Stetson and wearing the khaki sport jacket with an emblem on the breast pocket said, "Ma'am, I'm Sheriff Wilt Masterson. This is Deputy Doss."

He pulled out a small notebook and read from it.

"Are you Sukhon Jiao from Hong Kong?"

"That depends," Suki replied wryly. "Is this a social or an official visit?"

"Official, ma'am."

"Then yes, that is my name."

"Do you know a woman by the name of Genevieve duCoeur? I think I said that correctly."

"Yes, I do."

"Well, she's apparently a significant figure in your part of the world, and…"

"My part of the world?"

"Suki, work with them," Toot cautioned.

"You're not from here, are you ma'am?"

"No, I have dual citizenship in China and Thailand."

"Then I suggest you cooperate in the fullest manner possible. It'll make things a lot easier."

"Cooperate? Is that anything like bend over?"

"Suki!" Toot said. "Be respectful of these men."

"Forgive me. I forgot I am supposed to subordinate myself to all men, especially cowboys like Toot."

Masterson didn't care for Suki's attitude.

"Ma'am, I have no reason to dislike you, but the fact is you are under investigation as a person-of-interest in the disappearance of Ms. duCoeur. Apparently she has been missing for a long time, and it is assumed she is a victim of foul play."

"She's no longer apparently a victim—she's dead."

After looking at Toot, the sheriff asked, "You know this for a fact, Ms. Jiao?"

"Call me Suki, please."

"You know this for a fact, Ms. Jiao?"

"Absolutely. She was shot in the head at close range with a nine millimeter handgun. I am certain she died instantly."

"Did you shoot her, Ms. Jiao?"

"Suki, don't answer that question," Toot said, holding his hand up in the air. "Wilt, I want to get Roger Delaney involved before this goes any further."

"I think that would be a good idea, Toot."

"So, I thought you and your officers were called out by Paul Duke to investigate Diane's injury?" Suki asked, digressing to the other matter.

"We are, ma'am. I'm certain one of my investigators caught her just as she walked through the door. If her story ties with what Toot and Paul told me, I think it was all a misunderstanding. You, on the other hand, have big problems."

"And why do you say that, Officer Masterson?" Suki asked, trying to get a rise out of the visitor.

"I got a phone call from the district office of the Texas Rangers this morning. They were contacted by an official of Interpol in Bangkok who has been investigating the disappearance of Ms. duCoeur, and the trail leads to you. Now that I have verified that you are the individual he is looking for, this man from Bangkok will be here with a Ranger and myself day after tomorrow to question you about this matter."

"I will be gone by then. I was just asked to leave by the lady of the house."

"Well, you either need to remain here under Toot's supervision through the time of that questioning, or accompany me to the Sheriff's office where you will remain in custody until we are finished with the investigation."

"She'll stay here with me," Toot said emphatically.

"You're willing to take that responsibility?"

"No question, Wilt. She'll remain with me."

"Do I have any say in the matter?" Suki asked.

"No," was Toot's only response.

"One more thing, Ms. Jiao."

"Yes, officer?"

"Two more things. Number one, I suggest you show respect for authority. You're a guest in our country. I can change that with one phone call. Secondly, are you related to a man named Chi-feng Wu?"

"Yes. He was my grandfather."

"Was?"

"Yes, he is dead as well. He was murdered."

"Suki, stop talking now!" Toot insisted.

"You witnessed this murder?"

"More or less," Suki replied.

"Toot, I think you'd better have Delaney set up an office right here for the next couple of days."

"Looks that way, don't it?" Toot replied, not believing what he had heard.

Another man in uniform came out onto the patio from inside the house where he had been talking with Diane.

"Story checks, Sheriff."

"Good," Masterson said, nodding at Toot. "Looks like that matter's closed." Making sure he had Suki's attention, he finished with, "Remember Ms. Jiao, you must remain at this residence under the watchful eye of Toot until we return. If you attempt to leave, I will assume you are fleeing, and I'll have a warrant issued for your arrest. I would arrest you right now if it weren't for the fact that you are an acquaintance of Toot's. I also strongly suggest you seek legal advice immediately. Am I clear?"

"Absolutely clear," Suki replied sarcastically.

"Toot," the sheriff said. "I mean it."

With those words, the sheriff and his men departed, as did Paul and Austin Duke. Diane took Gigi to her room and closed the door. That left Suki and Toot alone on the patio.

"What in the hell are you doing, Suki? These guys mean business."

"There is an explanation for everything, Toot," Suki said, as she hopped off the wall on which she sat, and sauntered over to a chair where she took a seat. "Here is the part of the story only Mickey and I know about. You see, Diane was brutally raped by the two men she spoke of. Fortunately, she remembers only bits and pieces of the horrible event. Mickey, bless his little heroic heart, came to her rescue and shot both men while they were committing the act. He was then confronted by Genevieve duCoeur, and he shot her as well." Acting distraught, she continued, "He then turned the gun on me and told me to dispose of the bodies which I did. I saw what he could do in the fit of rage that consumed him at that moment. I was not about to disobey him. He shot and killed all three. I did not want to be his fourth victim."

Toot looked at Suki with squinted eyes as he recalled what he had heard earlier.

"Diane told me a slightly different story. Seems her memory is that 'someone'—and she specifically said it was not Mickey—came to her aid and shot the two men. I think there was someone else involved. Was there?"

A coy smile crossed Suki's face as she said, "Tell me, Toot. Were you lying between her legs when she told you this? Was your face buried in her breasts at the time?"

"You don't seem to understand, Suki. Masterson is an egomaniac and a politically-motivated man. We're talkin' about some high profile crime here involvin' law enforcement from overseas. He thrives on that kind of stuff 'cause it comes around only once in a blue moon. If he could get his name on page 95 in the local newspaper, he'd throw you to the wolves. He don't give a rat's ass about you."

"Just like you."

"Suki! The thing this afternoon with Diane—it was a mistake. I can't take back what I did. I can't take back the hurt I caused you."

"There is no hurt, Toot. Do not give yourself that much status in my life. You speak of the sheriff as an egomaniac? Consider yourself when you make such a judgment."

"Alright, I deserve that. What I want more than anything is for you to be treated fairly in this whole thing. I'll contact our attorney and he'll coach you through this."

"Oh, good. And be sure he has time to coach Diane as well."

"Why's that?"

"She is the person who murdered my grandfather."

"I can't believe that, Suki. Diane's not that kind of person."

"Really? Why not ask her yourself?"

"I think I'll go do that. Don't stray off the property."

"Of course not, Master. I am in your charge."

Toot had been around long enough to know that there was little to no chance of reconciling with Suki—at least not now. All he could do was try to get the facts straight and provide her with the services of a good attorney.

As Toot turned down the hallway to Gigi's room where he hoped to find Diane, Suki made a beeline to Mickey's office, making sure nobody saw her. It only took her a few seconds to get beyond the security on Mickey's desktop computer, and open up an application. He was sadly unoriginal, never changing the universal password—LuvMeMaria—he had confided to her years ago. She turned on a small transmitter that was hidden behind a framed picture on a bookshelf behind his desk, moved the cursor over a specific instruction, highlighting it, then clicked. She next ran just as quickly as before to the bar in the dining room, poured herself a quick glass of water, and took a seat on a sofa where she pretended to read a magazine.

"Suki!" Toot shouted, running back up the hallway to the patio.

"What, Toot?" she replied.

"It's Diane. I think she's having another seizure."

Chapter 39

The twin-engine Cessna rolled to a stop, shutting down its engines just outside the small group of offices that made up various private enterprises at the Harrison County Airport. The pilot got out of his seat, walked to the mid-section of the aircraft and helped his only passenger deplane. Carmen may have been simply going to retrieve Mickey and bring him back home, but she looked like she was on a hunting trip and she was the bait. After Diane ran off, Carmen took the initiative, or perhaps created a scheme, by which she was certain she could get Mickey back—one way or another. The short, strapless, bright red dress fit her tight body like a glove. The pilot handed Carmen her small travel bag and shoulder bag, and directed her to one of the buildings. A mustachioed, middle-aged man dressed in boots, blue jeans, and a cowboy hat met her at the door.

"Mornin' ma'am. I'm Lew. You must be Carmen, the young lady the folks from Rub-a-Dub called me about."

"That would be correct. Do you have my car ready?"

Lew was one who was inclined to make conversation. Carmen continued to get straight to the point.

"I'm in a terrible hurry, and I'm not one to chat it up, so can you give me the keys and be done with it?"

"Yes, ma'am," Lew replied, tipping his hat back and scratching his neck in reaction to Carmen's brusque attitude. "It's right over there," he said, pointing toward a blue Buick sedan.

Covering her mouth in disbelief, Carmen said, "There must be a mistake. I can't drive that."

"Ma'am, it's got automatic everything. Ought to do you just fine."

"No, you don't understand," she continued. "I am not driving that! Do I look like a woman who would drive *that*?"

Lew was beginning to get flustered at this point. He was caught between providing a service to a long-time friend and loyal customer, Toot, and taking Carmen across his knee and spanking her.

"No ma'am, you look more like a Lamborghini kind of gal, but I don't have one of those. I have *that*," he said nodding toward the blue Buick.

Scanning around the dozen or so cars on the lot, Carmen pointed toward an SLK Mercedes convertible that was the same fire engine red as her dress.

"What about that one?"

"That one's spoken for, ma'am, as are all of the rest of the vehicles here. The blue Buick is yours. That's the best I can do for you on such short notice."

"So, what will Toot say when I tell him this is the best you can do for me?"

Lew didn't want a confrontation, and there was nothing kind nor constructive he could say in response to her question.

"That's what I thought," Carmen said as she turned and walked to the Mercedes. The keys were in the ignition. After starting the car and revving the engine twice, she retracted the convertible top and pulled her hair back, fastening it with a scrunchy.

Lew made no attempt to stop her. He knew it would be futile. He'd take the matter up with Toot later.

Pulling up next to him, Carmen said, "My name is Carmen Julietta Emmanuel de los Santos. Don't ever forget that name."

She then sped out of the parking lot, her wheels squealing.

"Nice to have met you, ma'am. Name's Lew…"

IT WAS THE MORE or less fast and effortless drive that Toot had described from the Harrison County Airport to the small, unincorporated settlement called Gray. However, a vehicle involved in an overnight traffic accident at the intersection had knocked the directional signs down. Carmen knew one of the landmarks along the way was Potters Point. Off to the side of the road was a hotel and resort, a store called Potters Point Sundries, and what looked like a beer joint named Mick's Place. With two familiar names in one location, she had to be close and thought this looked like a good place to get directions.

Carmen pulled to a stop in front of the store and got out. A maintenance man stopped painting trim to stare, as did several men sitting in pick-up trucks in the parking lot. She knew she was being watched and made sure her walk caused each man to have immoral thoughts about her. Spotting a lone, nicely-dressed, attractive, middle-aged woman behind a jewelry counter, she headed over to ask directions.

"Hi," the woman greeted her visitor. "Can I help you with something?"

"Actually, I need directions."

"Okay, we give those. What are you looking for?"

"It's not so much a *what* as it is a *who*. I'm trying to find the residence off of FM 727 where I could find a man named Mickey Rollins. Do you know him?"

"Sure do," came a tentative answer. "I know all the locals up here," she replied as the phone began to ring. "Forgive me while I take this. I'm the only one here right now."

"Go right ahead," Carmen said, as she scanned the trinkets and souvenirs in the jewelry case.

"Potters Point Sundries. Yes, this is Laura. Drew! How ya been? Good...good. How's Katie? Pregnant? Again? Thought you two figured out what was causing that. Hey, hey, you go, man. Uh huh, uh huh. Twenty bags of ice, twenty pounds of hamburger, buns...okay, two dozen brats, four fryers, two sides of ribs...you want pork or beef? Tater salad? All we have is mustard. Two charcoals. Beer...my choice...thanks for trusting my taste. Man, when's the party? Thanks. Hey, I'll try to be there. I'll have all of this ready in a couple of hours. Say 'Hey' to Katie. Bye."

Turning her attention back to Carmen, Laura asked, "So, you're a friend of Mickey's?"

"What business is that of yours?" Carmen replied.

Boundaries

It was the wrong response, and it unsettled Laura to no end. It came as no shock that such a young and beautiful woman would be pursuing Mickey, but she wasn't about to have her face rubbed in it. The cat fight was on.

"Uh, there are a lot of things up here that are my business. Taking care of my friends and neighbors is just one such undertaking. I don't mean to be rude, but I don't give out detailed information unless I get a little in return. I don't know the first thing about you except that you dress like an Italian prostitute. On the other hand, my Dodge 3500 can drive right over your shitty little convertible. Oh, and did I mention that Mickey is a dear friend?"

Laura ended her sortie with a smile on her face.

"Yes, but of course I could tell by the way you dress that you are quite the fashion expert. And you say you are a dear friend of Mickey's? Oh, you must mean that you are another castaway. I've heard stories that he has left behind a long trail of female destruction."

That remark hurt. Carmen could see it in Laura's face.

"You wouldn't want me to miss his birthday party, would you? I'm jumping out of his cake."

"Considering his birthday is in July and this is March, you're either very early or very late. Which is it? Oh, I hope you're not *late*. Mickey doesn't want children."

"How odd? As his daughter's nanny, I never sensed anything but love between him, his wife, and his little girl."

Laura had enough.

"Look, sweet-cheeks, this could go on all day. I'm way beyond the point of not giving you any information about Mickey so I think you should leave. And please, don't come back soon."

"Have it your way. I'll find someone intelligent who can give me the directions I need. Too bad your experience with Mickey left such a bad taste. I always thought he…tasted quite good."

Gripping the molding on the counter as Carmen left, Laura shook her head in disbelief at the abrupt meeting and conversation that had just taken place as she told herself, "Lord, what did I do today to deserve this? I got up, I ate breakfast, I've been nice to everyone."

She picked up the phone and dialed Back East to see if Mickey was still there, but there was no answer. She wasn't about to show Carmen any trace of the pain she inflicted, but seeing two women involved with Mickey at a time when he had been so far removed from her life for so many years was a shock to her system. On top of that, he was now supposedly married and a father.

Laura watched as, instead of driving off, Carmen flagged down a local cop who had just driven into the store's parking lot.

"Come on Gerome, don't tell her anything. Tell her to get lost."

No sooner had Carmen come within a few feet of the patrol car than she dropped her keys on the pavement, bent over to pick them up, and deliberately put on a lingerie show for anyone looking at her from either direction.

"Unbelievable!" Laura said out loud. "What a slut!"

It wasn't long before Carmen was making conversation with the deputy, and he was pointing down the highway in the direction of Back East. Having acquired the information she set out to get, Carmen gave the deputy a brief pat on his shoulder, evoking a smile, and then returned to her car. Moments later, she took off in the SLK heading south. The deputy got out of his vehicle, chatted and laughed with a couple of guys in the parking lot who got the other end of the show and then headed into the store.

"What's up, Laura?"

"Gerome, do you ever think with anything but your dick?"

"Oh, did you see that show out there?"

"I saw a grown man make a jackass out of himself."

"Come on, Laura. She just wanted some information."

"No, she wanted directions to Back East. I refused to give them to her. Did you tell her how to get there?"

Gerome lost his silly grin, rocked back and forth from leg to leg for a moment, and said nothing.

"Dork!"

He hung his head low, acknowledging his misdeed.

"Go after her, and see what's going on. I'm stuck here until Lisa gets back from lunch. I called the cabin, but nobody answered. She said she was looking for Mickey, but her story didn't hang together. She fabricated his birth date. She told a whopper of a lie that he was married. She even said she was a nanny for Mickey's kid."

"Mickey's got a kid?"

"Of course not! The only thing Mickey hates more than marriage is children."

"She hasn't done anything wrong, has she?"

Laura squinted at Gerome. He realized, once more, why he should never question her judgment.

"Go after her or you can stay here and mind the store. What'll it be, Gerome!"

"Alright, Laura. I'll do it for you. But, you owe me."

"Yeah, right. Go do your job. If she's on my place, shoot first and ask questions later."

The deputy dutifully departed and headed out after his quarry. Once he was gone, Laura picked up her phone and dialed.

"Roger Delaney, please. Tell him it's Laura Chase. I don't care if he's on the phone, go get him."

She paced back and forth nervously behind the counter until a familiar voice got on the phone.

"Laura, it's Roger. How can I help you today?"

"Guess who's back in my cabin?"

"Oh, that's an easy question—Mickey."

"Do you know something?"

"I'm on the other line with Toot right now. There's some big problem at the ranch, and Mickey's at the center of it."

"How can he be at the center of something there when he's up here?"

"You actually saw him?"

"No shit! And with some naked woman at Back East!"

"Oh dear, then what Toot said must be true—he said he might have gone to the cabin with…a girlfriend."

"Roger, you're a lousy liar. On top of that, I just ran into another bimbo on her way out to see Mickey, dressed like I-don't-know-what, and telling me a bunch of bullshit."

"That's Carmen, his…nanny."

Laura held the phone away from her head and stared at it for a moment as if what she heard was unreal.

"His nanny? You mean, he has a child?" Laura asked, her heart torn open.

"Are you sitting down?"

"Just tell me, Roger!"

"Well, he came back to the ranch some time ago with a woman he claims to be his wife, Diane, an Asian gal, and a little girl who he claims is his daughter, Gigi."

Seething, Laura said, "Roger, he can't be married. We both know…"

"Laura, let me get back to you. I think Toot's got a problem that needs immediate attention. You just sit tight and don't do or say anything you'll regret. I'll call you back within the hour."

"Who are you working for, me or Mickey?"

"Now Laura, you know I represent the entire estate, and to the best of my ability, I try to take care of all interested parties. We've all done well for many years, and I don't see why we can't sort all of this out. So, just be calm. He's never produced any of the documents I have asked him for to verify matrimony or paternity. She may just be the current lady in his life and her child."

"What about the Asian gal?'"

"She seems nice enough. Mickey says she's some sort of physical therapist helping his wife who is rehabilitating from a traumatic injury of some type."

"And you believe all of this?"

"Let's just say I've given Mickey the benefit of the doubt."

"Roger, we're talking about Mickey…Mickey Rollins.

"Laura, like I said, I'll get back to you."

Boundaries

"Don't bother, Roger. I'll be in Kerrville tomorrow."

"Laura…"

She hung up on him and threw the phone across the store.

THE DIRECTIONS THE DEPUTY had given to Carmen were spot on. He obviously was very familiar with the location. After driving down the freshly-travelled road and pulling up to the front of the cabin, she honked the horn twice to see if anybody was there. No one responded. Either nobody was home, or someone was inside, and that person was occupied. Hoping to make an impression on Mickey if he answered the door, Carmen let her hair down, quickly ran a brush through it, touched up her make-up, and donned some glossy red lipstick. It took her all of thirty seconds.

It was a good thing she wore flat-soled shoes as the boards on the front steps had plenty of gaps through which to poke a spiked heel. There was no doorbell, but there was a knocker in the shape of a small metal oil derrick, and it was heavy enough to make a loud thump each time Carmen let it strike the door plate. When she was sufficiently convinced nobody was home, she used the key that Lupita had given her to let herself in.

"Hello, Mickey? Are you here? It's Carmen." She slowly made her way into the kitchen where she set down her bags on the island. Looking around, she said to herself, "Not bad…not a bad place at all." Walking to the bottom of the stairway, she again called out, "Mickey?" Next to the stairway was another door. It opened to an empty garage. "Huh. Guess nobody's here. Drat!"

Seeing a backpack on the floor in the living room, Carmen walked over, picked it up, and rummaged through it. Finding a hidden pocket, she unzipped it and felt something solid. Her face lit up as she pulled out Mickey's iPad. She turned on the power and in short order an icon appeared in the center that read PicoPoint. Holding the device close to her chest, she began spinning around jubilantly.

"Okay, got to be quick," she said as she reached into her shoulder bag and pulled out a tiny laptop computer. After powering up, she linked to a wi-fi connection on the laptop, launched an application and began transferring the contents of Mickey's most recent life's work. Suddenly, there was a knock on the door. All Carmen could see through the etched glass was a tall figure wearing a hat.

"Yes?" Carmen answered.

"Hello. It's Deputy Deslatte from the Sheriff's Department. Can you open the door, ma'am?"

Quickly grabbing the laptop and iPad, Carmen put them in a cabinet above the bar. Seeing a series of family photos, she took out a picture of herself that was in her introductory folder, removed a picture of Ruby from its frame, and replaced it with hers. After quickly hiding Ruby's picture, she placed the frame next to Mickey's on a bookcase beside the bar.

The deputy knocked again. "Ma'am, is everything alright?"

"Yes, just a moment. I'm getting dressed."

She quickly took off her dress leaving her in only her bra and panties. She then put on a man's button-down dress shirt that she found draped over the living room sofa. She left a few strategic buttons unfastened, allowing the shirt to gape open at the top, then went to the door.

Opening it slowly, she said, "Hello, again. I was hoping you were Mickey."

"Ma'am. Right about now, I wish I was Mickey. Since I'm not, if I may ask, what's your relationship to Mr. Rollins?"

"She sent you, didn't she?"

"Beg your pardon?"

"The lady back at the store where you gave me directions. I don't think she liked me."

"Don't worry about what she thinks, ma'am. So, your relationship with Mr. Rollins?"

"If you don't mind telling me first, who was that woman back there?" She seemed a little bit protective of Mickey."

"That's Laura, his ex-wife."

Carmen hadn't heard that part of the family history yet, and it took her by surprise. Thinking quickly, she said, "I suspected it was her. Mickey's told me of her, but I've not seen any pictures or met her before."

"Ma'am, your relationship?"

"Please, come in and make yourself comfortable," Carmen suggested, heading away from the deputy and into the kitchen.

Deslatte had no option but to follow.

Opening up the refrigerator and taking an instant inventory, she offered, "Can I get you some water? A soda? Perhaps some juice?"

"No thanks, ma'am. Do you have any identification?"

Carmen walked over to the bar and stood in front of it where the deputy could see her picture on the bookcase with Mickey's.

"I'm Mrs. Rollins. Is there some sort of problem?"

It worked.

"No, Mrs. Rollins. I think there's been a misunderstanding. Did you tell Laura you were the nanny for Mickey's child?"

Giggling, Carmen replied, "Yes. Look, I thought she might be his ex-wife, and I didn't want to hurt her feelings. I mean, look at me. How do you think she would have felt like if I told her I was Mickey's wife?"

The deputy smiled, understanding the compliment Carmen had just paid herself. Tipping his hat back on his head asked, "Is Mickey here?"

"Not right now. He doesn't know I'm here. I'm surprising him and you'll blow it if he sees your car here. I was just about to park mine in the garage." Putting on her final touch of charm, she walked up to the deputy and asked, "What was your name again?"

"Deslatte. Gerome Deslatte."

"French, am I right?" She was standing so close he could feel her breath when she spoke, and he began to fidget nervously.

"Cajun. Born in Louisiana, ma'am. Reckon I'd best be leaving. Wouldn't want to ruin a surprise. I'll just let myself out."

"Nice meeting you. Thank you for checking me out…I mean…you know what I mean."

"Have a good day," he said tipping his hat once again, then exiting. He closed the door behind him.

"What an idiot," Carmen said under her breath.

Rushing back to the cabinet, Carmen pulled out the laptop and iPad. The transfer was complete. She quickly disconnected the device from her laptop, turned it off, and returned it to Mickey's backpack, trying to return everything to the condition she found it. She then pulled her phone from her bag and dialed. Soon, a man answered.

"Hello?"

"Did I wake you?"

"Yes, that's alright. What's going on?"

"I have them."

"The files?"

"Yes."

"And the application?"

"Everything."

"Maggie, you're spectacular. I knew you could do it. What about the desktop files?"

"I don't have them yet. Those will be easy. I took advantage of Mickey's carelessness and got these files first."

"You need to get out of Texas before Carmen shows up. Be sure to transfer all the files to the secure IP address I gave you."

"Absolutely. I'll be in touch tomorrow. When are you…"

There was another knock at the door.

"Someone's here. I have to go."

"Be sure you protect that information until you send it off."

"Rest assured. Goodnight, my love."

"I love you too, Maggie."

Boundaries

Carmen looked at the figure through the glass once more. From the height, body shape and what she could make out of the clothing, she suspected it was Laura. Assuming she might need to turn up the heat in order to chase her off, she unbuttoned the shirt entirely before opening the door.

"Hello, again."

"You and I need to talk," Laura said, pushing her way past Carmen. "I spoke with Deputy Deslatte in the driveway. He says you're Mickey's wife. Is this true?"

"Yes, I'm Diane."

"I see Mickey's robbing the cradle now. How old are you?"

"Twenty-four."

"So you could easily be his daughter."

"And yours."

It took every ounce of self-control for Laura not to slap Carmen after that remark.

"You need to leave…now."

"But, I'm here to see Mickey."

"This isn't Mickey's place, it's my place. Now leave."

"Aren't you a little out of bounds asking me to leave? After all, I'm Mickey's wife."

Laura walked up to Carmen and delicately touched her face as she said, "I've got a newsflash for you sweet-cheeks. I'm still Mickey's wife, and you have a problem. Now, for the last time, get the hell out of my house."

Chapter 40

"Toot, help me get her back to Mickey's office so I can start treatment."

"No, we need to call 911. She's having way too many of these seizures, Suki."

"Toot! This is just the same thing she always experiences. She is stressed emotionally after what happened this morning. Stress can trigger a seizure."

"Momma," Gigi said, beginning to cry at the sight of her mother lying on the floor and sensing the tension of the situation.

Toot whisked her up into his arms and cradled her as he said, "Momma's gonna be alright, baby-girl. She's taking a nap right now. Suki and Toot need to help her get into bed."

He looked toward Suki for guidance.

"Take her to Lupita for a few minutes, then come back and help me."

"Suki, we need to call for help."

"If you bring someone from the outside into the picture, they are going to take Gigi away from here."

What Suki suggested was far from true, but she needed to put the fear of God in Toot so he'd obey her without question. After hesitating for only a moment, he left the room with Gigi. While he was gone, Suki dampened a washcloth and rubbed it gingerly over Diane's forehead and cheeks.

"You will be alright, Diane. I plan on taking good care of you, my friend."

Toot came back in what seemed like just seconds to find Suki holding Diane compassionately. It gave him a tenuous sense of reassurance that Suki was truly concerned about Diane.

"How's she doin'?" He asked in a breaking voice.

"She is as she always is when this takes place. We simply need to get her back to the table in Mickey's office so I can treat her."

"You can do that? Shouldn't we make an attempt to call Mickey?"

"Go ahead and try. I doubt he will answer. However, with or without Mickey, she needs to be treated. I know what I am doing. I have been assisting Mickey for a long time now."

Toot dialed Mickey's number and let it ring until it went into voice mail.

"Let me try Carmen."

Suki hadn't figured he would be that persistent, but had no choice other than to let Toot make the call. Her phone went unanswered as well.

"I thought you said she had specific instructions and would be in phone contact!"

"Toot, focus! Help me get her to the table."

Reluctantly, Toot did as asked, and carried Diane to the table in Mickey's office. Laying her carefully on it, he asked, "Now what?"

"Now I need you to leave."

"You're kiddin', right? I mean, I'm not leavin' her."

"Well, Toot, I am not proceeding with treatment while you are in the room. What she undergoes is a personal matter. The therapy is not something Mickey wants to share beyond me. He will not even discuss the particulars with the Oversight Committee. She has a seizure, we administer a therapy, and she recovers. It is all very simple. Besides, someone needs to look after Gigi. I think she needs you more than anyone right now," she said, appealing to his strong feelings for the youngster.

"Whatever you say," he said hesitantly. "But, promise me you'll come get me as soon as you're done." Reaching out to touch Suki, he continued, "I want to talk to both of you."

To put him completely at ease, Suki leaned over and kissed Toot on the cheek and said, "She will be alright, I swear."

He smiled and gave a sigh of relief—unaware of what was about to take place.

Once Toot was out of the room, Suki closed and locked the door. She then walked back over to her unresponsive friend.

"Well now Diane, we have some unfinished business to take care of," she said, squeezing Diane's cheeks in such a manner that her lips puckered. Turning her head to the side, she continued, "There is just so much to do...so much to talk about. Mickey always talks to us when we are treating you."

She began undressing Diane.

"First, he hypnotizes me. Oops, somebody forgot to tell him that I can no longer be hypnotized. I simply amaze myself each time we administer his therapy. We go through this same bullshit routine. It is mind-boggling that he has not discovered my ruse after all this time. He hypnotizes me, then he tells me what to think about in order to focus my emotions and thoughts. Then *I* decide what messages I want to send to you, irrespective of what he wants. That is when he 'lights you up.' Yes, 'lights you up,' is what he calls it. Then it begins—our minds blend.

"Why am I undressing you? Because he always takes our clothes off. Mine first, needless to say. Do you know he has sex with us each time we go through this process?" Throwing Diane's blouse and bra on the floor, she continued, "It is really quite pathetic. After all, he thinks we are both unconscious—and for that matter, you are. Sometimes he just has sex with me. He is getting up there in years, Diane. Yes, at times he has just enough energy for one of us, and I am always the one who gets him. Did you hear me? You are second—always. He thinks he is such a spectacular lover. What he does not realize is that I am a ten-times better actor. He does not realize I am cognizant of his actions. I think that is why I enjoy it so much more than when he makes love to me when he knows I am awake."

After throwing Diane's shorts and panties on the floor in the same pile, Suki removed her own clothing, folding them neatly on the chair. She then got out some massage oil and began rubbing it all over Diane's body.

"He never does this to you any more, does he? No. That is up to me. All the touching, all the passion you feel comes from me. You are generally quite deprived of affection, but then, you do not need to experience it, do you? Of course not, I provide all of the emotional nourishment you need to lead a satisfying life. Yes, you heard me…I give and give, and you take and take. To be honest with you, Diane, it is getting very old…very old indeed. I think it is time to bring this partnership to an end.

"I realized when I undertook this endeavor that it was a major commitment of my life. But, remember what I told you on the plane that time we took the shopping trip to Bangkok? I said something to the effect, 'There are some men and women who do not always hold life as sacred, especially if it stands in the way of wealth.' I never knew I could describe myself so succinctly."

After putting some oil in both of her hands, Suki began rubbing it delicately all over her own body as she went on to say, "You have been useful, Diane. Oh yes, you have earned the attention I pay you. You see…Genevieve was another such individual. She was quite the nemesis, actually. I had to find a way to first use her, then trap her, then kill her. When Mickey called me and suggested the vacation, the plan just fell into place. True, I have had to improvise on occasion, but for the most part we have been executing my plan the entire time I have known you. It would have been impossible to reach the point where we are without such a perfect victim as you."

Suki once again began to gently caress Diane.

"I had to dump Bates. He did not hold up his end of the deal. At one time, he was one of the best transporters of human cargo in Asia. I used him frequently, but not as much as Genevieve. I feel that is why his loyalty toward me suffered.

"This will really come as a shock to you. You have probably heard the adage, 'What a small world it is in which we live?' Speaking of small, do you know how I discovered Carmen for you? She had a sister, Magdeliene, who was, how should I say it, troubled. She had an awful rebellious streak, not to mention she was also a drug addict. But, she was beautiful, as was her twin sister. That is the perfect profile for one of my girls. She brought me four hundred fifty thousand Euros. You say 'what?' You heard me, nearly half a million Euros. The high bidder was a gentleman from Silicon Valley in California. He was an entrepreneurial type named Constantine. Mickey gave me his name.

"Anyway, continuing with Bates, he began to exhibit human qualities that did not serve us particularly well. One, in particular, truly offended me—I think he fell in love with you. He had sex with you, then he fell in love. I simply do not understand. He had sex with so many of the women he transported for us. Why did you affect him differently? Anyway, I paid him well, and he is sworn to silence for life. He is out of the picture, sailing the seas alone, carrying with him the knowledge of who truly killed Genevieve. Maybe you will meet him again someday after you are released from prison or whatever institution you end up in. It would be a proper ending for Gigi to know who her father is. What? You did not know? Well, maybe I should tell you that my little bit of detective work proved that Mickey's DNA did not match up with Gigi's whatsoever, and she doesn't look a bit Asian like the two men who raped you on Maribella—that would leave Bates as the father. Mickey should never have left obstetrics in the hands of a bunch of mad scientists. The likelihood of them giving him accurate information about your pregnancy, when I could influence the course of events with a few thousand Euros, was infinitesimally small. I wonder how Mickey will take to the news that he is not a daddy?"

Suki's massage strokes began getting heavier.

"Right after I had you kill my grandfather, I thought to myself, 'this is a relationship that has possibilities.' What? You do not remember? Oh, that is right. You were still recovering from your injury. It was so perfect. My grandfather and his 'hands-on' approach to therapy—so arcane, so passé. Ricardo was right, he had all the information he needed to diagnose your injury, but my grandfather could not keep his hands off of the patient. It was an ideal set of conditions. I could not believe it, and I certainly was not going to pass up the opportunity to end the torture he put me through."

Suki leaned over and rubbed her chest on Diane's. Their breasts slid across one another's several times. The movement ended when Suki kissed Diane on the lips.

"I enjoyed you as a lover, Diane. You really were quite the companion. My grandfather was about as close as we are now when you killed him. Did you feel his breath? Did you smell his breath? He always had atrocious halitosis. It could make me gag. Oh, not that way...the bad way. How many times he would be lying on top of me, and all I could think of was how bad his breath smelled.

"I listened as he began to step back. He had a habit of retreating, then advancing toward the patient again and repeating what he had just done. He was absolutely predictable. That was when I had you grab the scalpel. It was pretty good, am I right? I mean, you got him in the heart with just one thrust. I did it all with my eyes closed because you were my eyes. I do not think either Mickey or Ricardo believed what you had done—they had created the perfect monster. I could never have stabbed him myself. After all, I loved him. He was my grandfather."

Suki took a soft towel and rubbed the oil first off Diane's body, then off of her own. Going to what Mickey called his control table, she clicked on an application that was on the monitor. A message window popped up that said 'connected to primary.'

"How is that, Diane? Does this hurt you at all?" Suki asked, stroking Diane's forehead. "I never feel it, but then, I am on the other end of the messaging. Mostly I am sending, but you know what? Occasionally I take from you. You heard me. *I* take from *you*. Mickey does not know about it. He has never learned that aspect. He is so behind the technology. I can feel your need, your euphoria as I send you my thoughts and memories. Then the cascade kicks in, but I deprive you of what you want. You want more and you want it faster, but I will not let that happen. That is when I feel your pain the most. It is utterly exhilarating.

"So now, Diane, we need to rewrite some history, so pay attention to what I am saying. We need to, let me think...yes, we need to make it clear to Sheriff what's-his-name that it was you who killed Genevieve. There is a lot of detail you are missing, but I can make the picture absolutely unambiguous. And as for my grandfather, you killed him too, I am afraid. All of those moments, all of those memories, they will soon be restored. You will be so thrilled that you now have recall of all those times, there will be no way you will be able to withhold that information from the authorities. I am afraid, Diane, you may be in serious trouble with the law.

"Oh, and as for Toot, sadly he raped you. Yes, I am afraid he took advantage of you after the attack at The Falls. You paid him with your body for your salvation. I will make certain that is what you recall. You will threaten to press charges. After all, you are full of his DNA. His attorney will make up some story challenging your memory and stability, and Toot will go free. That said, the damage in your relationship with Toot will be done. He will no longer love you. He will probably not even like you. He will, however, join a growing faction that is certain you are crazy. That will leave it up to me to console this poor, wrongly-accused man. He will once again be mine, Diane, and he will remain mine. Then, when Mickey finds out you were violated, I suspect he will no longer want anything to do with you either. And we both know Mickey. He may despise Toot, but you will be the one blamed for his impropriety. He is such a jealous and selfish man. Oh my, I may have both of them when I am done, and you will have neither. I like that. Yes, I really like that.

"And speaking of crazy, the little voice you hear? The vision of the young woman you see—Sylvie? That is working out spectacularly. Yes. Hearing voices; seeing imaginary people. I need orange juice...no, keep the OJ away. The Committee is going to think you have totally lost it. I think it is called schizo-effective disorder mixed with a little bipolar mania. Yes, dear Sylvie is about to tell you all kinds of secrets. Of course, they will all be wrong. But then, we are creating a new history, so who is to say? You know what else, your handwriting matches mine identically now—or at least to the most casual observer, maybe even to the trained eye. I have this little journal that I am going to start for you. It will come in handy some day. Yes, some doctor will find it and he will think to himself, this lady is a complete basket case. There will be nothing you can do about it at that point. They may even lock you up and throw away the key."

After crawling on top of Diane's body, Suki laid on her face-to-face holding her head so that her face was pointing straight up at hers and said, "There is one final detail, Diane, that has to be settled once and for all. Gigi is mine. True, you and Bates are the biological parents, but I carried her in my body for eight months and twenty-three days. That is something you will never know about. I will never let you have any sense of my satisfaction. Do you know what it feels like to have a child grow inside of you? No, and you never will. Do you know what it feels like to be kicked from inside your womb? No, and you never will. Do you know what it feels like to hear a heart other than your own beating from inside your body? No, and you never will. Do you know what it feels like to push that baby out into the world and to hear her first cry? No, and you never will. Do you know what it feels like to breast feed a baby and deliver her first and most important nourishment? No, and you never will. Those are my memories, and all the emotions that go with those memories will remain with me. I am Gigi's mother, not you. You and Bates were nothing more than pistol and stamen. I gave birth. When the dust settles, Gigi will be in my care. You heard me. I will have your men and Gigi. You, on the other hand, will have the bare walls of your new habitat to look at."

Hopping off of Diane, Suki walked to the computer and clicked on the application command once more. A message window appeared that said, 'connected to host.' She then walked over to the head of the table to Diane, knelt down on a thick pillow, and placed her forehead against Diane's. A small red light appeared in both women's ears. The therapy was underway...for the final time.

Chapter 41

The small electric motor moved Mickey's bass boat slowly toward the cove at Back East. The headwind was strong enough that it kept him almost stationary. If it weren't for the fact that he was making a zigzag pattern as he made his way back, there would have been no forward progress at all.

In the short time he had been fishing, Mickey had managed to catch two nice-sized largemouth bass—one a four-pounder and the other at least a six. That was more than enough for him to eat tonight, which was a good thing considering he wasn't alone any longer. Laura was waiting for him at the dock.

"Like your black eye," she shouted. "Rough sex?"

"It doesn't get any better than this," Mickey replied to what he saw as provocation from Laura. "A man, his boat, fishing, a quiet, secluded cabin on a fabulous lake, and his ex-wife. God damn, you just don't get it, do you?"

"Do I need to remind you I spend more time here than you?"

"No, and please don't remind me now how much time *you* spend at *my* cabin."

"Do you like the colors of the new interior paint that I chose?"

Mickey was silent.

"How about the kitchen? New cabinets, new appliances, sub-zero fridge."

Mickey looked away from Laura.

"Let me quiz you on something you probably did look at. Did you see your mother's quilts on all the beds? They've all been recently dry-cleaned. I hope you took them off before you…"

"Alright!" Mickey cried out. "I give up! You're numero uno, okay?"

He threw her a rope.

"Here, tie me up."

"Do I get to pick the tree?" Laura replied, a coy smile growing across her face.

It took a few moments, but eventually Mickey smiled as well.

"I guess I walked right into that one."

Nodding, Laura agreed and said, "Uh huh…"

She tied the boat to a mooring before extending her hand out for Mickey to take. At first he hesitated—sort of a reflex as when Lucy would hold the football for Charlie Brown. But, after a few moments, he took her hand, and she helped him up to the dock.

"Why do I get the feeling you didn't come here to see if I had a fishing license?"

"It's been a long time since we talked about things, Mick. I wanted to talk to you…alone, and preferably in a pseudo-neutral setting like the cabin."

"In other words, you want to discuss our pseudo-marriage."

"At some point, we need to discuss our marriage. Right now, I want to catch up on your life, Mick. Maybe you would like to know about what's going on in mine. It's been a long time since we talked about anything at all. I remember you saying goodbye to me seven years ago while I was sitting in your old Land Cruiser. You shook my hand, Mick. I loved you all those years, and I got a freakin' handshake."

"I thought you didn't want to discuss our marriage."

"I'm not talking about our marriage, Mickey! I'm talking about feelings, emotions, and being a part of someone."

"So, you are talking about our marriage."

At that point, Laura put her hands up as if to say she had heard enough, turned and walked away. After taking about ten steps, she stopped and slowly turned around. Tears were beginning to run down her cheeks.

"I promised myself I wouldn't let you get to me this time, Mick. I had it all figured out. I know who you are and how you are. I was going to roll with the punches—hell, I figured I'd let you walk all over me just to spend some time with you again."

"I'm going to fillet these babies so we can have something to eat tonight."

"There you go. I hold out an olive branch, and you completely ignore me so you can fillet your stinking…" She shook her head trying to recall his exact words, then said, "Did you say, 'so *we* can have something to eat tonight,' as in the two of us?"

"Yeah, that's right. You wanted to spend some time with me, and I have dinner in the works. You might as well stick around."

"What's the catch?"

Mickey laughed as he said, "Nobody can do double-jeopardy like you, Laura."

Realizing she had put Mickey in a no-win situation, Laura decided to press on by asking, "Fine then. I want to spend time with you, but do you want to spend time with me?"

"Here, hold these," he said, handing Laura the fish. Instead of giving Laura a direct answer, Mickey reached into a small ice chest he had with him, pulled out a cold bottle of beer, twisted off the top and handed the bottle to her. He smiled as he walked past her, taking the fish as he intentionally brushed her shoulder with his. After he had passed, she raised her eyebrows acknowledging the fact that at least for now, she had some of Mickey's time. Quickly running to catch up with him, she came up to his side, matched his stride, and even slipped her hand into his rear pocket without any objection. With the arm of her free hand, Laura wiped the tears from her face—tears of joy.

"So, what's new with you?"

"You mean aside from the black eye and the naked woman I was with?"

"Look, Mick, I want to know about you. Work with me. I hear you're back at the ranch."

"Who have you been talking to?"

"Roger."

"What else did he say?"

Realizing they weren't in for any such thing as casual conversation, Laura answered truthfully, "He said you were married and had a daughter."

"Good old Roger," he said, reaching the back porch of the cabin

"What's he supposed to do, Mick? He's an attorney. Do you want him to lie?"

Walking up next to a large barbecue pit at the end of the porch, he tossed the fish onto a wooden slab with a splat, looked at Laura, and replied, "If that's what it takes to look after my interests."

"He's looking after *our* interests." After setting her beer down, she asked, "So how does Toot fit into the picture?"

"Toot runs the ranch. Toot's...Toot." Mickey hesitated a moment as he watched Laura's reaction to his short response. "But then, you know exactly what I'm talking about, don't you."

"What's that supposed to mean?"

Proceeding to cut the heads off of both fish as he spoke, he replied, "You know damn well what I mean."

And she did. She moved across from him so he had to look down in order to avoid making eye contact as she spoke.

"Does it bother you that I dated Toot a couple of times? Is that why you've avoided me all these years?"

Mickey stuck a knife into one of the heads, using it to fling the head across the yard.

"You're still pissed. I mean, right now, you're pissed, aren't you?"

Mickey stuck a knife into the other fish head and launched it twice as far in the opposite direction.

"Jesus, Mick, this isn't high school anymore!"

Still not making eye contact with Laura, Mickey stuck the filet knife into the belly of the headless fish near its tail and made three quick slices.

"Mark Mendelsoln," was the only thing he said in response to Laura's remarks.

"Mark?" Laura shouted, throwing her arms into the air. "Now, you bring up Mark? Mickey, we'd been separated for two fucking years by then. What did you want me to do, join a convent?"

Mickey scraped a handful of fish guts out with his bare hand and threw them to the side. Laura insisted on getting his attention, so she grabbed his wrist with her left hand while forcibly removing the knife with her right. She then stuck the knife at least an inch into the wood. It was only then that Mickey made eye contact with her.

"You didn't wait for me," he said. "You just jumped in the sack with the first rich Jew that came along."

Laura was speechless. She couldn't believe her ears. It wasn't long before she couldn't believe her eyes either.

"Are you crying?"

Mickey didn't answer, but he wiped his eyes with his sleeves.

Speaking slowly and deliberately, Laura said as she reached for his hand, "Mick, you walked away from me, remember?"

Struggling to remain composed, he replied, "I thought you needed some space so you could get on with your music. You were good, you know."

"Lame. Really lame, Mick. Don't even think of making our break-up my fault."

"Plus, I got tied up in grad school. And besides, you were different from me. We didn't click."

"No!" Laura shouted, now starting to cry herself. "We complemented each other you idiot! That's what was so beautiful about our marriage—that's what could be so beautiful about our marriage again."

It took a few seconds, but the two fell into each other's arms forming an arch over the half-filleted fish. Eventually, the two moved to the side so they could fully embrace one another. They rested their heads on each other's shoulder as they came to grips with an emptiness of nearly thirty years. After several minutes of holding one another, Laura began tugging at Mickey's memories.

"Do you remember those times we would go fishing at your grandparents' lake?"

"It was a stock tank, not a lake," he said in typical fashion, always needing to have the final say in everything.

"Whatever. Do you remember?"

"Oh, yeah. We did a lot more than fish, didn't we?" He answered, nodding his head.

"That's where we made love our first time, right on the bank," she replied, rocking her cheek against the curve of his neck.

"Do you remember the trucks driving by?" he asked. "Holy crap. What a place to do it—right on the bank of a stock tank next to the interstate highway. Thank God it was night."

"I didn't care," Laura said, laughing as she rubbed Mickey's back. "I do recall, however, getting a lot of mosquito bites in lots of strange places."

"You and me both."

There was a good interlude complete with chuckling.

"Do you recall my next period being late?"

"Yep. I also remember aging about six years during those seventeen days we waited. You never could do math."

"Hey, it wasn't math at that point. It was biology. We were just a couple of teenagers and my hormones were still all over the place. I never had a regular period until I got on the pill." Stepping back so she could see his expression, she asked, "Have you ever experienced an almost perfect moment in time?"

After reflecting for a moment, Mickey replied, "I've never given it a lot of thought."

"That time in our life—that was what I saw as our perfect moment in time. I've never felt closer to any man as I did at that time with you." Continuing to study Mickey's face, she continued, "I was madly in love with the man I thought was going to be the father of my baby. What would you have done if I'd been pregnant?"

"All I could think about was the licking Dub was going to give me when I told him you were pregnant. Mom would have simply passed out. They both thought you were the greatest thing—the daughter they never had. Admittedly, I was relieved when it turned out you were just late." Mickey took a moment to squeeze Laura tightly as he said, "I'm sorry if that wasn't the outcome you were hoping for."

"Well, at least I ended up with you…for a few years."

Mickey continued, "When I was nearing the ripe old age of fifty, I realized that there was something missing in my life—actually a couple of things. One was a child, the other was a companion."

"So, why didn't you just call me? We could have picked up where we left off," she said stroking his cheeks. "I never would have settled for anyone other than you, Mick. We could have adopted a child. Life would have been spectacular."

Mickey didn't respond at all, and Laura sensed the conversation had turned far too serious for him.

"Look at it this way, you already paid for one wedding, and we're still legally husband and wife. It wouldn't have cost you a cent."

Mickey released Laura, picked up the knife, and continued cleaning the fish. She thought for sure the exchange was over at that point and her heart fell into her stomach. Surprisingly, he resumed the tête-à-tête where they had left off.

"I'm not a very good catch, Laura. You deserve better."

Laura picked up her beer and took a drink, thinking hard about the best response.

"You can't make choices like that for another person, Mick. Individuals have to make their own—good and bad. Otherwise, there is nothing learned. Don't start thinking for others. The outcome is bound to be bad.

"I chose you when I was seventeen years old, Mick. I'm still yours as far as I'm concerned. The decision about where we go from here is up to you."

The pressure was too much for him. Glancing at his watch, he said, "Well, I guess I have twelve hours to think about it."

Laura set her bottle down on the cutting board with a thud, asking, "You're not starting this countdown shit, are you?"

"What do you mean?"

"Your infamous countdown to whatever. You always did that. We'd go on a two-week vacation, and you'd be saying, 'thirteen days left, twelve days left, eleven days left...' Semester break—you'd be saying, 'twenty days left, nineteen days left...' You drove me crazy."

"See, I'm not a good choice."

"No! What did that shrink tell you once? You just need to *be here now*. Everything you do isn't drawing you one step closer to an end. Everything you do is taking you toward a better tomorrow."

"Wow, that's profound. You should be a therapist," he said sarcastically.

Without thinking, Laura poured some of her beer over the four fillets, and Mickey followed her by sprinkling spices. For a moment, they froze as they both realized how naturally those small events happened. Even after all the years apart, making a meal together was still a part of their collective makeup. She put her hand on top of his and left it there for a few moments, igniting a lust and desire she hadn't experienced in a long time.

He looked at her just long enough to say, "I'm going to let these marinate while I take a shower. Can I get you another beer or a glass of wine?"

Mickey could see in Laura's eyes what she wanted, but he wasn't ready for that.

"Well, if you want one, help yourself. I'll be back in a short while," he said, slowly removing his hand from under hers.

She knew this might be her last chance to share all they once had, and she wasn't going to be denied that opportunity without a fight. Searching for another angle of attack, she asked, "Do you have a shirt I can slip into?" Turning around to display traces of blood and various fish remnants in the shape of handprints on her back, she added, "This one's a bit fishy."

"Sure, there should be something upstairs...but then you know that."

The two slowly made their way inside and, after putting the fish in the refrigerator, walked up the steps to the second floor, the pace set by Laura who was in front. Mickey studied her hips as they swayed back and forth with each ascending step. Her figure was as taut as it was when they were in college. At one point, she slowed such that he put his hand on her waist to encourage her onward. This time it was Mickey who felt the electricity.

Once at the top of the steps, Laura turned to the left toward one of the smaller bedrooms. Out of curiosity, Mickey followed. She opened the door to the walk-in closet in that room and looked about for a short while before spying what she was hunting for. She reached for an old rugby jersey and pulled it out.

"Remember this?" she asked, holding it in front of her and flipping it alternately from front to back then front again.

"My God. I can't believe that thing's still in one piece."

What Laura was holding was her team jersey. The men on the college rugby team had given one to each of their girlfriends. Over the right breast, 'Laura' was embroidered, and over the left was a Chief Illiniwek patch. Across the back was embroidered 'Mother Rucker.' The orange and blue striped shirt was as good as new. While Mickey stood mesmerized and speechless, Laura quickly removed her top, slipped the jersey on and pulled her hair out from under the collar.

"How's it look?" she asked while slowly twirling.

"You're beautiful."

Laura stepped back into the closet and pulled out another, much larger, orange and blue stripped jersey. This one was tattered and worn. It had the Chief patch on the left breast as well and the number '13' on the back.

"My old jersey," Mickey said, now thunderstruck. "Who kept all these things?"

"Your mom and I kept a lot of your belongings. I couldn't part with certain things, and those I could part with, she wouldn't. There are three closets full of Mickey Rollins memorabilia here at the cabin."

Mickey took the jersey from Laura and flipped it back and forth, smiling all the while. Pointing at a jagged tear about waist high on the right side, Mickey said, "Got that our last game against the Lions up in Chicago. Jersey ripped, I broke the tackle and scored the winning try." Holding the jersey close to his face, he said, "Still smells like beer and B-O."

Putting her face into the jersey, Laura said, "It smells like you." The look on her face showed an unmistakable blend of adoration, affection, and devotion.

Mickey sat totally overwhelmed on the bed, holding the jersey. Laura pulled up a chair, sat in front of him and held his hands.

"Now it's time we talked about this woman you are calling your wife."

Mickey didn't argue. He knew it was time to talk.

"What's her name?"

"Diane."

"That's a nice name," Laura said, trying to sound conciliatory. "Did you really marry her?"

He evaded giving a response for a moment, ultimately answering, "No. She was injured before we could get married."

"Why would she think she's married?" Laura asked, furrowing her eyebrows.

"Because that's what I have her believing."

Sitting up straight, reacting to Mickey's answer, she continued, "You mean you tricked her?"

"No. It's a really long story. The short version is this. She sustained a head injury that resulted in significant amnesia and physical disability. I've essentially been, for lack of a better term, rebuilding her for the last several years."

"I'm afraid to ask what you mean by that," Laura said with a serious expression on her face.

"And it's best that I not go into a lot of details right now. Let's just say the work I am doing on…I mean *with* Diane, is groundbreaking. I'm on the cusp of changing how those of us in the medical field deal with brain injury."

"So, somewhere along the way, you told her you were married."

"Yes. I've also told Roger and Toot the same thing, as well as everyone else in the community for that matter."

"Mickey, why on Earth would you do such a thing? That's a boldfaced lie. You know it's just a matter of time before you get busted. You never made such a claim with what's-her-name—Maria—and you lived with her forever."

"It just made sense at the time. I needed to disguise our work to some degree with our relationship and provide myself with certain license to do what I was doing."

"Won't that taint the credibility of your work?"

Mickey became defensive and pulled away from Laura, saying as he stood up, "I'm betting that in this instance, the end for once justifies the means."

Shaking her head, Laura challenged his logic.

"It never works that way, Mick."

"It will! It has to!" he shouted, pounding his fists against the wall.

After digesting what he had just said, she asked, "So, do you love Diane, or is she only a test subject?"

"Don't doubt my devotion for Diane!" he shouted, his face turning beet red. "I've been to Hell and back for her. You have no idea the strain this has put on me. I'm mentally and physically near my breaking point over this. Why do you think I'm up here in the first place?!"

Quickly responding, Laura stood nose to nose with Mickey and said, "Devotion? All you said just now was I, I, me, me. What about Diane? What's best for her?"

Now clenching his fists, he responded very tersely, "This is the way it has to be, Laura." Swallowing his pride, he finished with, "I need your help. You're the only one who can do what needs to be done."

She was so afraid to ask, she had to look the other way. "What is it that you need from me, Mick?"

It took even Mickey some time to get up the courage to pose the request.

"I need you to tell Roger you will go ahead with the divorce."

Laura cringed and bit her lip to keep from crying out.

"It has to be discreet. He's the only one who knows we're still married."

Laura couldn't face him. She was unable to respond in any manner.

"I'll make it worth your while. You'll get your percentage of the estate as well as mine. I don't want it. Just leave me my place in Sausalito and my financial assets that are separate from the estate."

Laura was still unable to reply.

"Of course, you get to keep everything Dub and Mom left you here."

That last offering finally got a reaction from Laura. She turned to him with tears streaming down her face.

"Mickey, this place was for us—you and me. That's what your parents wanted. That's all I ever wanted. This was a shrine I maintained in the hope that someday, we could once again be the man and wife we once were. You have just desecrated all the expectation, optimism, faith and love the three of us poured into this abode. I hope I never have to set foot in this place ever again!"

With those words, Laura ran down the stairs and out the front door. Mickey made no effort to stop her.

HALF AN HOUR PASSED during which Mickey stood motionless under the hot spray of the shower, his arms resting against the tiled wall until they tingled. He was lost in one of his numb moments—his thoughts racing between Laura, Sarah, Suki, and Diane; love, lust, and betrayal; freedom, subordination, and domination; fantasy and treachery; good and evil; the past, present and the future. It didn't bode well for the man who had such lofty dreams.

One of his arms finally became fatigued to the point where it buckled at the elbow, and he fell forward against the wall at the same time the hot water ran out, jolting him back into reality. No problems had been resolved, and his skin was well-pruned. After shutting the water off and drying, he dressed in some clean cutoff blue jeans he found in a dresser. He didn't bother with a shirt.

It wasn't long before he unexpectedly smelled something—something delightful. It smelled like food cooking. He ran down the steps thinking perhaps he had mistakenly left something on the stove or grill. What he found took him by surprise. Laura had returned and was baking the fish. She was wearing the unbuttoned man's white dress shirt Carmen had earlier tossed back on the living room sofa. Her powder blue panties were exposed and she also sported a devilish look.

"I figured I had you for ten more hours. I wasn't going to waste it over a petty argument about our marriage."

"What's this countdown shit?"

"Shut up," she replied in a feisty tone of voice. "Like the shirt? You wore it on a couple of interviews. I like wearing it when I'm here."

"It looks a lot better on you than it ever did on me," Mickey said with an approving grin. "I never was a suit and tie sort of guy. So, what'd you have in mind?"

Stopping what she was doing at the kitchen island, Laura answered, "Oh, booze, dinner, debauchery, and classic rock 'n' roll. Have any drugs?"

She walked over to Mickey and embraced him so their flesh met. It hadn't met in such a manner in a very, very long time.

"Either the tabloids can read, 'Man Raped by Estranged Wife After Thirty Years,' or you can simply give in to my desires one more time. What'll it be?" she asked.

Making no effort whatsoever to move away from Laura, he replied, "A while ago, you said something along the lines of, 'Where we go from here is up to me.' What happened?"

Shrugging, Laura replied, "I realized you're thoroughly incapable of making such a decision, so I made it for you."

"We're still getting a divorce, Laura."

"Yeah, right," she said as she wriggled out of the shirt, tossing it to the floor. "We'll see what you say in the morning."

Chapter 42

Roger Delaney was a punctual man who also made house calls, an unusual practice that was beneficial the next morning when he had arranged to meet with Toot, Suki, and Diane at Rub-a-Dub. His hope was to get as much accomplished as possible in the matters that concerned them before he was confronted by Laura. He had avoided coffee this morning, and took his stomach medicine in preparation for what was expected to be a stressful day. Accompanying him was one of his paralegals, a fact that, in and of itself, underscored the magnitude of problems he felt he would be facing. His knock on the door was quickly answered by Lupita.

"Mr. Delaney, how are you doing this morning?"

"Oh, pretty good for an ol' dog," he replied, giving Lupita a hug as he entered. "Have you ever met Tracy?"

"No, I don't believe I have," Lupita replied.

"Tracy Ost, this is Lupita Flores. She and her husband Lupe run the ranch."

Tracy stepped forward and shook Lupita's hand.

"Mr. Delaney, don't go saying things like that. I'm pleased to meet you, Ms. Ost."

"I'm pleased to meet you, too, Lupita"

"Tracy's one of my paralegals. She does all the work, and I get all the credit. Ain't that right, Tracy?"

"I don't believe that's quite the arrangement, sir."

All three took turns chuckling at the vague attempts at humor, after which the two guests entered the splendid home, following Lupita to the dining room table where they would be working.

"Will this be enough space for you, Mr. Delaney?"

"Oh, it's enough space, alright. I'm just worried about all the blood, tears, and crap we're gonna be wading through getting all over the furniture."

Lupita stood shaking her head indicating to Delaney she had opinions on all that was going on.

"Are we alone?" Delaney asked.

After looking down several hallways, Lupita answered, "Yes, for the time being anyway."

"What's your take on all that's going on here at the ranch, Lupita? I mean, you've been here a long time. You've seen the boys grow up. They've been in and out of trouble occasionally, but I get the feeling life here has really changed—and not necessarily for the better."

"To be honest, Mr. Delaney, I don't like what I see."

"How's that?"

"Life was so normal until Mickey showed up again. He's like a dog that brings in ticks and fleas, and makes a mess on the floor. I know he thinks this place is his birthright, but it should belong to Toot. He's the one who made this ranch what it is today. He's carried on the legacies of his father and Mr. Rollins...Dub, that is. Mickey hasn't contributed much at all since he got back. All he worries about is Diane and her problems."

"What are all of her problems, Lupita?"

"I think her biggest problem is him. She seems like a normal, pleasant woman. She's intelligent, gracious, beautiful, a good mother. He simply dominates her. He controls every aspect of her life. It's creepy, to tell you the truth."

"What about Suki?"

"She's very nice, and she helps a lot with everything. However, I think she and Mickey are...you know..." Lupita finished her remark by wrapping her arms around herself.

"Yeah, I know. What about the little girl?"

"Oh, how I do enjoy having a child in the house. I just wish Mr. and Mrs. Rollins could have seen her. She is everything they wanted in a grandchild. She just came too late."

"Does she seem normal to you?"

"What do you mean?"

"I don't know. Does she seem like a normal kid for her age? Does she fit it with the family here?"

"Oh my…she's sharp as a tack. And, oh, what a sweet personality. There is one thing, however."

"What's that?"

"Well, it's sort of odd, but Toot treats her more like a daughter than Mickey does, and she clings to Suki more than her mother."

"Did I hear my name?" Toot asked, coming in from the kitchen. "Mornin', Roger."

"Toot, I won't ask how you're doing," Delaney responded, shaking Toot's hand.

"Good. Don't," Toot replied. Reaching over to shake Tracy's hand, he asked, "How are you doin' this mornin', Tracy?"

"I'm doing fine, Mr. Teudi."

"Damn, I feel old, Ms. Ost," Toot replied with one of his big smiles. "Has everyone had breakfast?"

"No, we just loaded up and got over here as soon as we could. Figured Lupita would probably have some kind of spread for us, and then we'd have to eat two breakfasts 'cause we sure as heck wouldn't pass on Lupita's cooking."

"Right you are," Lupita said proudly. "I have a breakfast casserole in the oven and it should be done in about ten minutes. Would you like some coffee?"

"Coffee sounds good," Delaney answered. "How about you, Tracy?"

"Mr. Delaney, you said you were going to stay off the coffee this morning."

"Yeah, guess I did. But, what the hell. I'll take a cup anyway. Least I can do is sniff it. Coffee's like a good cigar—can't partake anymore, but sure can savor it. So, youngin', you gonna have coffee or not?"

"I'd love some," Tracy finally replied.

"Bet you ain't never had coffee with chicory before, have you?" Toot asked Tracy.

"No. I've heard of it, though."

"Well, you're in for a treat then," Delaney said. "Better sit down and put your seatbelt on. Nobody, but nobody, makes coffee like Lupita."

Tracy took Delaney's remark literally, sitting down at the table. She was followed by Toot and her boss. The veteran attorney pulled out a legal pad with notes scribbled all over it from his briefcase, put on a pair of narrow reading glasses that rested on the end of his nose, and began to peruse what he had written earlier.

Without looking up, Delaney began, "It's both a blessing and a curse that Bangkok is half way around the world. You know I spent half the night talking to people? Hell, it was the middle of the day over there. I need to talk to you about my retainer. I'm too old and not paid well enough to stay up all night."

The conversation stopped for a short while as Lupita set out her coffee service for everyone. As soon as she was out of the room, the dialogue continued.

"Get us out of this mess, and we'll discuss your retainer. How did you know who to talk to?" Toot asked.

Delaney smiled and looked over his glasses as he replied, "Masterson."

"Did you call him up?"

"Hell no. Went over and sat in front of him at his office. I could tell by the bulge in his boxers he was up to no damn good—like a cop right out of the academy getting his first big bust."

"Did he give you the name of that Interpol guy?"

"No. Not at first." Delaney took his glasses off and chuckled as he said, "But, I reminded him of the mess he got himself into with that Mexican gal down in Juarez a few years back, and how I happened to give him a believable alibi. It wasn't long before he was singing like a mockingbird."

"You blackmailed the sheriff?" Toot asked.

Tracy looked on with anticipation of an interesting answer to Toot's question.

"I don't call it blackmail so much as I consider it 'encouraging an elected official to come to his senses about a particular matter.'"

"Gotta hand it to you, Roger. You get the job done."

"Like they say on those reality shows with the crazy motorcyclists—don't try this at home. Best leave it to the professionals."

"Like an attorney," Toot said, pointing at Delaney.

"Damn right." Looking directly at Tracy, he added, "You didn't hear anything that was just said, youngin'."

"No sir, Mr. Delaney."

"Anyway, this guy in Bangkok…" Delaney put his glasses back on and scanned his notes for a moment. "His name is Tik Boondesud. Sounds like a bug of some sort. I called the number Masterson gave me, and I'll be damned if the son-of-a-bitch didn't answer his own phone. He even speaks English pretty good—hell of a lot better than I speak Thai."

"So are we in trouble?"

Removing his glasses again, Delaney answered, "Long story short, no. Here's the deal. That Genevieve duCoeur woman who Mickey supposedly whacked is, or was, a piece of work. She made Bonnie Parker look like Princess Diana. She was into prostitution, drug dealin', human traffickin', gamblin', illegal this and that all over Southeast Asia, India, and parts of Europe. I'd estimate her worth to be about two-and-a-half fortunes. She was revered by many, and disliked by more. The law enforcement people hated her and wanted to take her out, but she paid 'em all too well. She had puppets in all levels of government, too."

"So, what do they want?"

"Let's just say that nobody's crying 'cause she's gone. All kinds of vultures have swooped in to take over her surly businesses. I think the authorities simply want a reliable story that confirms her demise. Then somebody in an official capacity over there is gonna take credit for knocking her off, get a medal, and they'll all sing '*Ding-Dong the Witch is Dead.*'"

"So, they don't want to arrest anyone."

"Surprisingly, no."

Toot sat back in his chair and breathed a sigh of relief.

"You never actually thought Mickey could shoot anyone, did you?" Delaney asked.

"Hell, no. He's such a bad shot," Toot replied with a chuckle. "He couldn't shoot the floor with the gun pointed down. You know what's funny? He's so bad with guns—I mean truly unsafe—that for everyone's safety, I put empty shell cartridges in the .357 he carries in the glove box of his Range Rover. And he doesn't even know it."

Delaney cleared his throat, then said, "There's more to this story, however, and this may not set well with you."

"What's that?" Toot asked tentatively.

"Mickey's friend, Suki…she was in cahoots with Ms. duCoeur at one time."

Toot stared at the table for a while, saying nothing. He was clearly disturbed by Delaney's comment.

"I got the feeling from talking to this Tik fellow that she's moved on to other endeavors. Problem is, nobody knows exactly what those endeavors are, or if they're any more legitimate. He basically told me we need to be careful. There's no doubt who is 'number one' in her mind. He said she's left behind a trail of human carnage for which they believe she's personally responsible."

Toot took a long drink of his coffee before asking, "What about that deal with her grandfather?"

After putting his glasses back on, Delaney checked his notes, then replied, "His name was Chi-feng Wu. Supposedly, he was a world-renowned doctor who dealt with matters concerning the brain. He died under mysterious circumstances, and the body was reportedly cremated."

"When was this?" Toot asked.

"About the same time Mickey and Diane were over in Asia, and she got hurt."

"So, is Diane a suspect?"

"No. The officials don't seem to be overly concerned about it. The guy was old. He could have died of natural causes. The family—who I understand consists solely of Suki—never raised a concern over his death. I think the authorities just want to know for certain if this guy is dead or not, and then they'll move on to something else. It's the fact that the circumstances are unclear and that he was associated with Suki that bothers them."

"So, basically what you're tellin' me is life is good once more, and I spent last night pacin' the floor for no reason," Toot said with a look of relief on his face.

"Breakfast is served, everyone," Lupita interrupted with her singing voice as she came back into the room. She set the breakfast casserole on a large trivet on the table in front of the three, then set out a basket with rolls and a bowl of fruit. As she was passing around some plates and tableware, she asked, "Do you want me to serve it up for you, or do you want to do it yourself?"

"I'll take care of it," Tracy replied.

"Alright, then. Let me know if you need anything else. I'll bring out a carafe with some more coffee." Lupita stepped out of the room, and, once again, the discussion continued.

Picking up where he left off, Toot again asked, "So, Roger, are we in the clear?"

"I think so, Toot. This fellow was fixing to leave on a plane, and he's supposed to be here tomorrow. He'll ask a few questions, and that should be that. I do want to talk with Suki, Diane, and Mickey about what they know before this guy shows up. There are things I want them to say and things I don't want them to say, if you get my drift. No need giving out information that isn't asked of you."

"I hear you," Toot said, the stress having left his voice.

"You know when Mickey's gonna be back?" Delaney asked, starting to eat some of the breakfast set before him by Tracy.

"Who knows? We sent Carmen up to Caddo to fetch him, but she called me last night sayin' she got chased off the property by Laura before she could tell him to get his ass back here. I tried callin' Laura, but she's not answering her phone, nor is Mickey...still. Maybe Laura and Mickey killed each other, and we can get on with our lives."

"That'd end a lot of suffering," Delaney said with a chuckle.

"That's not a nice thing to say, Mr. Delaney," Tracy countered.

"Oh, just a figure of speech, youngin'."

"Anyway," Toot continued, "Carmen was goin' to find a hotel in Marshall, spend the night, then fly back this mornin'."

The three ate some of the casserole and drank coffee for a while, discussing more benign, local issues. Once Delaney was finished with his breakfast, however, he got a serious look on his face.

"Somethin' wrong, Roger?" Toot asked.

Delaney cleared his throat, ran his hands over his head, then said, "I gotta tell you some news about the estate—something I've known about for years, but never needed to tell you about until now."

Sitting back and trying to look relaxed, Toot asked, "Can't be that bad, can it?"

Delaney nodded.

"Well, what is it?" Toot asked impatiently.

"Is Diane around?" Delaney asked.

"No. I think she's still asleep. She had another seizure last night. Suki spent the night with her and I haven't seen either of them yet. Do I need to get her?"

"No. You need to hear this first."

After waiting impatiently for Delaney to finish what he had started, Toot pressed him, "Come on, Roger, what's up?"

In a relatively quiet voice, so as not to be heard by anyone, Delaney replied, "Laura and Mickey are still married."

Through the closed swinging door to the kitchen, Toot and the others heard the sound of dishes crashing to the floor, followed by Lupita shouting a tirade in Spanish. Apparently, Roger's voice wasn't soft enough to elude Lupita's keen hearing.

It seemed like an eternity, as Toot's face took on a multitude of changing expressions. He tried speaking several times, but words never left his mouth. As Toot sat with his tongue pressed against the inside of his cheek, Delaney elaborated.

"Dub swore me to secrecy, Toot."

Toot just stared at Delaney, until he finally responded with, "This is some sort of sick joke, right?"

"'Fraid, not, my friend."

"So, you kept this from me all these years 'cause of Dub? I mean, he's been dead a long time. Didn't you think it was time to…"

"And Laura," Roger continued. "She didn't want it known either—didn't want to make waves."

"So, they really never got divorced?"

"You know how Mickey is. He's not a very thorough man in some regards. Genius in some ways, idiot in others."

"But, she changed her name and everything."

"Name, yes. Everything else, no. Laura refused to divorce him, and he simply never pursued the matter. They just lived separate lives. It never became an issue because Laura never asked for anything except for what Dub and Ruby left her. Those two always hoped Mickey'd find his way back to her, and for that matter, so did Laura."

As calmly as he could, Toot asked, "So what's changed?"

"Laura found out about Diane yesterday. She's coming here today, and I think shit's gonna hit the fan. I'm pretty certain she's gonna make certain Diane never makes any direct claim on the estate."

Shaking his head, Toot asked, "Is she with Mickey?"

"I'm not sure if she's *with* him, per se, but they certainly had an encounter. She ran into him up at Caddo with…another woman. That got her fired up, and you know how she can get when she's mad."

"Did she say who it was?"

"I think you and I know who it was."

Toot finished his coffee, then asked, still shaking his head, "Roger, why is it people can commit murder in Asia and get away with it, but that doesn't work here? Because right now, I desperately want to take Mickey out of the picture. He's really made a mess of things, and I've truly had it up to here with his bullshit," he ended, holding his hand above his head.

Delaney poured Toot another cup of coffee, then said, "As much gratification as that might bring to all of us, sadly it would cause more problems than we now have."

"Hello, everyone," Suki said, joining the others at the table as she carried Gigi in her arms.

"Heddo," Gigi repeated in a meek, little voice.

The little girl reached out for Toot, which was a good thing. That was probably the only act anyone could do that kept him from exploding in an outburst.

"Hey, baby girl, come to Tootaroo," he said taking her from Suki's arms.

"Tootaroo," Gigi echoed. Everyone at the table laughed at her.

"So why all the serious expressions when I walked in? Is there bad news? Am I in trouble with the Sheriff?"

"Twubbo wishref," Gigi sang, relishing the attention.

"No. You're not in trouble," Delany replied. "I need to speak privately with you after a bit."

Lacking all sense of tact and diplomacy, Toot jumped in with both feet and asked, "So, you and Genevieve were business partners?"

Suki knew how to make nice and how to make love, but she also knew how to fight, how to lie and how to manipulate. More to her advantage, she knew when. If Toot wanted to go down this path, so be it.

"And I suppose you have never had a business partner who at some point you decided was wrong for you?"

"Toot, we oughta…" Delaney interjected, trying to defuse the situation.

"Business partner? Yes. Partner in crime? No."

"Are you the type of person who does not believe in such a thing as reform?"

"So you're not denyin' you had dealin's with her?"

"Toot, I really think this matter needs to be…"

"We were close friends and school mates when we went to university. After that, we were in business together for several years."

"You call drugs and prostitution work?"

"Why don't I take Gigi into the kitchen for breakfast?" Tracy offered.

The truce was going to be short-lived so Toot took Tracy up on her offer.

"Hey, sweet pea, go show Ms. Tracy how you can fix your own breakfast."

The little urchin happily hopped off Toot's lap, toddled around the table to Tracy, and took her by the hand to the kitchen.

Once the room was clear from young ears, Suki continued, "Everything you have heard about Genevieve is probably true. I could tell you stories that would horrify you. If evil was her goal, she was at the top of her game. Having said that, I realized quite some time ago that she and I had very different aspirations in life, and most certainly I had different ideas about how to reach my goals. When we reached that fork in the road—she chose to continue her ways, I chose a different life. We parted amicably. Today, I stand before you, a reformed woman. Have I ever done anything to you that you would remotely consider malevolent?"

Toot looked at Suki peculiarly, and she realized he didn't understand what she was asking.

"Evil? Wicked? Immoral?"

"No, but I'm just not sure how much I really know about you. And what I'm findin' out is pretty shocking."

"You knew me well enough to make love to me."

"That didn't require a lot of thought."

"Just like when you did not think about the ramifications of seducing Diane?"

The room was silent for a few moments until Delaney said as he exhaled, "Oh, shit."

"You know what she's tryin' to do, Roger?" Toot asked, standing up defensively. "She's tryin' to divert attention from her to me."

"She's done a good job, too."

"Roger! What's the crime here?" Toot asked, pacing nervously around the room. "Is it murder and drugs and whatever, or is it the fact that I slept with her," he finished, pointing at Suki.

"It ain't her I'm worried about. It's Diane," Delaney said, keeping the focus on Toot.

"Look, Roger. That was an error in judgment. What do you want me to say?"

"You'll have to do better than that," Suki said. "She told me this morning that you took her against her will."

"Rape? She says I raped her?"

"Well, what would you call it when you force yourself on a woman—especially the wife of the man who is almost your brother?"

"This is nothin' but bull, Suki. Besides, haven't you heard the newsflash? Diane and Mickey aren't married!"

"That's enough!" Delaney shouted, slapping his hand on the table. "None of this—I repeat, none—leaves this room. Do both of you hear me?"

Ignoring Delaney's plea, Suki asked, "What do you mean, they're not married?"

"They can't be. Mickey's still married to his first wife, Laura! And you probably knew all about it!"

Simultaneously, out of the corner of their eyes, all three saw a figure standing at the end of the hallway that went to the master wing. It was Diane. There was no point in wondering if she had heard what had been said. Her facial expression made clear she had heard everything.

Chapter 43

No bed had ever felt softer, and no quilt ever felt more comforting than those Laura experienced the morning after her long sought-after reunion with Mickey. It was shortly after daybreak, and the flapping of the curtains against the window sill had awakened her. The spot that Mickey had occupied next to her overnight was still warm, and she could still feel his heat as though he were still there. When she opened her eyes, she saw him sitting in a chair by a desk, a few feet away…simply staring at her with a smile on his face.

"You look like a happy man," Laura said as she yawned. "I sure hope you are, because I'm in heaven."

"The coffee's done. I got up a while ago and made some—weak, and with a touch of vanilla like you used to like it. Would you like a cup?"

"You remember how I used to take my coffee?"

"I remember a lot of things about you, Laura, and I don't have to tuck them away in a closet."

Pulling the sheet over her head, she replied, "I know. I'm pathetic, aren't I?"

Chuckling, Mickey answered, "No. It's sort of cute, in an obsessive-compulsive sort of way."

"You think I have OCD?"

"I *know* you have freakin' OCD." He walked over, pulled the sheet back, kissed Laura on the cheek, then said, "Let me get your coffee. I'll be right back."

Mickey trotted quickly downstairs, whistling as he went. Laura got out of bed and immediately found herself standing in the buff in front of the mirror mounted above the dresser. She convinced herself, as she turned side-to-side looking at her reflection, that she looked fifteen years younger than when she went to bed the previous evening. After using the bathroom, she returned to the bedroom wearing her panties and the unbuttoned shirt she had taken off—hoping the view would again remind Mickey of what he had once left behind and what he might be fortunate enough to have in his life once more. He was waiting for her.

"I'm never wearing this shirt again after today," Laura said, jubilantly. "It's being retired to the closet."

"Speaking of OCD… So, why are you retiring it?"

"It's a commemorative shirt, now."

"In honor of what?" Mickey asked, handing Laura her coffee.

"Last night, of course," Laura replied, not understanding why he would even be asking the question.

Laura returned to the bed, lying propped up on an elbow in such a way that her shirt gaped open provocatively. Mickey took a seat in the chair.

"Laura?" Mickey started, setting the tone for a disappointing message.

"What?" She asked, bracing herself.

"We're still not getting back together."

After taking a sip of her coffee and swallowing with difficulty, she replied, "So, last night didn't mean anything to you? Was I wrong this morning? You looked like a happy man."

"I'm happy in as much as I think we can put some things behind us. But, as for the future, we're still going our separate ways."

Trying not to sound desperate, or for that matter, angry, Laura persisted, "So, what's wrong with me?" she asked as she sat up on the edge of the bed in front of him. "Am I that hard to look at?"

"No, you're beautiful."

"Have I done something to offend you?"

"No, Laura. It's the simple fact that I'm married."

"No shit! I'm the other half of that deal!"

"I mean, to Diane."

"You're…not…legal!"

"You know what I mean, Laura. I made a vow to myself some years ago that Diane was the one with whom I wanted to settle down, and I'm going to remain true to that conviction. For all intents and purposes I belong to Diane, and vice-versa."

"Which is why you've slept with two different women in the last twenty-four hours?" Laura asked with greatly exaggerated waving of her hands and arms. "Did she actually take part in any vows, or did you make that decision unilaterally?"

"There was some history between myself and the lady from yesterday. We had to put some things behind us as well."

"Oh, I'll bet there was some history, alright," Laura responded, her arms folded in disgust. "Admit it, Mick, you just can't keep your cock in your pocket."

After letting the dust settle from that last salvo, Mickey replied, "I really enjoyed last night, Laura. It's simply too bad you had to end it like this."

Mickey's remark and his complete failure to take responsibility for any of his actions, took all the wind out of Laura. Arguing was useless—the marriage between her and Mickey was over, plain and simple. She had just one last thing to say.

"You know what I find so sad about your farce of a marriage to Diane? It's that you robbed the cradle. It's one thing to fuck over a mature, adult woman who should have enough sense to run the other way at the very sight of you, but to take advantage of someone her age is just…is just…" She couldn't finish the sentence with words, ending it with her hands up in the air in surrender. "How old was she when you knocked her up, Mick? Was she still a teenager?"

Looking puzzled, Mickey asked, "Who are you referring to?"

"Diane!"

"I'll admit she's younger than you, but only by a few years. What the hell are you talking about?"

"Either she's been soaking in formaldehyde for the last twenty years, or you have yet another wife. I met Diane yesterday. She told me she was twenty-four and she looked it."

"Diane was here?"

"Yep. She came up to get you, though I can't understand why."

"Why didn't you tell me?"

"Possibly because I thought you might want some quality time with your wife—your *real* wife. You even said as much at the boat dock, if you remember. Furthermore, she was a total bitch to me at the store. She asked for directions to this place, but by that point in our conversation I was ready to strangle her, so I blew her off. An idiot with a badge and an erection told her how to find the place, so I came here and told her to take a hike."

"What did she look like?"

"She looked twenty-four!" Laura replied, quickly holding up both hands twice, followed by her two middle fingers pointed straight up...twice.

"No, I mean hair color, size, shape."

"Uh, brunette, size 2, Cosmo material in a vampy sort of way. Now does she sound familiar?"

"That's not Diane," he replied. "Diane's not supposed to be alone. Suki wouldn't have let her come here by herself."

"So, you're sleeping with yet another woman!" Laura shouted.

Heading back down the stairs once more, Mickey said, "I need to call the ranch. Something's not right."

Laura followed.

Mickey walked around the rooms of the cabin where he had been, looking for his phone. Finding his backpack, he rummaged through it, but came up empty-handed.

"Have you seen my phone?"

"Nope," Laura replied tersely.

Without hesitating, he asked, "Can I borrow yours?"

"I don't have it. It's in pieces back at the lodge after I threw it at your wife! I wish I did have it, though, so I could tell you, no!"

"Does the house phone work?" Mickey asked, pointing to the phone on the bar.

"I suppose," Laura answered reluctantly. "I unplugged it yesterday, so you'll have to plug it in."

Boundaries

Mickey grabbed the plug for the phone, and reached behind the bookcase at the bar to plug it in. In the process, he knocked over several framed pictures sitting on top of the bookcase. He set them back up, then grabbed the last one and held it in front of him.

"What the hell is this?"

"That isn't Diane?" Laura asked, referring to the picture Carmen had earlier substituted for Diane's, and that Mickey now held in his hand.

"Hell, no. This is our nanny, Carmen."

Shrugging her shoulders, Laura said, "Well, that's the chick I saw here yesterday. She told me, before I chased her away, that she was your wife, Diane."

"Why would she say that?"

"I'm supposed to know what's going on with all the illicit women in your life?" Laura asked sarcastically. "Oh, and by the way, I think having a nanny who dresses and acts like a Washington escort, is in poor taste. But then, we're talking about the nanny employed by Mickey...Mickey Rollins."

"Bitterness is unbecoming of you, Laura."

"Just as intelligence is unbecoming of you."

Mickey turned away and dialed the ranch number. After three or four rings, Lupita answered.

"Good morning. This is Rub-a-Dub ranch." Her tone of her voice sounded stressed and Mickey thought he heard shouting in the background.

"Lupita, it's Mickey. Is Diane there?"

She gave him no answer, choosing instead to carry on in a tirade in Spanish.

"Lupita! Let me speak with Suki!"

There was a crashing sound as the phone apparently landed on the floor. Mickey thought he could tell from the diminishing shouts that Lupita was leaving the room. Soon, he heard footsteps getting closer to the phone.

"Mickey, where are you?" Suki asked.

"Caddo. Where's Diane? Is she alright?"

"She is here. She had a seizure last night after the police left."

"A real seizure?"

"Yes, a real seizure."

"What's with the police?"

"Just get home as soon as you can. Everything is a mess right now."

"Tell me what's going on!"

"Not over the phone. Diane is already upset."

"Upset over what?"

"You and your betrayals. For that matter, I am upset, too. How come you never told me you and Laura were still married?"

Putting his hand over the mouthpiece, Mickey looked at Laura and angrily asked, "Did you tell Suki that you and I were still married? What about Diane, did you tell her?"

Defiantly, Laura replied, "I told 'teen queen' yesterday that we were still married. I also spoke with Roger Delaney."

Mickey banged his head several times against the bar cabinet, before answering Suki, "We'll talk about it when I get back. Did Diane come up here yesterday?"

"No, we sent Carmen after you."

"Do you have any idea why she would pose as Diane?"

"It is not my job to explain the actions of all the women in your life, Mickey."

"Yeah...I keep hearing that."

"What?"

"Never mind. Diane's alright after the seizure?"

"Yes, I gave her some medication after it happened. She slept all night, but she just found out about you and Laura, and it is all Roger, Toot, and I can do to keep her from completely erupting."

"Would it do any good for me to talk to her?"

"You have to be kidding."

"Well, give her some more sedative. I'll be home as soon as possible. It looks like some bad weather is rolling in so I don't know if I'll be able to fly. Worst case, I'll be back mid-afternoon."

"Bye, Mickey. Please hurry back."

"See you shortly," he said, then he hung up the phone.

Looking at Laura, he asked, "Why on God's green earth would you tell anyone we are still married?"

"Because I'm honest."

Mickey thought for a few moments, then realized he still needed Laura.

"Sarah left in my vehicle yesterday. Can you give me a lift back to Tyler? She was supposed to leave it there."

"You are freakin' unreal, Mick," Laura responded, shaking her head. "There is no limit to your gall, is there?"

"Look, the quicker I get home, the quicker we can resolve a lot of issues."

"Issues...that's all our marriage is to you, isn't it? It's an issue..."

"One of many, at this moment. Now, will you give me a lift?"

She let him suffer a few moments without an answer, then replied, "First, tell me. Who is Sarah?"

"Is that relevant?"

"Do you want a ride, or not?"

"She's a neighbor."

"She isn't just anybody, is she?" Laura asked with confidence. "Roger seemed to know who she was."

"Why did you tell Roger about her?"

"It's my fault your boots stink after you step in crap? I'd be really careful, if I were you, Mick. Someday, there will be a husband holding a gun pointed your direction. Surely you wouldn't want to take a bullet before you resolve the 'issue' of our marriage?"

There was a long pause as the two contemplated their next moves, and silently reflected on their brief interlude together.

"Please, Laura. Do this one last thing for me."

"It'll cost you," she replied after thinking about his request.

"You name it."

She held her arms open. He walked into them, and she closed her arms around him one final time. He did the same.

Chapter 44

Stormy weather around north and east Texas prevented Carmen from flying back to the ranch. It also prevented her from getting more than a couple of hours of sleep. Having had a little shut-eye, a shower, and a change of clothes, she took off on her own, driving herself back to Hunt. She made remarkable time in the SLK, arriving shortly after the hurricane that had been Diane.

Tracy met Carmen outside the back door of the house and quickly handed Gigi off to her. Carmen could tell by the expression on Tracy's face, and by looking through the panes in the French doors, that there had been a commotion. Gigi, remarkably, appeared not to be the worse for wear, but she was not her happy, outgoing self as evidenced by the way she clung to Carmen's neck.

"What on earth happened?" Carmen asked, peering about, shocked at what she was seeing.

"We've had a conflict arise here, and the news wasn't taken very well, I'm afraid," Tracy answered.

Lupita was busy sweeping up broken glass and debris. There was also broken plaster and sheetrock from where heavy objects had been thrown against walls. Most of the furniture that had been upset in the commotion had been set back upright, but many of the pieces showed scratches or damage of some type. The wreckage continued down the hallway toward Mickey's office and the master bedroom. As Carmen passed by Mickey's office, she could see complete disarray. Worse yet, his computer chassis was laying smashed under a large decorative piece of polished agate from his collection.

"Mama mad," Gigi said.

"It sure looks that way, baby. Are you alright?" Carmen asked.

"Uh huh. See horses?"

Hopeful that Gigi hadn't witnessed the disturbance as it was taking place, Carmen agreed to Gigi's request.

"Sure. I think we should go see the horses now. Would you like that?"

Gigi nodded.

As soon as Carmen turned to leave the room, she encountered Suki standing in the doorway.

"What are you doing in here? I told you this part of the house is off limits."

Before Carmen could answer, Toot appeared.

"Is everythin' okay?"

"I found Carmen in Mickey's office. Access to this wing is supposed to be restricted, as you know."

"I wasn't doing anything," Carmen said, surprised by Suki's tone. "I'm sorry, but I was just…I guess…shocked by what's happened. Who did this?"

"We got some news this mornin' that upset a few of us," Toot offered, "Some more than others."

"I hope nobody is hurt," Carmen said, showing what appeared to be legitimate concern given the magnitude of the mess.

"Why did you not tell Mickey to return immediately?" Suki asked sternly.

"Look, I did my best," Carmen replied, now upset at Suki's persistent unpleasantness. "I had to get directions when I got close to the cabin. Imagine my surprise when I happened to run into Mickey's ex-wife—who, mind you, nobody told me about—and she basically ambushed me before I could see him. He wasn't at the cabin when I arrived, and he hadn't returned by the time she forced me to leave."

"It was a very simple message. I do not understand how you could have…"

"Suki," Toot interrupted. "She's right. I know how Laura can be, and Carmen is no match for her. We should have handled it differently.

"You know, this works out perfectly," Toot continued. "Now that Carmen's back, you can go with Roger and give that statement he was askin' you to do."

"I cannot leave Diane in her condition. For that matter, I do not trust Carmen. I would prefer to remain here."

"You don't trust me?" Carmen argued.

"No, I do not. There is something about you...I just cannot put my finger on it, but I have a problem with you."

"That's not fair..."

"Oh? Tell me, why would you tell Laura that you were Diane?"

"I introduced myself to her as Gigi's nanny," Carmen said truthfully. "When I got to the cabin, a policeman showed up, and I was afraid I wasn't supposed to be there. He kept asking questions about who I was. That is when I told *him* that I was Mrs. Rollins. I guess *he* believed me. He must have met this Laura person on the driveway and repeated what I had said. I apologize if this caused any confusion."

"Ladies!" Toot interrupted. "We don't have any choice, Suki. Diane chose Carmen to be Gigi's nanny, and that's all there is to it."

"Gigi nanny," Gigi mimed.

"Right! The woman who just threw a fit and tore the place up is capable of making rational decisions."

"Suki!" Toot shouted. "It's not right to judge Diane after the news she heard. You'd be freaky, too, if you'd had that bomb dropped in your lap."

"Feeky," Gigi repeated.

"Guys," Carmen said, "We shouldn't argue in front of Gigi. I'm perfectly capable and willing to take care of Gigi as well as Diane while you're gone. If you have some place to go, I suggest you leave and take care of your business."

"She's right, Suki," Toot said, siding with Carmen once again. "I'll drive you in. We need to get this over before Laura and Mickey show up this afternoon. Who knows what'll happen after that?"

Reluctantly, Suki gave in to Toot's suggestion, but not before adding, "I am not finished with my questions, Carmen. When I get back, you and I need to have a talk."

With that, Suki went to the living room where Delaney was waiting.

"I'm sorry about all this, Carmen. Suki's just really upset right now. She and Diane are terribly close, and this has affected both of them equally."

"What got everyone all worked up?"

"That lady you met up at Caddo."

"So, it's true…"

"I'm afraid so."

"Wow…" Carmen replied, shaking her head.

"Wow," Gigi repeated.

Toot took Gigi into his arms for a few moments, hugging her while he finished with Carmen.

"Diane's restin' in her bedroom. Suki managed to get some meds into her. She'll probably sleep the rest of the day…maybe all night."

"Do you want me to clean up in here?" Carmen asked, with peculiar interest.

Sensing it was best that she not, Toot replied, "No. Leave that for Lupita and Suki. Just look after Gigi for us. We'll be back this afternoon some time. Call me if anything comes up."

"What about Mr. Rollins? When is he coming home?"

"As I said, he'll be back in Kerrville this afternoon. As for comin' home…" Toot finished by mouthing, "Probably never," so that Gigi couldn't hear him.

"Oh," Carmen mouthed back as she reached for the little girl.

"You take care of Miss Carmen, got it?" Toot told his favorite pixie.

"Okay!" She replied with enthusiastic naivety.

TOOT CAUGHT UP WITH Suki as she sat waiting in his truck. Delaney and Tracy pulled out of the driveway ahead of them. As he started the truck, he noticed Suki was very distant.

"What's on your mind?"

"Oh, nothing…nothing at all," she replied very sarcastically.

Toot knew that was a lie, but he was reluctant to pry. Obviously, Suki was upset at everything that had taken place in the previous twenty-four hours.

Eventually, he had to ask, "Did you know Laura and Mickey were still married?"

Suki's flabbergasted look told him 'no.'

"Did you?" She asked derisively.

"Nope. Surprised the hell out of me. I thought I knew every aspect—big and small—about this ranch until about two hours ago."

"I suppose it is justice in some fashion," Suki continued bitterly. "First, you fuck a man's wife, then he fucks you back."

Toot reached for Suki's hand, but as quickly as his hand got close to hers, she pulled it away. The relationship that had been between them was obviously destroyed by his unfaithfulness.

After driving close to half an hour without saying anything to each other, Suki began asking Toot some questions about Carmen.

"Toot, do you remember the first time you and Mickey saw Carmen in the window of her room?"

"Hey, like I said, that was a complete accident."

"I know. I do not care about that. Did you happen to see a tattoo on her?"

Toot looked first to see the expression on Suki's face, then asked, "Is this some type of trick question?"

"No. It is a simple question. Did you, or did you not, see a tattoo?"

"Well, I saw a lot, obviously."

"Spare me the details, Toot! All I care about is a tattoo."

He thought a while, then answered, "Now that you ask, I think she had a tattoo or a birthmark of some kind on her chest. It was above her left breast if I remember correctly. It's always been concealed when she's dressed."

Suki grimaced and bit her hand anxiously.

"What's the matter?"

"Nothing. We need to hurry home. I think I know what is wrong with Carmen."

"What do you mean, 'what is wrong?'"

"You will not believe me even if I tell you."

"You're kiddin', right? After what we've been through today, I'd believe anything."

After hesitating a moment, Suki said, "Carmen is not who she says she is."

"What do you mean?"

"Remember, she told us that she has a twin sister?"

"That's right. She never said anything more, though."

"I am very familiar with her sister. Her name is Magdeliene."

"Yeah, so?"

Looking at Toot, Suki continued, "I am fairly certain our Carmen is actually Magdeliene."

Toot pulled his truck off the road and stopped.

"Aside from the deception, is that a bad thing?"

Suki put her hands over her mouth, obviously frightened in a manner unlike Toot had ever seen.

"It is no longer a secret that I used to arrange to have young women sent from Asia and Europe to anyone with enough money who wanted to procure a wife."

"Like Genevieve used to do, right?"

"Yes, we were partners."

Suki began to cry so Toot handed her his handkerchief.

"What's this got to do with Carmen?"

"It was really a bad thing to do in so many ways. I found Magdeliene in Bangkok a few years ago. She was really a mess at the time and an embarrassment to her family. Her father was familiar with Genevieve and her business. He told her he wanted Magdeliene gone, and he would pay handsomely if she were to successfully orchestrate an arranged relationship for her with respectable circumstances."

Putting the truck in park, Toot asked, "And…?"

"Genevieve asked me for help, and I found a man for Magdeliene. It was a good deal for me. The buyer paid Genevieve, me, and Maggie's father."

"So, I don't follow you. What does this have to do with now?"

"Well, I think Magdeliene must have somehow managed to swap places with Carmen. You see, aside from the tattoo, the sisters were absolutely indistinguishable. They went through university together and, as I understand it from the father, Magdeliene frequently usurped Carmen's place in life causing a great deal of trouble. Carmen is a sweet, caring, loving, intelligent person. Magdeliene can exhibit all of the same qualities, when she cares to."

"So how do we figure this out?"

"Look for the tattoo. If she has it, she is Magdeliene."

"Is there anybody we can phone to see if Carmen is lost somewhere?"

"Yes, I have contact information. But, it is back at the house."

"Do you have any way to contact the man who paid for Magdeliene?"

"Yes. I have that information as well."

"Who is this guy, anyway? Is he from around here?"

"No. But, he is a business acquaintance of Mickey's. That is how I located him in the first place."

"You mean, Mickey helped broker the deal?"

"Yes. This man is a very wealthy financier. Mickey was hoping to persuade the man to back some of his work. He thought an arranged marriage might be the ticket to his success."

"What's this guy's name?"

"Constantine Strokas."

"Never heard of him. What the hell would he want with us anyway?"

"It is not us he is after. He wants Mickey's technology. Strokas has dealings with many people who would pay dearly for what Mickey has developed. He has no allegiance to anyone except the person whose face is on any form of currency. I suspect Strokas has managed to infiltrate our home with Magdeliene posing as Carmen."

"Is Magdeliene dangerous?"

Suki nodded.

That was all it took. Toot put the truck in drive, made a U-turn, and headed as quickly as he could back to the ranch. There were a few minutes without conversation while Toot pondered the information Suki had just given him. His mind was overloaded by the discovery of multiple shams people close to him had unveiled. Suki was soon to reveal yet another.

Shaking his head, Toot inquired, "I have to ask you, Suki, why would you recommend hiring Carmen in the first place. You must have known there was some risk given just the facts you know."

"Carmen is exceptional."

"Right, but she has a nutcase for a sister."

"I honestly expected Magdeliene to be out of the picture by now."

"Why? If anything, she's even more of a threat because she's already in the States."

"Because women like Magdeliene have an extremely high mortality within a very short time after their spouse takes them in."

"What do you mean? They get sick and die?"

"No…they just…go away."

Toot nearly ran off the road as he absorbed the true meaning of what Suki had told him.

"Can we call Lupita and warn her?"

"Bad idea. First of all, Lupita wouldn't know how to handle the situation. Besides, we have no phone service until we get out of these canyons and up onto the plateau." Toot pressed hard on the accelerator. "Hold on."

ONCE DIANE WAS CONVINCED anyone who posed a threat was out of the room, she sat up in bed and spit out her chewing gum that she had managed to wrap around the two tablets Suki had given her. Her idea had worked—she had ingested only a tiny amount of the medication. She also realized something else…there was nobody she could trust. Carefully peeking around corners, she soon became aware of the fact that she was free of anyone menacing. She saw Carmen with Gigi down with the horses at the corral and Lupita cleaning up the living and dining areas. When the coast was clear, she made her way to Mickey's office.

Diane knew she had to find out more about her condition and treatment if she was to have any legitimate claim that she was endangered in any way. Such findings would be necessary if she was going leave to Mickey and also if she wanted to pursue any other medical treatment once she was gone. Unfortunately, her greatest source of information—Mickey's computer—was for all intents and purposes destroyed during her earlier outburst. If there was to be any tangible evidence that would help her, it had to be physical.

She took a seat at Mickey's desk and visually scoured the room from his perspective looking for anything that might prove useful to her. As she glanced down, she saw a box pushed back under the desk so it was out of plain view. Diane pulled it out and noticed right away that it was marked with a corporate logo and name Medico Techniq. Diane recognized the name from her meetings with Rajeev Munshi and others who worked at or for that company. Given the type of interactions of late that Diane had with Medico, it was very likely the contents of the box bore some connection to her. The box had never been opened—that was about to change.

The first thing Diane encountered after cutting open the top of the box was a letter from Rajeev to Mickey. Its content stunned Diane:

Dear Mickey,

As per my conversation with you last week, I am sending you Diane's personal effects from the office she once kept here at Medico. I understand your wish not to give these items directly to Diane at this time, but I insist that at some point in the very near future, you give these to her. They represent important milestones from her past. If you choose not to give these to her, please return them to me.

I hope all is going well with Diane's treatment. Your work appears to be near completion. The committee looks forward to our meeting next month.

Regards,
Rajeev Munshi
CEO, Medico Techniq

Boundaries

Now Diane understood why Rajeev was so curious about Diane's recollection of Medico. She had worked there. The former executive continued removing wrapped items one at a time from the box. Each one evoked increasingly powerful emotions as well as increasing resentment for what had been kept from her for so long.

The first item she unwrapped was her business card holder—full of her cards. They read: Diane L. Alders, Executive Vice-President, Medical Product Technology.

The next bit of treasure Diane unwrapped was two diplomas. The first was her Bachelor of Arts Degree from the University of California at Santa Cruz—the name on it, Diane L. Fontaine. She now had a maiden name. Immediately, images of her mother, father and brother came to mind—images she had long forgotten. The second diploma was for her Master of Business Administration from the University of California at San Diego—the name on it, Diane L. Alders. There had been a name change...a marriage.

The third article Diane removed took her breath away. It was the framed picture from her office bureau—the one of her and Bruce taken by a friend while they were in college. Tears began to well up in Diane's eyes. She now knew.

"Bruce?" She muttered quietly as she stroked the picture. "How could I have forgotten?"

She clutched the picture to her chest and broke down crying.

Lupita heard the commotion and came to Mickey's office where she found Diane with her face down on Mickey's desk sobbing uncontrollably.

"Diane, what's the matter?"

Diane leaned back in the chair, held up the picture and pointed to it as she screamed at the top of her lungs, "This is my husband!"

Lupita wasn't sure what to do, but she tried to convince Diane otherwise.

"No, ma'am. Mickey is your husband. You are Mrs. Rollins...Mrs. Mickey Rollins."

"No! This is me!" Diane shouted as she threw her business cards at Lupita. "This is me!" She shouted again, as she tossed one diploma onto the floor in front of Lupita, "And this is me!" She shouted one last time as she threw out the other. Finally, she held up the picture one last time and said, "This is my husband, Bruce."

Lupita picked up the diplomas and set them back on the desk as she said, "Honey, I don't know what to say." As she looked at Diane, she spotted an envelope taped to the back of the picture of her and Bruce. "What's that?" Lupita asked, pointing to it.

Diane turned the frame around and removed the previously opened envelope. It contained a short, hand-written note on personal stationary, a small photograph, and a business card. Diane read out loud.

Diane,

I found this picture that I took of you and Bruce back in college. Hard to believe that was ten years ago. Carol and I love you guys.

Call if you ever need anything. We owe the two of you our perpetual happiness together.

Regards,
Joel

The business card read: Joel Wakeland, Attorney-at-Law, with an address in Durango, Colorado and a telephone number. The photo was a 3"x5" color photograph of two couples on motorcycles in the mountains. On the back side was inscribed, 'Wakelands with Alders, Pike's Peak.'

Lupita recognized one of the women on the motorcycle, as well as the one in the larger photograph, to be Diane. Not being a strong ally of Mickey, and certainly not willing to overlook what he had done, she said, "Call the number on the card."

"What?" Diane asked.

Lupita picked up the phone from its cradle on Mickey's desk and handed it to her.

"Call that man…Mr. Wakeland. He's a lawyer. He's a friend. He'll help you."

Diane looked at the phone for a moment, then at Lupita.

"Go get Carmen for me. Tell her to pack two days of clothes for herself and Gigi. She needs to be ready to go in twenty minutes."

"Yes, ma'am. I'll pack some food and drinks for you to take."

Before Lupita could leave, Diane stood and gave her a hug. Tears ran down their cheeks.

After taking a seat, Diane grabbed a pad of paper and a pen from Mickey's desk drawer, then dialed the number on the business card. Soon, a receptionist answered.

"Law Offices, how may I help you?" asked the woman on the other end.

"Joel Wakeland, please."

"One moment. May I tell him who is calling?"

"Diane Rollins…No! Tell him, Diane Alders."

"Certainly, Ms. Alders. Just one moment."

Diane listened to a recording of 'Born to Be Wild' over the phone during the short time she was on hold. It wasn't long before a familiar voice picked up the phone.

"Diane?"

"Joel?"

"Diane, where are you? How are you? I thought you had fallen off the face of the earth. Rajeev would never tell me anything except that you had been in an accident."

"Joel, I need help. Please. I need help now," Diane said, sobbing as she spoke.

"Are you safe?"

"No. I need to leave and I need a place to stay. I need to meet with you."

"Do you need money?"

"No, I have money. We need to hide from a man who says he's my husband. He's done terrible things to me."

After a brief pause, Joel asked, "Did you remarry?"

"I don't know. He says we're married, but I don't remember anything."

"You said 'we'. Who else is involved?"

"I'm leaving with my daughter and her nanny. I want to leave in the next fifteen minutes. I'm afraid they'll come back and stop me."

"Can you call the police?"

"No! I think they believe I committed a crime, plus we live in the middle of nowhere. It would take too long for them to get here."

"Are you being investigated, or have you been charged with a crime?"

"They haven't charged me with anything, but they think I had something to do with...a homicide."

"Did you?"

Crying, Diane answered, "I don't know."

"Have you been asked not to leave your locale?"

"No. They want to ask some questions, but they didn't tell me I couldn't go anywhere."

"Do you have safe transportation?"

"Yes. I have a vehicle I can leave in immediately."

"Where are you?"

"Hunt, Texas...near Kerrville."

"Where the heck is that?"

"About eighty miles from San Antonio."

"That's a good nine hundred miles from Durango. Maybe I should come down there."

"No!" Diane shouted. "I need to get far, far away from here."

"Do you know how to get to Durango?"

"I'll find it."

"No. I'll tell you what roads I want you to take. Stick to that route in case something happens. Do you have a phone I can call you on?"

"No. I'm not taking it. He may have a way of tracking me with it. I'll call you along the way to give you my progress."

"Good idea. Here's my number. Call me every few hours. If I don't hear from you, I'm sending the police out looking for you. Got it?"

"Thanks, Joel."

Wakeland gave Diane final details and instructions, then the two disconnected. Immediately thereafter, Carmen appeared.

"What's going on? I thought you were asleep."

"Right, as did the others. We're going to Durango."

"Why?"

"I'll tell you along the way. Are you packed?"

"Give me ten minutes. What vehicle are we taking?"

"The FJ. I'll meet you in the garage." Diane reached for Gigi. "I'll get her ready."

Quickly, Diane disappeared down the hallway.

Carmen wasn't about to neglect her other responsibility. Before she finished packing, she stood up the broken chassis of Mickey's computer, opened it, and removed the hard drive.

Chapter 45

Delaney had waited impatiently for Toot and Suki to arrive. His repeated attempts to contact either of them by phone had been futile, and he was about to get in his car and retrace the route they had taken when his cell phone rang. Caller ID showed it to be Toot's cell phone.

"Toot, where the hell are you?" Delaney asked over the phone. "You were behind us 'till we got to Smith Crossing, then you disappeared."

"Roger, we got trouble," Toot responded.

"I know, God dammit! That's why you were supposed to follow me to the office."

"No. I mean more trouble…Diane's gone."

"What?" Delaney said, nervously running a hand over the top of his head.

"She bailed on us. She left with Carmen, and she took Gigi."

"How'd she do that? Suki said she had her drugged up."

"I know! Suki found a piece of gum in the trash that contained the pills she gave her."

"That was clever," Delaney said with a snicker. "It appears to me we have a serious trust problem. Where the hell did she go?"

"I don't know. Tell you what, though, she's got a good head start on us. I think Lupita has an idea where she was going, but she's mum."

"Sounds like we got us a whole bunch of trust problems. What's she driving?"

"She took Mickey's black FJ. Do you need the license so we can get troopers to look for her?"

"Give me the license, but don't go telling the law about her being gone. I know the intentions of this Interpol guy, but Masterson's been out of the loop. As far as he's concerned, Mickey, Suki, and Diane are suspects in an international crime, and if he finds out she flew the coop, it'll get ugly."

"Roger, there's somethin' else. Suki thinks Carmen may be a threat to Diane and Gigi."

"What kind of threat?" Delaney asked, flopping down into his chair.

"She may actually be Carmen's psycho twin sister—a gal named Magdeliene. She apparently poses as Carmen on occasion. Suki just phoned Carmen's home, and her mother said Carmen got delayed gettin' out of school, and hadn't made it over here yet. We were supposed to have been notified. The real Carmen is scheduled to arrive next week after she finishes a requirement for graduation or something. The family thinks Magdeliene is the one here takin' care of Gigi."

"How the hell did you people get mixed up in this baloney? Cattlemen and oil men don't get in trouble like this." Delaney said, pounding his fist on his desk. "I'll say it again—I'm too old and I don't get paid enough to put up with this crap!"

"Roger, stay focused. I need you to send Mickey directly to the ranch if he shows up there."

"Mickey? He's come and gone. I filled him in on what was happening with Diane, and he tore out of here. He, too, tried calling you and Suki, but nobody answered."

"When was that?"

"Oh, probably around two o'clock or so."

"He should have been here by now. Are you sure he was comin' here?"

"That's what he said."

"Was he with Laura?"

"No, she hasn't arrived yet. She just called a bit ago and said she'd be here shortly."

"Well, if you hear from him, tell him to give me a call and get to the ranch. Don't tell him Diane's gone. I want to do that personally."

"I'll sure do that. Keep me posted about Diane."

"Mr. Delaney?" Tracy interrupted.

"Hold on a second, Toot."

"I'm on the phone right now, honey."

"I have Mickey Rollins on the other line."

Nearly falling out of his chair, Delaney sat up quickly saying, "Toot, I got Mickey on the other line. I'm putting you on hold."

Delaney changed phone lines, then answered, "Mickey. Where are you?"

"I'm at the County Sheriff's Department. I've been detained."

"What? Who told you that?"

"Some guy named Masterson."

"Son-of-a-bitch."

"You know him?"

"Unfortunately," Delaney replied, pulling out one of his forbidden cigars and sticking it in his mouth

"I need you to get me out of here."

"I'll be there in five minutes. Don't say shit to the man. He's an idiot."

Mickey hung up his phone. Delaney reconnected with Toot.

"Toot, Masterson took Mickey into custody."

"He what?"

"Don't worry. I'll get him out. Meanwhile, see if you can figure out where Diane ran off to."

"We're trying to do that now. Talk to you later."

TOOT HUNG UP HIS phone and took a seat across Mickey's desk from Suki.

"What is wrong?" Suki asked.

"Masterson took Mickey into custody."

"Mickey has been arrested?"

"I guess. Roger was pretty vague. All he said was he'd get him out of trouble." Toot popped his knuckles, then asked, "Any more clues about Diane?"

"No."

Boundaries

As Toot crossed his legs, he bumped the desk, knocking the desk phone receiver from its cradle. When he put it back, he accidently pushed the 'redial' button. Hearing the phone dial a number, he looked at the number on the display, then showed it to Suki.

"Do you recognize this number?"

"No. I guess we will find out whose number it is in a moment."

A voice answered, "Law offices. How may I help you?"

Toot handed the receiver to Suki.

"Uh, yes ma'am. I am not sure if I have the correct number. Who is this again?"

"The law offices of McMurray and Wakeland."

Suki had to think quickly if she was going to find out anything at all.

"I am trying to find your office. Where are you located?"

"We are at 111 Pine Street."

Writing as she spoke, Suki continued, "I apologize for not making myself clear the first time. I am coming in from out of town. What city are you located in?"

"Durango, Colorado. Your name please?"

Unsure if she should answer, Suki cautiously responded with what she thought might get her the information she needed. "This is Diane Rollins, Diane Rollins-Alders."

"Hello, Ms. Alders. Mr. Wakeland said you would be checking in with us. He's with a client at this time. He wanted me to ask you if everything is alright, and if you are still on your way?"

Suki grinned, satisfied that she had at least a destination for where Diane was heading.

"Yes. Everything is fine."

"Do you need to speak with Mr. Wakeland? He gave me instructions to break into his meeting if necessary."

"No. That will not be necessary."

"Good, then. He'll look forward to your next call in a few hours."

"Thank you."

"Good day, Ms. Alders."

After Suki hung up the phone, she handed Toot the sheet of paper with her notes.

"The good news is that we know where she is likely going—Durango, Colorado. Do you know where that is?" Suki asked.

"Yeah, about nine hundred miles northwest of here. She's definitely on the run."

"They knew who Diane was. She must be seeking help from this attorney named Wakeland."

"I'll get Roger on it. Maybe he knows the guy. What's the bad news?"

"She is apparently calling in on a regular basis. That means the next time she calls in, she will know that we are onto her, and all bets are off after that."

Suki flipped a pen in her hand as she contemplated what to do next.

"If she is driving straight through, how long would it take her?"

"She might be able to get there in fifteen hours if she goes through West Texas and New Mexico. I've driven to Durango before, and it's a long day's haul, especially with Gigi in tow."

"What is between here and there?"

"Nothin' but highway, desert, and some small towns. Once she takes the cut north out of Pecos through New Mexico, it's just you and the stars except for Carlsbad, Artesia, and Roswell. Santa Fe would be on her route, but that's ninety percent of the way there." Toot waited for Suki to digest what he had said, then added, "If you're pretty certain that's where she's headed, we could fly there tonight. We could get there before she arrives and get to her before she goes into this Wakeland guy's office."

"Oh, that would be real smart. Snatch a client from the doorstep of her attorney's office. How far do you think we would get with that plan?"

"Do you have a better idea?" Toot asked.

"I think we will have to ask Mickey to intervene with Diane."

"What do you mean? She's gone."

"I mean, Mickey has the capability of tracking and locating her. With any luck, he may have another way of stopping her."

"What are you talking about?"

"He controls her, Toot. Have you been blind all of this time? Part of Mickey's treatment includes total control. If she fails to do as he wishes, he creates an event that shuts her down."

"You mean, like a seizure?"

"Would you ever have figured it out on your own, Toot?"

"So, you and Mickey are together in this? You somehow have taken control of Diane, and if she doesn't do what you want, you make her have a seizure?"

Suki shrugged her shoulders as if it shouldn't matter.

"So all this time, those episodes Diane had, have been bi-products of something you're doin' to her?"

Suki shrugged her shoulders again.

"You people are sick. This ends now…I mean, right now."

"No, Toot. It can never end. If it ends, Diane dies."

"What are you talking about?"

"I am not about to give you a lesson in higher cerebral control, emotional transpondence, and nanotechnology. I will tell you this much, Diane and I have a bond that cannot be separated. She is undergoing a therapy that can never cease. She will always be exactly what I allow her to be. Take me out of the picture, and Diane becomes a fond memory. Piss me off, and I'll guarantee you the same result."

With a look of anger Suki had never seen before, Toot replied, "I'm headin' to the airport."

"You do not know what you are dealing with, Toot," Suki said in a threatening tone of voice.

"Just try and stop me."

A minute later, Suki could hear the squealing of tires as Toot sped out of the driveway.

IT TOOK MUCH LONGER than expected for Roger Delaney to free Mickey from the long, egotistical arms of Sheriff Wilt Masterson. By the time Mickey arrived at the ranch, it was dark outside, and he wasn't in the mood to mince words. As soon as he got in the house, he immediately set out to find Suki. She was waiting for him, lounging comfortably in the living room and sipping a glass of chilled Chablis.

"We are alone. Would you like to have some fun?"

Clenching both fists, Mickey said, "I called Toot. He told me Diane was gone and that he was on his way to Durango to get her."

The only response Suki gave him was a nod.

"He also said you told him a great deal about my work. I certainly hope you didn't."

"What is he going to do with that information, Mickey? He is a stupid cowboy. He is no match for us."

Exasperated, Mickey responded, "All you had to do is watch out for her. That's all. 'Just don't let her out of your sight'—that was all I ever asked."

After taking another sip of wine, Suki said, "I think you need to change your tone of voice, Mickey."

He walked over to the chair where Suki was sitting, put his hands on the armrests, and got up to Suki's face, at which point he said ominously, "I'll speak to you in any manner I want."

His bad-boy behavior didn't faze Suki.

"Have you ever given any thought as to what you were going to do with your life, Mickey, when Diane discovered what we have done to her?"

"You forget…such a discovery is only temporary. I control her memory."

"No, not this time," Suki said boldly.

"You forget…I call the shots," Mickey replied, trying unsuccessfully to remain dominant.

"No, that, too, is no longer the case, Mickey."

He was not accustomed to such defiance.

"What's the matter, Suki? Did Toot ignore you last night?"

Smiling at the irony of Mickey's remark, Suki replied, "As a matter of fact, he did ignore me. Because, while you were away, he found a new piece of ass— Diane."

Laughing with disbelief, Mickey said, "Toot wouldn't do that. He's too wholesome."

"Toot was wholesome. Diane took *him* to bed."

The two stared at each other, waiting for the explosion. Suki decided it required another nudge.

"Face it Mickey, you…are…just…simply…not…Bruce. He was the only man she ever loved, and he is the only man she ever *will* love."

In a split second, Mickey slapped Suki across her face. In the next split second, Suki knocked Mickey off of his feet and had him face down on the floor with his face pushed against the hardwood floor and his arm pinned painfully behind his back. He struggled in vain to break free from Suki's grip, but the diminutive, yet formidable woman had him exactly where she wanted him.

"I will ignore what you just did to me, Mickey. I will chalk it up to a fit of pique. Besides, I would not want a little physical violence to put a damper on the next chapter of our lives together."

"I love Diane," he responded.

"Of course you do, as do I. She has been an asset to our work together, as well as our relationship. You and I most likely would not be here right now if it were not for her. And we certainly should not discount the fact that she conceived our little Gigi, now should we?"

"Let me correct you, my little Asian bitch. Diane and I are fine together, with or without you. Secondly, it's been my work, not ours," Mickey said, grunting as he strained. "You're the surrogate, nothing more." Again trying to wrestle free, he said, "Finally, Gigi is one-hundred percent Diane's; zero yours."

Suki laughed for a moment as she reveled in what she perceived to be her total domination of him. "She's also zero percent yours."

Chuckling himself, Mickey replied, "I'll bet you think I didn't know that?"

That was not the reaction Suki expected to get from Mickey. She was fully anticipating an uproar fed by jealousy—in fact, she was hoping for one.

"Just so you don't bother trying to get my dander up any more about Toot and Diane, that doesn't matter to me. I figured the powers-that-be would dole out this type of justice someday. I guess it was about time."

Suki realized Mickey had taken the advantage, and she slowly released her hold on him. As he rolled over onto his back, she remained straddling him. Nonetheless, her situation had changed from domination to submission.

"Mickey, you can no longer trust Diane. She has feelings for another man."

"No, she had sex with another man. Believe me, I know the difference between having sex with someone and having feelings for that person."

The expression on Suki's face told Mickey that his punch had connected.

"So, how did you gain this wisdom?" Suki asked, doubting Mickey's epiphany.

"A beautiful, inspiring, wonderful woman who lives near Caddo Lake taught me."

"Laura?"

"Of course."

"And what would Diane think about your behavior?"

"Well, after we find her and things have settled down to the point where we can have a conversation, I plan to tell her about Laura. I guess at that point we'll know."

"She will leave you. You know that, correct?"

"If she does, she does. She's an adult. I'm not going to stand in her way."

"But, she cannot be apart from me for more than forty-eight hours. You would let her die?"

"You mean traumatic separation? That won't happen. You see, I plan to halt PicoPoint. I know what it can do, and I'm afraid the dangers outweigh the advantages for now."

"How can you stop it? You told me that was impossible!"

"And you believed me? You're talking to Mickey…Mickey Rollins. Why on earth would you ever believe anything I say?"

He watched as a mixture of expressions filled Suki's face, matching the torrent of emotions passing through her heart.

"I will not let you. I will not cooperate!" Suki said desperately.

"I don't need you. After I find her, I'll place her in stasis and disengage. The algorithm is already written."

"So if she leaves, does that mean that we…"

Managing to crawl out from under Suki, he responded, "Suki, there is no 'we'. There never was. Let me say this one last time—you were the surrogate, nothing more. You're free to leave at any time. Send me a bill."

Those acidic words were so far from what Suki wanted to hear. She couldn't imagine life without Mickey, not after all she had longed for. She hoped there might be one final trick left up her sleeve…

"Have you seen your computer? Diane destroyed it."

Reaching for his iPad, Mickey replied, "All I need is this."

He made several motions across the screen before putting the device back in its case.

"What did you just do?" Suki asked anxiously.

"I issued a simple command. Without my computer, I'm unable to issue complex instructions, nor am I able to track Diane's location. Fortunately, Toot told me her destination, and I can rebuild the workstation. All I need is the hard drive. If that's damaged too, I still have everything backed up."

"And you think she will trust you with this disengagement process? To use your own words, why on earth would she ever believe anything you tell her?"

Mickey realized Suki was probably right. It would take some more slight-of-hand in order for him to be able to come close to Diane at this point, let alone convince her to participate further in any of his science.

"What was this command you sent to her?"

"It's called Stop-on-Yellow. She'll see something yellow in color and she'll drop."

"What is special about yellow?"

"It's in the middle of the visible spectrum, and it's a color we see in the sun. There's always a reflection of sunlight in something. The command should be executed fairly quickly."

"Mickey," Suki said with a grin, "Look outside. It is night."

Her last move worked. She could tell by the look on Mickey's face she once again had his king in check. Mickey turned and headed for the door.

"Where are you going?" she asked.

"Durango," he replied without turning around.

"I am coming with you," she said frantically.

"Suit yourself…"

THE EFFECTS OF A combination of the stress of the day, hours of riding in the car, Gigi's impatience with confinement in an infant seat, nightfall, and the growing clinical symptoms of being away from Suki had taken its toll on Diane. She was tired, nauseated, and had a splitting headache. As they reached the southern edge of Roswell, New Mexico, the three happened to come across an unremarkable motor lodge. It was comprised of about a dozen identical, small bungalows, all painted white. They surrounded an empty swimming pool that, like the motel itself, was long past its heyday. The neon sign flickered as if it belonged in some type of horror movie. The office was in a larger building that also served as a diner. Regardless of its condition, this was as far as Diane could go, and it was on the route chosen by Wakeland.

Pointing at a phone booth just outside the office, Diane instructed Carmen, "Call Wakeland for me. Tell him it was a long distance between phones and apologize for the delay. Tell him where we are, and let him know we'll be spending the night here."

"Certainly Diane. Do you mind if I first walk Gigi around for a minute? She's about to jump out of her seat."

"No, go right ahead. I'll get us registered."

Diane got out of the FJ and headed slowly inside.

As soon as Diane was out of sight, Carmen picked up Gigi and practically ran to the phone booth where she placed her call. The phone rang on the other end only twice before a man answered it.

"Hello?"

"It's me again. Now, we're stopped for the night at some dump called the Red Planet Inn. It's south of Roswell on 285. Diane's not feeling well enough to continue."

"Do you still have the hard drive?"

"Yes, of course. It's packed in my bag."

"Keep it hidden. We'll continue as planned. Once Diane gets to her attorney's office tomorrow, she's bound to meet with him privately. That's when I'll meet with you, and we'll be on our way."

"What about the kid?"

"Leave her some place safe. Somebody will realize she's lost and take care of her until she's reunited with her mother."

"Okay, I have to go. I'll try to call you tomorrow while we're on the road just like I did today."

"I love you, Maggie."

"I love you, too."

While Carmen was on the phone, Diane was taking care of the business end of things. She only hoped she had enough stamina to make it to bed before she fell. After making her way to an unmanned registration desk, she tapped the bell next to the sign that read, 'ring for service.' Soon, a scruffy, older man appeared. A lit cigarette dangled out of the corner of his mouth.

"Help you?" he asked half-heartedly.

"Right…" Diane replied tentatively. "I need a room for one night."

"That'll be forty dollars for two hours, or sixty dollars for the night," the man replied tapping the ashes of his cigarette onto the floor behind the desk."

"Uh, it'll be for the entire night."

"Then that'll be sixty dollars cash."

"Cash?"

"Cash."

"Does that include tax?"

"The man studied Diane for a moment, then asked, "You with the government or something?"

"No," Diane replied.

"Then what I do with the money is none of your concern. That'll be sixty dollars cash."

"Right," Diane responded, as she handed three twenty dollar bills to the man.

"Do I need to register?"

The man returned a blank stare.

"You know, do I need to fill out a card or a registration book?"

It took a few moments, but the man finally answered, "Nobody fills out no paperwork here. Enjoy your stay. Dial "0" if you need anything. Diner's open another hour," he said, nodding in the direction of the dimly-lit eatery.

"Great. Would you recommend anything from their menu?"

The old man grinned, took a drag on his cigarette, and replied, "No." With that, he handed her a key to bungalow #4, then returned to his room.

Diane hadn't realized how hungry she was until she smelled…whatever it was that was cooking. In any case, it smelled wonderful. Being a little apprehensive about the conditions of the restaurant, she walked over to peek in. At the door, was a sign that read, "Martians get 15% discount." Next to the sign was a four foot tall effigy of a little green man—your stereotypical Martian. As she walked up to the entrance, the Martian squeaked, scaring Diane and drawing her attention to it. At the same time, its eyes illuminated a bright yellow. Diane immediately crumpled to the floor.

She lay there unconscious and unnoticed for some time until Carmen walked into the office and spotted her on the floor. Carmen had more than one reason to avoid making a scene and drawing attention to them, so she began to drag Diane out the door. Diane, though fit and trim, proved to be a load for Carmen to move, and she bumped into a magazine rack, knocking it over. It wasn't long before the old man at the registration desk came out to see what the noise was.

Boundaries

Seeing Carmen trying to remove Diane's unresponsive body, he yelled, "Hey, what's going on?"

Carmen didn't say anything, she just moved quicker, eventually getting Diane out into the parking lot. The motel clerk, meanwhile, telephoned for help.

Carmen was just about to lift Diane into the passenger seat of the FJ when a deputy arrived...then another. Approaching Carmen, one of the deputies asked, "What's going on, Miss?"

Frightened, Carmen released Diane, and tried to run away. She was quickly apprehended by one of the deputies, while the other called for an ambulance. It was only then that the deputies found Gigi curled up and frightened in the backseat of the vehicle.

One of the deputies asked the other, "Ain't this that FJ we got a bulletin about?"

"Yep, plates match and there are two women and a kid."

Book 7

"How do you know about Sylvie?" Diane asked.

"Is there someone you deal with on a regular basis named Sylvie? Answer my question," Mason pressed harshly.

Diane began to rock back and forth nervously. Madden didn't know where Dr. Mason was going with his question and couldn't understand why this person would be so important for him to push Diane toward the brink of a breakdown to get an answer.

"Loarn, maybe this isn't a good time for such a question. Maybe you're taking the matter too personally?"

"You're damn right I'm taking a personal interest in this. So, Diane, Sylvie?"

"She talks to me," Diane reluctantly replied.

"Where does she live?"

Continuing to rock nervously, Diane looked out the window for diversion.

"Where…does…she…live?" Mason pressed.

"She's in my mind. Satisfied?" Diane replied, defiantly.

"So, she's not a sentient being," Mason said.

"That depends on how you describe sentient. At least she's nice to talk to."

"Oh, so you have conversations with this person you are imagining?" Mason asked.

"That's it! Let me out of here," Diane said, angrily trying to wiggle past Madden.

"Sit down!" Mason barked. Fortunately, the restaurant was empty except for the three of them.

"I don't have to put up with your shit, Dr. Mason. If you want to help me, that's fine. But, if you're going to berate me, then fuck you!" Diane shouted, again trying to wiggle past Madden.

Boundaries

Mason reached out and physically grabbed both of Diane's wrists, then said, "Sit down and cooperate, or I'll contact the police, we'll get an emergency detention order, and keep you until I say otherwise."

"You can't do that!" Diane shouted.

"Oh, I can, and I will," Mason replied with certainty.

There were a few anxious moments, followed by a slow release of tension between Diane and Mason. He slowly released his grip on her.

Just as peace settled at the table, Joan returned. "You want me to call the cops, Dr. Mason?"

Slowly turning to look at Joan, Mason replied, "No. What I would like is for you to leave us alone for a while."

Joan managed to reply with a "Humph," before storming off.

Surprised at Mason's behavior, Madden asked, "Loarn, why are you acting like this?"

"I have good reason, Bev. I do believe my chickens have come home to roost."

"What do you mean by that, Loarn?"

"Diane," Mason began, "Tell me, did Sylvie ever tell you her last name?"

"Yes. I think it was de Beers."

The cringe on Mason's face was one of both gratification and pain.

"Do you think you would recognize her if you saw her?"

"What do you mean?" Diane asked.

"Loarn, what's wrong?" Madden asked.

Mason pulled out his wallet and took out a photograph. After looking at it himself and smiling, he showed it to Diane.

"That's Sylvie!" She exclaimed.

He then showed the picture to Madden.

"Loarn, that's…"

"I know…my Sylvie."

Now it was Diane's turn to ask questions.

"This is way too creepy. How do you know *my* Sylvie?"

"We are connected via our mutual acquaintance, Dr. Mendoza."

"I don't follow you, Loarn," Madden said.

Mason leaned into the table and rested on his elbows.

"Let me tell both of you about a little dark secret I have been keeping. In all honesty, I know a lot more about PicoPoint than I have led both of you to believe. In fact, I too have experienced the full impact of the technology and its wrath."

Holding a hand up to her mouth, Madden said, "Loarn, surely you didn't…"

"You see, Diane, de Beers was an alias I used for my wife when she underwent a prototype therapy similar to that which you are undergoing now. Sylvie…my Sylvie…acquired a rare neurological disorder that was quickly, and painfully, robbing her of her memory and physical strength. She had always been a vivacious and brilliant woman. On top of that, she was a research scientist who held dear to her conviction of helping others, even if that meant taking risks—personal risks.

"As I told you earlier this evening, I was brought in by a venture capital group to examine the merits of PicoPoint. I could not throw my support to the work because of the very real dangers involved with human testing. Sylvie and I shared everything during our forty years of marriage. We knew exactly what the other's needs were. It was an intimacy I suspect few have enjoyed. When I told her about my objection to the work, with complete understanding of the potential consequences, she suggested that she become a test subject for the therapy and that I participate as well. After all, what better surrogate could one ask for than a life mate.

"After Sylvie's condition took a dramatic turn for the worse, we entered into the project with Dr. Mendoza. The timing must have been just immediately prior to Diane's accident and prior to the perfection of Mickey's nanostructures and the algorithms Mendoza is using today. Most likely, what they learned from their work on Sylvie was directly applied toward Diane's therapy. In Sylvie's case, there were no surgical procedures. Information was passed between host and surrogate using more external means that proved to be far less effective and very poorly controlled.

Boundaries

"I'll spare the two of you the graphic details, but the therapy was a failure and it cost Sylvie her life, as it nearly did my own. If there is any virtue in what took place, it appears the improvements they made to the therapy post-Sylvie worked, at least to the degree that we see before us today with Diane."

There was a long period of silence. The only sounds were the sobbing and sniffling of Dr. Madden, and Joan, who had managed to eavesdrop once more.

Diane sat expressionless and unable to speak until she managed to ask, "How does this link to me?"

"Do you have a photograph of Suki?"

After thinking for a moment, Diane reached into her bag, pulled out her wallet and removed a picture of Suki holding Gigi. She held it in front of Mason.

Having been the victim of a ruse himself, Mason grinned and said, "She called herself Maribella. She was present during the entire time Sylvie was being treated. She said she was Mendoza's assistant. I had no reason to doubt her. She was remarkably knowledgeable in the field. Of course, that stands to reason now that you have told us that she was essentially the author of all Dr. Wu's published research."

Turning to Dr. Madden, Mason continued, "I'm sorry, Bev. I know you and Sylvie were close friends. I apologize for never having told you the truth about what happened. It was a promise Sylvie asked me to keep, regardless of the outcome of her therapy."

Madden sat in stunned silence as tears streamed down her cheeks. Wiping her nose with a napkin, she asked, "Why now, Loarn? Why did you wait until this moment to tell us everything? Wasn't this valuable information I should have had when we began Diane's treatment tonight? You acted tonight as if you knew very little about this technology. You're as much of a fraud as the rest of the people in this project."

"I couldn't compromise my pledge to Sylvie," Mason said with a long face.

Looking puzzled, Diane asked, "Why would Suki use the name of the island as her alias?"

Mason gently touched Diane's hand as he asked, "It's hard to say. Maybe she was attempting to see if anyone could connect the dots once you arrived at the island. Is it possible Suki conspired a long time ago to create a situation in which you would become the next test subject of this project? Could you be the victim of an elaborate scheme that deliberately put you in harm's way, so that you would potentially suffer the injuries you sustained, resulting in an opportunity for Mickey and others to carry out their work?"

Diane turned pale, and got up from the booth as she said, "I think I'm going to be sick."

"I'd better go with her," Madden added.

"I'm right behind you, gals," Joan said as the three rushed to the ladies' room.

Chapter 46

From within a darkened truck parked off in the brush in front of Rub-a-Dub, two figures watched as Mickey and Suki left the ranch in his Rover. The passenger dialed a number.

"Sheriff? It's Doss. The subject's vehicle just left the ranch with two occupants."

"Well, we know Toot's waiting for an aircraft to arrive at the airport and Delaney told us Mrs. Rollins already skipped town. It's got to be Mickey and that Sukhon Jiao lady. She ain't supposed to be out of Toot's sight, let alone leave the ranch. Which way are they headed?"

"West on 39."

"That's the wrong way as far as I'm concerned. Sounds to me like they're taking off—probably trying to catch the interstate off of 83. Do you have them in sight?"

"They're about a half mile ahead. There's nobody else out on the road so they're easy to tail."

"Don't let them get out of the county. Pull 'em over and bring her in. Are you alone?"

"No. Chandler is with me."

"Watch yourselves. That Asian lady is nothing but trouble."

"Got it."

Doss pointed to Mickey's vehicle in the distance, and the deputies began to close in on it.

MICKEY WASN'T SPEAKING TO Suki, but that wasn't going to stop her from trying to persuade him to change his course of action.

"Mickey, what if you and I were to start over—just you and me? We could go anywhere you want. Between the two of us, we have the means to be comfortable forever."

There was no response.

"I think you are correct. We need to let PicoPoint come to an end. Diane can go her own way. We'll move and take Gigi with us. We could put all of this in the past and have a fresh beginning."

There was still no response.

"Someday, if you want to begin your work again, I will be there by your side to help you."

There continued to be no response from Mickey and Suki was getting frustrated.

"Fine. Have it your way. You and I can go our separate ways, but there is always Mendoza. He will appreciate what I have to offer. He and I will take up where you left off."

Finally speaking, Mickey replied, "You have no idea where I left off, or began for that matter. You were always hypnotized."

"If that is what you wish to believe, go ahead and fool yourself. But, I was never hypnotized, Mickey."

Mickey grinned, but certainly didn't appear to be threatened.

"That is correct, Mickey. All of your wondrous technology you take from me and give to Diane pales when matched against what I am able to do with nothing more than my mind. I worked around it all of the time. I am the one who transformed Diane into the person she is today, not you."

Again, Mickey let Suki have her say.

"So, you see, you need me. If your work is ever going to go anywhere, if PicoPoint has any hope of succeeding, you need me to do it for you."

That was the final threat Mickey was going to tolerate. He jammed on the breaks, pulling off the road.

"Get out," he said.

"You are making a terrible mistake, Mickey. You will not make it without me."

"Do you think I would put the project in such jeopardy? Suki, you haven't always been able to avoid hypnosis. That was a skill that took a while for you to acquire, correct?

Suki didn't respond.

"Right I am. You should know that one of the first things I transferred from you to Diane was your memory of your grandfather's writings…the ones you transcribed. A copy of that information is neatly tucked away in her mind, along with the keys to your encryption, waiting for me to tap when I need them. I found it to be good reading, actually. Your grandfather's discoveries are what gave you the ability to control your mind during hypnosis. To make a long story short, I created a warning utility that notified me whenever you deviated from my script during hypnosis. That allowed me to intervene as necessary—even from a distance…like Caddo. Be certain, Suki, I will make it without you."

Suki was too shocked to react.

"Now, get out!" he repeated.

Before either could say another word, the deputies pulled up behind Mickey's vehicle and turned on the bright take-down lights on top of their vehicle.

A voice shouted over the public address system, "Driver, step out of the vehicle with your hands over your head, and lay face-down on the pavement. Passenger, remain in the vehicle with your hands on the dashboard where we can see them."

Looking cocky at Suki, Mickey said, "Guess you're not going to have to walk back to the ranch after all."

Mickey stepped out of the vehicle and got down on the road as he was asked. Quickly, Chandler had Mickey in handcuffs and placed him standing between the two vehicles.

Next, Doss shouted, "Passenger, step out of the vehicle with your hands over your head and lay face down on the ground."

Suki was out of ideas. It was clear she had lost the only thing she had ever wanted—a fairytale life with Mickey. She pounded her fists on the dashboard causing the glove box to open. Suddenly, she saw the gun that Mickey carried in his vehicle.

"Passenger, step out of the vehicle with your hands over your head, and lay face down on the ground."

Suki grabbed the pistol, checked that it had rounds of ammunition in it, and stepped out of the Rover for the last time.

"Mickey, I love you!" she shouted, aiming the gun at him.

She pulled the trigger, but nothing happened.

"Gun!" Doss shouted.

Suki tried to shoot again. The clicks of the hammer were unmistakable. Both deputies drew their weapons defensively and opened fire, striking Suki repeatedly. She fell to the ground.

"Suki!" Mickey shouted as Chandler took him to the ground. "Suki!" Mickey screamed again and again.

Doss walked up to Suki who was mortally wounded, bleeding badly from her wounds and barely breathing. Doss removed the gun from her hand which then flopped back onto the dirt. Slowly, and with great effort she drew in the soft, brown dirt the letters E-V-O-L, drew a circle around them, and then a line trough it. Immediately after finishing, she took her last breath. Mickey was dragged screaming to the deputies' vehicle locked in the back seat while they waited for assistance to arrive.

DIANE SPLASHED WATER ONTO her face while Dr. Madden paced back and forth, both reacting in different ways to what they had heard from Mason. As Diane stood up and looked into the mirror, she saw her reflection. Suddenly, standing next to her appeared an eerie image of Suki that lasted only a few seconds. What followed was the worst headache Diane had ever experienced—the pain so intense, she fell to her knees screaming.

"What's wrong Diane!" Madden asked.

"No EVOL!!" Diane screamed.

"Joan, go get Dr. Mason," Madden ordered.

"No EVOL!!" Diane screamed again. Moments later, she collapsed into Dr. Madden's lap.

Having heard the screams from where he sat in the booth, it was no time before Mason was at their side.

"Bev what's wrong?"

"She began screaming and collapsed holding her head."

Madden began to assess Diane for vital signs.

Shaking her head as she looked up at Mason, Dr. Madden shouted, "Loarn, she's not breathing. I don't feel a pulse."

Mason paused, overwhelmed for just a second by the memory of what had taken place during his wife's therapy and of her death.

"It's traumatic separation," he said with absolute certainty.

"What?" Madden asked, laying Diane face up on the floor.

"The surrogate separated unexpectedly. Joan! Bring us as much ice as you can in one of those large tubs you use to bus tables."

"Is she's going to die, Loarn?" Madden asked.

"Not of I can help it!" Mason yelled. "We need to do CPR and pack ice around her head to keep her cold until we can get back to the hospital."

Epilogue

Today…

Tracy thought she would be at the office early enough to surprise her boss with her return from a six month hiatus as a political operative for a senatorial candidate. Such was not the case. He was already there, and it was barely six forty-five in the morning. The door was unlocked so she didn't have to fumble for her key. Entering the law office, she was overwhelmed with the familiar smells of dark roasted coffee and cigar smoke. She found Delaney hard at work, pouring over a document file.

"I thought you gave up cigars?" she said, leaning against the frame of the door.

Looking up, Delaney smiled as he said, "I thought you quit being a pain in the ass."

The venerable attorney stopped what he was doing and got up to greet his comrade with a kiss on the cheek.

"Sure is good to have you back. So did you learn anything from that yahoo you were working for?"

"Possibly. He told me you could be charged with harassment for calling me youngin' all the time. He said you're creating a hostile work environment."

"Is that a fact? Well, come on over here, youngin', we got a helluva lot of work to do."

Tracy smiled at the familiar environ. It felt good to be back after six months on the road.

"I see you don't have any coffee, can I get you a cup?"

"Please do, and help yourself to one at the same time."

"Still like it black?" Tracy asked.

"I beg your pardon?" Delaney joked. "You know if you'd been campaigning for the Republican candidate, you'd still be gone. I guess there is some benefit to having you throw your support for a Democrat."

After getting the coffees, Tracy joined Delaney at the oval, mahogany table. "So what are you working on?"

"Gotta couple of friends of yours coming in after a while—Mr. Teudi and Ms. Chase…soon to be Mr. and Mrs. Teudi."

"Naw…you're kidding?"

"Pretty soon, according to my tea leaves. They haven't formally set a date yet, but I suspect it'll be before the holidays. See what you miss when you're gone?"

"That's wonderful. So what are they coming in for?"

"Wrapping up the estate. As you remember, just before you left Mickey admitted he wasn't married to Diane. He took off, Laura and Mickey officially got a divorce, and transferred all of his estate assets to Laura. She can buy herself that new set of pots and pans now."

"How much are we talking about?"

"High eight figures in cash and securities. Then, there's all the producing assets in the form of oil leases. That's one rich little gal."

Delaney smiled coyly as he glanced over at his assistant and reached into his pocket. He handed Tracy an envelope which she hastily opened. It only took a moment for her to tear up.

Giving her boss a hug, she said, "Thank you, Mr. Delaney."

"Rub-a-Dub's been pretty good to the firm this go-around. After taxes, that ought to pay for two year's tuition."

Tracy took a sip of coffee to clear her throat, then asked, "Whatever became of Diane?"

"What's the last thing you remember?"

"She practically died, and they revived her at the hospital. Is she alright?"

"That depends on your definition of 'alright.' Diane experienced something called traumatic separation. At first, I thought they were describing Mickey's divorce. Anyway, she lost all memory of everything that had transpired in the years after the instant her original injury occurred. In fact, according to her doctors, her last memory before waking up in a hospital in Albuquerque was making love in a waterfall with some guy we know only as Captain Bates. Sadly, she had no memory of motherhood or Gigi, or any part of her life in Texas for that matter. Her doctors, lawyer, and friends felt the best course of action for now, was to give Diane's mind time to heal, and allow her the opportunity to get back into some kind of normal life. They're supposed to monitor her for signs should she recall any of the more recent events she experienced."

"How did they save her life? Is she, I don't know, normal?"

"Some fellow named Dr. Mason was able to save Diane's brain from suffering massive cellular destruction by cooling her brain. To paraphrase the reports that were given to me as part of our discovery, Diane has these things called canals and nanocells in her brain. They're all entirely organic and they ceased to function and appear to have been absorbed back into her body. The volume they filled was slowly replaced by Diane's normal brain tissue and fluid and Diane was allowed to slowly come out of her state of hypothermic sedation. As far as anyone could tell, there were no clinically significant physical or mental deficits with Diane aside from her retrograde amnesia, and the fact that she remains right handed, multi-lingual, and her emotional responses all remain intact."

"Is she still seeing Dr. Mason?"

"Nope. Once Diane's case was closed, Mason retired from practice and returned to his home in Santa Fe. His colleagues at the Trauma Center in Albuquerque reportedly received a letter from him stating he and a female associate named Dr. Beverly Madden, who also participated in Diane's treatment, were enjoying themselves on a cruise around Greece and in the Mediterranean."

"What about the other ranch?"

"Well, not long after Diane got out of the hospital, she sold her family ranch in Gilroy. The money Diane made with the sale was put toward the creation of a scholarship fund for undergraduate architecture students in memory of late husband, Bruce Alders. Now get this—the buyer of the ranch was a man from Texas she had never heard of—Marque Teudi. All she knows is that he seemed to show a genuine interest in the ranch, though she couldn't understand why. After all, he's a cattleman. According to Toot, Diane thought his fiancée, Laura, seemed quite nice. He showed her pictures of Gigi, and all she said was that it appeared he was a dedicated family man. Toot renamed the ranch Grace Place, after Gigi, which Diane found quite poignant given that 'Grace' was her mother's name as well. She has no recollection at all about the kid."

"Oh, my gosh. That's so tragic. Did Diane ever go back to work?"

"Well, her boss brought Diane back to work at her old company, Medico Techniq, but a lot of time had passed, and there was no longer a particularly good fit. She seemed to be happiest working at a Dippin' Dots kiosk, of all things, at a park near San Diego called Torrey Pines. Strangely, just as she seemed to be standing strong on her own two feet again, she left the country with the help of her attorney and friend, Joel Wakeland—her whereabouts known only by him."

"That's unreal. What a story. So what's happened to Mickey?"

"Laura gave him the divorce he wanted, and they have remained friends. Though they keep in touch, Toot forbids Mickey from returning to the ranch, and vows to have nothing to do with Mickey ever again. Lots of bad blood between the two boys. Tell you what, Mickey was lucky. Although prosecutors tried to establish wrong doing in his treatment of Diane, Suki's death, and his unethical medical research, a Grand Jury no-billed the cases, all charges brought by the state against Mickey were dropped, and he was allowed to return to California."

"Scumbag."

"Get this, he had a visitor every day he was behind bars for three months—his old live-in housekeeper from Sausalito named Maria. When they returned to Sausalito, she drove him home in her new car—Dub's old yellow Jag. Life for them picked up where it had left off, as if Mickey had left for vacation just a few weeks before."

"I'll bet he marries her. He probably always had a thing for her. What about Gigi?"

"It was determined that Mickey had no legal rights to the child since he was not her father...a point that he did not contest. Perhaps being honest for the first time in his life, Mickey admitted Toot would be a much better father for Gigi than he could ever hope to be. She's a perfect fit in the new family, since the ranch is for all practical purposes the only real home she had ever known. Toot and Laura agreed, for now, to remain designated as her foster parents until a determination is made regarding Diane's parental rights. Their hope is that Gigi will become their daughter someday."

"So, if Mickey wasn't the father, who was?"

"Nobody knows. Might be that Bates fellow, but he lives on the other side of the planet so a hair sample for DNA testing is a little hard to come by."

"And Carmen?"

"Missing in action. Police in Roswell discovered a stolen hard drive in her bag and returned it to Mickey. There were conflicting stories about a twin sister named Magdeliene, but she never materialized. Neither Mickey nor Toot pressed charges, and she hadn't done anything wrong with respect to Diane, so Carmen—or Magdeliene—was released and immediately disappeared."

"I hate to ask. What about Suki?"

"Tragic ending, to say the least. An investigation called what Masterson's people did a justifiable shooting. There is no family, so her remains were cremated."

"What happened to her remains?"

"Diane has them. Can you believe that? She lost all memory of Suki's sinister side. She still thinks she was a dear friend."

"You ought to write a novel about all of this."

"Nope. Youngin', I'm too old, and I don't get paid enough to write that kind of tabloid fodder."

After laughing at Roger's humor, Tracy asked, "So, what are we doing this morning with Toot and Laura?"

"Well, we need to sign all the necessary documents. Both sets of articles deal with the final disposition of the estate. Laura, having been the wife of Mickey, and first spouse between the two 'boys', receives not only her share as designated by Dub and Ruby in their will, but also Mickey's portion of the estate as he had promised."

"Toot's alright with the disposition?"

"Toot's more than satisfied with the outcome, especially since he and Laura have become reacquainted. She's selling off her assets at Caddo, including Back East, and has moved into Rub-a-Dub with Toot."

TOOT STUDIED THE DOCUMENTS set before him for quite some time, occasionally asking a question of Delaney, or Laura who sat next to him.

"So, all I gotta do, Roger, is sign next to the little yellow arrows on these pages, and Rub-a-Dub takes on a whole new future. Is that right?"

"Future looks good, don't it?" Delaney asked, a large Texas grin covering his face. "Y'all set a date yet?"

"Probably October," Toot responded cheerfully.

"That's right around the corner."

"I know, Roger," Laura replied. "But, we want to make it all official as soon as possible so we can move forward with adopting Gigi, if and when that becomes a possibility."

"She's a doll," Delaney said as he mulled over something in his mind.

Toot signed on the designated lines, closed the folder, and handed it to Tracy who was sitting next to Delaney. The gleeful attorney then pulled out two Cuban cigars in aluminum tubes.

"To the two principal owners of Rub-a-Dub, may I offer my congratulations."

"And we kept the Trust in place for the others," Tracy reminded everyone.

With his fingers interlocked behind his head, Toot grinned as he said, "Yeah, boy. There's fixin' to be one helluva party up at Eight tonight."

"I have two more cigars if you ladies would like to join us in celebrating?"

"No!" both Laura and Tracey replied in unison.

"I'm gonna pass, too, Roger. I'm not a cigar kind of guy."

"Suit yourself," Delaney replied as he clipped off the end of a cigar.

"You told me just two hours ago that you were going to stop smoking cigars," Tracy said.

Defiantly, Delaney replied, "What'd I tell you about opinions?"

With a deep sigh, Tracy replied, "You told me the only ones you listened to were those you paid for."

"Right, so stop nagging me," he said as he lit the cigar. "I'm too old, and I get paid too much to put up with that sort of thing from a paralegal."

If Delaney hadn't been smiling and playfully squeezing Tracy's shoulder when he said that, she might have taken him seriously.

Resting his arms on the table, Toot said, "A little bit ago, it looked like you wanted to say something about Gigi."

"Well, it's the whole mother thing with Diane. She was nothing but a victim in this whole fiasco Mickey created. It don't seem right to keep Gigi and her mother apart."

Responding for Toot and herself, Laura replied, "We agree. There will be a time when they need to be introduced. But, for now, Rajeev says Diane's therapist and attorney want to keep Gigi out of the picture. Diane's simply clueless about being a mother—she doesn't even suspect she had a baby. Since Suki bore Gigi, Diane has no physical marks of pregnancy or childbirth."

Toot stood up abruptly and began walking around the conference room.

"I can't believe what a turd Mickey became. I mean he's a big ol', sun-dried cow patty," he continued, making a circle with his hands. "It's an evil person who would do what he did to Diane and Suki."

Shaking his head in disagreement, Delaney argued, "Look, Mickey's got a long list of faults, but when he got mixed up with Suki, it all took on a whole new dimension. You need to read the synopsis put together by that Interpol guy. Mickey was the gasoline, but Suki was the match. She knew exactly what she was doing and she played him like a fiddle. Dr. Mason said, after he read some of Suki's journals, had her grandfather's book translated, and talked to that Tik fellow, that Suki knew nearly as much about the project as the original three partners combined. She'd been playing all three guys against each other without them knowing it, and all along lining up potential buyers from places that have names too long for this old boy. Talk about the ultimate terrorist—and here she was living in central Texas."

Not ready to buy into Delaney's argument, Toot countered, "I think you're discounting what Mickey knew. I'd bet a bunch of Ben Franklins that he knew exactly what Suki was up to. It's just a matter of time before he comes out on top and gets exactly what he wanted. Mickey ain't no fool."

"Let's please not talk any more about Mickey," Laura requested.

After a moment, Toot concurred, "She's right. Besides, he's not welcome back here anymore. He's a menace to society, and since he don't own any piece of the ranch or any other business for that matter, I think he's out of the picture."

"You did send him all of his computers and electronic gadgets he listed in that letter from his attorney, right?" Delaney asked.

"All accounted for and gone as of twelve days ago. But, nobody's counting," Laura replied.

"So, who do you have watching Gigi?" Tracy asked.

"Lupita's daughter. She started a few months back watching her two or three afternoons each week. Other than that, she's mine...all mine," Laura answered adoringly.

With a sinister look, Delaney proposed, "I could probably arrange for you to meet a few au pairs if you'd like me to…"

He couldn't finish his sentence before both Laura and Toot vigorously declined his offer.

"So Laura," Tracy began, "You'll be back here on Thursday at ten o'clock to sign the closing papers for everything up at Caddo, correct?"

"Yep. I'll miss the lodge, beer garden, and the store. I have a lot of friends up there, but I can't pass up my chance here. Toot's too good of a man to go to waste."

"You apparently don't know you're supposed to say mushy things like that out of earshot of the person you are complimenting," Delaney joked.

Disagreeing, Toot said, "No, I think she's dishin' out just the right amount of flattery. A little goes a long way with me," Toot ended as he put his hands on Laura's shoulders.

"What about Back East? Does that Houston couple want it?" Delaney asked.

"They're supposed to send you a contract in the next day or so. I'm sure it's a slam-dunk given how low I priced the place."

"You really want it gone, don't you?" Delaney asked.

"Like a bladder infection," Laura replied, tongue-in-cheek. "It's all cleaned out. The items I thought we might want here some day—a lot of Ruby's and Dub's legacy furnishings and her quilts—are in storage. I'll integrate them into the ranch once things settle down. But, as for all of Mickey's crap, I boxed it up and shipped it out to him along with the remnants of his computer. He and Maria can deal with it."

"So you heard?" Tracy asked.

"You mean that Mickey's back with Maria in Sausalito? I'm not surprised. They were all but married for years and years until he ran off with Diane. She certainly knows what she's getting into, and she still chose to let him come home. He said she was the only person on the planet he could trust anymore, and he's probably right. Anyway, I wished them both the best and that's that."

"Hopefully, she keeps him penned up," Delaney said.

Chuckling, Laura said, "You know, when I called Maria the other day to tell her about the shipment? I asked her what Mickey was up to. She said he was locked in his office—he was working on the Big One."

DIANE SAT IN A chair on her porch at L'il Daba, sipping her espresso. Rajeev sat next to her watching as she stared off in the direction of the ocean, mesmerized by its sound. Two place settings of tableware, both with partially eaten muffins and fruit, dotted the tabletop.

Finally ending a long silence, Diane said, "It's time for me to move on, Rajeev."

He knew she was right, but nonetheless countered her remark by saying, "No. We can make this work. It just takes time."

Putting her hand on his, she said, "No, I mean it. My heart's just not in the business anymore, Rajeev. Be honest with me. I mean, I've been away for so long. The chemistry isn't there. I'm not current with the technology. You have better things to worry about than trying to help me fit into the organization when I'm simply not motivated."

Rajeev was only able to reply with a kind, understanding smile.

"There's something out there for me," Diane continued, looking out toward the ocean. "I can feel it."

"Have you spoken with your doctor about work?"

"Which one?" Diane replied sarcastically. "The shrink, the neurologist, the surgeon, the ear guy? I'm so sick of being evaluated and tested and poked and prodded and this and that. Yesterday, I told my psychologist that I'm taking a six month break from all doctors. These people have no boundaries when it comes to the invasion of my life and my body."

"That's a serious step, Diane. Are you sure? I think you are taking way too many radical steps all at the same time."

"Like what?"

"Well, like you sold your family ranch. That was a big deal. Then, you tell me you no longer want to work at Medico. Next, you stop seeing your doctors. Finally, you stare off into the ocean like that is where your future lies. Quite frankly, you're scaring the shit out of me."

"You think I'm suicidal, don't you?"

"If you tell me you are not, I will believe you, Diane, because you have never lied to me...ever. I simply think you should take things a bit slower. Let life catch up with you."

Diane leaned over and gave her friend a hug. Looking into his eyes, she said, "Rajeev, I'm not suicidal. Life excites me again—just not life here. There's a part of me out there someplace. I have to find it."

"Where will you go?"

"I can't tell you."

"Oh, now that reassures me."

"Seriously, I've made arrangements through Joel. He knows where I am going and who I will be with. He made me promise to keep in touch with him weekly. But, I told him he had to keep my whereabouts confidential. He said he would do that for me."

"What about your home here?"

"Rosario said she'd take care of it for me. She did a good job while I was gone the last time."

"So you've made up your mind. You're going to simply vanish once again. I won't stand for it, Diane. I won't let you do it."

The look on Diane's face told Rajeev to back off.

"Rajeev, nobody will ever take over my life again…nobody. And that includes you. I'm sorry if you don't like my choice, but it's *my* choice, not yours."

Realizing he had been out of line, Rajeev reluctantly said, "Of course, Diane. I need to step back and let you spread your wings once again. You realize I only want the best for you, don't you?"

After hugging Rajeev again, Diane replied tearfully, "I know you do, Rajeev, I know you do. That's why I want you to oversee Bruce's Foundation while I'm gone. Would you do that for me?"

He gave his long-time friend a warm embrace, immediately overwhelmed by what he felt was the most personal, and generous offer Diane could possibly make

MICKEY'S BREATHING WAS PACED to his running stride as he finished the last mile of his morning run along the winding roads in the hills above the Banana Belt near his Sausalito home. After rounding the last turn, he came up behind his neighbor, Mrs. Grady, and her two golden retrievers just like he did nearly every morning he went running.

"Beautiful day today, isn't it Beth?" Mickey was still conscious of letting unsuspecting walkers know he was passing them rather than startling them.

Boundaries

"Beau, Gracie, don't jump on Mr. Rollins!" Beth shouted as her dogs lunged toward Mickey, wagging their tales frantically. He reached down to pat their grey muzzles as he breezed past. Beth pulled on their leashes, "Like always, Mickey. Are you doing okay?"

"Just dandy, Beth. Just dandy."

When he got to the top of his driveway, he was met by Maria in her Prius. She rolled down the window to speak with her born-again house mate.

Mickey leaned through the window, kissed his old friend then asked, "Where are you headed off to?"

"I need to get some flour for the rolls I'm baking for tonight's party. I forgot to get it yesterday. Do you need anything?"

"Just you, Babe. Just you."

Smiling ear to ear, Maria replied, "You should have come home a long time ago."

"You're right, but then you were always right," Mickey said sincerely.

"Oh, my. This is going to be a wonderful."

Mickey leaned in for one more kiss. Afterward, Maria drove away.

The market was only about a mile from their house at the bottom of the serpentine road. Instead of pulling up to any of the many empty spaces close to the entrance of the store, Maria parked near the back of the lot away from the door. It wasn't long before a bronze-colored Jaguar pulled up next to her. The passenger rolled down her window. It was Magdeliene. She reached out her hand and into it Maria deposited first a box that contained Mickey's old hard drive, then Wu's manuscript. An older man leaned forward from his driver's seat to peer over at Maria. It was Constantine Strokas.

"Be discrete when you spend your money. You don't want to draw attention to your new wealth."

Maria felt guilt unlike anything she had experienced before. But, the feeling was short-lived. After a few moments, she held up an airline ticket and said, "Where I'm going, nobody will think a thing of it."

With that, Maria got out of the Prius, hopped into a small rented vehicle she had parked there earlier, and left the parking lot, heading north.

Strokas and Magdeliene headed south toward the Bay Bridge. Constantine reached over to his phone and dialed a number.

"Yes," answered a man on the other end.

"I have them," Strokas said.

"What a traitorous bitch. I knew I couldn't trust her."

"So now what, Mickey?"

"Did you line up the funding?"

"Yes, just like you asked. The money will be deposited overnight. They're absolutely ecstatic about the new phase of testing."

"Were you able to get Rajeev on board?"

"Medico was the largest investor. So when do we begin?"

"Probably in a few days. The updated satellite tracking is working like a charm. Next, I need to light up the structures again and run some diagnostics."

"You're certain they can be salvaged."

"One hundred percent. They were designed to be switched in and out of stasis. We'll have Diane back on line by the end of the week."

"What do you want me to do with this old disk drive and the manuscript?"

"Just toss the drive. There's nothing important on it anyway. I only used it occasionally as a red herring. But, whatever you do, don't lose that book."

"You scare me sometimes, Mickey. I like you, but you scare me."

"Dandy. I'll be in touch." Mickey disconnected.

"Get rid of it," Strokas said, looking over at his passenger.

Magdeliene rolled down the window and threw the drive out, sending it crashing into the channel below. Afterward, she asked, "Why did he go through so much trouble having Maria take this book and a useless disk drive, then pay us to pay her off? I just don't get it."

"Mickey's smart. There are others who want his technology—in particular, a gentleman named Mendoza. He was a partner of Mickey's at the onset of the project, but was forced out when his mistress, Suki, changed allegiances. With the death of Suki's grandfather, the balance of power shifted in favor of Mickey. All was not lost. Mendoza, too, is a smart, young fellow. He told an associate of mine once that Dr. Wu challenged him regarding the quality of patience. Once he lost his place in the project, he decided to allow Mickey time to finish all the hard work before stepping back in. Mickey knew it was only a matter of time before Mendoza came back into the picture. Word has it he's about to make his move. Maria is one of Mickey's red herrings. From the outside, it appears she stole the goods and disappeared. That will keep Mendoza busy for a while. I wouldn't want to be in her shoes when Mendoza's people find her—and they will find her."

"Me either."

"You're certain your sister has done her part?"

With a diabolical look, Magdeliene replied, "She told me last night that Bates has everything ready. She said she's looking forward to having some quality sister-time during our charter cruise."

A week after leaving San Diego…

THIS WAS THE MOMENT Diane had been dreading. She cradled the urn that held Suki's ashes for a long time while she chanted one of the songs Suki used to sing in her ear a long time ago. It was hard to let go of such a dear friend. She meant more to Diane than any other woman. But, she knew she was the one— the only one—who could rightfully dispose of Suki's ashes. What better place than the sea where they had enjoyed such a beautiful vacation together.

Diane stood on the stern of the boat, opened the urn, and cast the ashes into the wind. They blew around for a while before settling onto the water. She then tossed the urn into the sea.

Tears filled her eyes as she returned to the helm of the schooner where Bates was piloting the boat. She wrapped her arms around him, and buried her face into his bare back—the talons of his Wedge-tailed Eagle tattoo 'gripping' her. He held her arms tightly as they sailed toward the setting sun.

"You're certain this is the direction you want to be going, love?" Bates asked.

"Absolutely," Diane replied.

"And why is that?"

"I just know…"

~~ The End? ~~

About the Author

Doug Carlyle grew up in Urbana, Illinois where he graduated from the University of Illinois with, of all things for a novelist, a degree in electrical engineering. After a circuitous journey that took him through 26 glorious years in the semiconductor industry, he began writing great fiction. He also married, raised a family, and relocated to the Central Texas Hill Country.

Against this backdrop of mountains, valleys, live water, and wildlife, he is writing fiction intended to touch all of his readers in a very special way.

Never being able to choose just one pastime, he continues to practice his 30-year long medical ministry as a paramedic, while filling in the gaps in his calendar writing, signing, or selling his books.

Doug is a member of the Writers' League of Texas and the Houston Writers Guild.

*You may learn more about him at **www.dbcarlyle.com** .*